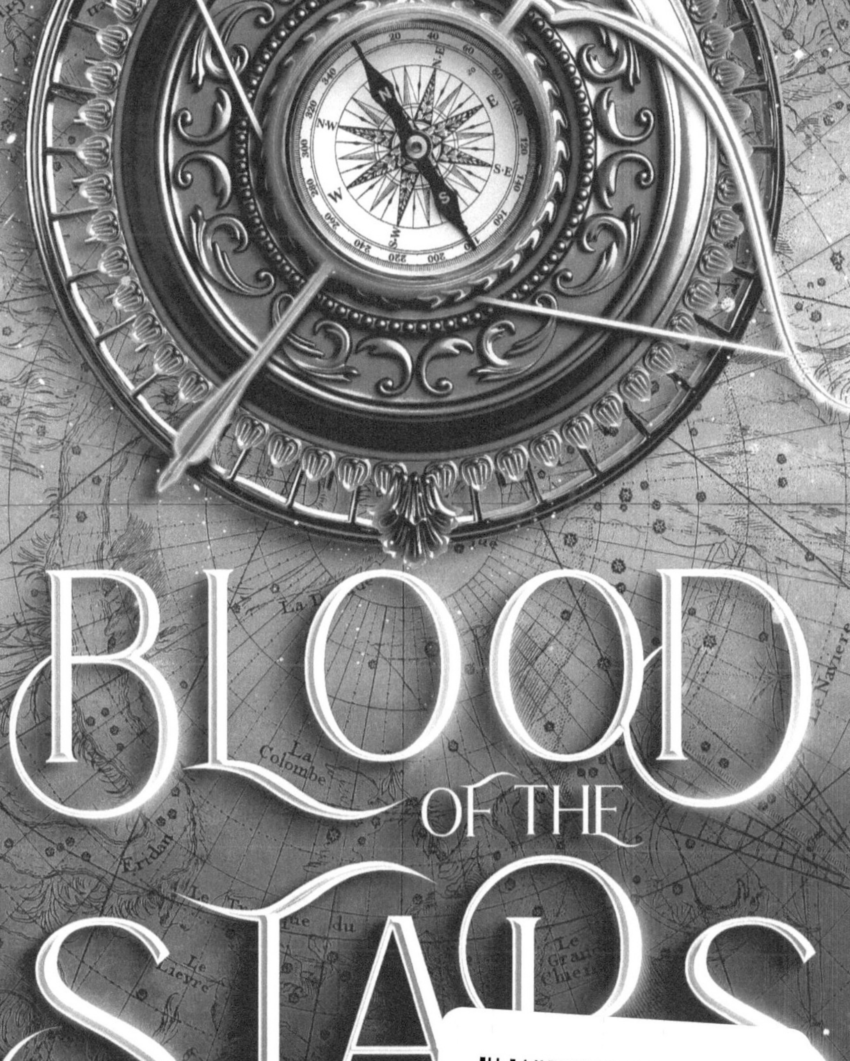

BLOOD
OF THE
STARS

KARYNE NORTON

BLOOD OF THE STARS

THE HALF-LIGHT CHRONICLES
BOOK ONE

FIRST LIGHT
PUBLISHING

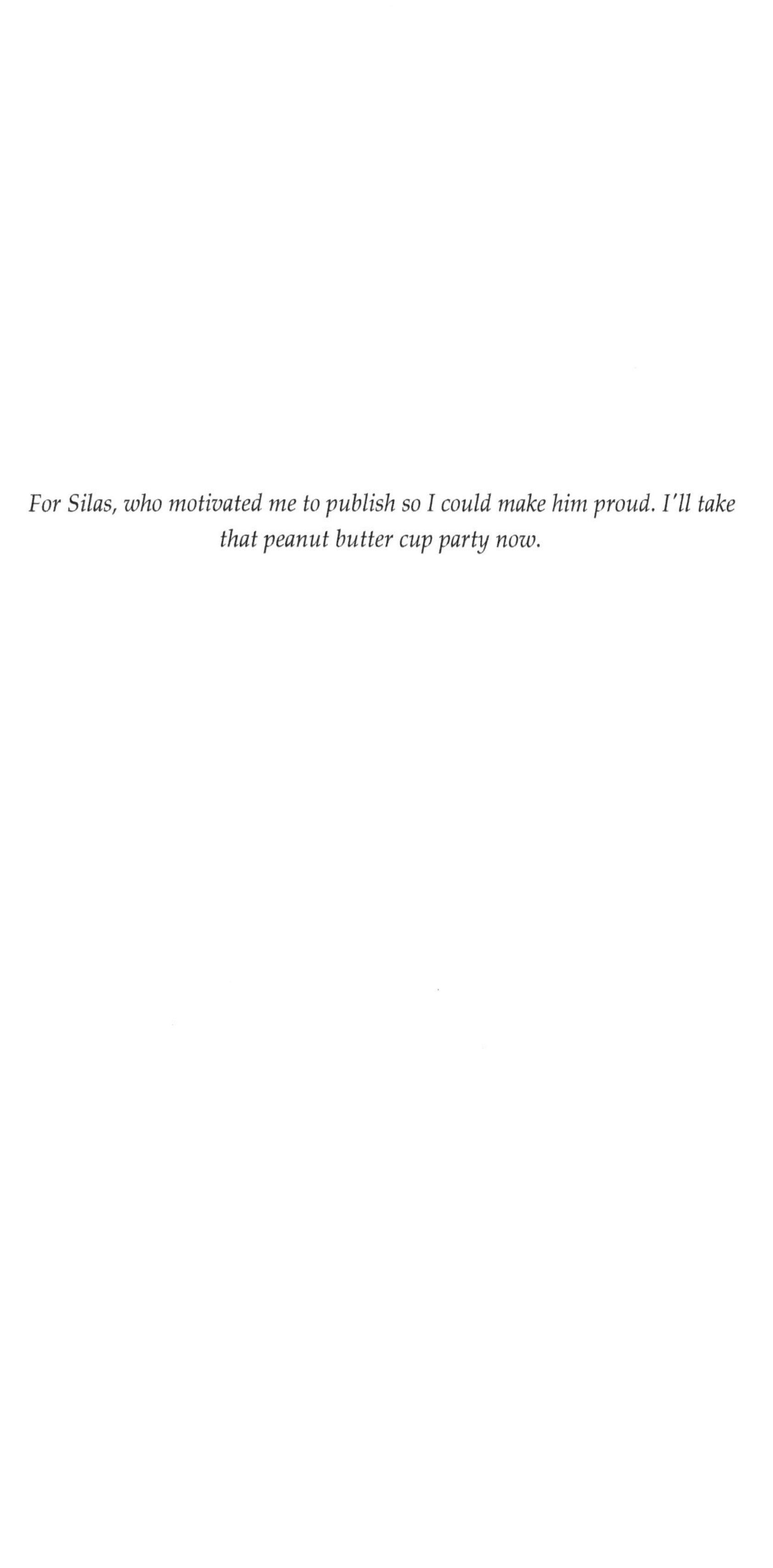

For Silas, who motivated me to publish so I could make him proud. I'll take that peanut butter cup party now.

ILIONA
LAST CHANCE
SERENDELLAN
STARHAVEN
LUHMEN MOUNTAIN
MAHLIC
GAHLDRIC VALLEY
VELSPETZ
ELANESSE
WEST HARBOR
LORVANDAS
BOLSPA
RYKARN
ISLARA
FAIRMOOR
DAHLVAS
DARKWOOD
BAMBOO ISLAND
SAYHLA PORT
VALORIAN
SEER'S SANCTUARY
ANDEL
TIDEHOLM
SAYHLA ISLAND

THE LANDS OF
RHYSTAHN
AHMRANAS
ST VALLEY
HEART'S HOPE
ELANDRA
LAND'S END
SELAHSTRA
MAHRAGLEN
NORTHPOINT
MYNDREN
DRAGON'S ROOST
VENDARAS
SUNSHROUD
WINDMERE INLET
WYVERN WATCH
CELANOFT
GALGOTTA
EASTHAVEN
DEHVLON
BURROWER BEACH
SEAGLASS PORT
IRONSPIRE
ASHENWOOD

ELANESSE
MT. VESCANO
RYKARN
ISLARA
DAHLVAS
BAMBOO ISLAND
LOVERS' FALLS
VALORIAN
ANDEL
THE CONTINENT OF
VENDARAS

THE NORTHERN SEA
NORTHPOINT
AHLRIC DESERT
MYNDREN
MYNDREN MOUNTAINS
SUNSHROUD
WINDMERE INLET
CELANOFT
DEHVLON
SEAGLASS PORT
THE DARKWATER CURRENTS

The Wheel of Magic

THE WHEEL OF MAGIC

The Wheel of Magic is made up of a hub, six spokes, and a rim.

Hub: The simplest form of magic that only requires movement of energy to manipulate things. It manifests during adolescence, but fades if not developed.

Spokes: Once a progeny earns their starlock during their Awakening, they can progress in developing their magic from the hub out to a spoke. There are three sets of spokes (somatic, noetic, pneumatic) each with a constructive and destructive side. Typically progenies develop a specific skill along one spoke, which they can sometimes mirror on the opposite (constructive or destructive) side.

Rim: Advanced progenies can develop additional skills along their spoke, but the most advanced develop skills along a second neighboring spoke. This then gives them access to the elemental magic found on the rim between their two developed spokes. Rim magic can also be accessed through blood magic.

Somatic: Progenies who adjust the body (heal, harm, disguise, etc)

Noetic: Progenies who tune into the mind (thoughts, memories, emotions etc)

Pneumatic: Progenies who sift through the soul (motives, past, future, etc)

For other terms please see glossary in back of book.

BLOOD OF THE STARS

CHAPTER 1

AELIANA HELD her breath as she stood on the threshold of the Stargazer's gate. It was the third place she'd tried that week—the thirteenth that month. She was running out of Stargazers.

A priest stood before her, guarding the gate as if the property held boundless treasures. Instead, it contained a modest stone tower and a freshly tilled garden, just enough for two servants of the Stars. He stared at Aeliana, his bushy white eyebrows furrowing in thought.

"A golden arrow?" he asked.

"It would fit in your palm," she said. "It's meant for decoration, not as a weapon."

He shook his head. "Can't say I've ever seen one. Not since I've been here."

Aeliana bit her lip, and the old man's frown shifted to a fatherly smile.

"I've only been here thirty years, though. I could be wrong." He patted her shoulder. "Come in from the cold. Just because the Stars aren't out doesn't mean we can't pray over what ails you. The Stars are more likely to help than an old arrow."

She tried to refuse, but he tugged on her arm, drawing her into the sanctuary of the tower. Stone walls interspersed with narrow windows rose high to reveal a small opening at the tower's zenith. At night, it would reveal the dance of the Stars, and worshippers would come to bow and pray, but for now, it showed blue sky and the edge of the Sun.

"So many priests and priestesses put stock in old artifacts," the priest mumbled. "Too much stock. They're objects, nothing more. Here is where you can find comfort and aid."

He gestured at the dirt floor, and Aeliana reluctantly kneeled.

She wasn't opposed to the faith. She'd spent a fair amount of her youth in Stargazers because her guardians had no intention of raising her. Back then, she'd thought Arvid and Vera were lazy. She hadn't realized they'd been biding their time, waiting for her to become useful. In the meantime, she'd grown to love the priests and priestesses who'd guided her, or really saved her, from the darkness her guardians sought. Those years of Arvid and Vera's neglect had been peaceful compared to the last four years.

"Sometimes I find my daytime worship even more restful without all the crowds," the priest continued, half grunting as he kneeled beside her. "There's something magical about it."

Aeliana choked back a bitter laugh. If he only knew.

They both bent their heads, Aeliana's wavy bronze locks wrapping around her like a blanket from head to elbow. The Sun warmed her skin even through the windows and her thin blue dress, its power flooding her blood, though she wished it wouldn't.

Despite her agitation, the priest's murmurs left her sleepy, and soon she sensed the Sun's warmth flowing not just through her, but also out of her.

Aeliana peeked between her lashes. Green shoots poked through the hard earth. White petals unfolded from a fresh stem by her knee, far too early for the long winter and far too fast. She swept her skirt over them, then squeezed her eyes shut again, as if she could hide the involuntary magic not just from the priest but also from herself.

After several long moments, the priest rose. When his back was turned, Aeliana reached under her skirt, plucking the half-dozen daisies that had grown around her, eager to dispose of the evidence of her wrongness.

"Oh!" The old man turned.

Aeliana shoved the bouquet behind her back.

"You might wish to try Gahldric Valley's Stargazer," he said. "I hear they've received dozens of shipments of artifacts. So many Stargazers in the eastern provinces are closing down. Not enough worshipers." His eyes grew troubled, even though he still offered her a small smile.

She gave a half curtsy, careful not to reveal the flowers, and backed up toward the open door. "Thank you, Father. May the Stars bless you for your guidance."

She slipped through the doorway before he could keep her longer, then tossed the daisies behind a cluster of wintergreen bushes. It would have been bad enough for the priest to discover her magic, but it would be even worse if Arvid and Vera discovered she'd used magic without them. Not that Aeliana had any control over it.

She raced to the nearby woods, ducking between pine trees and around the remaining patches of snow. Under the cover of the trees, she was no longer warmed by the Sun, and she rubbed the goose-bumps forming under her thin sleeves.

She was careful to retrace the miles back to where she'd camped the night before with her guardians. For the millionth time, her mind and body warred over whether to return. Aeliana could continue the search on her own and use the golden arrow to cross the barrier back to Vendaras, the land where half-lights like her lived. Descendants of humans and Stars with starblood in their veins. People with magic. She'd leave behind Lorvandas and its fragile humans and be rid of her guardians once and for all.

But they would keep searching too. What if they found it first?

She wasn't even sure she could escape them. Supposedly, they'd saved her as a child from the witch burning that had taken her parents, but they'd told too many lies for her to believe that. They treated her more like a prisoner. Every time she'd tried running, she always ended up right back with them. Sometimes they tracked her, but more often, she returned. They needed the energy in her blood to do their magic, but Aeliana needed them to pull the energy out before it tore her apart, or worse.

She tripped over a root and caught herself on the sharp branch of a tree, the cut across her palm bringing fresh pain, followed by a hint of relief. The scent of iron met her nose, and she shook away the desire to examine the wound, to squeeze out more blood for more relief. As the energy built in her blood, it was like steam rising to fill a room. Releasing it would be like lancing a boil. The pain would be worth it.

But that was Arvid and Vera's way, not hers.

She tore off the hem of her skirt, wrapping it tight to cover the wound and stem the flow. Her hands trembled with the effort, more from the mental control it required to staunch the flow of energy than any physical pain. She sat for a moment, closing her eyes and counting out ten shaky breaths.

Accidentally growing daisies was one thing. Her blood was fairly harmless when contained in her body. But once the blood was removed? She shuddered. Her guardians had used it for unspeakable things. And when she'd tried running, she'd unwittingly done far worse.

"What are you doing?"

Aeliana started at the sharp voice, the familiar tone filling her with hatred. She tucked her injured hand behind her back as she turned to face Vera, who stood several feet away, arms crossed over her ample chest.

"We've been waiting all morning. It shouldn't take that long to check one measly Stargazer." The older woman grunted as she turned her stout frame back toward their camp.

Aeliana bit back her retort. They'd slept within two miles of each of the Stargazers her guardians had checked, but Aeliana's had been twice that distance. She slowed her pace to match Vera's shorter legs.

"Well, did you find anything?" Vera asked.

"Nothing," Aeliana said, hiding her smile. If Vera had to ask, that meant they hadn't found it either. "I was hoping to try Gahldric Valley next."

Vera squinted up at her. "Why's that?"

They topped a small hill, and Arvid came into view, sprawled out on a blanket in the middle of a clearing. His eyes remained closed, a half-eaten loaf leaving a trail of crumbs from his hand, across his belly, and up to his beard.

"It's not too far. Seems logical," Aeliana lied, then mentally begged the Stars for forgiveness.

They crossed the clearing until Vera could kick at Arvid's girth. "Get up."

The old man jolted awake, pawing at the crumbs. "What is it?"

"Aeliana wants to go to Gahldric Valley." The way Vera said it made Aeliana tense. "Said it 'seems logical.'"

"She did?" He stood, towering over both women, his eyes narrowed.

Her guardians were opposites when it came to height and girth, but they shared enough other features—a rounded nose, pale blue eyes, and black hair lined with grey—that Aeliana suspected they were siblings. After being stuck with them for fourteen years, she knew better than to ask.

"No other reason?" he asked.

Aeliana shook her head, even though she knew it was the wrong answer. It was too late to back out now.

"Don't lie." Arvid slapped her across the face, jolting her head back.

Her eyes stung with tears, and her cheek was like fire when she touched it. Before she could respond, he grabbed her hand, holding it out palm up to reveal her torn hem and hastily tied bandage.

"What's this?"

"A cut," she whispered.

"You used your blood?" His face took on a red hue, and he squeezed her hand tighter.

Aeliana winced. "No. You know I don't know how."

He yanked off the fabric, stretched at the edges of the wound until it reopened, then pressed his thumb over it, drawing energy from her blood and into himself. He stood straighter and rolled his neck, bouncing from one foot to the other like a young man ready to enter a street fight.

That same sense of relief flooded through Aeliana as the pressure inside her lessened, and she hated herself for it.

Arvid dropped her hand and sucked in a long breath through his nose, closing his eyes. "We leave for Gahldric Valley now. Seems we found similar leads."

Night fell as they approached the valley. Buildings fanned out as far as the eye could see. Light flickered to life like fireflies as home after home lit their torches. The path they traveled split, one way heading east and winding down into the valley toward the city. The other forked west, extending around the far side of the city's Stargazer to eventually meet up with the main traveling road.

They took the path to the west, heading toward the Stargazer, which stood on the edge of the hill overlooking the city in the valley. The path that led through its gates was already occupied by worshipers trickling in. Aeliana drank in the sight of the simple stone buildings. Several small chambers held what was likely the quarters of the current priests and priestesses and their few servants. Moss and ivy climbed up the walls, filling the dead nooks and crannies with life.

The holy quarters surrounded the grandest building of all—the Stargazer itself, its roof left open to provide worshipers a constant view of the heavens. It towered over the grounds, higher than four of the buildings stacked together. Windows the height of a man broke up the stone exterior all the way to its apex, and Aeliana craned her neck to take in their stained glass. Candlelight from within lit up the displays depicting dancing Stars, a mix of their lithe human forms and their distant sparkling existence in the sky.

Small clusters of people crowded the garden, which met up with groves of trees extending far beyond the land directly surrounding the buildings. Somewhere past the trees, out of sight, the walls of the property stretched out to encompass and protect the Stargazer.

Clouds threatened rain in the distance, but for now, the Stars were out. She leaned farther back to take in the Stars' dance, their movement and brightness distinguishing them from the plain static stars they darted between. They shot through the sky, spinning in patterns that held a rhythm desperate for a melody.

"Move it," Arvid muttered, pulling her past the Stargazer.

"But I thought—"

"Not yet," Vera said.

They kept to the dirt path that wound west of the property. Eventually, they stopped to settle against the boundary wall between two large oak trees, the roots rising like a nest of snakes.

They waited for what felt like hours, the task of walking so much in one day taking a toll on Aeliana. Her eyelids drooped, and her head listed to the left. Hardly anyone came from this direction, but each time someone did, Arvid and Vera tensed, studying the stranger before leaning against the wall once more.

As the clouds rolled in and blocked their view of the Stars, they all donned cloaks. The wall did little to protect them from the rain, and Aeliana wasn't about to huddle with her guardians for body warmth.

Finally, a girl approached, maybe a year or two younger than Aeliana's seventeen years. Arvid and Vera stood, pulling Aeliana to her feet with them. The girl hesitated, her eyes widening as she took in three strangers blocking her path. Without warning, Arvid snatched Aeliana's hand and took a knife to her palm, reopening and extending her wound.

The girl screamed, but Aeliana only sucked in a breath, too shocked to notice the pain, then too overwhelmed by the mix of fear and euphoria that always came with a larger loss of blood. It pooled in Arvid's hands and with it, her magic—magic Arvid would harness.

Aeliana's mind dimly registered that the girl's scream had cut off, blocked by Vera's hand. Not that anyone was out here to hear her anyway.

"No," Aeliana murmured, her focus hazy with the internal shift. She tried pulling her hand from Arvid's grasp, but he tightened his fingers around her.

"You want to get back home, don't you?" Vera dragged the girl closer. "Be with your own kind?"

Aeliana's vision swam, and she reached for a branch from one of the oak trees to steady herself. "Not… not like this."

Arvid scoffed. "You think these humans matter? The Stars separated them from us for a reason."

He stepped away from Aeliana, bringing himself closer to Vera and the girl.

The whites of the girl's eyes flashed in the moonlight as she screamed against Vera's hand and thrashed to get out of the older woman's grip.

"We're human too," Aeliana said.

Or she thought she did. Her words came back to her muffled. Maybe she'd only said them in her mind. She let go of the tree and instinctively pressed against her palm to staunch the flow of blood. Blinking rapidly, she tried catching up with Arvid's intentions.

When he reached a bloody hand toward the girl's throat, Aeliana lunged for his back, pawing at his arm to pull him away. His arm was like a rock, fueled by her blood, and her efforts were like clawing through sludge. In moments, the girl went limp in Vera's arms, eyes just as wide but absent of life.

Arvid shrugged Aeliana off with a glare. "Be grateful I kept it painless. Next time you interfere, I won't be so kind."

Aeliana's shock pulled her from her stupor as they lowered the girl to the ground. Rain splattered on the still, pale face, tears twinkling in the moonlight. Arvid placed bloody hands on the tree roots, which came to life, slithering around the girl like the snakes they'd resembled. They wrapped around the body and drew it down into the rain-soaked earth. Despite the hard, icy ground, the body was buried in moments, the leather satchel the girl had been holding the only proof of her existence.

Aeliana wanted to ask why, but even if they answered her, she couldn't trust it to be the truth.

Arvid ran his thumb over her right palm, healing her wound with her magic. A faint pink scar remained, one of many on her palms. Arvid frowned, using his cloak to wipe away the smudges of blood that remained on her skin. She jerked her palm away.

"You need to look presentable." He nodded toward the Stargazer.

Aeliana scratched at her scar, then ran her thumb across the tear-shaped patch of skin that was raised and deep red on her left palm. It was more like her other scars than the permanent ink she'd seen others use for tattoos. They'd never cut over that mark, and she'd had it as long as she could remember.

A cold rush of blackness swept across her arm, even through her cloak. She shuddered, wrapping the fabric more tightly around her, glancing around for the shadows that might be the dark spirits drawn to her tainted blood. Arvid and Vera would welcome them like old friends, which was reason enough to hate them. She begged the Stars to protect her, to keep the dark spirits from fusing with her guardians. She couldn't bear another night of that.

Vera rifled through the girl's bag, pulling out a set of papers. "Looks like you're Celeste now." She held the papers and the bag out to Aeliana. "Celeste, the future priestess-in-training."

Understanding dawned, and Aeliana swallowed hard. "You knew she was coming. You planned this."

It wasn't the first time her guardians had killed using her blood. But it was the first time they'd done it for her. Her stomach churned, the broth she'd had earlier threatening to surface.

"You get in, you find the golden arrow, and you get out," Arvid said.

Aeliana shook her head and crossed her arms. "They would have let us in. They're letting everyone in. You didn't have to—"

Arvid grabbed her arm, making her wince. "You think they would have let us rifle through their artifacts? No. This is the fastest way. You'll have access to everything now. The sooner you bring us the golden arrow, the sooner we can take you home and leave all your precious humans alone. Don't waste the girl's sacrifice."

He snatched the bag and papers from Vera before shoving them into Aeliana's arms, forcing her to take a step back. She glared at him, hating the way he put the blame on her shoulders, the way it even felt right. He'd used Aeliana's blood—her magic. The reminder stung, but it also gave her hope. He needed her blood. He needed her magic.

She slung the leather bag over her bony shoulder and folded the papers, tucking them inside her sleeve to keep them from getting too wet. She gripped the strap against her cloak, hoping her guardians wouldn't notice how her hands shook. "I'll find the golden arrow."

"The one that hums at your touch," Vera reminded her.

"And then we'll take you home," Arvid said. "We're giving you two weeks to do this your way, but if you haven't found it by then, we do things our way." He didn't have to explain how many would suffer in that scenario. By then, without any bloodletting, the Sun would have filled her blood with energy ten times over. She'd be so bloated with her magic, releasing its valve would create a deadly geyser.

Aeliana clenched her jaw and nodded, turning her back on them.

She would find the arrow, and she would take it home to Vendaras without them.

She prayed to the Stars for strength. Celeste never should have been killed, but Arvid and Vera were right about one thing: Aeliana wouldn't waste the girl's sacrifice.

CHAPTER 2

THREE HOURS INTO THE PARTY, Gaeren eyed a fork near his parents' anniversary cake, weighing the risks and benefits of stabbing himself. A significant enough injury could get him removed from the obnoxious crowds filling the palace rooms, but it would be hard to make it look like an accident.

Besides, he hadn't found his sister yet. If Enla didn't see him, he wouldn't get credit for attending. And he needed credit before he could leave. He glanced out a window, eyeing the angle of the moon. He was running out of time.

Dozens of familiar faces, plus many others he didn't recognize, swam before him, all decked out in their finest suits and dresses as they mingled in the main hall. Enla had spared no expense. Lanterns lined the hall, making the extravagant floor-to-ceiling windows gleam like obsidian, reflecting and doubling the already full room. Calla lilies, native to their swamps, were placed strategically throughout the room. Chrysanthemums, symbolic of loyalty and honesty, lay nestled in the dual purple vases Gaeren had fetched all the way from Andel. Fish, fruit, cheese, and several delicacies that had likely given their cook grey hairs filled the tables. More lanterns floated through the room, a display of both power and opulence, highlighting the royal family's abundant access to magic—their blessing from the Sun.

Gaeren closed his eyes, blocking out the flashy fabrics competing for attention. The buzz of nobles attempting to outdo one another put him on edge, so when he opened his eyes again, he focused on the door his sister should walk through.

Lenda pressed up against him, wrapping a possessive hand around his arm.

Gaeren held his breath against her noxious perfume, but his attention veered from the doorway, lingering on her blonde ringlets and red lips. He scratched at the bond mark on his left palm as if he could pick it off and break the connection that had been forcing them together since childhood. One of the many curses of royalty.

"Hardly anyone is dancing," she said. "And the desserts are melting. Do you see how awful they look?" She peered around a noble-woman to examine the contents of a table and shuddered.

"I'm sure they're still delicious. There's chocolate in them." He reached over and grabbed a piece of candy, popping it in his mouth. He hummed his satisfaction. "See, it's perfect."

Lenda didn't even pay attention as she scanned the crowd, offering judgmental frowns for the gowns she didn't like. "It's a wonder everyone's still here when your parents haven't even shown up."

"You're welcome to go home if you'd like," he offered.

She stuck out her lower lip. "You know that's not what I meant."

"No," Gaeren agreed. "But what you really meant sounded a bit judgmental of the king and queen, so…"

Her face blanched.

"I just—I wish they'd come, that's all." She stood on tiptoe, craning her neck to see the dais at the edge of the main hall. "Oh, Enla's dress is to die for."

Lenda's voice grated on his nerves, even as another part of him was drawn to it. He followed her gaze across the dancing guests until he found his sister. She'd finally arrived and was, in fact, wearing a stunning gold gown, symbolic of the crown she would one day inherit from their father.

Her bondmate guided her up to the platform, where they sat, barely touching, to watch the remainder of the event. Croft's stiff black hair, rigid limbs, and hovering attention gave him more of a guard's appearance than a bondmate's—unlike Enla, whose grace and beauty practically embodied a glowing Star.

Enla and Gaeren shared their father's Sun-kissed brown hair. Gaeren kept his tucked away under his ridiculous hat, but her chin-length strands were intricately braided away from her face. It left the heart-shaped charm of her starlock exposed where it dangled across her forehead on a delicate chain.

Gaeren frowned, wishing she kept the source of her power tucked out of sight.

Only two other chairs graced the dais, confirming that Enla didn't expect him to fulfill any hosting duties. He sighed in relief.

Enla and Croft scanned the haughty nobles lining the room as if looking for someone worth their attention. Really, they waited for the King and Queen of Elanesse to arrive for their own party. Everyone did.

Gaeren supposed fifty years of bonding was a big deal, but he and Lenda had been bonded for twenty years already, since he was a toddler, and he didn't think that was anything worth celebrating.

Gaeren raised a hand, waving it like a ridiculous child over the heads of the people. Several around him covered their mouths and whispered, but along with the gossip, his efforts had the desired effect: Enla's gaze flicked to his.

"Isn't it gorgeous?" Lenda tried again. "I love how it brings out the highlights in her braids."

Gaeren scanned his sister's dress once more, then hummed his agreement with Lenda as Enla's eyes narrowed in his direction. Enla was a pneumatic progeny, gifted with the ability to sift through a soul's future, but as his sister, she also had the uncanny ability to read his every emotion. He forced a grin and blew her a kiss, stepping closer to Lenda.

Enla hesitated, clearly warring between approval of his presence with Lenda and irritation with his antics. Eventually, she nodded, and her gaze moved on.

Now that she'd seen him in attendance, his duty had been fulfilled.

Gaeren slipped his arm out from Lenda's grip, placing his hand on the small of her back. He bent close to her ear. "Why don't I go get you a drink?"

She preened under his attention.

The bond mark on his palm twinged at the lie, but as usual, it never manifested into actual guilt. He hadn't chosen this bond any more than he'd chosen to be born into the royal family, and yet he'd been saddled with the titles of bondmate and prince. He slipped through the crowds of people all eager to get a glimpse of the king and queen, who had made fewer public appearances over the last several moons.

No one cared about the wayward prince who spent more time at sea than in the palace, which made it that much easier for him to escape.

Instead of making his way out the back to the gardens, where all the guards would see him, he snuck through a servants' door, stopping to wrap up half a dozen rolls and pastries in a napkin. He wound through the narrow corridors until he reached a wider public hall far from the festivities, where he climbed the stone stairs to his chambers.

With everyone down in the main hall, it was eerily quiet, and Gaeren was tempted to stop and breathe in the silence. But he was already late. He slipped through his rooms, tossing his pompous overcoat and hat on the bed and shaking his hair loose around his ears.

He opened the door to his balcony just enough to slide through with his stash of food. The moon was blocked by clouds, so he slipped his legs over the railing and found the lattice by memory. When his boots hit the dirt, he raced past the statue of the first Queen of Elanesse in the gardens, giving her his customary mocking bow. Then he slipped through a gap in a hedge, which he'd made several years before. The stables loomed before Gaeren, but instead of skirting them, he ran to the barn door, where he knocked three times, paused, then knocked again.

Furtive whispers came from the other side, making him grin. The door slipped open just enough for him to shove the napkin full of food through for the stableboys on the other side.

One green eye showed through the slit. "Thank you, Master Gaeren."

"That's Captain Elanesse to you, Erech," he said. "Won't be long before I expect you on *Starspeed* as my cabin boy."

"Yes, sir—I mean, Captain Elanesse." The boy choked on a laugh as he slid the door shut once more.

When Enla had found out he brought the stableboys extra food, she'd increased their wages. Then the boys said that meant they could send more money to their families, so he kept bringing the food. Next time he got caught, she'd probably make him start a donation program instead. It wasn't a bad idea for the future, when he was stuck in Elanesse all the time.

Beyond the stables, Gaeren was mostly free, but still, he had to be cautious. It wouldn't do for a couple's evening stroll to reveal the prince sneaking out for black market trade.

He slipped across a creek and deeper into the woods, taking random turns so as not to form a trail. Slipping his dagger from his belt, he entered the wetlands, wrinkling his nose at the rotten swamp stench. With the mangroves' canopy and the dark night, it was nearly impossible to see. He cocked his head as he drew energy from his blood to tune in to his surroundings. Just because there weren't usually people around didn't mean there wouldn't be hippos or crocodiles. As a noetic progeny, he could tune in to the mind, or more specifically, the memories of a mind, even one that had come and gone, leaving traces of their recent memories behind.

The heat of his silver tear-shaped starlock warmed against the skin beneath his shirt, where it hung from a leather cord. Reassuringly close to his heart. Like all progenies, he'd earned the small charm that housed a lock of a Star's hair during his Awakening, and now it heightened the power already flowing in his blood.

Small pinpricks of memories stood out between mangroves as if discordant notes settled into harmony in the spaces recently inhabited by creatures. One in particular was brighter and hotter than the rest— the memories not just remnants left behind, but memories from an active mind.

As he'd hoped, there was one man out here, if that was what Riveran could still be called.

Gaeren let out a low whistle. When Riveran returned his signal,

Gaeren couldn't help grinning as he picked up his pace, heedless of the water soaking through his boots and pants. He didn't trust the traitor any more than the hippos he sensed grazing a hundred yards to the west, but if Riveran was here, that meant he'd found what Gaeren needed.

"I didn't think it'd really be you." Riveran's timbre brought a rush of memories flooding through Gaeren's mind.

Gaeren paused, shin-deep in water reeking of sulfur, and closed his eyes, involuntarily filtering through his memories of the other man. Swimming in the lake as boys, hunting baby winex together, giving and receiving bloody noses in their first childhood fight. The nostalgia was ten times stronger than when his progeny mentors made him tune in to someone else's memories, because these memories came mixed with pain. His nose even twinged where it was still bent from being broken.

At one time, he and Riveran had been meant to become brothers.

The bright spots in his childhood shifted to later memories, marred by the truth of Riveran's betrayal. Enla's tears, the burn on her palm, the desire for revenge. It had only been two years since they'd severed ties. And yet it felt like ages.

"I figured you wouldn't show up for anyone else." Gaeren stepped out of the shadows so the little light from the moon could reveal his minimal weaponry. He lowered his dagger to a semi-dry stump, then raised his empty palms.

Riveran eased out from behind a mangrove, weaving between the tangled roots like a dance. Even though his head was nearly shaved, Riveran's dark beard reached the middle of his chest. Gullet, his ever-present hawk, rested on the leather trim of his shoulder. The bird's beady eyes watched Gaeren with even more distrust than Riveran.

"You're right. I wouldn't have." Riveran's last step off the roots brought them eye level, a strange sensation since Gaeren usually towered over everyone else.

"Did you bring the book?" Gaeren asked.

"I'd heard you'd taken to treasure hunting since I'd left. Did you grow into your family's greed?" Riveran's sneer was punctuated by hard lines and fresh scars on weathered skin. He'd traded his easy life among the nobility for a hard one, aging him far faster than Gaeren. Or maybe he looked like he'd been to the Deep and back because he'd cheated on Enla, been stripped of his starlock, and fathered a child with his new bondmate.

Gaeren bristled at the accusations coming from his former friend but didn't bother correcting them.

"Or maybe you're still looking for the girl." Riveran's face softened. "After all these years."

Gaeren pursed his lips. "Do you have it or not?"

Riveran's eyes narrowed, but he didn't answer right away.

Riveran was the only person Gaeren had told about Daisy. He hadn't even told Enla, mostly so she wouldn't search for the girl in his future. He wouldn't be able to accept it if she wasn't present in any possible paths.

When Gaeren was eight years old, his mother had sent him to a Sungazer on the eastern shore for his dedication year. The priestess watching over him had been well loved by the people, but more importantly, kind. While living in her home, Gaeren had sworn to protect Aeliana, the priestess' barely weaned daughter, whose love of daisies had sealed her nickname.

Daisy had been Gaeren's constant companion that year—until she'd been taken by a bright light.

Riveran pulled a small volume out from his leather satchel. Gullet's brown and white wings flapped as he leaned over to peck at it, but Riveran kept the book out of the bird's reach. Gaeren forced his hands to remain relaxed at his sides, even though he itched to grab it out of Riveran's grasp.

Riveran frowned at the book. "You think she was taken across the barrier, don't you? To one of the other lands? That's why you're looking for information about the Great Divide."

Gaeren stiffened, not wanting to rehash his plans with an enemy. Even if he was the only one who might understand.

"The bright light you saw when she disappeared," Riveran said. "You think it was from a starbridge?"

Gaeren's silence was as equally condemning as his answer, but he stubbornly kept his mouth shut. What did it matter if Riveran knew his plans?

"The Sun split our land for a reason," Riveran continued. "Even if the starbridges are real—even if people and places exist across the barriers, it's not likely a child could survive what you witnessed. You might not like the answers you get on the other side of the barrier."

Gaeren tried not to care what Riveran thought, but part of him felt hope that his old friend took his quest seriously. Most people didn't even believe the starbridges existed. They were the only objects that could supposedly cross the barriers. Legends of their existence had been passed down orally, growing until no one knew if they'd ever been real in the first place. Feathers that turned a man into a bird so he could fly over the barriers. Scales that turned a man into a fish to swim under the barriers. Entire contraptions that housed a person and took them to another land. Tiny objects the size of a button that served as a conduit to a matching object in the other lands, with instantaneous transport.

But every known story of starbridges included mention of a bright light. It was the only way Gaeren could explain what he'd seen so many years ago. So far, every lead had had a dead end, but he'd hoped this book could change things.

Riveran rubbed the back of his head, eyes hard. "Fine. Keep your silence. The book won't tell you anything you don't already know, anyway."

Gaeren raised his brows. "Then you won't mind lowering your exorbitant price."

"On the contrary. I've raised it. On top of the regular risks I took to procure the book, you picked a location rife with death traps."

"If a croc found you, it would be more merciful than how I've envisioned your death." Gaeren's words finally broke through Riveran's confident demeanor, but he wasn't sure if the other man's pained expression was from guilt or fear.

Gullet squawked in the awkward silence, and they both flinched.

After haggling over the price, Riveran finally passed the book off to Gaeren, who counted out and tossed a bag of coin at his former friend.

The clink of silver felt like the close of their conversation, so Gaeren turned on his heel.

"How is Enla?"

The soft question made Gaeren pause, heat billowing through his body. A cloud of hatred rose around him like steam releasing from Mt. Vescano when it threatened to erupt. He didn't bother turning around to respond. "If I ever hear her name leave your lips again, it will be the last word you speak."

CHAPTER 3

Instead of heading back to the dry lands, Gaeren grabbed his dagger and traveled northwest until he reached an especially tight grove of trees. He squeezed through a narrow opening, then climbed higher until he reached a hole in the canopy that let in the fresh air for his hideout.

The perilous deck he'd crafted a few years ago during summer's peak was comprised of twelve boards. It held a small table and chair with a dozen books, a pillow and blanket, and a few other bare necessities for him to escape. Enla would be hurt if she knew he considered this home. She worked harder to make their parents' palace a home for Gaeren than she did for her new bondmate, which made no sense since she and Croft were next in line to rule. The palace was their future home, not Gaeren's. Thank the Sun.

He settled in a hammock made from discarded fishing nets and examined his newest book, *The Sins of the Stars*, which was softly lit by the light of the moon. As he rocked back and forth, he flipped through the pages, studying the drawings. The maps and art revealed nothing new, so he started back at the beginning to read the words.

It detailed the Great Divide, an event that had occurred over a thousand years ago when the single continent of Rhystahn had been divided into five, separated by water and shimmering walls. Most retellings defined it as a punishment from the Sun, but this one had a different take, marking the event as a solution sought by a handful of Stars for the people's tendency toward intolerance and oppression. The unusual intervention had been led by a Star named Sheen, a name Gaeren had never seen anywhere else in holy literature.

Gaeren snorted. If all that were true, the rebellious Stars had fixed nothing. Intolerance and oppression had carried on amongst the Vendarans just fine. Either way, the book lacked the specifics he needed. There was no mention of how exactly the barriers were formed—or how they could be removed.

There was also no mention of the fabled starbridges.

Few people cared about the starbridges or other lands now that they were so far out of reach. Since people hadn't been spotted across the barriers for centuries, the Vendarans were content to believe they were the only ones left. But Gaeren believed the starbridges—and full-blooded humans—still existed. His entire crew had turned last year's sighting into a ghost story, but he held on to the truth. He'd seen a ship full of humans across the barrier. If people still lived in the other lands, Daisy could still be alive, just out of reach.

He had to hold on to that truth. It was his last hope of finding her.

He frowned as he reached the end of the book with no new information, and then he slammed the book shut. The holy Stars danced above, their joy as they flitted amongst the static stars mocking his frustration.

"Where are you, Daisy?" he murmured.

He turned to the beginning of the book for one last scan, and his eyes fell on handwritten notes on the inside cover. He squinted, pulling the scrawl closer, and saw a tiny arrow with the phrase "Lorvandas - Bamboo Island?" followed by an oval and triangle with the question "Sayhla?" A miniature sword or knife with the word "Falls" and a circle with "Ahmranas?" completed the odd collection of words and images.

He frowned and tossed the book on his table. A few birds flew from the nearest trees, startled by the noise. When Gaeren stilled, his senses tuned in to something he'd missed when he'd been distracted by the book. Someone had been here today. The books he'd left scattered on the desk now had an order to them, a purpose. Traces of magic lingered in stronger ways than those left by the monkeys and birds he often shooed away.

He drew energy from his blood, sending it through the swamp, waiting for it to tune in to the memories of whoever had been here before, and looking for the magic's source. Strangely, no memories appeared, as if the person had known his spoke on the Wheel of Magic and purposely blocked him. He crept down from his hideout, warily leaping from root to root.

Instead of tuning in with his noetic spoke, he stuck to the basics, the hub of the Wheel of Magic, and drew more energy out from his blood to alter his strength and agility to easily maneuver through the mangrove trees. He could practically hear his progeny mentors lecturing him about not draining his power source during the night. *A starlock only takes one so far, and the Stars are just as dependent on the Sun as we are.*

As he drew closer to the edge of the swamp, where the wetlands met the royal grounds, the traces of magic dimmed, becoming like trails of stardust. He concentrated so hard on the residue as he swung around a mangrove that he nearly smacked into a pale gold blur of gauze before realizing it was Enla. He caught a branch with his right hand but still had to bring his left around Enla to steady them both instead of knocking her over.

Enla sucked in a breath, then patted her short hair, the tiny walnut braids lining her head still perfectly in place.

"Mother and Father noticed your absence. You couldn't wait to go on your silly adventures until after they turned in for the night?" Her eyes narrowed, and the silver starlock shifted a fraction on her forehead, the heart leaning to the left. She shoved his arm away and took a delicate step back, her effort wasted since her slippers and gown were already soaked with mud. She lifted a hand to her nose, likely trying to block out the sulfurous stench. "What are you doing out here, anyway?"

"Nothing the future queen would approve of." He grinned and glanced behind her, tuning in for any guards. She'd come alone. "How did you find me?"

Guilt replaced anger on her face, making him wary.

"We talked about boundaries, Enla. I don't tune in to your memories and you don't sift my soul's future."

"Father made me." She spat the words out, her anger back full force. "You're lucky I told him you snuck off with Lenda. Even luckier that she was willing to cover for you after you abandoned her at the party."

He rubbed the dark scar on his palm when it twinged.

"It's a wonder Father believed me. You've completely ignored her since your childhood ceremony." Enla's dry tone used to make him grin, but now it meant she'd lost her temper enough to slip out of her pretentious royal act.

Gaeren stepped past her, over mangrove roots, working his way toward drier ground that would lead them back to the palace. "You're one to talk. It's not like you and Croft have become best friends."

"Have you even set a date for your wedding?" Her breath hitched as though his pace was too fast, but her words only made him march faster.

"Why rush it? Unlike you, I don't need to produce an heir." He gave her a pointed look over his shoulder.

"What's more important than sealing a bond? An expedition to Lovers' Falls?"

He stopped short, making her crash into him. She swore, shoving him harder, as if he'd been the one to bump into her.

"You saw my request?" He turned to face her, all irritation forgotten. He dropped to his knees, heedless of the mud soaking through his trousers. He grabbed her hands and channeled his best begging face from their childhood. "Please promise you'll approve it. Please?"

"Oh, stop." She pulled her hands away, but her lips bloomed into a smile. She'd never been able to resist his adventurous requests when they were little.

He stood. "You won't regret it, Enla."

He bent forward to kiss her cheek, but she turned away, the moon giving just enough light to reveal her face tight with regret. "You know I can't approve it."

"An expedition to Lovers' Falls could serve us twofold," he pressed. "We could ask the sprites for support. Even if they say no, I can stop in Valorian on the way there or back. I heard talk of Wyndrens that I want to check out." He didn't really care about rumors of their family's oldest enemy, but Enla might. Supposedly, generations back, the Wyndren family had come from a distant cousin who never quite gave up what he thought was his right to the throne.

She batted his words away with her hands. "There are no more Wyndrens. Grandfather took care of them fifty years ago."

Gaeren cocked his head. "Isn't it my job to figure that out? Every three generations, the line seems to pop up again, pushing us off the throne. We're due for some usurpers."

Enla gave him a scathing look. "You can send out hired investigators. No need for you to sail there yourself. Besides, the sprites are just as likely to curse us as they are to aid us." Enla folded her arms across her chest. "They're too unpredictable. I'd much rather you rode inland to Islara. They've been threatening to defect with the Recreants in the southern provinces for the last year."

"I have no interest in going on some diplomatic mission, especially on land." Gaeren grimaced. "I'm also the worst person to send on a mission like that. I'm more likely to widen whatever rift has formed between us."

"Sailing as far south as Valorian and trekking to Lovers' Falls would take weeks. I need you back here as my throne warden."

This time, Gaeren looked away. He couldn't hold her gaze when she assumed his mission centered on him helping her uphold her place on the throne. Throne warden was yet one more title he'd been given without being asked. Defending Enla would always be second nature, but it wasn't the same as protecting the throne.

He couldn't tell her those things. And he definitely couldn't tell her why he really wanted to go to the sprites. Even if Enla knew about Daisy, she wouldn't approve of him asking the sprites to help him find a girl.

He closed his eyes, recalling the feel of her chubby little arms around his neck, the tiny crown of daisy chains in her hair. An innocent soul he'd sworn—and failed—to protect.

Someday, his title of throne warden would become official, but how could he protect the queen of his nation if he couldn't protect one little girl? The last thing he wanted to do was to abandon his search for Daisy, and that was exactly what he'd have to do if he settled in Elanesse as throne warden.

Before he could come up with a decent argument for taking his voyage, a burst of light shot through the night sky. They both paused, their focus swinging left to right to follow the trail of stardust. Gaeren sent an automatic prayer to the Sun on behalf of the progeny who'd either received a starlock or recently died. The sight was both sobering and inspiring, and Gaeren's starlock burned warm against his chest, knocking all the fight out of him.

Enla sighed, placing a hand over her starlock, and she gave him a sheepish smile. Her eyes were a perfect match for their mother's: a blue so deep it could only be caught in certain skies or seas. So were Gaeren's, but that was where the similarities ended. He was tall like their father, his bulk from days at sea the forerunner to the paunch he'd probably inherit from his father, whereas Enla had gained their mother's short and slim frame. His skin, which had always been darker than hers, almost had the warm brown hue of the southern Vendarans after his time at sea, and hers seemed even paler with the additional council meetings these last moons.

It wasn't worth adding to her stress. Not when they'd never come to an agreement anyway.

The croak of frogs and the chirp of crickets were the only sounds in the night as they resumed their walk past the hedge wall and through the side gate. Magnolia and gardenia scents replaced the sulfur lingering in Gaeren's nose, but he still longed for the salty wind of the sea.

The guards nodded at Enla and Gaeren's approach, their darting eyes the only hint at their surprise. Tomorrow, the king and queen would be sure to hear about Enla and Gaeren's excursion sans guards, and Gaeren would likely have extra attendants for the following moon.

"I still expect you up with the Sun's morn to weigh in at the council meeting," Enla said as they took the stairs to the side door.

He made a face, earning him a light tap from her fist against his jaw. A second pair of guards opened the door, giving the siblings another set of curious glances. When the door shut behind them, firelight from the hall sconces lit up Enla's eyes, and they paused where their paths through the palace diverged.

"If you can't learn to love the council," she said, "at least learn to hide your thoughts."

"Father never had to."

They both grinned, and the memory of the king's face turning a deep purple over the council matters he found so trivial sprang to Gaeren's mind. It was the one way he and his father saw eye to eye.

"See you at the Sun's morn," Gaeren promised, the lie tightening his throat as he planted a kiss on the top of Enla's hair.

She headed toward her rooms, seemingly satisfied, even though if she used her pneumatic spoke to sift through the future of his soul, she'd see it wasn't true.

He didn't want to plan the trip to Lovers' Falls behind Enla's back, but he had to go, with or without her permission. It was his best chance at finding Daisy. Which meant tomorrow he'd have to prepare *Starspeed* if he wanted to be on the seas within a quarter moon.

Enla expected him in the council meeting at the Sun's morn, but she was going to be disappointed. He'd be deep in the heart of Elanesse securing crew and cargo long before then.

CHAPTER 4

Aeliana flinched at the greeting. A wrinkled woman in a simple brown robe held out the customary cup of water blessed by the priests and priestesses. The woman's hood remained lowered as she stood in the dry space under the eaves of the outer building. Most of her grey hair formed a simple wreath braid, and the remaining locks nearly reached her knees.

"Yes—and no." Aeliana took the offered cup, trading it for the paperwork falsifying her admission as a priestess-in-training. She drank the water, watching the reaction of the priestess over the rim of the cup. The woman's eyes lit up, her smile creating more wrinkles that somehow softened her face. She scanned the paperwork, her lips moving as she read.

"Celeste?" She lowered the papers. "What a beautiful name. Are you from the southern provinces?"

"Eastern." Who knew where the other girl had been from? But Aeliana's guardians had spent the last five years in the eastern provinces, which meant she could stick closer to the truth when she inevitably had to lie.

The woman clucked her tongue, tucking the papers in the folds of her robe. "So many Stargazers closing down in that region. We get shipments often with artifacts needing a home." The woman placed a hand on Aeliana's back, guiding her farther into the gardens. As the rain ceased, Aeliana pulled back her hood, soaking in the gentle murmur of worshipers and croaking frogs.

"I'm Della, second to Bartholem, this Stargazer's High Priest." The woman leaned in to add wryly, "Who also happens to be my husband."

Aeliana attempted a smile, assuming a real priestess-in-training would find the comment amusing.

Della led Aeliana through a side courtyard, where a dozen doors led to various back entrances for the Stargazer and its connected buildings. The quiet sounds were left behind, replaced by a pure silence that made Aeliana step lighter. The temperature rose instantly as the walls surrounding them provided shelter.

"First, I want to introduce you to Cyrus." Della knocked on the door three times. "He arrived last month. Since we only have room for two trainees, you two will be spending a lot of time together."

The door flew open, making them both jump. The man before them had wide green eyes surrounded by a shocking amount of freckles. Priests and priestesses were known for never taking shears to their hair once they took their vows, but it seemed as if Cyrus had taken his vows at birth. His thick red hair was tied at the nape of his neck, extending well past his elbows.

"Forgive me, Gams." His words rushed together with the awkward crack of a voice recently deepened. "I don't know how I slept past the fifteenth bell. I mean, I know how. I just thought today would be different because I left my window open, which let in all the rain, too. So on top of being late, I have a colossal mess to clean, and you wouldn't believe how much—"

"Cyrus." Della's calm interruption made him clamp his jaw down tight. "We can discuss your tardiness another time."

His entire body slumped with relief. "I'll take an extra shift or do an extra round of—"

"Cyrus."

Aeliana's lip lifted as the young man's face reddened.

"Right, right." He bit his lip as if it was the only way for him to stop talking.

"This is Celeste," Della said.

Aeliana winced at the use of the dead girl's name.

"She's our new priestess-in-training."

Cyrus' eyes widened once more, and before Aeliana could guess what he might do, his hand was clasping hers with a grip that made her wince.

"It's about time you got here." He studied her face with such intensity that Aeliana couldn't hold his gaze.

She tried to imagine what he saw besides her thin frame and pointy chin. Dark brown hair matted to her face and neck. She hadn't seen herself in a mirror for several months, but Arvid and Vera always said her eyes were soulless, waiting to be filled by the dark spirits.

He turned her hand over, examining her arm. "Your skin is so brown, like the tanned leather hides Gamps brings from ranchers. You probably never burn out in the Sun." The last words came out wistfully as he patted his own pale cheeks.

"That's why I thought she might be from the south, but she's from the eastern provinces," Della said.

Aeliana tried smiling as if she hadn't been caught in her first lie. Her olive complexion had nothing to do with the southern or eastern provinces and everything to do with her half-light heritage.

Cyrus' grin widened, turning lopsided. "When Gams said they sent for another, I hoped it would be for a priest, but a priestess is just as good."

"Who is Gams?"

Della laughed. "Cyrus is our youngest grandson. I was meant to be Grams, but he had a speech impediment, and by the time he outgrew it, the name had stuck." As Della spoke, Cyrus' light blush turned a deep shade of red.

"Next, she'll probably tell you how I wet the bed until I was ten," he muttered.

Della's eyebrows rose. "There's no need for me to spill your secrets. You do that just fine on your own."

Cyrus ignored the mild jab. "Gamps said the best friend he ever had was the one he trained with. They ate together, learned rituals together, hunted together—they spent every waking moment side by side." He grinned at Aeliana. "That will be us."

His words stirred a deep longing in her. Before her blood revealed its power, Arvid and Vera had let her spend countless hours in Stargazers across the country. The priests and priestesses she'd met had been distant holy figures, occasionally a temporary parental figure. None of them had offered friendship.

If Cyrus knew who she was—what she was—he might not be so eager.

"Don't scare her off on day one," Della said. "I have a good feeling about her."

Aeliana swallowed hard, tuning out the farewells as Della led her toward another room. She wanted to return Cyrus' excitement, to share Della's confidence, but they spoke in terms of years, and she had only two weeks. The only feeling she had was that her blood would likely be the cause of their deaths.

"I'm sorry we don't have a bigger room for you, but at least it's your own." Della gestured to a straw mattress and shelf, empty except for a stack of bedding. There was space on either side for Aeliana to walk, but little else.

Aeliana held out her bag. "I don't have much, so it's perfect."

"You're welcome to join us for worship, but I understand if you're not ready until tomorrow." Della held back a yawn as she spoke. "Most of us rest between the eleventh and thirteenth bell, just before dinner and the Sun's sleep, which is when the worshipers first start coming. Then we take our full sleep around the twenty-first bell, once the worshipers have gone. Working through the night and sleeping through the day will take some getting used to, but it's for the Stars' glory."

Aeliana smiled, but her heart pounded as she calculated her best opportunities to hunt for the golden arrow. "The journey has been long, so I might rest now if that's all right? Start my duties tomorrow?"

"Of course, dear. There's a washroom in the next building over, shared by all the priestesses. Rest well, and may you always be blessed by the Stars." Della wrapped an arm around Aeliana's shoulders and squeezed her in a side hug.

Aeliana flinched. Her guardians only touched her when they wanted blood.

After Della left, Aeliana unpacked Celeste's few belongings, her nausea intensifying as she placed each one on the shelf. She settled on the mattress, not bothering to change clothes. The small window was too high for anyone to see in, but it allowed her to glimpse the quarter moon among the dancing Stars.

Despite her exhaustion, she didn't sleep well. Visions of the dead girl filled her dreams, the horror of her buried body a mere hundred feet away almost palpable. If she wanted to search for the arrow while the others slept, Aeliana needed to be up before the first bell with the Sun's morn. Her body remained tense, as if falling in too deep of a sleep would make her miss her chance.

When the moon was no longer visible through her window, Aeliana rose, stretching out her anxious muscles. She stood on tiptoe, then gave up and perched on the bed, peeking out the window. The grounds were empty save a single priest. He ambled over to the gate, locked it up, then returned, disappearing through the door of another building like hers. She counted to three hundred without seeing any more movement, then pulled open her door with a soft click of the handle.

She passed the washroom, hoping she could pretend ignorance of its location amidst all the uniform stone buildings. When she glanced back, she squinted at the line of wooden doors. She might actually have trouble remembering which room was hers when she returned.

A bird screeched in a nearby tree, and Aeliana instinctively dropped to her knees. The thump in her chest was almost painful with its ratcheting speed, but silence settled in the courtyard once more. When the frogs resumed their croaks, Aeliana ran to the Stargazer.

It was locked.

Not willing to give up, she started in the outer buildings. After two bells of tearing apart and reassembling the kitchen and pantry, she had nothing to show except dark grey bags under her eyes. As the fourth bell approached, she knew she had to give up or get caught by the others rising for the day. She headed for her room, nearly tripping over her feet, then hesitated before the bedroom doors, bleary-eyed and uncertain. When footsteps sounded behind her, she jumped, but it was only Della rounding the corner to the courtyard.

Della sucked in a startled breath. "Oh, you're up already." She collected herself and smiled. "That's wonderful. We can get started on your first lesson."

"Now? I thought priestly duties happened at night. Didn't you say you usually slept through the morning?"

Della laughed. "Usually we sleep a little later than this, but whoever's up first starts the bread."

"Bread?" Aeliana frowned, her mind fuzzy from lack of sleep.

Della eyed her strangely. "It takes a lot of bread to feed all the servants of the Stars. Plus extra for the beggars who find our gate. There are a dozen men and women living as priests and priestesses under these roofs. We live to serve the Stars, but we still need to eat." She hooked an arm around Aeliana's elbow, pulling her back toward the kitchens. At least Aeliana already knew where to find measuring cups and flour.

She gave one last longing look over her shoulder at the door she thought might be hers. She'd let herself rest with the others at the eleventh bell, but during the night, she'd have to resume her search.

CHAPTER 5

After Gaeren's lengthy carriage ride to the docks, his first stop was Larkos' office, his first mate's tiny room over the shipyard.

"How in Rhystahn did you get your crazy sister to approve it?" Larkos leaned back in his chair, propping his boots up on the rough table. The Sun's morning light filtered in through a dirt-smudged window, casting a dingy glow about them.

Gaeren flinched. "She may be uptight, but she's still my sister and your future queen."

Larkos grinned, unconcerned over the reprimand. "So she didn't approve it?"

The already tiny office felt smaller. "I don't need her approval for everything I do."

"Ask for forgiveness instead of permission?" Larkos' grin turned to a chuckle. As long as he got paid what he was promised, he seemed to find everything about their arrangement amusing, most especially how Gaeren's role as prince conflicted with the older man's penchant for Recreant ideals.

"Something like that," Gaeren mumbled.

Larkos rubbed the stubble covering the lower half of his face, one of the rare bits of skin not already covered by his tattoos. His barrel chest and thick arms belied the agility he had on a ship, and he kept his black hair knotted at the nape of his neck. Most Vendarans kept their hair no longer than their shoulders, leaving the honor of long locks for the holy Stars, who reflected the Sun's glory.

Larkos wasn't like most Vendarans.

"So," the older man said, "we sneak out of harbor in the dead of night, aiming south for Valorian for a trade. Lovers' Falls is several days travel inland. How am I supposed to convince a dozen sailors to join our crew when their time on land might be longer than that at sea?"

"Money." Gaeren folded his arms across his chest, prepared to start the bartering process.

Larkos lowered his feet. "You know, when you pay the men from the royal coffers instead of giving them shares from that voyage's trade, they're less motivated to do well. Plus, it's a slap in the face after all your talk about favoring democracy."

Gaeren frowned. This was not the direction he'd thought the conversation was going. "I can't exactly change things overnight."

He didn't mind talk about dissolving the throne. Leadership didn't need crowns or bonded bloodlines involved. But he also didn't know how those things were supposed to change without war or harm to his family, two things he could never support.

"Let's start with one thing at a time." Gaeren pulled several notes out of his pocket, slapping them down on the table. "I'll pay the men from the royal coffers, and they can use it to spread their ideas of democracy."

Larkos reached for the notes, counting them out. "I'm just saying you're going to need to take some action soon if you want the Recreants you've wooed, including your crew, to continue believing in you. For the last year, you've walked a fine line, and now the men are anxious to see you do more than talk. You're halfway to being a Recreant, but as long as you live off the taxes your family collects, you're still holding on to your old ways as a Loyalist."

The advantages and disadvantages of Gaeren's position danced in front of him. The Recreants had been fighting for democracy since before he was born, which meant he had to prove himself to them instead of the other way around. As a part of the royal family, it was assumed he was a Loyalist. Was he loyal to his family? Of course. Was he loyal to the throne? That was where things got a bit more complicated.

"I know," Gaeren admitted.

Larkos' gaze flicked to him in surprise.

"I'm just not sure what to do about it." Gaeren stood, his chair legs scraping against the wood floor. To his relief, Larkos let the topic drop.

"In half a moon?" his first mate asked.

"Or less—a week, if possible." Gaeren stuck out a hand, gripping Larkos' forearm. "Even that might be too long. Enla will find reason to keep me here."

"Sailors are superstitious. I can't guarantee many of the men will follow you through to Lovers' Falls." Larkos said the words without apology, the statement more of a fact than a dig at the quality of men on their ship.

"I don't expect them to. In fact, the more that stay on board the ship, the faster my trip inland will go. Make sure they know they'll receive the same payment either way."

"How generous..." Larkos raised an eyebrow as their hands dropped. "Or secretive."

Gaeren lifted the corner of one lip. "We'll see whose curiosity outweighs their superstition."

By the time Gaeren's carriage brought him back to the palace's sprawling estate, the Sun was past its peak and his stomach growled. Beyond the guarded gate, overarching oak trees bordered the lengthy driveway, which felt miles longer than usual—until Enla came into view on the veranda, her slippers tapping an irritated beat on the top step. The stone arches dwarfed her figure. She wore a flowy white dress, and her hair was pulled back to reveal her starlock, which meant she had either just finished a meeting, or she had more to attend. If her queenly activities were done for the day, she'd be back in trousers, hair down, although he'd been seeing her that way less and less as their parents passed over more and more duties.

He took the steps two at a time, planting a kiss on her stiff cheek.

"I'm impressed at how early you rose from bed," Enla said.

Gaeren flinched at the icy quality of her words. "Someone told me I need to be more responsible. I'm proving them right." He gave her an easy grin, but she didn't break.

"I want you at these meetings, Gaeren. Not for you. Not even for the people. For me." Her porcelain exterior cracked, just for a moment, and she looked away, probably to check for an audience of house staff. Besides the two of them and her guards several paces away, the veranda was empty.

"I'm sorry." Gaeren ran a hand through his hair, scratching the back of his head. And he was. It pained him to know she felt abandoned, but that didn't change the fact that she was more than competent to handle council members. "I never talk at those things, anyway. Even Mother and Father don't bother attending because you've got it under control."

This time, her mask cracked to show narrowed eyes and a look that burned. "When's the last time you saw our parents take part in anything? If you'd stayed for the party last night, you'd have seen them make a show of standing by the cake, giving a wave, then returning to their rooms. I'm worried—" She pressed her lips together and turned away. The crease between her eyes deepened, shifting her starlock where it delicately draped across her forehead.

"Worried about what?"

She held his gaze again, reaching out to smooth the hair near his cowlick. Her voice softened. "I'm worried they're sick. Or that one of them is sick. That they don't want us to see how bad it is. Their futures are murky, like they're not guaranteed to exist."

This made Gaeren pause. Their parents had always been healthy, and they weren't old. Plus, there were plenty of somatic progenies on staff who could heal most ailments.

But not all.

He glanced through the open door even though the Sun's light only showed the curved stairs and a small distance down the hall. His parents' bedroom and offices were on the second floor in the west wing, far from his own rooms. He rarely saw them on any given day, so it would be impossible for him to know if they were out less.

"Has Mother been taking tea with friends?"

"Not for the last moon."

Alarm sliced through Gaeren. "Have you sent in healers?"

"They refuse to see them. They refuse to see the priest for prayers. They often refuse to see me."

Gaeren wrapped an arm around her, pulling her against him for a hug. She stiffened, always aware of how her actions might be perceived. But this wasn't a weakness, and many of the staff had been around long enough to have seen her tantrums as a child. He refused to let go, and eventually she melted into him, taking the comfort he offered.

"Well, there's no point in me trying, then, is there?"

She gave half a laugh against his chest, and while he'd said the words to lighten her mood, the truth behind them was a little stab to his chest. Enla had always been the preferred child. The oldest, the highest concentration of starblood. The one ready to obey and please, even before she understood the role she would take on.

Maybe it should have made him jealous of her or caused a rift between them. But it wasn't her fault. Instead, it made him despise their parents, who should have loved them equally.

That didn't mean he wished either of them ill.

"Maybe you should try," she said, pulling back. Her eyes begged him to agree. "We could go together. I need to know if I'm imagining things."

He winced, glancing through the doors once more as if he could see his parents beyond. "Of course. Anything for you."

"Anything except attending council meetings?" She gave him a wry look, then straightened the seams of her dress until she realigned into her prim and proper statue.

As they passed through the main doors, a set of guards fell in line, shadowing them through the west wing corridor and up the stairs to their parents' chambers, where soldiers not only guarded the entrance but blocked Enla and Gaeren's access to the door.

One guard cleared his throat. "Permission to speak, Your Majesty."

"Of course." Enla dipped her head.

"His Majesty, the king, has requested to not be disturbed after last night's festivities."

Gaeren snorted, then leaned past the guard to pound on the door anyway.

"We don't need lunch!" The sharpness of their father's reply didn't surprise Gaeren, but the man had never refused food.

"It's me, Father," Gaeren called. "I've come seeking your blessing for my voyage to Valorian and Lovers' Falls."

Enla jostled his arm. "I already rejected that request."

"Then my request will rile him up and bring him to the door. Or he'll overrule your authority." Gaeren grinned. "Either way, I win."

"It's no wonder I'm their favorite," she murmured as the door clicked open.

The king's brown eyes blazed with health, and his girth showed no signs of slimming as he glared down at the two of them. "Enla said she wants to send you as an ambassador to Islara." He pulled the door open, allowing them in.

"She also says she wants me here to act as throne warden." Gaeren stepped past his father, scanning the sitting room for the queen. "She can't very well have it both—" He cut off when his eyes landed on his mother's slight frame perched on the edge of a settee. Her blue eyes glazed over as if she were Enla sifting through visions of his soul's future.

Only his mother was a noetic like him, her magic allowing her to project emotions on others. She was a perfect match for their father. After he created chaos in a room, she calmed everyone down. Now she sat perfectly still, either unaware of their presence or uninterested. Her dark brown coils with hints of grey were still done up from the night before. Enla sat next to her, causing the cushion to dip, but the queen didn't move. Their father remained in the doorway, making it clear they were only allowed a brief visit.

"Mother?" Gaeren stepped forward, kneeling until his face was in her line of sight.

Her focus shifted, and a smile brightened her face. "Hello, dear. So good of you to come." She clasped his hand between her gloved fingers. Had he imagined her odd behavior?

"We're both exhausted," his father said. For the first time, Gaeren noticed they were in their nightclothes, breakfast trays still on the tea table.

"You hardly even attended last night's party." Gaeren released his mother's hand and stood to face his father. Enla stood too, pinching his arm through his sleeve. He held back a wince.

"Have you come to lecture us on our social life?" the king snapped. "Your sister knows what's best for you. If she wants you in Islara, go to Islara. If she wants you here, stay here. There's no reason to come whining to me like a petulant child asking for extra sweets." The exposed bits of skin above his beard took on the purple hue Gaeren and the council members were so familiar with.

"She could send anyone to Islara," Gaeren insisted. "And Uncle Dantoran still serves as the throne warden. I'm not needed yet, and I have leads of my own."

His father's color darkened further. "Dantoran serves me, not your sister. Go on. Can't you see you're upsetting your mother?"

Gaeren glanced at the queen, whose eyes had glazed over once more. "What's wrong with—?"

"I'm sorry, Father." Enla said, dragging Gaeren toward the door. "We'll let both of you rest."

"It's not you who should apologize." The king scowled at Gaeren as they headed back into the hall. "The Sun knows you're not the reason our rest has been interrupted. Send him out to spar with Dantoran. He needs to burn off more of his youthful arrogance."

The door slammed shut, cutting off any reply Gaeren might have had. His father's rejection had been filled with the passive aggressive statements he expected, but there was an unusually blatant bite that delved too close to Gaeren's heart. Why did his father always blame him? Why did he always see Gaeren as the plague on their family?

His chest burned with the battle cry held within. "Well, Father seems to be doing fine."

"Is that how you test his health?" Enla asked. "Push him until he snaps?"

"That's pushing? Showing up and asking a question is pushing? I'm surprised he didn't break my arm to keep me from sailing." It wouldn't have been the first time their father had used his destructive somatic skills for discipline.

All four guards stared straight ahead, avoiding eye contact.

Enla turned her back on Gaeren, walking away. She hadn't been wrong about their mother seeming sick.

"Maybe I can find some of that red bush tea Mother likes when I make port in Valorian. On the way to Lovers' Falls," Gaeren offered as he followed.

"I have not approved that voyage," she threw over her shoulder. "It's too far. We have too many important events in the coming moons. You're needed here." Her chin raised higher with each objection.

He placed his hands on her shoulders, preventing her from walking away, then gently turned her to face him. He bent until they were eye level. "*You* have too many important events. *You're* needed here. I'm more useful out there."

He waved a hand in the general direction of the city of Elanesse, the harbor, the rest of Vendaras—all the places and people he felt burdened to protect. In the back of his mind, he included all of Rhystahn, but he couldn't include the lands on the other side of the barrier until that was breached. Until he'd proven himself capable of protecting one little girl.

"I'm better at observing, interacting, changing things with my hands," he continued. "What you do is valuable. But what I do has a different value. I want to protect all Vendarans, not just the House of Elanesse. I can't do that unless I learn more about them."

Enla took a step back. "You should be here, courting Lenda, befriending the council members, wooing the nobles."

Gaeren shook his head, too spent to argue further. She'd never see things his way. Not unless he got her out in the world. She rarely left the walls of the palace, let alone the city of Elanesse.

"Come with me," he begged. "We can discuss all the council matters you wish with the sea breeze in our hair and filling our lungs."

The noise in her throat reminded him of a wild animal ready to charge. "Don't make me ground *Starspeed*." The abruptness of her threat left him speechless. "If I search your future, will I find you disobeying your eventual queen?"

He frowned. "You might find me disagreeing with a selfish and obstinate sister."

"Selfish?" All anger drained from her face, along with her color. "Everything I do is for the good of this land, our people. You don't even know everything I've had to give up." She scratched at her palm once more—the scar, not the new bonding mark. She couldn't possibly consider Riveran something she had to give up for the throne. He'd broken their bond. He'd chosen someone else over her.

He shuddered as he remembered her pain, the way he'd tried to take those memories from her before he understood his magic, before he knew how he could damage her mind. His progeny mentor at the time had saved both their lives that night, but even his mentor's skills hadn't been able to erase the shared pain from either of their minds.

"Maybe you're right." The half apology exited Gaeren's mouth from habit. "Maybe I would understand if you told me more. If you could. But maybe part of the problem is that this is your burden to bear, not mine. I should be free to serve our people in different ways, not be penned up here as your shadow."

"You think you're my shadow? You think you could do better if our roles were reversed?" Her voice shook, but Gaeren couldn't tell if anger or pain fueled the emotion in her voice.

"No! I want nothing to do with the throne. I want to sail away from it." He gestured toward the docks far beyond the royal land, wishing he were already there. "I'm grateful it's yours."

Her eyes closed, her face tinged pink. "I need you here."

Her lids opened, the apology in her pools of blue not enough to compensate for the loss he felt. She left without another word, making it clear he couldn't ever expect support for this mission. Maybe not any mission anymore.

Larkos had been exactly right. They'd be sneaking out of the harbor in the dead of night.

CHAPTER 6

"How exactly is this helping me become a priestess?" Aeliana spun in a half circle, wrestling to pull the bow from its sling on her back.

Cyrus laughed and helped her retrieve it. "Servants of the Stars still need to eat. Gams and Gamps will likely spend more time teaching us how to bake and garden rather than have us reading the holy books or meditating on the Stars' light." He pulled an arrow from her quiver, passing it over with the ease of familiarity. "Besides, many times while out on a hunt, I've had my deepest conversations with the Stars, alone amidst all they've created."

He scanned the surrounding forest, and Aeliana followed his gaze, taking in the trickling brook at their feet and the pine trees blocking the Stargazer. Her guardians were probably camped somewhere out here, waiting, watching for her. She couldn't imagine coming out here alone to find peace.

"You have a distinct advantage, having been raised to this from childhood." Aeliana thought of her own childhood—being carted from town to town while her guardians sought the golden arrow. Fending for herself like a street rat most days. Until they tested her blood and her magic showed. For the last four years, she'd been more of a prisoner, a daily source of power they weren't willing to give up.

Aeliana adjusted the arm guard before nocking the arrow the way he'd shown her earlier that morning. Her shoulders resisted, her agitation at an all-time high. It had been a week since she'd replaced Celeste, and she sensed her body fighting to release its power, making her head ache and her muscles tense.

"It's not a competition." Cyrus adjusted her grip on her bow. "There. Now, aim for the tree across the water." He pointed at a tree a dozen feet away.

She emptied her quiver, with only a single arrow grazing the tree. As she and Cyrus bent to gather the fallen arrows, Aeliana let out a sigh of frustration.

"You're trying too hard. Relax and enjoy the morning. Don't worry about hitting the tree." He handed her several arrows.

She shoved them into her quiver with a short laugh. "How am I supposed to aim for the tree and not think about hitting it?"

"Aim for the tree, then close your eyes and imagine it striking the wood, right at its center. But don't look to see if you made it. We're practicing form today. I don't expect you to hit targets yet."

She frowned at the bow and arrow in her hands. After seven days, she had nothing to show for her efforts except the added stress of hiding the magic building in her blood. She'd searched the unlocked Stargazer storerooms when it was her turn for private prayer, then the stables and even the refuse piles during the night. Now, instead of hunting for the golden arrow, she was shooting cedar ones.

When Cyrus gestured for her to try again, she sighed, then pulled the string taut and anchored her hand at her cheek. Her fingers and arms burned from the repetitive motions, and she let the arrow fly before she'd had a chance to truly aim. It barely cleared the brook. She nocked another arrow, avoiding Cyrus' eyes.

"Della said we get shipments of artifacts. Find anything interesting so far?" She held her breath while waiting for his response and found her arms steadier, her aim truer. Sure enough, when she released that arrow, it bounced off the tree.

Cyrus jumped from his rock and clapped for her, like she'd just won a tournament.

"It didn't even stick," she mumbled.

"Doesn't matter." He grinned. "You just need more energy behind it, and that will come with time. The stronger your arms get, the more force you can put behind it." He sat back on his rock, crossing a foot over the opposite knee. "And yes, the artifacts are always interesting, especially the books and weapons."

She dropped an arrow in her relief. She bent to grab it, going through the motions of aiming again, the strain on her muscles worth it to keep him talking. Not that he needed much encouragement. The harder part would be ensuring he didn't tell Della or Bartholem about all her questions.

He knotted his long red hair at the nape of his neck, then grabbed his own bow and arrow. When he stood beside her, he took aim for the same tree. "It's sad how many Stargazers are closing, though."

His shot stuck in the center, mocking all the arrows Aeliana had left littered at the tree's base. He jumped across the brook to gather them up. "Training under Gams and Gamps has made me see how little regard people have for the Stars. It's made my faith stronger, which is probably good, since I was always destined to be a priest. I think you and I are meant to bring about a revival in our generation."

Aeliana's guilt bloomed, spreading and swirling in her chest. He'd already latched onto her like a leech, not knowing her blood was poison. She tried not to think about the danger she was putting him in. The closer they became, the more likely he'd get hurt.

Even if they didn't get close, what would happen to the people here if she left Arvid and Vera behind? They had stores of her blood hidden away, and they wouldn't be afraid to use it.

She squared her shoulders and clenched her jaw. Removing herself —and her blood—from Arvid and Vera would save countless others. And if she could reach Vendaras, surely there would be another half-light who could teach her how to rid her blood of its magic. She had to find the arrow, and she had to leave.

"Why were you destined to be a priest?" she asked as Cyrus hopped back across the brook.

"I have six younger sisters, two older sisters, and two older broth-ers. My oldest brother inherits my father's land, but the next one became a sailor, which left me or my sisters to take over the Stargazer." Cyrus handed the arrows to Aeliana.

She took a deep breath, aiming for the tree once more. This time she closed her eyes like he'd suggested. The loss of vision encouraged her other senses to take over. Crisp mountain air with fresh pine scent flooded every breath. Birds twittered and trees creaked. Warmth surged through Aeliana's veins as she imagined the arrow hitting the tree's center. She willed her energy to pass through the arrow, giving it the force to stick.

She let the arrow fly, and Cyrus gasped.

"You did it!" He slapped her back the way she'd seen children do in the market, excited over a shared toy.

"Did you not expect me to?"

"Not on the first day. Do it again."

She hit the tree five more times in quick succession, each time giving herself over to the senses flooding her mind and the will to prove herself. When she turned to see Cyrus' reaction, his jaw hung open, but his freckled brow bunched in confusion.

Her gut tightened. Her success hadn't been normal, which meant she'd done magic.

She hadn't meant to. Hadn't even realized that was what she'd been doing. She scanned the skies for dark spirits, even though she was almost certain they came for the blood, not the magic. But the power that had swelled within her left her breathless with need, her body and mind warring over how much harm her magic could really do. But also how much better she might feel if she gave in to the desire to use it. She gritted her teeth, digging the bow's lower limb into the soil where newly grown blades of grass poked through the earth, evidence of her crime. She glanced back toward the Stargazer's wall, where an unmarked grave lay. She was unwilling to forget the price.

"Beginner's luck, huh?" Her words came out strained.

"You don't have to pretend to be new at this." Cyrus' brow lowered, his confusion giving way to disappointment. "I won't hold it against you if you're better than me."

"I'm not pretending." She bit her lip, wishing she could bite back her words. It would have been easier to let him believe the lie.

"Then how did you do that?" He didn't wait for an answer. "There! See the squirrel in the tree?"

Aeliana followed his pointing finger, her heart sinking as the tiny creature settled on a branch just a few trees away from their original target.

"Let's take that home for dinner."

Aeliana's stomach churned. "I can't kill a squirrel."

"The Stars gave us animals for food." Cyrus gestured toward Aeliana's bag, which held the food Della had packed. It contained salted meat and brown bread, a combination Aeliana had been eager to roast over a fire, but which now left her nauseous.

"But it's wrong to kill." She still argued, even though she was no longer sure if she should.

Cyrus crossed his arms over his chest. "If a man walks by, and I shoot him, yes, it would be wrong to kill him. If he runs at us with an axe, bloodlust in his eyes, killing him would be the exact right thing to do."

Aeliana laughed. "I don't think any squirrels are going to be galloping at us with weapons."

"True." Cyrus smiled, picking up his bow and arrow and anchoring his hand against his cheek. "I'm just saying right and wrong lies more in our intentions. There's a difference between using a bow to hunt for sustenance and using a bow to kill without purpose. The bow itself is not evil. It can be used for good or evil by the person who wields it. It's a choice." He let the arrow fly, and it struck the squirrel through the eye, making Aeliana wince.

His words sank deep into her soul, digging at truths and lies she wasn't ready to dissect, and the rest of their time, she was too distracted to hit a single tree. By the time they returned to the gate, it was almost the eleventh bell. They passed through the gardens, the flowers all in a state of hesitation, nearly ready to bloom.

She paused at the Stargazer's threshold, scratching at the scars on her hands, never feeling worthy to enter the place of worship. Cyrus nudged her forward, forcing her in so he could follow. He scanned the other clergy, but his eyes lit up when they landed on Della, who stood precariously on a ladder where she replaced candles in windows in preparation for the nightly worshipers.

"We're back, Gams." He held up the strung meat as if offering his grandmother a bouquet instead of a squirrel's carcass.

Della turned and smiled. "How were archery lessons?"

"She's a natural when she's focused."

Aeliana started at the compliment.

Della climbed down the ladder, then brushed off her hands as she joined them in the middle of the room. The small dirt circle there was the center of a starburst of benches leading out to the edge of the room. Tonight, like every night, worshipers would gather and sit here, faces angled up to take in the Stars' beauty.

"I'm glad to hear it. I'm sure you'll sleep well for your rest time this afternoon." She took the squirrel from Cyrus. "Oh! A new shipment came today. From Luhmen Mountain's Stargazer." Her face grew troubled even as Aeliana's heart soared.

"Luhmen Mountain? I thought they would never close." Cyrus elbowed Aeliana. "Celeste was just asking about the artifacts. She wants to see them."

Aeliana grimaced, both at the false name and the direct request.

"The two of you can sort them tomorrow. I'll have Bartholem help. He can show you some of the older ones we're preparing to put on display. They're in the storage room." She gestured with the squirrel toward an oak door amidst the curved stone wall.

It was one of the two locked doors Aeliana hadn't been able to get past during her searches. Now Della used her free hand to pull a key from her pocket, and Aeliana's breath hitched.

"I hope to sleep late since I'm last to bed tonight. But the two of you can start early in the morning." She held the key out toward Cyrus.

Aeliana clenched her hands together to keep from snatching it.

Cyrus held out his hands, smeared with squirrel blood. "I cleaned them after I strung it up, but I tripped and nearly dropped it halfway back. I'd better wash up first."

Della gave a small snort and turned to Aeliana. "Celeste? Can you hold it for my uncoordinated grandson? He's likely to lose it before the Sun's morn, anyway."

Aeliana licked her lips, glancing at the key, then back to Cyrus and Della's faces. Was this a test? Or could it really be this easy? She slowly took the key, her fingers numb. "Of course."

Deep gongs sounded from the bell tower just north of the Stargazer, drawing Aeliana's attention to the emptiness of the room.

"Oh, dear," Della said. "Is it already that time? I'll take care of this. The two of you should head for your beds."

Cyrus nodded, but Aeliana hesitated, tucking the key in her pocket.

"Would it be all right if I took an extra hour to pray?" she asked. "I know the Stars aren't out, but I find these quiet times without the crowds to be the most rewarding."

Della beamed at her. "That is a request I will always be willing to grant."

Aeliana could hardly believe her luck when the two left the Stargazer, and she shut the door behind them. Without wasting a moment, she rushed to the storage room, raising the key with trembling hands to fumble with the lock.

As the door opened, wood scraped against the floor like a grindstone sharpening an axe. Aeliana froze, straining her ears for anyone who might not be resting to come investigate. But then she caught sight of the artifacts, and her mouth swung open. The closet extended the length of her bed before wrapping around the curve of the wall like a corridor, farther than she could see. Shelves lined both walls, and a third set of shelves ran down the middle.

Carefully placed holes in the outside wall let in enough light for her to see, but not enough for others to see in or even notice the miniature windows from the outside. At first, the collections looked erratic: weapons next to robes and books next to jars. But they were all carefully labeled with the Stargazer they'd come from and their estimated date of origin.

Golden figurines were scattered throughout, some in the shape of five-pointed stars, some resembling humans. She ran her hands over a stack of books that had come from Velspetz, a tiny seaside town in the eastern province. If she closed her eyes, she could still smell the salt in the air, feel the thickness of it blowing across her neck. It had been her favorite of all the towns. The priestess had snuck her candy and shown her an alcove overlooking the sea where she could come and sit anytime she liked.

An entire bell passed before she got through a quarter of the shelves. She quickened her pace, not sure if she'd have the key tomorrow. The farther she walked back in the closet, the older and more decrepit the items got. Several books looked like they might crumble to dust if she touched them, and some metal objects were too rusted for her to define.

The Sun was nearly ready to sleep when she found a basket of trinkets labeled "starlocks" in the back of the room. Her guardians had never specified the arrow's size—maybe it was tiny. Aeliana bent low to dig through them, but before she could look closer, her gaze landed on a golden shaft tucked back behind the basket. She gasped, moving the basket aside and rubbing dust off the arrow's label.

There was no date, but the tag read "Golden Arrow of Lorvandas."

Aeliana's palms grew damp with sweat. She wiped them on her robes, then inched shaking hands toward the arrow. An inscription in the ancient tongue danced across its golden surface, the shaft as thick as her finger and half the length of her arm. She bent closer to make out the words. Cyrus had introduced her to the archaic symbols the other day, but they still looked indecipherable.

The thirteenth bell rang.

"What are you doing?"

Aeliana jumped at Cyrus' question, her head bumping into the shelf above her. She stood quickly, turning to face him as her cheeks grew warm. His brow bunched in uncertainty, or maybe hurt, and his gaze drifted between the shelf she'd abandoned and her empty hands.

"I couldn't sleep," she said. "I thought I'd get started on the artifacts that came in."

He chewed on his lip, glancing back toward the main room. "The new artifacts are by the door."

She squeaked out a laugh. "Ah, I must have walked right past them. Then I got distracted by all the amazing things." She spun in a circle like a child testing the flare of a new dress.

"Well, no one's allowed to be in here by themselves. Not even Gams or Gamps."

"Of course," she said, nodding soberly.

He turned and stepped away, trusting her to follow. She bent down and reached blindly for the arrow, begging the Stars to keep him from turning around.

Smooth, warm metal met her fingers, and as she tightened her hold on the arrow, it thrummed with energy.

CHAPTER 7

ORRA'S EYES flew open even though she'd just lain down to rest. The blond braid tied around her wrist warmed against her skin, its touch like the vibration of a cat's purr. She sat up straight, nearly falling from the crudely hung hammock. Her bare feet sought the rough edges of the rotting deck of Gaeren's hideout, even though her shock made it impossible to stand. She'd been squatting there for the last week, searching through his books and keeping track of his plans, but she hadn't expected this.

She grasped the braid, using the energy flowing through her blood to reach out beyond the mangrove trees into the night air, past the deep waters under the dancing Stars, even beyond the barrier. Reaching for the long-lost piece that called out to her, that spoke to her. Its signal grew stronger, closer, the woman grasping it acting as a conduit.

Orra grew blind to the mangrove forest, lost awareness of her own slight frame and slender limbs. The eyes of her mind sought someone new, someone powerful, someone who might be able to help her.

Someone who'd touched the arrow.

CHAPTER 8

AELIANA COULDN'T HELP the whimper that escaped her lips. When Cyrus turned, it was impossible for her to hide her bent posture, the arrow in her hands. She clung to it like a lifeline even as she feared the power feeding it.

"I'm sorry," she whispered.

"For what?" His eyes dropped to her hand, to the flash of gold. His brow furrowed, then understanding dawned. "Are you stealing from the Stargazer?"

The accusation stung even though her true purpose wasn't any more noble.

She waited for its power to work, for the arrow to remove her from this place—from Cyrus' disappointment, which was far worse than anger. When nothing happened, she ran, pushing past Cyrus and out to the Stargazer's atrium.

By now, the other priests and priestesses had risen, gathering in the Stargazer for a group prayer before dinner. She skidded to a stop, unable to control her gasping breath or darting eyes. The only door out was blocked by Della. The Stars were just beginning to be visible through the open roof, witnesses to her downfall. Whether the servants of the Stars meant to help or stop her, they all took a step closer, hedging her in.

The buildup of energy in her blood left her taut, like a bowstring pulled to its maximum tension. The only way to let the arrow fly would be to release her blood—to release uncontrolled magic. Even though it would draw in the dark spirits, the temptation was strong. But without knowing how to use it, she'd be more likely to kill them all than to escape with the arrow.

"Please," she murmured, grasping the arrow tighter in both hands, her palms growing numb from its vibration.

"Wait." Della's voice rang out through the room, drawing everyone's eyes to where she stood, hand raised.

Aeliana's gaze flicked toward the door behind her.

Della took a few steps forward, squinting closer at Aeliana, completely ignoring the humming arrow in her hands.

"Aeliana?" she whispered.

Aeliana went still. "How do you know my name?"

"Rildan, your father... He asked me to guard the arrow for him, to hold it until he—or you—came back for it."

Aeliana straightened. "I have no father." Still, her pulse raced a little faster at the mention of family—the impossible thing she'd never let herself want.

Della hesitated. "Something got lost over the years, didn't it? Either your father or your memory... maybe you." She scanned Aeliana's face, her eyes troubled, but Aeliana shook away the hope rising in her chest.

"Then you'll let me leave?" Aeliana asked.

Tears welled up in Della's eyes. "It would be an honor to watch you use the starbridge."

Gasps spread through the room, followed by murmurs.

"Celeste?"

She turned to see Cyrus' face pink and blotchy, his eyes darting between her and Della.

She opened her mouth, unsure which lie to tell. Would he hate her less if he discovered she wasn't stealing? Or would he despise her more for keeping her secrets?

The arrow's hum deepened until it was audible, the glitter of its edges shifting to a glow that slowly grew to fill the room. It seemed to sense her power, absorbing it for its own use. Aeliana froze, her mind screaming that she should drop it, but her body was unwilling to obey the command.

The priests and priestesses around them gasped. Several ran from the room, tripping over each other in their panic. The light became blinding, and Aeliana threw an arm over her eyes to block it out, too disoriented to even use the distraction to run for the door.

When the light receded, the atrium still shone as if the Sun's light filled the room. The handful of servants of the Stars remaining all bowed before a figure now standing with Aeliana. The woman's short dark hair swung across her face, framing her round cheeks. One moment she looked as old as Arvid and Vera, another as young as Aeliana, but her dark eyes held an ageless quality, like they'd seen a thousand lifetimes. The transparency of her slim form made it difficult to determine the shade of her skin, and the details of her appendages grew fainter the farther out they were from her core, making her clothing and figure unidentifiable.

She tilted her head, taking in Aeliana for a mere moment before eyeing the golden arrow. Her eyes slid shut, her lips moving with words Aeliana couldn't make out.

"Who are you?" Aeliana's fingers trembled as she shielded herself, as if the woman might lash out.

The woman ignored her question, inching forward, hand stretched out toward the arrow. "Do you know what you hold?"

Instinctively, Aeliana pulled it closer to her chest. "I thought—I thought it was a starbridge." She glanced down at the arrow, which still hummed in her hand. "Instead, it brought you?"

The woman hummed noncommittally. "Perhaps it's a starbridge. Or perhaps it's so much more."

"That light," Aeliana murmured, noticing the way it blotted out her view of the Stars. "My guardians will see it. You all need to run!" Her voice rose to hysteria, inducing panic that sent the last of the servants of the Stars from the room, save Della and Cyrus. She reached out a hand for Della's robes, clenching the fabric in her fist to pull the priestess toward the door. Now that the moment had come, she couldn't leave them. Not like this. "They'll destroy everything in their path to reach the arrow."

Della's face paled, but her voice remained calm. "Then you must use it. Now."

Aeliana gaped at Della. "And leave you at their mercy?"

The old woman's eyes were clear, with a defiant confidence. "Your father left it for you for a reason, for a greater purpose."

That same hope unfurled in Aeliana's chest, but it was too complicated to grow.

"The Stars will protect us." Della stood a hair straighter. "Or they will honor us in the next life for our sacrifice."

The strange woman shifted, her eyes alighting with interest. "Yes. Use it to take yourself back home."

"Back?" Cyrus asked, wedging himself between the woman and Aeliana like a shield. "Back to Vendaras?"

The woman raised a brow at him, her form flickering. "Loyalty is an admirable form of faithfulness."

Cyrus seemed to grow several inches at her words.

"Does that mean she's a half-light?" He turned to Aeliana as if seeing her for the first time.

His words left her exposed. She didn't want him studying her in this way any more than she wanted Arvid and Vera using her blood for their purposes. She craved invisibility, anonymity, even more now that a label had been put on her strangeness for all to see. She needed to be among other half-lights where she could blend in. She needed people who could show her how to tamp down the power in her blood and live like a human.

"Read the words, Aeliana," Della urged, gesturing at the inscription on the arrow.

"I don't even know what they say." Aeliana frowned down at its shaft.

The strange woman hummed as if they had all the time in the world. "They go back to a time before the Great Divide. A time before half-lights and humans. In today's language, it would be something like 'divided in war, united in hope, reconciled in love.' Or maybe 'separated by strife, merged by faith, restored by sacrifice.' Nothing is ever just one thing." Her eyes closed, and the foreign words slipped across her lips like water on river rocks.

The temptation to repeat them was strong. It was what Aeliana wanted on so many levels. But that was also how magic felt. Something she wanted to use, even though she knew it was wrong. She could practically taste the acrid stench of her plans going up in flames around her. There was only one solution she could consider. She had to wait for Arvid and Vera and take them across the barrier. It was the only way to protect these people who had welcomed her into their home and, if Della's story could be trusted, had guarded a relic for her for over a dozen years.

With the resignation came relief. Finally, she was doing something to save lives instead of take them.

"Hand it over, Aeliana."

Aeliana cringed as the familiar deep voice rang out from the back of the atrium. Arvid shuffled through the door, squinting in the apparition's bright light. Vera followed, and the servants of the Stars who had fled peeked in through the door behind them. There were still too many people here who could get hurt.

"Come. Let's use it together." Aeliana held the golden arrow out with a shaking hand toward her guardians.

It was all the invitation they needed. As they stepped forward, several priests and priestesses snuck into the room, eager to watch history be made.

"Don't do it," Cyrus said.

"I have to go." Aeliana pressed her lips together.

"Then you go alone," Della said. "Your father made no mention of these two."

Vera laughed, edging her way to Aeliana's side. "Her father? You mean the thief who stole the starbridge? We brought her to Lorvandas. For her protection."

"You brought her here?" The suspicion coloring Della's tone matched Aeliana's own doubt.

"She was a helpless baby." Vera turned beady eyes toward Aeliana. "There was talk of killing you because of some curse or prophecy. We brought you here to save you."

Aeliana held back a snort. Maybe some of that was true, but definitely not all of it.

"What about you?" Della rose as she spoke, her voice ringing through the now nearly full room. She gave a respectful incline of her head toward the strange woman, keeping her eyes lowered as she directly addressed her. "What do you have to do with all this?"

"More than even I realized." The woman's eyes narrowed in consideration as she took in Arvid and Vera's proximity to Aeliana and the arrow. "I'm here to make sure Aeliana crosses the barrier."

"Who are you?" Cyrus dared to repeat Aeliana's question.

"You may call me Orra." She gave a serene smile but offered nothing more.

"I know what you are." Arvid waved a hand through her form, the vague parts of her disintegrating before reforming, like a cloud trying to retain its shape. "You can't do anything to us. You're not even here."

His taunts only made the woman calmer, quieter. "Perhaps not." She turned to Aeliana. "But you can."

Aeliana hesitated before turning to her guardians, tucking the arrow in against her chest. "Why do you want to go back?" She'd never asked them, but suddenly it mattered. Did they have far worse things planned for Vendaras?

"You think you can cross on your own?" Vera's laugh grated on Aeliana's nerves. "What will you do when you get there? You'll either bleed to death or summon the dark spirits, and then who knows what kind of havoc you'll wreak?"

Her words stirred up a different fear in Aeliana, fear that she could never be free of her guardians, not even in Vendaras. Her magic could be monstrous, but at least her guardians managed it enough to keep her from unleashing its full power.

"Don't go with them," Cyrus pleaded.

Everyone assumed the choice was up to her, but she had no choice. If she didn't bring them, it would be Cyrus and his family who had to pay.

Della stood tall, gently pulling Aeliana away from Arvid and Vera. "The decision isn't up to you or Aeliana. She has made a commitment to the Stars and is under my care as a priestess-in-training. Her training will best be completed if she travels to Vendaras alone. I'm sending her as an ambassador from the people of Lorvandas. May her path bring glory to the Stars."

Cyrus inched to his left, ignorantly stepping in front of Aeliana as if his mortal body could defend whatever onslaught her guardians might bring.

Tears pricked at the back of Aeliana's eyes at Della's words and Cyrus' tangible show of support. Della didn't know what she was saying. She didn't really understand what Aeliana was, what terrible things her blood could do, but her words held a depth of love Aeliana had never experienced before. She wished it was enough to keep them all safe.

Before she could turn down the offer that had been more of a command, Arvid shoved Cyrus to the ground, then yanked Aeliana closer. He nearly pulled her shoulder out of its socket as Vera tugged on her sleeve and sliced Aeliana's free hand without ceremony. More cries echoed around them as the servants of the Stars once again scattered.

Aeliana winced, but as the blood pooled out, she sighed, the relief overpowering all her fear and concern. The tightness of her skin and muscles slowly abated, as if the pressure her blood had been building was released like with an opened valve. She tried to tamp down the euphoria that built in its place, horrified as always as the relief grew to satisfaction. She didn't want this, and yet...it was exactly what she wanted.

Arvid cupped his hands under hers as Vera squeezed.

Aeliana blinked, dimly aware that Arvid lost more blood to the floor than he gained, but their sloppy efforts were an act of desperation and impatience, not calculated precision. Arvid had no interest in being careful as he turned to the boy curled up on the floor.

Arvid's eyes rolled back in his head as the energy of her blood seeped through his skin.

Aeliana snatched her hand back from Vera's grip to tug on Arvid's wrist and draw his attention back to her. "I'm going with you." Her words spilled out in a slurred rush. "Take me to Vendaras without harming him, and I'll do whatever you want. Please."

His lips curled in a snarl, and Aeliana knew she'd lost. He'd already tipped over the line of sanity. Aeliana launched herself on top of Cyrus, lying face down and spreading out as far as possible, bracing herself for the pain that was sure to come. Instead, she heard a high-pitched scream that cut off abruptly.

She turned back to find Arvid's bloody hand grasping Della's throat, her eyes bulging as she clawed at his grip. The sight was sobering, pulling Aeliana from the drunken stupor of her blood being spilled.

"Gams!" Cyrus pushed Aeliana aside so he could rise, but Aeliana pulled him back down. He would only get Della and himself killed.

Even if the handful of remaining people all worked together, they couldn't stand against Arvid using her blood.

"Let me help her," Cyrus ground out.

Aeliana latched onto his legs, nearly dropping the arrow, then turned to Orra. "Please, stop this!"

Orra's eyes grew troubled, the crease returning to her brow. "Even if I could, interfering is not my way."

If the woman had been solid, Aeliana might have slapped her. As it was, it took all her effort to hold Cyrus back, and still he was making ground, dragging her across the dirt with him.

"Arvid," Aeliana called, her voice hoarse as fear crawled up her throat. "Leave Della alone. She's a simple priestess who can't harm you. She can't enforce the authority she claims. It's me you want. Take me with you to Vendaras, and be done with this part of the world. Killing her won't gain you anything." She held up the golden arrow, now splattered by her own blood, fearing how close the dark spirits might be, how eager Arvid would be to let them fuse with his soul.

Cyrus broke free from her grip, but before he could reach Della, Vera's hand snaked out around his upper arm.

"That's where you're wrong." Vera's other hand reached for the arrow. "You need a reminder of what we're willing to do."

Arvid released his grip, and Della fell to her knees, gasping in air and rubbing her neck. She looked old and frail, nothing like the strong priestess Aeliana knew. But then Della's gaze landed on Cyrus, her focus intensifying until it seemed Cyrus would combust.

"Protect her," Della rasped out. "Don't let—" Her words cut off with gasps as Arvid smeared Aeliana's blood down the front of Della's robes, his touch almost gentle as her body convulsed with pain. Her gasps turned to cries as her body flopped to the ground and fresh blood seeped through her robes.

This time the blood wasn't Aeliana's.

"Gams!" Cyrus called again, but Vera's grip was like iron on both his arm and Aeliana's golden arrow. Orra might have whispered an apology, but her words were lost to Della's sobs echoing off the atrium walls.

Without another glance, Arvid reached for the arrow. His massive hands enveloped Aeliana's and Vera's as he uttered the foreign words barely visible beneath the blood. The brightness of the Stargazer engulfed them, the walls closing in like a vise that squeezed the breath out of Aeliana before everything went black.

CHAPTER 9

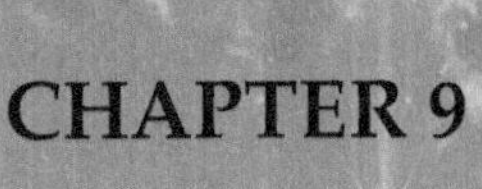

ORRA KNEELED, her face a handsbreadth from the woman called Della. She wouldn't be on this world much longer, but at least Aeliana had used the arrow. She'd brought it to Vendaras. It was finally where Orra could reach it.

Della was scrunched up in such agony that Orra felt her own muscles tense. Orra held out a hand, itching to ease the woman's pain, to heal her or even just numb her, but Orra's hand was a mere wisp of shadow and light. There was nothing she could do with her physical body hundreds of miles away.

Instead, she sang. She started out low, more of a hum.

Della's cries turned to whimpers. Her eyes latched onto Orra's, as if drawing strength from the melody. The pure tone held the sorrow of a thousand lifetimes, the joys of hundreds more. A man rushed into the atrium, the panic on his wrinkled face tightening Orra's gut. Not a bondmate in the traditional Vendaran sense, but threads of love tied their souls all the same.

He dropped to Della's side, hands clasping hers. The motion brought the woman out of the near stupor she'd been in as she listened, her pain resurfacing even as Orra sensed the comfort brought by the man's presence.

Orra picked up the pace of her song, engulfing them both. The man held Della, careful not to aggravate her wounds, tears streaming into his white beard as he whispered words only for her.

Orra wished to comfort them both. To wrap her arms around them and infuse them with love and hope beyond this lifetime. The limitations of this form left her agitated, and her volume increased until the man winced.

She cut off her song, the silence that followed bringing the woman's eyes open a mere slit.

"Do you see the light of the Sun?" Orra asked.

The woman's whimper gave no indication of an answer.

The man stroked her brow, his lips moving, the sound too low for human ears. But Orra heard the prayer, guiding the woman to the Stars.

"Look to the Sun," she told the woman. "Do you see its light? It will hurt, even more than it already does. It hurts to look upon the Sun's brilliance."

The woman's eyes were unfocused, her gaze resting somewhere behind Orra.

Orra imagined the woman's view beyond this earth to the Sun's presence on the other side. Orra longed for it in a way that left her weak, vulnerable to losing her hold on this place. She sucked in a breath, focusing on the frail humans around her, the wooden benches and stone walls.

"The Sun will draw you into its presence, give you greater life than the one you've known. May the Sun ever shine upon you." Her voice caught as she forced the words to be for the woman and not for herself. No matter how much she desired these truths to be her own, this moment was for the human. "May you never lose its light."

Della's breathing slowed, the muscles on her face relaxing. The man's breath hitched as her lips lifted, her gaze still focused beyond Orra. When she took her last breath, the entire room paused with her. The life left her body, her pain along with it.

Orra's shoulders slumped. Now the woman was safe. The woman had what Orra could not obtain. The hold Orra had on this place disintegrated, her light bursting out around her as her essence was pulled back across the water and through the mangrove trees.

CHAPTER 10

Gaeren had just reached the swamps when the light came, shooting from the distant west toward the southern provinces. He froze, allowing the matching memory to saturate his entire being. That hadn't been the light of a starlock being delivered from the Stars or retrieved from Rhystahn. He'd seen this light only once before—fourteen years ago.

He climbed the nearest tree, reaching for his starlock's power to imbue himself with strength and speed. Then, willing the memory of the light to remain, he tuned in to its source. With his bird's-eye view, the most he could see of the light's memory was a silvery fog extending down the western coast of Vendaras. If someone had used the starbridge, that was where they'd ended up. But how far exactly?

His need to set sail intensified tenfold.

He scrambled back to the ground and had made it a hundred paces toward the palace when he remembered the book. It was the reason he'd headed for his hideout in the first place, and he couldn't leave it behind.

Eagerness made Gaeren reckless, so he was only ten feet from the right grove of trees before he finally tuned in to his surroundings. He sensed the same strange magic, absent of memories, that he'd noticed the last time he'd been out here. Removing his dagger, he slowed his pace, nearly choking on the swamp gas stench but unable to escape to higher ground with cleaner air. Not until he knew what awaited him.

He took a cautious step forward, preferring to climb the crude ladder one-handed than release his hold on his dagger. His starlock warmed against his skin as if preparing to enhance his magic. A peek over the boards revealed a woman slumped over his desk, her body too still. He tuned in to his surroundings, wary of a trap, and yet she didn't breathe.

He hopped onto the landing and took a step closer. Who was she? Why was she here? And what in Rhystahn would he do with a dead body?

As he scooted closer, debating his options, she gasped in a deep breath, her light brown skin taking on a glow that infused her body with life. Painful life, if the tightness of her features was any indication. The light faded, and she attempted to straighten, dark strands of hair hanging in her face. She doubled over the desk once more as if she might be sick.

"Sun's fire," Gaeren murmured, reaching out a hand to steady her.

She lifted her head, eyes slitted with her discomfort as she tried to focus on him. "Help me."

The pitiful request snapped Gaeren into motion. Intruder or not, he wasn't about to let her suffer. He reached for his waterskin, holding it out as a peace offering.

"I'm sorry; I can't heal you. I'm not a somatic progeny. But I have water."

When she didn't move, he slowly lifted the flap, then tipped the skin forward as she tilted her head back. As she drank, he automatically scanned her neck for the cord of a starlock, but there was none.

Her vulnerability confused him after he'd watched her still form, frozen as if dead, be saturated with light and…life. There was no other way to explain it. Her body had been temporarily lifeless, and then her soul had returned.

The light…

It was too coincidental that her strange magic had brought her to life just after the light he'd seen as a child. Did she know something about the starbridge?

"Bamboo Island," the woman croaked out once she'd had her fill.

Gaeren stood a little taller. The small island was one of many stops he made along the western coast of Vendaras. It wasn't as far as Valorian or Lovers' Falls. And it had been handwritten in *The Sins of the Stars*.

He squinted toward the southern provinces, mapping out the trajectory of the light he'd seen. It could have gone to Bamboo Island.

"Is Bamboo Island where the light went?" he asked.

She nodded, licking her lips. "Can you—can you get me there?"

The desperate request gave him certainty. She wanted to find the starbridge just as much as he did.

"Who are you?" he asked. Underneath a faded cloak, she wore a simple wool dress unlike the silky layers of the nobility but also unlike the trousers of the commoners. Her short hair hung loose, her wrists empty of jewelry except for a strange braid of tawny hair. But her hands and face didn't hold the rough wear of a working woman.

"Orra."

"Where did you come from? And how did you… come back to life?"

"I wasn't dead. It nearly killed me, but it didn't." She glanced away, her eyes flashing with pain. "I won't do it again."

It wasn't an answer, but it might be all he was going to get right now. He had every intention of tracing down that light. It didn't matter if it went to Bamboo Island or all the way to Andel. Dragging this woman along might slow him down, but if they had goals that aligned…if she knew more than he did…

"What will we find there?"

She closed her eyes, exhaustion lining every feature on her face. "The things we seek."

He frowned, her answer putting him on edge. "How do you know what I'm looking for?"

She gestured to his books without opening her eyes. "Your research. You may have tried to keep it quiet, but word gets around."

The words sent a chill down his back.

"It's a good thing," she reassured him. "We can help each other."

"So we're looking for the same thing?" He wasn't going to name it if she wasn't. The thought felt petty, like a game he and Riveran might have played as children, but it also felt prudent.

She grunted, maybe a laugh that her body didn't have enough energy to produce. "You can't possibly be looking for the same thing as me."

Coughing spasms wracked her body, and he offered her water again. She trusted him with her frail body, but not with her knowledge —which meant she knew too much or too little.

He reached out, tuning in to her mind, attempting to find a memory that could give him a sense of whether he could trust her. But her mind was blank, her memories blocked so thoroughly it was like she had none.

"What is it you think the light meant?" she finally asked.

They stared each other down for a few moments. He should be skeptical of a stranger, but her magic outstripped his by miles. She wasn't a simple thief or squatter, which meant he needed to find out what all she knew. Finally, Gaeren threw caution to the wind. "Someone used a starbridge."

She looked away. "Perhaps. Or perhaps it means more."

Her words stirred hope he hadn't realized he'd been guarding. "But you're saying that's part of it. That someone came across the barrier?"

"Four someones." Her eyes rolled in her head, as if she might pass out. Even so, the hope in Gaeren's chest grew, blossoming into some-thing big and fragile, making him feel far too vulnerable.

"Who? Humans? Half-lights?" He leaned forward, supporting her even as he wanted to shake the answer out of her.

"Two beasts using blood magic. A young woman named Aeliana—"

He sucked in a breath, nearly dropping her as she slumped against him.

Daisy.

"Ah, perhaps I was wrong about what you seek." The woman's eyes fluttered open, her head lolling back so she could look at him. "A 'someone' is a far more motivating goal than a 'something.'"

Daisy was back. The idea flipped all of his plans on their head. He no longer needed to cross the barrier. He simply had to find her.

Except… he'd been there when her mother sent her across the barrier for her protection. He'd seen the couple Orra referenced, the ones who used blood magic. He'd always suspected and feared they'd been too powerful for Daisy's father to keep her safe. If the people using blood magic had brought her back, that wasn't good. Because something, or someone, on this side of the barrier was even more dangerous for Daisy.

Suddenly the questions surrounding Orra didn't matter. If she could help him find Daisy, he could put up with her mysterious magic and presence.

"I'll take you." He helped Orra into his hammock as her eyes closed. When his hands brushed her skin, he tuned in to her soul, fumbling with his less developed skill along the pneumatic spoke.

Few progenies developed a second spoke. With all of Gaeren's and Enla's mentors' training combined with their high concentration of starblood, the royal siblings each had one. Still, neither of them had developed their second spoke enough to consistently use it. Someday it would give them access to the elemental magic on the rim of the Wheel of Magic. For now, it was more like a trick they could occasionally pull out.

Gaeren's starlock burned with the effort to discern if Orra was lying, but he sensed nothing. Either his second spoke was too underdeveloped, or the mental wall she'd erected was too difficult to breach.

The woman's hand gripped his arm, her nails digging in until Gaeren winced. "Don't ever try that again."

"I wanted…I was just trying to help you." Not exactly a lie. If he trusted her more, he'd be more likely to help her.

She relaxed her grip. "Take me to the island. That's the only thing I need from you." Her eyes closed, and her hand fell back in her lap, her body limp. He couldn't just leave her here, unguarded and half dead.

He stared at her a moment longer in indecision, then pulled the desk closer so his waterskin would be within reach. He patted down his pockets, pulling out some of the honey bars Enla insisted he keep on him. They weren't much better than hardtack, but they'd saved him from hunger on more than one occasion when he avoided socializing with nobility.

Her eyes darted beneath her lids, but it didn't seem like a restful sleep. What if she was sick? He reached out a tentative hand, placing it on her forehead. The same instant, her hand circled his wrist, and her eyes flew open, the warm tone of her skin carrying that eerie glow.

"Don't touch me. I only need you to get me to Bamboo Island. Nothing else. I'll be fine by the Sun's peak."

He lifted his hands in surrender, stepping back and straightening to his full height. It went against everything in his nature to leave a woman alone, injured, but if that was what she wanted…

Besides, he needed to get moving if he had any hope of bumping up their departure. Larkos had done well finding a crew on such short notice, but he'd been expecting three more days to secure stragglers and supplies. Somehow, they'd have to get out of here tomorrow. Well, tomorrow night. They'd still have to leave in the middle of the night to avoid Enla's wrath.

He swore under his breath. His parents had made a lot of foolish decisions lately. Giving his sister increasing authority was not one of them, but placing him under that authority as the future throne warden? It was like they wanted a family feud.

Unless… Enla might agree now that the circumstances had changed. Now that he'd seen the flash of light and met this woman. Both carried unknown magic, and any unknown power was a potential threat to the throne.

"Stay here," he told the woman's still form. "I'll come back for you when I have things ready."

Her fingers lifted in acknowledgment. "Thank you, Gaeren."

He paused at the use of his name, which he'd never given. The question hung on his lips for a moment, but then her breathing shifted as if she already slept.

CHAPTER 11

AELIANA'S STOMACH churned after the transition from solid earth to emptiness back to solid earth. She reached out, grasping only empty air, unsure which way was up or down. She lost her grip on the arrow, uncertain if Arvid or Vera ended up with it. Her eyes attempted to adjust to the lack of light, and awareness of her surroundings trickled in like her senses were being awakened one by one.

Muggy, stale air with a hint of sea salt filled her nose and drenched her in sweat. Her cloak became suffocating instead of warm and protective. Dense foliage lay before them, with wooden shoots poking out from a carpet of moss.

A fresh ocean breeze, still almost too thick and wet to breathe, provided a brief respite from the heat. To her front and sides, a forest of unfamiliar hardwood trees mixed with bamboo came alive with exotic bird calls. Strange vines twitched as unseen creatures moved through them, and leaves and moss carpeted the ground. To her back, beyond a cliff's edge, water stretched on as far as she could see, which meant little with the full moon barely visible between clouds in the night sky.

The soothing and rhythmic flow of waves contrasted with the light sobs escaping Cyrus, who dropped to his knees. She bent down, rubbing his back, her throat clogging with tears she felt unworthy to shed. He shrank away from her touch, further magnifying her own anguish, the wall between them now as impenetrable as the barriers.

Which they'd now breached.

"About time," Arvid muttered. He yanked on Aeliana, forcing her to stand in front of him. "Remember our annual test?"

Aeliana shuddered but held still. If she fought him, it would only take longer. "You told me it was to check the quality of my blood."

He pulled back her cloak and tore at the collar of her blouse, exposing the top half of her back. "I don't suppose you'll believe that anymore."

"I never did." The breeze on her sweat-soaked skin made her shiver. Sharp pain followed as Arvid carved into her skin, sending waves of heat through her torso. She pulled away, but her blood still covered his hands, her own energy holding her prisoner as he finished his task.

In the past, he'd left it there for a day, sometimes more, until she cried out in pain as her magic carved a second mark. She'd tried countless times to see what marked her back, but he placed them strategically where her eyes couldn't reach. After the second mark came, he always claimed she was holding out on them, threatening to take more blood if she didn't behave. Then he removed the marks until the following year.

"What are the marks really for?" she asked through ground teeth, but neither of her guardians answered.

"Gams." Cyrus' tortured voice brought Aeliana fresh grief.

"Hush." Vera jabbed him in the side with the toe of her boot, but her eyes scanned the skies.

"You killed her. She would never hurt anyone, and you killed her." Cyrus' voice grew louder, his words too frantic to be directed at any one person. Still, Aeliana felt each one aimed at her heart.

"What don't you understand about being quiet?" Vera hissed, her attention shifting to the surrounding forest.

Arvid finished his handiwork and stepped to Aeliana's left, eyes narrowed as his focus intensified between two trees. He rubbed his hands together, the congealed blood covering them still far too potent. The air around him practically hummed with the energy of it, but this time he held back, waiting for the right moment.

The change in tactic left Aeliana more wary than when he used the magic freely. She took a step away, gingerly letting her shirt and cloak fall against her back even though it stung. She'd need to leave it open to the air that night so it could scab over. Whenever Arvid had to treat it for infection, he blamed her.

Cyrus wiped his cheeks and stood, eyes blazing even through his grief.

Before Aeliana could question his fresh determination, a blinding light exploded, bringing them all to a crouch. It held more color and heat than Orra's light, and the scent of singed fabric and hair lingered in the air even as the heat receded. It had come from the space Arvid studied.

There was something else out there.

Arvid grunted, and as Aeliana's vision normalized, the sight of charred flesh on his arm made her stomach turn.

Despite his earlier rejection, Cyrus pushed Aeliana behind him, protecting her from the new threat just as Vera reached out a hand. Instead of finding Aeliana's arm, Vera trapped Cyrus in her iron grip. Undeterred, Vera pulled out a knife, slicing Cyrus on the palm.

The heat of Aeliana's wound flared, then sent a cold bite sliding down her spine. The sight of his blood spilling was like a deadly omen. "You can't even use his blood."

Cyrus' howl nearly drowned out her panicked words. The knife shifted dangerously close to his neck while the flow of blood poured uselessly from his hand to the moss as he squirmed and groaned.

"Maybe not, but if I slice a little deeper, a little higher, he won't have much use for it either," Vera said. "But if you give me some of yours, I can use it to heal him. Blood for blood."

Aeliana bit her lip in consideration. Vera wouldn't heal him, but she might trade Cyrus for Aeliana's blood. Cyrus' eyes begged her to respond, but she wasn't sure which answer he wanted her to give. He squeezed his good hand over the injured palm, applying pressure to lessen the flow.

Arvid took several steps toward the tree line, leaving Vera to deal with Cyrus and Aeliana while he dealt with whatever was in the woods. He roared, releasing his own rush of heat and fire, the blood on his hands like oil fueling flames. Aeliana had never seen him use magic so openly, the wildness of it terrifying and limitless. Even when he had welcomed the dark spirits, letting them fuse with his body, it had been done surreptitiously. But here, he had no reason to hide.

A figure emerged from the forest line, lit up but unharmed by Arvid's fire.

"Sylmar," Arvid hissed.

The other man, Sylmar, had greying hair and a short beard, and he gripped an intricately carved staff. He appeared more beast than man, the deep scars covering his face and arms like gouges cut from a craggy mountain, far different from the snake-like lines marring her palms. As he held out the staff, his gaze watched for Arvid's next move.

Now Aeliana knew why Vera wanted the blood trade, why she needed it now more than ever before. They'd left all their stores of her blood back in Lorvandas. They were running out, which meant Arvid's magic wasn't as limitless as it seemed. Understanding flashed on Cyrus' face as well.

"Run," Cyrus whispered, waving Aeliana on toward the tree line, distracting her from the tense words Arvid and Sylmar exchanged. Cyrus gasped as small drops of blood beaded down into his collar from the knife cutting his skin.

"If you run, he dies." The cold truth in Vera's voice made Aeliana shiver.

Sylmar adjusted his staff, using it more like a cane as he drew closer, his stance appearing too vulnerable to be the source of the sparks she'd first seen. A deep belly laugh rose from his throat, leaving Aeliana pained that the old man must be oblivious to the threat flowing in her veins.

She wanted to warn him away. He was no match for Arvid.

"Surely you knew I'd come." Sylmar's words came out raspy, like his insides held the same scars as his face and hands. "Where's Rildan?"

"In the Deep."

Aeliana's heart dropped to her stomach. Had Della's story been right? Had her father left the arrow for her? And died because of it?

Arvid widened his stance, elbows out, bouncing on his heels as if ready to pounce.

Sylmar made no move to defend himself or prepare for his own attack. "You never were a good liar."

Arvid scanned the skies, making everyone else glance up as well. The dark spirits couldn't follow them here, could they? If he gave control over to one, the battle would be finished before it had begun.

"Gone for fourteen years, and you're still doing her bidding?" Sylmar's taunt was like the flick of a switch.

Arvid's body tensed, the blood on his hands nearly glowing in the moonlight, as if to remind the enemy he hadn't completely used up his stores. "Mayvus rewards her faithful servants."

Sparks erupted from Sylmar's staff, which then shifted its shape to a sword. Arvid began throwing flames instead of words once more, and stray sparks grazed Cyrus and Vera. The brunt of it smoked Cyrus' arm, and he screamed, taking Vera's focus off Aeliana. Still, her hold on the knife remained steady on Cyrus, his life held in her unpredictable hands.

"Time's up," Vera said, using her free hand to toss a glass bottle at Aeliana's feet, where it bounced in the moss. "Just one more bottle. Then we'll leave you two to survive the jungles of Vendaras."

"I'm not worth it." Cyrus winced as Vera adjusted her grip on the knife.

They would get her blood either way. They always did. But at least she could save his life. She bent to retrieve the glass bottle, then eyed his wound, still seeping despite the pressure. Hopefully, she could still save him.

Vera pulled a second knife from her boot, tossing it in Aeliana's direction.

The decision felt wrong. There was a reason they wanted her blood, and it couldn't be good. But nothing was more valuable than a life, and the life in front of her was the life she could save right now. Aeliana yanked the stopper from the bottle with renewed purpose.

She couldn't watch Cyrus die. Not when she could do something about it.

She picked up the knife and sliced the skin of her palm, letting the blood fill the tiny jar. It was nothing compared to the blood they'd taken in the past.

She dropped to her knees, and the muggy air turned chilly, goosebumps rising on her flesh. A sense of euphoria mixed with shame flooded through her as a desire grew to spill more blood even once the bottle was full. Green shoots rose from the ground, and her eyelids fluttered, her mind losing control over her body. The power of her blood filled her, taking over her senses. The urge to give in to the blood's demands hit harder than ever before, as if freely giving it made it stronger than when it was forcibly taken.

The only thing that brought her back to her senses was Cyrus' mournful cry.

She stoppered the jar, then pressed the wound hard against her thigh, standing and stomping out the daisies that had grown. Her breath came out ragged, her muscles limp like she'd run to Gahldric Valley and back. A dark shadow flitted across the sky, black against the moon's light. Maybe the dark spirits could cross the barrier. Or maybe these were different dark spirits, unique to Vendaras.

"Now let him go," she demanded, her voice almost as hoarse as Sylmar's.

"Give me the blood first." When Vera held out her hand, the edge of the golden arrow peeked out from inside her cloak.

For a moment, Aeliana wanted to barter for that as well, but it was too risky. She reached back and flung the bottle high above Vera.

Vera pushed Cyrus out of her way as she lunged for the blood. Aeliana reached for Cyrus to stop his fall, but he pulled her down with him, the moss breaking their fall even as tiny bamboo shoots dug into their backs. For a moment she let herself feel the crash of anxiety and relief, and she leaned over to bury her face in his shirt.

Sweet Stars, she hoped she'd made the right choice.

"Why would you do that?" The frustration in Cyrus' voice was softened by his arm wrapping around her. "Gams sacrificed herself for you to escape them. She told me to protect you. Not the other way around."

He had every right to question Aeliana, but she had no answer.

The plain stars above twinkled in the sky, and the heavenly Stars did their dance as if unaware of—or maybe uninterested in—what took place in this tiny clearing. Vera ignored them as she cradled the vial of blood in her hands, and Sylmar and Arvid were locked in battle, sparks and fire flying as they danced in and out of the other's reach, both surprisingly spry.

"Come on. Let's go," Aeliana whispered, rolling away from Cyrus. They crept through the brush, and Aeliana was thankful for the return of shouts and flames, which drew attention away from their escape.

Another distant glow of fire shone at their backs, briefly lighting up the night and forest before them. It revealed a lanky man with black hair sheared close to his head. Aeliana gasped, and Cyrus tripped, falling to his knees. The stranger leaned against a set of particularly thick vines a dozen feet away.

"Where do you two think you're going?" His voice was smooth, like a storyteller's polished timbre. A lazy grin split his face. "Honestly, I leave Sylmar alone for mere moments, and he gets himself into all sorts of trouble. I'm gonna enjoy holding this over his head for years to come."

He pushed off the vines and ambled their way, his manner easy and unthreatening. Still, Aeliana backed away, tugging Cyrus with her. If the stranger was with Sylmar, he probably didn't intend to kill them, but that could just mean they wanted her alive for something far worse.

Striking blue eyes stood out from laugh lines even in the low light. Fish hooks hung from his ears, and despite the rebellious tilt to his smile, he seemed old enough to be her father. His tight breeches and simple vest over a bare chest and deep brown skin seemed more suited to a sailor. When he clapped a hand on Aeliana's shoulder, water immediately soaked through her cloak and tunic, and he removed his hand with a suction noise.

"The name's Velden, but I should really go help our friend before we finish introductions. He might come in handy someday." His words held a soft lilt, like his consonants were lighter and his vowels longer. Even Sylmar's throaty rasp had held the same strange enunciations. It was a tiny difference, but Aeliana realized if Arvid's and Vera's voices hadn't been so harsh and overbearing, she might have caught the hint of an old accent, further proof that she'd been brought from this foreign land.

Cyrus struggled to rise with his injured arm, and the man held out webbed fingers, easily pulling Cyrus to his feet. A slimy, wet residue clung between their hands as the man let go.

Cyrus made a face and rubbed his hand on his cloak. "Thanks?"

Before Velden could run off, Sylmar hobbled their way, leaning on his staff far heavier than he had when he'd first arrived.

Aeliana tensed, peering around him for her guardians to follow, but for now, he came alone.

"Where in Rhystahn did you go?" Sylmar's rasp made Aeliana's skin crawl. He drew closer, his glare resting on Velden. "The one night I truly need you, you're nowhere to be found."

"Ah, so you *do* like having me around." Velden beamed at him. "I'm never sure with all your grumbling. Kendalyhn's stew didn't agree much with me." He made a face and rubbed his belly.

"Oh, for the Sun's fire," Sylmar muttered. "Just lead the way back to camp."

"Of course, Wise One." Velden's low bow matched the drip of sarcasm in his tone.

"What about Arvid and Vera?" Aeliana asked.

"They gave up after you left. Rushed for the valley." Sylmar's furious glare didn't fade. "But who knows what kind of reinforcements they have?"

"They just left?" Aeliana frowned, her gaze still scanning the forest behind Sylmar. She supposed that was what Vera had said she'd do if she got Aeliana's blood, but it wasn't like them.

"Probably to get help," Sylmar reiterated.

It made sense, but it still seemed too easy.

"Come on," Velden called as he wound his way deeper into the forest. Sylmar gestured for Aeliana and Cyrus to follow.

"You want us to go with you?" Cyrus asked, hunching over his injured arm.

Velden turned, his amusement contrasting Sylmar's impatience.

"Of course," Sylmar said.

"You're the reason we came here," Velden added, his gaze resting on Aeliana.

CHAPTER 12

"How can you be here because of me?" Aeliana asked, stepping back from Sylmar and Velden.

"You're the daughter of Emeris Wyndren, the high priestess," Sylmar said. "After fourteen years missing, she's still the hope of the Vendaran people, who have been under tyranny for far too long. We've all made a promise to protect you for her sake." He glanced back over his shoulder as if expecting Arvid or Vera at any moment. It was a legitimate concern, but following strangers into the woods seemed equally concerning.

Still, what if he could tell her more? Aeliana let her mother's name roll around in her mind, trying to decide if it fit the woman she couldn't remember. She joined it with Rildan as if their names alone could bring back knowledge lost long ago.

"She sounds… important," Aeliana said.

Sylmar studied her but didn't expand on her family history.

"She's also just a really nice person. Everyone loves her," Velden added, then frowned. "Except for the king and queen. And Mayvus. And anyone who serves them."

"Which is why we need to leave," Sylmar said. "Now."

"That still doesn't explain how you knew I'd be here." Aeliana crossed her arms over her chest. "Tonight."

"We didn't," Velden said. "Not exactly. It's the drop-off point for the Lorvandan starbridge, and we knew you'd arrive here sometime between your seventeenth and eighteenth year. Your parents always planned to have your father bring you back sometime this year. Only… he didn't bring you back. Arvid and Vera did. So we got a bit lucky on the timing."

Their answers only stirred up a dozen more questions, reminding her they could be telling just as many lies as Arvid and Vera.

"Run to safety now, answer questions later," Velden said. He tugged on Cyrus' sleeve and angled his head toward the woods, but Cyrus let out an awful moan.

Velden released his grip, and Cyrus pulled back his sleeve. The gash on his hand seemed longer, stretching into his wrist and continuing to pool blood. Aeliana gasped, closing the distance between them.

"Oh, Cyrus." She held out a hand, but he flinched back from her touch. "I'm so sorry." He never should have crossed the barrier. He should have been worshiping the Stars under the watchful eyes of his grandparents, who should both still be very much alive. Why in Rhystahn had every little detail gone wrong to leave him here like this?

Sylmar kneeled down in front of Cyrus, who still held his hand protectively against his chest. Velden stood behind him, placing his hands on Cyrus' shoulders, holding him in place.

Aeliana's skin prickled. "What are you doing?"

Sylmar positioned his hands on Cyrus' arm, eliciting a whimper that elevated to a cry.

"You're hurting him." Aeliana yanked on Sylmar's arms, but he was like a rock, eyes closed, hands sliding along Cyrus' exposed flesh. She pulled harder, but her efforts only brought Velden around to pull her away.

"Just watch," the man whispered as his sticky fingers held her wrists.

Cyrus' cries settled into a sigh, his eyes closing. This time, when Aeliana pressed forward, Velden let her. Beneath Sylmar's hands, Cyrus' flesh melded together, the line of the cut more stain than wound. It was sloppy, but effective, and the bleeding ceased.

"Thank you," Cyrus murmured.

"I can only do so much. We need Lukai." Sylmar opened his eyes to half slits and rubbed at the scruff of his beard. "Wrap the skin. It will be tender." It seemed like he wanted to say more, but he sat back in a slump.

Velden reached into a bag tied at his waist, pulling out what looked like dried seaweed. It expanded before Aeliana's eyes, dripping with water coming from Velden's webbed fingers. He wrapped the moist plant around Cyrus' hand like a bandage, the seaweed clinging to itself as if growing into one solid mass.

"That should help some with the pain, too," Velden said.

"But you—you healed him," Aeliana said.

Velden glanced up at her, his smile shifting to a smirk as he stood. "What did you think we were doing?"

She clamped her lips down, aware her mouth had hung open like a child's on Winter Solstice.

Velden turned to Sylmar, not waiting for an answer as he bent over the older man to assess his strength.

She'd expected Velden and Sylmar to act as Arvid had. To use Cyrus' vulnerability to their advantage. But healing him…with magic?

That idea had never occurred to her. It made even less sense than her assumption, and yet she'd seen it with her own eyes. She supposed that was what Arvid did on a much smaller scale each time he cut her and then sealed her skin. From Arvid, it had seemed like self-preservation, to ensure no one knew what he'd done, but from Sylmar it had seemed…kind.

She scratched at the edge of the marks on her back, the ones Arvid had placed when they first arrived. She was tempted to ask them to heal those wounds but wasn't sure she trusted anyone to use any kind of magic on her. What would happen when her magic made its second mark in a few days? Would the marks go away on their own, or would she have to ask someone to remove them?

Out of habit, she scanned the skies, but there were no dark spirits.

"You're half-lights." She said the words slowly, as if drawing the truth out of them with each syllable. "And you use your blood for magic?"

Velden's head bobbed back and forth as if weighing her words. "We use the energy in our blood, yes."

She glanced at his hands, both exposed and fully intact. "Where do you draw it from?"

Velden's brow furrowed, but it was Sylmar who responded with his own question, his voice wary. "When did Arvid and Vera take you from your father?"

"My father?" She hated how the word rekindled that same hope. It was like they knew the mention of the parents she thought were dead was enough to get her to stay and hear them out. "I've never met my father."

Velden's eyes widened. He reached for her hand, pulling her sleeve back to reveal the scars crisscrossing her palm, along with her current wound, which still oozed.

Aeliana surprised herself by being slow to cover the scars, unsure if she was still in shock over the events of the night or if she maybe wanted him to see. Wanted him to understand without her having to explain. But why didn't he and Sylmar have the same scars as her?

Sylmar swore under his breath. "She's been trained in blood magic."

"How often do you draw your blood?" Velden asked.

"They took blood almost daily. Stored what they didn't use."

Velden and Sylmar exchanged a glance.

"She'll need to be weaned," Sylmar said.

Velden grimaced. "We don't have time for that."

"We'll have to make time."

"What are you talking about?" Aeliana asked, rising from the moss.

Distant shouts carried on the wind, and they all stiffened.

"We can't stay here. It's not safe." Sylmar stood as well, leaning heavily on his staff, which now appeared solid again. "Come with us. We'll have Lukai heal your friend. We can teach you about your magic. All the things Arvid and Vera probably left out."

Velden nodded, then gripped Cyrus' elbows to pull him to his feet. Something shifted between them, as if the motion brought Cyrus awake and made Velden tired. Like energy had been passed or shared between them. All three turned toward the forest, but Aeliana held her ground.

"Can you teach me how to get rid of my magic?" she asked.

Velden stilled, and Sylmar glanced back, squinting at Aeliana. "Get rid of it? Whatever for?"

"The magic in my blood…" She hesitated. "It's done unspeakable things."

Sylmar grunted his disagreement. "Arvid and Vera have done unspeakable things using your blood."

He turned once more to lead them through the forest.

"I killed an entire family," Aeliana blurted out.

Cyrus' mouth dropped open, and she lowered her eyes.

"I ran from Arvid and Vera and hid in a barn, but the pain—I couldn't take it. I used leeches to drain my blood, but it wasn't enough. When I finally released my blood"—she shuddered—"the owners and their children…they were all dead."

The repetitive call of an exotic bird was all Aeliana heard for several long moments.

"You remember killing them?" Sylmar asked.

Aeliana shook her head. "There are gaps in my memory. When the magic builds and finally releases… I'm not always in control."

"You probably invited in dark spirits." Sylmar's voice held a rebuke.

"She didn't know," Velden said.

"It still makes the weaning process that much harder." Sylmar studied her like a wild animal he debated putting down or trying to tame.

"What dark spirits?" Cyrus asked.

Sylmar ignored his question, turning back around. "You couldn't have killed the farmer's family without help," he called over his shoulder as he resumed walking. "Not without a starlock."

Aeliana pictured the barrel of trinkets she'd seen in the Stargazer, but she still didn't know what they were. Even so, his words gave her pause. If her blood alone hadn't killed the family, what had?

When she followed Sylmar, Velden and Cyrus took up the rear.

"Was it the dark spirits?" she asked. The idea wasn't any more palatable, not if she was the one who called them by spilling her blood, but it helped her understand how it had happened.

"More likely Arvid," Velden muttered from behind.

They fell into line, and Aeliana mulled over Velden's accusation, afraid to hope that it could be true. She still wasn't completely innocent if Arvid had used her blood, but maybe there was a chance she could learn to neutralize it.

If Sylmar and Velden weren't concerned about the dangers of her magic, then she'd go with them, for now. Not because they offered to teach her magic, and as terrible as it was, not even because they had someone who could heal Cyrus.

They claimed to know her parents, and, if her parents still lived, she wanted to find them.

Sylmar led them to the other side of the clearing, then down a path through the rainforest. His pace was slow considering the urgency he'd expressed.

Aeliana lifted her hair off her neck, wondering if this heat was why both men kept their hair so short. Random questions like that mingled with more complicated questions about magic and starbridges and… her parents, making it difficult to focus and grasp the most important ones.

"Are you still looking for my—my mother?" The familial word felt strange, yet welcome, on her lips.

"There's been no need to search." Sylmar turned, his face twisted in what she thought was a grimace but might have been sympathy. "When your father took you across the barrier, Mayvus kidnapped your mother. We haven't had the resources to rescue her until recently, but we knew she would want us to ensure your safety first."

One truth stood out from his dire words: her mother was alive.

"And my father? Rildan?"

"Time will tell. I don't believe Arvid was telling the truth, but I didn't have magic to waste on sifting his words."

"Who is Mayvus?" Aeliana asked.

"Mayvus is another high priestess," Velden said. "She wasn't as popular as Emeris, so she took out the competition."

Sylmar grunted from up ahead but didn't comment.

"That's not—" Cyrus straightened, affronted. "What kind of priestesses do you have over here?"

"Most are harmless," Velden said. "Mayvus is her own kind."

"Now that you've found me," Aeliana asked, "are we going to rescue my mother?"

"It's not that simple, but yes." Sylmar's voice ebbed and flowed with the wind.

"It can be that simple," Velden said. "But not if Sylmar's explaining it."

The older man rested his glare on Velden. "We have a handful of progenies hidden in a cave. Our group's mission was to retrieve you. Now that we've accomplished it, we'll head out to join the others. Make our way to Mayvus so we can rescue your mother."

"What are progenies?" Cyrus asked.

"Half-lights who can do magic," Velden said.

"That's not exactly precise if—" Sylmar started.

Velden let out a theatrical gasp. "I forgot," he said, raising his hands in mock defense. "No one but the master may instruct the students."

Aeliana felt the tug of a smile on her lips, a strange sensation after all they'd been through. Then she caught sight of Cyrus studying her, as if applying their words to who she was and what she could do. There was a hint of admiration in his gaze that she didn't want.

She rushed to catch up with Sylmar. "What did you mean when you said I needed to be weaned?"

"Your body is used to the release of blood," Sylmar said. "It's like a cow that needs milking. The more the cow is milked, the more its body supplies milk to meet the demand."

Velden groaned from behind Aeliana. "Have some tact, my friend. You just compared the lady to a cow."

Cyrus laughed uncomfortably, but Aeliana wasn't amused or offended. The words touched on the truth of her experience too much for her to feel anything other than understood.

"It builds," she agreed. "Like a boil needing to burst."

Velden made a noise of disgust. "That's even worse."

"But apt." A smile was evident in Sylmar's voice, like a teacher pleased by his student's success.

"Can my blood be neutralized?" Aeliana asked.

"You can learn to control its energy," Velden said.

Aeliana shook her head. "No. I mean, remove it."

Sylmar paused, half turning to study her face. He cleared his throat. "If you learn to control it, there will be no need to remove it. But our priority will be weaning you from the blood magic." He faced forward again, picking up his lumbering pace among the thinning foliage.

She didn't quite agree, but less supply and demand of magic was a step in the right direction.

"What about Arvid and Vera?" Cyrus asked. "Why didn't they just use their own blood?"

"They did," Aeliana said. "I mean, when I was younger. Around thirteen, they tested mine and never went back. I used to think they didn't want to cut themselves, but now I'm guessing theirs isn't as strong."

"Exactly," Sylmar said. "They have so little starblood they probably never even had the basic skills in the hub of the Wheel of Magic."

"What's the Wheel of Magic?" Cyrus asked, his voice breathy.

"Now you've done it," Velden muttered.

Aeliana glanced back, tripping over a root jutting out of the rich soil. Cyrus' eyes glinted in the moonlight. She thought she'd sentenced him to this foreign existence after watching his grandmother murdered, but he almost sounded eager to be here. She supposed it was like the books in the Stargazer's library coming to life for him.

"If the source of our magic is the energy in our blood, the Wheel of Magic is the product." Sylmar's voice gained volume, the gravelly quality thicker and more obvious. "The simplest magic only requires that energy—the movement of small objects, the infusion of that energy into muscle. It enhances what our bodies and the things around us already do on a daily basis by speeding it up or making it more. That type of adjustment is the hub of the Wheel, and most half-lights who have enough starblood can make those adjustments during their puberty years."

Waves crashed against a rocky beach they'd almost reached, the sound overriding everything else. The surrounding bamboo had been replaced by ferns, which were thinning as the soil grew rockier. Light finally filtered through the clouds as the moon's descent shifted to the Sun's morn. There wasn't a boat in sight.

Despite everything, there was something about the sea that calmed Aeliana, something about the salty scent that put her at ease.

"And then they're trained to control it?" she asked. If that was the case, she was several years behind.

"Not quite." Sylmar paused to lean heavily on his staff. "If they don't earn a starlock, they outgrow their skills. Only the progenies go on to train. So even though you have magic, you won't be a progeny until you earn your starlock."

"What's a starlock?" Cyrus asked.

"It's a lock of hair sent down by the Stars." Sylmar reached under his tunic, pulling out a metal staff hung from a leather cord, an oddly detailed miniature of the weapon he carried. "They're encased in metal, each a unique shape. They enhance a half-light's magic, guiding and controlling it along one of the three spokes on the Wheel of Magic —pneumatic, somatic, and noetic. But starlocks are becoming more and more rare. It's not even one in ten anymore."

"They're earned during an Awakening," Velden added. "Usually some life-threatening experience that's never spoken of."

"Unless you're Velden," Sylmar muttered.

Velden turned and winked at Aeliana. "I fought off a giant squid that had just smashed an entire ship in half. How could I not talk about it?"

For a moment, both she and Cyrus chuckled, but when their eyes met, his smile dropped, his face taking on the heaviness of grief.

Sylmar cleared his throat. "Awakenings are both feared and desired. Not everyone survives, but if you walk away with a starlock, you are chosen—a progeny—handpicked by the Sun to tap deeper into the Wheel of Magic."

Aeliana shivered. It sounded like the exact opposite of what she was asking them to teach her.

"The Sun?" Cyrus asked. "You mean the Stars?"

"The Stars are created beings just like us," Sylmar said. "They serve the Sun and do its bidding, same as we do."

For a moment, Cyrus looked like he might argue, but thankfully, he kept his mouth shut.

They followed the shoreline around until it looked like they'd be forced to stop where the water met a cliff.

"A starlock functions like the axle of the Wheel," Sylmar added. "It gets it turning, allowing the progeny to develop stronger magic along one of the spokes. There's a constructive and destructive side to each of the three spokes, giving six possible paths out from the axle for each progeny."

Aeliana's heart pounded, pushing the blood she'd always seen as a danger faster through her veins. Sylmar talked of it all almost lovingly, but to Aeliana it sounded no better than the magic her guardians had used.

"How does blood magic fit in?" she asked.

His face grew grim as the scars puckered his eyes and lips into an even deeper frown. "Blood magic skips from the hub to the rim of the Wheel, giving half-lights access to uncontrolled elemental magic. It's a distortion of magic's design. A cheat. And it comes with great consequences. I'm grateful they didn't teach you to perform the magic with them, but rather stole your blood for their own use."

Velden snorted. "They weren't protecting her. They were protecting themselves. They knew she would grow into a progeny who would surpass their skills."

Sylmar lifted a shoulder. "And yet I'm still grateful. The addiction to her blood's release will be hard enough to break as it is. It would be far worse if she were also addicted to the rush of using it. It would be much harder for her to resist the pull of the dark spirits."

Despite the warm air, Aeliana's limbs felt like ice. She'd rather give up the minimal good that might come from using her blood's power than risk giving in to its darker pull.

Sylmar stopped near an outcropping, and they halted with him, water lapping at their heels. He then tapped against thick vines growing along a rock. The leaves muted the sound of his staff until his tapping revealed a small gap in the vines.

"Here we are," Sylmar said.

From inside the cave, hands split the vines to reveal a man's shocked face.

"Sun's fire, you found her." Morning dew from the vines fell into his golden hair, the short ends curling slightly around the crown of his head. The upturn of his nose gave him a playful look despite the worry pinching his features.

Heat spread across her cheeks when he studied her in return. It was as if he was evaluating her worth, but unlike the inebriated men Arvid spent time with, this man's pale blue eyes were clear. And instead of drunken lust, his freshly shaved face held admiration.

The longer he stared, the more uncomfortable Aeliana grew, and yet there was something almost familiar about him. Like she'd known him years ago, and if they spent a single day catching up, they'd be the best of friends.

"Welcome home, Aeliana." His voice softened, as though it were just the two of them standing at the mouth of the cave. He held out a hand, not in greeting, but in invitation. Was he going to pull her in for a hug?

Aeliana bristled at the familiarity, but it also stirred something inside her, unlocking some dormant part of who she'd been long ago.

Cyrus leaned in to whisper. "Do you know him?"

Aeliana blinked, the spell between her and the stranger finally broken.

Velden chuckled. "Aeliana, meet Lukai—your bondmate."

CHAPTER 13

By the time Gaeren reached town, he had to hunt Larkos down in a tavern to round up their crew and supplies early. The loyal man grumbled at the inconvenience until Gaeren handed over his family ring. The royal seal would open every door as well as every mouth, but Gaeren was more concerned about missing whatever remained at Bamboo Island than he was worried about people's assumptions and interpretations of his purpose and sanity.

With Larkos managing the final tasks, Gaeren returned home to get his bags packed and affairs settled. Half his wardrobe lay spread across his bed when the dreaded knock came at his door.

Enla barged in without waiting for a reply.

"What is the meaning of this?" She held out a paper with the family's seal, but Gaeren didn't bother taking it before stuffing more clothes in a bag.

"A request to procure an artifact." He had to give some credit to Larkos. He'd worked fast in one night.

"Yes. I can read." His sister raised her eyebrows. "I already told you no."

"You said no to Valorian and Lovers' Falls. Now I want to go to Bamboo Island." He didn't care as much about the starbridge anymore. Not if Aeliana had crossed the barrier with it, but Enla didn't need to know all that.

Gaeren left her standing open-mouthed as he closed his last bag and headed to the next room, where a steaming bath with lilac soaps and fresh night clothes waited.

"Do you think it's Lovers' Falls I'm afraid of? I need you here, Gaeren."

"We both know you don't trust me enough to give me any responsibilities you aren't overseeing. You'll take care of things while I'm gone." He pulled his shirt off and threw it at Enla to give him space from her glare.

She sputtered and flung it off her shoulder, then spun on her heel as he tugged down his pants. "Gaeren Elanesse! You're impossible. Mother and Father already think you're a lost cause. It's like you don't want me to convince them you can be more."

Gaeren smiled as he eased into the bath, letting the steam and flower scent invade him. He'd hoped stripping for a bath would make his sister leave, but it was easier having this conversation with her back, so it was still a win. "You shouldn't have to convince them. They should see that all on their own because they see what I'm doing and they understand. Not because you've made me do what you would do if you were me."

Some sort of huff met his ears, but he dunked under water, grateful he couldn't see her expression. When he surfaced, she was mid-speech.

"—the one person I trust. You're my one ally. What does it say to Mother and Father every time you hop on a boat? What does it say to Lenda every time you leave without even a goodbye? That's not how you should treat your bondmate. And what about me?"

Gaeren rested his arms over the tub's edge, the break in his sister's voice finding that little nerve in his body that knew how to twinge with guilt.

"We have meetings with the council," she continued, "dignitaries coming from Mayvus—"

"Mayvus?" Gaeren asked. An image of the high priestess and her wicked grin, more teeth than lips, floated through Gaeren's mind. "I've never trusted her. Why do we need to meet with dignitaries from the eastern provinces anyway?"

Mayvus' control as a high priestess over the other servants of the

Sun in the Sungazers had been growing in the east. Between her subtle shift in power and the Recreants' outright demand to bring down the monarchy, he didn't know which was the bigger threat to their family's rule in Elanesse. But for some reason, his sister and parents weren't concerned.

"Don't you pay attention to anything? Mother and Father want to seal her authority as a spiritual leader for the nation in order to differentiate their governing authority. Plus, there are the Recreants in the south to deal with. I need you around when things get hard."

"I'm not abandoning you. I'll be back well before the dignitaries arrive. If you trust me as much as you say, trust that this is something I need to do. Not just for me, but for you, for our people." His words weren't lies, but he wasn't sure he could explain their truth. Daisy was important. He'd known it as a child, and his certainty had only grown over the years.

Enla's hesitation gave him hope. He lathered up with soap, waiting for her response, but the longer her silence went on, the more his hope soured into dread.

"Who is she?"

He stilled, the water suddenly too cold, too suffocating. "You sifted my future."

It wasn't a question. It was the only way she could know. He'd never spoken about Daisy with Enla. Normally she had to be near the person whose future she sifted, but with Gaeren, she had other means —objects that contained elements of his essence. Over the years, it had progressed from childhood trinkets to locks of hair and letters. Now he was fairly certain she'd gone back to using the pyramid-shaped bead they'd made with Riveran years ago. Sometimes the older and more meaningful objects were better conduits.

"Every path I sift has you leaving on that boat. Not every path has you returning." Her soft words held pain.

He winced. "You shouldn't search that much."

When she went down multiple paths, it left her weak, and not just because it drained the energy in her starlock. There was a confusion that came with seeing so many options, almost like having a memory play out a hundred different ways until she couldn't remember how it really happened. Only worse, because the memories were mere possibilities.

"If you're honest with me, I won't need to search so much."

He studied the slump of her shoulders, the way her feet scuffed at the tile. She wore the soft pants and tunic reserved for sleeping, and her hair was loose around her ears and forehead as if hiding her starlock could hide the weight of her role. She was his sister once more instead of the future queen. Older than him, but always smaller, needing protection. Protection he didn't feel fit to provide.

"What did she look like?" he asked. It could be the stranger he'd met, but he suspected it was Daisy. Or maybe he hoped. Knowing she was in his future only spurred him on to leave sooner.

"Strange." Enla's voice gained the faraway tone that never failed to make Gaeren squirm. Her visions were always disjointed. Their accuracy had grown with her trainer's influence, but they were still too unpredictable to be anything other than a suggestion. "Like she's from another time. Russet brown waves to her waist, piercing green eyes. Regal grace in humble rags. Remember your bond. You forget in some paths."

He snorted at the idea. He was chasing a child, an innocent life he'd always felt responsible for. But the warning in Enla's voice was unmistakable. He did the math, realizing the girl would be approaching eighteen, more of a woman. The five years that separated them in childhood would feel far less now. Gaeren shook his head to clear his thoughts. Bonded or not, he didn't have time for distractions.

"Her name is D—Aeliana." He supposed he should learn to call her by her real name. It wasn't likely that she still made daisy chains into crowns. "She's the daughter of my dedication priestess."

Enla shifted, as if she might turn around, then caught herself. "Mother said you came home early because the priestess died."

"Huh. Interesting." He'd always wondered what his parents had been told. He stood and grabbed a towel off the stool to wrap it around himself. Enla still didn't turn as he stepped out, dripping on the rug. Maybe if he told her the truth, she'd let him go. "I don't actually know what happened to the priestess. Maybe she died. I hope not. But people came to steal Aeliana away. A bright light took her, along with her father and two of the strangers. They crossed the barrier with a starbridge." He spoke with confidence, but Enla still laughed.

"Starbridges aren't real. They're part of the ancient myths."

"Fernandus would be horrified to hear your heretical words." He knew she smiled even though she still didn't turn. The old priest was half-blind and mostly deaf, but he doted on them both as if they were his grandchildren. Gaeren's faith had far more to do with Fernandus' care and convictions than anything Gaeren had learned from his parents.

"Something else probably blinded you as they ran off. You were young. You can't trust your memories." Her voice hitched. She knew all too well that he could trust his memories. Tuning in to memories was his strongest point on the noetic spoke. He'd relived the memory a thousand times, the small girl's wide green eyes, her pudgy hands reaching out to him even as her father took her away. The starbridge was supposed to have taken them to safety, but the strangers had used blood magic. Crossing the barrier wouldn't have kept Daisy and her father safe from that.

Gaeren ran a hand through his wet hair, then shook his head like a dog, more to splash Enla than to dry off. "Earlier tonight, there was a light across the water."

She stepped away, glaring over her shoulder as he grinned.

"I've heard. It's all the servants can talk about. Some light from the southern provinces. They think it had to have been a high priest or some other extremely powerful progeny who died. Either that or someone who's about to come into a lot of power. There are rumors it was more than one Star who must have delivered or removed a starlock."

Gaeren let out a derisive snort. The Stars no longer communed with people, but they still came to deliver and remove the charms blessed by the Sun. When a progeny passed on to the Sun's brilliance, their body and starlock were left on the rooftop to be burned up by the Stars. Both the delivery and removal left a streak of light in the night sky, but neither matched what Gaeren had seen.

"I saw it with my own eyes from the mangrove trees. It's not a star-lock. It was identical to the light I saw as a child."

Her skeptical gaze faltered. "Meeting Riveran again?" She almost sounded jealous.

He held back his surprise. "No. I haven't seen him since Mother and Father's party." Might as well come clean if she already suspected.

She bit her lip and turned away. "I've heard he's in trouble."

"Trouble?" He grabbed the stack of clothes and stalked back to the bedroom.

"That's all I know. You'll have to ask him for details."

"I don't want details." He pulled on his shirt, and Enla settled by the door, her back turned again.

"Fine. Tell me more about the light."

"It came from across the water and traveled east to the southern provinces. Near Bamboo Island."

"Impossible."

He laughed as he pulled on pants. "You still don't believe humans exist across the barrier? I told you I saw them a year ago when—"

"You've always told me you've seen things. Ever since we were kids. You've made every effort to trick me into believing the most ridiculous lies, so forgive me if I don't believe everything you say anymore."

He tapped her shoulder, and she turned, unable to hide the hurt in her eyes.

"Everything I'm telling you now is true. No lies and no jesting. There's another woman in the mangrove trees. Her name is Orra. Short dark hair, skin a shade lighter than mine. She's young, I think. But her eyes are…ancient, weighted. Was she in your visions?"

Enla frowned. "No. What is she doing out there?"

"Hopefully recovering. When I found her, I thought she was dead, but then she sucked in a breath, and it was like her skin glowed. It wasn't purely somatic energy. No one can bring themselves back from the dead like that."

Enla shook her head slightly. "That's not—I've never heard of magic like that."

"Exactly."

"Do you think it could be blood magic?" Enla whispered, her face draining of color.

He'd be lying if he said he hadn't already thought of it. "There was no blood. I saw no brands on her hands. Unless she had vials of it stashed somewhere, but she was clean. I don't see how she could have used it that way."

Enla nodded, the relief on her face mirroring his own. Most blood magic was detested by all Vendarans, even Recreants, but the royal family had outlawed all forms of it two generations past. Recreants still fought for the right to do tracking spells, claiming their use was no different from the innocent amounts of blood mixed for a bonding ceremony. But if they decreed those forms of blood magic lawful today, tomorrow the Recreants would ask to use it for branding, then rim magic—or even to call the dark spirits.

It wasn't worth the risk.

"She wants me to take her to the starbridge on Bamboo Island," Gaeren said. "Friend or foe, I need to see this through to understand what she can do. With her advanced magic, maybe she could even help Mother." It was a low blow to drag their mother's health into the equation, but it was also the truth. "You won't even know I'm gone."

She chewed her lip, eyes on his neck. "You'll return within a moon's cycle?"

"Maybe sooner." He grinned, even though it was unlikely with or without favorable winds.

She smacked his shoulder. "I meant what I said. I need you around."

"I know." He tried to wipe the smile off his face so his words might be more reassuring. The anticipation of being on the open seas, finding answers to his oldest questions, and discovering new magic made it impossible to contain his excitement.

"I need you to promise me that this is your last trip." Enla wrapped her hands around his forearm, her face pinched with the anxious weight of all her responsibilities. "Even if you don't find what you're looking for. It's time for you to settle down with Lenda and be my throne warden."

Most throne wardens took on their role at eighteen, and she'd let him roam the seas until twenty-three. She'd given him far more time than he deserved, and yet it would never feel like enough. Not unless he came back with Daisy.

"I promise," he said, hoping it was true. Not because he truly agreed, but because this time he would find her. If he didn't, he might never get another chance to look.

Enla's eyes lost focus again, visions plaguing her in ways he'd never understand. "You can go to Bamboo Island. Trust Riveran to have your back."

"What does Riveran have to do with anything?"

She ignored his question. "And stay away from Lovers' Falls."

"All right." He wasn't planning to go to Lovers' Falls anymore, anyway.

"I have one more condition." Enla crossed her arms over her chest.

Still buoyant from his success, he let a dangerous word slip from his mouth. "Anything."

"Take Lenda with you."

CHAPTER 14

"BONDMATE?" Aeliana frowned, no more certain over who Lukai was now than she'd been before the introductions.

"Yes, yes, now get inside the cave." Sylmar drew the vines back farther. He ushered them all into the dark until the vines could swing back in place behind him, effectively hiding them from view.

A small lantern rested on a rock, the dim light from its fire casting more shadow than glow.

"What's a bondmate?" Cyrus asked.

Lukai held out his right hand, but this time he angled it palm up to reveal a dark mark, like a teardrop. Aeliana gasped, holding out her hand with its matching mark before she could think the action through. Lukai locked his fingers with hers, and warmth spread between their palms as if the marks conducted heat when they touched.

He smiled, his eyes never leaving her face. "When two people are bonded, it strengthens the connection between them the more they're with each other."

Sylmar huffed, picking up the lamp to lead the way through the cave.

When Aeliana broke away from Lukai's gaze, Velden's features were tight. "Don't mind Sylmar's pessimistic views on love."

Aeliana dropped Lukai's hand like a hot coal. "Love?"

Velden's tension dissipated as he laughed. "Bonds were originally used for protection. Sometimes for a parent and child or comrades in war. The desire to protect a bondmate overruled any fears. When used between spouses, the bond gained a depth unlike any other. Over time, it's evolved into something shared mostly between couples, either as a part of their wedding ceremony or their betrothal."

"Which is why you should have let me swap watch with Velden tonight," Lukai called out to Sylmar, bending forward to grab his bag. "I sensed she was in danger. It was driving me mad."

"You've sensed it almost daily for the last four years," Sylmar grumbled, his voice echoing back to them against the cavern walls.

"Considering she was with Arvid and Vera," Velden said, "she probably was in danger daily."

Lukai frowned, and the lamp's light caught on a silver object hanging from a leather cord around his neck. A starlock? He tucked it under his shirt and followed Velden, his broad back blocking most of the light. Aeliana and Cyrus quickly joined the procession.

"The royal family is one of the few left who use bonds from childhood," Lukai said over his shoulder. "The older a bond, the stronger it is. It's meant for protection more than love, but the two often go together like starlocks and progenies. Your mother knew from the start that you would be in danger. Bonding is only one of many things she did to protect you."

"Was the starbridge another?" Cyrus asked from behind Aeliana, his tone unreadable. Was he bitter? Or merely curious?

"Yes," Velden said.

What had originally sounded loving now felt selfish. Aeliana's mother had put protective measures in place for her, but at the cost of so many other lives.

"Our bond allowed me to sense your well-being, even across the barrier." Lukai turned, placing a finger on his matching mark.

The same sense of warmth that had been present when Lukai held her hand returned. She rubbed at the mark, a wariness settling at the edges of any comfort she might feel. She'd felt that warmth before, several times over the years. Now that she knew he'd been checking on her, she wasn't sure if it felt reassuring or invasive.

Lukai sucked in a breath. "I can sense you even more."

His excitement wasn't contagious.

"Now that we're not divided by the barrier, I'm guessing the bond will work far better."

"Sensing my well-being isn't protection," she said. "You didn't do anything even though I was in danger all the time."

"True." He winced. "Before you returned, I couldn't protect you. The bond simply would have told me if it had been broken."

The question sat on the tip of her tongue, but she was too afraid to ask what it would take to break a bond. Death? Was she now tied to this stranger for life?

The ground sloped downward, the temperature growing cooler despite the thickness of the air. The layer of sweat Aeliana had built up outside the cave cooled her down too well. She shivered, pulling her cloak tighter around her waist.

A mix of voices came from ahead, the light from Sylmar's lantern shining brighter around Lukai's form. Only the light wasn't just coming from Sylmar's lantern.

"Welcome to our Bamboo Island base," Sylmar said.

The cave's path opened up to a small cavern. Half the room held bedrolls, and snores drifted from a large lump in the middle of one of them. In the center, a petite young woman with light brown skin and short black braids frowned at biscuits cooking over hot coals. An equally short older man ate slightly blackened versions of what was on her pan, which explained the acrid stench in the air. Aeliana's stomach growled, reminding her the night was nearly over and it was probably close to breakfast.

Another woman, pear-shaped and aged with laugh lines, sharpened swords and arrow tips on whetstones in the corner, sparks dancing at her boots. The sight of a white bow leaning against the cave wall made Aeliana's arms itch to hold it, to feel the firm wood in her hand, the reliable tension in the string. There'd been something peaceful about learning to shoot from Cyrus, even though she couldn't imagine using the skill to hunt.

From the look of this group, these weapons were meant for war, not food.

At first, all eyes turned to Sylmar, Velden, and Lukai, but it was the second look taking in Aeliana and Cyrus that made everyone go still. The room grew quiet except for the sizzle of batter on a pan, then broke as the sleeper gave a violent, choking snore.

Velden sent a flick of water from his webbed hand toward the woman cooking. "I'll need at least four of those, so don't you dare burn them, Kendalyhn."

Her pretty face screwed up into a scowl as she turned back to the biscuits, wiping away the water glistening on her long lashes.

"Our mission has been accomplished," Sylmar announced. "We head for the mainland immediately."

"Does Mayvus know she's here?" The booming voice startled Aeliana when it came from the small man near Kendalyhn.

"I assume so." Sylmar sighed and tugged at the short strands of his beard. "Arvid and Vera came with her."

Murmurs spread through the small entourage.

"And Rildan?" the man pressed.

Sylmar hesitated. "They said he was dead, but it felt like a lie."

The room grew quiet, faces troubled.

The woman sharpening arrows dropped the one she held and approached Aeliana, a hand outstretched. She scanned Aeliana as if starved. "You look so much like your mother, Sun protect her." She placed a hand on Aeliana's cheek, then chin.

Aeliana took a step back, eyeing the woman's strangely cropped hair and trousers.

"Iris was your mother's maidservant in Celanoft's Sungazer." Sylmar rushed through the introduction while grabbing a pack from the wall's edge. "She witnessed your crossing. She's one of the few survivors of the old Celanoft."

The others went back to their duties, this time with a sense of urgency. Even the man who'd been sleeping rolled up the bedding as he yawned. But their eyes strayed toward Aeliana, and their conversations became hushed whispers.

"I can help you get ready, love. Your skirts will slow you down, as will this." Iris gently pulled on Aeliana's hair. "I have extra clothes you can wear. Would you like me to cut your locks, too?"

"No." Cyrus answered for her, his hands flying to his own long hair.

Iris laughed, the sound echoing through the chamber in an easy way that defied everyone else's haste. "We'll see how long you both last."

"What happens when we get to the mainland?" Aeliana asked. Traveling with half-lights might be safer in one sense, but this small group seemed likely to attract trouble. Aeliana watched as Lukai folded up dozens of arrows and knives in blankets and tied them together in bundles. Or maybe they went looking for trouble.

Aeliana shuddered.

"Now that you're here, we'll head north—join the rest of the new Celanoft. Those of us who survived Mayvus' rampage years ago went underground." Iris rifled through a bag, pulling out fine, unfamiliar clothes and passing them to Aeliana. "We thought you'd be here moons ago. It's a relief to know you're all right."

She patted Aeliana's cheek, then nudged her toward a sheet hung up as a makeshift dressing screen.

Was that why they had so many weapons? Had they been prepared to fight for her? Aeliana watched the others more closely, noting that in addition to Sylmar and Lukai, the shorter man and Kendalyhn had matching cords tucked into their shirts. Only Iris, Velden, and the larger man had bare necks, and yet Sylmar had said starlocks were becoming rarer. They'd not only been prepared to fight for her, but they'd sent several progenies.

All because she was the daughter of a well-loved high priestess? It didn't seem to fit. Vera's strange story about curses and prophecies came back to Aeliana. She couldn't trust anything that woman said, but these people weren't telling her everything either.

Aeliana changed, then rounded from behind the screen, pulling at the trousers as if they might grow a skirt. She quickly pulled her robe on over it.

Iris fussed over her a moment longer, then stood back with a critical eye. "Well enough. You won't pass for an average Vendaran with all that hair. Some will think it disrespectful to the Stars, but we can braid it and hide it in your hood."

Aeliana ran a hand over her waves. Disrespectful seemed like a bit much. "I thought you didn't worship the Stars."

Iris' hands went to her hips. "Doesn't mean we don't respect them."

Aeliana didn't want to stand out, but she wasn't sure she could cut her hair. Not yet. It was the pride of a Lorvandan. During desperate times, men and women cut a lock of hair to lie out in the Stargazer as an offering to the Stars. Otherwise, it was shameful to have hair as short as Iris'.

The man who had rolled up the bedding stood, towering over Aeliana until she took a step back. He bent to give Iris a peck on her cheek.

"I'll load your herbs up next." His voice held a gentleness Aeliana hadn't expected.

"Don't be rude," Iris said, swatting his arm. "Aeliana, this is Holm. Holm, this is Aeliana."

"Good to meet you," Aeliana said, unsure how the Vendarans greeted one another. A handshake? A curtsy?

He ducked his head in her direction but said nothing more before ambling toward a stash of supplies in the corner.

Iris leaned close with a grin. "He's formidable in battle and intimidating at first glance, but don't let him fool you. He's a giant puppy."

Aeliana's gaze swept over the room, taking in their varying shades of skin. In Lorvandas, she'd stuck out with her copper tones, whereas Cyrus' pale skin had been more common. Here, he looked almost sickly against the warm browns.

"What about the shorter man?" Aeliana asked. The stranger still chewed biscuits as he bent over a map, his trim grey beard belying his youthful frame.

"Jasperus," Iris said. "Loud and a bit of a know-it-all, but he tells the best stories. He missed his calling. Could have made a fortune with a traveling troupe."

Aeliana smiled, even though she was already forgetting names. They seemed like an odd bunch, but with only seven of them besides Cyrus and herself, maybe she would find her place among them.

Cyrus sat on a large rock, where Lukai's hands slid over Cyrus' wound. Lukai took his time, his touch gentler and more exact than Sylmar's had been. Every place his fingers brushed on Cyrus' hand and arm showed pale, freckled skin. If scars remained, they were almost impossible to see. Cyrus stared in wonder, but at this rate, it would take all day for Lukai to finish smoothing out the scars left by Sylmar's healing. After a moment, Lukai patted Cyrus on the back, then stepped away to pack his bag.

Cyrus walked over to Aeliana, holding up his hand and examining it in the low light in wonder. "He said he'll finish tonight."

Aeliana's hand grazed the back of her neck. She longed for that kind of relief on her wounds, but the idea of volunteering for someone to use magic on her felt like madness.

"Which route are we taking?" the short older man called out to Sylmar, his focus still on the map. Hadn't Iris called him Jasperus?

"We may need to take the Pass."

The room went still once more.

The larger man stood, his hair nearly grazing the cave's ceiling. He'd been the one to kiss Iris, and Aeliana thought his name might be Holm. "We can't get an army of ten thousand men through the Pass." His eyes darted everywhere in the room but on Sylmar, his tone still soft despite his urgency.

"Army?" Cyrus' voice rose. "Are you at war?"

Aeliana tried imagining a group that large. On Harvest Day last year, she'd seen, from a distance, a thousand gathered in a town's square. But ten times that? Aeliana couldn't even picture it.

"We're starting one," Velden said. "It's the only way we can rescue Aeliana's mother from Mayvus."

"Meeting up with the army to take the trade route would be ideal," Sylmar said, "but we might have to take it slow for now. The Pass is a shorter way through the mountains, and it will allow us to meet up with the army farther east beyond the mountains without having to keep their pace. Traveling with Aeliana will require extra stops and training periods." Sylmar turned to her, his scars deepened by the shadows in the lantern light.

She squirmed under his attention.

"She'll need to be weaned from blood magic."

A wave of gasps traveled through the others, Aeliana's uneasiness deepening. Sylmar glared at them, and the flurry of activity resumed. Even Iris and Velden moved away to help pack.

Sylmar turned to Aeliana and Cyrus. "I'll do my best to answer what questions I can, but some will have to wait for the road. I'm not sure what reinforcements Arvid and Vera have here. The island has seemed empty this last year. But Mayvus always seems to be a step ahead of us. If she doesn't already know you're here, she will soon. We need to be long gone before that happens."

"Why? Aren't you trying to go after her?" Aeliana asked.

"We need to meet with her on our terms, not hers. With our army behind us." Sylmar hesitated, his impatient gaze scanning the group's progress. "You should know that Mayvus and Emeris are sisters."

"Sisters?" Aeliana echoed. "So this woman is my aunt?"

"Yes. An aunt who imprisoned your mother to gain more power. She's risen to control all the Sungazers in the nation by the unholiest of tactics, including blood magic—more specifically, branding."

"She imprisoned her sister?" Cyrus asked, his face screwed up in horror. With his ten siblings, he probably had a better understanding of family than Aeliana, but even she found the news disturbing.

"I'll admit it's not a widely accepted story." Sylmar's eye twitched in irritation. "Emeris has been missing as long as Aeliana. Anyone who claims to have seen her in the eastern provinces also goes missing, which only confirms the rumors instead of putting a stop to them. The rest think your mother's grief over losing you and Rildan made her go mad. They think she's dead, or that she's run off. But that's because they don't know she sent you both away for your safety. And they weren't there to witness her capture."

"But you were?" Cyrus pressed.

Sylmar's scars puckered with his frown. "Some things don't need to be witnessed to be known. The point is, we are on the brink of war. Mayvus' supporters couldn't care less if she kidnapped Emeris. In their minds, their high priestess can do no wrong. They'll find a way to justify her actions. They tell the royal family they're Loyalists, but the Recreants know they consider themselves Zealots."

"Recreants?" Cyrus asked.

"That would be us," Sylmar said. "Loyalists think of Recreants as dissenters and traitors. It's a bit of a political term for people who oppose the Elanesses—the royal family. It may have started out that way, but as Mayvus rose to power, the Recreants supported Emeris' efforts to stop her sister more than they opposed the Elanesses."

"How is she rising to power if there's a royal family?" Aeliana asked.

Sylmar snorted. "The royal family is too busy levying taxes and planning parties to see what Mayvus is up to. They consider her a spiritual influence for the country, but they'll probably hand over their crowns before they realize what's happened. Most Loyalists are honest when they support the Elanesses. They just don't realize the royal family is slowly relinquishing power to Mayvus and her Zealots.

"Before Emeris disappeared, she was working on a way to suppress Mayvus' growing power. She'd discovered something just before Mayvus kidnapped her. We were hoping Rildan could tell us what it was." He frowned again. "Either way, she knows how to defeat Mayvus. We're determined to rescue her and expose Mayvus for the fraud that she is."

"You and the ten thousand soldiers you mentioned?" Cyrus asked. "What kind of army are you up against?"

Velden joined the group, slipping a pack on Cyrus' back without waiting for permission. The others followed, having already made quick work of packing up the entire camp.

"Mayvus' supporters are nearly equal to ours," Velden said, "but there's probably five times that in the eastern provinces who have no interest or opinion on the matter. If we could expose her and sway them…"

A few others grunted their agreement, showing they'd all been carefully following the conversation.

"Well, it's not likely," Velden said. "I don't know what Lorvandans are like, but Vendarans prefer turning blind eyes to the trouble at hand until those eyes are ripped out and eaten by Durriken." He pressed two fingers together near his eye, then popped them apart with a squelching sound.

Cyrus shuddered, making Velden laugh.

He smacked Cyrus' arm with his sticky webbed fingers. "By the time all of Vendaras admits there's a war, it will be too late." His humor faded, and the others grew somber as well.

Cyrus took a step closer to Aeliana. "Who's Durriken?"

Velden leaned in to whisper, "You don't want to know."

"Time to go," Sylmar said.

Aeliana still hesitated. She trusted these people more than she did Arvid and Vera, but there were too many gaps in the story. "So we rescue my mother, and she stops Mayvus?"

Sylmar grunted. "It's a bit more complicated than that, but that's the plan. Mayvus has been delving so deeply into blood magic that she can't return from it." Instead of anger, Sylmar's face held something closer to pity. "Emeris is one of her brands. We'll need to cut out the brand mark. Otherwise, Emeris won't be able to leave Mayvus, let alone stop her."

"What's a brand?" Aeliana asked.

"We can discuss it more on the road," Sylmar said, guiding them toward an unfamiliar path out from the cavern.

"It's similar to a bond," Velden said as she and Cyrus fell in line behind him.

"I thought those were for marriage." Cyrus narrowed his eyes. "Wait, no—protection?"

"Mmm, how to explain the difference…" Velden's profile faced them as he tapped a finger over his lips, eyes squinted in thought. "In the case of marriage and betrothals, servants of the Sun bond couples with the tiniest drop of blood. It's fused to the palm with heat and light from a somatic progeny."

"The half-lights who adjust the body?" Cyrus asked.

Aeliana turned to him in surprise. He'd taken in more of Sylmar's lessons on magic than she had.

Sylmar spoke over his shoulder. "Yes. They basically grow the bond between the couple using the blood as an anchor. It connects the couple emotionally and spiritually, even when they're not physically near each other."

"And that's not blood magic?" Aeliana scratched at her palm, the dark red bubble suddenly more ominous than it had ever been.

"It's a fine line," Sylmar admitted, "defined more by intent than the presence of blood. Mayvus—when she uses someone's blood as a brand, she fuses their blood to her skin but doesn't share any of her own. The connection is still just as powerful, but it only flows in one direction, allowing her to steal their power if they're a progeny and use them to do her bidding. Bonds are a mutual decision made by a couple or the parents who care for them. It's a sharing of power that's unable to be abused. Brands are often forced on someone. The recipient doesn't even need to be present for the brand to take effect."

Cyrus and Aeliana exchanged a nervous glance.

"I suspect she took Emeris' by force and branded her for her power," Sylmar added. "She was always jealous of Emeris' noetic abilities. At most, a progeny can master two spokes without blood magic. I can't help wondering if her goal is to master all points on the spokes of the Wheel of Magic through the brands she controls."

"Can she do this with anyone's blood?" Cyrus asked.

Sylmar nodded. "If she wanted to. But people aren't exactly offering their blood. It's a sacred thing to trust someone with your blood."

Velden shuddered. "Sun's fire. I would hate to be her brand. They're essentially puppets."

Arvid and Vera's torture would seem like a game in comparison. Aeliana reached out to grip the cave wall, her knees suddenly weak as she held up the line of travelers behind her. All this time, she'd thought her guardians were building up her blood for their own use, but what if they'd been grooming her for something bigger, something far worse?

"Aeliana?" Lukai called out from behind her in concern.

Velden and Sylmar turned back, the lamp's light highlighting the question in their eyes.

"I know why Arvid and Vera were willing to leave me." Aeliana swallowed hard, forcing herself to look Sylmar in the eye. "They're taking my blood to Mayvus."

CHAPTER 15

IT WAS ALMOST the Sun's peak when Larkos sent word that *Starspeed* was ready to set sail. *Starspeed* had been gifted to Gaeren when he'd turned sixteen, more of an offhand attempt at making him feel special since the year was more about Enla's induction ceremony as queen-in-training when she turned eighteen. A silly celebration, considering she'd been training for it her whole life. It was just another year. Another reason for his parents to waste money on a party.

But he did like the boat. The three-masted barque had been brand new, tested only by the builder, with polished timber and watertight melted pine-pitch caulking. Every time the tightly woven sails snapped in the wind, it brought Gaeren back to her maiden voyage. He'd taken her out almost a hundred times in the seven years since, whenever Enla agreed to spare him.

And sometimes when she didn't agree.

In a surprising show of solidarity, Enla rode with Gaeren in a horse-drawn carriage to the docks. His hopes were tentatively high because he still hadn't heard from Lenda, but when they rounded the corner where the main street met the wharf, Lenda stood in front of *Starspeed*. She beamed, three trunks and four maidens by her side.

Gaeren groaned as he slid from the open carriage. "You realize how much she's going to slow me down?"

"One small woman has the power to take the wind from your

sails?" Enla's composure remained queenly atop her seat as hordes of people crowded around to see what the royals were up to. Gaeren still caught her smug tone.

"If she hasn't found sea legs since we were children, she'll spend the entire voyage puking down in the hold."

Enla laughed, then hunched forward to whisper, "Lean into the bond. It's a blessing from the Sun, not a curse."

Gaeren clenched his jaw. He'd known this was the reason Enla wanted Lenda to go along. Time spent together would enhance the bond. It would feel natural, and as Gaeren fell for Lenda, he would probably wonder why he'd ever resisted in the first place.

He waved off the footman and pulled his bags from the back of the carriage, slinging them over his shoulder. The mark on his palm itched as he wrestled with his sister's plea.

There was something that felt off about bonding. Like a love potion that took away his choice or control. Leaning into it sounded like giving up all of his desires and dreams.

"She'll be a distraction."

"For you or your crew?" Enla's smile still didn't falter.

Was she trying to make him jealous? He glanced at Lenda. Her eyes were like a baby winex's, large and unblinking, taking in the barque's height as she leaned back. Short blonde locks curled all around her head, an artistic creation that would be ruined within moments aboard *Starspeed*. She wore an impractical blue silk dress that wouldn't last through the voyage, but it matched her eyes, which were now in front of Gaeren, as if his perusal had drawn her close.

"I'm looking forward to our time together." Red lips parted in a smile he knew to be falsely humble, a practiced look with fluttering lashes.

Still, his heart picked up its pace as she toyed with the cord of her starlock where it dipped below her low neckline. He turned back to Enla, cursing the bond's ability to work even when he didn't want it to.

"I'll return soon. Hopefully, with answers." He gave his sister a knowing look. She wanted answers about the strange woman's magic, maybe something to quench his curiosity and help him settle back at home as throne warden. He wanted so much more.

"May the Sun's light always shine upon you," Enla said.

Gaeren stiffened. It was a common farewell among the nobility, especially for long voyages. But it had also been a daily adage for Enla, Gaeren, and Riveran in their youth. With the gathering crowds, he couldn't hold back the reply, even though it had been two years since he'd used either phrase.

"And may the Stars' light always guide you." The words came out stiff, but Enla nodded her approval.

Gaeren turned around sharply, the farewell suddenly tainted by memories of Riveran.

He nodded at Lenda like he would a member of his crew, then walked to the planks, already feeling some of the tension leave his back as he boarded his home away from home.

"Larkos can show you to your room," he shouted over his shoulder. It was just as well that Lenda take the captain's quarters. He preferred sleeping on deck with the crew, under the Stars. The twinge he felt over her safety was short-lived, as usual. Lenda was a destructive somatic. She could protect herself far better than Gaeren could protect her.

By the time Lenda's trunks had been brought on board and three of her four maidens dismissed by Gaeren, despite Lenda's protests, the last of the sails had been unfurled and the anchor raised.

"Good to see you, Erech." Gaeren ruffled the stableboy's hair, letting loose a few stray pieces of hay.

The boy grinned, then schooled his features as he glanced at the other sailors. "You too, Captain Elanesse."

Gaeren leaned in. "I had your wages sent to your mother this morning. Figured the baby might come before we're back."

Even as Erech thanked him, the boy's features pinched, and he glanced back toward land.

Gaeren made a mental note to check on the boy's homesickness in the coming days. The first voyage was always the hardest. For now, he took the helm and guided the ship out of the harbor, the practiced motions calming. Instead of passing the wheel off to Larkos, he remained, partly to avoid Lenda, who hovered as though ready to pounce the moment he was free, and partly because he hadn't told Larkos about their first stop in the marshes.

The Sun was nearly ready to sleep when they left the major inlet to Elanesse and rounded the western coast. Gaeren shouted orders to drop anchor and lower a boat port side. Larkos raised an eyebrow, but the crew knew better than to argue or ask questions. Lenda, on the other hand…

"What are we doing? Where are you going?" Her hands twisted, a crease forming on her brow.

"We have one more stop. It's your last chance to go back, if you'd like." Gaeren smiled, the thought too good to be a true possibility. "I doubt you want to deal with sickness and storms."

"But I…" She turned to study the men as they worked, gnawing on her lower lip.

"We're actually closer to the palace now than we were at the docks." He tried not to sound too hopeful. "You're already looking a little green."

Her face sagged as she temporarily lost her hold on the serene smile she maintained to maximize her beauty. Strangely, he found the vulnerability more attractive. He clenched his jaw and looked away, hating that their bond could make him feel an attraction he didn't want.

"My maid brought herbs." Her voice held a stubborn determination.

"Very well." He threw a leg over the ship to catch the rope ladder.

"But why are we stopping?" she pressed.

Even Larkos leaned over to hear Gaeren's reply.

"I have additional cargo to pick up."

After leaving Larkos in charge, Gaeren had a couple of men row him inland, where he hopped from the roots of one mangrove tree to another until he reached his hideout. The swamp gas was particularly bad in today's heat, forcing Gaeren to cover his nose to hold back a gag. He expected to hear light steps on the wooden boards, maybe even the woman's voice if she was one to talk to herself.

Instead, he heard heavy footfalls and a deep baritone.

He unsheathed his dagger, cursing himself for not tuning in to his surroundings earlier. Before he could get a read on the situation, the woman called out. "No need to skulk, Gaeren. You're among friends."

He straightened, not ready to believe her, but then a familiar bearded face peered over the boards. Riveran held out a hand in some sort of greeting, but Gaeren hardly noticed. His gaze rested on the black X newly tattooed and bleeding on Riveran's forehead.

The humiliating and permanent mark of a criminal.

CHAPTER 16

"Is it that noticeable?" Riveran's joke fell flat as his hand brushed the tattoo on his forehead.

Fresh blood smeared, making Gaeren wince. How long ago had he gotten it? Riveran held out his clean hand once more, and after briefly hesitating, Gaeren took it, allowing Riveran to haul him up to the platform. It felt too crowded with three people. And one bird.

Gullet adjusted his grip on Riveran's shoulder, his left eye drilling into Gaeren.

"Riveran was just filling me in on your childhood," Orra said from where she sat in the hammock. The glow of her skin had receded, and now her skin actually looked a shade deeper than his sailor's tan.

Gaeren shot Riveran a questioning glance. That could mean a lot of things, but no matter what it meant, Gaeren didn't want any of his personal matters discussed with a stranger.

Riveran shrugged. "I haven't been able to talk to anyone besides Gullet for a few days." The hawk squawked his agreement.

"Why are you even here?"

Riveran couldn't hold his gaze. "I didn't know where else to go."

Gaeren's focus strayed to the mark again. This was the trouble Enla had been referring to. Whatever Riveran had done to earn the mark had been public enough that there was no going back. Tampering or removing the mark with magic would escalate his penalty to death.

And yet Enla had said to trust him.

Gaeren was tempted to search the other man's memories, but he was too afraid of what else he might see. "You've had it for a few days? It shouldn't be bleeding anymore. Is it infected?"

"It was." Riveran glanced at the woman. "Orra lanced and cleaned it, so the wound is a bit fresh again, but at least it's not likely to kill me."

She smiled and patted his arm.

For a moment, Gaeren had a strange pang of jealousy. He had no attraction to Orra, but something in her expression spoke of wisdom and experience, a maternal quality. It was more like he was fighting a sibling for the attention of a parent.

That, he was used to.

"We should get going." Gaeren turned his back on Riveran. "The boat isn't far from here." He rummaged through the books on his desk until he found *The Sins of the Stars* and tucked it in his coat pocket.

Orra raised her eyebrows. "You don't want to know why your friend has been marked a criminal?"

Gaeren winced. "Our friendship ended long ago. I have a good guess as to the reason for his mark."

Riveran scoffed but held his tongue.

"It's never wise to settle for an assumption." Orra gracefully sank back into the netting, as if they had all afternoon to rehash the history leading up to the inevitable result of Riveran's mark.

"Maybe he can tell me about it after you and I get back. It's important that we get out of these waters before the Sun's sleep. There are too many places to run aground."

Orra studied him for long enough that he fought the urge to squirm. How was it that this woman's silence commanded authority when it was his ship that would take her to Bamboo Island? He was doing her a favor.

"How about he tells us both on the boat?" she suggested. "It's an eight-day voyage. There should be plenty of time."

Both men eyed each other warily for a long breath. Gaeren spoke first.

"I can't bring a traitor aboard my boat."

Orra snorted. "I'm not sure it's always clear-cut who betrayed whom. Riveran only has his mark because he's been forced to partake in black market trade. And now he can't even do that. Which leaves him no way to support his wife and child."

The surge of pity that flowed through Gaeren ended at the mention of Riveran's family. Perhaps if he hadn't broken his bond with Enla, he wouldn't have needed to deal in the black market.

"Riveran needs a job, and you can provide him one as crew aboard your boat."

Gaeren's mouth swung open to protest, but Orra went on. "It's the only way I'll come with you. If you won't provide him means to support his family, I'll need to hire him to escort me to Bamboo Island instead of you." She eased out of the hammock, standing tall while brushing off her fading cloak, as if allowing Gaeren time to recover his pride.

He clenched his jaw. The idea of agreeing to her demands burned, even though Larkos *had* lost two crewmen because of the rushed departure. What would the others think about Riveran? Those who didn't know him would be horrified at the idea of a marked traitor coming aboard. Sailors were superstitious enough that they'd see it as all sorts of bad luck. And those who knew Riveran would be sure to spread their opinions over Gaeren's supposed acceptance of the man who had betrayed their family.

And yet Enla had warned him to trust the traitor.

"I could cover it." Riveran's gaze ended somewhere around Gaeren's elbow. There was a flicker of hope on his face, surprising Gaeren. Riveran wanted to come.

"No," Orra said. "That's the reason you developed the infection. It needs to heal in the open air."

Gaeren swore, running a hand through his hair. He didn't have time for this. "Fine. But keep in mind that sailors found committing acts of treason on the high seas are judged by the captain and crew. You won't be given the mercy of waiting to disembark for a trial on land, especially not with that on your forehead." He gestured at the ugly brand.

It was possible the men would set Riveran up for failure, wanting him to be keelhauled. Eight days was plenty of time for them to lay any kind of blame at Riveran's feet.

"I'll take the risk." Riveran's agreement came quickly, his mouth very near to a smile. Even Orra's lips tilted up in something resembling satisfaction.

The whole walk to the shore, which was slow thanks to Orra still being weak, Gaeren couldn't help feeling tricked.

Sure enough, the two men who rowed them back to the ship glared daggers at Riveran and Gullet while sneaking the occasional peek at Orra. Gaeren boarded *Starspeed* first, reaching out a hand to help both Riveran and Orra up the ladder. Gullet took to the skies, aiming back toward land as if showing his irritation at their plans to be at sea.

When the rest of the crew saw Riveran's forehead, the unsurprising mix of fear and dark hatred left Gaeren defeated. No one dared question their captain, but whatever clout Gaeren had earned with the men had just gone down several notches.

"Who is she?" Lenda's question brought everyone's gaze to Orra as she swung her legs over the edge of the ship. Expressions shifted; backs straightened. A few men used their fingers to comb back their hair. The older men's eyes shined with interest, but the fresh recruits' faces held longing and homesickness, which Gaeren didn't usually see until they'd been at sea for weeks.

"Orra and Riveran will join our voyage. Riveran will take over swab so Breeve can focus more on cooking. Maybe actually make a decent meal while we're out here."

A few men laughed or grunted, some elbowing the young man whose pimply face turned pink.

"Orra will bunk with Lenda and her maid. She's our tracker, and her duties begin once we reach Bamboo Island." Gaeren bristled as the elbowing started up again. "She's here as a guest of the family of Elanesse when she's not in my employ."

Orra strode to Lenda, either purposely ignoring or unaware of the crew's leers. She gripped the younger woman's hands, whispering something that relaxed Lenda's clenched jaw into a hesitant smile. The two headed toward the stern, bending to enter the captain's cabin and shut the door behind them.

The men's distraction disappeared with the women, and their hateful eyes trained back on Riveran.

"Weigh anchor and man the sails." Gaeren passed in front of Riveran, drawing his crew's attention away from the traitor's mark. "The Sun's sleep will be here soon, and *Starspeed* doesn't need to run aground because of childish grudges and superstitions."

He grabbed the mop from Breeve's hands, passing it over to Riveran without ceremony. The men broke into action, including Riveran, who shot Gaeren a look, his eyes more grateful than his stiff salute.

Gaeren turned away without acknowledging it, determined not to let Riveran's circumstances garner any more pity. He joined Larkos at the helm, arms folded, gaze across the water. High laughter drifted from the captain's quarters below him, making him wonder how Orra had won Lenda over so fast. Probably the same way she'd had Riveran spilling secrets about their childhood.

In the night, taking her to Bamboo Island had seemed right, like a spot of good fortune. Now her presence felt too large, like she'd taken over his entire mission and made it her own. He'd have to be cautious.

He'd wondered if she was a noetic when she knew his name. Maybe she'd tuned in to his thoughts when he'd tried tuning in to hers. Then he'd thought she might be somatic, since she'd cleaned out Riveran's infection. She could have used supplies from town, but few people knew such skills without being somatic progenies. Perhaps she had a rare secondary spoke and she was both. But what spokes, or even rim magic, would allow her body to return to life the way it had the night he'd found her?

"You never fail to surprise me." Larkos grinned lazily even as his focus remained on the water, his hands guiding the wheel with a precision Gaeren couldn't help admiring.

"Who wants to be predictable?"

Larkos laughed. "I think there are plenty of people who want you to be predictable."

"That wasn't my question."

"True."

They inched out from the wetlands until the wind caught the sails, and then they picked up speed. The wind whipped through Gaeren's hair, calming him as he let the tension of the day ease out from his limbs.

"For what it's worth, I think it's noble of you to give Riveran a second chance."

Gaeren frowned. "Your opinion's never been worth much."

Larkos laughed again, ignoring the jab for the lie that it was. Enla never understood why Gaeren trusted Larkos, with his gruff presence and thinly veiled hatred of the crown. She'd also never sailed through a hurricane or along the Western Horn with him. After years together at sea, there was no one else Gaeren trusted so completely.

"It wasn't my idea to let him come." Gaeren turned, studying the men as they worked. Breeve ducked into the galley to prepare what was likely to be an awful dinner, and the rest all manned their stations without complaint.

Riveran kept to himself, swabbing the deck until it sparkled. Then he picked up where Thallahan, Gaeren's second mate, had left off strengthening a spare sail that had loose threads. Erech watched Riveran more than he helped, but if his work ethic from the stables held, he'd be climbing the rigging tomorrow.

"Is she really a tracker?" Larkos asked.

Gaeren thought about the label he'd given Orra. The way she'd known immediately where they should go. "Of sorts."

It didn't seem advantageous to explain how little he knew about Orra or her motives. Or her magic. She could still be an enemy, and he needed to remember that. But he didn't necessarily want others suspicious of her. Not yet.

"The missus thanks you for her extended vacation from my presence." Larkos' change of subject dripped with sarcasm.

Gaeren grinned. "I suppose she'll tell me all the ways I've made her life miserable when we return." As a young swab, Gaeren had been taken under Larkos' wing, and the old man's wife and bondmate, Calia, had treated Gaeren as one of her own. Being so easily accepted by near strangers had highlighted the dysfunction of Gaeren's own parents' favoritism, and the strength of Larkos and Calia's bond had been the reason Gaeren had first doubted the success of his own.

Their bond came after a foundation of love, and Gaeren's... well, his could never be anything more than a farce. Not when they'd been assigned to each other since birth.

"Of course she will. We'll both get an earful. Along with a bowl of stew and some of those berry tarts we love." Larkos rolled up his sleeves, drawing Gaeren's attention to a fresh tattoo.

"What's the story behind that?"

Larkos grinned. "Glad you asked."

Gaeren grimaced, bracing for a lecture.

"It's just the Wheel of Magic." Larkos held out his arm, displaying the basic hub with six spokes. The constructive and destructive somatic spokes were on opposite sides of the hub, their focus on adjusting the body evident by the symbol of a healing hand on the constructive side and skeletal fingers on the destructive side.

The opposing pneumatic spokes were represented by black and white hearts, a symbol for sifting through souls that Gaeren never understood until he saw his sister weigh the intentions and desires that would play out in a person's future. It broke her heart every time to see all the ways people could hurt each other—or love each other— even if it never came to pass.

The noetic spokes showed an eye, closed in concentration on the destructive side and wide open on the constructive side, which still didn't make sense to Gaeren. Tuning in to thoughts, memories, and emotions wasn't only something that he saw. He experienced it with all of his senses. Too many times, his progeny mentors had had to pull him from the memories, which had swallowed him whole and threatened to trap him.

It was the standard Wheel of Magic, but a tattoo was never just anything if Larkos made it permanent on his body. Gaeren looked closer. Usually the ends of the spokes connected to form a perfect circle, the rim of the Wheel holding the elemental magic few ever obtained, but the rim on Larkos' tattoo was faded, like it was old or needed a second layer.

"It seems unfinished." Gaeren bent over to study it further, but that was the only difference.

Larkos grinned. "So it is. Just like our world is incomplete without the Stars."

"I didn't take you to be a very religious man." Gaeren couldn't keep the wry tone from his voice as he backed away and leaned against the bulkhead. He doubted the other man knew where to find the nearest Sungazer. If anything, Larkos worshipped the ground Calia walked on more than he did any deity.

Larkos feigned offense. "I may not be devout, but I still believe. Besides, this is less about faith in a discriminatory Sun and more about the fate of our world." He gestured at the ink on his skin. "The longer the Stars stay away, the more creation's balance breaks down. If you run a wheel without the rim, your spokes will bend and break. The Stars are what once held our world together."

"They're still involved," Gaeren argued. "The Stars might not commune with priests in the Sungazer anymore, but how else do you explain the honor of starlocks? Even though we're chosen by the Sun, it requires a lock of hair from a Star." He gestured to the teardrop hanging from his neck even though Larkos couldn't see where it rested beneath Gaeren's shirt. The shape of a starlock either represented the events of a person's Awakening or some other event, past or future, that would be even more significant. Until Gaeren knew what his meant, he kept it out of sight of prying eyes.

"Have you compared records of starlocks?" Larkos raised his eyebrows. "Of course you haven't. In the last hundred years, the number of people being gifted with starlocks has gone down by almost half. In another hundred years, will anyone be getting them?"

"Half?" That couldn't be right.

"None of your crew has them. When's the last time you saw a commoner in the market with one? The progenies are all swept off to your schools, where they become part of the nobility, which is why you still think there isn't a problem." Larkos' jaw tightened, and his hands turned white where he gripped the wheel.

Gaeren wasn't sure how this conversation had suddenly become political again. He supposed it made more sense for Larkos' tattoo to be a political statement than a religious one. For all Gaeren knew, this symbol could now be the mark of a Recreant, their slogan changing from "Bring down the Elanesse" to "Save the Wheel of Magic." But the royal family had no power over the Wheel of Magic.

"So you think we need to call on the Stars to commune with us again? Is that even possible after they put up the barriers?" His recent read of *The Sins of the Stars* had recounted the event in detail. Whether the barriers had been put in place by Sheen and her fellow Stars like the text claimed or by the Sun in its divine justice, the barriers had also cut off the people's access to the Stars.

According to this book, the Stars blamed themselves for the state of the world. The varying cultures were a result of the Stars' interference as they not only communed with humans in Sungazers but also started families with them, creating half-lights with starblood. The Stars had attempted to right their wrong by pulling out from the lands and leaving the people to their own devices.

Which were just as bad as before.

Larkos shrugged. "I have no clue if we can commune with the Stars again. Like I said, I'm not that devout. I'm more about preparing for the inevitable breakdown of the Wheel. The need to function as a society that will eventually lose magic."

Gaeren's hands tightened on the bulkhead. He'd grown so used to his magic, even dependent on it, that he forgot some people had no experience with it. A world without magic would still go on, but it would feel bleak.

Lenda and Orra chose that moment to exit their quarters and take a turn around the deck, followed by Lenda's maid. Lenda's face was too pale, her grip on Orra's arm too tight. By the Sun's sleep, she'd likely be trapped in her quarters, too sick to even come out for fresh air. In some ways, it was a relief for the women to have each other. Gaeren wouldn't have to entertain either of them, which would have been frustrating for vastly different reasons.

The entire crew's stances shifted, their hands slowing in their work as their gazes lingered over the women.

"You know, it's bad luck to have a woman on board," Larkos grunted.

"Maybe having three cancels it out?"

Larkos shook his head, but there was a tilt to his lips. "What do you expect to find when we reach Bamboo Island?"

Gaeren tensed, then pulled out his dagger, running his thumb over the daisy engraved in its pommel. Sometimes the answer felt simple: he wanted to find Daisy. Other times it felt much bigger, like finding her and solving the mystery of his childhood would open up a hundred doors to his future. He wondered if that was what it was like for Enla when she sifted through souls. Doors waiting to be opened.

He'd told Larkos about the light, how he'd wanted to investigate its source, but that was all. Orra's presence clearly clued Larkos in to the fact that there was more to the story. Except Gaeren still didn't really know what he expected to find. He tucked his dagger back into his belt.

"Hopefully, the truth."

CHAPTER 17

AELIANA TAPPED her boot against the cave wall. Her frustration grew as she watched the mouth of the tunnel for any flicker of light signaling Sylmar's return. He'd chastised her for letting Arvid and Vera take her blood, then shifted plans. He took all the Vendarans except Iris to comb the island for her guardians. She supposed the more accurate term was kidnappers, or maybe even Zealots, but it was hard to think of them as anything else.

The Recreants had left at the Sun's morn, and after three meals, two fitful naps, and infinite rounds of pacing, Aeliana suspected it was past the Sun's sleep.

"Everything will be fine," Iris said for the hundredth time. She handed over hemp, instructing Aeliana how to braid it into a sturdy rope while she did the same. The activity was meant to be distracting, but it only left Aeliana more agitated.

Cyrus was better at keeping himself busy—or maybe he just had less to be concerned about. He sharpened a sword on the whetstone before testing its weight in his hand.

A low hum wound its way through the cave, momentarily rattling packs. All three of them paused, eyes meeting over still hands.

"What was that?" Cyrus whispered.

Without warning, Iris stood, grabbing daggers and heading for the cave's exit. Just before leaving, she turned.

"Please, stay here." Her eyes begged Aeliana and Cyrus with an intensity that didn't match her calm instructions. "If no one returns before another Sun's morn, take the north exit." She pointed toward the back half of the cavern, where they'd all started walking before Aeliana had told them Arvid and Vera had her blood. "It slopes down under the channel and will take you through to the mainland. Follow the coast south until you reach the sound. Catch the ferry and take it to Valorian, then go straight to the blacksmith. He'll get you to the Recreant army. Don't trust anyone else."

She was gone before either of them could ask a question.

The sound of her boots faded along with her candlelight bouncing off the wall. For a moment, Aeliana and Cyrus stared after her, the sudden silence more foreboding than a clash of weapons would be.

Aeliana scratched at her back. The mark made by Arvid had scabbed over, making it itch.

"Could you look at my back?" She swept her hair to one side and undid her top button just so she could pull the collar of her blouse down on her shoulder, angling the back of her neck toward Cyrus.

His face turned red even though nothing inappropriate was exposed. Still, he leaned forward and pulled it down more, letting the cool cave air rush across the wound and provide momentary relief. Maybe Velden could make one of those seaweed poultices for her.

"Aeliana, what is this?" Cyrus' voice was low, his words urgent.

"I don't know. They make the marks once a year, but I can't ever see them. Is it infected?"

"No, it's—they wrote words."

"Words?" Aeliana turned to face him, doing her button up once more. "What does it say?"

"'Send Durriken.'" His face grew pale, his freckles standing out.

"What is—?" She cut off suddenly, remembering.

Cyrus answered the question anyway. "Something that rips out people's eyes and eats them."

"We need to go out there," Aeliana said.

Cyrus gaped at her. "Did you not hear Iris?"

"Of course, but we need to know what they're up against. What could come for us." She grabbed a torch, and after a moment's hesitation Cyrus took a sword.

"What?" he asked when she raised her eyebrows at the weapon. He strapped on the belt and slipped in the sword, gauging its weight against his hip.

"Do you even know how to use that?"

He shrugged. "It's not the same as the sabers my brother trained me with, but I know how to parry and thrust." His eyes seemed wide in the torchlight, and Aeliana suspected he wouldn't actually be able to stab the sword into another person. She almost told him to leave it behind, worried the added weight would slow them down, but decided it might give him confidence.

Besides, they were just going to look.

They picked their way back through the cave's tunnels, hesitant to get caught but nervous to be left too far behind. When they reached the vines concealing the cave's entrance, Aeliana peeked through, blinking into the inky blackness of the night. The moon had already risen high.

"Do you see anything?" Cyrus whispered from behind her.

"Just the deserted beach." Her gaze traced the path Sylmar had brought them down. "Wait, I think Iris is going back up into the forest. We won't be able to see anything from here." She stepped out of the cave, ignoring Cyrus' protests.

She snuffed out the torch, then traced their steps back from the night before, guided by memory and the imprints of the others running before them.

"I think we should go back," Cyrus said for the tenth time.

Aeliana shushed him, wary of how their voices might carry now that they'd reached the forest line. It was harder to find the trail, so she settled for making her own, using the moon as a reference point.

A rush of air mixed with thunder swept over them, rustling the leaves of every tree. The silence that followed was too complete, as if every creature from the tops of the trees to the snakes burrowing underground had paused in fearful recognition.

"Was that the same thing we felt before?" Cyrus whispered.

"I don't know." Aeliana's words came out on such a shallow breath that she wasn't sure if he heard them. When she counted to one hundred with nothing happening, she resumed her trek. At any moment, they would break through to the clearing they'd been in with Arvid and Vera. Hopefully, they could see something from that position. Once she knew exactly what the others faced, she would be willing to turn around and hide like Iris had asked.

But she couldn't run until she knew what she was running from.

Sharp pain sliced across her chest, making her trip. Panic came on the heels of the pain, but it was panic for Lukai, not herself. Was he injured? Had she sensed his pain? The unknown drove her forward faster.

The break beyond the trees came so quick that Aeliana had to step back to keep herself from being visible in the clearing, stepping on Cyrus' toes in the process. He leaned over her shoulder as they scanned where the bamboo forest's edge met the field of grass. At first, it looked empty, but then lumps that were rocks became people, and nightlife sounds became hushed whispers. Sylmar crouched five paces away, his body shaking as he bent over Jasperus, the smaller man's eyes squinting in pain.

"Hold it," Sylmar hissed.

Their forms flickered once more, and they were rocks again. Cyrus' sharp intake of breath near Aeliana's ear made her jolt.

"Jasperus' masking them with an illusion," he said.

Aeliana scanned the clearing, making out four other rocks with suspiciously human-like shapes. Then her attention caught on Arvid and Vera, a dozen paces farther than Sylmar and Jasperus, their eyes trained on the skies and faces twisted in triumphant grins.

The golden arrow poked out of Arvid's pocket, and Aeliana caught the glimmer of glass in Vera's hands. From this distance, it was hard to tell for sure, but it seemed as if only half the vial remained. Had they used the other half to fight off the Recreants? She squinted until she could make out black swirls like smoke drifting from Arvid's ears and nose.

She shrank back against Cyrus. Arvid had invited in a dark spirit.

They were all doomed as long as Arvid had her blood. Unless…

"What if we can get them to use up all my blood?" Aeliana murmured. It would be just as good as getting it back.

"No." Cyrus tugged on her arm. "You said you just wanted to look. Let's go back to the cave."

"Where did Iris go?" Aeliana counted the rocks under her breath. There wasn't enough for her mother's maidservant to be one of them.

"Maybe she's circling around to surprise Arvid and Vera?"

The illusion flickered once more, and this time Aeliana recognized Lukai's form sprawled in the moss. She gasped at the red slashes on his chest. On instinct, she pressed a finger into the mark on her palm, desperate to know if their connection held. Pain seared through her, and she grabbed on to a bamboo shoot, her knees nearly giving out as she moaned.

"Are you all right?" Cyrus asked.

Aeliana sensed Lukai's pain, shared his anguish, but the bond remained intact. He was alive. The sense of relief surprised her. He was a stranger, and while she didn't wish him dead, she also shouldn't care so much that he wasn't.

As Aeliana's pain faded, she gained a new sense of awareness. Arvid's eyes narrowed in her direction.

"Come out, Aeliana. Before I make you," Arvid called.

"No," Cyrus hissed, grabbing her arm to hold her back.

Vera stepped closer to Lukai, who was a rock once more, and Aeliana stiffened. The older woman bent down, placing her hands on the rock. The illusion dissipated, leaving Lukai hunched like a newborn baby, his face bunched in agony.

"He's a pretty boy," Vera said. "It would be a shame to leave him less than whole." She ran the flat of her knife's blade over the smooth skin of his face.

"No." Cyrus tightened his grip on Aeliana's arm.

"They already know I'm here," she argued. "They'll make me come out. It's just a matter of whether it's before or after they've hurt him."

"That's backwards. You're falling for the same trick they used before. They'll hurt him whether or not you come out. It's a matter of whether they get you, too."

She bit her lip in indecision. "Maybe, but maybe I can make them use up the rest of my blood." She shook off Cyrus' hand and stepped forward into the clearing.

Arvid grinned, and another low rumble met their ears. The skies remained clear of clouds or lightning, but a fiery glow spread across the forest to the left. In the light, blue and purple scales briefly glittered across the sky before disappearing beyond the treetops.

"Perfect timing," Vera said. "Our ride is here."

Without warning, Aeliana's legs flew out from under her, a smoky black rope dragging her by the foot across the moss. Random clusters of fresh bamboo shoots scraped her back and hip, and her vision blurred with the passing trees. Still, she caught a glimpse of Sylmar's face, his scars puckering in grim determination. Vera and Arvid raced between the trees, dragging Aeliana behind them, her blood and the dark spirit fueling their escape.

Another rumble and another glow in front of Aeliana turned Arvid and Vera to silhouettes running between the trees. Now she could see flames, slow to engulf the bamboo thanks to the perpetual wetness around them. Still, a portion of the land had been cleared to blackened ash. Other figures appeared behind her, but Aeliana quickly lost the ability to identify the people chasing her as she was tossed and turned by Arvid's and Vera's blood magic.

When Aeliana abruptly stopped, she let out a grunt, her entire body aching. She rolled over with a groan. Smoke filled the air, and ash clung to her trousers and cloak. They were in a new clearing, unnaturally widened by fire or some kind of brutal force. The trees that weren't blackened were uprooted and cracked in half, shoved to the side as if by giant hands.

On her left, Arvid and Vera argued near the center, their harsh voices making her wince, but their distraction left her free of the rope they'd used to bind her. She crawled backward away from them, her efforts likely futile.

"I won't give you more." Vera's voice rose and fell, only allowing Aeliana to catch snippets of their fight as the older woman tucked the vial of blood in her cloak's pocket. "We've already...half the bottle. Mayvus will...if—"

"There's more blood in the girl, you idiot." Arvid reached his hand into Vera's pocket, but she slapped it away. His eyes burned red, and the black trails leaking from his ears and nose billowed faster, like a furnace being fed more coal.

Panic rose in Aeliana's chest. Her hands stung, but she flipped to her knees, then shifted her crawl to a low run that took her to the tree line so she could hide. Footsteps crashed behind her until the thunderous roar returned. A massive creature flew overhead, giving Aeliana a clear view of its soft pale underside, its length from head to tail tip rivaling the height of a Stargazer. Its wingspan was as wide as it was long, the transparent cerulean skin of its wings revealing the Stars still at their dance in the sky above. Flame and smoke, pouring out across the northern edge of the clearing, hid its snout.

Aeliana couldn't stop the scream escaping her mouth, but it was muted by the roar of fire and flap of wings. The humidity that had absorbed her shifted to a blazing dryness in a matter of moments. Arvid and Vera gave one last look toward Aeliana's hiding place, then turned and ran to the center of the clearing once more.

"Meet Durriken." A familiar voice cut through the night.

She turned to find Velden crawling up behind her with a grimace. Blood trickled from a wound at his side, which he stuffed with seaweed as he spoke. "Some say he's the last dragon."

Aeliana squinted through the smoke and flames to her left, but the beast was gone. Vera and Arvid huddled in smoldering ash, waiting like bait for the dragon to return and squash, eat, or burn them.

Sylmar and Cyrus joined Velden and Aeliana, followed by Iris and Kendalyhn, whose pretty face broke into a frown as she helped Aeliana up.

"Come here, love." Iris fussed over Aeliana, smoothing her hair and cloak even as she admonished her for leaving the cave.

Sylmar's staff changed to a sword in his hand, its burning glow resembling coals. Except Aeliana realized the staff had always been metal, its shape shifting as if it were still in the blacksmith's furnace.

The dragon chose that moment to land in the newly blackened clearing less than a hundred paces away. The weight of his body touching down sent a shock through the ground that left Aeliana disoriented. Smoke swirled from his nostrils, then faded as he sucked in a breath. His jaw widened, revealing sharp yellow teeth, charred flesh caught between molars. More flames erupted on Aeliana's right, and fire licked deeper into the forest on both sides. Soon there would be a wall of it cornering them in closer to the dragon.

Cyrus gasped, then grabbed her hand and pulled her back out into the clearing. The others followed, taking up a defensive stance—swords raised, arrows nocked. Matching determination set all their faces in stone, but Aeliana sensed a futileness behind their actions. One by one, they loosed their arrows, but the targets were out of reach.

Vera and Arvid climbed onto the dragon's back, slipping over scales and regaining their foothold as if they'd been riding dragons all their lives. The dragon shifted impatiently, claws digging at the earth like a dog pawing the ground. He turned an eye on Aeliana, cocking his head as if intelligently assessing her from a distance.

He didn't even glance at the small force of Vendarans, whose weapons couldn't do any damage to his thick skin. Instead, he stared Aeliana down, as if daring her to come and claim what was hers. Aeliana's eyes narrowed as the true situation sank in. It didn't matter that the beast could take her out with fire or claws or a single bite. Vera had her blood, and if what Velden said was true, Aeliana had no other choice but to get it back.

Without a second thought, she ran, closing the distance between her and the dragon.

CHAPTER 18

DURRIKEN SNORTED as if entertained by Aeliana's attempt at heroism, then turned in a circle like he might settle down for a nap. Arvid and Vera screamed their protests, and a sparking cough left the dragon's snout. Durriken's amusement only served to make Aeliana wary, but she was too close to turn back.

He stilled enough for Arvid and Vera to get situated, which also allowed Aeliana to get closer. Horns jutted out from Durriken's neck, possibly natural, but more likely some sort of collar. The horns gave her guardians something to hold on to, and gaps in the dragon's scales provided footholds—footholds that were close enough to his underbelly that Aeliana felt certain she could reach them.

If she could live that long.

As she sidestepped Durriken's tail, he stood, stomping in a circle to test the security of his cargo. His tail bent and curved, the scales nearly brushing Aeliana aside, which probably would have been her death. From the top down, the scales appeared shiny and slippery, but Aeliana got the sense that if she could run her hands from the bottom up, their delicate edges would be as sharp as knives. Vera screamed her irritation, scrambling to regain purchase when her hand slipped. Heart thudding in her chest, Aeliana used that moment to leap up and snag Vera's boot, pulling the woman down to the ground with her.

Vera screamed again, this time in pain, as something snapped with her landing.

Aeliana grimaced at the sound as she rolled to the side. She had no time to be shocked or even proud of her success. Strange metal spikes grew from the ground, wrapping around Durriken's paws like some sort of trap, nearly catching Aeliana along with him. The beast growled and lifted his feet, forcing the metal to bend. Aeliana rolled even farther from Vera to avoid getting trampled, then glanced back at the others.

Sylmar's hands rested on two large rocks, his face a mask of concentration as the metal in the surrounding land bent to his will, sliding to the surface and wrapping around the dragon's paws once more, reinforcing the traps. The others lowered their swords and bows, as Aeliana's proximity to the dragon made it more likely they'd injure her than Durriken in a physical attack.

Spirals of smoke shot out from Arvid's hands, snapping the metal chains to free Durriken without difficulty. The beast readjusted, causing Aeliana to bump into his soft underbelly. He grunted and turned as Vera stood, nursing her wrist against her side while looking for another foothold. Aeliana could take the woman down again, but she didn't need Vera. She just needed her cloak.

She stepped forward, but Durriken let loose a thundering rumble that shook Aeliana's insides and knocked her to her backside. Vera used the distraction to climb up on his back once more, accepting Arvid's help and wincing as she adjusted her grip to accommodate her wound.

Aeliana followed before she could think through the consequences. She jumped on Durriken's tail, the scales as slippery as she'd expected. Reaching for purchase only sliced her hands more as Durriken flared out the edges of the scales to flay her skin.

The blood trickling down her hands made it that much harder to think, the temptation to use it in some way almost impossible to resist. But giving in now would mean giving herself over to Arvid and Vera, to the dark spirits, and most likely to Mayvus. She took shorter breaths through her mouth, avoiding the coppery scent's pull as long as possible.

Durriken circled again, and Aeliana nearly lost her grip. She yanked one of his scales off, slicing her palm in the process, releasing even more blood. She climbed higher, managing to reach the edge of Vera's cloak as Durriken picked up his pace, which jostled Aeliana to the precarious edge of his back. At any moment he would take off, and Aeliana would either be swept away with the enemy or dead.

The fleeting thought that her death might be the safest thing for everyone else crept through her mind, but she shook that darkness away.

With a burst of adrenaline, she launched herself at Vera, grabbing the woman's cloak and swinging low to the ground. Aeliana's weight pulled the cloak down, nearly ripping Vera from the dragon's back, but Arvid held Vera tight. Instead, Aeliana was dragged along the charred earth, flaming skeletons of trees whipping across her face.

She reached up with the scale she still gripped and blindly sawed at Vera's cloak until the small tear she formed caught the momentum of her weight, ripping completely and sending Aeliana tumbling to the forest floor. Durriken's back legs nearly trampled her, and his tail snapped back, its tip slapping her back and rolling her through embers that singed her along with Vera's cloak.

Bright white light flashed, blinding her; then there was a crack as her head hit rock.

The blackness that came over her felt expected. A hit like that should have knocked her out. But her racing mind wasn't right. Neither was the pain. Hot and searing, like something spliced through the center of her head, striving to be released as the pressure built. The pain fell away as quickly as it came, her mind no longer connected to her body.

Was this death? Would she join the Stars?

The blackness shifted to the deep blue of water, but instead of the Stars winking before her, Cyrus' lifeless face floated by. She wanted to scream, to reach out for him, but the water shimmered, quickly replaced by the image of the dead girl outside Gahldric's Stargazer, her accusing eyes trained on Aeliana even as Arvid's magic buried her body. The foliage shifted into the dragon's sneer, its neck red and raw, stripped of scales but also the collar. A creature with glassy eyes and red wings fluttered past, replacing the dragon.

Aeliana fought the images, trying to pull herself from the strange dream, but instead saw herself behind prison bars, eyes full of contempt, face half-hidden by stringy hair. It morphed into a far more pleasant face full of freckles splitting for a grin, a moment when Cyrus laughed so hard tears streamed down his face. Then a man, his face in shadow as he bent to kiss her. A silver creature writhing on the ground. A muscular woman rising from the water. Crows pecking at her eyes. A battle, too full of blood and smoke to make out individuals. A heavyset man handing her a sword. A city stretched before her. A young man lying on a table, chest open with heart and ribs exposed. An arrow protruding from her own chest.

The visions came and went until Aeliana no longer tried to make sense of them. When the last image faded—a silver heart embedded in a pale woman's forehead—the blackness took her once more.

She woke to the pain spreading as she regained awareness of every cut and burn on her body. With the pain came the reminder of her purpose. It felt like she'd been out for ages, living entire lifetimes through the visions she'd seen. Visions that were already beginning to fade in her memory. But the dragon still ran across the clearing as if no time had passed.

Despite the dried-up plants around her, Aeliana lay in a thick bed of daisies.

She bolted up, fighting through the throbbing ache to slide her hands over the singed fabric of the cloak, aware of Velden, Sylmar, and Cyrus all yelling and running in her direction while the others chased the dragon, wasting arrows on its armored hide.

"Where is it?" she mumbled over and over, more desperately as her hands came up empty. Could the vial of blood have been in Vera's dress pocket? Or a pocket higher up by her shoulders? She'd cut off as much of the cloak as she could, but it hadn't been enough. She felt like weeping.

The blood wasn't there.

She turned to find Cyrus' shocked eyes on her.

"Are you all right? What were you thinking?" He patted her down, making her aware of tinier cuts and scraped skin, like she'd rolled through broken glass. It was worth it to see his body relax in relief as he found her whole. To see him care.

"Vera still has the blood," Velden said, eyes closed and hands fisted around the remnants of her cloak. In the distance, the dragon's wings expanded so he could leap into the air.

"He's too heavy for me to bring down," Sylmar said. "And too far." Each flap brought a rush of wind that nearly knocked Aeliana over, and then the backdraft seemed to suck the fire even closer. They spoke as if they still had a chance, but Aeliana knew it was too late. Vera still had her blood, and the dragon was flying away.

"Then just bring *her* down," Velden commanded, his former jesting tone a distant memory. He passed the cloak to Sylmar. "Quick!"

Sylmar gripped the fabric, then pulled his arms back as if yanking something over his shoulder. In the distance, Aeliana heard a scream. She sat up, eyes on the dragon shrinking in the sky where a body tumbled from his back. It was both an eternity and a blink in time as she watched Vera's fall. Her mouth went dry at its abrupt stop on the distant forest floor.

Sylmar's face relaxed in grim triumph as Durriken and Arvid flew farther into the distance without their prize. He dropped Vera's cloak as Jasperus and Kendalyhn raced through the smoldering forest in Vera's direction, maybe to check for the vial. Maybe to check if Vera was dead. Aeliana shuddered.

Velden reached for a large man's boot caught in a blackened bush. The brown leather was familiar to Aeliana from years of scrubbing it clean for Arvid. She could imagine his anger over its loss. How much more would he hate her for Vera's death? Would he turn around for revenge? To get her blood?

"The Zealots tricked us." Velden groaned, slamming the boot against the dirt.

"What?" Sylmar's scars puckered once more as he leaned heavily on his molten staff.

"Vera gave the vial to Arvid." Velden turned a pained expression on Aeliana. "Arvid has your blood."

CHAPTER 19

Everyone's gaze shifted to the dragon, now a mere dot in the sky where the pale moonlight glanced off scales.

Aeliana reached for the half cloak, patting it down once more, begging it to hold the missing vial. Instead, she found a tiny golden star. It was heavy, more like a ball of lead with spikes—some trinket Vera had probably stolen. She chucked it at the ground, drawing the others' attention.

Sylmar's eyes widened, and he limped her way.

"So..." Velden's eyebrows lifted, and he bent down to pick up the star. "You earned your starlock. I suspected as much with that flash of light."

Cyrus gasped, leaning in to see it. The others around them smiled; Holm even clapped.

Aeliana shrank away. "That can't be right."

"Yes, it can." Sylmar's eyed the starlock. "That act of bravery could have easily initiated your Awakening. Now your blood will answer to your starlock. They'll work in tandem to make your magic even stronger."

Aeliana shivered.

Sylmar's gaze traveled over Aeliana, most likely taking in cuts, bruises, and singed hair. Then he studied the strange bed of daisies surrounding her.

Had she done that while she was unconscious? Had her starlock?

For the first time, Sylmar's lips lifted. Aeliana thought it might be a smile, but the way his scars shifted with his beard left her anxious.

"Tonight wasn't a loss; it was a sacrifice," he said. "And with sacrifice comes gain."

She glanced back toward the others, silently counting them off. Holm's arm wrapped around Iris, and Cyrus, Lukai, and Velden all studied the starlock. With Jasperus and Kendalyhn checking on Vera's body, they were all accounted for. At least her blood had been the only sacrifice that night.

Velden held out the star. "Congratulations."

Aeliana backed away. "I don't want it."

Sylmar's back straightened, his face darkening as the knot of scars once again bunched together. "You don't get a choice. It's the Sun who chooses the half-light, not the other way around."

He turned, stalking off toward the others to bark out orders, once again leaning heavily on his staff.

"I think you offended him," Cyrus said.

"Everyone's mere existence offends him." Velden stepped forward, turning Aeliana's hand palm up. He dropped the thimble-sized star in her hand and closed her fist around it. It felt heavy and warm like the golden arrow had. Alive.

"It's an honor to be chosen." His smile softened the rebuke. "Whether you use it or not is up to you, but it's still a gift from the Sun that you should accept."

She glanced at Velden's neck—void of a starlock even though she'd seen Velden do magic. He joined Sylmar before Aeliana could work out the inconsistency. Aeliana held back, knowing that if she continued on with these people, she was making a choice to join their war and learn their magic.

The object that had previously felt harmless now seemed sinister, a snare lying in wait to trick her into using it. They made it sound like she'd done something to earn the thing. Like they expected her to use magic almost out of reverence for the Sun. She didn't even know what to think of the Sun. She wasn't sure what the Vendarans believed about it or how that lined up with the Stars she'd worshiped all her life.

She squeezed the object, letting it dig painfully into her palm as a reminder of its danger.

Cyrus stepped away, his actions momentarily seeming like a rejection. But he spoke with Lukai, gesturing back at Aeliana. Lukai nodded, then handed over his own bow with the white wood Aeliana had admired, along with a leather quiver and several arrows.

Cyrus returned, holding out the bow. Aeliana hesitantly grasped its wood, but Cyrus didn't let go. "Is this bow evil?"

The soft question ushered in the memory of their archery lessons. Aeliana pressed her lips together, still not ready to face the deeper truths of his analogy.

"The magic in your blood is no more evil than this bow," Cyrus said. "Your guardians used it for evil, but you can use it for good. The motivation behind it can change the outcome." He released the bow.

Aeliana hugged the weapon close, unable to hold his gaze.

The wind picked up, bringing heat and the threat of flames with it. The events of the night passed over Aeliana in a wave, weighing her down with exhaustion. Clouds covered the moonlight, bringing the fresh clearing into deeper shade, the glow of the dying fire at their backs their only light.

When Jasperus and Kendalyhn returned, the slight shake of their heads seemed to propel the others into action. Lukai checked everyone's injuries while Kendalyhn and Jasperus gathered fallen arrows. Sylmar and Velden held back, watching Aeliana and Cyrus.

"Look," Cyrus whispered, his eyes following Sylmar and Velden's approach. "Gams' dying wish was that I protect you." He looked away, his jaw tight. "The truth is, you probably don't need my protection. You've got all these progenies and your magic. But maybe I'm not meant to protect you from external threats. Maybe she wanted me to protect you from yourself and your own doubts. You don't believe your magic can be good? Prove it. Let Sylmar train you. Let him teach you how to control it."

Her heart pounded with his words. "I need to learn how to get rid of it."

"It sounds like the same thing to me. If it's as bad as you say, they'll be eager to teach you how to get rid of it. Besides, it's no longer just about your magic. These people can help you find your mother."

Her gut clenched as Cyrus hit on the one thing Aeliana couldn't refuse: the chance to find her family.

"Besides," he added. "If they're trying to get back your blood, they can probably help us get the golden arrow that started all this. We—I—could go home."

She blinked back tears. "I'm so sorry, Cyrus. I've taken so much from you."

His fist tightened around the hilt of his sword, which looked odd against the singed priestly robes he'd refused to exchange for the Vendaran leathers. "The Stars saw fit for me to do without. Gams wouldn't want me to waste these opportunities blaming someone else, especially when that someone is just as much a victim."

"You're a good friend, Cyrus." Aeliana swiped at the wetness in her eyes. "I don't think I've had one before now."

His smile bloomed, and he elbowed her in the side. "Gamps said we would be the best of friends. I can't make a liar out of him."

Despite everything, she returned his smile. She even wanted his words to be true.

She'd wanted freedom from her magic—she still did. But she couldn't expect to be free from something she didn't understand. Finding her mother and a way home for Cyrus had to be her new priorities.

Even if it meant learning magic.

As Sylmar and Velden approached, one more objection rose to the surface, a dark thing that tainted any acquiescence she might have leaned toward.

"Is it safe for me to stay with the group?" she asked the progenies. "If Mayvus uses my blood to brand me, is there risk of me turning on you at any point?" The question felt ridiculous, the idea of her being used as a weapon against these people almost arrogant, but it had to be asked.

"Of course there's risk." Sylmar's straightforward answer made Aeliana's stomach drop. "But that could happen even if you strike out on your own. At least if you're with us, we'll have the hope of restraining you or even cutting out the brand mark on your skin to reverse it. The safest place for you to be is with us."

Aeliana chewed on her lower lip, still not convinced.

"The brand can be reversed that easily?" Cyrus let out a long breath, his body slouching.

Velden winced. "Reversed? Yes. Easily? No. Everything inside Aeliana will fight us, including her blood and that starlock she just earned." He tapped her fist, reminding her it was clenched so tight her palm had grown numb.

She relaxed her fingers, then tucked the charm in her pocket and rubbed the feeling back into her hand. When she scratched at the mark on her palm, she couldn't help glancing at Lukai. His left arm was wrapped in seaweed, and he limped as he approached Kendalyhn. Aeliana was starting to feel a pull, a heightened awareness. Not exactly the attraction Velden had suggested, but a desire to help and a need to prioritize him. Was that what Mayvus' brand would feel like?

Probably a lot worse.

"When can she use my blood?" Aeliana asked.

Sylmar's brow furrowed. "Once she has it in her possession, she could use it at any moment, but my guess is that she'll wait for Summer Solstice. It's what she's done in the past because with the longest hours in the Sun's light, the brand will be the strongest."

"Many bonding ceremonies are held then for the same reason," Velden said.

"Plus, they're not aware Aeliana's already had her Awakening," Sylmar said. "They'll want to give her time to earn her starlock to make sure her magic is worth stealing."

Aeliana bit her lip, watching the others disappear from view as Jasperus led them around the dwindling flames toward another rocky path. It would take them back to their cave and away from the smoke and stench of dragon. And based on Iris' earlier directions, it would also take them toward the other Recreants in Valorian. Toward unknown dangers and threats.

Only Iris and Lukai remained at the path's edge, a faithful servant and bondmate, as if their roles held them there, unable to move on without her. It made her want to be worthy of their devotion.

"You know we're the good guys, right?" Velden cocked his head, then sprayed her face lightly with water from his hands.

She wiped her face. "You just killed a woman. I don't know what to think of you."

"Hmm." He glanced across the clearing as if Vera's body might be just beyond their view. "Fair point. Does it help if I remind you we're in a war? She was the enemy, whereas you"—he gestured toward her and Cyrus—"are not."

"I could become the enemy, with or without Mayvus' brand. There's something wrong with my magic." Aeliana glanced at Sylmar, who didn't disagree. Was she the only one who felt the pull of darkness? It was less about whether she trusted these people and more about whether she could trust herself.

"Then let us help you," Sylmar said, both hands balanced on his staff. "You let me teach you about your magic, wean you from the blood magic, and then, if you still want me to get rid of your magic, I'll teach you that too."

"Sylmar—" Velden started to protest.

"Do we have a deal?" Sylmar held out his gnarled hand, the thick scars drawing Aeliana's curiosity once more. She glanced at Velden, who glared at Sylmar but said nothing.

"What's in it for you?" she asked. "Why did you bother waiting for me in the first place? It can't just be a favor for a priestess everyone loved."

Sylmar's hand hung in the air, but his confidence didn't wane. "Just like your mother is the key to defeating Mayvus, you are the key to rescuing your mother. The way Mayvus uses her brands, well, it leaves them imprisoned in their mind almost as much as their body. After all this time, if you aren't with us when we find Emeris—if you aren't safe —I'm not sure she'll ever escape that prison."

Aeliana stared at Sylmar's outstretched hand for a moment longer.

"Deal." She grasped his forearm, surprised by his strong grip as he returned the gesture.

Without further deliberation, he turned, passing Iris and Lukai, clearly expecting them all to follow.

Lukai stepped forward, rubbing the back of his neck as though flustered. "I'm sorry I couldn't come fast enough. I sensed your pain—I wanted to be there, but my injuries needed tending. Plus the injuries of the others around me." He closed his eyes. "I should have come to you first."

She placed her hand on his arm. "No. Never abandon someone else in need to save me. Regardless of our bond."

His brow furrowed, but instead of commenting, he turned her hand over, gently running his fingers over her forearms and palms. The motion felt surprisingly intimate until she sensed a coolness over her burns and her pain receded to something far more tolerable. Her heart raced, but she couldn't tell which made her more anxious—his magic or his touch. He repeated the motion over her face and neck, but this time her cheeks were too warm for the coolness to ever come.

"Ready?" He reached for the bow and quiver, but instead of taking them back, he helped her strap them on like she was a child. "They suit you better anyway."

The gift was extravagant, and she should thank him, but she was still too flustered by his touch. She adjusted her hair where it got caught under the straps, wincing as he tightened them on her back where Arvid had carved his message.

"Oh, love." Iris shook her head, mistaking the reason for Aeliana's pained expression. "You should have let me cut your hair."

CHAPTER 20

THE BOAT ROCKED, the light sway more natural to Orra than the heaviness of walking on land. A salty breeze left strands of short dark hair blocking her view, but it was too soon to see Bamboo Island against the rising Sun anyway. She closed her eyes to assess its place in the world by feel instead of sight. The sliver of magic needed was an extravagance when it had once been like breathing.

Her body was still weak from her efforts to trace the arrow across the barrier. She couldn't regret singing the priestess to sleep, but she still paid for that choice. It could take weeks to get her energy stores back to the level they'd been. If they could even be replenished. Every year, she faded a little more.

Out of habit, Orra ran her fingers over the braid at her wrist, the smooth hairs a reassurance even though they represented her greatest loss. She still remembered how it had thrummed even though the sensation had died down to a slight tingle against her skin. She'd only felt that thrum a handful of times in her life. Each time, it had led her to a new piece she'd lost, and each time, she lost it again. Now that the golden arrow had been used, it could be hundreds of miles away, or it could still be on the tiny island that grew closer as the Sun rose higher. Its power was too dim to sense.

She'd have to use the girl. She was grateful she could use her. She'd sensed her connection to the girl's blood, but she couldn't let that truth matter. The golden arrow mattered more.

The arrow would always matter more.

CHAPTER 21

GAEREN WATCHED Orra perch on the prow of the boat, eyes closed as she played with the blond braid she wore as a bracelet. Her own dark hair fluttered around her cheeks, the short strands caught by the wind. Even her skin seemed a shade darker, as if being on the water brought renewed health.

There was an unnatural quality to the way she stood, leaning forward as if she might dive over the edge at any moment, and yet her balance never faltered as her skirt tangled around her legs. He was surprised Lenda hadn't given her a nicer gown to wear, more so Lenda wouldn't have to bear the out-of-date peasant look. But maybe Lenda was too… preoccupied.

Sometime during the night, she'd given in to her seasickness, refusing to leave her quarters and not letting anyone except her maid, not even Orra, by her side. It was a relief for Gaeren to not have to address their bond, but without Lenda, Orra's strangeness became more apparent, leaving the men more unsettled.

They eyed her warily as they worked, whispering amongst themselves. Gaeren stepped to the middle of the quarterdeck until the main mast blocked his view of her trance-like state. Perhaps he was as superstitious as the men, but pretending she wasn't on board made his shoulders loosen and his stance relax.

"Will she come back with us from Bamboo Island?" Larkos asked, his hand on the wheel of the ship.

"Doubtful." Gaeren glanced at his first mate, whose curiosity was only apparent in the slight narrowing of his eyes. "Depends on what happens when we reach it. I expect she'll part ways with us there."

Gaeren ran his thumb over the daisy on his dagger, relishing its solid weight and reminder of his goal.

"You have no idea what you're doing." Larkos laughed, the star-shaped tattoos near his eyes crinkling in a dance. "How long has she had you doing her bidding? Was this entire voyage her idea and she roped you into offering your boat?"

"I only met her two nights ago." The moment the words were out of Gaeren's mouth, he regretted the admission.

Larkos' eyebrows nearly reached his hairline. "Two nights ago? Then she must have bewitched you into bringing her."

Gaeren shrugged off the accusation. Any excuse he gave would only confirm such a theory. Besides, he wasn't entirely sure that she hadn't used magic to persuade him. He still questioned the sanity of bringing her on board.

"There's something I lost," he finally said. "She knows how to find it. If I hadn't brought her, she would have hunted it down for herself. She might have beaten me to it."

"Nothing's faster than *Starspeed*," Larkos scoffed, his grip on the wheel tightening. Gaeren's mind tuned in to his own memories, honing in on the way Orra had looked dead, hunched over his desk. The way life had suddenly infused her. He was no longer sure of anything, least of all *Starspeed's* ability to beat a woman with mysterious magic to Bamboo Island.

He didn't want to answer any more of Larkos' prying questions. In fact, he needed to get his own questions answered. As he made his way across the deck and back up to the bow of the ship where Orra still balanced, he debated if he would lose face by speaking to the woman on the ship or gain ground by showing a lack of fear. Either way, it was too late. The men had all watched his approach, and backing down now would make him look like a fool.

"Are you able to sleep standing?" he asked.

She smiled softly, opening her eyes. "Who could sleep with the Sun's light on them?"

Gaeren paused, squinting toward the rising Sun. Perhaps she was still weak, but he didn't think so. She must be as devout as their priest for a phrase like that to leave her lips without a hint of a mocking tone.

"When we reach the island, what will you do?" His heart beat faster at the question, unsure what he hoped her answer would be. If she wanted to use the starbridge, he would be willing to give it up for Daisy. But what if she was also looking for the girl?

She leaned forward, eyes on the water where it parted for *Starspeed* to cut through. "I can sense things better on land."

He waited for a real answer, but she kept her eyes on the foam, oblivious to his impatience. "Will you use it if we find it?"

She stiffened, then pulled herself away from the boat's edge to face him. "Use what?"

He hesitated, wondering again if they really were looking for the same thing. She'd said it was a starbridge, maybe something more. "Aren't you wanting to cross the barrier?"

A short laugh escaped her lips. "No."

She turned back to lean over the water, frowning. "It seems the barriers have only served to make men more curious, more desperate." Her words came out mumbled, like she was no longer aware of his presence. It felt like a dismissal, but he hadn't learned anything about her magic or her true motives. If he'd been able to touch her, he could use his weaker second spoke to determine if she told the truth, but she'd already warned him against that. Besides, the last time he'd tried, she'd been a blank wall.

He reached out, tuning in to her memories for some hint, but it was still like none existed. He frowned, unsure how she was blocking his intrusion so completely. Usually when he met resistance, flashes of images still broke through.

"How did you know my name the night we met?"

She watched the water long enough that he thought he wouldn't get an answer. When she finally spoke, her words came out slow and measured. "Everyone knows the Prince of Elanesse."

He made a face at the title. Those who knew him well knew not to use it.

"But I started paying attention when I heard you wanted the book *The Sins of the Stars*." Her eyes found his, burning into him with an intensity that made him feel exposed. When her gaze shifted to his coat pocket, he knew she'd seen him studying it between tasks, poring over it for any detail he might have missed.

He'd put out requests for that book several moons ago. Did that mean she'd been watching him that long? "Why?"

She sat precariously on the boat's edge, a single rogue wave away from being thrown to the sea. Against his better judgment, he felt no fear for her safety. Somehow, Gaeren suspected she was immune to such a simple end.

"The handwritten notes inside are peculiar, right?" she asked.

He stilled, thinking of how he'd first found her camped out in his swamp hideout. It bothered him that she'd been following him so closely, even going through his things. But his need for answers overrode that. What did she make of the strange symbols marked with references to various people groups and locations? Were they places the starbridges were hidden? Places they were last seen? The people who'd been given charge of them? Those were the questions he wanted to ask, but they felt too vulnerable.

"How did you see them?"

She shook her head slightly. "I wrote them."

His mouth swung open before he could stop himself, and he clamped it shut before any of his men could see. He glanced around, making sure none were within hearing range while closing the distance between him and Orra.

"Have you already found some of the objects?"

Her lids lowered, and she ducked her head. "They've slipped through my fingers over the years."

His knees felt weak even as his heart rate picked up its pace. He crouched beside her. "Which ones? When? Where did you last see them?"

"When we reach the island, what will you do?" She turned his own question on him. "Will you use *it*"—she spat the word out—"if we find it?"

He hesitated, unsure which answer she wanted to hear. It was only fair that she wanted to know his motives just like he wanted to know hers, but one of them had to show their hand first. He didn't want it to be him.

Besides, he didn't know. He'd wanted to find the starbridges to find Daisy. Now that she was accessible without the starbridges, the drive to find them had weakened.

Orra studied him while the spray of the salt water misted against their arms. When he didn't answer, she let out a stilted laugh. "Two types of men seek the starbridges. One who wishes to make the world bigger, to fill it with all sorts of wonder created by people far and wide. And one who wishes to make the world smaller, to fit it in the palm of his hand and hold it in his fist." She closed her eyes, her lashes suspiciously wet. "Which one are you?"

The answer seemed obvious, but her vulnerability made him truly ask himself the question. Why did he want the starbridges?

His hand slipped to his dagger once more, the hard lines of the grip swirling to the pommel, where the ridges of the daisy gave him focus. This had all started as a way to find out what had happened to Daisy. A small part of him wondered if the starbridges could still be useful for protection. He didn't know why Emeris had sent Daisy away. Maybe he'd need to use a starbridge to take her back to Lorvandas to continue protecting her.

Beyond that, the adventurous side of him relished the idea of exploration. Finding the starbridges could unite the people, not just in Vendaras but all of Rhystahn. He thought that would make the world bigger—breaking down the barriers and bringing people together again. It would be a far better way for him to spend his time as throne warden than sitting in a stuffy palace.

But what if the people across the barriers didn't want unification? What if war broke out the same way it had before the barriers had been put in place? Whether he wanted to or not, it was possible he could eventually use the starbridges for control, to make the world the place he thought it should be even if others disagreed.

The idea left him nauseous, like Lenda's seasickness had suddenly become contagious. Deep down, he knew Larkos was right. Gaeren had been raised to see progenies as better, more valuable than half-lights who couldn't do magic. He tried to work with his men and see them as equals, but even his authority as captain made it impossible to truly see them that way. It made it impossible for them to see him as anything other than someone who controlled them.

Orra waited for an answer, but the time he spent working it out seemed to already be answer enough. She turned away, her face impassive.

"I want to be the first man, the one who makes the world bigger," he said, letting the words hang in the air as an unfinished sentence. *But I don't know if I am,* or *but I'm probably the second* were both viable endings. Did that mean he should give up the search? Was she saying he wasn't noble enough to use the starbridges?

"Perhaps you will be." Her lips twitched, like she had a secret.

She was a mystery and clearly wanted to remain one, but she didn't feel like a danger—yet.

Still, he wanted to know more about her notes in his book. He opened his mouth to ask again, but her gaze shifted over his shoulder, her smile deepening with amusement.

"Your bondmate has graced the deck with her beauty. You should go see her before her jealous rage mixes with her sensitive stomach."

He turned to find Lenda glaring at them from the doorway of her quarters, arms wrapped around her stomach like she held its contents at bay. The men all paused in their work, gazes volleying between Gaeren and Lenda like they expected an entertaining showdown.

Guilt swarmed through Gaeren's chest, and he stepped away from Orra before he could evaluate why. He hadn't done anything wrong. Why should he feel guilt just because Lenda misread the moment? He ran his thumb over his palm, tracing the bond mark with his nail as if he might be able to dig it out.

He should apologize and tell Lenda about the starbridge, give her peace of mind that she was the only woman he was interested in. His feet propelled him forward, but halfway across the deck, he realized it was the bond urging him to do and feel those things, so he jerked to a stop. With a bow small enough to possibly be a snub, he acknowledged Lenda's presence above deck, then made his way to the quarterdeck, where Larkos' shoulders shook with held-back laughter.

"It's like you want to have a miserable marriage," the older man said.

Gaeren took the wheel, knowing the need to display his authority was as childish and privileged as Larkos had accused him of being.

"Lenda's suspicion is only a quarter of your problem, though," Larkos warned. He leaned back against the bulkhead and retied his sleek black hair in a knot at his neck, drawing Gaeren's attention to his Wheel of Magic tattoo once more.

Something about the tattoo bothered Gaeren, and he couldn't put his finger on what.

"I can only do so much to keep the men supporting you." Larkos crossed his arms and frowned. "Orra draws the men in while simultaneously repelling them. They think you've brought a witch on board."

At least Larkos wasn't bringing up Riveran. Maybe no one cared about the traitorous X with the threat of a witch. The hidden progenies, witches to most, were driven mad by their aspirations for more magic. They worshipped the Stars' power more than the Sun's light, and their blood magic and sacrificial practices were barbaric—murderous acts that Gaeren hoped Enla would abolish once all the threats of war had passed. The witches' obsession matched Mayvus', and for a moment he wondered if the power-hungry priestess could be from the witches' coven, secretly rising to power. It would fit the strangeness about her that he couldn't quite explain.

Something about Orra seemed different, though. Maybe her motivation or the way she held back her power instead of displaying it for the world to see. But maybe false humility was part of her strategy.

"Perhaps I have brought a witch," Gaeren murmured.

Larkos' gaze snapped to him. "Don't let the men hear you say that." Then he laughed. "Or Lenda."

CHAPTER 22

THE TUNNEL the Vendarans took Aeliana and Cyrus through was more like the scratched-out remains of a mole's burrow. At various points, the paths veered off into dead ends, as if the person digging out the tunnel hadn't been able to decide which direction was best. When it sloped downward, the mud often gave way to water, but when it angled back up, the ceiling didn't necessarily adjust, forcing the entire party to bend at the waist until the ground gave way again.

Aeliana couldn't fathom their position beneath the sea.

Supposedly, most of the tunnels had been formed by lava tubes thousands of years before, and progenies had used magic to break through the rest of the hard earth while stabilizing and connecting them. Velden had given that explanation as if it might comfort the newcomers, but it only made Aeliana more uneasy. In addition to picturing the tunnels collapsing beneath the weight of the water above, she imagined fresh lava at their backs.

She forced herself to relax, to think of the open air on the other side. They were almost through the twelve-mile trek that would bring them out from the caves to the main land around the time of the Sun's sleep, but after she had traveled across the barrier by using a starbridge, spent a restless day debating if she made the right choice, then attacked her guardians on a dragon, she was ready to fall asleep on her feet.

Even the Vendarans seemed unsettled, but Aeliana suspected that was related to the lack of light. She sensed her own blood craving replenishment but found it more like the ache of hunger versus the nausea of satiety—far more manageable.

For the most part, the shuffle of boots against rock was only joined by the *drip, drip, drip* of water. She shivered in the dank air.

"Would you like an extra cloak?" Lukai asked.

Aeliana shook her head, then glanced in Cyrus' direction. He spoke animatedly with Kendalyhn, whose face remained bunched up in irritation. The other woman had yet to smile, at least when Aeliana was around.

Maybe Aeliana should engage Lukai more, ask questions about her homeland, discover more about this man who was her bondmate, but her eyes fought to stay open, and placing one foot in front of the other for the remainder of the day was all she could manage.

By the time they reached the surface and Sylmar instructed them to make camp, every muscle in Aeliana's body demanded that she sit or lie down, but she refused to be seen as a weak link. She dropped her quiver and bow to the earth, still ridden with bamboo shoots, and assisted Holm in laying out the bedrolls in the small clearing they'd found amongst the thick trees. Their variety was unfamiliar to Aeliana —large leaves and larger trunks that soaked up the perpetual wetness of the rainforest. Lukai and Jasperus used the trees' limbs to replace the foliage hiding the lava tube entrance, their easy banter drifting across camp.

Holm rose from the last bedroll and leaned back slightly, as if that particular stance was the only way to balance the large gut before him.

"You should rest," he offered, gesturing to the bedrolls they'd just laid out. Despite his girth, there was a formidable thickness to his limbs that should have left her on edge. Instead, his quiet manner made him more approachable than Jasperus, whose theatrical voice still startled her when it came from his small frame.

"I'm not sure I'd be able to get back up for the evening meal." Her gaze shifted to the nearby fire that Kendalyhn had built and stoked. The other woman flitted around the flames, her tiny frame almost child-like, but there was a beauty in the way the glow shone over her light brown skin, the way her black hair had been braided across her crown. It made Aeliana reconsider Iris' offer to cut off her locks.

As Kendalyhn leaned forward, a leather cord slipped from beneath her tunic, and a small object flashed in the firelight. Kendalyhn's eyes swung in Aeliana's direction, as if she sensed her curiosity, but a vicious frown crossed her face, and she turned her back on Aeliana.

"Don't let her get to you," Holm said. "Had a rough upbringing and doesn't trust easily. Eventually she'll crack. She's all soft inside."

Aeliana smiled faintly as Iris joined them.

"Who's all soft inside? You'd better not be spilling my secrets." The older woman poked Holm in the gut, then pecked his cheek when he doubled over. During lunch, Aeliana had spotted their bond marks and had watched them ever since. If this was how things could someday be with Lukai, perhaps the bond wasn't such a terrible thing.

"He was talking about Kendalyhn," Aeliana said.

"Ah, give it some time." Iris' wrinkles smoothed out as her gaze softened. "I was a bit like her when I was young. Took a lot of time healing from old wounds."

"I might have helped things along," Holm said.

She swatted him, then turned back to Aeliana. "You'll have to earn her respect, love. Your starlock helps."

The word stirred up anxiety and fueled her curiosity. "How does it work?"

"It's a bit like oil in a lantern," Holm said, still rubbing his side with one hand while wrapping the other arm around Iris. "It keeps the fire of the magic lit. But eventually it runs out until it can recharge in the light of the Sun."

"So it's like our blood?" She tried not to let her disgust taint her willingness to understand.

Holm angled his head side to side, as if weighing the accuracy of her words. "In function, yes. But a starlock also strengthens the magic of your blood tenfold, maybe more."

Tenfold? Aeliana shuddered. This was what her guardians had been watching for. Not just for her to realize she could do magic, but for her to come into a far greater power. She stuck her hand in her pocket, testing out the tiny sharp edges of her starlock.

"How do the Stars decide who gets a starlock? And when?"

Iris clucked her tongue. "The Stars can only do what the Sun asks of them."

Aeliana winced, forgetting their differences in faith. "But why an Awakening? Why not just give them a starlock?" She really wanted to ask if others saw visions and memories in their Awakenings. But Iris and Holm didn't have starlocks, and Sylmar had made it sound like the experience of receiving one was something to keep private.

"Sometimes the Sun uses the Awakening to test the recipients character in the present," Holm said. "Or the Sun might use an Awakening to reveal aspects of one's future."

Aeliana squirmed, wishing she could remember more details from her visions. They'd grown more blurred in her mind, like a dream that faded the longer she was awake.

"Sometimes the Awakening is used to call them out on their past," Holm continued. "There's a purpose even if we don't understand it. Some half-lights are chosen but don't survive the experience. To be chosen and to survive…it's a gift."

Despite the muggy air and the warmth of the nearby fire, coldness swept through Aeliana's limbs. Out of habit, she searched the skies for dark spirits. It didn't feel like a gift. Still, even through Holm's quiet explanation, Aeliana sensed awe, maybe longing.

She glanced at his bare neck. "Can you not do magic?"

"No." He frowned. "I never developed any skills. Those who do often start training to prepare for their Awakening, but it's difficult to learn much before receiving a starlock. Only one in ten of us get them. Or we used to. It might be more like one in twenty these days."

Iris nodded her agreement at his estimate.

Aeliana raised her eyebrows in surprise. "So this group is unusual."

Iris laughed. "Very much so. Outside of the schools, there's probably not another group with this much training or experience."

"Maybe with Mayvus." Holm's face puckered in irritation.

"Well, I didn't mention the witches either, did I?" Iris pulled away from his grasp. "I thought we were talking about progenies worthy of respect."

"Witches?" Aeliana asked.

"Progenies who use blood magic and worship the Stars," Holm clarified.

Iris smacked him again with a guilty look at Aeliana. "You're nothing like them, love."

She nodded even though it sounded exactly like the way she'd been raised. Instead of evaluating her discomfort, she redirected the subject. "I thought anyone with starblood could be chosen."

"Most of the chosen have a higher concentration of starblood, but sometimes people have that and still don't receive a starlock." Holm shrugged. "My family has never had much. My mother's parents pushed her to marry a man with a higher concentration of starblood. They thought she'd have more chance of bearing children who would get chosen." His smile was more of a grimace. "That didn't work out so well."

"My guardians used my blood for its magic, but I never really developed any of my own." Aeliana bit her lip, trying to decide if that was a good thing.

"Sure you did," Iris said. "I saw the bed of daisies you grew. That's unusual. It hints that you might lean toward the earth elemental. Some progenies develop a second spoke, which then gives them access to the rim of the Wheel of Magic. The earth elemental falls on the rim between the constructive noetic and somatic spokes. I suspect those will be your strengths. Even if you only develop one spoke, you'll be surprised at what you can do now that you have your starlock."

Aeliana opened her mouth to protest, but the words died on her lips. The idea of using magic had always been so detestable, the concept equated with the horror of what her guardians had done. But her guardians didn't have starlocks; they'd just had her blood.

Could she simply choose to use it now? Especially now that she had a starlock?

She wasn't sure she wanted answers to those questions.

After dinner, Lukai and Cyrus pulled her aside.

"Cyrus says you have a wound that needs healing," Lukai said.

Cyrus gave her a sheepish grin. "If you're as tired as I am, it can't feel good to also have that pack scratching your scabs."

She sighed and undid her top button, turning to let her collar fall enough for Lukai to see the marks on her back. His intake of breath brought back all her fears, and she and Cyrus shared a grimace.

"Does Sylmar know about this?"

She shook her head.

"Arvid and Vera were communicating with someone, most likely Mayvus." Even as he spoke, he ran his hands over the scabs, a coolness settling into her skin that made her sigh in relief.

"I keep forgetting to tell him, but I will."

"I'll let him know," Cyrus offered.

"Thank you," she said as he headed for the cookfire. She wasn't sure she had the energy to deal with Sylmar's response. Lukai tugged on her shoulder so she could face him.

"All done," he said.

"Thanks." She buttoned her shirt once more, and an awkward silence hung between them.

"The last couple days have been"—Lukai fought to find the right word as he scratched the back of his neck—"strange."

She laughed, a light airy thing that made her inwardly cringe. "If it's been strange for you, a Vendaran, imagine how it's been for me."

He smiled, his gaze drifting over her shoulder, back at the others. A lock of his golden hair fell in his eyes, and Aeliana wondered if she should brush it away. The thought was so absurd she almost laughed.

"Look," he said. "I don't have any expectations for the two of us. I'm your bondmate, and I will protect you. But it doesn't have to be more if you don't want it. It's not fair to expect anything else from you when you didn't choose this." He gestured between them.

"You didn't choose it either," she pointed out.

He shrugged. "I know."

They stared at each other for a long moment.

"Let's work on being friends, for now," she said. "Friends who have this strange impulse to protect each other. I think that's all I can handle until we get my blood back anyway." She wrapped her arms around herself even though the forest air was still thick and warm.

"Fair enough." His smile seemed wider, lighter—a vast contrast from Sylmar's dark look as he headed their way.

After extensive questioning about the marks on her back, Sylmar finally let them all go to sleep. Aeliana's dreams were filled with blood and tears. It could have been memories of the last two days all squished together. It could have been what she feared might be the result of Mayvus having her blood. But when she woke in the night, she realized half the sobs she'd heard came from Cyrus.

Unsure if he'd welcome comfort from someone partly responsible for Della's death, Aeliana remained curled up on her bedroll, crying silent tears along with him.

The next two days passed in a similar fashion, only instead of trekking through lava tubes slightly improved by progenies, they walked through forests of bamboo and giant taro, still thick and untamed. Having caught up on rest, everyone was determined to take their turn walking with Aeliana and Cyrus, comparing Lorvandan and Vendaran history and culture—if nothing else because it got them out of the duty of hacking overgrown trees in their path.

Cyrus' excitement distracted him from his grief. It was like the text of *The Legend of the Stars* was coming to life before his eyes. Aeliana was glad he at least had that. Despite his tears during the night, he'd stepped away from the group to worship the Stars, had even invited her to join him. It didn't matter that the Stars hadn't stepped in to save his grandmother, he still called on them to guide him through his grief.

Aeliana and Cyrus drilled Velden and Jasperus about the landscape of Vendaras when they discovered Sylmar meant for them to cross most of it.

Jasperus gestured to the ferns and canopies of trees. "After we get through this rainforest, we'll spill out into the plains, which will be much faster, though more exposed, travel."

The air was still thick with the scent of rain and wet soil, but the edges of the forest rippled until fields of grass stretched before them, dotted by the occasional tree or water hole. After a moment, Jasperus dropped his hand and the illusion disappeared.

"Is that noetic magic?" Cyrus asked. "Are you tricking our minds?"

"Ah," Jasperus said. "That's a good guess, but these are more like physical masks. I adjust the elements before you to create something tangible. It's a temporary change, but still a physical one you can touch, so it's a somatic skill. Though touch often dispels the illusion. I can't hold anything for very long because I'm pushing against its natural composition."

Cyrus begged for another illusion, and Jasperus happily complied, narrating it with a fanciful story that likely held little truth. With his misleadingly small frame and grey beard, he was like a grandfather gathering children at his knee while his deep voice carried them across unknown mountains and waters.

Velden joined them, adding his own commentary to Jasperus' story.

"Do you know where my mother lived?" Aeliana asked. "None of this feels familiar to me."

"Celanoft." A small smile crossed Velden's face. "You come from the eastern regions, which is why your skin is lighter like Lukai's and Kendalyhn's."

Cyrus snorted and slid back the arm of his priestly robes to reveal an even paler arm with freckles.

"Ah, your human skin doesn't absorb the Sun's light the way ours does," Velden said. "It doesn't pull the warmth into the blood because you have no starblood."

"So the darker the skin, the stronger the power?" Cyrus asked.

"Not exactly. Just maybe stronger ancestral ties to the Stars. It's said their skin is a rich, deep brown, darker than the soil of this forest. The better to reflect the Sun's glory."

Cyrus frowned.

"What is Celanoft like?" Aeliana asked, eager to avoid the religious debate she sensed brewing in Cyrus' mind.

"It had a seaside Sungazer," Velden said, "resting on the eastern cliffs of Vendaras—a majestic place with a sharp drop to the sea on the east and a sloping decline to the city's valley on the west."

"I take it Mayvus destroyed it?" Cyrus asked.

Velden nodded, his smile fading. "Officially, she had it torn down because Emeris was in league with the witches. Not sure how Mayvus got that declared."

Aeliana's disappointment grew. "I loved being by the shore in Lorvandas. But I don't remember living by it as a child."

"What do you remember?" Jasperus asked.

It had been a long time since Aeliana had thought of her life before her guardians. The question stirred up a deep longing. She should have grown up in the safety of a Stargazer with her parents. Wait, no, a Sungazer. This place should feel like home, but it didn't. Not yet.

The rain picked up speed, pattering on the leaves around them. She let the rhythm of it bring in memories as fuzzy as the mist surrounding them.

"I remember feelings mostly. The presence of people, but blank faces. Arvid and Vera told me so many lies that they contradicted themselves. I don't know what's true, not even my memories, which are more likely a fabricated mix of truth and lies."

There were some things that stood out in her memory. A sense of belonging, being held. Warmth and security. A smile parting a brown beard and mustache. The sound of high laughter mixed with deep belly laughs. And daisies…so many daisies. The memories mingled together the same way the visions she'd received in her Awakening had overlapped in confusing loops and layers. It all felt too personal to share, too deeply felt.

"Kendalyhn could help you separate the truth from the lies," Velden said.

Aeliana shook her head. "Sylmar said he and Iris are the only ones who've met my mother. The vague memories I have probably can't even be confirmed by someone who knew her well. Maybe not even by her." Her throat grew tight.

"That's not what I meant," Velden said. "She and I are both pneumatics. My skills focus more on sifting through things in the present, but she's best at sifting through things in the past."

Aeliana shuddered at the thought of Kendalyhn digging through her memories, dissecting them for bits of truth.

"Or not." Velden laughed, and the fish hooks hanging from his ears shook. He still wore a mere vest over his chest, and Aeliana wondered if he would don more clothing when they reached cooler regions. Iris had helped him shear his hair close to his head the night before, once again offering to trim Aeliana's hair to what Iris called a respectable length.

"What's after the plains?" Cyrus asked.

"In a little more than a moon," Jasperus continued, "we should reach a mountain pass just east of Mt. Vescano, Vendaras' only active volcano. It's in the Myndren Mountains, but that will be our halfway point to Mayvus' fortress, which is built into the cliffs of Myndren on the northeastern shore."

"Do you think she knows we're coming?" Aeliana asked. "Or do you think she expects you to hide me?"

"I think she prepares for both." Velden shrugged. "Realistically, she probably assumes we're bringing you so we can protect you while we come. Which just means we have to come up with some amazing way to surprise her and catch her off guard."

"Can't pneumatic progenies see the future?" Cyrus asked. "Isn't that where she lands on the Wheel of Magic?"

"Think of it more like sifting through someone's desires and plans," Velden said. "It produces possibilities, but nothing certain. Besides, Mayvus' strength is similar to mine. She's sees more of what's happening in the present. She tends to sift through evil intentions of a person, whereas I tend to sift through the truth of a moment, like when I sifted Vera's soul using her cloak."

Their conversation with Velden was cut off by Sylmar, who saw their confusion as an excuse to run through the Wheel of Magic properties again and again until Aeliana could recite them and scratch the image from memory into one of the giant taro leaves.

Just when Aeliana thought Sylmar might let them stop for the night, sharp pain dug between her shoulder blades. She stumbled, pulling at her pack and quiver in an effort to get them off.

"Aeliana?" Cyrus took her pack, then helped her to the ground, where she kneeled, forehead against the soil. "What's wrong?"

"I didn't think it would happen," she said. "Not after we healed it."

Lukai fought his way through the line. "What's happening? Is she hurt?"

Aeliana squinted up at him, then took in Sylmar over Lukai's shoulder. "I think she's sending another message." Her hands trembled, but she undid her top button, then swept her hair to the side and bent forward.

Warm fingers brushed her neck, and the fabric was pushed aside. Several gasps rang out.

"I've never seen magic like that," Iris whispered.

"It has to be blood magic." Disgust tinged Kendalyhn's tone.

"I've seen it before," Sylmar said quietly. "But I'm not even sure I'd call it magic."

"What does it say?" Aeliana couldn't keep the desperation out of her voice.

For a moment, no one seemed willing to tell her. Then Cyrus placed a hand on her shoulder and kneeled beside her.

"It says, 'she belongs to me.'"

CHAPTER 23

"Again," Sylmar demanded, tapping Aeliana's taro leaf with his staff.

She scratched at her back even though Mayvus' message had been healed the night before. She still felt its presence, as if she'd been marked permanently. The entire group had remained somber, except for Sylmar, who had gained renewed determination to train Aeliana.

Which was why stopping for water and a rest now meant something different to him.

"Somatic progenies make up two opposite spokes, constructive and destructive," Aeliana said slowly, running a finger over the line on her leaf.

Sylmar nodded his approval. "And what do they do?"

"They adjust the body, their skills ranging from healing and growth on the constructive side of the Wheel to sickness and death on the destructive side." She cringed, wondering how progenies on the destructive side justified their work as blessed by the Stars. Or Sun…

Cyrus peered over her shoulder, his red hair falling across her arm. Despite his human blood, Cyrus was an eager pupil, catching on to the rhythm of the Wheel much faster than Aeliana.

"And who in our party has that skill?" Sylmar asked.

"You and…" Aeliana glanced around. "Lukai."

"Anyone else?"

She hesitated, eyeing the group once more. Her gaze lingered on

Jasperus. She remembered him creating the masks to hide people from Durriken along with the story-telling illusions. Hadn't he said that was somatic?

Sylmar followed her gaze. "Good. Jasperus is one. That wasn't really a fair question. We tend to hold our magic close to us. You probably haven't seen enough of it used. Tell me about noetics."

She couldn't decide if the idea of holding magic close sounded safer, like they might only use it when absolutely necessary, or if it meant they only used it secretively. Were any of them using their mind-reading skills right now?

Cyrus cleared his throat, angling his head toward her drawing.

"Um, noetics." She frowned at her Wheel. "Noetic progenies tune in to the mind: feelings, thoughts, memories—again on opposing constructive and destructive spokes."

"Correct. On the constructive side, they plant feelings, thoughts, and memories, which is what your mother does. On the destructive side, they receive them. It's much harder to see these progenies using their magic, especially in battle." Sylmar tapped his temple. "But a fight can be won in the mind before it's even begun. Same with the pneumatics, who do what?"

"They sift through the soul," Aeliana said, "discerning truth in the present and the future on the constructive side and discerning lies in the present and the past on the destructive side."

"Which spoke does Aeliana fall on?" Cyrus asked as Velden and Iris joined them by the spring's edge. They each found a rock to sit on or lean against.

"Her mother is a constructive noetic," Sylmar said. "So perhaps Aeliana will lean that way. Emeris is gifted at transferring memories. It's said she can allow someone to relive a moment from her own life with such clarity that they have difficulty grasping whether or not it actually happened to them."

"She holds back, though," Iris said, her gaze softening. "She waters it down because she wants her memories to remain her own as much as possible."

Aeliana drank in the glimpses she got of her mother, even though they centered around magic. They quenched her thirst far more than the water they'd stopped for and reminded her why learning the ins and outs of magic was worthwhile.

"What about her father?" Cyrus asked. "Or does it pass down from the mother's side?"

"Rildan is a great man," Sylmar said, the praise from his lips rare. "But he's just a man. As far as we know, he's the first human to use the starbridge from Lorvandas."

Aeliana leaned forward in disbelief. "He's Lorvandan?"

Cyrus frowned. "Wouldn't that make Aeliana have a low concentration of starblood? It sounded like it should be higher when Or—" He broke off, glancing at Aeliana, who shook her head slightly.

Her trust in these people grew every day, but she still wasn't ready to tell them about Orra.

"I just thought she'd have more starblood if her magic was so strong," Cyrus finished.

Sylmar leaned forward, peering at Aeliana. "I suspect she has more of her mother in her than her father. She even looks more like her mother." He settled back against his large rock. "Regardless, her guardians built up her body's demand for energy, which is why we have to wean her."

"Why don't all half-lights who aren't progenies do the same, then? Build up their energy through blood magic?" Aeliana asked, her hands growing clammy just from voicing the horrid question.

"Because it's a detestable form of magic," Iris said with a shudder.

At first Aeliana shrank back, regretting the question, but she supposed it was the reaction she wanted. If they despised blood magic as much as she did, they would never force her to do it.

"Do you already feel the energy returning?" Sylmar asked, studying Aeliana.

She nodded. The warmth of the Sun had overwhelmed her a dozen times already. By the Sun's peak, she felt rejuvenated, but the closer they got to the Sun's sleep, the more the energy started to feel strained, like her skin wouldn't be able to encase it this same time tomorrow. She knew she could go longer than that; she'd done it in the past. But it wouldn't be pleasant.

"Good," Sylmar said. "Even though spokes can be consistent

among family members, there are tests done in the schools of nobles to determine a progeny's spoke. We can simulate one of them this evening. See where your strengths lie."

Aeliana opened her mouth to protest, but Cyrus caught her gaze and raised his eyebrows. This was what she'd come for. She nodded, attempting to align her heart to agree even though the thought of voluntarily performing magic felt wrong.

Sylmar stood and brushed off his cloak, calling for everyone to resume their brisk hike.

Velden offered Aeliana a hand up, the residue from his webbed fingers feeling more like a lotion than the slime she'd expected. She subconsciously rubbed it in her hands, staring after Sylmar.

"You know, you and I are more alike than you might realize." Velden's grin widened. "My mother crossed the barrier probably a dozen years before your father."

"I thought Sylmar said Rildan was the first," Cyrus said.

"He was the first Lorvandan. My mother had a different star-bridge." Velden laughed, wiggling his webbed fingers once more before walking backward toward Sylmar. "Haven't you figured out where I got my webs and water from by now? She was Sayhleen."

"Half-fish?" Cyrus scoffed. "Sayhleen aren't real."

Velden held out a slimy palm and squirted him with water before turning around. "Believe what you want," he called over his shoulder.

"This first test is almost always right." Sylmar's gravelly voice came to Aeliana from the other side of her blindfold. "But we'll follow it up with a few others to be sure."

She nodded uncertainly, rubbing her sweaty palms on the trousers she still hadn't gotten used to. They'd stopped trekking through the woods earlier than usual, well before the Sun's sleep. Aeliana had been relieved to slide her assigned pack from her back—until Sylmar announced that they'd begin training while the others set up camp.

"There's something before you," he continued. "Without touching it, I want you to sense what it is. No matter how concerning it might be, you must leave your blindfold on and try to fix it." He let out a grunt like he had sat next to her. She imagined his beady eyes studying the object, waiting for her to alter it in whatever way he expected.

"Fix it? I'm not sure—"

"That's the only instruction you'll get."

She frowned. "I think you've forgotten that I didn't grow up learning the basics of magic. I've done everything I can to avoid it. I don't know how—"

"It's easier if you shut your mouth and make some effort."

Was Sylmar teasing her?

"I never shut my mouth." Velden's reassuring voice came from her left. "I still figured it out."

The smack of flesh on flesh met her ears, but Velden only chuckled.

She bit her lip, too nervous to laugh along with him. Nothing more than the distant sounds of camp assailed her senses. The rock beneath her backside was cool and a little pointier on the left. She wondered if she'd have a bruise by the time they were done.

The starlock warmed against her chest as if reminding her it was willing to help. Velden had strung it through a leather cord and fastened it around her neck. She'd been instructed to keep it hidden beneath her tunic, resting against her heart. The points that had dug into her palm now tickled her skin. The others made it sound like it would be a comfort, but it felt more like a reminder of how her blood and this starlock could be a deadly combination.

She supposed that was the point. They were training her so the combination wouldn't always be deadly. She took a deep breath and tried again, straining her senses for something, anything.

Laughter reached her ears, mingled with the clanking of dishes and the thump of bedrolls being laid out. Kendalyhn's voice rang out as she teased Lukai, and for once she sounded happy instead of bitter. Water splashed, and Aeliana imagined Jasperus fishing at the creek. He was almost as good as Velden, when his boisterous laugh didn't scare the fish away.

She tried to make out Cyrus' constant chatter, but he was unusually quiet. She frowned, straining her ears. It would be impossible for him to be quiet this long unless someone made him. She turned her attention to Sylmar's and Velden's breathing. Sure enough, there was a third intake of breath coming from somewhere between them.

Was Cyrus the object before her? Even if it was him, what would she need to fix? Did he have a loose button? A blister on his heel? She tried to lean into her other senses. Even though he no longer smelled of Della's apple blossoms, she felt certain it was him. Something about the space before her just felt like him. But how did that help her know what to fix?

She shifted, trying to hide her agitation, knowing Sylmar watched. She blew out a long breath, recalling all the times she'd accidentally used magic. When the daisies had grown, when she learned to shoot the bow and arrow. What had she been doing or feeling in those moments?

Usually anger or fear, but when Cyrus had taught her to take aim, she'd been calm. She'd held her breath and let her body go still, closing her eyes to tune out the rest of the world. In fact, it was eerily similar to the setup Sylmar had created now. Even though the blindfold did its job, she closed her eyes, honing in on the space where she heard extra breaths.

Without warning, an image of Sylmar filled her vision, as if he walked toward her in the giant taro trees and ferns surrounding camp. She felt herself smile at him, her lips spreading wide, until she saw the staff in Sylmar's hand flare to life with its ominous molten glow. Her smile dropped, and the old man growled, pulling her hand down and bending her wrist back, only it wasn't her hand or wrist. Freckles spattered her skin, and faint scars lined her arm, the result of Sylmar and Lukai having healed her—having healed Cyrus. She panicked, recognizing that the memory belonged to Cyrus but unable to stop it. Sylmar seared Cyrus' palm with the heat of his staff. Blood trickled down, and Cyrus screamed.

Aeliana stood, screaming with him, and the vision dissipated, leaving her panting. The starlock burned against her chest, making her wonder if it would leave a mark. She reached for the blindfold but remembered Sylmar's warning. If she didn't figure out how to fix Cyrus before taking off the blindfold, would they put him through it all again?

How could they have done such a thing in the first place?

Anger replaced her panic, feeding the energy that burrowed within her. It wanted a release, and she wanted to let it loose. She wished she could give Sylmar the same wounds he'd inflicted on Cyrus, maybe make him regret taking things too far.

The intake of breath from her right gave her pause, made her wonder if Sylmar could read her thoughts. She knew so little of what his magic could do. She was fairly certain he was a destructive somatic —the killing spoke, as she'd come to think of it—but he still had some healing abilities. What else could he do that she didn't know about?

Had he already healed Cyrus? Or did he expect her to try doing that now?

She sat down, back straight as a rod. Instead of picturing Sylmar wounded, she imagined Cyrus' wounds closing up and patching themselves, like holes in a sock, and then smoothing over, like Velden's seaweed bandages. Her starlock burned hotter, tempting her to rip it from her neck.

"What—?" Cyrus hissed from in front of her, but he was hushed by Sylmar.

Still, the little bit she heard from him gave her relief. He was all right. Did that mean she was actually healing him with her thoughts? Hope mixed with dread, leaving her stomach hollow. She didn't want to learn magic, and yet it was the only way forward. It was the right way, but it didn't stop her from breaking into a cold sweat.

The balance of right versus wrong left her on edge, but it wasn't just a matter of whether or not she should be doing magic—it was something else. It was almost like patches of hot and cold surrounded her, the cold trying to infiltrate the heat. It didn't belong, and she needed to separate the two. As she did, reality unfolded before her mind's eye, Cyrus sitting across from her, wholly intact, gnawing on his fingernails as he watched her sweat and scream.

"None of it's real," she muttered. A stillness settled over her, a rewarding peace even though she'd been tricked.

She whipped off her blindfold, frowning at Sylmar as her eyes adjusted to the setting Sun and her vision grew spotted. She ripped the cord from her neck, slipping the hot starlock into her pocket instead of letting its confusing burn settle against her skin.

Her entire body shook with relief and overexertion, like she'd chased the dragon once more. But then she took in the daisies at her feet, the blood-stained moss, the dark brown splatters on their clothes and skin—Cyrus' pale face.

"Sweet Stars, what did I do?" she whispered.

CHAPTER 24

"You passed your test," Velden said, clapping with his overdramatic flair.

"But the blood…"

"You didn't hurt me." Cyrus was quick to reassure her.

Sylmar's mouth was set in a line of grim determination, but his eyes shone with something like curiosity or…pride?

By now the others in the group had gathered, probably summoned by her mortifying scream. Their slack faces mirrored the shock Aeliana felt as they took in the mess.

She reached for Cyrus' bloody hands.

"What did *you* do?" she narrowed her eyes at Sylmar.

"Nothing." He held up his hands—which were also covered in blood—in surrender. "You're right; it was a mask for the truth, created by Jasperus. Ideally, if you were pneumatic, you would attempt to sift through the truth of it. If you were noetic, you would tune in to our minds or emotions to recognize how they didn't line up with the illusion. If you were somatic, you would adjust his body, attempting to heal him."

Aeliana turned her glare on Jasperus, whose weathered face held guilt.

"If it's not real," she asked, her heart still pounding in her ears, "where did all the blood come from?"

"I assume you tried to heal him," Sylmar said. "For a new progeny, attempting to heal a wound that doesn't exist usually produces a tingle, or maybe an insatiable itch. In your case…" He trailed off, eying the splatters.

"So I hurt him." The words came out flat.

"I'm fine," Cyrus said quickly, placing a hand on Aeliana's arm. "You startled me is all. Sylmar and Lukai healed me before I could even feel the pain of it."

His hand was far steadier than hers, his reassurance sustaining even as her guilt deepened. She closed her eyes, wishing she could block out the damage she'd done, but the evidence was burned into her vision, present even on the backs of her eyelids. Even when she used magic the right way, she caused harm.

"You might have been a wee bit overzealous with your test." Velden's teasing tone brought her gaze to his. He held up his thumb and forefinger, squinting at the small space between them. "You're like a baby scorpion that uses up all its venom in one sting."

Aeliana shuddered. This had been a terrible idea. What if she'd killed someone?

"Your power was unbridled." Sylmar's words came slow.

"Dangerous," Kendalyhn corrected, arms crossed. For once Aeliana agreed with the other woman's negative outlook. She pulled away from Cyrus, afraid that mere proximity could cause him more harm.

"It could be," Velden agreed. "Until it's tamed."

"So she's a somatic?" Cyrus asked.

Velden nodded, but Sylmar held up a hand.

"How did you know it wasn't real?" Sylmar asked, leaning forward. His arm nearly brushed hers, like he still held no fear after all she'd done. "Did you sift through the lies of the illusion?"

"I don't—I don't know." She threw the blindfold to the ground. The familiar sense of euphoria from the release of energy washed over her, triggering her disgust. She scanned the skies out of habit, but nothing blotted out the orange hues settling into purple dusk. She tried to remember that this hadn't been blood magic. It hadn't been wrong.

But this was how it felt when her blood was used. It still felt wrong.

She shook her ahead, attempting to regain focus. "I sensed hot and cold. An unevenness that didn't belong. But not until after I tried fixing him."

"So you first adjusted his body, attempting to heal it?" Lukai asked, almost eager. As a constructive somatic, he probably found that idea appealing. Maybe as bondmates, it was desirable to share a spoke.

"Maybe." Aeliana glanced at Cyrus' blood, unsure if *healing* was the right word for what she'd done.

"Regardless of which she did first, she sifted through lies and adjusted his body. It's evidence she can access both a primary and secondary spoke." Sylmar's beard and mustache split into what might have been a smile. "It's unheard of for that to be present in an initial test."

The others who'd gathered around all hummed their agreements, setting them off into excited chatter that made Aeliana's head ache.

"What's a secondary spoke?" Cyrus asked.

"Usually progenies can only access one spoke, and even then it's the constructive or destructive side that's more dominant, like your hands." Velden waved his in the air, involuntarily flicking water. "Every once in a while, a progeny is a bit ambidextrous. That's why Sylmar can do some limited healing even though he's a destructive somatic. He can use more points along his spoke. The most advanced progenies can access a second spoke, always adjacent to their primary."

"Velden and Sylmar are the only ones here with secondary spokes," Jasperus added. "It's why they can adjust water and metal so easily."

Aeliana eyed the water still dripping off Velden's hands. "I thought it had to do with the…"

"Being half-Sayhleen?" Velden laughed. "No. But I'm guessing there are more Sayhleens who wield water than fire."

Sylmar shifted, drawing Aeliana's gaze to his staff. "That's how you change the shape of your staff."

"Sylmar and Velden can probably access more points on the spokes than all the rest of us combined," Lukai admitted. "But they can access an element because of the connection between their primary and secondary spokes. Elements connect the spokes like the rim of a wheel."

"Or the crust of the piece of pie." Velden grinned at her, licking his lips and rubbing his belly.

Aeliana pulled her taro leaf from her pocket, examine the spokes again. "So Sylmar is a destructive somatic, and his secondary spoke is…"

"Constructive pneumatic," Sylmar said.

She traced the two lines out to the rim, then traced the line of the rim that connected them. "So anyone with these two spokes would have access to metal?"

Sylmar shrugged. "In theory. Magic is like a muscle. It needs to be trained and maintained. It's possible more progenies would be able to access a secondary spoke and rim magic if they trained harder."

A few groans spread through the group, and Jasperus headed back to the cookfire.

"What?" Sylmar's frown turned fierce as he stared the remaining progenies down. "Velden and I have dedicated our lives to training. It makes sense that we have access to the rim."

"They're also significantly older than most of us," Kendalyhn said with a smirk.

"But Aeliana's not." Lukai beamed at Aeliana. "And she can already access a second spoke."

Aeliana felt her face heat under his pride, along with something deep in her belly.

Kendalyhn rolled her eyes before joining Jasperus at the fire.

"It's true. It usually doesn't present until you've had significant training." Sylmar stroked his beard thoughtfully. "Some access a second spoke decades later. But we'll be able to train you on both right from the start."

Why didn't they see this as concerning instead of exciting? This was further proof that her magic was flawed. Dangerous.

The unease returned with a flutter in Aeliana's stomach. "I won't train unless we set some ground rules." She stood, limbs shaking. The coldness in her voice sobered the few who were left. She gestured at the blood splatters. "This method was wrong."

"It was an illusion," Sylmar said.

"Until I drew blood." Her voice broke, memories of Arvid and Vera cutting her overlapping with the memories of Cyrus being injured, first by Vera and again by Sylmar.

It didn't matter if the memories weren't all real. Maybe that made it worse.

"It was too much like blood magic," she said. "It was too real. Marking him along his scars, making him scream the same way he did that night. If you make me watch those things over and over—I can't—not after Arvid and Vera." Her voice grew hoarse as so much of her abuse lay exposed before people who, despite being friendly, still felt like strangers in many ways.

Lukai inched closer, wrapping his hand around hers. The moment their palms touched, comfort flooded through her, but it felt more like a distraction meant to keep her from addressing the real problem at hand. Iris covered her mouth, blinking furiously, and Velden and Sylmar exchanged wary glances.

"Are you saying—did you first tune in to the memory of the illusion?" Sylmar's face paled above his beard, the ridge of his scars going from a deep purple to a spidery pink. "Did you see it that clearly?"

Aeliana groaned in frustration. "Every word you say still feels like a test. I don't know if I'm sifting through lies or adjusting his body or tuning in to memories. I simply know that I saw you hurt him. It was as real as if I'd been there myself. I hated you for it—hated that you would put him through that just to teach me some sort of lesson. It made you no different than Arvid or Vera. It made me want..." She trailed off, her anger fading as she took in Cyrus, whole and unharmed. Humiliation filled the space that had housed the anger.

"What did it make you want?" Sylmar asked.

"I wanted to make you suffer in the same way." She shivered, surprised at her own honesty. But if these people thought they could turn her magic into something good, they had to realize what they were up against.

Sylmar held out his bloody hands, and for the first time, Aeliana noticed fresh pink scars. She bent forward to survey the damage, her stomach curdling with the truth. Not all of the blood had been Cyrus'. Did that mean she'd done blood magic? Was it possible to injure someone with starblood and not do blood magic?

She dropped Lukai's hand, wiping her sweaty palms on her trousers.

"I thought my cuts were a casualty of proximity, but perhaps your efforts were more focused than I realized," Sylmar mused.

"He won't use that type of test again, love." Iris placed a gentle palm on Aeliana's arm, her heated gaze resting on Sylmar like a mama bear protecting her cub.

"No, of course not." Sylmar shook his head, instantly contrite. "I didn't think—I've never trained someone who'd been—" He trailed off, ruffling his thinning hair until it stood up.

"So she can access all three spokes." Holm's low voice barely reached Aeliana's ears. "What does that mean?"

Finally, someone seemed afraid. Someone recognized the gravity of the situation.

"It means we have to wean her before we test her." Velden crouched next to Aeliana, placing a hand on her back. His touch was cool, and Aeliana sensed energy flooding back through her, but instead of refilling her like the Sun replenishing her supply, it soothed what energy remained, bringing its flare down to a tolerable heat. "She's still full of energy, despite having expended more in one night than the average progeny does in a single day. She's accessing all the spokes because her power is out of control."

"We can't know which are the false positives," Sylmar muttered with a frown. "Not until her energy stores are at a normal level, clear of the effects of the blood magic."

Velden's eyes held an apology. "We should have guessed it might be that way from the start. It could take a moon or more before she's ready to truly train."

Aeliana's gaze volleyed back and forth between the men. She couldn't believe her ears. "You still think I should be trained instead of subdued?"

"Either path starts with weaning you off blood magic. We start by teaching you basic alteration, just enough to ease your pain." Sylmar stood and headed for the cookfire.

Aeliana closed her eyes. She should be relieved at their persistence, at their acceptance, but it was hard to feel anything more than fear and exhaustion at the road ahead. Lukai squeezed her arm as he stood, and she opened her eyes to give him a weak smile. Cyrus nodded in sympathy before taking himself to the creek to wash off the blood. Holm guided Iris away, his arm wrapped around her. Only Velden remained.

"Give it a moon, and things will have turned around." Velden picked a handful of daisies at her feet and passed them to her before leaning against a cluster of bamboo.

"How can you be so sure?" She swallowed hard, fighting down the urge to rip apart the daisies he'd given her, the evidence of all she'd done wrong.

"Because by then you'll hate Sylmar more than you hate yourself. He's a tough trainer." He grinned, and in spite of everything, her lips tugged upward.

"If you dislike him so much, why do you follow him?"

Velden chuckled. "I don't mind the old grump. If he'd trained me, I'd probably hate him. I simply come for the adventure." He winked at her.

They were alone at this point, the others following their stomachs to the scent of cooked meat. Aeliana's appetite had gone with the sight of Cyrus' and Sylmar's blood. She glanced at the dusky sky, watching for the moon's rise, and with it, the shadows she expected to see.

"They won't come," Velden said, following her gaze.

Aeliana's face heated, but his candidness emboldened her. "Why not?"

"That wasn't blood magic. Blood magic has far more to do with the intentions behind it than the actual act of spilling blood."

His words should have produced relief, but they were just a reminder of how little Aeliana knew.

"We don't use blood magic," he added. "And we'll never ask that of you."

Her mind kept replaying the false sight of Cyrus bleeding out, then the real images of the blood covering the two men. She turned away from the blood still staining the moss and rocks.

"Tonight's injuries won't be the last caused by your magic. If anything, that's more reason for you to learn to use it, to control it. I

hadn't realized the depth of energy in you until I saw it for myself."
His gaze swept over her, and he shook his head in awe.

"I'm not sure I can do this," Aeliana whispered, twisting the daisies
in her grip.

He studied her, his normal laugh lines puckered in thought. "I once
knew a man who took to drinking far too much. At first he didn't
know any different. Had friends who drank just as much, or so it
seemed. The more he drank, the more he wanted a drink. Gave him
relief, but it was a trick, because the more he drank, the more he
became tethered to the bottle and the need to drink more.

"One day the man hit his wife, his bondmate. She nearly left him,
probably should have, but it scared him as much as her, and he swore
to drink less. At first he did, by sheer willpower. But certain friends
could convince him to have another one or two. Even having the occasional drink seemed to whet his appetite instead of taking the edge off
his cravings. He finally figured out the way to get ahold of his addiction. Know how?"

Aeliana shook her head.

"He gave it up. It was easier for him to swear it off completely than
to have even a single drop now and then. His bondmate was more
important to him than his drink, and he aimed to prove it." Velden
leaned forward, jabbing a webbed finger in Aeliana's direction. "Sometimes I think you see yourself like that man. By swearing off all magic,
you can protect those you care about. It's true. In that regard you're the
same. But you know who I think you're more like?"

Aeliana held her breath, afraid of the answer he might give for his
own question.

"His wife."

She let out her breath, more confused than relieved. "Why his
wife?"

"His wife was a victim of his addiction. Until he found a solution,
she took the brunt of his anger and violence. She dealt with the consequences of his actions."

Aeliana looked away, blinking back tears.

"When he gave up alcohol," Velden said. "She did too. She didn't
need to, but she thought it might help him."

"And did it?"

"It did," he admitted. "But Arvid and Vera aren't here. Using your magic in moderation won't tempt them to use blood magic. In fact, it will make you stronger to resist the temptation if anyone ever tries to use you for blood magic again."

Aeliana nodded, giving his words time to sink in. "Thank you, Velden."

He shrugged. "If you want to hear a better story, we need to go get Jasperus."

Aeliana smiled.

"You feel lighter than you did before the Sun's sleep?"

She nodded. "There's always a sense of relief when the energy leaves, whether it's through loss of blood or through…"

"Magic?" He grinned again. "No way getting around the word. Your guardians drained all your energy, making your body produce more. Tonight you took a lengthy draft, but tomorrow we merely skim the cream off the top. If we do that every night, your body will stop producing so much energy. It will recognize that you're storing it and that it doesn't need to work so hard to take in more from the Sun. Your starlock will help speed up the process."

Aeliana's hand automatically reached for the starlock in her pocket, its sharp edges welcome.

"Is your energy source different from other Vendarans?" She couldn't help glancing down at his neck, still absent of a leather cord.

Velden laughed. "Sayhleen are half-lights too, just like Ahmranans and Dehvlonians across the other barriers. Sayhleen just happen to occasionally have tails instead of feet. Most of them anyway."

Aeliana gave a faint smile. The legendary water creatures supposedly had bodies covered in scales, their lower halves having fins rather than feet. Knowing she and Cyrus had crossed a barrier, nothing seemed too far-fetched anymore. Besides how else could she explain Velden's webbed fingers and liquid secretions? The other night, he'd even shown her his webbed toes.

"Many progenies have been brought down by their enemies," Velden continued, "because they wear their starlock on a flimsy cord around their neck." He pushed off the tree and bent down, angling one of his fish hook earrings for her to see. "I hide mine in plain sight."

She sucked in a breath, eyeing the matching pair. "You have two?"

He laughed again. "No one can have two starlocks. Which is why no one suspects that's what this is. Its simple design was easy enough to replicate. Unless you hold them and feel the weight of the true starlock, you'd never know the difference. My mother suggested it."

The urge to hide her own starlock grew strong, but she wasn't sure if it was because she still found the idea of magic so shameful or if it was because she saw the wisdom in his methods.

"Where is your mother now? Did she return to Sayhla Island in Paelen's Waters? Or is she still in Vendaras?"

Velden's jaw tightened, and he turned away. "She's dead. A few years back, a fisherman caught her in his nets. Harpooned her like some sort of animal."

Aeliana sucked in a breath. "I'm so sorry."

He nodded, a faint smile crossing his features. "She was different, but there was nothing wrong with her. Just like there's nothing wrong with you."

He gave Aeliana a pointed look before pushing off the bamboo to join the others by the fire.

CHAPTER 25

THEY WERE STILL three days and three nights out from Bamboo Island, and Gaeren was beginning to wish he hadn't given up his cabin for Lenda and Orra. When the men weren't glaring at the women, they turned their suspicions on Gaeren.

He leaned against the main mast, watching the men laugh and eat their meal. Thallahan had pulled out his fiddle, and a few who'd had too much ale stomped their feet and danced without partners. The moon shone over the water, waning from the full moon. If Bamboo Island didn't hold answers, an inland trek would be treacherous with full grown winex out on the prowl.

The silvery beasts waxed and waned with the moon, their short lives balanced out by their infinite rebirth—if they survived each cycle. During a new moon, their newborn cries were annoying, but they held no danger. During a full moon, coming across a pack was deadly. They grew weaker as the new moon and their rebirth approached, but sometimes weaker meant more desperate.

Gaeren glanced at Riveran up in the crow's nest. Maybe that was why Enla insisted he bring Riveran. He'd always been able to manage the creatures the same way he'd managed horses.

Before he could think it through, Gaeren climbed the rigging, joining his former friend in the tight space. Riveran gave him a wary look before returning his gaze to the sea, his watchful eyes taking in any potential danger. Gullet blinked at Gaeren, then let his eyes slide shut. The bird spent most of the day on the coast they skirted, hunting and foraging, then joined up with Riveran at night.

Gaeren shifted his gaze to the X on Riveran's forehead, the scars forming an outline for the bold ink. Rather than keep staring, he pulled out his dagger, weighing its balance over his knuckles and testing its point against the pad of his finger.

"You haven't replaced that daisy yet?"

Gaeren's lip lifted at the surprise in Riveran's voice. "I told you. It doesn't make me look weak."

Riveran shook his head. "People are probably just saying it behind your back."

They'd argued over it when Gaeren had had the dagger made. It was a gift for Daisy—her dedication year dagger. Riveran thought it was fine for a girl, but he'd teased Gaeren mercilessly for carrying it around.

"The men think you've gone mad." Riveran's soft rumble put Gaeren at ease despite his words.

"Because of the women?"

Riveran nodded. "At first I thought Orra was the girl you've been searching for. But you're still hunting for something or someone. It didn't feel right."

Gaeren didn't say anything, unwilling to confirm or deny Riveran's line of thinking.

"The men won't talk to me either, but I still hear things. Thallahan defends you. Says its good for a man to keep his women close to keep them safe."

Gaeren cringed. "They're not 'my women.'"

"Lenda is in a way. Just like you're her man. But they've all latched onto that, and now they're heralding you as the prince with two bonds." Riveran's smirk stirred up Gaeren's irritation.

"Orra is twice my age."

"Is she?" Riveran's brow furrowed, making the X shift into a jagged squiggle. "She doesn't seem that old."

Gaeren didn't honestly know or care, but he wouldn't stand for rumors about the women. Just because he didn't love Lenda the way he should didn't mean he would cheat on her. "Lenda is my bondmate, and I will remain faithful."

His words silenced Riveran, and the air between them grew thick with the unspoken reminder and accusation. Why had Gaeren come up here? This would always sit between them. It wasn't like he could ever regain the friend he'd once had. No matter how much he might want to.

The realization that he wanted their friendship back was like cold sea water splashing overboard. Even wanting it felt like he'd betrayed Enla in some way.

He stood, throwing a leg over the nest's edge.

"I didn't tell you those things to rile you," Riveran said, eyes still trained on the horizon. "The point is that the men think you're besotted. Despite the bad luck you've brought on the ship, they understand. In fact, it makes you seem more like them and less like some inaccessible royal brat."

Gaeren paused, one foot on the rigging. "I haven't completely lost their respect?"

Riveran snorted. "It's not about respect. Well, it is, but not in the way you're thinking." He turned his gaze on Gaeren. "They're Recreants, not Loyalists." The admission was treasonous, but Riveran wasn't saying anything Gaeren didn't already know.

"I'm not asking them to be loyal to the crown." Gaeren frowned at Gullet, who fluttered his wings and turned his tail feathers toward Gaeren. "I want respect as their captain. I want them to trust me."

"You should want their camaraderie more than their respect," Riveran said. "They aren't willing to die for their superior, but they're willing to die for their friend."

Gaeren's chest tightened. He'd been willing to die for Riveran at one point. Nearly had when they'd gotten in over their heads with some fresh progenies who'd had a score to settle with Riveran. He'd loved him like a brother.

"That kind of love trumps respect," Gaeren said, "but it also goes both ways. I would need to be willing to die for them."

Riveran hummed his agreement, turning back to the water now that his point had been made.

Gaeren glanced down at the men below him, their laughter carrying out across the water. The carefree teasing reminded him of his childhood, even though most of the men were old enough to be his father or grandfather. He knew them all by name, even knew many of their families, but he'd purposely kept them at arm's length.

When he knew too much, he grew too frustrated with his inability to change their circumstances. Bringing bread to Erech was one thing, but Enla would never let Gaeren patch up the boy's drafty home or ensure his mother had adequate care from healers. Not unless Gaeren turned it into a program he could manage. And then he'd hear everyone's woes and feel even more helpless.

Was it so strange to want to know these men as friends? To be willing to die for men who served on his ship? He could practically hear Enla's frustrated voice in his head. She believed he was worth hundreds of their people. But wasn't that part of what he hated about his family's tyranny?

How could he say he valued democracy if he wasn't valuing the people fighting for it?

"Thank you," Gaeren said, unable to look Riveran in the eye. It didn't matter, because the other man nodded, gaze on the water.

As Gaeren made his way back down, he tuned in to the men around him, sensing their warmth. He rarely used his skills without first asking permission. It felt like a violation of someone's privacy. But all these men knew his spoke, and they'd all signed on to work for him, knowing their proximity alone put their memories within his reach.

His progeny mentors would scold him for needlessly using magic, especially at night without the Sun's energy to recharge. But maybe this exception to all the rules was more necessary than ever.

Erech stood on the outskirts, young enough to not know his place in the crowd. When Gaeren came close, the boy turned with a smile, then started upon seeing his captain. He ducked his head.

"It's good to see you having fun, Erech."

The boy smiled hesitantly.

"Was it hard leaving your family?"

Erech's smile faltered. "Harder than I expected." Images from

Erech's mind flashed through Gaeren's. His parents smiling down at his siblings, his mother's hand over her distended belly. Squalling infants being handed to Erech, one by one, as he met his siblings for the first time. The pang of loss over missing this newest sibling's birth.

"Probably easier to leave the horse manure, though," Gaeren suggested.

Erech laughed, and the edges of the sorrow blurred. "I promised my sisters I'd bring them seashells. Larkos says there are blue ones off the coast of Bamboo Island."

"Ah, the butter clams," Gaeren said. "Those are nice, but I bet we can find some Sundial shells that will really impress them. Or some of the tiny clams near Rykarn have pink and orange shells."

The boy's eyes lit up, and Gaeren ruffled his hair.

"Climb on up to watch the water for a bit with Riveran."

Erech fought for footing on the rigging before Gaeren could even finish his instructions.

He chuckled and moved on to Breeve, who was only a few years Erech's senior. He'd done his time as cabin boy and swab, and while he couldn't cook well, the job suited him.

"The chicken had good flavor tonight," Gaeren lied. "Have you been taking lessons?"

An image flashed through Breeve's mind, and Gaeren tuned in to it. A woman in an apron, smiling from behind the stove.

"Just helping Ma between jobs." Breeve's pimply face always had a red hue, but in the wake of Gaeren's compliment, the color reached the tips of his ears.

"Your mother probably worries too much, yeah?"

The young man's grin filled his face. "Of course. That's what Ma always does. She's got four others at home. You'd think they'd be enough to keep her mind off me." The other children's faces passed through Breeve's mind and then Gaeren's, their shapes taking form and movement. Shrieks of laughter, hay-filled hair, skinny legs wrapped around ropes, swinging in a barn.

Gaeren slapped Breeve on the back, letting his hand rest on the young man's bony shoulder. He didn't need to maintain contact to tune in to Breeve's memories, but they grew far more vivid this way.

He felt the emotion instead of just seeing it. It made his heart ache and his throat tighten. It made him long for home even though he'd never had a home with such carefree abandon. His parents probably didn't even miss him. Were they doing well? Or had his mother's health taken a turn for the worse?

He shook himself from his thoughts, focusing on Breeve once more.

"You're the oldest, right?" Gaeren already knew the answer after seeing Breeve's memories, but he waited for Breeve's nod before continuing. "What does your father do? Are you going to carry on his line of work?"

Breeve faltered. "I am carrying on his work. He died at sea when I was twelve. Aboard one of your father's vessels."

The image that came to Gaeren this time was fuzzier, faded with years and probably altered by the boy's grief and adoration. He didn't recognize the man, but then he would have been seventeen or eighteen when Breeve's father had died. Still, he felt chastened. He should have known this about Breeve.

"Well, it's an honor to have a second-generation sailor on my ship."

Breeve stood a little taller. "Fourth generation, sir."

Gaeren raised an eyebrow. "No wonder you climb the rigging like a spider." He slapped Breeve on the back once more.

He moved on to Thallahan, who had passed his fiddle off to an older sailor. He smiled as easily as Breeve, but his burly physique and shaved head made Gaeren think he'd be more like Larkos in a few years. He even had a few tattoos on his arms, working up to a fine sailor's collection.

As they watched the other sailors dancing, Thallahan's memories of a woman were so vivid they left Gaeren yearning to meet her. It didn't take much to get Thallahan talking about her, his mind recalling how they'd first met and where they liked to take walks. Gaeren pulled back on his starlock's power when the memories became too private.

"She's waited through three voyages for you?" Gaeren asked, stealing a glass of ale from on top of a barrel as they walked past. "Why haven't you proposed already? Not many women are patient enough to deal with the comings and goings of a sailor."

"I plan to." It was hard to tell in the moonlight, but Gaeren thought Thallahan's face might have turned a shade of pink. "You promised us enough this time around that her father should say yes."

Thallahan's words struck that same guilty nerve that Enla often hit. Gaeren paid his men well, far more than average, but he hadn't realized it still wasn't enough to guarantee supporting a family. He took a sip to hide his uncertainty over whether an apology or congratulations was in order.

"Must be nice to not have to worry about the father or the daughter saying no," Thallahan said, elbowing Gaeren with a cheeky grin.

Gaeren choked on his ale before glancing at the closed door to his quarters. Lenda had made more appearances over the last day, but he doubted she'd come out for tonight's revelry. A longing to sweep her in his arms for a dance flowed through him, and he frowned at the bond's insistence.

"Or not," Thallahan said, wincing. He rubbed the back of his neck and looked away.

Gaeren felt their easiness slipping away as Thallahan rebuilt the wall dividing their stations. He didn't want to lose the ground he'd made, especially not over his sour attitude toward his bondmate.

"Would it surprise you to know I envy your freedom?" Gaeren asked, tensing at his admission.

Thallahan's gaze swung to Gaeren, his mouth slack. He quickly closed his lips, licking them nervously.

"Yes." The word came out more like a question, a fear of saying the wrong thing. "Does this mean"—he lowered his voice conspiratorially —"that you really do wish to be bonded with Orra?"

Gaeren barked out a laugh.

"I guess that's a no." Thallahan's shoulders drooped.

"Correct. Orra is more of a business partner. Like Larkos." Gaeren took another sip. He could never break his bond, not after seeing it happen to Enla. But in some ways, wanting another woman made sense considering how much he resisted the bond. Instead, he was left wanting something he couldn't have with a woman who likely didn't exist.

Thallahan grunted his understanding. He would probably dispel the rumors later that night, and then what would the men have to speculate about?

"What's it like to fall for a woman of your own will?" Gaeren's gaze returned to the closed door as he mused out loud. "To know that she loves you, not because magic deems it so, but because her mind, soul, and body choose to?"

Thallahan didn't say anything for a while, and Gaeren didn't expect him to. They watched the men grow louder as they finished eating, more of them laughing and singing along with the fiddler.

"My pa once told me it was like earning his starlock." Thallahan's voice was so low Gaeren almost missed it. "He described it as a rush that left you equally empowered—invigorated by desire—and vulnerable. Deeply aware of your weaknesses. Except instead of growing used to it, growing into the feeling as you do when you learn to wield the source of magic"—he eyed the bulge beneath Gaeren's shirt—"love makes you feel the same old fool every time you lay eyes on her."

Gaeren let his eyes slide shut, the memory of his Awakening flooding through him. It had been his fifth time at sea with *Starspeed* and the worst storm he'd seen in his life. The boat had risen and fallen with every swell, filling faster than they'd been able to pump it out from the bilges. He hadn't felt brave climbing the main mast to untangle the sails. He had known it could snap at any moment, and it would be the end of him. He'd been scared senseless.

But he'd done it anyway. He'd seen the sailors beneath him cheer, but the wind had taken away the sound of their voices, and then the next wave had taken him away from the ship. He still wasn't sure how he'd survived the thrashing waves to wash ashore. But he would never forget the euphoria of waking with the silver teardrop squeezed so tightly in his palm that it drew blood. The grin that split his face from relief at having survived not just the storm but his Awakening. The warmth of the metal spreading through to his toes.

"At least, that's what he said about my ma."

Thallahan's voice pulled Gaeren from the memory, forcing his eyes to open and refocus on the man beside him.

"And when I met Fay, I understood. I have to take his word for it when it comes to the starlock." Thallahan's voice was laced with a wistfulness. "Having never experienced an Awakening."

Gaeren's smile felt strained. "It's a perfect description. And I'll have to take your word for it when it comes to falling in love." He couldn't keep the same wistfulness from tainting his words. "Having never experienced it for myself."

The men shared a rueful smile.

"Speaking of bonds..." Thallahan angled his head toward the stern, and Gaeren turned to follow his gaze.

The cabin door swung wide, revealing Lenda's silhouette as she stepped onto the deck. Gaeren's heart picked up its pace as she moved into the lantern's light. Her eyes brightened, and her hesitant smile deepened when she caught him studying her, but it was more like a winex reeling in its prey.

The rush he'd hoped to feel was gone as quickly as it had come without ever having reached a fraction of the euphoria he'd felt after his Awakening.

"I stand by my initial assessment," Gaeren muttered to Thallahan. "I envy your freedom."

CHAPTER 26

Gaeren made his way across the deck, gaze on Lenda. A quick glance at Orra revealed a matronly nod of approval, and he nearly laughed at the sailors' assumptions about him. Two bonds. What would he do with two bondmates when he couldn't handle one?

Lenda held out a hand.

He lifted it for a kiss, clenching his jaw at the way it made his heart pound. "You're looking refreshed."

Her face wilted slightly at his words, like she'd expected more of a compliment.

He tried again. "There's a glow to your cheeks that was missing the last several days."

This time she leaned into him, practically purring. "I think life at sea is finally starting to agree with me."

"By the time we reach Bamboo Island, you'll be swinging from the rigging."

She glanced up, swallowing hard as she took in the full height of the main mast. "How about I conquer the sea on this trip and heights on the next?"

Her dry humor surprised and even enticed him, but there was an assumption of future trips together that left him sober. She was his future, whether he wanted her to be or not. He wasn't sure why he fought the bond. Lenda was shallow, but she wasn't cruel or hungry for power—a rare thing in a destructive somatic progeny. He could do far worse in a bondmate. And yet, even before Thallahan shared his experiences, Gaeren had always sensed there was something more to a bond. Something that his would always be missing.

The music stopped, drawing his attention to the men around him, some gawking without shame, others trying to clear their dinner mess to make room for the women. Orra gently pried the fiddle from the slack-jawed sailor's hands before settling herself on a bench amongst the men like she'd been there all her life.

With a pointed look in Gaeren and Lenda's direction, the strange woman started in on a complicated tune that immediately got boots tapping.

"Would you like to dance?" Gaeren held out a hand, nearly choking on the words. Enla would be pleased with Orra's interference.

Lenda took his hand, and together they weaved throughout the deck, spurred on by the men's shouts whenever they drew near. A second sailor pulled Lenda's maid out on the deck, swinging her around with little finesse, but her laughter proved she didn't mind. Even the men started partnering up, tripping over each other's feet and laughing. Thallahan sat near Orra, his eyes narrowed in concentration as he watched her fiddle.

Orra entertained them with two more songs, during which Lenda allowed herself to be passed from sailor to sailor before settling in Gaeren's arms once more.

"I think you made Erech's entire moon by dancing with him tonight." Gaeren laughed, taking in the flush of Lenda's cheeks and the wisps of light hair coming loose from her braid.

"He's sweet," she said, glancing back at the cabin boy still watching her with stars in his eyes. "A far finer dancer than all the men reeking of ale. It's a shame he'll end up just like them."

She wrinkled her nose, and just like that, all the ways he'd started to find her endearing dissolved. His arms suddenly felt stiff, the space between them too narrow. This was why their bond never fully took.

"I hope he ends up exactly like Larkos," Gaeren said. "A fine father and sailor. A loyal bondmate with a loving wife. A man free to spend his summers at sea and his winters by her side." He didn't bother hiding the hunger lacing his words, and Lenda missed a step to turn sharply his way.

Orra switched to a melancholy tune, and Gaeren and Lenda slowed. Eager to avoid Lenda's reproachful stare, he watched Orra's bow slide across the strings.

"I wonder where she learned to play," Gaeren mused.

"She told me she was raised on the seas. Gave me all sorts of tips on finding my sea legs because she's seen everything tried and knew what worked. I suppose she learned from a sailor."

The explanation made sense, and yet it felt off. Like every tidbit he learned about Orra, it only brought out more questions.

"Did you know her great-great-great-grandmother married Captain Moss after the Last War?" For once, Lenda's interest seemed sincere. "She told me all about how she saved his life."

"Captain Moss?" Gaeren narrowed his eyes as he studied Orra once more. She did resemble the portraits he'd seen of Lady Redwood. But in the version he'd heard, the ex-pirate had married the famous captain after he'd saved her life at sea, not the other way around. "Everyone knows that story. It's not very likely the woman was really her great-great-grandmother."

"Great-great-*great*-grandmother," Lenda corrected. She stepped away and grabbed a glass of ale, sipping at it daintily before making a face at its bitterness. "She added impeccable details, so she's either a professional storyteller, or the real story has been passed down in her family."

"You've grown to like her." Gaeren said the words like an accusation, noting Lenda's defensiveness as she watched Orra pass the fiddle back to Thallahan.

Lenda shrugged. "I wonder if it's possible for anyone to not like her. There's something about her..." She turned a haughty gaze on Gaeren, slipping back into her familiar facade. "Except for maybe you. You find a way to dislike everyone and everything."

Gaeren laughed, drawing the attention of the men around him. Even Orra glanced his way with her secretive smile, like she'd planned this whole evening for the sake of his bond. She was as bad as Enla. But she wasn't the only one who could manipulate situations. She'd been tight-lipped earlier, but if she was so forthcoming with Lenda, maybe he could use that to his advantage.

"Lenda tells me you have famous kindred." He let the words ring out, guaranteeing the sailors would pay attention. "I'm sure everyone here would be eager for tales of Lady Redwood."

A few of the men gasped while others gave Orra incredulous looks.

To her credit, she showed no concern about being found out. In fact, she closed her eyes and tilted her head as if calling up a memory. Gaeren leaned forward, recognizing her actions from his own efforts to tune in to memories.

Her eyes flew open, a new spark of life shining out from deep within her. "I know there's wild debate among sailors as to whether Captain Moss saved Lady Redwood or whether Lady Redwood saved Captain Moss, but I guarantee you the pirate saved the naval officer."

"That version says she made a fool of him too. He never would have married her if he'd been made a fool by her," a sailor shouted.

"No?" Orra's eyebrows rose in disbelief. "How many of you have been made a fool by the woman you love?"

The men all eyed each other as if daring someone to admit such a thing.

"It may not have been as public, but I guarantee it happened. Love makes a fool out of every man eventually." She shrugged. "And every woman."

"My pa hammered his thumb while staring at my ma one day," Erech admitted.

The other men chuckled, and Orra smiled. "Thank you for that perfect example. Lady Redwood made a fool of Captain Moss several times, and then she saved his life. It's possible he returned the favor, but by then he was smitten anyway." She stared at the moon, pausing long enough to make everyone shift uneasily. Her smile slowly faded to something forlorn and haunted. Like someone lost in a memory. Gaeren felt certain at that moment that she had loved someone deeply —loved someone and lost them.

She cleared her throat. "Forgive me. Where was I?" Her grin turned almost wicked as she leaned forward. "Oh, yes! It all started when the Fearsome Pirate Redwood plundered Captain Moss' ship."

As Orra continued spell-binding the men, Gaeren bent toward Lenda. "Did you notice the way she called up the memory?"

"Hmm?" Lenda responded, her attention on Orra even though she'd already heard the story.

"She must be a noetic. I would bet my life on it."

Lenda finally turned to look at him, letting out an unladylike snort that surprised him. "Well, then one of us should be dead, because I'd be willing to bet my life that she's a somatic. She healed me, Gaeren. I've never been able to function this soon on a ship. I've never been able to function at all. And I get the impression I'll never have such awful seasickness again."

Gaeren frowned. If that was true, Orra definitely had to have a second spoke like Gaeren and Enla. It was rare outside the royal family. It usually only manifested in those with higher starblood concentration, those who would have shown up as potential bond-mates to keep the royal family's bloodline as pure as possible. Could a second spoke give her the power to leave her body the way she did?

She was too old for Gaeren, and he suspected she was too young to have been matched with his father. Still, Gaeren had three uncles also in line for the throne who had been bonded at young ages. As far as he knew, none of his aunts had secondary spokes. Shouldn't Orra's blood have been chosen before those women's?

"Is it possible to avoid being in the running for a royal bond?" He asked the question of Lenda, but only because she was close enough to hear. Really, he wanted to ask Enla or his parents. People who cared far more about those details than he ever had. He assumed it was an honor and privilege, that everyone would register their children's blood in the hopes that their child would become the next king or queen. But what if not everyone wanted that responsibility?

After all, he hadn't wanted it.

He glanced around at the men aboard the ship. None of them even wanted a king or queen, so why would they force their child to be considered for a role they hoped to usurp?

"What are you talking about?" Lenda asked.

"Never mind," he muttered. He listened to Orra's story half-heartedly, his thoughts swirling too much to focus. The idea that Orra might have avoided bonding or that some people might despise the throne enough to keep their children from the pool of bondmate applicants was like a punch to his gut. It didn't matter that he'd supported the people's desire for more rights or that they wanted more of a say in their laws and where their money went. This felt more personal, like they rejected the Elanesse family as people, not just their titles and crowns.

He could almost understand it when it came to his parents. For the most part, they were fair rulers, but Gaeren knew they weren't perfect. They'd upheld laws that should have been done away with years ago —taxes for money they didn't need, unnecessary authority over business structures that didn't impact their roles. The list was endless according to Larkos, who'd been ranting about it again just that afternoon.

But Gaeren and Enla were still growing into their roles. They were moldable, and the people should see that as an opportunity. The fact that they didn't made Gaeren spiral right back into the teaching he grew up with, the idea that the people wouldn't know how to rule themselves, which was why they needed kings and queens in the first place.

He rubbed his temples, hating where his thoughts were going but not knowing how to stop them. What would it take to prove to the people that he wasn't the same as the men and women before him? What could he do to let them give Enla the opportunity to make change instead of digging her own grave as the people grew more discontented?

"Do you know what Lady Redwood gave her beloved captain as a wedding gift?" Orra's question and theatrical pause drew Gaeren's attention. The story was coming to a close, and he'd hardly heard any of it.

The men all shook their heads, each on the edge of whatever barrel, bench, or space they could call a seat.

"The ancient cutlass she'd stolen from him on that first raid when they'd met."

A few men clapped while the others laughed. Lenda had been right about Orra knowing details that weren't included in the story sailors typically shared, but Gaeren wasn't sure if that made it truer or just a better lie.

"Ancient cutlass?" Gaeren asked. "How old was this sword, and where is it now?"

Orra's secretive smile returned, the glow in her eyes receding as she went from a lively narrator to her former mask of subdued wisdom. "Some say it was made by the Dehvlonians themselves."

Breeve sucked in a breath, excited at the prospect. Before the Great Divide and the rise of the barriers, the Dehvlonians had separated themselves from the Vendarans by claiming lands far east. They valued intelligence over physical strength, whereas the Ahmranans, who had settled in the north, were strong but simpleminded. Each race was the product of half-lights attempting to breed what they believed was the best of the best.

Collectors around Vendaras claimed to have some of the rare Dehvlonian artifacts that had survived the Great Divide, but somehow the number of artifacts grew each year, making Gaeren suspect each one's authenticity.

"Even their advanced metals would have corroded in that time," Gaeren argued.

Orra wrapped her arms around her knees, tucking them up under her chin like a child. She toyed with the braid on her wrist. "True. Which is why I suspect it has different origins." Her words felt heavy with meaning as they drifted over the heads of his men. Was she giving him a clue? "I suppose we'll never know."

She turned to Thallahan, requesting a song. Everyone else resumed their shouting and dancing, prepared for a long night that would turn into an even longer tomorrow at sea.

Gaeren still stared at Orra, ignoring Lenda's tug on his shirt sleeve. Orra had said she wrote the notes in the front of the book *The Sins of the Stars*. He pulled it out from his coat pocket now, his gaze landing on the miniature weapon with the word "Falls."

An ancient sword unaffected by corrosion. One with different origins. Perhaps celestial origins.

Lady Redwood's cutlass was one of the starbridges.

This time when he glanced back at Orra, she gave him a knowing look and a nod.

CHAPTER 27

THE MORNING after Aeliana's initial test, Sylmar had her sit just outside the campfire, eyes closed, instructing her to focus on each individual in the group. The others packed their belongings, and Aeliana wished she could be helping them instead of trying to understand what Sylmar wanted her to do. Light rain splattered against her trousers, a welcome coolness in the muggy heat of the jungle.

She felt hatred pouring out of Kendalyhn, but that had more to do with the glares she'd seen before closing her eyes than any magical intuition. Cyrus and Velden bantered over the safety of eating raw bamboo, their voices too energetic for the Sun's rise. Holm and Iris were closest, and Aeliana thought she might detect a heat from them that represented their energy levels, but what if it had more to do with the love she'd constantly felt between them? Jasperus was the farthest away, but she still felt his presence like the flare of fire. Although even that might have just been his loudness that she sensed more than any energy levels.

Sylmar had insisted that she see each person as a vessel requiring the extra energy she held, energy she could push into them to strengthen them for that day's climb. But it remained trapped beneath her own skin.

"Throughout the day, I want you to practice reaching out." Sylmar's commanding tone pulled Aeliana from her thoughts.

She opened her eyes to find him frowning down at her, leaning on his staff.

"You may have to place a hand on their arm to heighten the connection. Focus on altering their energy levels. It's the crudest form of magic, the hub of the Wheel. It's the type of alteration we teach children waiting for their Awakening."

Her cheeks burned, and she dropped her eyes.

"It's not meant to be an insult." Sylmar's rough voice softened a hair. "Until we know your spoke, it will be difficult to teach you the finer methods of tuning, sifting, or adjusting. For now, it's more of a large-scale alteration rather than a tweak. Even your efforts to assess the others' energy levels will help use bits of your energy and take the edge off your growing pain. We'll work on it more tonight whether you're able to do it during today's trek or not."

He awkwardly patted her back before turning to check on everyone's progress.

Aeliana sighed as Velden approached and held out fruits and cheese on a bamboo leaf.

"Cheer up," he said. "His face always looks like that. And don't take it personally—I never do."

Throughout the day, Aeliana made minimal effort to alter the other travelers' energy. Most of her efforts were attempted on Lukai, who entertained her with tales of cresting Mt. Vescano and made her mouth water when describing his mother's banana-leaf pouch holding shrimp and rice. She enjoyed talking to Lukai, but Sylmar's assignment put a damper on things.

Even if Aeliana had managed to succeed in transferring her energy, which she hadn't, the effort of imposing it on other people felt invasive. Her mind played tricks on her, and at times she swore blood seeped from cuts on her palms before they healed themselves. It was a vision she'd received hundreds of times over the years, especially when her blood grew bloated with magic, but it was no less disturbing. By the Sun's sleep, her feet dragged, less with the effort required by the walk and more with the weight of her blood having been replenished.

Later that night, Aeliana curled up on her bedroll, the familiar ache spreading through her body. It was like fire being pumped from her heart to every appendage, warning her that eventually the heat's pressure would be too much.

"Are you all right?" Cyrus asked from his place beside her.

"I've been through worse," she said.

"I'll say a prayer to the Stars for you," he offered.

She gave a weak smile of thanks but wasn't sure if he saw it. They still saw the Stars dancing above, weaving in and out among the plain stars in the sky. Their darting light should have been reassuring. Surely prayers could still be heard on this side of the barrier, even if the people here worshiped the Sun.

Most of the others were occupied setting up camp and making dinner. The last few days had brought them closer to the sound dividing their peninsula from the mainland, which would supposedly bring them to a ferry that would take them down the coast all the way to Valorian. The idea of sitting on a boat instead of walking sounded glorious. Sylmar and Jasperus bent over a map nearby, the smaller man's loud voice making Aeliana wince as they debated the safety of one road over another. When Sylmar was finally satisfied, he came to Aeliana, his intention to train written all over the scars on his face.

"I think she's ill." Cyrus bent forward, placing a hand on her forehead.

"She's in withdrawal," Velden said as he joined them, his eyes reflecting Cyrus' concern.

"How do we help her?" Cyrus asked.

"She needs to help herself," Sylmar said. "She needs to do magic."

Aeliana shut her eyes at the exhausting thought. She'd fought through this before when she'd run from Arvid and Vera. It had been almost two weeks that time. But she also hadn't been pushing her body to walk several miles a day with a heavy pack while short on rest.

She opened her eyes at a rustling sound near her head. Velden pulled more seaweed from his pack. It expanded in his hand as his water rehydrated it. He flung it in a bowl, mixing it with other herbs so ferociously that Aeliana winced, but his glare was aimed at Sylmar. Aeliana couldn't stop watching, his motions rhythmic and relaxing as he formed a paste, even while her insides felt stretched to bursting.

Without warning, he smeared the paste on Aeliana's forehead, then her hands. The concoction was surprisingly cool, like mint with recently thawed spring water, spreading through her body to provide a haze of relief around the areas that ached with her building energy.

As the pain relieved a fraction, her mind cleared enough for her to acknowledge that Sylmar was right. As agonizing as this process was, she couldn't give up. The only way to subdue her magic was to wean herself from it, and the only way to wean herself was to learn how to do it. She couldn't even think about saving her mother or finding the arrow for Cyrus until she'd accomplished those first steps.

"I'll try again." She sat up, closing her eyes at the dull throb invading her head. Sylmar would have to be content with teaching her here on her bedroll. At least she could keep her eyes closed. "Remind me how to transfer the energy."

She had to think of it like getting rid of her magic, just on a smaller scale. She wasn't getting rid of it all at once like she wanted, but she was getting rid of it bits and pieces at a time, passing it around to different people like sharing a bottle of mead around a room of friends.

Not that she had a lot of experience with friends.

"Let's try something different instead." Sylmar grunted as he lowered himself to the bedroll next to hers. "Kendalyhn! Come here."

His shout brought Aeliana's eyes open wide.

Kendalyhn came without question, but she eyed Aeliana warily. Maybe it was the strange paste coating her hands and face, but Aeliana suspected it was something else. Why did he have to choose her? The woman was probably only a few years older than Aeliana, but she was as intimidating as Sylmar. Beneath her tiny frame, Kendalyhn had a lot of bite that Aeliana didn't want directed her way.

"Sit across from Aeliana. She's going to place her hands on your arms and replenish your energy." Seeing Kendalyhn's apprehension, he added, "Velden will take over your duties by the fire for as long as it takes."

"You just don't want to eat her cooking," Velden muttered before ambling over to the cookfire.

"I heard that." Kendalyhn's eyes shot daggers at Velden, which Aeliana preferred over them being aimed at her.

Aeliana tentatively held out her shaking hands as if asking Kenda-lyhn for permission to touch her. Kendalyhn grumbled something unintelligible before holding out her arms.

While Aeliana closed her eyes, she gripped Kendalyhn's forearms as if they were locked in greeting. Kendalyhn's hands returned the tight hold, and Aeliana tried to sense the other woman's power, to envision it growing as it took on Aeliana's energy. The only thing she sensed was the croak of frogs nearby and the chirp of birds overhead.

"I can't—" Aeliana started.

"You have to give it more than a moment," Sylmar said.

"You can do this, Aeliana." Cyrus' encouraging words flooded through her, empowering her in ways Sylmar's sharp rebukes never did.

But still, her starlock lay cold against her chest. She tried to concentrate on it, willing it to send the energy in her blood toward Kenda-lyhn, but it was like her power had gotten too strong, clogging all the avenues of release. They sat in silence for so long that the clanking of pots and pans and the crackle of the fire started to hold a rhythm that made Aeliana's focus drift. Kendalyhn dug her nails into Aeliana's forearms, the pain pulling her fully awake.

"Are you using magic on me?" Aeliana gasped, eyes flying open.

"It doesn't require magic to sense you're falling asleep. You nearly fell into me." Kendalyhn's eyes narrowed, and she leaned forward. "Sylmar would have more luck training a rock to do magic."

The tremor in Aeliana's hands spread to her arms. "Don't use magic on me."

Sylmar hummed from beside Aeliana, reminding her of their audi-ence. "Kendalyhn, sift through Aeliana's soul."

"What?" Aeliana tried dropping Kendalyhn's arms, but the other woman's grip tightened, her lips curling into a smile as she closed her eyes.

Cyrus frowned, tugging on Sylmar's sleeve. "Isn't there another—?"

"There's a darkness," Kendalyhn murmured. "She carries it with her, holding on to it like a child's favorite toy."

Aeliana tried again to pull away, but Kendalyhn held tight. And as

Kendalyhn sifted through Aeliana's soul, it was like it was being laid bare before Aeliana in her mind as well. The darkness Kendalyhn spoke of spread through Aeliana's soul, painting it as black as the congealed blood her guardians had collected and used at their whim. Tiny winged creatures fed on the edges of her painful past, the image a shockingly perfect portrayal of the depths of pain Aeliana shoved down on a daily basis.

"Block her magic," Sylmar said, nodding at Aeliana, distracting her and dispelling the awful images still floating in her mind's eye. "Do you sense the invasion of her energy? If you don't want to use magic, perhaps subconsciously you'll at least be willing to use your magic to stop someone else's."

The idea rang with truth in Aeliana's mind, but it didn't help her know how to make it happen.

"Her past is full of lies, mostly fed to her, believed by her. Her self-loathing is almost…sad." Kendalyhn's eyes remained closed. "There's a sense that her existence is a mistake, something the Stars must regret." Her voice hitched, and she frowned with uncertainty as she spilled the secrets of Aeliana's soul. Maybe even she realized it was too much to reveal.

Aeliana closed her eyes, mortified as Sylmar and Cyrus listened in. She forced herself to become aware of the tiny bits of energy surging through her body, how they pumped with her blood and gathered in her heart. How her starlock rested over the well of energy.

Kendalyhn spoke again, but Aeliana didn't hear her words. She fixated on the starlock as a conduit, as the release of the dam holding in her blood's power. Heat stirred in her chest, and the starlock burned, but Aeliana kept her eyes shut, concentrating with an intensity brought on by the fear of losing focus before she could gain relief.

As the heat spread, she focused on Kendalyhn's arms, every place her fingers and hands touched Aeliana's skin. The touchpoints became targets for the energy. Hope rose in Aeliana with the realization that she could channel her energy, that she could control it, but it was quickly doused by the truth that she wasn't controlling it. She was simply letting it go.

Too late, she realized the energy she released was too much for the task at hand, too much to simply block magic. Her eyes flew open, and she tried jerking her arms back, but Kendalyhn gripped tighter, her sneer deepening for a breath.

Aeliana's energy left her body with a palpable rush, searing Kendalyhn's skin. The other woman's lips split open in a terrified scream as the force pushed the smaller woman across the clearing, where she barely missed the cookfire before slamming into a nest of broken bamboo shoots.

Kendalyhn slumped to the side, and her body went still.

Shouts erupted throughout the camp and weapons were drawn, everyone's gazes darting around for the unknown enemy in their midst. Cyrus gasped, leaning back from Aeliana as if more bursts of energy might escape her. She gaped at her uninjured hands, horrified at what they'd done.

Lukai and Velden rushed to Kendalyhn, leaning over to examine her.

Aeliana's mouth went dry, then flooded with saliva. She turned to retch, stretching across the bedrolls to hit moss instead of blankets, but the moss she'd expected was covered in a thick bed of daisies, which were now covered in her bile. Her hearing dulled and her vision faded, making the chaos that ensued a blur of panicked bodies and muffled shouts.

She'd killed Kendalyhn. She'd known it could happen, and she'd done it anyway.

"Aeliana?" Hands shook her arms, turning her. A cloth wiped her face, and her gaze finally took in Iris, her lips moving, the words like a foreign language.

"What have I done?" Aeliana asked.

"It's all right, love. You're fine. Everything will be all right." She punctuated each word as if that might be the one to finally get through Aeliana's head.

Aeliana looked beyond Iris, where Lukai lifted Kendalyhn and brought her to the bedrolls. Aeliana scrambled back, watching from a distance as Velden wrapped seaweed around the burns at Kendalyhn's wrists. Her heart rate slowed. Velden wouldn't heal wounds on a dead woman.

"She's alive?" she whispered.

"Of course." Sylmar's gravelly voice met her ears.

"Thank the Stars." Aeliana's weariness returned.

The flurry of activity around her calmed as quickly as it had begun, people returning to their tasks while glancing back at Kendalyhn, worry in their eyes. Kendalyhn woke with a brief moan, then quieted down as Lukai placed his hands over her arms. Still, her face remained pale, a grimace straining her features.

Jasperus and Holm glanced Aeliana's way, fear replacing their worry, but Iris continued fawning over her, tying back her hair and putting fresh cool cloths against her burning skin as if she were the one who'd been injured.

"I could have killed her."

"But you didn't," Sylmar said.

Aeliana turned to face him. For the first time, he looked tired instead of irritated.

"What if I had?" she asked.

"Then it would have been my fault." His words came out quick on the heels of her question, harsh enough to make her flinch. "It would have been my fault because I worked you too hard, too fast."

They sat in silence for a long moment, their shared guilt unexpectedly tying them together.

"Kendalyhn's parents were killed by Mayvus several years ago," Sylmar said. "Publicly the Zealots said her parents desecrated a Sungazer. Something that would have gone to trial in the west with the royal family as judge was settled by the high priestess in the eastern part of the country.

"Lukai's family took her in, but her anger runs deep, spilling out into her words and deeds. She's here for a reason that's much bigger than you. Every person here was handpicked, not just for their skill but for their loyalty. They're all ready to sacrifice anything and everything for this mission to succeed, even if there are bumps along the way."

She glanced back at Kendalyhn, who slept soundly, knocked out by whatever concoction Velden had given her. Lukai still bent over her, eyes squinted shut while he healed her wounds.

"We'll figure this out, Aeliana," Sylmar said. "We're here to push you to learn, but we're also here to help you."

"I'm trying," she said. "But I'm scared."

"I'm not asking you to not be scared. I'm asking you to fight through your fears."

She nodded and let out a shaky breath.

"Are your energy stores depleted?" he asked.

The heat still swirled in her, but instead of threatening to burst, it merely boiled under the surface. "Not absent, but less."

He studied her, his face impassive. "Good. Tomorrow we start again using inanimate objects until you're weaned." He sighed, leaning heavily on his staff. "It will take too long, but it's our only choice."

CHAPTER 28

GAEREN HAD NEVER FELT as relieved to see land as he did when his barrelman spotted Bamboo Island from the crow's nest. Between Lenda's flirting, Orra's eerie way of watching him, and Larkos' loud political opinions, he was ready for an escape. When they anchored *Starspeed*, Gaeren asked for volunteers to row him and Orra ashore.

Thallahan and Breeve were quick to step up. When the other men kept their eyes on the deck, Riveran was the final man to raise a hand.

"I'll go." His gaze rested somewhere between Gaeren's neck and chest. "Gullet could use some time on land."

Outside of orders, they hadn't spoken since the other night on the crow's nest. Gaeren had preferred it that way, but Enla had wanted him to stay close to Riveran. For the thousandth time, he wished his sister's visions were more specific.

Gaeren nodded his assent, and soon the five of them were rowing from *Starspeed* to the small island overgrown with bamboo. It wasn't large, and it was usually deserted. Sailors often made it a stop for repairs, but for now, the coast was empty. Beyond the initial beaches, the earth quickly turned black, the rich soil filled with exotic plants Gaeren could only vaguely identify as harmless versus suspicious. The sky had grown darker as the day progressed, confirming Larkos' prediction that a storm was brewing. The sailor always seemed to sense them long before Gaeren.

Gullet made himself at home, flying among the trees and diving down for various creatures he deemed worthy for a meal. He didn't return for a time, and it felt safe to assume his hunting had been a success.

When they reached the ridge, Orra gasped, holding her hand to her head. "Durriken."

Gaeren's sword was out in an instant, and he was grateful to see Thallahan, Breeve, and Riveran held their own daggers and swords even though their weapons combined could do very little to Durriken's hide. The last dragon had been spotted a dozen times in the last ten years, and it was rumored he was Mayvus' pet, but that only gave Gaeren more reason to run a sword through the beast's underbelly.

"No, no." Orra waved them off as if they'd overreacted. "Days ago. He was here." She crested the ridge, and they all followed, their gazes taking in the blackened earth, not from rich soil but from burnt foliage. The smoky scent drifted their way as if the fire had just finished burning out.

Gaeren tried tuning in to his surroundings but didn't expect much if the memories were days old. Even hours-old memories were often unidentifiable wisps without being attached to a person.

"Days ago?" Gaeren asked. "Like when the light was seen?"

Orra nodded. "It's no longer here." Her voice grew small, and her eyelids blinked rapidly as if holding off tears.

"Isn't that a good thing?" Gaeren asked.

Orra ignored him, bending down to thrust her hands in the soil.

"I don't think she means the dragon," Riveran said, putting away his daggers. The scabs on his forehead were nearly gone, but the X still stood out against his pale skin, drawing Gaeren's gaze. A healer could remove it, but if Riveran was caught hiding his status, not even Gaeren could protect him from the penalty of death.

Orra's eyes were closed again, face tilted to the clouds. Despite the lack of Sun, the deep brown of her skin almost glowed. Gaeren exchanged a baffled look with Riveran while sheathing his sword.

Orra twitched, her face scrunching as if in pain.

"Is this how she tracks?" Breeve's voice cracked as he leaned toward Gaeren.

Gaeren tensed. He had no idea. But he wasn't about to let Breeve know that. Despite Orra's willingness to entertain the sailors with dozens more tales from the far eastern seas, she'd hardly exchanged five words with Gaeren since she'd hinted at the sword's location. He still couldn't grasp why she'd written the "Falls" if it was last known to be in the possession of Captain Moss. It seemed more likely to be among a Sungazer's artifacts. Unless it had been passed down in her family, and she already had it. Or was it the same starbridge Daisy had used?

He'd listened closer to her cleverly crafted stories in case they held more hints, but they'd left him with more questions than answers.

She never answered questions about the stories, and after the legend of Lady Redwood, she'd never taken requests. Any inquisitions about herself were unmistakably ignored, including her stake in this voyage. When she'd finally answered his question about what she'd do when they arrived, she'd hummed and said, "Whatever the island tells us to do."

Now, Orra pulled her hands out from the ground, flecks of mud speckling her arms elbow to wrist, her light brown hands stained black, fingernails caked with dirt. "Southeast, across the channel and sound. Toward Valorian."

She brushed her hands together and strode across the ridge, headed for the scorched earth in the valley below.

"Wait," Gaeren called. "We can't just leave the ship."

She turned around. "Normally we could reach Valorian faster by taking Starspeed down the coast, but with the storm coming, it might be faster to travel on land. But as captain, of course, the decision is yours."

His mouth dropped open. Was she mocking him? "That's not what I—what if we've overlooked something? We should search here first."

Her eyebrows rose. "What do you think I just did?"

Sun's fire, she was driving him mad. "I have no idea."

"I told you I can sense things better on land. It would be best if you trusted me. The longer we stand here debating my methods, the farther the others get and the more we're delayed by the storm."

Thallahan snickered, elbowing Breeve as they all waited for Gaeren's decision. He glanced at the sky where even darker clouds rolled in. They'd had smooth sailing using the trade winds so far, but Bamboo Island was in the heart of the Dead Winds. If anything, a bit of a breeze would be welcome as they fought their way both to the southern trade route and then against its northwesterly winds. Besides, he'd rather face a storm at sea than on land any day.

"Let's sail." Gaeren purposely placed himself between Orra and the others, slowing down until the distance allowed a private conversation.

"What magic do you use?" It was a question that required tact, but he had no time to ease into the topic.

She sighed. "It's not blood magic if that's your concern."

It would be a lie to say it wasn't, but without seeing any blood spilled, it was hard to consider it for long. Was she somehow tracing the memory of the starbridge? Or Daisy's memory?

"How do you know where to go?"

"When you tune in to someone's memories, how do you find them?"

He spun around, forcing her to stop.

She stared up at him, her face too serene, almost uninterested.

"How do you know my spoke?"

"You tried reading mine when we first met. I sensed it then. Along with your affinity for sensing truth. It's dampened but still useful."

He'd never heard someone use the term "reading," like memories were a book to be explored. It gave him the uneasy feeling that she belonged on an entirely new spoke. Maybe an entirely different Wheel of Magic.

"Besides, you've continued trying to access my memories despite my advice to never use magic on me. It's not like you've been hiding your spoke."

He felt the warning in her words even as she glanced beyond him.

"We should catch up with the others."

"If you want me to help you, you need to start explaining things."

She frowned, swiping at the sweat dripping down her temples, leaving streaks of mud across her face. "When devouring the moon, small bites are digested more easily."

"That's not an answer."

She huffed, pushing past him on the path back to the beach. "It would be if you were listening. And until you truly listen, it's all you will get.."

He ran after her like a child chasing his mother. But he didn't care how desperate he looked. "How do you expect me to follow your directions if you're not willing to give me context?"

She glanced over her shoulder, her expression mildly amused. "The same way you expect your men to blindly follow you."

He caught up to her, but her words were too much an echo of Larkos' for Gaeren to feel like they were still having the same conversation. "It takes time to build that trust."

"Time." She snorted, the closest thing he'd heard to a laugh from her. "More like money, which is still symbolic of our working relationship. Only I'm delivering you the location of the person or thing you're chasing. Whichever it is you want, it will be at the end of this journey."

They'd nearly reached the rowboat where the others, even Gullet, had already settled in, but Gaeren still didn't have answers.

"And if it's not?"

She turned and raised an eyebrow at him. "It will be."

Without warning, she plucked a handful of red leaves from a nearby plant, then grabbed Gaeren's wrist, placing the leaves in his open palm. He automatically shut his hand around them before they could fall.

"Red bush leaves. They make a fantastic tea." She smiled, then turned her back and joined the men by the rowboat.

Gaeren's words to Enla came back to him, plans to bring back red bush tea for their mother. Did Orra expect this offering to somehow put her more in his favor? Or was it some sort of warning that she knew far more than any one person should? Still, he grabbed more of the leaves, stuffing his pockets to the brim.

No one spoke as they rowed through the choppy waves back toward *Starspeed*, probably because Gaeren couldn't keep a scowl off his face. Traveling to Valorian would be worth it if they found Aeliana, but if not, Orra would probably spit in the wind and say they had to take the Darkwater currents down to Andel.

Enla would be furious if he didn't make it back before the dignitaries arrived.

His bad mood stayed with him even as he gave the command to turn and set sail for Valorian. Several of the men whooped and hollered, as the town was known for its bawdy taverns.

"What did you find on the island?" Larkos asked, leaning against the bulkhead while Gaeren steered.

"Nothing." He spat the word out, his glare still resting on Orra, who perched on the bow as if willing the boat forward. He rested a hand on his dagger, rubbing the daisy on its pommel.

"There must have been something if we're moving on to Valorian. Especially with high winds. It's going to be a nasty one."

Gaeren pressed his lips together, irritated that Orra's unwillingness to speak was only serving to make him look like more of a fool.

The door to the captain's quarters opened, saving him from having to answer.

Lenda's pale face peeked out. Her brow furrowed in confusion as they sailed south from Bamboo Island.

Larkos' cackle raked on Gaeren's nerves.

"I'll take the wheel so you can deliver the bad news to your bondmate."

CHAPTER 29

Taking the ferry down to Valorian brought on a new form of torture for Aeliana. Sylmar had her alternate running through the properties of the Wheel of Magic and attempting to push energy to those around her, all while keeping her hair and face hidden under her hood. By the time they reached the Valorian docks she was nearly falling asleep on her feet.

In the distance, the Sungazer and city proper lit up with torch light, but Sylmar had them set up camp in the woods between the docks and the heart of Valorian. Holm, Iris, and Velden went into town to buy horses among other supplies. Iris even promised to find Aeliana a skirt, though she swore it wasn't fashionable or practical unless you were nobility. Even though a light rain fell, the group left in high spirits, knowing the days ahead would be easier on horseback.

Aeliana ached to lie down for the night, but Sylmar had other plans.

"Flame requires more than heat," he said. They sat beside each other, staring at the sticks Cyrus and Lukai had gathered. "There needs to be a spark. And that spark can come from you."

Aeliana glanced over at Lukai, who had remained at Kendalyhn's side almost constantly since Aeliana…well, since Aeliana had nearly killed the other woman. Kendalyhn was finally strong enough to assist in setting up camp, so she and Lukai had laid out all the bedrolls. Now, Lukai ran a finger over Kendalyhn's arm, assessing her recovery.

Kendalyhn had hardly spoken to Aeliana since that night, and Aeliana couldn't blame her. According to Lukai, Kendalyhn's burns had run far deeper than those Cyrus had received from the dragon's fire. It was almost like she'd been burned from the inside out. Aeliana shuddered, the motion only highlighting the way her body felt feverish and bloated with her blood's energy.

"Are you paying attention?" Sylmar's sharp tone startled Aeliana.

"I'm trying," she mumbled.

Cyrus gave her a sympathetic look from across the pile of sticks where he and Jasperus watched. Someone besides Sylmar always sat with her during each training session, as if their eagerness might translate into her success. But their presence only made her more nervous that their proximity put them in danger.

Sylmar sighed. "You're building energy faster than you're releasing it. Your mind is growing numb, like when people eat themselves into a gluttonous stupor. You must release your energy."

She nodded, even though that was exactly what she'd been trying to do for the last two nights. She had spent both evenings focusing inward, searching for the place where her energy could be channeled, where she could direct it down a path to the rock Sylmar wanted her to split or the tree he wanted her to help grow. Each time she sensed it, her starlock shimmered, sending a flutter of confidence through her. But then she'd remember Kendalyhn's pained scream, the way her body had flown across the clearing, the horror that had torn through Aeliana when she'd thought she'd killed her.

"What if I practice archery?" she asked, looking longingly at her white elm bow and its quiver of arrows. She'd carried them plenty, but Cyrus had only taken her out to practice once. It had been relaxing, almost fulfilling. "Or even sword fighting."

Jasperus shook his head. "You're too full of energy. You're more likely to injure yourself than make headway on those skills."

His words struck true. She was even more likely to hurt someone else. But the same was true of her magic. Splitting a rock could send the pieces flying, and the moment she imagined shards impaling people, her starlock went ice cold, the avenue that had once been cleared for her energy's release now blocked. Growing a tree could send roots up, wrapping around legs, arms, necks, just like the roots that had bent to Arvid's will when he'd buried the dead girl.

Without the ability to control her magic, every action Sylmar suggested was dangerous.

Even now, when pain left her gasping and she wanted freedom, it was like her subconscious had removed the possibility of accessing her energy. She couldn't sense any way to release it without erupting like the volcano they aimed to reach after Islara.

"Reach inside for that spark and send it to the sticks," Sylmar said, drawing her attention back to the place where a fire should be. "Use your energy to provide warmth for the people around you." It was his newest tactic. He sensed her fear of harming others, so he tried to turn it around into something good she could do.

But her blood was so full of energy that she was more likely to start an inferno that rivaled the range of Durriken's breath.

She closed her eyes and searched inward anyway. If nothing else, it felt good to take a deep breath and relax. With the loss of vision, her other senses grew stronger. She'd grown used to this, but still found the jungle sounds rewardingly peaceful. Even the distant howls that were too high to be wolves and too long to be foxes or wild dogs.

She imagined a wall protecting Cyrus and Jasperus, hoping that if she ever managed to create the spark, she would also create a barrier to keep them safe. Without warning, she was on the ground with Cyrus bent over her, cool hands applying one of Velden's pastes to her forehead and cheeks. Beyond his red hair, thick clouds rolled and lightning flashed.

"You're all right. You just passed out. You'll get it next time." His tight smile contradicted the encouragement of his words.

It took longer than usual for the paste to work, and by the time she sought out Sylmar to try again, he waved her away. "I've been told I'm pushing too hard."

"It's what I need, isn't it?" she asked. "I can do it."

He studied her but must have found something wanting. "Not tonight."

She wrapped her arms around her waist and turned away, heading for the small spring they'd used to refill their skins and traveling downstream until she reached a mossy bank. She removed her shoes, sitting down and slipping her feet into the cool water. Her entire body shivered even though she felt swollen and heated with the energy beneath her skin. She imagined the cool water slipping through to her veins, replacing the tainted blood, easing her pain and setting her free.

Cyrus sat next to her, passing over a helping of cooked fish on a stick. She blinked, noting how much darker it had already gotten. How long had she sat here?

"For the record," he said, "I agree with the others that you should learn magic, but there's something honorable in your resistance. Like you're subconsciously determined to avoid what's wrong even if it kills you. I think that tenacity will serve you well in the long run, when you have difficult choices to make and the wrong thing seems easier than the right." He gave her a sad smile before taking a bite of his own fish, then turned to the waning moon above.

She blinked. His words sounded like a compliment, but she didn't feel tenacious or determined at the moment. They sat in silence until he'd picked his first fish clean.

"Aren't you going to eat?" He nudged her arm with his elbow.

She should eat. But her stomach churned at the scent of cooked meat. She raised it to her lips and took the smallest of bites to keep him happy. As Aeliana chewed, the heat of her energy went cold so suddenly she broke into violent shivers. Cyrus wrapped his cloak around her, setting her stick and fish against a rock.

"Should I get Sylmar or Lukai?" he asked.

The heat returned in a wave that made her break into a sweat. "See if you can find more of Velden's paste?"

Cyrus nodded, jumping to his feet.

Cold paste slid over her skin, jolting her awake and making her realize she'd passed out once more. Her violent shivers started again as the medicine compensated for the volatile shifts of her body's temperature. This time it was Jasperus who crouched before her, wiping the paste on her skin.

"I'm sorry this has been so difficult for you," he said.

She sighed. "Is it possible she already branded me? That she's keeping me from learning?"

He shook his head. "No. You'll know if you've been branded. A mark will sear your skin, and you'll sense her."

"If brands are so terrible, why hasn't anyone else tried stopping her? Why hasn't the royal family labeled her a threat?"

He frowned and sat back on his heels, setting aside the bowl of paste and wiping his hands on a towel. "Those are good questions. Hopefully the royal family's silence means they don't know she uses them. If they're aware, it would say a lot about what they truly value. Although brands started out as innocent as bonds—a method to protect children. But removing them was painful, even traumatic, because it severed the connection between parent and child too deeply."

"It was cut out?" Aeliana asked. "How does that work?"

"Just like it sounds. It will leave a permanent mark, even when healed by magic, showing the person was at one time branded. But once removed, there's no more compulsion or attachment."

A spark of hope flared inside her. "How hard is it to cut out a brand? Velden made it sound…difficult. Maybe one of you should hang on to my starlock so there's not risk of me using it against you."

Jasperus shook his head. "You could lose moons of training if you avoid your starlock now—training that could save your life later. Cutting out a brand is difficult, but still possible. The problem is that your desires will match hers, so you'll either hide it from us or leave. I think it's far more likely for us to wake up and find you absent one morning than it is for us to fear you using your magic against us. Mayvus will want you by her side."

A shudder ran through Aeliana. "I suppose the night watch is meant to watch me as much as it's meant to watch for outsiders."

He grimaced but didn't disagree. The light rainfall that had started with the others' departure grew heavier. Kendalyhn and Lukai tied a tarp in the trees and pulled the bedrolls closer to the cookware.

"What about bonds? Can they be cut out the same way?"

Jasperus' smile was fatherly. "People don't usually want to remove bonds. Give it more time."

"That's not—I was just wondering." Her face heated, making her even more thankful for Velden's paste.

"They can be cut out. It's a painful process—not as much as a brand, but it still hurts both physically and emotionally." He glanced at Sylmar. "There's only one person I know of who's cut his bond mark out, and he won't ever talk about it. Supposedly it's like carving out a part of your heart. Even if you fall in love again, you can't quite gain that part back."

"Sylmar?" Aeliana had more trouble imagining the old man bonded than she did imagining him cutting out a bond.

Jasperus laughed. "If you don't believe me, you can ask him, but I don't recommend it. Most of the time, which is still rare, bonds are broken by infidelity. Bond marks have a way of encouraging faithfulness because even a kiss can sear the bond mark off."

"That seems—oddly powerful."

Jasperus laughed. "Yes, well, the bonds between couples are oddly powerful. That sort of thing can't be replicated with bonds between children and parents or siblings. I think it's possible—"

His words were cut off by shouts from around the main fire, then a high-pitched howl that made Aeliana cover her ears. Jasperus stood, drawing his sword out in one fluid motion. His face hardened with determination as he stepped in front of Aeliana.

"What was—?"

Jasperus' hush drowned out her words. She peered over his shoulder, taking in the sight of silvery figures darting between the others at camp. They hunched like wolves, crawling on all fours, but their smooth skin shone like glass and stretched taut over sinewy limbs. They resembled unfinished humans with child-like faces, their large eyes and delicate noses interrupting the smooth silver of hairless heads. When one paused long enough to growl and hiss at Cyrus, its mouth spread wide, revealing hundreds of tiny razor-sharp teeth.

Before it could attack, Sylmar's sword sliced through its chest, silver blood spilling out around the blade. Another took its place, and Aeliana counted at least eight more swarming Cyrus, Sylmar, Lukai, and Kendalyhn.

Instead of joining the fray, Jasperus pulled Aeliana toward the edge of the clearing and shoved her down under low-hanging branches, sending rainwater down her back. They crouched down, hiding while he remained guard over her. Gratitude warred with humiliation inside Aeliana. If she'd been training like Sylmar wanted, would she be able to defend herself? Would she be willing? Or if she'd spent more time learning archery with Cyrus, would she be armed and taking out the creatures along with her friends?

The mark on her palm twinged, and her gut flared.

Lukai.

She peered over Jasperus' shoulder, catching sight of Lukai and Kendalyhn, back to back as they fought off the animals. Kendalyhn nearly flew at one of the creatures with her dagger, all signs of weakness absent in the heat of battle. Lukai's sword flashed in the moonlight, spilling silver blood with frightening precision. They were still outnumbered.

"We have to help them." Aeliana tugged at Jasperus' sleeve, but he hushed her. In desperation, she scanned the ground, digging through wet leaves and ferns until her hand found a large rock in the mud. She scooted back away from Jasperus, then came around the other side of the tree until she could stand and aim at the nearest one's head. She held her breath, recalling the way she'd aimed the arrow at the tree, the way everything else could disappear as her vision narrowed. Only this time her target was moving, and maintaining that strength of focus made her dizzy. She let the rock fly, and it miraculously struck the center of the silver head.

Instead of doing any harm, the creature turned around, hissing. Its gaze darted around the clearing until it found Aeliana and locked eyes with her.

Jasperus swore under his breath, then bolted in front of Aeliana as the creature bounded toward them. Instead of swinging his sword, Jasperus tightened his grip on Aeliana's wrist. Just before the creature lunged, it skidded to a stop, a wrinkle forming above its eyes. After a long moment, it snarled.

"Magic," the creature hissed.

Aeliana sucked in a breath. "It can talk?"

"Of course; it's a winex." Jasperus' voice came out strained.

Aeliana had heard of the creatures that waxed and waned with the moon, but she'd thought they were fables.

It sat back on its haunches and howled, making the others pause in indecision. Half of them raced off into the night, but those who still fought were left at a distinct disadvantage. In unison, they all threw their heads back, letting a strange tinkling sound escape their lips. It almost looked like they were laughing. It left Aeliana and the others stunned, and through a sluggish haze Aeliana watched her comrades all hesitate. The winex each got in a swipe; one even snatched a dagger from Lukai's hand.

Her friends recovered and resumed their attack with renewed purpose. Sylmar's staff was once again molten, cutting through two of the winex like they were wax being melted. For being a healer, Lukai had no qualms about using his magic to drain the winex of health.

Aeliana stepped back, shocked at the sudden turn. It was as if they'd been holding back their magic, hiding it, and the moment they were found out, they let it loose. Kendalyhn's eyes grew haunted as she flung her dagger, like she was seeing a different dimension. Was that how Aeliana looked when she used her magic to aim?

Even Cyrus managed to draw blood, holding his own against the winex attacking him.

Despite its apparent howl for retreat, the winex before them leaned in, sniffing at Jasperus. "You smell wrong."

It sat back again, wiping rainwater from its eyes and bouncing on its hind legs like it itched to launch at them. Within moments, it was the last creature left alive in the clearing as it debated whether or not to attack. Soon it was whining, like its indecision was physically painful.

Sylmar approached from behind, then held his staff near the winex's head, the heat making the creature cry out in fear. Lukai took a rope, wrapping it around the winex's wrists. Finally, Jasperus dropped his grip on Aeliana, bending at the waist with a gasp.

The winex went wild, snarling and snapping in Jasperus' direction, but the rope held firm and the proximity of Sylmar's staff eventually left the winex still, heaving and glaring in Aeliana and Jasperus' direction.

Even Cyrus gawked at the two of them.

"What just happened?" Aeliana asked.

"You were a—you were winex," Cyrus said.

"Jasperus adjusted your appearance," Sylmar corrected. "He created the illusion that you were both winex, which made this one hesitate."

"Female," the winex added, then it clamped its mouth shut in regret.

Sylmar nodded. "Yes, he made you appear like female winex, which a male winex would never attack."

"Only we didn't smell right," Aeliana muttered, the creature's accusation coming back to her. She glanced at Jasperus. "Thank you."

He nodded, still breathing too hard to speak.

The creature's head fell back, his eyes squinting as his jaw widened, but before he could let loose that strange paralyzing laugh, Sylmar let his staff fall against the creature's skin. The winex howled.

"Who sent you?" Sylmar asked.

The winex frowned. "We don't work for people." He spat at Sylmar's feet, but Aeliana detected fear. They'd never get answers by intimidating him.

She eased closer. "What's your name?"

Sylmar shot her a scathing look.

The creature bared his teeth in her direction. "Felk."

Sylmar stepped between them. "If you weren't sent, why did you attack?"

Felk shook his head, then thought better of it as Sylmar drew the staff closer. "We scavenge. Two nights we took food. Tonight you were left. Ten of us, six of you." He glared at Sylmar. "But you have magic."

Kendalyhn, stepped forward, grimacing as she placed a palm on the creature's wet silver skin. He howled his frustration, but Sylmar's staff and Lukai's rope kept him still.

"He's lying about the food. They've taken some the past five nights. But the rest of what he said is true." Kendalyhn removed her hand, then rubbed her palm against her thigh with a shudder.

"Yes. We have magic." Sylmar leaned in, bringing his staff to touch Felk's cheek. The winex screamed in agony but didn't move. When Sylmar pulled his staff back, a small black mark marred the silver skin of the winex's cheek, like a black tear permanently bleeding from his eye. "Make sure your friends know we have magic. Do not follow us again."

The winex blinked mournfully. When Lukai removed the rope holding him, Felk tore out of the clearing in a blur of silver flesh.

CHAPTER 30

ORRA STOOD on the prow of *Starspeed*, closing her eyes and letting the wind rifle through her hair, praying for the Sun's light to fill her to the brim.

The storm had come and gone, taking portions of their foremast and mizzenmast with it. She'd known it would be the case when Gaeren chose that path, but there was little she could do about it. They'd been delayed four days already, and would likely be stuck on the coast of the sound for another two or three for repairs. Even now the sound of hammers on wood clashed with the peaceful warmth she absorbed.

Gaeren worked as hard as the others, gaining their respect in ways he couldn't have earned otherwise. The delay had purpose even if she'd rather be on the move. Her frustration was nothing compared to Gaeren's palpable agitation, which made Lenda and the younger crew avoid him.

To pass the time, she'd told the men more stories of her time at sea, making up ancestors instead of revealing her role in history. People had trouble understanding the weight of immortality. They had trouble accepting it. Even Orra hadn't understood its full impact until the last thousand years. Chasing what the people called starbridges while knowing the Stars watched—likely judged—gave her fresh perspective. She toyed with the braid on her wrist.

"Is there significance to your bracelet?" Gaeren's voice didn't startle her. She'd sensed him standing there for the last several moments, debating if and when he should interrupt her thoughts. Likely deciding if it was worth breaking his silence to get more answers.

Without opening her eyes, she nodded. "It was a gift." A gift, a farewell. A painful reminder. Nothing was ever just one thing.

"From a bondmate?"

In another time, she might have laughed. "Bonds are a trivial attempt to mirror an intimacy that goes beyond what the world offers."

She opened her eyes, flicking a meaningful glance in Lenda's direction. Their bond wasn't taking. Orra had tested it because she suspected as much. Gaeren fought it, and for that reason Orra respected him more than most men.

Gaeren's eyes widened, but he didn't say anything. It was probably the first time they'd agreed on something. She supposed she'd been hard on him, asking things she couldn't answer herself, questioning his motives when he could just as easily question hers.

She wanted the arrow, but she had no intention of making the world bigger or smaller. Was it wrong to want it for her own gain after all these years? Did it make it any more right if obtaining it also benefitted Gaeren or Aeliana? She glanced back at her wrist, where the soft blond strands shone in the Sun's light, wishing she could ask its owner for advice one last time. And yet, she didn't need to ask him. She already knew he would tell her to seek out the Sun.

"He was more than a bondmate," she said softly. "He was my other half." She wasn't sure why she revealed this detail. Few people knew the braid's significance. They were all long gone now anyway. Men she'd bonded with, women she'd confided in. Children who became adults then faded to dust, like winex aging as fast as the moon. Only they didn't return like the winex, and Orra no longer wished to distract herself from her true purpose.

"I'm sorry for your loss." Gaeren wiped the sweat from his brow, glancing back at the men still working. He showed promise. The light shining from him was the same as it had been for others in generations past. A hope that gave her love for people, even the misguided ones.

"Thank you," she murmured, pressing the braid to her lips, longing to feel its hum. To sense the starbridges once more. Gaeren returned to his work, rebuilding threads that joined him to his crew along with the masts that had kept them from sailing.

Was it too late to rebuild her threads with the Sun after all these years? She used to want to fix things to regain the Sun's favor. But the Sun wasn't the oppressive judge the Vendarans believed it to be. Her own shame and guilt kept her from claiming the Sun's full favor. She could sing a dying human to the Sun's light, but she'd lost her own right to that gift long ago. Hadn't she?

She was grounded to the earth, tethered in ways she didn't want by all the actions she regretted. But the Sun had left her here for a purpose. She might never be free again, but there were wounds she could heal, wrongs she could right.

She would put things back together even if it took her another thousand years.

CHAPTER 31

Aeliana found herself watching for Felk's return even though Sylmar insisted the winex were long gone. Now that they traveled on horseback, they had covered more ground, but it wouldn't be impossible for the winex to keep up.

"They fear magic. They won't be back," Sylmar said when he caught Aeliana squinting at the darkness beyond their campfire. "There's no need to be concerned."

"I'm not afraid," Aeliana said, and it was true. What she felt was more like curiosity, but even that was numbed by the energy filling her.

"They could come back with the new moon," Velden said. "They won't remember Sylmar's warning then." He offered Aeliana a biscuit, but she shook her head. Her belly felt too full to ingest anything. It had felt that way for the last day, and despite the energy growing inside her, she sensed her body getting weaker without nourishment.

"I'm more concerned about the sprites," Kendalyhn muttered, glaring at the creek, which had widened significantly as the day wore on. Sylmar had wanted to travel farther, but the others refused to camp any closer to Lovers' Falls. Supposedly it was the home of the sprites, who were just as likely to curse someone seeking their aid as they were to grant a wish. Instead of stopping, their party would skirt the sprites during the Sun's reign.

After dinner, Sylmar pulled Aeliana aside. She assumed it was for another lesson even though the previous night had ended with her falling asleep while trying to adjust the energy within her. They sat across from each other on two large rocks, the sounds of smothered laughter and chatter drifting from where the others remained by the fire.

"Your lessons aren't going well." Sylmar's blunt words were like icy wind on Aeliana's face. They stung, but they also brought her awake.

"I grew up believing magic was a tool for stealing, hurting, and killing." She pressed her lips together, knowing it still was for people like Arvid. "It's hard to instantly reverse my thinking." She wrapped her cloak tighter around herself even though it made her skin feel taut and raw.

He grunted, but it didn't necessarily sound like he disagreed. "I fear you're beyond lessons at this point. We may need to bleed you."

The heat enveloping Aeliana was near bursting, but something cold still slithered through her. "You said we wouldn't use blood magic."

He held up a hand. "You're right, we won't use it. But you need a release of the energy inside you. I'd prefer to wean you by having you expend small bits of energy, but if that's not possible, bleeding small bits is the only other way."

"What about the dark spirits?" she whispered.

"They won't come unless you use the blood for magic."

"They came the last time I bled myself. When I killed that family." Her words came out sharper than she intended, her fear tainting her tone.

He hesitated, making his previous confidence less reassuring. "It's a choice to invite them in. You didn't understand that, and you lost control. This time Velden and I will be here to watch you and protect you."

She bit her lip, her gaze on the others in the group. Who would protect them? Holm and Iris leaned into each other, the subtle, constant love between them proof of what a bond could be, what it should be. Holm didn't even need magic for his quiet, gentle presence to soothe Aeliana, which was why she preferred sharing chores with him each night. Would Iris still dote on Aeliana if dark spirits tore through Holm? How many people would be harmed if the spirits fused with Aeliana and drained the energy still growing within her?

She closed her eyes, attempting to block out the terrifying images of Cyrus' and Jasperus' bodies, pale and still like the family she'd killed at the farm. She couldn't imagine letting a single person in this camp suffer just so she could be free of the pain building up within her veins.

"It's killing you, Aeliana." Sylmar's words softened, and the shift nearly broke her. "I think anyone else would have succumbed to it by now."

His words rang with a truth she didn't want to acknowledge. She felt like her insides were near bursting. Is that how it would happen? Would she fill up with so much energy that her body would be unable to contain it?

She opened her eyes, holding his gaze. "Maybe it will kill me. Maybe that's the best way for me to protect everyone from Mayvus. When she brands me, she'll be able to override what's holding me back, and then I'll be a limitless resource to her."

"You think we'd bring you all this way just to let you die?" Sylmar's gravelly voice grew desperate, deepening to a hoarseness that made Aeliana want him to cough and clear his throat. "No. If we don't see any improvement by tomorrow, we should consider bleeding you. We have to at least try."

She nodded slightly, and he relaxed.

But she wasn't agreeing with his plan. She was agreeing that she had to try something.

He headed for the campfire, but instead of following him, Aeliana let her eyes drift shut while tugging at her blouse and the new split skirt Iris had bought for her in Valorian. She'd been grateful for the swap, since the trousers had felt even more constricting with the buildup of energy inside her. Sweat dripped down her temples, its constant layer something she was quickly becoming used to. But the sounds of the jungle filled Aeliana's ears like a symphony of foreign instruments. What had initially been soothing became more grating as everything in Aeliana ached, even her hypersensitive skin.

When Jasperus barked out a laugh, the others hushed him. Aeliana opened her eyes a crack, following the fearful gazes aimed toward where the waterfall must be. The sprites, who someone would have to be desperate to seek out for a wish.

This time Aeliana's eyes came fully open, her senses on high alert.

How desperate was she?

Which was more desperate: blood magic or sprites?

Sylmar's insistence that she bleed herself was already an act of desperation. The dark spirits would come. They would have her do blood magic whether she wanted to or not. But seeking out the sprites for a wish—even a wish to be rid of her magic—could have equally disastrous consequences. No. She couldn't go to the sprites. But she also couldn't stay here.

She let her gaze roam over these people she'd grown to care for. Friends she hadn't anticipated making. She wasn't willing to put them at risk.

Tonight's desperation had to be dealt with alone.

Aeliana rose, determined, and assured the others she just needed to relieve herself. While passing their stores, she snuck a knife and bandages from one of the supply bags, her heart pounding, expecting someone to shout and ask what she was doing. She strained to hold her head high and back straight as she walked upstream until she rounded a bend and stepped out of sight. Then she let her shoulders slump and her back hunch as if her torso nursed a wound. She wrapped her arms around her waist, stumbling through the water as she picked up her pace.

Eventually they would follow, so she needed to move fast. As the voices faded behind her, blending into the burble of the water, she breathed in as deep as her tight chest allowed, relishing the small taste of freedom. The dark shadows and lush leaves around her were more comforting than smothering, but she was grateful for the water. She'd never find her way back without it.

If she was able to come back.

Eventually the stream met up with a larger river, and the sound of rushing water beckoned her. This time she stayed on the mossy bank, wary of what creatures might rest in the deeper waters. A soft chirp broke through the constant splashing. She strained her ears for a few moments before the noise came again. It trilled like a bird, but the notes were too perfect and the sound too human. The third call gained a response—deeper, fuller, like a delayed harmony. Were those the sounds of the sprites?

The calls came closer, one on top of the other, forming a song with the percussive rush of water as its rhythmic chorale. Despite her exhaustion, the music drew her in until the water crescendoed to a thunderous roar and the river made one last bend to reveal a massive lake and waterfall feeding into it. The pool at the base of the waterfall churned hard and fast, its power frighteningly mesmerizing, while the water lapping at her feet seemed remarkably still in comparison.

She scanned the water and its edge, noting a small winding trail leading straight up the side of a cliff that had to be nearly two hundred feet high. Her heart sank at its steep and treacherous angle. This was where the sprites had to be. The melodious calls increased in volume as if confirming her suspicion.

She'd come far enough.

She pulled out the knife, testing its weight as if it could tell her how to proceed. If she cut her palm, she could try to resist the blood magic. She could bleed out just enough before wrapping the wound. If that didn't work, at least she wouldn't be around to hurt the others.

Before she could talk herself out of it, she used the knife to slice her skin along one of the many scars left by Arvid and Vera.

The knife fell from her grasp, blood dripping down after it. A sense of relief spread from her arm, through her torso, then out to her other appendages. The heady sensation left her light and airy until the feeling grew even stronger.

Why had she waited so long to do this?

She placed her right hand over the wound, ignoring the twinge of discomfort as the euphoria grew. She should bind the wound now, before too much blood was spilled. Or maybe she could heal herself. She'd never done that kind of magic before, but now she had a starlock. Maybe it would be instinctual, like shooting arrows. Maybe this time she could stop things before they got out of control.

But her body refused. Her starlock burned hot, almost as if calling the blood to a higher purpose, encouraging it to be used. The starlocks were gifts from the Stars. If the starlock burned for the magic in her blood, how could blood magic be so bad?

She sensed her mind being pulled along with her body, finding ways to explain away the wrongness, but she couldn't stop it.

She fell to her knees, her hands burying in the dirt. As the blood hit the earth, she knew she could send out its power, so she did. The ground cracked beneath her. Daisies sprouted in a wave from the soil at her fingertips out to the edge of the water, but there was a sinister air to the speed, like time passing by and aging her, taking life she could never get back. She tried to rein it in, tried to remember how Lukai had described the process of healing. The small stitches of the skin. She could seal it off and stop it all. It wasn't too late.

A moan met her ears, which turned to a scream. It erupted from her own mouth as she fought the blood magic's darker pull, but her body remembered too well that relief could come if the blood kept flowing. Her mind tricked her, telling her she could use this magic to get vengeance. To right all the ways she'd been wronged.

Over the rush of the waterfall and her own muffled whimpers, the shouts of her companions drew nearer. Far worse, and more subtle, were the flickers in the sky. Flashes of shadows blocked the quarter moon, hiding both the static stars and the dancing holy Stars.

Her friends were coming, and so were the dark spirits.

She couldn't control what her body did with this amount of magic. She'd already called the dark spirits without meaning to, and now her friends were coming. She squinted up at the sprites' trail, then back at the way she'd come, where her friends were surely looking for her. She couldn't let them find her. She couldn't let her magic hurt them.

The melodious notes rang out once more, beckoning her to climb the trail, to seek safety for her companions. That was when she finally knew how desperate someone had to be to seek out the sprites.

CHAPTER 32

BY THE TIME Valorian's lighthouse drew *Starspeed* in, the city's edge had come alive with its night life. Gaeren's men itched to disembark, but they didn't dare grumble about their duties keeping them from immediately entering the taverns. With Valorian's reputation, they'd still have plenty of time to gamble away the money they'd just earned.

Gaeren, on the other hand, felt time slipping through his fingers as they docked. It had taken far too long to reach the city. Where had Daisy gone in the last week? Had she stayed here? Orra stood at the edge of the boat with a proud serenity that only made Gaeren more anxious. The wind lifted the hair around her cheeks, billowing her skirt until she looked like some sort of sea goddess carved on the boat's prow come to life.

By her side, Lenda gripped the railing, fingers as white as her face. Despite gaining minimal sea legs, she remained weak. Gaeren fought the empathy rising in his chest, knowing it was a trick of the bond. He'd grown to care more for her in the last few days, felt urges to bring her food or extra blankets. Instead of giving in to those urges, he'd resisted them, swallowing down his growing interest in order to remain focused.

Sometimes it felt like more work than it was worth.

As Larkos hopped onto the dock to tie *Starspeed* in, Gaeren assisted Orra and Lenda across. By the time the men had secured the ship, had their fun, and returned to their duties, it would be morning, and Gaeren hoped to be back on *Starspeed*, questions answered—maybe even with a third woman on board to further annoy his superstitious crew.

When Riveran offered to come along, Gaeren only agreed because he could still hear his sister's haunted words reverberating in his mind. If he wasn't going to follow all her advice, at least he could heed this one pointless request. Riveran kept the healed X on his forehead hidden by a cap pulled low over his brow, which was a good thing because Gullet already attracted far too much attention.

Orra stiffly allowed the traitor to escort her through the streets, her awareness of the city's dangers most likely overriding her preferred solitude. Lenda clung to Gaeren's arm like a leech, nails biting into his skin even through his sleeve. Breeve's face was bright red as he escorted Lenda's maid. The deeper they walked into town, the thicker the crowds grew. The cobblestone roads echoed with the clip-clop of hooves and the tap of heels. Laughter rang out between fiddles and hornpipes, and Gaeren had to side-step more than one group of rowdy men sloshing more ale than they took in. They passed a dozen taverns and inns that Gaeren refused to consider, the ramshackle buildings held together with patches of grout and mismatched stones.

They all took a deep breath when they'd left behind the worst parts of town, entering the less lively but still awake areas. The buildings seemed to grow taller and straighter, their smooth surfaces evident of the tenants' affluence. The streets held half the revelers and half the volume, the celebrations muted in comparison.

Orra finally relaxed enough to stretch out a hand, tracing the buildings they passed as if feeling for the presence of the people inside. Gaeren bit his cheek to hold back his questions, knowing they would only make Lenda ask things he wasn't ready to explain. They reached the Night's Light Inn, where Gaeren sent Breeve back to his duties and Lenda half-heartedly fought Gaeren's insistence that she and her maid get checked in for the night. The moment the innkeeper's wife brought up a hot bath, Lenda's protests ceased. Even Orra's face took on a hint of longing, but the expression was quickly replaced by determination, and she left with Riveran and Gaeren.

"Where to now?" Gaeren asked, his tongue looser without Lenda's listening ears.

"The edge of town. I can't sense anything with all the noise." Orra's gaze drifted to the mountains in the east, the farthest range housing Lovers' Falls, which was barely visible even in the moonlight.

"You don't think they're here?"

Orra shrugged. "It's doubtful. Why come all this way just to find another tavern to get lost in another drink?"

Gaeren frowned, irritated by her nonchalance. He was starting to wonder if she spoke in riddles as a distraction. Maybe she didn't actually have all the answers.

"Is she still—?" Gaeren cut off, glancing at Riveran, who shoved his hands in his pockets and matched their long strides. He wasn't reacting, but Gaeren knew he was taking in every detail. He'd always been one to listen with little comment.

Gaeren leaned in, blocking Riveran out from the conversation. "Can you tell if it's still with the girl? Is she still with the two people using blood magic?"

She hesitated. "I can't—I'm not sure. I still sense the human and—"

"A human?" Gaeren's eyebrows rose.

"He was the fourth to cross."

How long would a human last in this part of the world? He supposed they were no different from the half-lights without starlocks —just men and women with powerless blood. But who knew for certain? Anticipation brewed beneath his compulsion to find Daisy. If it weren't for his obligation to find her and protect her, this was the kind of adventure that would distract him. Finding the starbridge and traveling to other lands—meeting long-lost people groups. He would still use it to protect Daisy, but maybe he could also use it to convince Enla she needed an ambassador to the other lands more than a throne warden.

If nothing else, she would see the starbridge as a desirable source of power and authority.

Orra's question came back to Gaeren, making him instantly contrite. Did that make Enla the kind of person who wanted to use the starbridges to make the world smaller? Did it make Gaeren that kind of person if he wanted to use them for his own freedom from the crown?

Orra would probably want him to think about what he could learn from the humans living in Lorvandas, or what he could offer them, instead of how he could benefit.

She stopped, turning slowly to look at him. Her eyes narrowed slightly, and without thought, he drew energy from his blood, wrapping it around his mind like a shield, certain she'd been listening to his thoughts. Her power's strength and place on the Wheel still remained a mystery to him, and he'd foolishly started leaving his guard down.

"She didn't pass through here," Orra whispered, her face growing troubled. Once again, she bent to her knees, shoving her hands in the earth, heedless of the wet soil soaking into her dress. They'd finally reached the edge of town, several fields the only thing separating them from the forest and eventual mountains.

Gaeren let out a breath. She'd been listening to something else, then. Except maybe this was worse. Had they lost Daisy and the starbridge completely? "So you were wrong on the island? Can you still track it?"

She tilted her head, eyes closed. Moonlight glowed soft on her skin, a strange trick of the light. Gaeren snuck a glance at Riveran, whose fascination mirrored Gaeren's own.

"It's faint. They're near Lovers' Falls if I had to venture a guess." She stood, brushing the dirt from her hands, but the uncertainty etched between her brows bothered Gaeren far more than the mud being flung on his pants.

"A guess?" Gaeren's laugh held no humor. "You expect me to abandon my ship and follow a 'faint trail' based on a guess?"

Her eyes flashed with anger, but her voice remained eerily calm. "I expect you to go after any chance if the price is right. How much do you want the things you seek?" She raised a brow, her question holding some deeper meaning. She wasn't just asking if he wanted to find Daisy and the starbridge. Whether she knew it or not, she was asking if he wanted to fix the mistakes of his past and secure protection for the future.

Enla's warning rang through his mind. He had no problem going to

Lovers' Falls, especially if it could help him find Aeliana, but somehow the warning held more weight if approaching the sprites was Orra's idea instead of his.

"If you have other methods of tracking," she added, "I'm more than willing to part ways. I no longer need your services." Her chin rose, a spitting image of Enla dismissing servants.

Riveran hid his face, but Gaeren knew he was being laughed at. By the traitorous fool who'd shunned his sister, no less. He clamped his jaw, unsuccessfully attempting to match Orra's cool.

"I just want to know how accurate your guess might be. I'm already going to be a week late returning home. If I follow your guess, I'm guaranteed to miss the dignitaries Enla wants me home for." Enla would never forgive him. His father would berate him as a sorry excuse for a throne warden. And what about his mother? Had her health improved or declined? How long could he safely stay away?

Orra gazed across the fields, her eyes locked on the mountains rising in the northeast, silhouetted by the quarter moon. "She was never here, which makes it more difficult. I sense she passed near here, and headed that way"—she pointed to the mountains where Gaeren knew Lovers' Falls to be—"but the trail will grow cold if we wait. I suggest we leave now."

"Now? As in tonight?" Riveran finally spoke, his wide eyes turning to Gaeren.

Gaeren swallowed hard. It felt like she was bent on making a fool out of him, seeing how far he was willing to go. Maybe even trying to get him to give up so she could resume the chase on her own. But what if this was his only chance?

"You think Lovers' Falls is their ultimate destination?" he asked, stalling.

"Perhaps. I sense their path veering from the well-traveled roads, whether for haste or concealment." Her gaze remained on the distant hills.

"I can't just leave," Gaeren said. A trip through southern territory and its Recreants required planning. Gaeren was just as likely to be recognized and assassinated as he was to get answers.

"Then stay," Orra said. "And I will leave."

Gaeren and Riveran exchanged a look.

Riveran leaned in. "What exactly are you tracking? Larkos made it sound like you were on a treasure hunt, but Orra's been talking about people. Is this about..." He trailed off, eyebrows raised. Even with their friendship long dead, he didn't give up Daisy's name in front of a stranger.

Gaeren bit the inside of his cheek. If he told Riveran everything, he wouldn't have to make the decision alone. But even if he had time to explain it all, he wasn't ready to share it with Riveran. Not now, maybe not ever.

He turned back to Orra without answering Riveran.

"I need to at least send word to Larkos." It wasn't a lie, but it also wasn't the only thing Gaeren planned to do.

Orra shrugged. "Be quick."

"Stay with her," Gaeren instructed Riveran even as he backed away toward town.

Riveran's surprise shifted to a glare, and he opened his mouth.

"That's an order." Gaeren took off in the night, not waiting for Riveran's protest. He couldn't completely trust Riveran, but he also couldn't trust Orra, which meant he had to verify her story. He pulled the hood of his cloak up, tight around his face, then headed for the taverns closest to the docks.

As he walked, he recounted in his mind his conversation with Orra, an unpleasant truth dawning on him. Riveran was right. Orra no longer talked about tracing the starbridge's location; she talked about tracing Daisy. So if Daisy was what the woman was really after, what exactly did she plan to do when she found her?

It took three taverns for Gaeren to get what he needed. After walking through the crowds and tuning in to the memories of dozens of people around him, he honed in on one young stableboy, whose excitement over the events of the week before still lingered in his mind. The boy's eyes shone as he watched a group of rowdy men sloshing beer and singing ballads, joining in for the parts he knew. Gaeren sidled up to the boy's table, allowing the crowd to jostle him until their arms brushed.

He apologized but didn't move his arm, leaning harder as if the crowd forced him off balance. The boy edged away, but in a distracted manner, like he was making room for Gaeren. Their contact didn't break, and Gaeren tuned in to the boy's memories, flowing through them in reverse until he hit the points he needed.

Three strangers approaching the blacksmith, leather cords around the one woman's neck. The boy's heart rate increasing as he inched forward, knowing this would be a story for his friends. The travelers exchanging coin for a dozen horses, maybe more. The boy hadn't learned his numbers well. Gaeren couldn't hold the memory enough to catch details on faces, but the boy remained fixated on the leather cord, hoping for a glimpse of the woman's starlock. It wasn't enough for Gaeren to be sure. He needed the boy to think of more details.

"You work for the blacksmith?" Gaeren asked.

The boy jumped, then nodded, his gaze darting around the room as if holding a job was a crime.

"I need three horses. Think your boss is still awake?"

The boy laughed, then tried to cover the action. "'Course. But not likely sober." He pointed across the room to where a bearded man downed half a glass of ale before belting out the last line of the song, slurring the words.

"Ah, I see." Gaeren smiled at the boy. "Are you able to help me, then?"

The boy shook his head. "He sold 'em all. That's why he's still celebrating." The boy leaned forward. "The buyer was a progeny, and one of the men with her had webbed fingers. Gave my boss double what they were worth."

"A progeny? And another with webbed fingers?" Gaeren didn't have to feign his interest. "Know what they were doing this far from the schools?"

The boy shook his head. "They weren't students. I guess maybe they could be teachers. They seemed worried though."

Gaeren tuned in to the memories the boy recalled as he spoke, honing in on the words spoken by the travelers. Despite their blurry faces and the boy's inability to recall much detail, Gaeren caught one phrase that took his breath away.

"She needs it for Aeliana."

Gaeren replayed the memory in his head, his grip tightening on the boy's arm until the boy wrenched free.

"I said let go!" The boy's cry rang out through the room between songs, and curious gazes turned their way.

"Forgive me," Gaeren said, half bowing as he backed away. He scanned the crowd, noting Thallahan and Breeve among the revelers. The two sailors stood a little taller, recognizing him as well. The crowd murmured, debating if they could safely return to their normal evening activities, and wary eyes followed Gaeren as he made his exit. How long would it take for someone to recognize him as prince? He stepped out into the night air, which was only a fraction less stuffy than the crowded tavern.

The travelers were with Daisy.

He bent over, hands on his knees. It proved that Orra was right. They'd passed by here, gathered supplies. It was just like Orra had said.

But there was a progeny in their midst. Not half-lights using blood magic. Had Orra been lying or just mistaken about that detail? He reached for his dagger, running his thumb over the daisy. He took a deep breath and let the grooves soothe his fears, as if the dagger's security was tied to Daisy's.

The door opened behind Gaeren, and Thallahan and Breeve tumbled out, brows furrowed.

"Captain?" Thallahan asked. "Is everything all right?"

Gaeren shook his head. "I'm not sure. I need to find Larkos, but I think I need to check on Orra first."

"We can come." Thallahan's response was immediate, reassuring. Not the bartering answer of hired help.

"Follow me." Gaeren took off through the town. Breeve and Thallahan weaved through the streets behind him, guided toward the edge of town by a sudden eerie wail.

"Is that a winex?" Breeve asked, voice hushed.

Gaeren wanted to say yes, but it sounded far too human. When they exited the last alley and found themselves at the edge of town Riveran kneeled over Orra, the woman curled up in a ball.

"What happened?" Gaeren ran the last several feet.

Riveran held up his hands defensively. "Nothing—I mean…I don't know. Her hands were in the dirt and she just—she let out an awful noise, and she hasn't moved since."

Gaeren dropped down next to Riveran, reaching for Orra, then hesitated, remembering how she didn't want him touching her. But this time she grasped his wrist, and her eyes flew open, a desperate fear transferring from deep within her to Gaeren, the sensation as forceful as a fist to his gut.

"It's consuming her," Orra said.

"What's consuming her?" Gaeren tried shaking off Orra's grip, but she held tight, too tight.

"The magic. It's killing her."

CHAPTER 33

THE TRAIL GREW muddy as Aeliana drew closer to the waterfall, and the spray of water soaked her legs, the sensation more refreshing than chilling between her hike and her body's blood still practically boiling with its energy. She pressed the hem of her skirt into her wound, staunching the flow, but her body refused to completely heal it.

Her mind still warred over all the ways she could use her blood for magic. Maybe she could use it to best the sprites. Maybe she could defeat the dark spirits. They still darted in the sky above her, inching ever closer, spurring her on faster. If she gave in to her desire for blood magic, she wouldn't be able to hold back its power. She'd give herself over to the dark spirits.

Without warning, a winged creature half her height hovered before Aeliana, red as the blood seeping between her fingers. A trill of notes came from the slits of its nose, and the fast flutter of its wings left Aeliana stunned, her breath hitching even as her lungs struggled to keep up with her efforts. The creature's small head and bulbous eyes resembled a butterfly's, but its body had arms and legs like the winex —shrunken and shriveled like a child not fully formed. Still…far too human-like.

The creature flew away faster than her eyes could follow, snapping Aeliana out of her reverie. It disappeared up the trail on the side of the waterfall, revealing a small alcove behind the spray almost halfway up. Mist soaked Aeliana's face and clothes as she hesitated. She turned away, rubbing the water from her face, wondering if the others might come around the bend at any moment in their pursuit.

She didn't have time for second thoughts. She continued the climb, practically blinded by the water's spray. Her entire body was soaked by the time she reached the gap where the wall of the cliff met the raging waterfall.

A wall of liana vines blocked her path, but after seeing the creature disappear here, she knew not to trust her eyes. She pushed against the ropey branches, careful to avoid their thorns. Eventually the vines had some give, and the branches swung like a curtain that she divided and stepped behind. The vines closed after her, the only source of illumination the moonlight peeking between the leaves.

Water dripped deep within, making it difficult to determine the size of the cave. A floral scent reached her nose—maybe an orchid or hyacinth—but was quickly overpowered by something rotting. She swept back the liana vines, wincing as thorns dug into her flesh.

The extra moonlight revealed two skeletons resting in an embrace. The lovers of Lovers' Falls. Inside their rib cages, something had formed a nest, the bones of recently picked-over animals mingled with shriveled plants. Cockroaches spilled out, escaping across her boots to a darker part of the cavern.

She jumped back with a gasp, her back bumping into the powerful yet tiny hands of the blood-red winged creature. It spun her around to face its big black eyes.

Cold fear swept through Aeliana. She no longer heard sweet music. On the heels of her fear, warmth seeped into her skin, heat from the starlock and blood, a reminder that she could use it to fight back.

Do you know what I am?

The voice held the same melody as the creature's song. Still, no mouth moved, the tones resonating more in Aeliana's mind. Its head simply cocked, waiting for her reply.

"Y-yes?" It had to be a sprite, even if it wasn't how she'd pictured it.

What is it you seek? Its eyes blinked, and a shiny film coated them. It blinked again, and the film disappeared.

Aeliana licked her lips. There were a number of answers she could give. She'd come to get freedom from her magic, but now that she was here, covered in her own powerful blood, with this… sprite, she wasn't sure if it was what she wanted anymore. There were far greater causes. She had a mother who was in danger, a friend who needed to get home, an entire people group who suffered from oppression.

Ah, do not lie. Everyone who finds the sprites is offered what they seek. Its head tilted the other way, the sharp motion leaving Aeliana uneasy. *It's not always what they want.*

The warning slid through Aeliana like a snake, unsettling everything it touched. Did it know what she was thinking? Maybe she didn't want anything from these sprites. She squeezed her hands into fists, relishing the sensation of blood dripping onto the mossy rock. Then hating herself for gaining any pleasure.

She'd tried weaning herself from the blood magic, but it was too dangerous. She could do more—for Cyrus, for her mother, for her new friends—if she didn't have to deal with weaning her magic. Holm and Iris contributed plenty without starlocks and magic. She'd never wanted magic to begin with.

"I seek freedom from the magic in my blood." She pulled the star-shaped starlock and its leather cord over her head, setting it on the ground between her and the sprite like some sort of offering. "I want to be rid of it all."

The request felt right as it left her lips. If she didn't have magic, Mayvus would never be able to use her blood.

The sprite tilted its head again. The space beneath its eyes shifted, like cheeks rising on a smiling face. The sprite seemed…pleased, which somehow made it more menacing.

Aeliana took a step back.

Freedom. The sprite bent to examine the starlock, its wings flapping to hold the creature in place at such an odd angle. *Such a noble request comes at a high price.*

Aeliana took another step back, but her boot crunched against bone. She shuddered, hands bracing for the edge of the liana curtain. Could she run from this creature? Did she dare try?

Ah, yes. The sprite blinked again, the film once more covering the glossy black of its eyes. *You can obtain your freedom at the cost of another's. I keep this trinket, and you never feel the weight of your magic again.* A blink, and the black eyes returned. The sprite breathed in deep, the slits between its eyes expanding. A rush of pain, then relief, flowed through the cut on Aeliana's arm until it was sealed.

She reached out to the wall of vines for support even though a thorn cut her other hand. The absence of the magic's pressure and temptation nearly made her crumple. It wasn't completely gone, not like when Arvid and Vera had drained her, but the surplus settled into a pleasant, controllable hum.

And it only costs the freedom of one mortal. The sprite's slim shoulder lifted and dropped. *Not even a powerful one.*

An image of Cyrus flashed before her, his innocent freckled face pale, lips blue. For a moment, she recognized it as a memory, a vision from her Awakening, but it was too vivid to be a recollection. The sprite had pushed the image into her mind, had given it to her as easily as she'd given it the starlock.

"No." She clenched her shaking hands. "The price is too high."

The sprite cocked its head again. *No?* Its cheeks lowered; its bulging eyes blinked once more. The film remained, the image of Cyrus growing hazier. The sprite leaned forward, draping the leather cord over Aeliana's head until the starlock settled around her neck.

For a moment, the creature's nearness had a sinister pause. Its wings beat like a loud drum in her ear, its hot breath drifted across her face from its enlarged nostrils, and its fingers tightened on the cord. It could kill her in that instant with just the leather around her neck. Maybe it wanted to.

A buzzing sound filled the space, followed by the iridescent glow of a dozen sprites rounding the corner from the depths of the cave. Their wings fluttered in a rainbow of golds, emeralds, sapphires, and rubies. She froze as they rushed toward her, realizing this hauntingly beautiful image was likely the last thing she'd ever see.

Instead, the red sprite spun her to face the vines.

The moment you asked for the deal, you'd already taken it. Its voice no longer held music, just a deep growl filled with hatred. *Your freedom or his.*

Dozens of little hands pressed on her back, shoving her through the vines, which sliced at her arms and face. Her boots slipped on wet rock, then lost purchase as the sprites pushed her through the waterfall and beyond.

The scream erupting from Aeliana's throat was drowned out by a mouth full of water. She spluttered as the shock of weightlessness overpowered her, and the black of night swirled with cerulean water and thick leaves. Before she could regain any sense of direction or reclaim more air, her body plunged into water.

It filled her nose, and her proximity to the waterfall pushed her deeper, churning her beneath its force. She fought against its power, lungs burning, but that only kept her revolving within the water. Her vision dimmed, the fight draining from her body. As she went limp, the current finally carried her out from under the waterfall, where she could sense up from down. Breaking through the surface, she sucked in fresh, hopeful air, hacking and spitting out water. The current took her nearer to the shore, her now bare feet scraping the sandy bottom.

But in the water, her hands brushed against fabric, skin, and hair, and her heart stilled.

Moonlight glinted off the water, leaving the heavy object before her in shadow. She blinked the water from her eyes, pushing aside familiar long red hair with trembling fingers.

"Please, no." Her words came out like a desperate prayer as she fought to turn Cyrus over.

Blue lips and wide eyes left her sick.

"Help!" The word left her mouth at a fraction of the volume needed, but her body couldn't produce anything louder. She hooked her arms under his and dragged him to the water's edge. His weight became unbearable as his body hit the sand, and she collapsed against his still form, water lapping at their legs.

"Sweet Stars, no!" She pulled at the fabric clinging to his chest, trying to remember the motions she'd once seen a healer do with a little girl who had drowned in the creek. Something to make the heart beat, to pump the water out. But she wasn't a healer. She didn't know what to do.

She bent forward, placing her forehead against his cold skin. It was her fault. He'd been doomed since the day they'd met. She'd always known it, and still, she'd led him into the trap like an animal to a butcher.

"This isn't what I wanted." She pulled back, the starlock miraculously still hanging from her neck, swinging between them.

The sprites had tricked her. She didn't want their deal. She turned to the waterfall, glaring at the space where she knew the creatures waited, probably watching.

"I told you no!" Her shout echoed across the water, her voice finally regaining its force. She turned back to Cyrus. "The cost of freedom is too high." She yanked the cord from her neck, and at her touch, the starlock pulsed, not unlike the blood pumping through Aeliana's veins.

Your freedom or his. The sprite's words came back to her, taunting her.

But also guiding her.

It was her choice. Her freedom or his. His life or hers. In order to save him, she had to give up the freedom she craved. She had to use her magic.

She closed her eyes, squeezing the starlock tight in her right hand while placing her left across her face, which oozed with blood from the vines that had sliced into her skin. Arvid and Vera had always spoken of manipulating the elements, forcing substances to obey their commands. It had sounded clumsy and imprecise.

Instead, she recalled Sylmar's words of altering the elements, enhancing them.

She focused on the beat of her heart, the pumping of her blood, the energy pushing through every drop in her veins. She placed her hands on his chest and willed the energy out from her blood and into the water around her, reaching for the water deep within Cyrus' lungs. She sensed it then, on a level deeper than knowledge or understanding, intuition that went beyond the senses. A need to pull the water out and replace it with air. To press the energy in until his heart could once more beat. To heal the parts of his body already damaged. Even with her eyes closed, they lit up in her mind's eye like points in a constellation, targets to direct the power constantly threatening to spill out of her.

For the first time, she purposely let her energy flow out uninhibited, the power expanding within her even as it left her body. It unfurled like a cat stretching, filling her veins before pumping out. She gasped as it wrenched through her, opening her eyes as her palm filled with heat.

When Arvid and Vera had drained her, the power only flowed out, but with the starlock, power also flowed in. The source felt frighteningly bottomless, and in her panic, she pushed the energy out faster. The heat of the starlock seared against her palm like the starting point of a string running through Aeliana's body and extending out to Cyrus' lungs.

Cyrus coughed and sputtered, his body wracking in the sand until he turned and retched, breaking the connection between them. Aeliana's sense of relief was quickly overshadowed by her inability to control the energy she released. It backed up along the string, filling Aeliana once more, bloating her with its painful presence.

She opened her hand and released the starlock, practically batting it to the pebbles on the shore. As Cyrus sat up, Aeliana crumpled to the sand, the pain now filling her lungs like the water had filled his.

A figure ran down the beach, slipping in the sand. Aeliana fought to stay awake, to know if the stranger would help Cyrus—or harm him. But the unfamiliar man rushed for her, bending to cradle her head with his tattooed hands, to say words she couldn't hear. The light of the moon winked out, hidden behind the dark spirits coming straight for Aeliana.

Her vision dimmed, her body too weak to warn either man of the coming danger.

CHAPTER 34

ORRA REMAINED in a ball on the ground, focusing somewhere beyond Gaeren, even past Thallahan, Breeve, and Riveran. Her gaze centered on the visions that would plague her every moment of every day if she didn't hold them at bay. Visions she'd ignored for much of the last thousand years as she preserved the magic threatening to slip through her fingers.

"What do you mean, it's killing her?" Gaeren asked.

"Prophecies have been set in motion," she said. "Curses…they're all colliding." She released his wrist, then shifted to her hands and knees, dizziness overtaking her.

Interfering was not her way. She was not meant to change outcomes. She was not meant to get involved. But how could she undo her wrongs without making change? Without interfering?

"What do you mean about prophecies and curses?" Gaeren kneeled beside her, the concern in his face not for her. It made him more endearing, to know that he felt so much for someone so far out of his reach.

She sat back on her heels, catching her breath. "It was put into motion generations ago." Orra fidgeted with the braid at her wrist, her focus shifting past Gaeren once more. "We couldn't stop what happened tonight. We can't stop some of the things that are coming."

"You're speaking in riddles," he hissed.

She flinched, then closed her eyes. It was easy to forget how hard it was to see things from a single point in time. She took several deep breaths before opening her eyes and speaking again. "Imagine a decision being made. Maybe to have a child. Maybe to start a war. Maybe to simply eat a meal. That action carries over into the future like how throwing a stone makes ripples in a pond. It can't be changed or stopped. The effects will be felt through future generations. But the things in the path of the ripple… maybe a lily pad or a boat. They can be moved. So the ripple effects them at just the right time in just the right place."

He shook his head. "You're still not making any sense."

She wasn't trying to make sense to Gaeren. She was trying to make sense of the confusing thoughts swirling through her. She had no right to interfere with stones being thrown. She'd done it before with disastrous consequences. Her decisions had changed the ripple to a tidal wave. She couldn't go back and fix that. It was impossible. But she could move things in the path of the tidal wave she'd created.

It wasn't quite the same as interfering. This was more like a gentle nudge. Like the shifts that came with her mere existence. It was impossible to be present for a thousand years and not have some impact, some change, on the world. Those gentle nudges were allowed.

"If we put things in the right place at the right time, we can heal things." She gazed up at Gaeren, her vision clearing, regaining focus. "We can put things right."

Something inside her burned with hope, with the knowledge that the Sun approved. Perhaps it was less about whether or not she interfered and more about whether or not the interference was guided by the Sun. The Sun didn't just want her to follow the arrow and gather the starbridges. The Sun wanted her following and helping Aeliana.

Gaeren stood, running a hand through his hair in agitation. "What does this have to do with"—he glanced at the others before leaning in close—"with her? With the starbridge?"

Dozens of possibilities flashed in the recesses of her mind. "Perhaps everything."

CHAPTER 35

GAEREN EXCHANGED a wary glance with Riveran, aware of Thallahan and Breeve watching a few paces away. They'd never seen Orra anything other than composed, but now, there was a madness in her that seemed to be crawling out. Larkos' suggestion about witches came back to Gaeren, unsettling him even more. He wanted to trust her. Especially now that the stableboy proved she'd been leading him the right way. But he needed her to speak clearly.

Gaeren leaned in to whisper, "Is she still alive? Can we help her?"

Orra peered up at him through watery eyes. "What did Enla tell you about Lovers' Falls?"

Gaeren stilled. He'd never told Orra about Enla's visions.

"What did Enla see?" Orra pressed.

Gaeren raked a hand through his hair. "She told me to stay away from it." He glanced over at Riveran. "And to keep Riveran close." He supposed he could add the bit about remembering his bond, but that felt irrelevant right now.

"And yet you're willing to go there." Orra's brow creased, but she didn't seem any more upset than she'd already been, just thoughtful.

"If there's a need to. Each of Enla's visions are only one of a hundred paths."

"Perhaps Enla doesn't want you finding Aeliana."

Gaeren's entire body tensed at Orra's accusation. He wanted to deny it, to say that Enla would only dissuade him from something that wasn't safe. But wasn't Enla trying to control what he did back in Elanesse? She was the future queen, and she would make sure that his actions protected Elanesse, not just him.

He glared up at the others until they took several steps back, giving him the privacy he needed. He bent forward once more with a heated whisper. "Why did you tell me Daisy was with a human and the couple using blood magic when she's with progenies?"

Orra gave a light laugh. "She was. Back on Bamboo Island. But now I suspect…she's with many progenies. I can't say for certain."

Gaeren frowned.

"But to answer your question…yes. We can still help her. If we go. Now." She stood, using Gaeren's shoulder to push herself up.

He followed, but while Orra seemed reinvigorated and ready to move forward, Gaeren felt even less confident. Going after Daisy felt right, but it would mean going back on his promise to Enla, which always felt wrong.

Orra turned once more to face him. "You think you're torn between two decisions. But you don't realize they're connected."

He stiffened. Was she reading his thoughts? When a noetic tried using their skills on him, he usually sensed the prick of the invasion, but he hadn't felt a thing.

"You're right not to trust Mayvus."

Gaeren stiffened. "Mayvus? What does she have to do with Daisy?"

"Mayvus is more of a threat to Enla than even you realize." Orra's gaze softened. "And Aeliana's the only one who can save your sister from Mayvus."

Gaeren's throat felt raw with his breath, his fears exposed. "So by protecting Aeliana I can protect Enla?"

"I can't guarantee that. There are always other factors."

"How do you know all this?"

She sighed. "We share the same power source. While you grow into your magic, mine is fading. But it's still stronger than yours. For now."

He nodded. It was one of the clearest truths she'd told him. "Are you still tracking the starbridge? Or do you track Daisy?"

"I track Daisy to find the arrow."

Gaeren frowned. "It's an arrow?"

"All four need to be found. Not just to help Aeliana and Enla. But to fix what's broken in the world."

Her words were as vague as always, but they made his heart pound. He'd always felt deep in his bones that his drive to protect Daisy was more than a childhood promise, that finding Daisy and the starbridge would lead to bigger things. He'd never imagined it would connect Daisy to the bigger things waiting for him back home. Or even bigger things that went beyond his family's rule. His family had never seen Mayvus as a threat, had never wanted to. Knowing his instincts held merit gave him validation, but it also made the threat feel ten times more real.

It was possible Orra was still leading him on, saying the things she knew would matter even if they were lies. But even without trying to tap into his second spoke, he sensed her words were true. He couldn't live with himself if he gave up now and crawled home to Enla without answers. He had to see this through.

He would find Daisy and protect her, but he would also find the golden arrow. He could even search Lovers' Falls for the cutlass while they traveled past it. Even if Orra was wrong about its location or importance, it was worth checking. Especially if it could all help him find proof that Mayvus couldn't be trusted.

His sister's warning flashed through his memory as if his starlock intentionally summoned it. *Trust Riveran to have your back. And stay away from Lovers' Falls.* Enla wouldn't approve of any part of this plan.

"So we head for Lovers' Falls, and you'll pick up their trail again?" He pursed his lips, mapping out the travel in his head. The road from Valorian would go through thick forests that might slow them down. At this rate, it would be better for Gaeren to travel inland from Lovers' Falls to Elanesse instead of trying to take Daisy back to *Starspeed*. Larkos could take the ship home.

The idea didn't sit well with him. Larkos was the one he trusted most. He'd much rather have the older man by his side than Riveran. But Larkos was also the only person he trusted to get *Starspeed* home safely.

Now he'd be fulfilling the worst of Enla's visions. The ship would return without him. Would it ease her fears to learn he stayed behind for a purpose? Probably not.

Gaeren would likely miss the dignitaries, but if he brought back proof of Mayvus' threat or aid in the form of starbridges, all might be forgiven.

"If we move fast enough, we should intersect their path before the trail has gone." Orra scanned the nearest buildings before letting her gaze fall on a large inn, then spoke loud enough to include Riveran, Thallahan, and Breeve. "They'll have horses there."

"You aim to steal them?" Riveran rubbed his forehead under his cap, and Gullet squawked, shifting as he sensed Riveran's nervousness. If they were caught stealing, even Gaeren's status couldn't save Riveran. He'd be hanged.

"Let me get coin from *Starspeed* while I give Larkos orders," Gaeren said.

"I thought you already did all that," Riveran said.

Orra raised her eyebrows, waiting for his answer as well.

Gaeren shrugged. "I may have gotten distracted verifying Orra's story. Can you blame me? She's not the most forthcoming."

Thallahan snorted, which made Breeve chuckle.

"We can pay for the horses and still be on our way before the moon's reign," Gaeren said.

Deep howls came from the forest, and Riveran shuddered. In the coming weeks they'd be traveling through those same trees with full-grown winex at their prime. Orra had better be right about this.

She kneeled on the dirt once more, this time like a stubborn mule waiting out its owner's patience. "I'll leave without you if the trail begins to fade." She closed her eyes, hands in the dirt, and with the backdrop of her stillness, it was like the moon began to rise faster, its zenith too imminent for Gaeren to return in time.

Riveran grabbed his arm before he could turn back to Valorian. "Is En—is your sister in danger?"

Gaeren stiffened. "My sister is fine as far as I know."

"Then who is she talking about?"

Gaeren glanced back at Orra's strange countenance, more to avoid Riveran's prying gaze. Why was Gaeren so desperate to keep it secret?

If they found Daisy, Riveran would know. But if they didn't find her, Gaeren couldn't bear pity from a traitor.

"No one you need to worry about." He yanked his arm out from Riveran's grasp before leading Thallahan and Breeve back to town.

Gaeren let the sailors choose their own path. It was no surprise that they chose the ship, but Gaeren sensed their relief at even being given the choice. All the sailors walked a thin thread, working for the prince they were supposed to want to overthrow as Recreants. It was one thing to make voyages under his authority, but it was another to follow him through southern lands in plain sight of all their fellow Recreants, marking themselves as Loyalists even if they weren't.

By the time they reached *Starspeed*, it was late enough that Gaeren only expected a skeleton crew left to guard it.

"Back so soon?"

Gaeren jumped despite his relief at Larkos' voice. Twice in one night, he'd been foolish enough not to tune in to his surroundings. The older man stepped from the shadows where he'd been leaning against the dock's post. A pipe rested between his fingers, and smoke billowed around his head. When he brought the pipe to his mouth, the motion drew Gaeren's eyes to his new tattoo. The Wheel of Magic and its faded rim taunted Gaeren as a reminder of all the ways Larkos had said the world was breaking down.

According to Orra, that brokenness could be fixed.

"There's been a change of plans," Gaeren said. "Tomorrow morning, you'll sail back to Elanesse without me."

Larkos raised a brow and sucked on his pipe. One glance at Thallahan and Breeve sent them scurrying aboard *Starspeed*, out of earshot.

"Riveran and I will return by land. Give Enla my regrets." Gaeren clenched his teeth before going on. "Tell her I hope to return before the dignitaries, but if not, it will be worth her wait. There are red bush leaves drying in my quarters. She can grind them up for tea leaves for our mother. Oh, and grab the Sundial shell from my shelf. I meant to help Erech find one for his sisters." Gaeren grimaced, wishing he'd had the time to follow through on that promise himself.

Moonlight reflected off the water, making the questions in Larkos' eyes dance. "What should I tell the men?"

"Thallahan and Breeve overheard enough to keep them talking for the entire trip back."

Larkos grunted and let out a puff of smoke. "Are they gonna say you're looking out for your men or for yourself?"

Gaeren tensed. "What's that supposed to mean?"

"You shirk your role as throne warden to your sister, but not because you think someone else has the right to step into that role. Be careful you're not still entrenched in the way you were raised—the way they hammered the lies into your brain until they sounded like truth." Larkos leaned forward, tapping Gaeren's temple with his stubby fingers. "If you're doing something that matters, Thallahan and Breeve will see that. If you're going off on treasure hunts, well, they'll see that too." His words held no bite, but they still stung.

"This isn't just about treasure hunts." Gaeren ran a hand through his hair and stepped away from Larkos. "This decision is best for everyone. For the men, for me, for our nation." He bit his cheek. Enla wouldn't like it, but that didn't mean it wasn't the best decision for her either.

"That's all I asked, then. Just making sure you're looking out for the men. It matters if you want them to look out for you." Larkos winked, unconcerned over Gaeren's irritation. He blew smoke out the side of his mouth. "Taking the lasses with you?"

Gaeren opened his mouth to agree, thinking of Orra, then froze. "Oh, Sun's fire. Lenda!" He spun to face the town as if he could see her beyond the town's revelry. Gaeren doubted Orra would wait much longer. There was no chance for him to warn Lenda or send her back to the ship. "I'll need you to send a sailor to collect her in the morning. Take her back to Elanesse."

Larkos chuckled darkly. "You really are determined to make her hate you."

Gaeren frowned, remembering Enla's insistence that Lenda go with him. What had Enla seen in the paths without Lenda? Something that wasn't good for Gaeren or for Enla's plans for Gaeren? He shook the thought away, hating that Orra's suggestion could make him question his sister's motives.

"She's not ready for this kind of travel," Gaeren insisted. "It's for her own good."

Larkos only laughed harder, waving Gaeren toward the ship to gather his supplies. Despite the older man's teasing, it would be hard for Gaeren to leave behind the father figure, especially knowing he'd only have Riveran and Orra for company.

Thallahan and Breeve offered their assistance, going so far as to help him find and load three horses. He headed for the place he'd last seen Orra with her hands buried in the soil, but when the fields came into view, Orra and Riveran were gone.

He rubbed his horse's side, hoping it would cancel out the agitation the black gelding was sure to be sensing. The gelding snorted and turned, showing off the white stripe down his nose like the fur on the back of a skunk. A howl whined in the distance, and the chestnut mare he'd taken for Orra and the roan gelding he'd taken for Riveran grew equally nervous, pulling at their bits. He'd attached their reins to his own horse, and the three started a strange dance.

He'd have to ride toward Lovers' Falls. Catching up wouldn't be an issue with them on foot. The bigger concern was passing them. Gaeren rode to the edge of the forest, where he let his mount lead, the horse finding the path familiar to him into the woods thick with bamboo and vines that looked threatening by the light of the moon. Another winex howled.

Gaeren heightened his senses, preparing to tune in to his surroundings for any danger when something swooped from the sky and dug claws into his shoulder. He readied himself to attack, pulling energy from the starlock burning over his chest before recognizing the bird nipping at his ear.

Gullet.

The hawk readjusted, its claws finding new places to make holes in Gaeren's shoulder. He winced as blood beaded up on his shirt.

"Am I supposed to be thankful he sent you to find me?"

Gullet's beady eye stared back. Memories poured through Gaeren without his permission. Finding the bird when it was just an eyas, his soft brown feathers tickling Gaeren's skin as he slept in Gaeren's arms. Helping Riveran feed him, then laughing as Riveran took to carrying him around like a baby. Riveran training him to hunt and Gaeren recalling the bird's memories to speed up recognition of Riveran's whistles. Gullet returning the favor by pooping on Gaeren's head.

"Yeah, you know I don't like you. I probably like you even less than I like Riveran."

The bird cocked his head, then took off, the scrape of talons when taking flight more painful than the initial landing. Gaeren followed the hawk as it flew from tree to tree, and before long, his senses caught the trail of heat, the memory of Orra and Riveran, just ahead of him in the woods.

He nudged the gelding's side, picking up the pace. When Gullet disappeared, Gaeren knew Orra and Riveran had to be around the bend.

"Took you long enough," Riveran complained the moment they were in sight. Still, he beamed at the roan before holding out his hand and complimenting the horse in hushed tones. Gaeren pictured Riveran in the royal stables, taking a hand from stall to stall, reassuring each animal individually. What could Riveran have accomplished if he hadn't been stripped of his starlock?

He shoved down the twinge of remorse. Riveran didn't deserve his pity. It was too close to understanding, and Gaeren could never understand how a man who had loved a woman could break the bond connecting them. Gaeren might not love Lenda, but he still wouldn't break their bond.

Gaeren winced as his bond mark twinged, a reminder of how he'd left Lenda back in Valorian. Breaking a bond was dishonorable, but was it any better than marrying a bondmate you could never love? A sense of longing flared in Gaeren, one that left him uneasy. He still hated Riveran for what he'd done to Enla, but a small part of him was jealous of the other man's freedom. It made Gaeren no better than the traitor.

Orra ran a calming hand along her mare before leaping astride her back and silently taking the lead.

Gaeren followed, not bothering to see if Riveran fell in line.

CHAPTER 36

As Aeliana's consciousness returned, fear pricked the fuzzy edges of reality. It made no sense, because for the first time in a long time, she felt almost no pain. The peaceful trill of birds met her ears, and bright light discouraged her from fully opening her eyes.

She gasped, sitting upright and blinking against the day's light. "Cyrus?" she croaked out.

"Hush, love, he's fine." Iris sat by her bedroll, urging her to lie back down. "He'll be back any moment. Sylmar and I stayed behind while the others went hunting."

As if summoned by his name, Sylmar shuffled from the cookfire to Aeliana's side.

"What happened?" Aeliana remembered the sprites and Lovers' Falls. She remembered Cyrus, dead, then alive as she pulled the water from his lungs with magic. Her starlock burned against her chest as if pulsing with the memory, but Aeliana reached for it anyway, reassured by its presence, its heat.

"We were hoping you could fill in some of the details." The gravel in Sylmar's voice seemed thicker. "You've slept straight through the night and half the day."

Aeliana turned, taking in the way he leaned against his staff even as he sat on a stack of bedrolls at her back. It was then she noticed the entire camp was packed up. Only Kendalyhn and Holm remained at the cookfire, but the supplies had all been tucked away for the journey. It was as if they'd been waiting for her to rise, and the moment she did, they'd begin their trek again.

"How do you feel?" Iris asked.

"Better?" Images of Cyrus floating in the lake flashed through Aeliana's mind. The moment the energy surged through her, drawing the water from his lungs. The instant relief, followed by the energy's return, the pain resurfacing. She shuddered as she recalled the dark spirits.

How had they survived?

"The man," she whispered.

"Hmm?" Sylmar leaned in, weary eyes sharpening at her words.

"There was a man who came. I didn't recognize him." The moment the words left her mouth, she realized they weren't entirely true. He'd been familiar, but her focus had blurred with his approach, and she couldn't remember many details.

Sylmar and Iris exchanged a glance.

"Cyrus said as much." Iris tucked the stray hairs of Aeliana's braid behind her ear, stroking her head like a child woken from a nightmare. "The man was gone before the rest of us arrived. We've searched the surrounding area, but there's no trace of him."

"It would seem he doesn't want to be found," Sylmar ground out.

"You say that like it's a bad thing." Aeliana couldn't help leaning into Iris, taking the comfort the older woman offered. The lack of pain made her aware of the exhaustion that couldn't be resolved with sleep alone.

"If the man could be trusted, why wouldn't he show himself?"

"Because there are nine of us?" Aeliana suggested. "Because he doesn't know if we can be trusted?"

Sylmar gave a dissatisfied grunt in response.

"Why did you leave camp?" Iris ducked her head with the question, but not quick enough to hide the wetness in her eyes.

"I'm sorry; I—" She hesitated, wondering how much they knew, how much she should say. Did they know she'd used blood magic and called the dark spirits? And then gone after the sprites? Or did they think she'd simply gotten lost and ended up near Lovers' Falls? She'd been desperate, but, in hindsight, her plan, or lack of it, had been foolish. "Did I—was anyone else hurt?"

Sylmar shook his head, watching her too closely.

"What about the dark spirits?"

"We saw them from a distance," Sylmar said. "They were gone by the time we reached you."

Aeliana frowned. She shouldn't have used blood magic to save Cyrus. There had been enough energy with the starlock, more than enough. But it had been instinctual to draw from her wounds. And she couldn't help wondering if it acted like a catalyst, giving her access to the rest of the power deep within her. But it had brought the dark spirits again. How had they not overtaken her?

Footsteps rustled through the trees on their left, and Cyrus and Lukai stepped into the clearing.

"Aeliana?" Lukai broke into a grin, then quickened his pace.

She stood, warmth filling her chest at the concern in his voice, the relief on his face. He pulled her into a hug, the sensation of his arms around her both foreign and strangely familiar. He pulled back to study her face, which felt tight with scabs. He brought his hands up to her jaw, cupping her face and running his thumbs over her skin.

Aeliana's cheeks heated at the intimate gesture, far too aware of everyone watching. But relief spread wherever his thumbs brushed, and soon her eyes were closed as she leaned into his healing touch. His hands lingered a moment longer after he'd fixed even the tiniest of scratches.

"Thank you," she whispered, then stepped back and cleared her throat.

He reached for her hand, turning it over to trace a finger along the mark of her bond. "I felt your pain when I searched for you. I thought —it felt like you were dying."

"She was," Cyrus said.

Aeliana's awareness expanded as she took in the return of those who'd been hunting. Holm and Kendalyhn had already started skinning the hide from some type of deer. Jasperus pulled Sylmar aside for an update, and snippets of their conversation carried back to Aeliana, the subject centering around whether it was too late in the day to travel farther.

Weapons had been dropped in a circle at the base of a tree that was wider than Aeliana was tall. The white bow and arrows Lukai had given her stood out in contrast to the green moss and brown trunks, beckoning Aeliana to come pick them up.

"Can you tell us what happened?" Lukai asked.

"I found Cyrus in the water. I was certain he was dead. The sprites told me—"

"You spoke to the sprites?" The disapproval in Sylmar's tone hurt more than Aeliana cared to admit.

She hesitated, catching more frowns and averted gazes from the others. "I thought the cost would be high to me. I didn't realize…"

No one spoke, not even those around the cookfire a dozen paces away. Only the sound of Holm's knife gutting the poor creature broke the silence.

"I'm so sorry. When Sylmar suggested I be bled to help the weaning process, I didn't want to endanger the rest of you. Only it was too much for me to do it alone. I grew desperate. I knew you were coming, but so were the dark spirits. It was the only way I knew to keep you safe." She covered her eyes with her hands, shaking her head as she tried to understand her own justification. "Only I still put you all in danger."

A hand rested on her back, and Iris' soothing voice murmured in her ear. "It sounds like you had two terrible choices, love. We'll never know if the other choice would have been worse. No sense dwelling on it."

Aeliana turned to Cyrus. "But you could have died because of me."

He shook his head. "I slipped into the water and hit my head because of my own clumsiness. You saved my life. The Stars watched out for us both. There's nothing to forgive."

She opened her mouth to protest more, but Iris interrupted. "What's done is done." She clasped Aeliana's hand between both of hers and gave a squeeze.

Kendalyhn snorted from her spot at the fire, drawing Aeliana's eyes up. Several others avoided her gaze, replacing the reassurance Iris offered with doubt.

"What did the sprites say?" Cyrus asked.

"They said I would have to sacrifice you if I wanted to be rid of my magic." When Cyrus' face paled, she quickly added, "Which is why I assumed that if I was willing to use my magic, I would be able to save you."

"You used your magic?" Sylmar stood, leaning against his staff. Still, a newfound strength emanated from him. Hope.

Aeliana squared her shoulders, shocked at the ripple of pride running through her. "I did."

She'd had to use blood magic, something that still left her feeling sick, but after tapping into the power in her blood—sensing where it resided and how she could access it—it was like a thread had been left behind, keeping her connected to it. She sensed that if she tried again, it would be easier to access, without the blood magic.

Sylmar's lips spread out, the motion probably a smile, but his scars twisted his face into more of a grimace. "Then we can start training again. You were motivated to heal, to save. That's as good a test as any for now. Even if that skill fades as you're weaned off blood magic, it's something we can start with for your training." He glanced at Lukai. "Your bondmate can help."

Lukai gave Aeliana an almost shy smile.

Aeliana turned to Cyrus. "After you…were revived, a man came. Who was he?"

"I don't know. He showed up out of nowhere, but it was like he knew you'd be there. I don't know how to explain it. It was like he breathed in your energy and then pushed it out toward the dark spirits. Sent them away."

"You told us he had no starlock," Sylmar said.

"I didn't see one. But Velden keeps his hidden. Maybe he did too."

"How was he able to send away the dark spirits?" Every muscle in Aeliana's body tensed. Her guardians had welcomed the dark spirits. She'd thought that if they came that close, it was impossible to resist inviting them in. Even Sylmar had sounded hopeless when he'd said they'd deal with them.

"It wasn't his blood that called them," Sylmar said. "If you'd been alert, welcoming them in, it would have been far more difficult. Still, it's an impressive thing he did."

She shuddered, knowing she'd almost welcomed the dark spirits. If they'd reached her before she found the sprites, would she have been unable to resist? Or if she hadn't used up all her magic to save Cyrus, would she have let them fuse with her like Arvid and Vera had?

"At first I didn't see you breathing," Cyrus went on, "but the stranger—it's like he was healing you. One moment he was gripping your arms so hard I thought he'd break them, the next he was barely touching your starlock, your wrist, your throat. When your breath came back, he nearly collapsed, but the others shouted from the opposite bank, and he took off."

"What did he look like?" Aeliana asked.

"My height, brown hair." He gestured toward Sylmar and Velden. "Somewhere between them in age."

"That doesn't narrow it down much," Velden said with a smirk. "Somewhere between youthful wisdom and declining senility."

Sylmar glared at Velden.

"Tattoos on his hands?" Aeliana asked.

Cyrus nodded, eyebrows raised. "You remember him?"

Aeliana hesitated, not quite sure if she was remembering him from that night or if she remembered him from one of her Awakening visions.

"We'll camp here a second night," Sylmar said. "Rest and recover."

There were mixed reactions around the fire, maybe because they were still so close to Lovers' Falls, or maybe because they'd already broken camp. But people dispersed, dragging out the equipment they'd previously packed away.

Sylmar turned to Aeliana, a question in his eyes. "Do we train tonight while it's fresh in your mind? Or rest and train tomorrow after the pressure has built?"

"Tonight." Aeliana straightened to her full height. It wasn't much compared to Cyrus and Lukai, who still loomed over her, but at least she was eye level with Sylmar's stooped figure. "But probably not how you're thinking. There's only one time I've used my magic with focused control."

She passed the horses, making her way to the tree to snatch up the white bow and arrows. She recalled the sensation of drawing the arrow back against her cheek, only this time she remembered the tug in her chest, the desire for the arrow to meet its mark combined with the energy to put it in its place. The pull of magic.

She hadn't carried these for days, even before they had the horses, because she'd been too weak. Even now, she lifted the bow and every muscle in her arms argued with her plan.

But it was the only plan she had.

Planting herself a fair distance from the others, she created targets in her mind, honing in on the distant node of a bamboo tree, then the large leaf of another. As they'd traveled, most of the bamboo had given way to lush forests, the trees' canopies blocking out all Sunlight. The leaves were as big as her body, and the flowers held intoxicating scents.

She picked each of these objects out, aiming for them like Cyrus had taught her, then pulling energy through her body and arms to create force behind the arrows like she'd accidentally done before.

She used such a minimal amount of energy it was almost laughable, but her aim was true every time. The physical energy required to lift the bow was probably more than the relief she gained from expending the energy in her blood. But after emptying her quiver, she thought she detected a change. An ease to her lingering pain.

A few daisies had sprouted by her feet. For the first time, she saw them as a mark of her power rather than a mark of her sins. She still slid her boot over them as she turned, wondering if Sylmar would consider this a waste of time.

The entire camp had stopped to watch, a few shocked expressions scattered amidst Sylmar's and Cyrus' pride.

"I taught her. Just last month." Cyrus beamed.

Velden chuckled. "Yes. Her skill is most definitely a product of your excellent teaching."

Lukai quietly gathered her arrows before dropping them in her quiver. He smiled, his gaze boring through her eyes until her soul felt bare. She didn't turn away, daring him to see her from every vulnerable angle. Almost desperate for him to find her wanting in some way.

His smile widened, and he nodded. "Again."

CHAPTER 37

To Gaeren's relief, Orra kept them riding at a fast pace. Still, it took them a week to reach the creek running from Lovers' Falls. Hints of the other group's trail became obvious to Gaeren: an old cookfire, prints in the soil from both man and horse. Orra's promise that they were gaining on Daisy no longer felt far-fetched.

"We'll camp up ahead," Orra said, surprising Gaeren.

They still had a fair amount of time before the Sun's sleep, and she'd been as determined to catch up as he was. Still, he was grateful. If they traveled much farther, it would be difficult to sneak out to the Falls during the night to hunt for the cutlass and return by the Sun's morn.

"Maybe we should go farther from Lovers' Falls," Riveran said. "Aren't the sprites close?"

"Close enough." Orra's murmur came so low Gaeren wondered if he imagined it.

Gullet took to the treetops as if he understood it was time to make camp, and when they rounded the bend, it was clear someone else had recently camped there. Flattened grass and evenly cut bamboo shoots surrounded an old cookfire, showing evidence of more than a half-dozen people having slept in the clearing. Gaeren's eyes narrowed at the surrounding trees filled with pock marks, like someone had been practicing archery.

He closed his eyes, searching for wisps of heat left from the memory of the people before him, but it had been too long.

"They must be at least a few day ahead of us," he said.

Orra nodded. "It should still be easy to catch them within a week or less. We can travel faster with fewer people." Her words were accurate, but something about the way she said them felt like a lie.

"I wouldn't mind riding later into the night," Riveran said even as he dismounted. His roan gelding stomped, eager to be freed for grazing. Riveran had taken to calling him Maw, claiming he didn't know which of his animals had the bigger mouth. "Get away from the sprites faster, catch up with the progenies sooner. Sounds like a win all around."

Orra glanced at Gaeren, her face passive. "No sense wasting a good campsite."

She knew. Of course she knew Gaeren's plans. Was there anything she didn't know? He slid off his horse, using the gelding to hide his irritation more than his guilt. Besides, she wasn't doing anything to stop him. She wanted him to find the cutlass. He paused. Did that mean he'd find it? How much did she really know?

The gelding turned, nipping at Gaeren's cheek, reminding him to keep working at the ties.

While the horses grazed, Riveran and Gaeren gathered sticks and dead grass, making use of the cookfire pit left by the group before them. Orra pulled out the bedrolls while mumbling to herself.

"You won't tell me who you're after, but you'll follow her blindly?" Riveran asked.

"She's been right so far." Gaeren shrugged, eager to change the subject and avoid more of Riveran's questions. "Besides, she's better company than Lenda."

Riveran laughed. "Lenda would be lying on the bedrolls moaning about how miserable she was. I would have put valerian root and winter cherry in her soup tonight."

Gaeren couldn't help grinning, remembering all the times they'd used the herbs' mild sedative properties to knock out Enla so she wouldn't follow them on their night excursions. Fed by emotion, the images grew stronger in his mind. Enla's frustration as Gaeren distracted her with a long, boring tale. Riveran's panic as the herbs got stuck in his pouch and wouldn't shake free. Enla's rage when she finally caught them. It was probably the real reason she employed a food taster.

"Do you actually have some out here?" The plants grew in drier areas farther north and east, but they could come in handy if he wanted to slip away from camp.

Riveran hesitated. "I've been taking it nightly ever since…"

Ever since Enla.

Gaeren frowned, different images flooding his mind. Enla's tears, the fresh scar on her palm, Gaeren's outrage. And then Enla's pleas, pleas for Gaeren to spare Riveran's life.

He probably would have killed Riveran that night if it weren't for Enla's request. And he would have hated himself for it the next day. He hated himself even now, knowing he'd wanted Riveran dead. And yet he still felt it would have been deserved.

He left Riveran to tend the fire by himself.

Orra had disappeared, so Gaeren took his time rubbing down his horse. The gelding nipped him again, but this time it didn't hold any urgency, and Gaeren felt like he'd earned some of the animal's favor. He ran a hand over the smooth white hair that stood out from the rest of the beast's black. "You smell like a skunk, too, so Skunk it is."

The horse whinnied, and Gaeren took it as acceptance of the name.

As the Sun finally slipped behind the trees, he rubbed down Orra's mare, figuring Riveran could take care of Maw. Orra returned, surprising them all with half a dozen fish.

"We'll need our energy for the tasks ahead." She set to work cleaning and cooking the fish, and if Riveran noticed that she gave double portions to Gaeren, he didn't say anything.

The evening stretched out long for Gaeren as he waited for the others to fall asleep. Finally, near the height of the moon's reign, he crept away from camp, following the creek as it widened, drawing him toward the deepening sound of rushing water.

He shivered, pausing to tune in to his surroundings at every rustle in the trees, every plunk from a fish in the creek. When he rounded the last corner and the waterfall came into view, he couldn't help stopping to admire it. A fine mist shrouded the base, and the drop had to be at least the height of two Sungazers, maybe three.

But where were the sprites?

Another rustle from the woods beside him automatically brought his hand to his sword. He tuned in to the noise, sensing a shape expanding until he recognized it as—

"Riveran?"

The other man stumbled out of the woods, taking in Gaeren's sword with a crease in his brow.

Gaeren sheathed his sword with a growl muffled by the roar of the water. "What are you doing here?"

Riveran shrugged, glancing back the way he'd come. "Orra woke me. Said I needed to come help you."

"That woman." Gaeren frowned, but it was Enla's face that came to his mind, Enla's words that returned to haunt him. *Trust Riveran to have your back. And stay away from Lovers' Falls.* Was there any point in following the first half of her advice if he was already ignoring the second? "Not a word, do you understand? Not to me or the sprites. Not to Orra when we return."

Riveran nodded, but his face had a sickly pale look under the moonlight. It contrasted the X on his forehead, which drew Gaeren's gaze.

"Come on," Gaeren mumbled, turning back to the path. Footprints led the way, small boots that probably belonged to a woman. His chest tightened with fear even though Orra swore Daisy was still alive, maybe even improving. What if Orra was wrong? What if she didn't actually know everything?

Because Gaeren only saw footprints leading up, not back.

Even if Riveran spoke, Gaeren wasn't sure he'd hear him over the water. When the path diverged, Gaeren hesitated, peering over the cliff's edge. One path seemed to lead straight to the waterfall. The other might have wound farther up to the waterfall's source. He wiped at the sweat running down his neck, but it was immediately replaced by warm mist from the falls.

He tuned in to the heat of his surroundings, but nothing stood out besides the critters and plants inhabiting the small caves and crevices on the cliff's wall. Riveran nudged Gaeren's elbow, pointing at a muddy boot track just beyond, on the path leading to the waterfall.

What if there was only a set of tracks leading this way because Daisy was still here? What if Orra had been willing to stop because she knew?

The fear in Gaeren's chest crawled up his throat, leaving it tight with worry. He rushed along the path, watching for more tracks, both terrified and relieved when they continued. When the path stopped at the water's edge, wet rocks hid any more signs of Daisy's steps, but scattered on the liana vines and dry portions of rock were sprinklings of dried blood.

Gaeren placed his fingers over the blood without hesitation. The images that came were blurry and rushed. Scratches on his face here, a shove in his back there. Pain and anguish. Betrayal. Despite the memories being incomplete, two things were clear to Gaeren: there was a cave beyond the vines, and the sprites had pushed Daisy off the cliff.

Gaeren unsheathed his sword, then slashed at the vines with unbridled fury, as if the vines were the sprites and not merely the door to their lair. Moonlight poured through the opening, revealing two skeletons so tightly wrapped it was hard to tell where one began and the other ended.

Riveran let out a sound of disgust and stepped away, but Gaeren was already walking through the remaining thorny vines, a small prick on his cheek reminding him of his own vulnerabilities. Inside the cave, the rush of water echoed from all directions, deafening Gaeren and leaving him on edge. He waited for his eyes to adjust, allowing time for Riveran to pull out his daggers. They moved as one, the years they'd spent apart vanishing as they came back to back like they'd trained, shimmying sideways through the cave.

Trust Riveran to have your —

Gaeren shook away the memory of Enla's words, not wanting to acknowledge the remainder of her advice. As the space grew smaller, Gaeren replaced his sword with the daisy dagger.

Nothing stirred, or at least nothing they could see. Moonlight faded behind them, but an iridescence came from the cave walls, some type of luminescent algae lighting their path with its eerie glow. The deeper they walked into the cave, the more the sound of rushing water faded, replaced by the plink of water dripping deeper within. Eventually, to Gaeren's relief, the space widened, and he swapped out his sword once more.

"Is this the end?" Riveran asked, his voice hushed. The cave extended to twice their height, branching out in a near circular shape that was as wide as it was tall. They turned in a circle, greens and blues reflecting off their blades, but besides the path they'd come from, there seemed to be no other entrance or exit. Piles of small critters' bones rested at the edges, blood dotting various parts of the ground and walls. There was more rock than soil beneath their feet, but, strangely enough, a handful of flowers grew from a small patch of dirt. The unnaturalness of it bothered Gaeren more than anything else he saw in the cave.

For a moment, Gaeren was disappointed. He'd wanted a confrontation. He'd wanted to pull information about Daisy out of the creatures who'd hurt her by hurting them back. He mentally shook himself. This was better. Orra had said Daisy was fine, and without the sprites here, it would be easier to look for the cutlass.

Gaeren drew energy from his starlock, pushing it out to form a small light in the palm of his hand until it grew to fill the room like a torch. He systematically searched through the bones, then palmed the walls of the cave until Riveran did the same.

"Maybe if I knew what we were looking for," Riveran said, "I would be able to help better."

"A weapon," Gaeren said. "You'll know it when you see it." He clenched his jaw, afraid the full answer might come tumbling out otherwise.

Gaeren wasn't sure how long they searched, but they left nothing unturned. He even pulled up the roots of the strange flowers, pawing at the soil in case the sword had been buried.

"It should be here!" He pounded a fist on the wall. Maybe there was a hidden room, a hollow space behind all the rock. He hit the solid surface until the sides of his hand were scratched and raw. Finally, Riveran pulled him to the center of the room, wrapping Gaeren in a bear hug from behind to protect them both from Gaeren's flailing limbs.

"Why did you come here? What are you looking for?" Riveran's words felt loud in Gaeren's ear as the other man pinned his arms at his sides. Gaeren went limp, and his starlock's light snuffed out, but still Riveran stayed at his back, clearly anticipating that Gaeren would get a second wind.

Trust Riveran to have your back.

"A cutlass." It was almost painful to admit the words out loud. "A starbridge."

Riveran dropped Gaeren's arms, coming around as if assessing his face for truth. "So you did learn something from the book."

Gaeren shrugged. "More like Orra."

"So she's leading you to the starbridges? I thought maybe it was the girl."

Gaeren sighed. Might as well come clean about everything. "She's leading me to both."

Riveran went still. "She found Daisy?"

"The light we saw last moon—it was a starbridge. Same as the light I saw when I was a boy."

Riveran's eyes flashed with understanding. "You think she came back."

"I know she did. Or Orra knows she did." He hated revealing these things to Riveran, of all people, but it was also a weight off his chest. A sense of freedom came with sharing the burden, especially with someone who already knew the history of his obsession.

"You finally figured it out." Riveran grinned, shoving Gaeren's shoulder like he had when they were friends. "Wait, then why are you still looking for a starbridge?"

"I'm being extra thorough?" Gaeren gave Riveran a weak smile, not really sure why he'd gotten so angry over the missing cutlass. It was like his inability to find the thing represented how much his hands had been tied in this whole hunt for Daisy. Just one more thing he couldn't reach. "Orra made it sound like the starbridges are important. Even if I can't figure out why Orra wants them, if I can get across the barriers, maybe Enla would see my itch to travel as an asset. I could form alliances with other nations on her behalf instead of being stuck back at the palace."

"Ah. Such a noble excuse to keep adventuring." Riveran's dry tone earned him a punch to his shoulder.

Then, trusting Enla's instincts instead of his own, Gaeren told Riveran everything, from the handwritten notes in his copy of *The Sins of the Stars* to Orra's suggestion that Enla was keeping Gaeren from Daisy. By this time, they'd settled comfortably in the cave, the glowing algae and the things it lit up or left dark no longer threatening.

Riveran traced his finger in the dirt, taking everything in with a frown. "Can Orra be trusted? It seems like you should trust your sister over a stranger. Orra has her own agenda, and like you said, she knows too much. She could be twisting everything to fit her plans."

"It's something I've considered." Gaeren shook his head. "I don't know. I'm just not sure how dividing Enla and me would fit into any of her plans."

"She's not exactly forthcoming with her plans," Riveran pointed out. "She just keeps guessing yours."

"She wanted me to come here, or, at least, she didn't stop me. Even though she knew Enla didn't want me coming here."

"Does Enla know why you wanted to explore Lovers' Falls?"

Gaeren flinched, both at his sister's name back on Riveran's tongue and the half-truth he'd had to tell Enla. "Initially I told her I wanted to ask the sprites for support even though I meant to ask them to find Daisy. Once I had Orra to track Daisy, I didn't need their help. But then Orra told me about the cutlass, and it seemed like an opportunity I shouldn't pass up. Not when we were so close to it."

"But Enla didn't mention anything about a sword," Riveran said slowly. "She would have seen and known, which means you probably don't find it."

"Or that she doesn't want me finding it." Gaeren groaned and rubbed his hands over his face. "Why can't her visions be more absolute?"

"But Orra told you the sword was here?"

"She wrote it in that book you gave me. And hinted at it in her story about Lady Redwood and Captain Moss."

Riveran shook his head slowly. "That peddler must have lied. He said the book had been in his possession since he was a boy. Close to fifty years. Unless—is it possible Orra's been setting you up?"

Gaeren frowned. "Setting me up for what?"

"Well, your sister didn't want you coming to Lovers' Falls, which means there's nothing good in her visions here. What if Orra knows what the sprites will do, and she wants you, her competition for the starbridge, out of the way?"

Riveran's words left Gaeren tense, itching to tune in to his surroundings, which suddenly seemed sinister once more.

"I mean, it's not like the sprites are known for their hospitality," Riveran added with a laugh.

Just as Gaeren sensed their heat, the weight of them in the room, one spoke, the words echoing through Gaeren's mind more than the cavern.

Such harsh words. We can be quite hospitable to guests.

Riveran and Gaeren jumped to their feet, hands on hilts. A creature moved from the shadows, its fluttering wings glowing green in the light of the algae, but Gaeren suspected they might be a golden yellow in different light. No mouth moved, but the room reverberated with the creature's words.

You, however, have come uninvited.

CHAPTER 38

DESPITE THE SPRITE'S veiled threat, Gaeren still didn't unsheathe his sword. Thankfully Riveran took his cue from Gaeren, maintaining a defensive stance. Sprites weren't known for being combative, just… tricky. He tried not to grimace at the creature's oddly human form, limbs all curled in like a corpse's. It blinked down at him, leaving behind a sticky-looking residue over its large black eyes.

"We apologize for intruding." Gaeren inclined his head. "We'll take our leave."

Leave? But you just got here. The sprite's tone held a childlike pout. *You haven't even made a request.*

Gaeren hesitated. At one time he'd wanted their help finding Daisy. A part of him still did. It burned to have so many obstacles when he was so close to finding her. Maybe they could help the process along, guarantee his success.

I thought so. What is it you seek?

"No, Gaeren." Riveran backed away toward the cave entrance, beckoning for Gaeren to follow.

The sprite glanced at Riveran, taking in the X on his forehead with mild curiosity. Then it turned more fully toward Gaeren, as if Riveran no longer mattered. *Go on. Tell me.*

Gaeren's mind raced, visions of both Daisy and the cutlass warring with common sense. Sprites couldn't be trusted. He reached out, tuning in to the sprite's memories, hoping for a hint of what happened to Daisy when she was here, but he met a wall as blank as the one in Orra's mind.

The sprites had power. Power to give him Daisy or the cutlass.

If he was being honest, he wanted to cross the barriers. To see the world. To make it bigger like Orra had suggested. Enla wanted to unite the Vendarans, but what if they could connect with the Lorvandans or Sayhleens? What if they could learn from the Ahmranans and Dehvlonians? What if they could unite all of Rhystahn?

He let his request roll around in his head, dissecting it until he felt sure the sprites couldn't turn it against him.

"I want to cross the barriers with Daisy," he said.

The sprite blinked again, the residue disappearing. It studied him for so long he wondered if it hadn't heard. Or if he hadn't heard its reply. Finally, the sprite cocked its head. *Unless you also seek an early grave, you will take her across a barrier in your lifetime.*

A rush of elation swept through Gaeren, but he held it in, waiting for the catch, for details—for the cost. But nothing more came. "That's it?"

The sprite's head tilted the other way as it blinked again, the cloudy film making Gaeren cringe. *Is that not what you seek?*

"I just—how will I cross? And what is the price for your assistance?"

Riveran shook his head slightly, a warning in his eyes.

We're not assisting you. It was already foretold.

Gaeren let the sprite's words run through his mind again. Gaining access in his lifetime could mean forty years from now. Was this one of their tricks?

"Foretold for when? I want to protect her now." He glanced at Riveran. Who knew how he'd interpret this request? Sun's fire, he wished he'd been able to come alone. "I want to cross the barriers to protect her and unite all of Rhystahn."

Riveran stiffened beside him, but Gaeren kept his eyes on the sprite, watching for any response.

Then you want to start a war. The words sounded cold and emotionless, but Gaeren detected a hint of morbid interest.

"What? No. I just want to make the world bigger." He winced, not sure if the sprites would see that the same way Orra did.

A strange tinkling sound filled the cavern as the sprite reared its head back. Was it laughing? *Assistance will be granted, but the cost will be high.*

"Don't." Riveran's hand gripped Gaeren's arm, but he shook the other man off.

"What's the price?"

The creature ignored his question. *You expected to find the cutlass. It's not here. A woman took it long ago. Gave it to her husband. It's a relic that's been passed on from collector to collector, each oblivious to its true value.* Another blink, and the film disappeared. *You're better off finding the fish first.*

"Fish?" Gaeren frowned, pulling out the book and flipping to the handwritten notes. He studied the symbols again. There was a sword, an arrow, a circle, and an oval with a triangle. There wasn't any fish. Unless…

He squinted at the oval and triangle, seeing how together they might make a fish. It even looked like there might have been a dot off-center in the circle, representing an eye. And next to the symbol was the question: "Sayhleen?"

His heart pounded so hard it felt like his starlock bounced against his chest with the reverberation. What if each starbridge was assigned its own land? The arrow took Daisy to and from Lorvandas. The cutlass and… whatever the circle represented would take someone to Ahmranas and Dehvlon. Which meant the fish would take them to Sayhla Island.

"Where is the fish?"

The sprite cocked its head once more, analyzing Gaeren like a calculative predator.

If you take the opportunity to cross barriers, you will lose much. Enla will lose more.

"No," Riveran whispered.

Gaeren took a step back. "Why Enla?"

The sprite blinked, and the residue returned. *A fisherman in Andel has the fish. He doesn't know what he holds. He mounted it on the wall of his ship's cabin, along with the hide of—*

"Stop!" Riveran flung himself between Gaeren and the sprite, daggers out, but not to defend against the sprite. His crouched stance and narrowed eyes faced Gaeren, ready for the offensive. "You can't play with people's lives. It's not your right to decide what Enla will lose. What if she loses her life? It's too high a price."

Gaeren hesitated. Riveran put a voice to his own concerns and fears, but they hadn't said she'd lose her life. What if they meant she'd lose her brother? Or her throne? If the Recreants got their way, Gaeren might need the starbridges to take Enla to safety too.

She forfeited her life the moment she aligned with Mayvus. Crossing the barrier won't change that.

Every nerve in Gaeren's body tingled with the sprite's words. "She's not aligned with Mayvus." Though as he said the words he recalled Enla's talk of confirming Mayvus' spiritual authority. Had the dignitaries already come? Was Enla already in danger?

The sprite lifted a shoulder. *Believe what you wish.*

Gaeren's hand twitched, brushing the handle of his sword. The fluttering of the sprite's wings intensified, drawing attention to movement around the perimeter of the room. A dozen or so other sprites came out of the shadows, all varying shades of green in the algae's light.

"They can't be trusted." Riveran inched toward Gaeren, forcing him to step back. "We need to leave. You don't want to owe them anything. The price they're extracting is too high."

It's not high enough. It's practically a gift.

Gaeren licked his lips, his mind racing as the other sprites crowded in. Riveran shifted his stance, no longer facing Gaeren but the sprites that were hemming them in.

"If Enla's life is forfeit, and crossing the barrier can't change it, what can?" Gaeren asked.

The sprites all paused in their advance.

You have a different request? The one he'd been speaking to shifted, its face bulging as if it had cheeks for a smile. *Usually these sorts of deals require one life for another.*

Riveran shook his head so violently his neck cricked. "No. We need to go. Now." He shifted both daggers to one hand like the X on his forehead and used his free hand to yank on Gaeren's arm, but Gaeren held his ground.

"How does it work? Whenever she would have died, I die in her place?"

The sprite bent in close, and both men held their breath, their fear reflecting back at them from the shiny bulbous eyes.

Something like that.

It appears he does seek an early grave. The second, higher, voice came from behind them, and both men turned. It was impossible to tell which of the new sprites had spoken. *So much for crossing the barrier.*

This is my deal. The first sprite's voice rose while it fluttered around the men as if shielding them from the others, then it turned to face them once more. *Which will it be?*

Gaeren shrank back, realizing the question was directed at him.

Your life for Enla's? Or access across the barrier at a high cost to Enla?

It wasn't much of a decision when the sprite put it that way.

"Neither," Riveran said, dragging Gaeren around the sprite's side, but the sprite shifted, hovering in their way.

Neither is no longer an option. Its wings beat faster, and the other sprites came even closer, the sound of all their wings almost deafening as it echoed through the cave. If Gaeren didn't take a deal, he and Riveran wouldn't leave the cave alive. Besides, he had to protect Enla. She would always come first.

"Take my life for Enla's," Gaeren said.

The sprite's cheeks rose again, making Gaeren wonder how a smile without a mouth could feel so sinister. *So be—*

"No!" Riveran lunged, driving his dagger into the sprite's chest. Its wings faltered, dropping it a foot, then another. Squeals erupted around the room, like pigs being slaughtered. When the sprite finally fell, the color drained from its skin starting at the tips of its wings and appendages and ending at the center of its chest, where the dagger still rested, drawing life from the creature's body.

Gaeren unsheathed his sword and cast a furtive glance at the other sprites, but all their eyes rested on the dying sprite, their wails of mourning still echoing off the cave's walls. The sprites were so caught up in their grief that it was like Gaeren and Riveran no longer existed.

This time Gaeren was the one to tug on Riveran's sleeve, pulling the other man from his shock. They slipped between two sprites, and Gaeren was surprised at the tears tracking down the creatures' faces. As they rushed to the cave's exit, a hiss erupted from behind them, like steam being loosed from a valve. Gaeren turned, and despite the algae being the only source of light, a clearly defined blackness rose from the now dead sprite, the stretching of a soul, filling the room and blocking their view of the remaining sprites.

It swept past them, through them, taking the exit before them, stealing their courage along with it. It left Gaeren's chest cold and his fears magnified, and when the blackness abated, a dozen pairs of livid eyes focused their filmy gazes on him.

As one, Riveran and Gaeren turned, running through the tunnel. Gaeren hoped the creatures' wings would hamper their progress. Screeches exploded from behind them, the echo making it impossible to tell how close they were. At any moment, Gaeren expected a claw on his shoulder, a yank on his foot. Maybe this was how it had gone for Daisy. Maybe the sprites were just waiting for Riveran and Gaeren to reach the mouth of the cave so they could push them off the edge.

He reached out, tuning in to the mind of the closest sprite. The memories were a blank wall, just like the other's had been, but its mind buzzed, like the hivemind of a colony of bees.

The gravel Gaeren had hardly noticed beneath his feet on the way in now felt like a slippery death trap. When Gaeren skidded, Riveran practically lifted him off the ground with one hand to right him. A glance back proved they'd made some ground, but the shrieks confirmed it wasn't enough. What would happen when they left the cave? Surely the sprites could fly faster than the men could run.

When the space widened again and distant moonlight lit the way, Gaeren's hope momentarily soared. Except the sprites could now use their wings more easily. This time when Gaeren turned, a deep orange sprite barreled down on him, hands spread with talons extended. Gaeren stumbled, falling on his hip, then backside, and before he could right himself, the sprite's claws raked across his chest. The pain didn't come at first, but it quickly turned to a debilitating burn, like acid that ate at the edges, then sank deeper and deeper.

By now Riveran was dragging him out the cave's opening, the dozen sprites still bearing down on them.

As a rainbow of arms and claws reached out for Gaeren, Riveran mumbled, "Sorry, friend."

The ground flew out from under Gaeren as Riveran yanked him up. Before Gaeren could get his bearings, the other man's arms were wrapped around him, pulling him over the edge. Together, they choked on water as they fell.

CHAPTER 39

"Do you ever get the feeling that we're being followed?" Cyrus asked, glancing over his shoulder. After a week of riding through rainforest, they were finally sloping down toward the grasslands. "Or watched?"

Aeliana tried to follow his gaze as she redid her braid while atop her horse. They were at the back of the pack with Lukai, and Aeliana only saw trees and the setting Sun behind them.

"Sylmar's always watching me," she said. "Like I'm going to sprout wings one morning."

"No, I mean over the last week."

Aeliana glanced at Cyrus. Worry pinched the skin between his eyes.

"Ever since Lovers' Falls?" Lukai asked.

"Exactly."

"No." Aeliana tied off her braid, flinging it back over her shoulder. "No one's following us. It's the dark spirits. Once you've seen them, they plague you. They can be hundreds of miles away, and it will feel like they're around every corner."

Cyrus hummed his disagreement. "I don't think they're interested in me. I don't have starblood."

Aeliana squirmed at the twinge of jealousy inside her. She wished she didn't have any starblood to interest the dark spirits either.

"Interesting." Lukai tapped his lips. "That actually gives me an idea for Aeliana's training."

Aeliana winced as he nudged his gelding ahead to catch up with Sylmar. The last several nights had been filled with theoretical and mental exercises from Sylmar, followed by hands-on physical training with Lukai, both of which came after archery with Cyrus. She reached her arms overhead, stretching out sore muscles.

"We'll stop here for the night," Sylmar called out from ahead. "Starting tomorrow, we'll be more exposed in the grasslands. This part of the country is still feeling the bite of winter."

Aeliana and half of the others were already sliding off their mounts, eager for the day of riding to be done. This was the hardest part of the day for her, when the buildup of her blood was most painful. Sylmar had made it clear that weaning would take weeks, but it was getting more manageable with each day.

Manageable didn't erase the panic and fear. She still scanned the skies, still tried to hide her scars. Guilt still plagued her no matter how many times the others reassured her she was doing nothing wrong. She wasn't sure if it was possible to unlearn those reactions. She wasn't sure she wanted to get comfortable enough to unlearn them. Not when she could slip back into blood magic.

"Ready to practice?" Cyrus offered her the white bow and quiver in exchange for her horse's reins.

Even after the day's ride, her arms itched to hold the bow, but the others pulled packs off horses and began setting up camp. "We should at least help with the bedrolls first."

"Your job is to train." Sylmar stepped between them, taking her horse's reins. "What happened to your arm?"

She glanced down at the bruise and cut on her forearm. "I'm not sure. I've always bruised easily. I never seem to remember what I bump into."

"Or what cuts you?" He reached out a hand as if he might touch the scab, and she jerked away.

"I didn't cut myself." Her words came out defensive, far more likely to sound like a lie even though they were true.

Sylmar's eyebrows rose. "That's not what I was suggesting." He paused, holding her gaze.

Aeliana forced herself to do the same even though shame coursed through her.

"After you're weaned, we can add you into the rotation for chores." He led the mare to a small clearing where the other mounts were tied.

Aeliana took the bow and quiver from Cyrus, and, despite Sylmar's probing, she smiled as she slid her hands over the smooth curved wood. As painful as this time of day was, it was also becoming one of her favorites. She wound her way through the eastern side of their temporary camp until the trees thinned and the edge of the grassy plains could be seen. She'd had to make do with shorter distances because of the rainforest's wild growth, but now she'd be able to practice longer ranges, challenging her skills, or really, her magic.

A breeze lifted her hair, the coolness stealing her breath. Deep in the thick, humid forest, she'd forgotten that it was winter, that back in Gahldric Valley spring would soon be announcing its return. But the higher they rose in elevation and the farther they got from the rainforests, the more the seasons would be apparent.

Choosing a tree as her mark, she pulled an arrow from her quiver and readied her bow. Her first shot hit the exact knot she'd been aiming for, at least twenty paces away. After several days of training, she could pull energy from her starlock without blood, and she could move the energy some, even if it was just to put more force behind her arrows.

Now Sylmar wanted her honing in on her senses, making slight adjustments to heighten her awareness of the sounds, smells, and movements around her. It felt impossible, but a week ago, she had said the same about pushing her energy out without blood. Now she felt like she had a loose hold on her energy levels, an awareness of when it was becoming too much and how to lighten the load.

"I'll miss the rainforest," Cyrus said, coming up behind her with his bow.

She let off a second shot, this time hitting the mark from thirty feet. Her starlock warmed its approval.

"I'm guessing you'll like Islara, too," Aeliana said. "Sylmar said it has pine and oak trees, fields of crops as far as the eye can see—a valley surrounded by majestic mountains."

"Sounds a bit like Gahldric Valley." Cyrus' wistful tone made Aeliana pine for something else, a sense of belonging, a family to make a place feel like home.

She grabbed another arrow. "We'll get you back home with Bartholem." She stumbled a bit over his grandfather's name, wanting to tag on his grandmother's name too, but Della wouldn't be waiting for him to return.

"After we get you to your mother," he said. "Somehow I think you need her as much as she needs you. And far more than I need to return to Lorvandas."

The priest in him found ways to see straight to her core. What might have been unnerving was more of a relief. Having him understand without having to explain was so much easier.

"Besides," he added, "if the Stars intend for me to return, I will."

She raised her arrow against her cheek. "Save that discussion for my training session with Sylmar. I like seeing him get worked up over your theology." Her arrow missed its mark, a testament to her lack of focus rather than a weakness in her magic.

Cyrus chuckled. "Jasperus gets adamant about it too. Tried telling me about a book called *The Sins of the Stars*. The title alone is so blasphemous I have trouble imagining what words it might contain."

"Velden told me it's their version of the Great Divide," Aeliana said. "Says it explains how the Stars went against the Sun's wishes by dividing the lands and putting up the barriers. That they thought it was for our good, but really it was their pride. They thought they knew better than the Sun."

Cyrus shuddered. "I find that scarier than those dark spirits of yours."

Aeliana grimaced as she let loose another arrow. They continued while the others set up camp, and before long, Holm and Velden came back with an antelope they'd shot in the grasslands. It was the largest thing they'd hunted since the journey had begun, and Aeliana couldn't take her eyes off the way it lay at an odd angle when Holm set it down by the fire, how the breeze ruffled the tuft of hair at its throat. Holm placed a hand on the antelope's flank, then surprised Aeliana by reciting some sort of prayer or blessing.

"We thank the Sun for your sacrifice. You were blessed with life and now you bless us with life. May the Sun's light always shine upon you." He paused for a moment, then patted the flank once more before pulling out his knife.

Aeliana turned away, catching sight of Cyrus' wrinkled brow. He'd spent so many nights out worshipping the Stars, while the Vendarans often said a quick prayer to the Sun when they rose. She tilted her face toward the Sun, which now hung low, nearly ready to sleep. She sensed it energizing her blood, her starlock. She could understand why the Vendarans, especially the progenies, worshiped the Sun.

While growing up, Aeliana's trips to the Stargazers had become fewer and fewer as Arvid and Vera had tightened their hold. Still, she'd grown to love the Stars even if she didn't understand why they would create things and people so bent on destruction. But it hadn't been her way of life like it had been for Cyrus. She didn't mind if the Vendarans served a different creator. It was how her parents would have raised her, and that alone was something she wanted to respect.

Holm and Kendalyhn made quick work of skinning the antelope and dividing up the meat to cook. Lukai raised his eyebrows and beckoned to Aeliana. The scent of food cooking was quickly becoming her cue for more training.

They settled at the edge of camp, where Lukai brought her through the same exercises Sylmar usually did: enhancing senses, pushing and pulling energy in and out of the starlock. The repetitive skills calmed her, putting her back in a better frame of mind. The chirps and chittering in the trees around her grew louder even without her enhanced senses as the Sun slid beneath the canopy of trees.

"Healing is simply taking things a step further," Lukai said. They sat on a bed of grass and leaves so thick that Aeliana was unable to tell if the trees had shed or if vines grew along the forest floor. "Instead of enhancing your senses, you enhance your awareness and understanding. As you become aware of what's wrong with a person's body, you can adjust it. Sometimes it takes the smallest of tweaks, a simple push or pull of the energy around it. Sometimes it's more like a yank or a shove. Think of it like bringing scales back into balance."

She nodded even though his words sounded too theoretical to actually apply.

"Cyrus," Lukai called over his shoulder.

Aeliana straightened. With her senses still heightened, she became acutely aware of her heart's increased rate. Cyrus grinned as he sat next to them, rubbing his hands together.

"Am I getting boils? A fever? A broken bone?"

Aeliana grimaced.

"A cut." With the flick of his wrist, Lukai pulled out his knife and made the slightest cut on Cyrus' finger. It was more like a needle prick than anything else, but still, Aeliana gasped.

"I told Sylmar no cutting." Her words came out on a growl.

"I don't even feel it," Cyrus reassured her.

"No." Aeliana moved to stand, but Lukai grabbed her wrist. For a moment, panic wove through her, but his touch was gentle as he kept her by his side.

"I will not torture him. I will not cut him in the ways you've been cut over the years." His hand moved to slide over her scars, and she couldn't stop the shiver that came at his touch. "But he's the best person for you to practice this type of injury on. You're still weaning from the buildup of magic in your system. But there's more to it than that. Starblood draws you to use it because that's how you were trained. Any time starblood is drawn, you'll sense its pull."

She yanked her hand away from Lukai's and glanced at Cyrus' finger. A tiny drop of blood beaded up around the broken skin. It didn't call to her the way her own had. Instead, there was a tug, a desire to find blood she could use.

This was the idea he'd gotten from their discussion earlier. To maim Cyrus because he didn't have starblood to tempt her.

"When you need to heal a half-light, you won't have time to wonder if you're using the magic in their blood or in your starlock. If you start developing your opposite spoke, you'll have the same problem in battle with the Zealots."

"My opposite spoke?"

"Healing falls on the constructive somatic spoke. You'll continue to develop that skill, but strengthening it will also open up the possibility for you to mirror that skill. It's how Sylmar's able to do minimal healing even though he's a destructive somatic. And I can injure—not like Sylmar can, but enough for it to be an advantage in a fight. Kendalyhn can sift through the lies of someone's past, understand the drive behind their actions, but she can also see a bit of the truth. It's like the Wheel's way of finding balance as your abilities grow."

Aeliana squirmed. "I don't want to learn to injure other people."

Lukai leaned to the side, bringing his face into her line of vision. "That's fine. For now, we're focusing on healing without blood magic. If we start with Cyrus, we'll know you're not using blood magic. Then we can work our way up."

She nodded, hating that he was right. If she was ever going to be of any use to this group, she had to get past this. Cyrus held out his finger, and Aeliana placed a shaking hand over his palm. She closed her eyes.

"Start by enhancing your senses," Lukai whispered, his breath hitting her ear in a distracting way as he leaned forward to watch. "Feel where his blood pulses, where the smallest parts of his body work. Do you sense the brokenness?"

She reached, pushing the slightest bit of energy from her blood through Cyrus' hand, its power tracing through to his finger, where there was a dissonance.

"Yes," she whispered. Without further instruction, she sensed the need to make it right, to adjust the wrongness. It was different from the time they'd tested her, when the need had been more of a feeling. Now it was like the need was a guide. She pushed her energy through his hand more, urging the broken parts to mend, the misaligned areas to weave together.

Cyrus inhaled sharply, and Aeliana opened her eyes.

The drop of blood remained, but Cyrus wiped it away, revealing the tiniest of scars, like a newly healed wound.

"Perfect." Lukai grinned, running his finger over Cyrus' to remove the scar. "At this rate, we can practice a dozen more times before Kendalyhn's done burning the meat."

CHAPTER 40

A MOAN WOKE Gaeren from a deep sleep, confusion making him slow
to realize the sound came from his own throat. Cool hands touched his
brow and cheeks, then water dribbled over his mouth. He let his lips
fall open, eagerly sucking down water dripping from a cloth.

"Take it easy." Orra's voice brought clarity with it, and the memory
of the sprites flowed through his mind. "There's plenty more to be had,
but it won't do you any good to bring it back up."

"Riveran?" Gaeren croaked the word out, cracking his lids open.
Sunlight blinded him, forcing his eyes closed once more.

"He's fine. Off looking for food and firewood before the Sun's
sleep."

Gaeren tried to process the last thing he remembered. He shifted,
pain shooting through his chest. The claws of the sprite, the deluge of
water, then nothing. He was dry, and it was daylight, so he must have
slept half the day away.

"Your fever was high all day," Orra said. "I'm glad to see it's
broken."

Gaeren's eyes flew open. He fought the Sun's glare to focus on
Orra's furrowed brow. "All day?" He adjusted, moving to sit up
despite Orra's protests. The world spun slightly, but he suspected the
pain in his chest prevented him from passing out. Deep breaths
brought his vision right again. "We lost a day of travel?"

"The sprite's poison spread through your body. We had no choice." Orra's lips lifted in that maternal smile, but it held a hint of curiosity. "I've never seen anything like it. The sprites are…complex creatures. I wish I'd spent more time studying them."

She sat back on her heels, bringing the rest of their camp into focus. A fire had burned down to near coals, but their bedrolls remained out, their supplies still unpacked. Had they completely lost track of Daisy due to his sickness?

"It would take a dozen lifetimes to parse out the sprites," Riveran said from behind Gaeren.

"Perhaps." Orra pushed off her heels to stand, twisting the blond braid at her wrist once more.

Riveran handed her an unfamiliar bird he'd shot and a basket holding mango and avocado. "There's not much in the way of meat to hunt in these jungles."

Orra's gaze softened as she scanned the trees. "Something I've always appreciated about the rainforest."

Riveran nudged Gaeren's thigh with the toe of his boot before sitting across from him. "You look better."

Gaeren frowned, already feeling sick from his short time sitting up. Bandages covered his chest, but blood still seeped through in various spots. "How did you get me out?"

Riveran shrugged. "You're heavier than you used to be, especially soaked in water, but I dragged you to the bank."

So much felt left unsaid, but as Riveran and Orra exchanged a glance over the fire, Gaeren suspected that was all he would get. Had he been that close to death? He watched as Orra plucked and cleaned the bird with practiced ease. Riveran stoked the fire to life before using his knife to peel and quarter the fruit.

Something had changed between them in the sprites' cave. Gaeren couldn't quite go back to hating his old friend. Not like before. Enla had told him to trust Riveran, and Riveran had saved his life. But the memory of Gaeren's hatred still plagued him. It left him staring at the other man for too long, contemplating how he could hang on to his anger, how he could reconcile the conflicting feelings.

"What?" Riveran frowned as if Gaeren's stare caused him physical pain.

Gaeren let his gaze drift to the fire. "Thank you," he mumbled. He could say more—he was sorry for dragging Riveran into that mess; it had been a mistake to meet with the sprites—but the two words had been hard enough after years of hatred.

From the corner of his eye, he caught Orra trying to hide a smile. Suspicion flashed through his mind. Had Orra somehow orchestrated this moment?

"What happened with the sprites?" Orra asked. "Riveran hasn't been willing to say too much." The question made Gaeren want to hold the information close. For once, Orra didn't know everything, and maybe that was a good thing.

"They chased us out of their cave."

Riveran's frown deepened, but he didn't contradict Gaeren's half-truth.

Gaeren shifted so he could lean against one of their packs, the motion making him aware of just how weak he was. He closed his eyes, the sounds of his companions preparing a meal almost musical enough to lull him to sleep. He forced himself awake, focusing in on Orra.

"Can you still trace her?"

Orra's gaze sharpened at his use of "her." She gave a slight nod of acquiescence. "Even though I sense them moving farther away, the pulse grows louder. She's gaining strength."

He didn't fully understand her meaning, but it was enough. Daisy was safe, for now. "Where to next?"

"You aren't going anywhere for at least another day, but then we take the roads north. They're headed for Islara, but they're taking the easier roads. We can keep your familiar face from prying eyes and catch up faster if we take the switchbacks out of the valley."

Gaeren frowned. Islara was safer than the smaller southern towns they'd skirted, but lately the Islarans hadn't been clear supporters of the Elanesses. Most southerners were Recreants who despised the royal family's rule; they had enough distance that they wanted to rule themselves. But the Islarans were far enough north to play both sides.

Throughout his parents' rule, they'd been docile, but as Mayvus' authority had grown, the Islarans had pulled back. Some had started defying the guards sent out for their own protection, while others refused to pay taxes from their hard-earned money.

Enla had wanted to send him as an ambassador, to feel out where their loyalties lay. But he would have arrived with an entourage of guards. Now, if they figured out who Gaeren was, they might not welcome him in their midst. Not without Larkos to defend his intentions at the very least. Still, he could assess the risks of them defecting and report back to Enla. It might appease some of her frustration at his change of plans.

Even Larkos would be grateful for the update. If the southerners gained support from a city like Islara, they could very well try to overthrow the throne. Gaeren appreciated their aim for democracy, but that would be a much bloodier end to the monarchy than Gaeren wanted, which left him a fine line to walk as he felt out loyalties.

"Enla's going to kill me," Gaeren muttered.

"Maybe we should go straight home, then," Riveran suggested without looking up from his task.

Did he miss his wife and child? The familiar hostility burned within Gaeren's chest, but it was tempered by curiosity. What kind of woman had taken Riveran's attention off Enla?

"I've likely already missed the dignitaries, but there will always be more of them to meet." Gaeren left the rest of the statement unspoken. There was only one Daisy.

He tensed as his memory retraced the horrible mistake of meeting with the sprites. Before they'd tried to kill him, they'd given him hints and clues to the starbridges, but who knew if he could trust them? Enla might not be ready to go up against Mayvus, but she certainly hadn't aligned with the questionable priestess. Had she? Her plans to define Mayvus' role as a spiritual leader had sounded more like a way to put Mayvus in her place.

He met Riveran's eyes across the fire. For once, he was more aware of Riveran's solemn gaze than the awful X tattooed on his forehead. Riveran had said the sprites couldn't be trusted, but he'd also believed they would exchange Gaeren's life for Enla's. He'd trusted them to exact a price even if he hadn't trusted them to give good information. And yet he'd stopped Gaeren from sacrificing his life for Enla's. Should Gaeren be grateful? It was hard to feel grateful when he would always pick Enla over himself.

He wished Larkos could have stayed with them. What would he give for the older man's advice right now?

Gullet stood by Riveran's boot, pecking at some entrails Orra had thrown his way. Gaeren frowned, recalling the way Gullet had found him in the forest outside Valorian.

"Does Gullet remember how to send messages to Enla?"

"I don't think he could forget." Riveran hesitated, glancing at his hawk. "But he's never traveled across a distance like this with a message. Would it be worth the risk?" His eyebrows rose, asking a different question.

Should they involve Enla?

Gaeren was tempted to ask Orra's opinion, but Riveran had already pointed out they had even less reason to trust her for true words. Even though she'd clearly nursed him back to health, he might not know how well he could trust her until they reached the starbridge and Daisy.

Until he saw what Orra wanted from her.

"Enla will want to know about the delay—and why." Gaeren said the words slowly. Orra might be fully occupied with preparing dinner, but she was also fully listening. "The sprites can't be counted on for support"—Riveran snorted at the understatement—"so finding Loyalists in Islara might make the additional stop valuable in her eyes. Besides, she's not just my sister; she's my future queen. I trust information with Gullet and Enla more than couriers."

Riveran stopped cutting the fruit, staring at the fire as though looking through it. He leaned toward Gaeren and whispered, even though both of them knew Orra could likely hear everything with her undefinable magical senses. "I'm not questioning Enla. I'm questioning you. What did you mean in the cave about uniting all of Rhystahn? About making the world bigger?"

Gaeren tensed, but Orra continued roasting the meat without pause. "Exactly what I said. I want to see Lorvandas and Vendaras together. Sayhleens and Dehvlonians, even Ahmranans. I want to see our world united again."

"Under whose leadership?"

Gaeren rolled his eyes. "Not Mayvus', that's for—" He cut off, tuning in to his memories. He hadn't actually asked the sprites to make sure Rhystahn wasn't united under Mayvus. Is that why they'd suggested he wanted war?

His heart rate picked up speed, his mind flying through their conversations. Which deal had the sprites taken? The one putting Enla at risk or the one sacrificing Gaeren? Would he cross the barrier with Daisy, or would he save Enla's life?

Or had Riveran's interference made both null?

"Your family rules over the people, not Mayvus." Riveran sat back, his brow furrowing. "She's just a priestess. A servant of the Sun tucked away in the mountains who has an unhealthy amount of influence, but she's not ruling."

"For now," Gaeren muttered. "The House of Elanesse is in trouble. If we're not overrun by Recreants, we're soon to be swallowed up by Mayvus' control."

"I think we should wait." Riveran's voice rose, drawing Orra's attention. "This is a conversation best had in person. It will be easier for us to see where loyalties lie."

Something in Gaeren's chest flared. "We? Us?"

Riveran flinched and looked away. "You."

Gaeren immediately regretted his anger, but he'd already thanked Riveran. He wasn't quite ready to issue any apologies. He reached into his pack, pulling out pen and parchment. "I'll keep it brief. I can't keep her in the dark even if I wanted to. She'll sift through my future. But telling her my plans at least shows her why I'm not doing everything she wants."

Riveran nodded. "You know your sister best." The words came out hollow, leaving Gaeren less confident in his choice.

His message was short, nothing more or less than Enla needed to know. She'd be too irritated to read more anyway, or she'd read into his words, thinking his actions far more sinister than they were.

Dearest Enla,

Going by land has proved difficult. Riveran has stayed by my side like you asked. I haven't learned enough to come home yet. We move on to Islara, like you originally asked. I'm sorry I didn't arrive in time to meet the dignitaries from the Myndren Mountains.

Your favorite brother,

Gaeren

By the time he was done, the meal was ready, and Gullet was cleaning his feathers, the entrails all consumed. Gaeren rose, grabbing a tree in a wave of dizziness, then ambled over to Riveran and Gullet. He bent down and pulled out his starlock, keeping his back to Orra, who still hadn't seen his starlock's shape. On either side of the teardrop was a wooden bead, one round and one square. He separated out the wooden sphere, bending even farther to put it in Gullet's line of vision. The hawk cocked its head, then tapped at the bead with its beak. After a moment, it grew restless, shuffling between Gaeren's and Riveran's boots.

"That's right, you dumb bird; you get to go on a long journey to find Enla." He tied the parchment to the hawk's leg, expecting Riveran to protest. But Riveran's gaze was fixed on the other bead, the square block—the bead Gaeren had used to send messages to Riveran. A strange expression crossed Riveran's face, and for a moment Gaeren felt embarrassed that he'd kept the beads all these years, like they spoke of an underlying trust he hadn't meant to convey.

But then Riveran toyed with his bracelet, which held the same wooden sphere for Enla and a pyramid bead that Riveran and Enla had used to direct Gullet to Gaeren.

Gaeren knew for certain that Enla still wore the beads. She'd moved her heart-shaped starlock to her forehead as a show of power when she'd come of age. She didn't fear people knowing its shape. But the leather cord remained around her neck because it still held their childhood trinkets. The three would always be tied together, and Gaeren didn't know what to do with that.

"What if we're both wrong about Enla? What if she really is aligned with Mayvus?" Riveran whispered, one hand on Gullet to delay his flight. Doubt settled in the lines of his face.

Gaeren glanced at Orra, who was busy dividing the cooked bird up onto large leaves for the three of them. If Orra knew what the sprites had said, would she forbid him from passing the message along?

"I thought you said the sprites weren't telling the truth."

Riveran's eyes blazed. "I was willing to say anything to get you out of that cave—alive. Maybe you didn't realize that whole thing was a trap."

"A trap?" Gaeren gave a short laugh. "It's not like they lured me in. I knew the risks. I went willingly."

"At least you can admit you made a stupid choice."

Heat flooded through Gaeren, leaving his fingertips tingling, itching to release his energy. "If we're discussing momentary lapses of judgment, I think some of your actions could stand to be examined."

"I've offered to let you search my mem—"

"You think I want to see how you betrayed my sister?" Gaeren stood, practically spitting the words out in his disgust. That kind of proof of Riveran's infidelity would make it impossible to hold back his rage, no matter what promises he'd made to Enla. "It's like you're asking me to put a knife in your back while you sleep."

"Why haven't you already?" Riveran stood too. "Your status would let you get away with murder."

"Now that you have that X, it wouldn't even be considered murder."

"That's enough." Orra's quiet words from behind Gaeren reached into some deeper part of his soul, pulling him out of his hatred with the shock of ice-cold water. "Even at this distance, the sprites play with your minds, twisting your words and your thoughts until you turn on each other. The food is ready, and then Gaeren needs to rest. If we're ever to get away from this place and its hateful inhabitants, we must eat and sleep."

The two men glared at each other until Gullet nipped Riveran's finger, making him wince and glance down. With a sigh, he released his grip on the hawk, and the bird launched from his arm, making a beeline for the northwest. Gaeren would never admit it out loud, but the hawk was smart. Or he had some small bit of magic in him.

It would take the bird a few days to reach Enla, probably arriving a couple days before Larkos and *Starspeed*. It would take twice as long for Gaeren to reach Islara. He patted down the bandages on his chest with a grimace. Maybe longer with his injuries.

He watched the sky long after Gullet was out of sight, munching on the food Orra had given him without really tasting it. Riveran settled on the edge of camp to keep watch, and Gaeren's stomach turned as the food tried settling.

"You think he's been bringing out the worst in you," Orra said quietly, tossing her leaf and bones in the fire with a sizzle. "But you've chosen to be this way around him. There was a time when he brought out the best in you. It can happen again if you allow it."

Gaeren frowned. Just how much of their history had Riveran told her? That wasn't why he was irritated though. He was irritated because she was right. Over the last moon, his mood had soured. He wanted to blame it on Riveran, but it had far more to do with his fear for Daisy and Enla. And now, for no good reason, he'd just thrown away all the progress he and Riveran had made in the cave. He wanted to be angry with Riveran for Enla's sake. It felt like the honorable thing to do as a brother.

But selfishly, after having his friend back even for one night, he couldn't help wishing he cared a little less about the young queen's feelings and a little more about the ex-friend who had been like a brother.

CHAPTER 41

THE OPEN GRASSLAND soon gave way to woodlands with thick red oak trees and bushy white pines, which gave Aeliana more opportunity to practice archery and made Cyrus more homesick. Days in Vendaras had turned to weeks, and with them the last bit of winter had shifted to spring, leaving their early mornings swathed in fog. That transition meant Aeliana had reached her eighteenth year, a date that had once held potential freedom from her guardians but now seemed far less important than her Awakening had been.

During the day, they trekked northeast toward Islara, and in the evenings, after setting up camp, Aeliana trained with Sylmar or Lukai. When Cyrus wasn't helping her train, he settled just outside camp to worship the Stars. One day out from Islara, Aeliana felt more equipped but no more prepared.

"What happens after we reach Islara?" Aeliana and Sylmar sat on stumps beside each other. She was supposed to be focusing on drawing energy from one side of her body to the other, but she'd already done it ten times.

"We join the army there and march toward the Myndren Mountains," Sylmar said, keeping his eyes closed. "They'll take the wider trade route through the mountains to the north side of Myndren, but we'll cut through the Pass. It's a shorter path that will allow us more time to train, but it's too narrow for the army. After the Pass, we follow the base of the mountains, and it will lead us all the way to the Valley of Krahn, which is the closest place we can gather to Mayvus' doorstep in the Myndren Mountains." He opened one eye to peek over at her. "Now, where do you have your starlock sending all its energy?"

She huffed and closed her eyes again.

Sylmar had a textbook approach. He made her map out the Wheel of Magic, plotting out how the ability to grow things would fall under a constructive somatic, or how a destructive noetic could plant thoughts and emotions in someone's mind. Anytime she struggled with similarities to her guardians' blood magic, he turned it around to something positive. They spent a lot of time sitting like this while she felt for the energy pumping through her veins, practicing drawing it from the starlock and giving it back. She opened her eyes again, catching the last rays of the Sun dipping behind the mountains.

"And then what? We just start shooting arrows at her gate?"

His left eye cracked open. "Something like that." His beard shifted in what looked suspiciously like a smile.

Taking advantage of his rare good mood, she pushed further. "So the army swoops in and clears a path for you to go straight to Mayvus?"

He shook his head. "The army is a distraction. We don't expect to be able to defeat her soldiers or even her. We're outnumbered. So we'll sneak in while our soldiers draw them out. Then we'll steal back your mother and your blood."

He made it sound so easy.

"Who exactly is 'we?'"

"The men and women in this group."

Aeliana watched the others still preparing food. It was the one chore Sylmar hadn't ever assigned her because her training time only lengthened each night. The more she trained, the more comfortable they all got with her, most likely comforted by the false security that her magic was now under control. Even Kendalyhn had warmed up a bit, though Aeliana was often still the recipient of her icy glares.

"They're among the most loyal Recreants. Iris served your mother before you were even born, and Holm was often out being your parents' eyes and ears. Lukai's family sacrificed much of their freedom to bond him to you as a child. Kendalyhn's mother was a priestess who worked alongside Emeris for years, and you know Lukai's family took her in when her parents were killed by Mayvus. Velden and I have spent the last fourteen years training for this moment. And Jasperus…" Sylmar glanced over at the only member of the group who might be older than him before closing his eyes once more. "Well, you should ask him to tell you his story sometime. It's the only one of his I care to listen to."

"So it's this group of nine who will go after the blood?"

"Eight."

Aeliana snorted. "There's no way Cyrus will stay back after all this."

Sylmar opened both eyes, giving up the pretense of concentration. "I was referring to you."

Aeliana's heart picked up its pace. "Why wouldn't I go? She's my mother. It's my blood."

"Exactly. Mayvus will use you to keep Emeris under her thumb. Or she'll brand you and use you against us. Either scenario is bad."

"I thought you needed me to rescue her. You said those who are branded need a connection like that to come out of the prison in their own mind."

He hesitated, and for a moment she thought she'd won.

"Yes, we'll need you to help rescue her from herself, but first the rest of us will rescue her from Mayvus. If seeing you safe and sound away from the Myndren Mountains doesn't recenter her, seeing you in Mayvus' lair certainly won't."

Aeliana scowled but had no argument. Especially when she had so little to offer. Sylmar and Velden concluded she was nearly weaned, but she wasn't so sure. Her pain was minimal and only present near the Sun's sleep, but she sensed herself holding back. When the other progenies practiced, they only did so during the day, draining their reserves and letting the Sun replenish them. She trained at night and never felt herself scraping the bottom of her blood's energy. Not since the night when the sprites had forced her to save Cyrus.

She constantly feared she might use too much.

Still, she sensed her power more clearly—when it was running low or building too high. With the increase in control came confidence and even eagerness. Instead of fearing her power, she wanted to understand its limits. She wanted to know how she could use it to help the others save her mother and get back the golden arrow.

Lukai left the fire and cautiously approached. "Does that frown mean you're ready for combat?"

Sylmar grunted as he stood. "It means she's not getting anywhere with me. She's all yours."

Lukai grinned and held out a hand. The moment he pulled her up and against his side, she felt a blade at her waist.

"What did I tell you about always being prepared to defend yourself?" he whispered. Her bond mark warmed along with his breath on her neck.

"I believe you said something along the lines of 'assume every Vendaran is out to kill you, except for me.'"

He stepped away, the loss of his heat making Aeliana shiver.

"Hmm, I take that back. Assume every Vendaran is out to kill you, including me."

She raised her eyebrows, then pulled a heavy dagger from her belt. He'd instructed her to wear it all the time, to get used to its weight and to practice removing it in one fluid motion.

"Again. Faster," he said.

They moved through several defensive maneuvers before Lukai called over Cyrus and then Jasperus, having her practice on them while he watched.

She preferred his hands-on approach—until it came time for magic.

"Let's see how you do at healing tonight." Lukai held out a hand, slicing his palm with a knife.

He and Aeliana both winced. He claimed he was able to numb his pain for their practice, but with every flinch, Aeliana wondered if he lied to keep her from worrying. The ability to heal was coming easier, but the sight of his injuries only became harder to stomach. And still, the starblood called to her.

"This time try to do it without touching me."

She sighed, knowing it would take longer, if she could even do it at all. But she pulled on the energy from her starlock, drawing it into her body, letting it spread out. When the pressure became too much, she focused on Lukai's arm, as if there were a thread of energy connecting her hand to his skin. This was where she often failed. Without the physical contact, sometimes the connection was never made.

Or worse, sometimes she connected to his starblood. He always sensed the change, describing it like a coolness opposite the starlock's heat. She began sensing it too, which made it easier to reverse directions and find the starlock's heat once more. At first she'd been embarrassed, but he never once berated her for the wrongness of it.

She did that enough to herself.

"There you go." Lukai grinned even though his arm continued bleeding out. She hated the sight of his blood even more than Cyrus'. It poured down his arm, practically begging for her to draw in its power to supplement her own. Healing Cyrus was faster, because with Lukai, instead of adjusting his body with all her focus, she had to reserve some of her power for resisting the temptation of blood magic. Or at least for maintaining awareness so she didn't accidentally use it.

She adjusted his tissue, sensing it beneath his skin as it reconnected. She hadn't hurt anyone since Kendalyhn, and she no longer had the sense that there was this wildness inside her, waiting to crawl out, but that didn't mean she'd never see the dark spirits again. It didn't mean she'd never lose control.

"You're getting so much better at this." Lukai ran a finger over her poorly crafted seam on his skin, smoothing it out. The dried blood remained along with its distracting pull, so when he leaned in, her reaction time was too slow.

Aeliana pulled out her dagger, her grip slippery with sweat after the complicated adjustments she'd done. Lukai would probably make her practice a hundred times more after this embarrassing display. She fumbled to angle it toward his waist, then gasped as his eyes went wide, his body still. The point of her dagger rested a hair from his rib.

"I was—I'm giving you a hug." Lukai's laugh came out strained.

"Oh." Aeliana let her hand drop. They stared at each other for a moment, and Lukai leaned in again, wrapping his arms around her shoulders and bending until their cheeks brushed. There was a rightness to the warmth of his body against hers, but there was also an awkwardness. She didn't know where to put her hands, especially since one still held a dagger. Sylmar and Lukai hadn't trained her on what to do when the enemy gave a hug instead of a swipe.

"Good work," he whispered. "And next time I'll warn you so I don't get stabbed." He pulled away, his lips lifting in a teasing smile. Her breath hitched as the blue of his eyes seemed to expand until they were the sky before her, the firelight's distant reflection like the Stars doing their dance.

When his gaze dropped to her lips, the fire in her belly grew larger, threatening to rise to her chest.

"Lukai?" Kendalyhn called, her steely voice breaking them apart. "I sliced my finger cutting carrots. Could you come help?"

Aeliana lowered her dagger before finally getting it settled back in her belt.

"Let's let Aeliana try." He glanced between the two of them, oblivious to Aeliana's panic.

"I'd rather wrap it up and let it heal naturally." Kendalyhn's eyes narrowed.

"Well, then, it must not be that deep of a cut. I'll look at it after we finish training." He turned his back on Kendalyhn, whose mouth hung open, then sliced his palm and held it out to Aeliana. "Again."

* * *

The next morning, they saddled the horses amidst a chorus of pitiful howls from the winex in the forest.

"I thought they only lived in the rainforest," Cyrus said. "I haven't heard them since we left, and it's been well over a month."

Velden hummed his understanding. "They weren't in the grasslands, and by the time we reached the woods, they had cycled through another life and aged enough that most had fallen silent. These ones are at their life's end, their cries like an old man dying. They go through their entire life with the moon's cycle, then they're reborn again with the new moon. In a couple of days, you'll hear them mewling like kittens."

"How do they survive as newborns? Who takes care of them?"

Aeliana imagined hundreds of miniature Felks lying on rocks like abandoned children.

"Half of them die for that exact reason." Sylmar waved away her concern. "They breed like rabbits during the full moon and bury their eggs like turtles, doubling their population all over again just in time for the new moon. In one sense they're immortal, but in another they're expendable."

Aeliana flinched at his harsh words, but no one else seemed bothered. She supposed that meant Felk was long gone, along with his pack. And wasn't it just as well? He'd wanted to kill her. And yet… he'd spoken. Talking about winex like turtles and rabbits felt demeaning for such an intelligent creature.

The farther they traveled, the more the cries faded to whimpers, but Aeliana suspected it wasn't because they gained distance from the creatures. Rain clouds had come in, the cool scattered showers likely to speed up the dying process for the winex that wouldn't survive this cycle or make it to the next.

It seemed a cruel trick of nature, but would saving them be worse? Having twice as many around at the full moon would be twice as dangerous for humans and other potential prey.

"We'll be there soon," Lukai said as he rode beside her. "Warm baths and beds plus dry clothes for all of us thanks to the faithful Recreants. We all have friends in the city and family in the army. So many people will be eager to meet you. I can almost smell the fire they'll have cooking for us." His grin was contagious, and despite how overwhelming the introductions sounded, Aeliana couldn't help looking forward to the image he'd given her. Her cloak kept her mostly dry, but her hands and face were chilled to the bone.

"I smell it, too," Velden said.

"That's because it's just around the bend," Sylmar confirmed from atop his horse behind them.

"We've heard that before," Cyrus muttered from her left.

"I think I see smoke from Matrina's cabin!" Kendalyhn urged her mare forward, and the horse complied, as if it knew there'd likely be endless grazing and even oats beyond the hill. The road they took from

Valorian brought them in from the east, where a Recreant lived outside town and could connect them with the growing army.

Aeliana rolled her neck, which cracked, then stretched her aching limbs and pruney fingers. It would feel good to get off her horse and have a solid meal and a real bed for the night. A dry bed.

But when Kendalyhn reached the peak, she let out a sharp gasp, reining her mare in.

Moments later, Aeliana and the others crested the hill, several giving their own cries of dismay. The cabin just over the hill was a pile of smoldering ruins hissing from the rain's touch. Beyond it, Islara spread out through the valley far past what Aeliana could see both in width and length.

The entire city had been razed.

CHAPTER 42

Amidst the sprinkling rain, Gaeren breathed in the scent of something smoky, like a campfire. Their proximity to Islara was almost palpable, and every new hint at civilization raised his spirits.

"Gaeren," Riveran whispered.

Gaeren glanced up to where Riveran sat astride Maw, a few paces ahead of Gaeren and Skunk. But Riveran's eyes were on Orra, a smile playing at the corner of his lips. Gaeren swiveled the other direction, turning Skunk so he could get a better look at Orra behind him.

She sat atop her horse, eyes closed, face tilted to the clouds, rain splashing on her face as she twisted the braid on her wrist. Her lips moved, the mutterings unintelligible. Gaeren swore under his breath.

"That's five nights in a row you've gotten stuck with kitchen duty," Riveran said, his voice rising with glee. "Want to go double or nothing? I'm willing to wager that tonight she'll have some sort of vision that requires shoving her hands in the mud."

"I swear you're putting her up to this." Gaeren couldn't help smiling. After a day of forced rest, it had taken them a quarter moon to catch up, but they were in good spirits knowing Islara was around the corner. According to Orra, Daisy was within their reach at last.

Gaeren and Riveran had gotten used to Orra's strange ways over the last few weeks—more so than they'd gotten used to each other.

They both knew some things would always be unforgivable. Still, the humor they found in watching her antics had somehow reformed a tentative and fragile friendship between them.

Orra sucked in a breath, leaning forward to grasp her mare's mane for support.

"Stop," she murmured. "Please."

Orra pulled back on the reins, and the horse came to a standstill just as she slid off. She let herself fall to the muddy earth, then plunged her hands into the dirt, ignoring the way it splattered and clung to her dress.

Riveran let out a snort. "You took that double or nothing bet, didn't you?"

"No way," Gaeren hissed, pulling Skunk back around toward Orra's mare. "Orra? Are you all right?"

Her eyes opened, her gaze almost on his face. She blinked and shook her head.

"She's either in the city or just beyond. There's just..." She trailed off.

Skunk pranced with impatience as Orra's face remained passive, her darting gaze the only evidence that she still followed her connection to Daisy.

"Will you still be able to trace her in Islara?" Gaeren asked.

"I'm not sure. There's something..." Orra broke off again, eyes unfocused. Every time she lost her words, Gaeren suspected it was a symptom of a greater sense of loss, maybe in time or place. The woman still kept her secrets, so he would never really know.

She stood, brushing the mud off her hands, which only served to spread it further. She wiped her hands on her equally sullied dress before mounting her mare. "Something blocks me even now. Probably just the weight of Islara. All those people and the things they've made. They interfere."

Gaeren and Riveran exchanged a glance, and Riveran's lips pursed as he tried holding back his grin.

"We're so close." Gaeren ran his thumb over the daisy on his dagger. "Once we find Daisy and the starbridge, we can get out of this rain. Maybe get rooms at an inn. But we need to catch them before they leave." His grip tightened on his reins as he urged Skunk past Maw. The two horses nipped at each other, taking their cues from Gaeren and Riveran.

Gaeren set a faster pace, his frustration and exhaustion finally tempered by the promise of reaching his goal. His recovery had been slow, and his pace and stamina in the days following had been even slower, but soon his tenacity would pay off. Gullet had returned too, Enla's irate response tied to his leg. She demanded that he come give their mother the red bush tea himself, insisting that she would never forgive him or let him set foot on *Starspeed* again, which only made him certain he'd made the right choice. His chest tightened. What if that really had been his last voyage on *Starspeed*?

Now the hawk kept to the trees, waiting out the rain. They probably wouldn't see him until they left Islara because of it. They headed for the closest entrance to Islara's valley at the west gate. As they reached the edge of the rim that would lead down to it, Gaeren pulled his cloak tighter around him and let the hood fall down over his face, just in case there were some radical Recreants who recognized him and felt burdened to do something about the royal family.

But when Islara came into view, he no longer worried about hiding his identity.

Every structure was blackened; every crop destroyed. Not a single living thing remained, whether plant or person. Pockets of fire and glowing embers flickered, but the rain had taken care of the worst of what had to have been an inferno. It was eerily similar to the sight that had greeted them on Bamboo Island. Except this had once been a thriving city.

Gaeren gave the skies a quick scan, but the clouds made it difficult to see any possible threats.

Riveran sucked in a breath, reining in Maw as they all took in the damage.

"You think Daisy is in there?" Gaeren asked Orra.

Orra's mouth hung open for a moment, and Gaeren's panic surged higher the longer she took to respond.

"I didn't—it's everywhere. No wonder I couldn't sense..." She brought her hand to her forehead, rubbing her temple with her thumb. "It wasn't just interference. It was fading."

Gaeren's fear spiked. He patted Skunk's neck, leaning forward and tapping the horse with his heels. "Let's go, boy."

"Gaeren, wait," Orra called.

Another set of hooves followed, but Gaeren didn't look to see who it was. As Skunk picked his way down the slippery hill, Gaeren kept his eyes on the sky. At one point, he swore he saw the outline of outstretched wings in the clouds, but the sky darkened as a heavier storm brewed, and soon the figure disappeared, taking on the full grey of a storm cloud ready to let loose. He didn't have much time before the scattered showers would turn to a torrential downfall.

By the time he reached the city's edge, the rain had picked up. The shops nearest had been gutted, revealing their remaining contents. At one point they'd held clothing and kitchen supplies, salted meats and hard tack for those heading out of town. There were also vases and pottery in impressive swirling shades of blue and green, at least the pieces that hadn't been smashed or melted—souvenirs for arriving travelers. Farther down the street, Gaeren entered an area with better-preserved buildings.

Buildings that might hold survivors. Answers.

Skunk fought Gaeren's lead, attempting to back out of the city and all its wrongness. Eventually Gaeren dismounted, then patted Skunk on his rump. "Go on. You won't find any food here. Go find Walnut."

The gelding took off on the hunt for Orra's mare, leaving Gaeren alone on the cobblestones. Only he wasn't alone.

Riveran stood beside him, daggers unsheathed, while Maw and Skunk wound their way back up the path to where Orra waited.

Appreciation flooded Gaeren, but he only gave the other man a quick nod. He took out his sword and tuned in to the memories around him. The sheer number of them made it impossible to follow any one trail, but they all held traces of fear, panic, and pain. There had to have been hundreds of people on this street in the last several hours for this mess of memories to remain. Had any of them been able to flee? Or had they all died?

Giving up on garnering valuable information from the memories, he entered the home before him. In its prime, it would have been for an affluent family, the cobblestone of the street spreading up the building's side in an elaborate pattern that created an ocean landscape with colored glass adding depth and detail. Now, half the building was completely missing, like it had been cut in two with a knife.

Wind whistled through the wall, and rain splattered furniture newly exposed to the elements. No one remained. Three more blackened houses revealed the same abandoned atmosphere, the same eerie quiet. It wasn't until they reached a fourth house that they found the first body.

"Stop." Riveran pulled on Gaeren's arm, preventing him from taking a step forward. Wind picked up what little ash hadn't become black mush, stirring it into tiny tornadoes but also revealing bones.

Gaeren kneeled to wipe away wet ash clinging to bone. The body was hardly more than a skeleton with blackened additions that might have once been flesh. Gaeren scanned the sky again, taking a raindrop directly in his eye.

He flinched and wiped his eye before placing a hand on the skull, hating what he needed to do.

He closed his eyes anyway, reaching out and tuning in to the ghost-like memories around him. The faint pull of them all grew easier to distinguish. Most of them were too old to be complete, too distant to be detailed. But one grew finer-tuned as he connected to it through the bones he touched.

A man, terrified and running. Only Gaeren wasn't just watching the man—he was reliving his memory. The lack of control made it his least favorite way to use his magic. It was like trying to wake or even move in a dream but having no command over his body. Normally, in order to tune in to someone's memories, they had to first be recalled by the person they belonged to, but Gaeren's progeny mentors had pushed him to take his abilities a step further for instances just like this. It drained him far too quickly and forced him to experience a memory with far too much perfection, like he was taking in an essence of who they were instead of just recalling their past.

Even now he felt the heat of the creature behind him, the sweat dripping down his neck as he ran. He prayed to the Sun for mercy and deliverance even though he knew it wouldn't come. Others screamed in the streets around him, and the rumble of destruction chased him along with the burning air. Then the heat overwhelmed him until he screamed in agony. His screams continued even after Riveran wrenched his hand from the skull.

"You're fine. We're fine." Riveran shook Gaeren, bringing him back to the present reality.

Gaeren glanced at the sky again, panting, but the rain clouds covered everything now, blocking out any sign of the Sun. It had been close to sleeping moments ago, but in the memory, the Sun had reached its zenith. Hours old. Surely the dragon was gone.

He stood shakily, tuning in to more memories around him, the heat of them rising from the cobblestone like steam in the rain. Hundreds surrounded him, even in areas they'd already explored. Now that he knew what to look for, he sensed the origins of them all: bodies that had been destroyed so thoroughly there weren't enough remains to mark them as people.

"They're all dead," Gaeren whispered. "Everyone in the city."

Riveran shook his head. "They must have evacuated. It's not possible that—"

"I see them." Gaeren's curt interruption silenced Riveran. "Their memories permeate the air. All of death."

He strode forward, finding the source of one memory, grasping the skull and letting himself enter another. A woman huddled over her children, as if she could absorb the creature's fire and somehow her babies would live. This time he was able to pull himself from it in the midst of her pain. Another revealed a couple sharing one last passionate embrace before their inevitable end. He tortured himself going from skeleton to skeleton, letting his energy drain as if reliving their memories somehow gave more value to their lives. He wanted to grieve them all, to experience it all for their sake.

The memory of a man hiding his child in a basement was cut short as Riveran slapped him across the face.

"No." Riveran's voice brought Gaeren's focus back to the present, but his former friend wasn't angry. His face was drawn tight with fear. "Your sister would get that look in her eyes when she let them overtake her. The visions of the future were too much. They would have killed her. Visions of the past will do the same to you."

Gaeren clenched his jaw, his gaze on the X covering Riveran's forehead. Riveran had still been with Enla when she'd first learned her magic. He'd seen her overdose on the addiction of prophetic visions. He'd been the one to ground her, to bring her back to the present. Until he betrayed her. It had taken Gaeren and her mentor weeks to get her centered once more. Riveran was right; he'd nearly lost himself to the memories thick with sorrow pervading every part of this graveyard.

Not that he would admit it to Riveran.

"I'm not like my sister." He placed his hand on the skull once more. "And this memory was different." He watched it again, paying closer attention. Watching the path the man took until his demise on the street where Gaeren stood. He shook himself free, then turned, tracing the man's path in reverse. He picked up his pace, nearly running through the ash that now clung to his boots.

Riveran followed, and the slap of their boots echoed off the empty buildings in the abandoned street. When they reached the house the man had left, Gaeren paused. Since the memory, the house had been smashed in two. It was unlikely anything had survived. And yet Gaeren had seen the child placed in the cellar.

Instead of going through the door, he picked his way through the remains, trying to make sense of the layout, trying to map out where the cellar door had been.

"Here." He pointed at a space where stone had fallen on wood floor. Wordlessly, Riveran helped Gaeren uncover the floor until they found the handle and the door had been cleared. Gaeren wrenched it open. Muted sunlight revealed a well-stocked storehouse, its contents practically pristine compared to the destruction aboveground. His hope soared.

"We're here to help," he said into the darkness. "The dragon is gone."

A sniffle sounded from the corner. "Da?"

Riveran stiffened beside Gaeren, then rushed down the steps.

Murmurs met Gaeren's ears, but they soon drew closer. When Riveran emerged from the cellar, a tear-streaked little boy gripped his hand. Riveran's other arm held a sleeping infant, his protective grip so natural Gaeren had a sudden image of him at home with his wife, snuggling a baby before tucking it in its crib.

He wanted to hate the memory he'd inadvertently tuned in to, but there was a fierce love behind it that left him breathless.

The boy began shivering as the rain hit his skin. Riveran tucked the baby deeper under his cloak before making sure his X was hidden, so Gaeren reached forward, beckoning the boy toward him.

"Where's Da?" the boy asked, still gripping Riveran's hand.

Riveran and Gaeren exchanged glances.

"Your father asked me to get you to safety," Gaeren lied.

Riveran frowned, but at least the boy came to Gaeren. He lifted the boy in his arms, surprised at how light he was. The boy instinctively snuggled against Gaeren, allowing Gaeren's cloak to wrap around them both.

"How old are you?"

"Three. I'll be four next moon. Da's going to teach me to ride his horse."

Riveran looked away, swallowing hard. Even Gaeren felt a lump in his throat. Hopefully there were other survivors who could take on the task of explaining what happened to his father. For now, they had to find a safe place. But where was a safe place in the midst of all this death?

A low rumble interrupted Gaeren's thoughts. The boy whimpered in his arms, and Riveran's eyes widened.

"The southern gate," Riveran suggested, nodding toward the edge of the forest. They'd come almost halfway through the city, and the gate to the south was closer than the east or west. But were the woods any safer? Durriken hadn't touched them yet, so Gaeren had to believe they could be.

The two men ran, tripping over debris, and soon the infant's cries drowned out any warning they might have of the dragon's approach. As they squeezed through the fallen gate, Gaeren glanced back. A dark figure loomed in the sky, finally below the clouds, but far enough away that they should be safe.

They climbed the valley's edge until they reached the tree line, grateful for the cover—not just from the dragon but from the rain. Riveran paced, hushing the baby and singing to it, distracting Gaeren for another surprising moment.

"This is the road to Grandpa's." The boy gazed down the path deeper into the forest.

"How far away does he live?" Riveran asked.

The boy shrugged. "We always get there before lunch. Mama doesn't even have to stop to feed Adella."

Gaeren glanced back at Islara. There was nothing there for them anyway. He needed to get to Orra. He needed Orra to trace Daisy again.

"I could take them and meet you back here," Riveran offered.

"What if I don't stay here?" Gaeren asked. "I have to keep going if Daisy keeps going."

Riveran frowned in thought, but a flutter of wings exploded from the trees, and Gullet landed on his shoulder.

Gaeren couldn't help grinning. Despite all that had just happened, the hawk had found them. And solved their problem. "He's making it harder for me to hate him."

A strange look crossed Riveran's face, and Gaeren realized he could say the same about his old friend.

"We can regroup tonight," Gaeren said, passing the little boy off to Riveran.

"I'll send Gullet as soon as I reach the cabin," Riveran said.

"May the Sun's light always shine upon you," Gaeren murmured.

Riveran's eyes flashed with hope at the farewell. "And may the Stars' light always guide you."

Gaeren turned before he could examine the meaning behind the words too closely. The dragon still circled the town as if it sensed there had recently been people there, alive. Gaeren eyed the woods to the west, wondering if he could skirt Islara and meet back up with Orra without having to go back through the city's remains.

A flash of movement in the distance caught his eye, and he

squinted toward the blackened city. Several forms darted in and out of the buildings. More survivors? He tensed as the people progressed deeper into the city. They weren't trying to escape, so maybe they weren't from Islara.

"Daisy," Gaeren breathed out before taking off down the hill, back toward the city and the dragon that had demolished it.

CHAPTER 43

Aeliana and Lukai entered the fourth building on their street and still found no survivors. Panic clawed up her throat at the massive devastation. Holm had said thousands lived here, and thousands more had been gathering on the eastern edges to form an army. Were they all dead?

Lukai's shoulders slumped as they met back at the front door. Only the frame remained around it, but habit and the obstacle of surrounding rubble had still made them open the door and walk through. Lukai's face held weary lines, drawing Aeliana out of her fears enough to remember that Lukai knew these people. Maybe he'd been to this home before its destruction.

Somehow his grief made her braver. She had no right to be swallowed up in anxiety when everyone else here had lost so much more.

"How did Sylmar communicate with the army?" Aeliana asked.

"Messengers." Lukai scanned the street, but he didn't move forward. "But his last contact point was in Valorian. That's why we went out of our way to check in. Iris and Holm said everything was on schedule."

"Did their contact send a message on from there? To go ahead of us?"

He shrugged, every movement becoming more listless. "Even if it was intercepted, it was always in code."

"Codes can be broken," she said.

He sat on the front step and dug his palms into his eyes as if he couldn't physically go on anymore. She debated putting an arm around him, but comforting others didn't come naturally to her. It made the idea feel fabricated, forced by the bond between them, and she wasn't sure what to do with that.

Holm and Kendalyhn stepped out from the house across the street. Kendalyhn reached out a hand, pulling Lukai to his feet and then wrapping him in a hug. A strange sense of heat rushed through Aeliana as Lukai leaned into the other woman, both of them shaking with silent sobs. It shouldn't bother her, not when they had a shared loss after years of friendship.

But the feeling didn't go away, and beneath it, something else simmered. A sense of wrongness. Like her bond had more influence over her emotions than it should be allowed. She turned her back to them, facing Holm, whose stricken face resembled a lost child's.

"She knew we were coming, didn't she?" Aeliana asked. "She knew I was coming."

Holm shook his head, his mouth opening without any words coming out.

"She broke Sylmar's code," Aeliana continued, "and beat us here, crippling us in the easiest way she knew how."

"You don't know that." Lukai's words came out weak. There was no other explanation to offer.

"I'm endangering you all." As Aeliana said the words, the truth of them washed over her like a wave of sorrow. It reminded her of her days under Arvid and Vera, when her energy and pain had come in undulating ripples.

No one argued, which spoke volumes to Aeliana. The four of them cut through the remains of an alley to meet Sylmar, Iris, Velden, and Cyrus on the next street over.

"We'll stock up and head farther north," Sylmar said, his gruff tone thicker than usual. "If we catch wind of the army, we can meet up with them on the trade route. Otherwise, we'll make for the Pass."

The word "otherwise" held too much heaviness. It meant the army would have all perished. It meant they'd be on their own, performing a stealth mission to retrieve Aeliana's mother and blood instead of being one small part in a much larger plan.

"If Mayvus knew about the army," Velden said slowly, "wouldn't she watch both the trade route and the Pass?"

Silence grew as even Sylmar couldn't argue with his point.

"How else could we reach the Myndren Mountains?" Aeliana asked.

Lukai shook his head. "We'd be better off returning to the coast and taking boats around the Western Horn."

"We'd never make it before Solstice," Iris pointed out.

"So despite being terribly dangerous, the Pass is our only option?" Cyrus asked. As they all waited for someone else to confirm their dire circumstances, a low rumble came from the north.

The others reached for weapons, making Aeliana realize she should probably ready her bow and arrow as well. But she'd seen how little good arrows did against Durriken's hide.

"How certain are we that the dragon is gone?" Cyrus asked.

"About as certain as we are about making it through the Pass," Velden said.

Iris shot him an irritated look.

Aeliana scanned the skies, the memory of Durriken's massive scaly body so vivid she worried she wouldn't be able to tell the past from her present reality.

"There." Holm pointed to the east, where a dark shadow broke up the grey clouds.

"Change of plans," Sylmar growled. "We're no longer stopping for supplies."

They all followed his lead, darting between buildings and heading farther south. When Sylmar veered left, Cyrus pulled up short.

"We're heading straight for Durriken."

"We're going east," Sylmar corrected over his shoulder. "If the dragon gets in our way, so be it."

"I guess it wouldn't be the first time Aeliana took on a dragon," Cyrus muttered.

"I did not—" Aeliana broke off, not wanting to waste the energy on such a pointless argument. As her thoughts turned to energy, the starlock around her neck grew warm, a reminder that she had more in her arsenal this time around. It might be a fairer fight.

But what good would stitches and basic healing do in the face of a dragon whose breath would make them ashes on contact? It made all their efforts to teach her seem like such a waste of time.

Aeliana's anxiety grew as they moved slower and slower through the rubble, occasionally having to turn back to find a clearer path. The rumbles grew louder and the sky darker. When they finally reached the city gate, a thunderous crash resounded behind them. Aeliana fell against Lukai as she turned.

The dragon perched on a tower, some building that had once been a grand five- or six-story structure but was now crushed into the semblance of three, its base threatening to topple as the dragon rearranged his grip on the turrets. His wings spread out for balance, so thin that Aeliana could see through them to the hills behind them in the distance. Iridescent scales shimmered all over his body and down the tail that wrapped around the tower for stability.

The beast huffed, black eyes scanning the group with far too much intelligence. When his eyes landed on Aeliana, he snorted, holding her gaze with a strange combination of hatred and respect. Atop Durriken's neck, a man clung to the spiked collar. The distance was too far to make out facial features, but the lanky form and dark hair was unmistakably Arvid.

Sylmar held out his staff, which took on its molten glow before rearranging into a metal spear. "Velden and Holm, head to the north side of the square to help block them off. Kendalyhn and I will stall them in the center. Iris and Lukai, get Aeliana and Cyrus to Jasperus and the horses."

The others all split off to obey, Iris and Lukai dragging Aeliana and Cyrus with them. From the corner of her eye, Aeliana caught sight of Velden's hands spinning, drawing in water from homes and the earth around him. Even amidst the danger, he grinned, relishing the challenge. If he survived, he'd turn his fight with the dragon into some tall tale that made Sylmar look the fool.

Or maybe not. A glance back showed Sylmar's face lit up with fury by the glow of his staff. Kendalyhn and Sylmar stood in the center of the square as if beckoning the dragon to come down and take them out like he'd done to all the buildings around them. What if that was exactly what he did? Was that their plan? Stall by self-sacrifice?

Aeliana stopped running. "There has to be a better way."

Iris tugged on her arm. "We're not prepared to fight a dragon, love. So we run."

"You wanted to fight him before," she argued.

"When he had your blood," Iris said. "Now the cost is too high for the reward."

By this time Velden and Holm had made it to the north side of the square, and Aeliana and the others had reached the gate. Jasperus waited on the other side with the horses, but the dragon watched, his lip curling to reveal the hundreds of teeth Aeliana remembered from before. Arvid bent forward, as if whispering instructions to the creature.

She stopped again. "Arvid and Durriken will kill them all. Look at them. They're devising a plan. They know what they're doing."

Tears streamed down Iris' face, and she wouldn't hold Aeliana's gaze. She knew. She knew those who stayed behind were going to die, and she'd accepted it.

Aeliana refused to do the same. Arvid and Durriken wouldn't win if there was a surprise they hadn't factored in. How could she get the upper hand?

"Jasperus," she shouted through the gate. "How far away can you project an illusion?"

His brow creased. "It's best when I can touch you, like when we fought the winex."

"But is it passable from a distance? Can you make it look like I'm standing with Sylmar?"

He glanced back at Sylmar and Kendalyhn, both adjusting their defensive stances as the dragon leaped down from the tower, scattering cobblestones in his wake. But then understanding dawned on his face.

"I could make Kendalyhn appear enough like you to the dragon. Maybe confuse Arvid. It wouldn't fool Sylmar, and if Durriken got too close…"

"Good enough. Do it. Once Arvid or Durriken seems to realize she's a fake, change it up. Make me be in as many places at once. They came for me. Make them find me."

Without waiting for a reply, Aeliana scrambled into the building on her right, to the south of the square. She heard footsteps behind her as she rushed up unsteady stairs.

"What are you doing?" Cyrus caught up to her as she hunted for a window that might give her access to the roof. "This is insane."

"I won't let these people risk their lives for mine. If I die, I'm actually saving everyone the trouble of worrying about Mayvus having my blood. Mine is the only life worth risking here." Finally, one window had a secure enough hold on the building's facade for her to step out and hoist herself up onto the roof. The building trembled beneath her, and for a moment she thought the whole structure would collapse, but another shudder made her realize Durriken was on the move.

She distantly registered Cyrus calling her name, but she ignored him, crawling across the roof until she could look down on Arvid, who sat astride Durriken just beneath her, and Sylmar and Kendalyhn, who faced them from the center of the square. The creature's eyes were wide with agitation, his snout dripping with water. From the north, across the square, Velden kept a steady stream, nearly drowning the beast before it could take to the skies or send flames on the others. Aeliana hesitated, momentarily reliving all the ways she'd almost died the first night she'd encountered Durriken.

But then Kendalyhn—who had a strange mix of Aeliana's long hair and Kendalyhn's petite frame—shrieked, a flame from Arvid's hand igniting her cloak.

Aeliana stepped to the edge of the roof and leaped. She aimed for Arvid, her boots hitting him in the side and knocking him off balance to the ground. Her momentum tried pulling her along with him, but she reached for the dragon's collar. Only one hand caught the collar's loop, and instead of giving her purchase, the awkward angle jerked her left shoulder. A sickening pop with searing heat made her yelp, and her body dangled from the collar, her legs closer to the dragon's chest than its back. Durriken turned sharply to assess his attacker, which miraculously swung her legs back up toward his back. She momentarily gained purchase, freeing the arm that now hung uselessly at her side.

Arvid's shouts were drowned out by a threatening rumble in Durriken's throat, but they proved he'd survived the drop.

Aeliana yanked another scale from the beast's back, then launched on top of his paper-thin wing, dragging the scale through the translucent skin the same way she'd used the scale to slice through Vera's cloak.

A strange howl escaped the dragon's mouth, instantly flooding Aeliana with remorse.

Until the gap she'd created in his wing widened, and she fell through. She landed hard on her side, unable to catch herself on the ground with her injured arm.

Arvid glared down at her, his bloody hand outstretched. His blood had never given him as much magic as hers, but she supposed he had access to many more half-lights' blood now. Maybe even more powerful blood. She flinched when his fingers twitched, but his scowl only deepened.

"That was my ride you just damaged." He backed away a step, his eyes glancing down at her neckline, at the proof of her starlock's presence. "She won't let me kill you, but it will be worth it. You're on borrowed time. And when you belong to her, she'll do far worse than kill you." As he reached the edge of Durriken's wingspan, a dark cloud swept through him and in him, his eyes turning black.

Aeliana's mouth went dry, images flooding her mind of the people he'd killed, the villages he'd destroyed, all under the influence of a dark spirit. She didn't have time to warn her friends. There was nothing she could do to stop him.

But Arvid didn't fight. He simply pointed at her and grinned. "Your time's almost up." He released flames from his bloody palms, where they were met by Velden's stream of water, and he ran off in steam as thick as fog.

She turned her attention back to Durriken, who was no longer nursing his injured wing. A deafening roar left his open maw, mere feet from her. A paw lifted off the ground, his talons extending. He let the paw drop over her chest, one talon drifting to a finger's breadth from her eye. As his weight shifted, the breath left her lungs until she thought he'd crush her.

Then the weight released, and Durriken shook his head as if clearing his mind. He studied her, then glanced at Kendalyhn, whose illusion flickered. The dragon backed away, freeing Aeliana to scramble backward and stand. He cocked his head, eyeing her one more time, as if waiting to see if she would change like Kendalyhn had.

He wouldn't kill her. He knew who she was. Or he at least knew that Mayvus wanted her alive.

Before she could process what that meant, she caught sight of Cyrus above her, slicing through the dragon's other wing.

"No!" she cried out.

Lukai dragged her away from the dragon, blocking her view of Cyrus.

"We have to get out of here." Lukai shoved her forward. She tripped over rubble, and they drew closer to the gate.

"Stop. Please!" She turned, and his forward momentum brought them both down. She cried out at the strain on her arm. "We have to go back for Cyrus. I have to go back. The dragon won't hurt me."

She shoved Lukai aside.

"That doesn't mean Arvid won't," he called after her.

Fire and water rained around her, forming a smoky mist where they collided, but she kept her focus on Cyrus, who now lay beneath the dragon's wing just like she had moments earlier.

"Durriken!" She held out her right hand, steadily walking toward the beast. He looked up, distracted, just like she'd wanted. He blinked as he took her in, shaking his head with that same eerie recognition.

Everyone in the square went still. Even Sylmar and Velden kept their rim magic at bay, as if they knew using them now could send Durriken over the edge. There was no sign of Arvid.

"Cyrus. Get behind me." Aeliana kept her voice low. "He won't hurt me."

Cyrus didn't hesitate but clambered back as Aeliana moved forward, steadily getting closer to the beast until her hand was in arm's reach of his snout. There was a strange sense of power that came with being so close to something so deadly. She supposed it might be considered courage, but it felt a lot more like stupidity or pride. Still, cautious fear held her back, watching, waiting to see what the dragon would do.

Once Cyrus was behind her, she knew she should step back, inch her way to the gate and make her escape, but the creature before her almost seemed broken with his tattered wings. His head tilted, and he let out a slow breath like he might lie down and cover his snout with his paws and have a good cry.

"You won't hurt me," she whispered. She took another step forward, heart pounding in her ears. Her name hissed across several lips from behind her, but she kept advancing, holding her trembling hand out for the dragon to smell.

He did, snorting air hot enough to burn. Then he nosed at her hand and let her rub her fingers over his snout like a horse.

Images flooded Aeliana's mind, and for a moment she was back at her Awakening as the disjointed visions took over. But these visions were muted, blurry. Flying over forests and deserts, a collar being wrapped around her neck, a brand being seared into her paw. Her mind balked at that one, reminding her she had hands.

The strangeness of it all allowed her to step outside the visions enough to realize she was seeing Durriken's memories.

CHAPTER 44

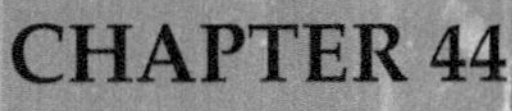

Orra rode Walnut but kept her eyes closed, watching the events play out in her mind as if she were present for them all.

Islara's eastern gate was almost in view, but she was still up on the forested ridge, slowly making her way around the destroyed valley. Orra had seen Gaeren and Riveran rush out the southern gate. She'd sensed more than heard Durriken long before she'd caught his shadow. It had all happened faster than Orra had expected, and yet as it happened, the possible paths grew narrower.

When Gaeren had run back, she'd smiled at his perfect timing.

He wasn't a mere boat or lily pad needing to be placed in the path of a ripple.

He was a stone, about to create a new ripple. One that might form a tidal wave as massive as her own. Only this time she sensed the Sun sanctioning it.

Now, Skunk came up behind her, huffing as if he'd worked hard to catch up.

Orra opened her eyes and hummed her disapproval. She pulled Walnut up short, then reached for Skunk's reins.

"He needs you. You know that, right?" she murmured. The horse whinnied, pulling against her grip. "Yes, you knew. Now go get him. Go get Gaeren." She dropped the reins and let Skunk go free.

Orra smiled as the gelding disappeared down the trail leading to the eastern gate. "This is how we put things in the paths of ripples."

CHAPTER 45

GAEREN HELD his breath as the fearless woman left her hand on Durriken's snout, eyes closed as if she fully trusted that the beast wouldn't snap her hand—or head—right off. Her long brown locks blew out around her in the breeze of the dragon's breath, like she was a Star dancing in the wind, her cheeks pink with the heat of it. In the mere moments he'd been watching, she'd stepped forward, eyes fierce with determination and a steadiness that held more courage than any man he'd seen preparing for a pirates' skirmish.

This couldn't be Daisy.

Gaeren shifted in the rubble where he hid, his gaze scanning the rest of her companions, but the only other woman whose age seemed right had short black braids and an upturned nose. Enla's description came back to him: russet brown waves, piercing green eyes, regal grace. The woman attempting to tame a dragon was a perfect match in one sense, but in another she was all wrong.

Daisy had been a child, an innocent toddler who needed saving. Someone he was ready to scoop up and dash to safety.

This woman did not need saving.

The complexity and confusion surrounding her entire identity left him frozen in fascination, allowing him to catch her small gasp when her eyes went wide. She dropped her hand and took several steps back, muttering something only for Durriken's ears.

The steps back were all her companions needed. A volley of arrows came from the edges of the square. A man nearly knocked Daisy to the ground in his effort to drag her away. The dragon roared, spreading his wings, but the sound died off to a whimper as his sliced wings shuddered. He turned to the side, directing fire at two people on the north side of the square. One had to be an advanced progeny because a wave of water doused the line of fire, including the dragon's snout. The dragon backed away, inching closer to where Gaeren hid.

They'd grounded Durriken.

Gaeren almost laughed with his shock, but then the beast's tail swung, forcing Gaeren to scramble backward before it crushed the place he'd been hiding. He made his way through the back of the building until he came out farther east, nearer to the group protecting Daisy.

A surge of disappointment flooded through him, leaving him mortified at his petty thoughts. He'd wanted to save her. He'd failed when he was young, and this was his chance to put things right. Only he'd been stupid enough to think she was still like the child in his memory, incapable of protecting herself and without aid from others.

He'd been a fool.

Somehow, he suspected Orra knew all this, and it made him feel like an even bigger fool.

By the time he rounded the buildings to the eastern gate and caught sight of Daisy's group again, half of them were missing. Had they left through the gate? Would they attack Gaeren if he went out the same way?

Daisy and a much older man remained, both holding out their hands as if to ward off the advancing dragon. A couple of others picked their way through the rubble, everyone taking care not to anger the dragon further.

Gaeren frowned. This time Daisy looked smaller, weaker. Had he imagined her strength and courage before? Or had the balance shifted that quickly? Maybe the magic she'd used was too much for her. Even her skin seemed paler.

He hesitated, watching as the dragon drew closer. Maybe she did need help.

He debated what he might do, but the older man's molten staff seemed far more useful than Gaeren's ability to steal memories. Even his skill with a sword was useless against the scales of a dragon. A noise behind him made him start, and when he turned, a horse nuzzled his cheek.

"Skunk?" Gaeren glanced up at the ridge, but there was no sign of Riveran or Orra. "You're a good boy, aren't you?" he murmured, glancing back at Daisy and her companion. The dragon had nearly reached them, and this time Durriken snarled, sure to bite off any hand held out to him.

Did Daisy know that? Or would she reach out again anyway?

He couldn't risk it. Maybe she hadn't needed saving before, but she clearly needed it now. He launched onto Skunk's back, then kicked the horse with his heels, rushing for Daisy.

When he drew close, he had a moment of panic, recognizing that the dragon could easily take him out before he ever reached Daisy. He imagined Enla having seen this potential future, having hoped it wouldn't happen. He could hear her telling people afterward, explaining how Gaeren's pride was the thing that had taken him out in the end.

His progeny mentors had always taught him that courage without fear was pride. The only time one wounded Gaeren in a duel was because he was proving that very point.

Which was why Gaeren knew Enla would be wrong in her assessment. It couldn't be pride rushing him closer to death, because he was terrified.

Durriken's gaze snapped to Gaeren, the beast's eyes narrowing. As Gaeren reached Daisy, the beast opened his mouth. Gaeren leaned over, grabbing on to Daisy by the arm and yanking her up over his horse. She screamed in protest, but it sounded like she spoke the name of her companion.

Gaeren felt the heat of Durriken's breath, the roar of fire erupting behind him. He didn't look back to see if Daisy's friend survived.

She twisted on top of the horse, attempting to pull herself upright on the horse.

"You're an idiot! I can't believe you interfered like that."

His mouth swung open, and his fear flipped to irritation. "What? I just saved your life."

Skunk practically flew through the eastern gate in his rush to escape the dragon.

The woman finally got herself seated as if riding one of Enla's ridiculous side-saddles, and the brown waves surrounding her face shifted to short black braids, her upturned nose lifted even higher with her disdain. "You probably killed Sylmar. Maybe Aeliana too, not that she really matters." She muttered the last part, forcing Gaeren to strain to hear her words.

"You're not…what happened to Dai—Aeliana?"

The woman eyed him strangely. "The dragon probably just ate her. Who are you, anyway?" They reached the forest line, and the woman launched off the horse's back before Gaeren could answer her question or come to a full stop.

Within moments he was surrounded by half a dozen armed men and women. When arrows trained on his chest, he held his palms up in surrender as Skunk did a nervous dance.

"Well? Who are you?" the woman asked again. "And why are you here?"

"I'm a friend. I've come to rescue Daisy, daughter of the priestess Emeris." He directed his answer to the woman but spoke loud enough for everyone to hear. "I was charged with her safety over fourteen years ago, and I mean to see it through." Admitting the truth out loud felt good, but it also sounded childish, symbolic of the age he'd been when he'd made such a promise.

"I recognize you," another woman called out, her voice filled with disdain. "He's Prince Gaeren of Elanesse."

The first woman's eyebrows rose, and Gaeren gave her a sheepish grin. "Doesn't mean I'm your enemy."

A man stepped forward, crossing his arms over his vest and nearly bare chest. Fish hooks hung from his ears, and his head looked newly shaven. "Tie him up."

Two others rushed to do the man's bidding, pulling Gaeren down off his horse.

"We'll let Sylmar decide what to do with him," the man said. "I have five silver notes that say he'll feed him to Durriken."

The last thing Gaeren saw before a bag was thrown over his head was the man holding up a webbed hand ready to collect money, and the last thing he heard before losing consciousness was the man's laughter.

CHAPTER 46

"Run, Aeliana." Sylmar's growl forced her head back around to face Durriken, whose flames had barely missed them both. "The dragon will take you to her. Run!"

Aeliana blinked, shaking her head. She still saw the image of the blur of a man on horseback stealing away Kendalyhn, who remained cloaked in Jasperus' illusion. "He can't take me. He can't fly."

She held out her shaky right hand once more, the ache in her left shoulder throbbing even worse than before. But now that Kendalyhn was no longer posing as Aeliana, Durriken's wary gaze rested on her. Sylmar inched his way to the side, and the dragon flicked a lazy glance the old man's way.

"He knows what you're doing," she said. "He's smarter than you think." After seeing his memories, it was clear he wasn't the mindless beast bent on destruction that they'd made him out to be.

Sylmar didn't respond, just crept his way closer to the dragon, who no longer seemed to mind. It was as if he'd given up when his wings were torn.

"Promise me you won't kill him," Aeliana begged. Her hand nearly brushed Durriken's snout once more, and the dragon sniffed again, probably unsure if he could trust his eyes after Jasperus' trickery. "He's branded by Mayvus just like my mother. It's not his fault."

When Sylmar reached for the dragon's side, Durriken jerked upright, growling and snapping as he turned toward his right wing.

"No, Durriken!" Aeliana reached for his snout, but the beast had already moved. He inhaled deeply, Aeliana's only warning for what was to come. She screamed, launching herself at Sylmar, who had dropped to the ground. Her sessions of self-defense, healing, and archery came back to her, all a waste in this moment when none of those things could help. She drew every ounce of energy from her blood, her starlock— even the deep well within her that she was always too afraid to access.

Without any place to push it, without any purpose to guide it, she hunched over Sylmar and flung it out wildly behind her, unsure if it was her power or Durriken's fire that burned into her back. Bright light flashed, blinding her, but even after the heat and the dragon's roar were gone, the light shone.

She and Sylmar turned.

A shield of light burned between them and Durriken, a wall like glass. It shimmered and faded but didn't completely disappear. Beneath it, a field of daisies grew, blossoms popping up in a wave around their feet and Durriken's tail.

Aeliana watched both the light and the flowers, sensing the way they ebbed and flowed with her breaths, like they were tied to her, like they were a part of her.

For the first time, the energy within her abated, its end within sight. And for the first time, Aeliana worried what it would feel like to not have it. She reached out, tugging back against the flow, struggling to rein it in. But its pull was too hard, the control she'd thought she'd had absent.

She could only guide the energy out, so she did, pushing it into the shield until it was bright once more, sending it through the flowers until they grew, twisting unnaturally like vines, taking over the rubble and remains, even crawling up over Durriken's paws.

In a panic he pulled, making the vines snap, but more grew until he tripped and came down with a thud that shook the ground. Sylmar bolted forward, straight through the glassy light, placing a hand on Durriken's foreleg. Before Durriken could attack or even assess his enemy, his eyes rolled back in his head, and he collapsed in a heap against the earth, rattling the few remaining windows of the neighboring homes.

The shield collapsed, and Aeliana sucked in a shuddering breath, rushing to check the beast, unsure where she would even hear a heartbeat.

"Did you kill him?" She ran to the beast's belly, watching for the rise and fall of his chest. When it came, faintly, she sighed out her relief.

"I'm not sure I could if I wanted to." Sylmar came around from the creature's other side, face pale as he warily eyed Aeliana. "Kendalyhn can sift his soul. See if it gives us answers."

Aeliana swallowed hard, afraid to ask what Sylmar might do once he had his answers.

"Is Arvid gone?" she asked.

Sylmar nodded, his gaze still on the clusters of daisies. "Ran off during the chaos. Hard to say if he'll stick around for vengeance or run back to Mayvus."

"He'll go back to Mayvus." Her voice came out hollow. "Told me I'd be under her power soon."

Sylmar was instantly alert. "Did he see you do magic?"

She shook her head. "I don't think so, but he probably saw the cord of my starlock." She reached for the leather around her neck.

Sylmar's eyes closed, his face a mask of concentration. "When were you going to tell me you can do a shield?"

The accusation in his voice left her startled.

"I can't—I haven't been able to before. I didn't know what I was doing."

Sylmar still stared at her. "You shouldn't progress that fast. Your skills should have tapered off when we weaned you, giving you just the one strength on your spoke. The others can be built up, but it takes time and effort."

With Aeliana's energy drained, the loss of what had filled her for so many years made her snap. "You make me practice every night. I have been putting forth time and effort."

Sylmar remained unperturbed. "And you stopped the blood

magic?"

She glared up at him, then turned on her heel, stomping through the rubble toward the eastern gate. How dare he accuse her of continuing the blood magic. She hadn't wanted to do any magic, and now they'd convinced her to try, and she was suddenly suspect for doing well at it?

"I've seen the marks on your skin. They're not all old," he called after her.

Her anger rose. She didn't know where the fresh cuts came from. She'd started wondering if she did it in her sleep. But that didn't mean she was doing blood magic.

"It's a temptation that never really goes away," he continued. "There's no shame in acknowledging that weakness. But if you've stopped the blood magic like you say, then you've been holding out on us."

She stumbled with his words, refusing to be baited, but they still rang in her ears like a memory stuck repeating. As the sting of the accusation faded, it was replaced with a hollow pang. Sylmar hadn't just accused her of doing something evil; he'd suggested they'd all come to trust her, to see her as one of them. And now they couldn't.

Lukai waited for her on the other side of the gate, his face relaxing into a slightly less concerned frown when she came in sight. "Is Sylmar—?"

"He's fine." She cut Lukai off, continuing her march past him without another word. Beyond the tree line, Velden, Iris, Kendalyhn, and Cyrus anxiously watched the gate. Aeliana singled out Kendalyhn. "Sylmar wants you to invade the dragon's soul."

Kendalyhn's eyes narrowed. "Sympathizing with the enemy?"

"The dragon isn't our enemy. Mayvus is."

The others exchanged glances, but no one dared get involved. Kendalyhn snorted and pushed past Aeliana, heading back into Islara.

Aeliana's gaze roamed the others, doing a silent census to make sure everyone was accounted for. Jasperus and Holm were missing, but an extra man sat, slumped against a tree with a sack over his head and his hands awkwardly tied behind his back.

"Since when do we take prisoners?" Aeliana asked.

Velden shrugged. "I'm just waiting until Sylmar can talk to him. He claims he's here to protect you."

The man they spoke of didn't move. His chin rested oddly on his chest. No tattoos marked his hands, so he wasn't the man from Lovers' Falls. "Is he unconscious?"

"It's just an herb in one of my seaweeds. Lukai can revive him when Sylmar is ready to question him."

She knew her friends hadn't mistreated the man, but after reliving Durriken's memories, something about seeing the man tied up left her raw. She stepped forward and pulled off the sack. The man's golden-brown hair hung in his eyes, and days-old stubble covered his jaw. She kneeled at his side, lifting his chin to see if he looked remotely familiar.

He was younger than she'd first thought, only a few years her senior if she had to guess. His nose had a slight angle, like it had been broken once in his youth, but every other feature seemed perfectly chiseled from marble. Still, he didn't wake.

Sylmar hadn't been completely wrong. She'd been holding back. She realized that now, after being forced to use her power to its fullest capacity. It hadn't always been intentional. Holding back had been her method of survival for as long as she could remember. She couldn't decide yet if that was a good or bad thing. Even her uncertainty was proof that she'd changed since coming to Vendaras.

Before she could evaluate it more, she pulled at the remaining energy in her starlock, drawing it through her arm and into her good hand where it held the man's chin. Her starlock grew warm, and then cold as the energy drained. She fed it to him, not knowing if it would work but eager to try. The others might be content waiting for Lukai and Sylmar, but this man had been looking for her.

She wanted answers for herself, now.

He drew in a deep breath, then his eyes fluttered open. Deep blue, like Durriken's wings, stared back at her. She dropped her hand, suddenly flustered at his nearness, that she'd been touching his face. She sat back on her heels, cradling her injured arm against her and giving them space to study each other.

For a moment, no one spoke. The others might have been too shocked at her use of magic. Or maybe they, like her, were waiting to hear what the stranger had to say. He seemed to study every feature of her face, taking it in like a man starved. Then he finally settled on her eyes. Her entire body screamed at her to look away, but instead she stared back, feeling oddly stripped and vulnerable before him, despite the fact that he was the one caught and bound.

His lips twitched, then the right side of his mouth lifted, like he was laughing at her.

"Sun's fire. You're not the Daisy I remember." His words brought up images of the daisies wrapped around Durriken's paws, along with the dozens she'd involuntarily grown over the years. The things she'd always tried to keep hidden. And now he teased her with it, like it was some sort of thing they shared.

She frowned. "I'm Aeliana, and I doubt we've ever met."

Now he really did laugh, and with their audience, Aeliana regretted reviving him.

"I taught you to swim," he said, "and you showed me where to catch tadpoles in the creek. I carried you around on my back half of every day for almost a year, just because you liked being taller. Your mother cheated on my training because it gave us more time to play."

Mention of her mother finally made the others stir. "You knew my mother?"

"I lived with your family for my dedication year. I knew you both. And your father." His smile only grew, still holding a mocking air. "You were my Daisy."

She stiffened at the familiarity. All his words felt foreign.

Iris stepped forward, almost between Aeliana and the stranger. "That's not possible. I recognize you. You're the Prince of Elanesse."

Her presence gave Aeliana space to breathe, to consider his words. It couldn't be possible, could it? She'd been three when she left Vendaras. So maybe it was possible, but definitely not likely. Not if he was the Prince of Elanesse. Her Recreant parents wouldn't have brought a member of the royal family to their home, allowing him to befriend their daughter.

"Iris?" He shifted against the tree to turn toward Iris more, but his bound hands were in the way. "You haven't changed a bit, have you? Yes, I'm Gaeren, but you knew me as Henri. My parents weren't exactly going to announce to everyone where I was for my dedication year."

Iris bent forward, studying the man like an insect she needed to identify. "It could be him. He has the name right, but... I thought he was a merchant's son from the village."

Gaeren snorted. "I guess my disguise worked."

The others started whispering, but Cyrus drew closer to Aeliana. "I don't like it."

Aeliana nodded. Sylmar would likely have Kendalyhn examine Gaeren next. It shouldn't be difficult for her to verify the truth. But what if he was lying?

Her gaze strayed back toward the Islaran gate. What was Kendalyhn seeing in Durriken's past right now? Were they going to kill him?

"Someone took the dagger off my belt. You'll want to see it," Gaeren said. "Although I still have another in each boot, which means you all didn't search me for weapons. Fine job you're all doing protecting Daisy."

She bristled at the accusation, unsure if she was offended that he felt she needed protection or that he was belittling her companions. Or that he still called her Daisy.

Lukai stepped forward, pulling the daggers out of Gaeren's boots before producing a third.

"There's a design etched in the pommel," Gaeren said, wriggling to sit taller and lean forward. "Do you see it, Daisy?"

She started once more at the name, then recoiled from the dagger that Holm tried passing to her. A simple daisy glinted up from the metal, large enough for others in the circle to see and start whispering about it.

"Do you remember the daisies?" His question was almost a whisper, the eagerness on his face suddenly stripping away his years to make him a boy.

She took the dagger from Holm, running her thumb over the grooves of the flower. It looked no more familiar to her than anything else in this part of Rhystahn.

"No." She handed it back to Holm, barely catching the way Gaeren's face fell before he could school his features.

"You chained them together," he murmured, shifting his gaze to the grass at their feet. "Wanted me to teach you to make crowns. You made a dozen of them that night while we hid—before you disappeared." He closed his eyes then and leaned back against the tree.

"You saw me disappear?"

"Yes." The single word held as much pain as the cries Arvid had wrung from Della. If she had been three, he had been, what—six, seven? In Lorvandas, dedication years for the nobility occurred when a child turned eight. Was it the same here in Vendaras? With his eyes closed, all his features were soft again, and she could imagine him as a boy, trying to protect a toddler.

What would it do to a child to witness something like that at eight years old?

"I've been looking everywhere for you." He held her gaze once more, the sensation unnerving. "To make sure you were safe. Do you feel safe here?"

She hesitated, not because she was uncertain about her answer, but because she wasn't sure how he might use it against her. "Being with these people is the safest I've ever felt."

Hurt flashed in his eyes, but then he gave a short nod. "That's— that's good. I should have known you wouldn't remember. You were so young. I could show you, but I doubt anyone would let me. It's my opposite spoke. I'd have to touch you to give you the memory."

Velden pushed off the tree he leaned against, shaking his head.

"Come here, love." Iris pulled on Aeliana's arm even though she was already out of Gaeren's range of touch.

Aeliana was opening her mouth to argue that she wanted the memory when the sound of approaching footsteps made everyone turn toward the Islaran gate once more. She sluggishly pulled her gaze away from Gaeren, still not sure what to think of him.

Kendalyhn and Sylmar approached, the old man hobbling forward with his cane. His skin hadn't regained its color. Knocking out a dragon must have taken everything out of him.

"It's clear Durriken came here against his will." Kendalyhn's gaze lingered on Aeliana as she announced her assessment to the group.

Aeliana nodded, grateful that the other woman could see the lies of his past. If there was a way to disagree with Aeliana, Kendalyhn would have managed it, which made the information even more reliable to their companions.

"He still killed all those innocents," Lukai said.

"As Mayvus' puppet." The words slipped out of Aeliana's mouth before she could think them through. "What if my mother had been on Durriken's back instead of Arvid? What if she'd attacked right alongside him?"

No one met her eyes. Cyrus shifted beside her as if he might say something, but even he kept his gaze fixed on the so-called prince.

"I know what you're all thinking right now. You're not deciding whether to let him live." She stared each of them down, her gaze landing on Sylmar. "You're deciding how to kill him."

"Of course he needs to die," Gaeren said.

Aeliana whipped around to find the stranger staring at her incredulously.

"He killed an entire city," Gaeren added.

All sympathy she might have felt for the tied-up prince vanished.

"It doesn't matter if it was on Mayvus' orders," he continued. "If anything, that's more reason to kill him. What else could she order him to do?"

"He's branded. It's not his fault."

"Branded? By Mayvus?" Gaeren had the nerve to snort. He shook his head. "I shouldn't be surprised that she does blood magic."

"Who are you?" Sylmar asked.

"Prince Gaeren of Elanesse." He said his own title with a mocking lilt, then gave an exaggerated and awkward bow from his seat on the ground.

"We can deal with him—" Aeliana started, but Sylmar stepped in front of her.

"Lukai. Take her." Sylmar's arms spread until his cloak hid Aeliana from view.

Lukai yanked on Aeliana's arm, but she shook him off. "Stop being ridiculous. He came to protect me."

"Is that so?" Sylmar asked. "Then why do his parents have a reward out on your head?"

CHAPTER 47

THIS TIME, Gaeren laughed so hard he coughed. When he finally caught his breath, he squinted up at the older man, the pock-mark scars resembling destination points on the maps in *The Sins of the Stars*. He'd thought all those points led to Daisy, but now he didn't know what to think about anything.

"If my parents had a reward on her head, do you think I'd march in here and announce my name?"

The man's glare didn't falter. "They may revere you in the north, but your image gets more distorted the farther south you go. They say your sister will be the queen to save Rhystahn, second only to Queen Amaya, the first queen of Elanesse, who united all of Vendaras under the Sun."

The stranger waved his arms out in mock praise, making Gaeren's gut clench. He couldn't argue with the man for thinking the northern people were overly obsessed with having a perfect monarch, but it wasn't Enla's fault they'd put her on a pedestal.

"But you…" The man bent forward, tapping Gaeren's chest with a gnarled finger. "They also speak of you. They say you can't take anything seriously. That you look pretty enough beside your sister, but you're not good for anything else."

The words shouldn't have stung, but they did. Gaeren took the things that mattered seriously. Those close to him knew that. But most of what went on in Elanesse was pomp and ceremony. If he didn't laugh at it all, he'd grow depressed over the waste.

"If I'm not good for anything else, why am I tied up like I'm a threat?"

The stranger straightened. "Do you know why your parents are after Aeliana?"

Gaeren let his gaze flick over the old man's shoulder, taking in Daisy as she gnawed on her lip, her brow crinkled. The man next to her took a step closer, as if to shield her, but Gaeren noticed she stepped away, rejecting his protection. For some reason, it made Gaeren smile.

"You find this amusing?" the older man barked.

"I try to find something to be amused about every day. You never know when it might be your last. I'd like to be happy whenever I join the Sun." He rested his head back against the trunk. It didn't matter what he said. They wouldn't believe him. Besides, maybe his parents did have some sort of reward out for Daisy. It wasn't like he'd been home recently to check.

But if that was the case, the man's question was a good one: why?

Shouts came from beyond the small crowd of strangers, causing everyone to turn and further block Gaeren's view.

"We found two more of them coming from the southwest." The crowd parted for the petite older man who spoke, finally revealing Riveran and Orra marching Gaeren's way, their wrists bound in front of them.

Gaeren grinned in relief, the humor of his reaction not lost on him. A few weeks ago, he hadn't been particularly fond of either of them, and now they were a welcome sight.

"Did you find their grandfather?" he called.

Riveran's face brightened as he sought out Gaeren among the strangers—until he saw Gaeren tied up.

"Yes." His surly response was all Gaeren got before they were hushed.

A much bigger man nudged Riveran forward, his voice soft. "The criminal claims to be his oldest friend"—Riveran avoided Gaeren's eyes—"and the woman refused to answer any questions until she saw Aeliana."

Daisy craned her neck around her personal guard, and to Gaeren's surprise, her face turned a fascinating shade of pink.

"You." In a blink, Daisy rushed at Orra, her attack blocked by Riveran as he stepped between them. She beat a fist weakly on his chest and continued shouting at Orra despite the wall between them. "You stood by and did nothing. She died and you just—you just watched."

Gaeren frowned, noting for the first time that Daisy favored her left shoulder. She cried out, then slumped to the ground. Despite her bonds, Orra stepped around Riveran, crouched, and placed her hands on Daisy's shoulder. The younger woman flinched, then gasped. Several of the strangers started forward, but Daisy rotated her shoulder, raising her eyes to meet Orra's.

From this distance and angle, Gaeren couldn't see her expression, but he imagined it mirrored the sensation he often got around Orra. Surprise, distrust, hope, curiosity, wonder…confusion.

"I would have healed her if I could have." Orra whispered, but her voice still carried through the silence. "I wasn't truly there. For that moment, I was even more ethereal than the dark spirits your blood summoned." She shut her eyes, the pained expression making her look far older. "I did the only thing I could and sang her to sleep. I sang her to the Sun."

"The song of the Stars." The awestruck words came from a man with unseemly long red hair, his face covered in freckles. His eyes took on an understanding that passed through the others listening in, and he dropped to his knees in a bow.

Gaeren held back a snort. Orra? A Star? She'd hardly left his side, let alone taken to the skies. And if communing with a Star was the same as talking in circles with that woman, he wasn't interested in regaining that benefit in the Sungazers.

Orra wiped her eyes, then stood, awkwardly pulling the freckled man to his feet.

"I deserve no such honor." Her clipped words seemed to wake everyone up, but the damage was done. Reverent and curious gazes followed her every move, even the swipe to catch the stray tears on her cheek.

"You have my honor and gratitude anyway," the freckled man said. "If you sang Gams to her eternal sleep, her end was far more peaceful than I imagined." The man's throat bobbed as he swallowed again and again, the skin around his eyes turning red.

Orra refused to look the man in the eye. If anything, that made Gaeren consider the possibility more. Having her secrets exposed might be the only thing powerful enough to subdue her.

"Why do you travel with the Prince of Elanesse?" The old man hobbled away from Gaeren, his inquisition shifting to Orra.

Orra straightened under his scrutiny. "When I saw Aeliana use the starbridge, I knew it would take her to Bamboo Island. Gaeren agreed to give me passage. We've been working together to find Aeliana and the starbridge ever since."

The man with the scars turned his glare back to Gaeren. "Is that true?"

He nodded, sitting up a little straighter. "When did my parents put out the reward for Dai—Aeliana?"

"Half a moon ago." The man frowned as if disappointed that Gaeren couldn't possibly know about the warrant.

For a moment, Gaeren felt relief that his mother was well enough for his parents to issue an edict.

"They're falling further under Mayvus' control," the man said.

"Control?" Gaeren's heart pounded. "What are you talking about?"

Several others exchanged glances. The old man hobbled back. "Don't you pay attention to your politics, boy?"

"I do when they matter. It's always been more of Enla's thing." He knew it was the wrong answer the instant the stranger's face twisted into a deeper sneer.

"They always matter. It won't be long before your parents relent to Mayvus, and then your sister won't have any throne to succeed. Or if she does, it will be in name only. Mayvus will see to that." He bent down and untied Gaeren.

Others in the group drew weapons, but Gaeren merely rubbed his wrists.

"What? You trust me now?"

The old man let out a snort that reminded Gaeren of Skunk's whinny. "Hardly, but you weren't part of that decree. You're foolish and young, oblivious to the ways of the world and the things going on in your country, right beneath your crooked nose. Stupidity isn't a crime... yet." His glare softened to pity, which was somehow worse. "Kendalyhn will still sift your soul's past, but you're as harmless as your critics say."

Humiliation flooded Gaeren, trapping him amongst the strangers more than the rope had. The moment the old man turned his back on Gaeren, the others slid their weapons back in place, shifting their attention to Daisy, who removed Orra's binds, then Riveran's. Orra and Daisy stepped to the side, clearly planning to have a private conversation, but the freckled man joined them. Maybe this had this been part of Orra's plan all along. To get to Daisy before Gaeren could. What did Orra want with her? And where was the starbridge?

The short woman with braids whom he'd accidentally saved planted herself in front of Gaeren, arms crossed. "Let's get this over with."

"Get what—?"

She grabbed his hand and closed her eyes. Gaeren automatically threw up mental shields, blocking her invasion with his starlock's energy the way his progeny mentors had taught him.

This must be Kendalyhn.

"If you don't cooperate, the shackles go back on," she murmured.

"Right." He closed his eyes, pulling back on his starlock's power, willing the shields to recede. He tried opening up his mind for her to excavate, but his self-defense training had almost been too thorough, and it took a few attempts. Once she made it in, he squirmed as he waited for her to finish her perusal. His mentors were the only ones who'd had this kind of access to Gaeren's mind, and it felt backwards to give in so easily.

Especially when she started laughing.

"She's not as innocent as you think." She dropped his hand and shook her head in disbelief. "Your mind is like a child's, categorizing people as good and evil, right and wrong. It doesn't work that way."

He glanced around at the others, but most had cleared out, leaving Daisy, Orra, and the freckled man to their privacy. Even Riveran had gone to let their horses join the others at grazing.

"I don't know what you're talking about."

Kendalyhn raised her eyebrows. "There's a purity around her in your mind. Like she can do no wrong. You know she does blood magic, right?"

Her words took the breath out of him. Blood magic? He thought back on Orra's comment about the dark spirits being drawn to Daisy's blood.

She'd done blood magic.

"Yeah, we've all been disappointed. Sylmar made it sound like she'd change everything." She glanced at the man with thick scars. "If Mayvus wants her, we should too, right? Only it seems Mayvus just likes collecting her family members and keeping them close. I wouldn't be surprised if the two of them join up and rule the world together." She turned to go, but Gaeren grabbed her arm. Something about her smile made him hesitate. There was a predatory hint, like when Lenda tried manipulating him to get what she wanted. Kenda-lyhn was goading him, but he didn't know why.

"They're family?"

"I thought you lived with the priestess for a year." She gave him an incredulous look. "Surely in that time you heard Emeris talk about her dear sister, Mayvus?"

He frowned, trying to remember if there'd been any talk of an aunt. He'd known Daisy's parents were hiding her, but he didn't know what, or whom, they were hiding her from. He hadn't even known who Mayvus was back then, but that didn't mean she hadn't already been climbing her way into power. He'd been eight, and he'd cared even less about politics then than he did now.

Kendalyhn narrowed her eyes and folded her arms across her chest. "You don't know who she is, do you? You don't know who any of them are." Her eyes softened, then lost focus, like when Enla saw a vision.

"What are you talking about?"

Kendalyhn's focus snapped back to the present. "She's a Wyndren. They're all Wyndrens."

Gaeren took a step back. His face stung like her words had slapped him. He sought out Daisy, but he couldn't reconcile the woman talking to Orra and patting the freckled man's back with the family line he'd been raised to hate.

Enla had been so sure that none of them existed anymore, but she'd also been insistent that Mayvus wasn't after more power. She needed to know Mayvus was part of the line contesting their throne. That their line hadn't died out but had been hiding, biding their time until they could get themselves in a position of power. This was the proof he needed. It could change everything.

But how would that change things for Daisy? And should it? A throne warden would take out every threat to the crown. And anyone who could produce more Wyndren heirs was considered a threat. His mind tried to wrap around the idea that the woman he'd been hunting to protect was now suddenly someone he was supposed to hunt as a threat.

"I thought Recreants don't want a ruler. But you all want her on the throne instead of my family?"

Kendalyhn snorted. "Aeliana? No. She would be a terrible ruler. Sylmar hasn't even told her that her family has claim to the throne. She's too weak to handle that kind of information. The southern and western Recreants push for democracy because they've been under your family's thumb for too long. For those of us in the east, we're still open to a ruler, and Aeliana's mother is our first choice. We'd like the other Recreants to see this option as superior to your tyranny, but for now, we all simply agree that Mayvus needs to be removed. We can figure out the rest later." She raised her eyebrows. "If you want Sylmar to keep you around, you should make that your focus as well." Then she walked off, leaving Gaeren to digest everything she'd said.

He closed his eyes, picturing Daisy's dimpled smile and curly locks. He wanted that simple, sweet toddler back.

"Kendalyhn says you wish Aeliana no harm." Sylmar's scratchy voice brought Gaeren's eyes open.

He stared at the older man, knowing he should agree but too confused to say the words and mean them. "I came to protect her."

"But now?"

Gaeren shook his head. "Now… I don't know. She doesn't need my protection. I shouldn't even want to protect her if she's a…"

Sylmar swore, glancing over his shoulder at Kendalyhn. "That girl needs to learn to keep her mouth shut. She's supposed to find your secrets, not spill all of ours."

"Well, like you said, I'm young and stupid." Gaeren clenched his fists. "I don't have secrets. I wanted to protect her because it was my childhood promise. She may not need my protection, but I'm not going to hurt her." The words coming out of his mouth didn't sound right. He still wanted to protect her, but deep down, it was like he'd been betrayed. Like she'd fooled him into caring about her for this very moment. So she could throw it in his face that he'd fallen for it.

Protecting her was the thing he'd held on to all these years. It was the one thing he'd needed to fix. And if he could fix this one thing, maybe it would get easier to fix the next thing.

He'd been a fool. All his life, he'd fought to avoid the drama of court and the pain of politics. He'd used his travels as a means of escape, not because he cared too little, but because he cared too much about the people around him, about the things he couldn't change. Only now he realized it had made everyone think he didn't care at all.

Maybe it didn't matter whether or not he could change something. Maybe it only mattered that he tried. He should have tried harder.

Sylmar hummed, breaking through Gaeren's thoughts.

"There are Recreants who would kill you just for being an Elanesse."

Gaeren nodded slowly, his heart racing. "I'm hoping you're pointing that out because you're not one of them."

They stared at each other for a long moment.

"Kendalyhn also says you have it out for Mayvus almost as much as we do."

"I've been warning Enla about her for years. She's a threat my family refuses to consider, like she's too far away to be a concern and too holy to be a fraud. After seeing what she's done here…" He waved his hand in the direction of Islara, his mind traveling through the hundreds of deaths he'd seen and relived. "And after learning she partakes in blood magic? I'm as committed as you are to removing Mayvus. She's a threat to Loyalists as well, whether or not she's a Wyndren."

At least this much was true. He could say it with confidence. He could fight alongside these people to take down Mayvus, but after that? His stomach twisted like he might throw up. Hopefully he would have a better idea of what he was supposed to do then. Maybe even that was too much. Clearly Daisy didn't need him. Maybe it was time to just… let her go.

His stomach churned at the thought.

Sylmar slowly nodded. "And what about the starbridges? Kenda-lyhn says you want those too."

Gaeren shrugged. "Originally I wanted them to cross the barrier and find Daisy. Once she returned, I knew they'd still be valuable. I figured Enla might want them." He clenched his jaw. He didn't want this man to see him as a threat, but he wasn't about to share his desire to be an ambassador, to potentially unite all the people groups of Rhys-tahn. It was exactly the kind of thing Sylmar would use to support his opinion of Gaeren as naive.

Sylmar coughed out some sort of laugh. "A treasure hunt?"

Gaeren nodded even though the description wasn't accurate. At this point, seeing how organized the Recreants were made securing the starbridges less of a treasure hunt and more of a necessity. If they could all go after Mayvus, what would stop them from coming after the Elanesses next? As throne warden, having an escape option might be his only way to protect his family.

"Maybe I don't need the starbridges anymore," Gaeren said, "but after hunting them for the better part of a year, they're still something I want. Orra wants them too, and I'm willing to work with her to find them."

"Oh, I already know she wants them. She'll probably use you to get them." Sylmar's gaze shot to Orra. "The question is… why?"

CHAPTER 48

AELIANA TRIED PAYING attention to Orra and Cyrus as Orra recounted Della's last moments. She even rubbed Cyrus' back as he relived his grief. But her attention kept straying to the prince as Kendalyhn invaded his mind the same way she'd invaded Aeliana's and the dragon's.

There was something vulnerable about the way he closed his eyes after Kendalyhn left, something disarming about the way he let Sylmar confront him.

Curiosity warred with irritation as she remembered the way he'd spoken of their childhood, the way he'd spoken of her. And then the way he'd so easily condemned the dragon to death. That last one fit more with the image she'd been given of the Elanesses.

"The starbridge isn't here, is it?" Orra's voice broke into Aeliana's thoughts, and she turned her attention back to the other woman. The question had been directed at Cyrus, but his tears had started up again.

"No," Aeliana said. "Arvid took it to Mayvus."

Orra's eyes slid shut, but she nodded her understanding. "She wishes to use them for power. To make the world smaller."

Aeliana frowned. "I thought it was to keep it away from me. So I couldn't go back."

"Perhaps." Orra shrugged. Beyond the clearing, Sylmar gathered Lukai and Holm, gesturing back toward Islara. Back toward Durriken.

"Thank you," Cyrus said. "For everything." He barely got the words out before he rushed away from the camp. Maybe it was worse that Orra had come. Maybe she'd torn his grief wide open again.

"Are you really a Star?" Aeliana had imagined them brighter, more powerful, then immediately worried her thoughts were blasphemous.

Orra's gaze turned sharp. "I can't take to the skies. I wouldn't be a very good Star if I was one."

It felt like a riddle. A non-answer. But before Aeliana could question her further, Kendalyhn joined them.

"You're last," Kendalyhn said, holding out a shaking hand for Orra. The younger woman's eyes darted around the camp, and Aeliana supposed it might be nerve-wracking to try sifting through the soul of someone who might be a Star.

Gaeren stood nearby, probably within hearing distance. The corner of his lips lifted, more like he found Aeliana amusing than he was actually smiling at her.

"The other two are harmless," Kendalyhn went on when Orra didn't take her hand right away. "Turns out the criminal isn't even very dangerous. He stole bread to feed his family. Not exactly a crime worthy of the traitor's brand."

Aeliana still watched Gaeren, and his face slackened with surprise at Kendalyhn's words. His gaze sought out the man they'd called Riveran, and his brow furrowed. Good. Whatever disagreement those two were having could end his childish staring contest with Aeliana.

When Orra finally took Kendalyhn's hand, Kendalyhn frowned. "You have to let your guard down; otherwise, Sylmar will want you bound for the rest of our travels."

"I'd like to see him try." Orra's face softened into something more like amusement than irritation.

"The rest of our travels?" Aeliana asked. "He means to take them with us?" She glanced back at Gaeren, whose curious gaze was irritatingly back on her.

"The prince wants you or maybe the starbridges, so he also wants to go after Mayvus." Kendalyhn's voice rose, making Aeliana's face heat. "And the friend will go wherever the prince goes. Some sort of childhood promise or vow or something. I'm guessing Sylmar is keeping them close to watch them, not necessarily because he trusts them."

"Does it ever feel wrong knowing so much about people when they haven't willingly given you the information?" Aeliana asked, her words sharp with her frustration. The other woman didn't have to spill everyone's secrets just because she knew them.

Kendalyhn's eyes flew open, all efforts to sift Orra's soul gone. "You'd be surprised at how willing people are to be seen. It takes little effort on my part. When you sift through someone's soul and their darkest and brightest parts and still love them? There's nothing to match the sensation of being seen and loved."

It was more than Kendalyhn had ever shared with Aeliana, but it felt like an insult. Or at the very least, a reprimand. Kendalyhn had seen Aeliana's darkest parts and held no love for her.

"True words, even when spoken so harshly," Orra murmured, surprising both women out of their anger.

Kendalyhn closed her eyes and squeezed Orra's hand once more.

Aeliana stepped away, not wanting to witness another display of Kendalyhn's magic.

Gaeren straightened, his eyes still on Aeliana, but she wasn't ready for whatever he might say. Her throat felt raw after facing Durriken, after defending a beast and reviving a stranger only to watch the stranger turn on the beast. She didn't trust herself to accurately evaluate anything Gaeren might have to say.

Besides, Sylmar, Lukai, and Holm were leading Jasperus and Velden toward Islara. She picked up her pace to follow, but Sylmar saw her coming and shook his head. "It needs to be done."

Her insides grew cold. "No. He's branded. There has to be a way to undo the brand. Jasperus told me they could be cut out."

Sylmar hesitated, then let the others get ahead of them. "He's a dragon. We don't know if it works the same way. We don't even know if he has magic for her to control."

The memories she'd seen from the dragon flooded her mind. He definitely had magic, but she wasn't sure if knowing that would make Sylmar more or less likely to kill him.

"Besides," Sylmar added, "it's nearly impossible to get close enough. He won't let us cut it out."

"You left him unconscious. It should be easy. If cutting out the brand could remove his connection to her, don't we have to at least try?" She let her gaze bore into Sylmar's, willing him to consider it.

He hesitated, making her hope rise. "Do you want to risk the lives of everyone you love on a possibility?"

She looked away, hating his logic, hating how the memories she'd received from the dragon defied his logic. Gaeren stood only a few feet away, far too interested in their conversation. She frowned at him, but he stared back, undeterred.

Sylmar turned to catch up with the others, and Aeliana watched him go. She couldn't save Durriken, but she could stay with him. It was better than facing Gaeren. Maybe like Orra, she could sing the dragon to the Stars or the Sun or whatever awaited them all beyond this life.

She rushed to join Sylmar, stumbling over her thoughts. She hadn't cared to evaluate what the servants of the Stars taught when she was growing up, but now she felt a burning desire to know the truth. Were the Stars worthy to be worshiped? Or were they created by something greater, like the Sun? She supposed Cyrus' faith hadn't wavered like hers.

The sky that had been dark with clouds now grew black with the setting Sun. The Stars and moon remained hidden, the only light coming from the torches carried by the men.

They entered the gate, weapons drawn. From a distance, the dragon looked almost like a large dog, curled up and passed out from an afternoon of play. His chest rose and fell as hot breath escaped his nostrils, his black tongue lolling out the side of his open mouth.

Without hesitating, Sylmar walked up to the beast's side and laid his staff and hands on the dragon's scales. Aeliana closed her eyes. Would it be peaceful? Or would the air be rent with Durriken's shrieks of agony?

She sensed a warm presence at her side and opened her eyes to find

Gaeren observing Sylmar's work. Gaeren's focus remained on Durriken, but his body angled toward Aeliana, his hand on the hilt of his dagger, as if ready to defend her should the need arise.

Aeliana almost laughed. That dagger couldn't protect anyone from Durriken.

Several long moments passed, and Lukai, Holm, Jasperus, and Velden huddled together, whispering. She slipped around them, making her way toward Sylmar. The old man sucked in several gasps of breath, turning his frustrated glare on Aeliana. She expected him to send her away, to make some comment about her reckless behavior putting herself in harm's way.

He bent over, hands on his knees. "I can't…"

"You can't kill him?" Hope bloomed in her chest.

He shook his head, wiping the sweat from his upper lip while squinting up at her. If his destructive somatic skills couldn't kill Durriken, it wasn't from lack of effort. "It's possible I could after resting, maybe recharging in the Sun." He straightened, then leaned on Durriken for support. "I've drained too much energy today. My starlock resists. But Durriken's likely to wake before I'm ready."

"So we debrand him instead? Remove his collar?" Every one of her limbs felt lighter.

Sylmar sighed. "For now. To weaken him. And we tie him up for the remainder of the night. Tomorrow we try again. He's too powerful a weapon to give back to Mayvus."

Aeliana frowned, but she couldn't argue. The men went to work tying Durriken's paws and snout. His wings remained shredded, but Aeliana noticed several areas had begun to heal. Perhaps it was another form of the dragon's magic. Once he was secured, Jasperus and Holm stepped forward and began slicing at the mark on Durriken's paw. Its shape was uncomfortably similar to Aeliana's bond mark but far larger and raised like a black blister, taking up a quarter of the dragon's paw.

Despite being unconscious, the beast groaned, pulling his paws from their grip. As the men's agitation grew, so did Durriken's.

"Stop," Aeliana hissed.

Jasperus and Holm froze just as Durriken's eyelids rolled open, revealing large purple irises with a cat-like gleam. Durriken reared back, attempting to open his mouth with a roar. It provided the men enough time to scramble away, but Durriken quickly snapped apart the ropes holding his snout, the frayed blackened edges making all their ties laughable.

He didn't bother with the ropes around his paws. His eyes followed Aeliana as she stepped forward, shielding the men.

"I have to be the one to do it. He won't hurt me. I don't think he can." She glanced back to find Gaeren once again on her heel. Before he could argue, she snatched the dagger from his hand, then took three tentative steps forward, ignoring Lukai's—and maybe Gaeren's—hushed protests.

Durriken shifted, eyeing the dagger warily.

"You want to be free of Mayvus?" Aeliana asked.

The dragon went rigid, his gaze even more intense.

"Should I remove the brand or the collar first?"

He cocked his head. Had he understood? His paw remained face up, bleeding from where Holm and Jasperus had started working. Aeliana shivered at the sight. Would his blood tempt her as much as a half-light's? Would it tempt her more? Still, she pressed on until she was close enough to touch the dragon.

"Brand?" She gestured at his paw. "Or collar?" She moved her other hand within biting distance of his snout.

Whether he understood or not, he shifted on his side, lying back down, eyes still studying her. He settled his bound paws back in front of her, then closed his eyes. The vulnerability of the action made her throat clog with sympathy. How could Sylmar think Durriken wanted anything other than his freedom?

She held the dagger over the dragon's paw, inhaling the stench of his blood. The headiness of it made her grasp his paw to steady herself, and she sensed him tense beneath her. As she began gently carving the brand out from the creature's paw, he squirmed and flinched, letting out the occasional growl or moan as he tried to pull away. A few times he snapped his jaws as if he might stop her, but Aeliana suspected that whatever compelled him to keep her alive was stronger than whatever compelled him to fight her efforts to remove his brand.

As she worked, the clouds rolled back, revealing the waning moon, which shed light on Durriken's paw as Aeliana worked. The Stars did their dance, as if celebrating this turn of events. Eventually, the branded skin lay flayed at her feet. She placed her hands over the wound, squirming at the sticky sensation of raw flesh and blood. Durriken inhaled sharply, and Aeliana braced herself for the expected fire from his breath. When it didn't come, she refocused, attempting to draw energy from her starlock.

The starlock remained cold against her chest, having had no opportunity to recharge since she'd used it. For the first time, the lack of magic frightened her. She'd grown used to it.

"My magic," she said. "It's gone. I'm sorry."

Durriken cocked his head, then tensed along with Aeliana as Gaeren placed a hand on her shoulder. Warmth rushed through her, and for the first time she experience the sensation of being on the receiving end of someone's energy. It felt oddly comforting, and a small part of her wished it had come from Lukai, or really anyone, instead of Gaeren.

In turn, she pushed the energy out through her hands, weaving and stitching Durriken's skin together, growing it until the stickiness underneath her hands was more scab and scars than open wound.

His blood called to her, but not in the same way a half-light's did. She suspected she could use it, but it was easier to resist.

Gaeren stepped back when the job was done, but Aeliana stayed, relishing the vulnerability of her hand on Durriken's paw.

Healing him, her supposed enemy, was like a balm for her soul. She'd come across the barrier wanting to be rid of magic. Because of that single-mindedness, she'd held back, just like Sylmar said. Now it seemed impossible to separate the magic from who she was, from who she was becoming. And for the first time, she didn't want to separate the two. She didn't want to hold back. Even saving her mother and returning Cyrus to Lorvandas felt small in this moment. She could do so much more with her magic if she let herself try.

Healing Durriken was more than putting together skin and flesh.

The wounds went far deeper, and so did her magic. She had the potential to heal wounds, bond rifts, or reconcile broken relationships. And she was doing it without using blood.

"How much more could I do if I lean into my magic?" she whispered, grateful only Durriken could hear. She shivered at both the thrill and fear of the answer, and her starlock warmed against her skin in its own encouraging way.

When Durriken's breath finally came, it was warm and soft, tickling her neck as it blew her hair out around her.

"That's enough, Aeliana," Sylmar hissed. "We can finish tomorrow."

She stepped forward, ignoring Sylmar. She placed a hand on Durriken's snout, and the same memories that she had seen earlier flooded her mind. Sylmar's idea of finishing would be to take the dragon's life—remove him as a threat. But Durriken was no more a willing murderer than she had been.

"We can fix this," she murmured. When she brushed Durriken's collar with her hand, the cold metal shocked her, but she kept running her hands along what felt like ice until she reached the clasp. It took several tries to find the right place to press and release it, but when she did, Durriken let out a small moan of relief.

She'd been as trapped as Durriken, but now, instead of being held back by fear of being made a brand and fear of her own power, she felt free from everyone's expectations. She was free to figure out who she could be with her magic.

The metal fell away from his neck, leaving behind a strip of raw skin where the scales had been rubbed off, exposing a leathery expanse of flesh. Her mind flashed to her Awakening, her visions. She'd seen this moment. This had always been a part of her future. Somehow sensing that truth made her giddy with relief. She had always been meant to free Durriken.

"Daisy!"

She flinched, then turned to see Gaeren drawing his sword. The other men had been too scared to startle the dragon, too afraid of putting her at risk. But now they followed suit.

"Move," Gaeren shouted as he ran toward her. "It's his only vulnerability."

She turned back, taking in the sight of Durriken's neck, the exposed skin creating a clear target to behead the creature.

"Fly," she whispered, momentarily forgetting the beast no longer had functioning wings. "Run! Get out of here!" Even as her voice rose to a shout, Durriken summed up the situation and pulled at the ropes tying him. He breathed out tiny sparks, disintegrating the ties, then tucked in his wings, rolling back out of Gaeren's reach.

His hiss came out like steam, and he opened his mouth, but Aeliana stood in front of Gaeren.

"Go. Please, just go!" she begged.

The purple irises flicked their focus between the two of them. At first Aeliana thought he was debating whether to stay or go, but then she saw his wings slowly healing, like a tapestry's gaps being repaired and tightened.

"What are you doing?" Gaeren growled.

"Saving your life," Aeliana said.

Durriken spread his wings, then ran at both of them. For a moment, Aeliana thought she'd been wrong.

Gaeren pulled her down to the ground, wrapping himself over and around her until she was tucked beneath him, as if his body might be made of armor. But his self-sacrifice was unnecessary. Over his shoulder, she glimpsed Durriken wink before taking to the darkened sky.

CHAPTER 49

GAEREN WAITED for the flash of searing pain, expecting to be engulfed like the memories he'd experienced on Islara's streets. A rush of air brushed over his back, ruffling his clothes and hair, but the heat didn't come. He became aware of the soft body beneath him, the short breaths in his ear, his arms wrapped around Daisy's neck, pulling her in to his chest.

Heat rose to his cheeks, and he released his grip, leaning to the side to give Daisy space to scoot out from under him.

Her eyes narrowed as she stood and brushed off her blouse and skirt. The men around them still watched the skies, wary for the dragon's return, but the beast was long gone, and only the Stars still darted through the sky.

"You let him go." His statement came out defeated. He'd meant to ask why, but the absurdity of it all left his tongue tied. His heart still thudded at their dance with death, and his head still swam over the fit of Daisy in his arms. The mark on his palm itched.

"He wasn't mine to hold back." She reached down to grab his dagger.

Gaeren couldn't stop the scoff from rising in his throat. "He was a murderer."

"He was a pawn, played by Mayvus." Her words took on a dangerous tone even as she held the dagger out for him.

If she'd been Enla, Gaeren might have been smart enough to shut his mouth, but she wasn't Enla. She was supposed to be his little Daisy.

But she wasn't her either.

He grabbed the dagger, shoving it in his belt. "He razed this entire town. He killed thousands." He swept his arm out, forcing her to take in their destitute surroundings. His throat grew tight as the people's memories flooded through him again. "I felt them die. He'll kill again. But this time you'll have played a role in it."

Something flickered on Daisy's face, but too quickly her face became passive once more, every part of her remaining a mystery. For all he knew, she'd used blood magic to keep the dragon at bay.

The man who had guarded her earlier came to her side, gently checking her over for injuries, but she ignored him, even brushed him aside to refocus her glare on Gaeren. "Kendalyhn says you're coming with us. Why?"

He opened his mouth, ready with his automatic response. He had vowed to protect her. But watching Daisy face a dragon and live, hearing her scold him for wanting the dragon dead? Her power was beyond anything he'd seen, and he'd been a fool to think she ever needed his protection.

His promise now felt childish. Even showing her memories of their childhood would seem like a pathetic attempt to sway her. And what were his memories? The leftover pain of an eight-year-old boy who'd watched a toddler get taken. Those memories would mean little to her now that they were adults.

But he couldn't just walk away. He finally had proof that Mayvus was the enemy he'd believed her to be. As long as they were against Mayvus, he would fight with them.

"I want to stop Mayvus," he said.

Daisy held his gaze as the others around them gathered their weapons, their eyes still glancing toward the sky. Sylmar hobbled between Gaeren and Daisy, taking in their stand-off.

"Do you have armies to help us?" Daisy asked.

"Maybe," he lied.

She rolled her eyes and turned to the other man, slapping his hand away from her arm. "I'm fine. It's just a scratch." Then she turned to Sylmar, effectively dismissing both Gaeren and her guardian. "Will Mayvus know we removed his brand?"

Sylmar nodded, also turning his back on Gaeren, whose mouth swung open. Even in Enla's meetings, when she held everyone's attention, he was never ignored.

"So on top of knowing we were headed this way, she now knows we've arrived?" Daisy crossed her arms over her chest with a frown. "Is it still safe to use the Pass?"

"It was never safe." Sylmar's gravelly words were barely decipherable.

"But is it even realistic?"

Sylmar hesitated, and Gaeren found his in.

"I have a ship," he blurted out. The others turned his way, the surprise on their faces almost insulting, like they'd already forgotten he was there. "We could take the road to Elanesse and board my ship to sail across the Northern Sea right up to Mayvus' back door."

Daisy stepped around Sylmar, her eyes finally alight with interest. If nothing else, he kept talking to see the green gleam he'd been envisioning all these years.

"While we're there, I might be able to convince my sister to send troops with us. She won't stand for Mayvus' attack on an innocent town."

"You're offering a potential fleet to go after Mayvus?" Sylmar's voice rose, his face as angry as ever. Somehow Gaeren suspected he was more interested than irritated.

"I can guarantee safe passage for eight to ten of you. And yes, maybe a small fleet." He was even starting to convince himself. His parents and Enla couldn't ignore what had happened. Mayvus had led a direct attack on a city in their kingdom. It couldn't go unpunished.

"And what about the warrant for Aeliana's arrest?" Sylmar asked.

Gaeren shrugged. "I'll find out what it's for. But my family doesn't need to know she's involved. They'll be responding to an attack on the city of Islara, that's all."

"What's in it for you?" Sylmar asked.

"Protection from Mayvus is what's best for the people of Elanesse, for all of Vendaras. Our goals align." Gaeren cocked his head, aware that his motivation sounded too noble for their opinion of him. "I'll want the starbridges too."

Daisy let out a huff and muttered something under her breath.

Gaeren smiled and shrugged. Being an ambassador instead of a throne warden still sounded good, but he was starting to wonder if the better plan was to collect them all for Orra. To see why she needed all four. But he was fine letting the others think he was on another silly treasure hunt.

Daisy's guardian slipped his hand in hers.

Gaeren's breath hitched as he saw their matching blood red marks slide together like a puzzle, the squeezing motion of their hands directly transferring to his chest. The man was her bondmate, then. It shouldn't have surprised Gaeren. He'd seen the mark of a bond back when she was a toddler.

His own mark itched again, and he rubbed at it in irritation.

"When you use the golden arrow to go to Lorvandas," Daisy said, "I want you to take Cyrus with you."

Gaeren raised his eyebrows, glancing at her bondmate.

"Not me," the man said. "The human she brought over with her. Long red hair, priest's garb."

Gaeren glanced back toward their camp even though he couldn't see the man they spoke of from this distance. The one who'd practically worshiped Orra. Did humans worship the Stars like witches? "You want me to take him back?"

"Safely." Daisy's response came out like a warning, and it stung. It appeared she trusted him as little as he now trusted her.

"You have my word."

"Can we make it there by Summer Solstice?" Daisy turned to Sylmar.

"Why? What happens on Summer Solstice?" Gaeren asked.

Sylmar's glare bore into Gaeren over Daisy's shoulder. "Nothing."

Gaeren swore he heard the old man mutter, "If we can help it."

"We should be able to," Daisy's bondmate said. "If Gaeren already has a ship available to take to the Northern Sea, we won't have to waste time finding a captain willing to take us."

Daisy didn't look convinced, but she nodded her understanding.

By now, the rest of the group had cleared out from Islara's wasteland. Weariness swept over Gaeren as the events of the day caught up to him. His exhaustion reflected back to him from Sylmar's and Daisy's long faces.

"We'll rest tonight," Sylmar said, leaning hard on his staff and heading for the gate. "Tomorrow Gaeren will lead the way."

Daisy and her bondmate followed Sylmar without another glance at Gaeren.

Everything he'd been so sure about before entering this city was now uncertain. He'd found Daisy, but she didn't remember him. She didn't even like him. She was a Wyndren—the sworn enemy of his family line—and she did blood magic. He couldn't support any of the things she stood behind.

So where did that leave Gaeren?

Giving up the goal he'd had for the last fourteen years felt like a betrayal of himself, of Daisy. But this woman wasn't really Daisy. She was Aeliana Wyndren, and he needed to remember that.

He followed Daisy's footsteps, knowing that as much as the events of the day should change things, they didn't. Not exactly.

He would still fight to protect his people from Mayvus' impending rule. He would still seek out the starbridges. He would even still watch over Daisy, partly because he couldn't quite let go of the habit but also because somehow, enemy or not, she was key to both of those goals. Besides, if she was going to keep making terrible decisions, like freeing deadly dragons, she needed someone looking out for her.

If anything, now he needed to protect her from herself.

CHAPTER 50

ORRA LAY AWAKE, listening to the sounds of the others sleeping around her. Aeliana and Gaeren were both restless on their opposite sides of the camp. Lukai shared their agitation, as if it carried through his bond. Perhaps it did.

She rubbed the space on her palm where her bonds had once been, the memories of the attachments like a phantom pain. She'd sensed her bonds' sharpest pains and regrets along with their deepest hopes. Today's events might have carried that same weight for these people and their bonds.

The braid at her wrist twinged with its own longing, reminding her of her primary purpose. The starbridge wasn't here. The disappointment burned deep in her gut. They'd been scattered throughout Rhystahn for the last thousand years. What made her think she'd gather them within a few short moons?

Still, she felt she was on the right path. Aeliana needed her, and it seemed as if the arrow's absence allowed Orra to continue pursuing it while helping Aeliana. It reminded her of the days when she'd walked in the Sun's blessing.

Orra rose from her bedroll and made her way to the edge of camp. As she passed Cyrus, she sensed his dreams still plaguing him with his grandmother's death. She bent down and placed two fingers on his temple, smoothing the sharp edges of his dreams, like blending water with light to allow joy to seep in.

He sighed in his sleep and turned, the lifted burden making Orra feel lighter too, even as her draining power weighed her down. She paused at the forest line, exactly between the two sentries on either side of the camp. They each glanced at her in turn but made no motion to stop her, especially when they caught sight of Sylmar joining her.

"You knew I'd come," he said.

"I suspected." She didn't bother looking at him but smiled as she gazed out over the lost city.

"Kendalyhn couldn't sift through your soul."

"No half-light can. But you knew that before you sent her to me."

"I suspected." His tone remained light, and for a moment Orra allowed herself to think of him as a teasing friend.

The silence between them lengthened until flashes of light popped in the sky, shooting down to the earth like meteors. Sylmar held up a hand, shielding his face, but Orra kept her eyes open until they watered, breathing in the sight of the Stars coming down to honor the dead progenies and take back their starlocks.

The sentries called out in their excitement, waking most of the others to watch. The lights came and went in such vast numbers, the broken city illuminated like it was filled once more. Until suddenly all the starlocks were gone, and with them all the Stars. Tears streamed down Orra's face, the loss of their presence too deep to ignore.

The others settled back in camp, still murmuring over the shock of such a sight, speculating over how many progenies had died by Durriken's fire.

"I know who you are." Sylmar shifted closer, as if daring her to look him in the eye. "I know what you did. The others might think you're too holy to lead us astray, but I know how selfish you truly are."

Orra's smile faded, and she blinked up at the Stars, the pain of watching their dance from the earth a welcome feeling. A grounding sensation. "Few have recognized me over the years. It takes someone who pays attention. Someone who knows what to look for—and when."

His laugh came out harsh. "Don't expect me to be flattered. I won't forget your mistakes, no matter how much you pretend to help us."

"I would think less of you if you did." She finally turned, watching him closely.

A flicker of fear crossed his face, and he tightened his grip on his staff. She didn't want his fear, but she appreciated his vigilance. It would serve their mission well.

"Even so," she said, "you don't know the whole story. So often we acknowledge that good intentions can be the difference between an action being right and wrong. But sometimes good intentions can lead to action that still has negative consequences. Someday my sins will be revealed to all, along with the Sun's glory." Her voice dropped to a whisper. "The time is soon." She turned back, her focus resting on Aeliana.

Sylmar shifted, following her line of vision. "You leave the girl out of your mischief." His words came out low in warning. When she didn't respond right away, he straightened. "Did you hear me?"

Orra nodded even though she couldn't make promises. "I made my choices long ago. I have to bear the consequences." She twisted the braid at her wrist. "Aeliana will have her own choices to make."

CHAPTER 51

"Who do you think will stop glaring at me first?" Aeliana asked. "Sylmar or Gaeren?"

Cyrus grinned from beside her, his teeth flashing in the sliver of moonlight. After one day back on the road, they'd gotten stuck with night watch, and Aeliana was glad. The day had been a strained, silent one, everyone too wary to say anything they shouldn't. Now she and Cyrus still sat mostly in silence, but it was a peaceful one with the fire crackling and Holm softly snoring.

This far from Islara, the forest no longer carried the scent of smoke, but Aeliana could still smell it on her clothes, like the ashes of the city's residents clung to her skin and stained the fabric.

"I think most everyone has glared at you today," Cyrus said. "Except for maybe Orra and me."

She made a face, knowing he was right. Her desire to free Durriken hadn't been a popular one, which wasn't fair considering cutting out his brand had ended up being their only option anyway. She thought about sharing the memories Durriken had shown her as proof that she'd made the right choice, but she feared confirming the dragon's magic would only fuel people's insistence that he was too dangerous to have let live. Gaeren even gained some ground with the Recreants when word got around that he'd tried to slay Durriken.

"Do you think his story is true?" she asked.

"Whose? Gaeren's?" He shrugged. "Kendalyhn tested him, and Iris vouched for his past. What does he have to gain by lying?"

Aeliana bit her lip. Access to her mother? Inside information on the Recreants? Sylmar, Velden, and Jasperus had held a hushed meeting after dinner instead of discussing their plans with everyone at the fire like usual. The caution didn't surprise her. If anything, she wondered why they hadn't been doing that from the beginning, knowing that at any point she could be branded and under Mayvus' control.

But it still left her confused. Gaeren was arrogant and foolhardy, but he hadn't shown any signs of being a danger to her or their mission to save her mother. Gaeren had ridden into Islara to save her from a dragon. He'd shielded her with his body when he anticipated Durriken's fire. And his words about their childhood stirred up that same longing she'd had for home, like he was the tie she'd been looking for to her past.

What if she asked to see his memories?

She ran her finger over the fresh scabs and bruises lining her arms. She couldn't remember getting them, but a lot had happened in Islara. She tapped into her starlock's power, letting it feed her magic as she healed them one by one.

"Has your magic replenished?" Cyrus asked.

She shook her head. "Not completely. Sylmar said it could take a few days. It's why they use their magic so rarely."

"I would have liked to see your shield."

She smiled. She was eager to try it again, too. "You know, slicing Durriken's other wing was both wildly brave and stupid."

He grinned. "I couldn't let you always be the one to save the day."

She snorted. "I never save the day."

"I thought I was going to die when I did that." He shook his head, his gaze unfocused, likely reliving the moment. "But I was more worried that you would."

Aeliana's throat grew tight. "You know you've already fulfilled your vow to your grandma a dozen times over."

He smiled. "I didn't protect you because Gams told me to. I'm not even sure I protected you because of how important you're supposed to be to the Vendarans. Maybe that should be my motivation. It sounds more like a mission from the Stars. But it's more instinctual than that. More simple. You're my friend, and I care about what happens to you."

Aeliana didn't trust herself to speak, so she reached out and squeezed his hand in thanks.

Cyrus leaned back, angling behind her to see deeper into the woods. A line of leather stuck out from his collar, and she tapped it.

"What's that?"

He sat up, placing a hand over his neck. "Nothing, it's just—the last time we stopped in a town for supplies, I noticed people treating the progenies differently. I thought it would be good for me to have a fake starlock."

She grinned. "That's actually brilliant."

"You think so?" He beamed at her.

"What did you pick for the charm?"

His hand went back to his neck. "Just a thing. Something to weigh it down."

She let him awkwardly avoid her eyes for a bit longer before letting out a snort. "You're a terrible liar, but I guess that makes you an excellent priest."

He frowned, glancing back at the lumps of blankets containing their friends. "Do you think an excellent priest would want to read a copy of *The Sins of the Stars*?"

Aeliana followed his gaze. "You saw Gaeren reading it when we stopped for lunch, didn't you?"

He nodded, his face clouded with shame.

"I think an excellent priest would do his best to learn as much as he can, even about teaching that could be blasphemous." She nudged him with her elbow, and he smiled faintly. "Then he would compare it to all the things he knows to be true about the Stars. Weigh the information out and ask the Stars for guidance."

He nodded and opened his mouth, but then his focus darted beyond her, his eyes squinting as his muscles tensed. "Are those—?"

Aeliana turned around, expecting nothing but darkness. Instead, silvery figures crept out from the brush dividing the road from their camp. Aeliana reached for her bow. Tomorrow was the new moon.

Surely these dying winex weren't reckless enough to stage an attack now. Aeliana jumped to her feet, pulling an arrow from her quiver while Cyrus unsheathed his sword. She tried to remember Velden's instructions. Winex had weak joints, so she should go for the knees. But if it came down to it, neither of their close combat skills had improved enough for a fight.

"Sylmar, Velden, Lukai!" Aeliana shouted. She didn't need stealth like the winex. She counted ten of them, but even if they'd had twenty, it wouldn't have been a fair fight in the creatures' emaciated condition.

The others rose from their bedrolls, barely grabbing their weapons before the winex were upon them. Two of the winex brandished sticks, and Aeliana gawked as they went after Sylmar and Velden, who batted them away like flies. Two more were met by Kendalyhn's and Jasperus' swords. Unfortunately, the two who had actual swords and seemed to know how to use them came for Aeliana and Cyrus.

Aeliana struggled to pull out her heavy dagger, barely managing to hold it out and block the winex's thrust. Her dagger was no match for a sword, and the momentum pushed her to the ground. Before the winex could thrust again, Gaeren was standing between them, blocking the attack and countering it with his sword. With his and Riveran's help, the two strongest fighters went down fast.

Three others went straight for the packs, digging for food, but Holm and Iris were waiting, the slice of their daggers mercifully quick. Orra stood off to the side, eyes closed and brow pinched as if mentally warding off the intruders. The fight was nearly over before it began, but the final winex raised his arm over Lukai, the glint of metal making Aeliana finally take aim and loose an arrow. The surge of energy in her blood made her aim true, but she pierced the creature's arm instead of his heart, making him drop the weapon and stumble.

Aeliana ran forward just as Lukai knocked the winex to the ground, his sword lined up to plummet through creature's chest.

"Wait!" Aeliana's cry startled Lukai, staying his sword. "His cheek. Look at his left cheek."

The others gathered around too, while the winex mewed pitifully. He scratched at the arrow in his arm, too weak or scared to pull it free. His big, mournful eyes studied them all as he squirmed, far too aware of his fate. In the center of his left cheek, a black mark stood out against his silver skin, a tear-shaped scar.

"Felk?" Aeliana asked.

The creature froze, then cocked his head at her. "You know me?"

Sylmar growled and lumbered closer. "He's been following us all this time." He whipped out his knife, but Aeliana blocked him with her body.

"How do you remember your name?" she asked the winex.

"We always know our names. It's written in our minds. Like breathing or scavenging for food. We can't forget the things of survival." Felk shifted warily, taking a step away. Lukai grabbed the winex's injured arm before he could bolt, and the creature let out a howl.

Aeliana frowned. She hadn't anticipated the scar transferring across his rebirth. So their bodies weren't entirely new even if their minds didn't hold their memories.

"We need to kill him," Sylmar said.

Aeliana frowned. "Tomorrow is a new moon." She studied the winex as he studied her back. "Doesn't that mean he'll die tonight anyway?"

"It means he'll be reborn tomorrow," Velden corrected. "With the Sun's morn."

"But he won't remember us?" Aeliana asked.

Velden hesitated, glancing at Sylmar.

"He followed us once already," Sylmar said. "Do you want to take the risk? For all we know, there are dozens of eggs planted between Valorian and here. We don't need an army at our front and another at our back."

"He had fewer winex with him than the last time he attacked," Aeliana said. "And clearly these weren't a problem. He doesn't seem like much of a threat."

"Things might have gone differently if the moon were full," Sylmar said.

"Might have?" Felk's eyes squeezed shut, and he threw his head back in that all too familiar laugh, a tinkling sound like a wind chime. It left everyone in the group momentarily stunned. Aeliana's mind felt fuzzy, and her actions slowed. Felk used the distraction to bolt away from Lukai, but Holm and Jasperus each grabbed an arm, holding him back despite his even louder howls.

"What was that?" Cyrus asked.

"A laugh," Sylmar said. "They often use it to reel in their prey."

"Let's tie him up," Aeliana suggested. "Let him loose in the morning."

"Whatever for?" Sylmar huffed out, then stalked off toward his bedroll, mumbling under his breath.

"It does seem…unwise," Velden said, rubbing his webbed hand over the back of his head.

"I'm curious about their transition," Aeliana said. Cyrus' eyes lit up with his agreement. "I'd like to watch it. And as a newborn, he won't be a threat to us."

Felk's tongue slipped out from between his rows of teeth to swipe across his lip. "I might not even survive." His interest in her plan probably confirmed it was a bad one.

"Maybe we'll make sure you don't survive," Lukai muttered, following Sylmar. The others slowly dispersed as well, not bothering to hide their disapproval. Jasperus and Holm forced Felk to the ground before tying his hands and feet.

"First the dragon, now a winex." Kendalyhn shook her head.

Gaeren and Riveran stayed, the faithful friend taking his cue from the prince.

"Is he a threat to your crown, too?" Aeliana asked, unable to stand the judgmental silence.

Gaeren ignored her question, holding out her dagger, grip first. "This is a terrible weapon for you. You need something light with a sharper edge."

She yanked it from his hand and shoved it in her belt, nearly missing its sheath. Gaeren smirked, the laughter in his eyes far more condemning than his earlier silence and stares. He turned back to his bedroll, and Riveran followed.

At the edge of the group, Orra stood, a serene smile on her face. She gave the slightest nod to Aeliana before finding her bedroll as well.

"I bet they've all done it once in their life," Cyrus said quietly. He and Aeliana remained, watching the winex squirm.

"Done what?" she asked.

"Caught a winex before a new moon and watched it be reborn. It's probably a rite of passage as a child here."

Aeliana smiled, then pulled out some dried meat, offering it to Felk.

"Wait a—that was supposed to be our snack." Cyrus glared at Aeliana, snatching the remaining meat from her hand.

Felk grinned as he chewed, his eyes closed to mere slits.

They dragged Felk to their original lookout, watching for more intruders while also watching for his transition. As the night wore on, Felk grew more still, his breathing turning shallow. Even his skin turned an ashy grey instead of silver.

"Are you sure he's not dying?" Cyrus asked, nudging Felk with his boot. Felk no longer moved, and Aeliana couldn't be sure he still breathed.

"Maybe it was the arrow in his arm." She bit her lip. She should have healed it, but she'd been worried it would make him too strong.

Exhaustion seeped in as Aeliana realized in their desperation to see Felk's transition, they'd never woken the third watch. The others stirred around camp. Kendalyhn rebuilt the fire, and Holm began packing supplies. Lukai led the horses to a new place to graze while they prepared to move out.

The Sun peeked over the horizon, and Aeliana started when Cyrus hissed her name. When she turned to look again, Felk's ashy skin looked mottled, and flecks of it blew away in the morning breeze. In moments, his entire body had dissolved to dust, the remnants of him floating away on the wind—except for a tiny figure left where his ribs had once been, half covered by the rags that had kept Felk somewhat modest—or maybe just warm.

A tiny yawn rose from the fabric, followed by a mewling noise, making Aeliana's breath hitch.

She stepped forward, adjusting the fabric to see those same mournful eyes looking up at her, the single tear marking Felk's left cheek. He blinked, and his lip quivered, revealing a mouth empty of the ferocious teeth he'd had moments before. Tiny hands balled into fists, and silvery legs poked out through the rags as he kicked. Aeliana squeezed her eyes shut, wanting to block out the pitiful sight, but it couldn't be unseen.

"No, Aeliana," Cyrus warned even as her hands reached for the bundle.

She picked Felk up, adjusting the rags tighter around his small form until he was snuggled between her arm and chest. She reached for her water flask and tipped it up to the tiny creature's parted mouth.

"You can't possibly bring him with us."

"He'll die if we leave him." Aeliana set her jaw, refusing to look at Cyrus. She stared at Felk, who studied her between slow blinks.

"It's their way," Cyrus said, but his words no longer held conviction. He leaned forward, reaching for Felk's tiny fist, which relaxed just enough to grasp Cyrus' finger instead. "By tomorrow, he'll be a toddler; at the end of the week, he'll almost be full grown."

"He won't stay with us that long. Just a couple of days at most. Until he can take care of himself."

Cyrus snorted, startling Felk into a cry.

Aeliana hushed him, then stroked his face and cheek until his eyes slid shut once more, and his mouth twitched into a gummy smile.

Aeliana smiled in return, but Cyrus backed away, shaking his head.

"Sylmar is going to kill you."

CHAPTER 52

BY THE TIME the Sun was high in the sky, Aeliana was forced to ride nearly a half mile behind the others. Instead of heading northeast, beyond Mt. Vescano and toward the Pass, Gaeren led the group northwest, angling toward the main roads that would give them the quickest path to the wetlands he called home. Lukai and Cyrus took turns keeping her company, but even they grew weary of the screeches coming from Felk's mouth.

Aeliana jostled the quickly growing winex in her arms, trying to hush him as she offered water and bits of food. "Come on, Felkie, you need to eat."

"Felkie?" Lukai asked with a grimace.

"Would you like to be the one to hold him?" Aeliana snapped. Lack of sleep hadn't improved her mood. Sylmar had told her that if she couldn't get Felk to quiet down before nightfall, he'd kill the winex himself. He wasn't willing to risk their safety by attracting all the predators in the surrounding area.

"He'd probably be better off if you left him on the ground and rode away," Lukai said.

Felk gave an especially loud cry, and Lukai rubbed at his ears.

"It's like calves," he added. "If you carry them around, they don't learn how to walk and get their own milk. You're weakening him by making him dependent on you."

"Maybe you should swap with Cyrus. Felk seemed to enjoy him singing." It wasn't true, but she'd rather listen to off-key lullabies than Lukai's opinion on raising winex.

Her bondmate didn't waste any time riding ahead, and when Cyrus returned, Riveran came with him. Aeliana had hardly heard two words out of Gaeren's right-hand man—hadn't even seen the two of them talking. The bird on his shoulder squawked as they approached, its eyes on Felk.

"Can I hold him?" Riveran asked.

Aeliana stiffened, glancing between him and Cyrus, who shrugged.

"What are you going to do?" she asked.

He reached out his hands, the distance impossibly far between their horses. "I don't have magic. I can't hurt him."

"There are plenty of ways to hurt him without a starlock."

"Please?" The calm patience in his tone and eyes won her over. That and the fact that she'd reached her limit. As she passed Felk over, he squirmed, looking around for her in a panicked frenzy, but Riveran wrapped him tighter, pulling the winex in against his chest. Then, to Aeliana's shock, he stuck his finger in Felk's mouth.

The winex immediately start gnawing, his cries replaced by strange gummy noises and something reminiscent of a purr.

"How did you—what did you do?" Aeliana leaned over, watching as Felk's eyes drifted shut.

"Back home, my son would cry when he was teething. I spent dozens of hours walking him back and forth during the night, letting him gnaw on my finger."

"He's teething?"

Riveran shrugged. "The first day of a winex's life is the most painful. The amount of growth they have is hard on their bodies. Considering how many teeth they have, I figured it was a safe assumption." He passed Felk back, and the winex whimpered until Aeliana got him settled with her own finger between his gums.

"What about when his teeth come in? Won't it hurt to let him bite?"

"Guess you'll find out." His smile showed through his facial hair. "No, don't worry. I'll whittle some wood for him to chew on instead."

"Thank you," Aeliana said.

"Yes. We all thank you," Cyrus said. "Except maybe Sylmar. I think he was hoping for an excuse to—" Cyrus cut off when he took in Aeliana's glare.

As the day wore on, Aeliana finally found a routine with Felk, and in the evening she requested a night off from training, insisting she'd have time the next night when Felk was older. Kendalyhn refused to include him in the meal she made, but Riveran and Aeliana ate smaller portions, sharing their food with Felk, who toddled around the campfire.

When he tripped and fell, tears pooled in his eyes, his wail drawing everyone's attention.

"Mama," he cried, reaching out for Aeliana.

The others exchanged horrified looks as she scooped him up, driving her to her bedroll even though it was far too early for her to go to sleep. Felk rubbed his eyes, so she nestled him against her while he sucked his thumb and drifted to sleep. A glint of moonlight danced on his silver skin, and his mouth fell open to reveal the new teeth he'd sprouted.

A shadow fell over them, and Aeliana looked up to find Orra kneeling next to her, smiling.

"I thought I'd seen everything possible under the Sun, but you've proved me wrong."

The next three nights, Riveran offered to play with Felk while Aeliana trained. The evening air filled with tinkling chimes of winex laughter as Aeliana and Cyrus practiced archery at the edge of camp. With each laugh, they paused, as if the sound were a toxin leaving them stunned.

"Maybe this is good for us," Cyrus said. "Think we'll become immune if we listen to him laugh enough?"

"I still don't think that would convince Sylmar to let him stay," Aeliana said.

During the day, Felk rode with Aeliana. She winced as his elbow dug into her stomach, but she refused to complain. Sylmar would be sure to offer a solution with his blade, and Kendalyhn would make some remark about her being more princess than priestess.

"Mama," Felk hissed. "There's not enough room." He elbowed her again as he readjusted on the saddle. He wasn't wrong. Five days into the moon's cycle, he was almost as tall as Aeliana, mostly because he stood straighter than any winex she'd seen, tall, like a man.

She glanced at the others, wary that they might have heard. She'd told him to call her Aeliana, but he couldn't make it stick.

"Let me run alongside you. I can keep up." His pleas grew louder, making the others glance back in irritation.

She hesitated over Felk's request, then nodded, more for the sake of their poor horse. At first Felk ran beside them, upright, but as the day wore on, his gait changed to a lope, where he used his hands almost as much as his feet. More than once, Aeliana caught her companions brandishing weapons, either because they saw him as a threat or because they wanted him to see them as a threat.

He ran on, oblivious, bringing pinecones or rocks he found in the woods to Aeliana, eager for her praise. Despite everyone's complaints, no one had a problem with his keen sense of smell, which enabled him to gather dozens of strawberries that afternoon.

"He looks more like the first Felk we met," Cyrus said as they picked up their bows and arrows to practice once more.

Felk danced near the fire, his tinkling laugh making more than one person turn his way, dazed by the sound.

Aeliana knew what Cyrus meant, but she couldn't agree. She remembered the hatred burning in Felk's eyes, but now they were lit with excitement and hope. He looked nothing like she remembered from the attacks.

Gaeren sauntered over, leaning against a tree just out of hearing range. He watched long enough that she took aim for a spot over his head, but he didn't even flinch when she let it loose. He moved to a stump when it came time for her to spar with Lukai, his lips twisting in his constant smirk, but when Lukai had her practice healing and growth, Gaeren's smirk disappeared, his brow pinched as he watched their every move.

"Should I injure Gaeren and have you heal him?" Lukai asked, his tone strangely cautious. "You're spending all your time watching him anyway."

Aeliana tried to laugh it off. "You might get tried for treason."

"It might be worth it."

"Ready for a break?" Sylmar hobbled their way, standing between them and Gaeren, which conveniently blocked the prince's view.

"Yes," Aeliana breathed out.

"I meant Lukai." Sylmar angled his head back toward camp. "Go on. I'll finish up with her tonight."

Aeliana slumped as Lukai took his leave.

"We haven't talked much about what happened with Durriken." Sylmar's eyebrows rose as he leaned on his staff. "And I don't mean you letting him go."

Aeliana tried to think about what else happened that night. "Cutting out his brand?"

"The shield you created."

The memory came back in a flash. The unbridled release of magic. The heady sense of the lack of control. The eagerness to do it again. "I don't know how I did that."

"I don't either, but we need to push you to a point where we can find out."

She swallowed hard, glancing at Kendalyhn, who sat by the fire with Lukai. "What about testing me again? Why am I able to heal and create a shield?"

Sylmar shook his head. "There's no need to test. Both are on the constructive somatic spoke. It's rare for you to have both skills, but even weaned your power is stronger. I can't explain that, but I'm confident in your spoke."

"And what if it's too dangerous? Too unfocused? I don't want to hurt anyone again."

"That's what I'm here for."

She nodded. After seeing what Mayvus was willing to do, Aeliana knew she needed to be willing to push herself more. To find out just how much good she could do even if it required some risks.

"Healing someone is a bit more basic because it's fixing an injury that's already happened," Sylmar said. "Creating a protective barrier is more complex, almost predictive in how it prevents the injury from ever happening."

"I just thought it was a shield. Made of light."

"Is that what you envisioned creating that night?"

She frowned, trying to remember. "No. I just envisioned all of my magic going out from my body, blocking whatever Durriken might send our way. I'm not sure I could recreate that unless someone was truly in danger."

Sylmar's staff shifted to molten. "Who would it have to be for you to be the most motivated? Yourself?" He let the staff hover over her arm, and she backed away. "Lukai? Iris? Felk?"

Aeliana's eyes narrowed. "You wouldn't torture someone just to scare me into using my magic."

"Felk!" Sylmar called, addressing the winex for the first time.

Felk's hairless silver head popped out from behind a tree where he and Riveran were playing hide-and-seek, his eyes scanning for who might have called his name.

"No." Aeliana clenched her fists to stop them from shaking. "Use it on me."

"Fine, but you need to set him free," Sylmar said. "He's old enough now to survive on his own."

She watched as Felk darted around camp, accidentally knocking over food supplies and unsettling the horses. "Tomorrow."

Sylmar nodded. "Otherwise, he'll take part in our lessons. Now, try to block my staff."

That night, Aeliana shifted in her bedroll, unable to sleep. Felk squatted on a stump, his long limbs folded up until he looked like a ball in the shadows. Gaeren and Velden were on watch, but Felk stayed up most nights, his nocturnal nature overriding the schedule he followed with them.

Aeliana stood, tugging her cloak around her. She couldn't imagine sending him away, but she wasn't willing to let Sylmar use him against her.

"Hi, Mama," Felk whispered as she approached.

Her throat tightened. How was she supposed to tell him to stay behind? She wrapped an arm around him but still couldn't find the right words.

"Why did you let Sylmar hurt you?" he asked.

Aeliana's arms tingled where she remembered the burn of his staff, but it had been worth it. She'd produced small shields of light, and while they weren't anything like the one she'd created with Durriken, the process became more familiar, the ability to create one faster like her muscles' memory with aiming an arrow.

"It's the same as when you and Riveran wrestle," she said. "He's teaching you to be able to defend yourself if something attacks you."

The silence stretched. She turned to study Felk's profile, his large eyes scanning the skies, darting as he watched the Stars in their dance.

"Why do they hate me?" Felk asked.

Aeliana stilled. "What? Who hates you?"

"The others. Riveran and Gaeren play with me. Even Cyrus likes me. But the rest don't. They won't eat with me or talk to me. They don't even smile." His lips quivered.

Aeliana sighed. "They don't hate you. They just don't understand you. We've talked about how other winex are different. How they don't like people. It's hard for them to forget that."

He nodded but seemed unconvinced. Probably because she wasn't convinced of her own words. All the friendships she'd formed with her companions had halted their growth. If it had just been Durriken's release, they might have moved on, but now Felk was a constant reminder that she might not be trustworthy. The distance was painful after she'd tasted the sweetness of friendship.

Which made what she needed to do even harder.

"You know how to fish now. How to find food in the forest."

"Riveran says I'm a quick learner." He grinned, his dozens of teeth flashing.

"You are. You're the smartest winex I know."

He rolled his eyes. "I'm the only one you know."

She hesitated. "I think it would be good for you to meet more winex. We've taught you all we can, and now you need to be with other winex. To learn from them."

Felk's eyes widened, and he stood, shaking his head violently before she even finished speaking. "I can't. I won't."

"If you don't, Sylmar will make you go."

A tiny growl escaped Felk's lips before he shut them tight. His gaze flicked over Aeliana's shoulder, and she turned to find Gaeren at her back.

"Everything good?"

She shrugged.

"My mama doesn't want me anymore." Felk's voice grew louder, threatening to wake the rest of the camp.

Aeliana pressed her lips together. Maybe it was best he believed that lie.

"I doubt that's what she meant." Gaeren approached Felk, hands out cautiously. "She's just trying to do what's best for you—and us." His hand wrapped around Felk's wrist. At first Felk tried pulling away, but then he went still, his eyes glazing over.

Aeliana stepped forward. "What are you doing to him?"

Felk gasped, finally jerking out of Gaeren's grip. He landed on all fours, snarling at Gaeren. With all his teeth bared, he finally looked the way Aeliana remembered seeing him, and she shuddered.

"That's not real," Felk said, his voice rising in panic. "That didn't happen." His eyes volleyed from Aeliana to Gaeren.

"What did you show him?" she demanded.

"Did I try to hurt you, Mama?" Felk's voice cracked, his eyes filling with tears. "Did you shoot me with an arrow?"

Aeliana glared at Gaeren. "Why would you show him that? He was different then. It's in the past."

Felk took a step back, shaking his head. "But it's true?"

Before she could say anything else, he loped off into the night, a mournful howl escaping his lips.

Aeliana didn't even realize she'd run after him until Gaeren's arms and chest blocked her, a solid wall that she beat against.

"It was for the best." He tried wrapping his arms around her, whether to comfort or subdue her, she didn't care. Instead of reaching for her heavy dagger at her hip, she pulled his from its sheath directly in front of her. Its familiar light weight from that night in Islara brought back the desperate emotions swirling through those memories. She held the dagger at his throat, the power she felt when he went still making her sicker.

"Don't touch me," she hissed.

He raised his arms and backed away. "I was just trying to help." The remorse in his eyes almost made her believe him.

She tossed the dagger at his feet. "I don't want your help."

CHAPTER 53

"You're staring again," Riveran said.

Gaeren shifted his eyes away from where Daisy sat atop her horse. "I expected her to hate me for being an Elanesse. I didn't expect her to hate me for helping her free Felk. At least not for this long."

"Women are complex creatures." Riveran grinned. Gullet squawked his agreement from Riveran's shoulder. "And it's only been six days."

A dozen retorts rose to Gaeren's mind, but for once he let them slide. An argument would only lead them back to stony silence, and if he didn't have Riveran to talk to, his options for conversation on the long rides grew slim.

There was always Orra, but half the time she was in her own world, far away from Rhystahn. Cyrus had borrowed *The Sins of the Stars*, so now the strange almost-priest only wanted to discuss theology with Gaeren. Every night, Velden left camp, returning after Daisy's training for a meeting with Sylmar and Jasperus. Those three never spoke to Gaeren, probably afraid he might pull the memory of their conversation right out of their head if they got close enough.

Kendalyhn hardly acknowledged Gaeren's existence, but she seemed to treat Daisy the same, so he didn't take it personally. Holm and Lukai had started sparring with him in the evenings, and Iris was gracious enough to give him a long-overdue haircut. She'd finally decided he was the same boy she remembered and fussed over him more than his own mother ever had. Sometimes they reminisced about life at the Celanoft Sungazer, but that usually ended with Iris in tears as she questioned how much Emeris had known about Gaeren's identity versus how much she had intentionally kept secret.

He would have liked to talk to Daisy some. He hadn't seen her do any of the blood magic Kendalyhn mentioned. He hadn't heard her making plans to overthrow the royal family. Maybe if they had a conversation, they could get to the bottom of what had happened that night when she'd left, or what she'd been doing since, or why their families had to hate each other when they'd been so close as children. But the connection they'd had as children was gone. Instead of being overjoyed at their reunion, he felt like the Daisy he'd known had died, and now he had to grieve the loss.

With no other options, he was left with Riveran for company.

Gaeren tugged on Skunk's reins to keep him from snapping at the horse's tail in front of him. The larger roads allowed for a faster pace, but to Gaeren's and Skunk's dismay, the size of their group still slowed them down.

"You should try talking to her," Riveran said. "Clear the air a bit. Maybe you two could be friends again."

Gaeren snorted. "That's easy for you to say."

"Seriously, go on. Take Gullet with you. She likes animals."

Gullet squawked as Riveran forced the bird off his shoulder. When Gullet landed on Gaeren's arm, they both eyed each other with distaste.

"Are you going to make this situation better or worse?" Gaeren asked.

Gullet readjusted, digging his claws through Gaeren's sleeve and into his skin. Gaeren tugged on his reins, guiding Skunk past Sylmar and Velden until he was lined up with Daisy's mare.

At first Daisy glanced up with a ready smile that took Gaeren's breath away, but as soon as she saw who approached, her face went blank. She sat straighter, channeling Enla's regal grace even though she wore the same homespun split skirts that Orra insisted on wearing.

He held back a frown at the oddity, certain she'd misinterpret it.

But even the peasant women in Elanesse chose practical trousers over skirts. How did these two women expect to defend themselves properly?

"Gullet was hoping to cheer you up a bit," Gaeren said, holding out the hawk as an offering. "He usually comes with earsplitting squawks and bird droppings. Otherwise, he makes everyone smile."

Daisy stared at the bird, then Gaeren. "Did Riveran tell you to bring him?"

Gaeren glanced over his shoulder, where Riveran leaned across his saddle's horn to get a better view. He grinned at Gaeren.

"He did, actually." Gaeren turned back around. "So maybe you should pet the bird and make everyone happy. Then you can go back to hating me."

"I don't hate you," she mumbled, leaning over to line her arm up with his. Their hands brushed for the long moment it took Gullet to make the transfer, making Gaeren's bond mark tingle.

"Really? Then how do you treat the people you do hate?"

She shrugged. "Annoy me a bit more and you can find out." Her gaze softened as she ran her fingers down Gullet's feathers.

To Gaeren's frustration, Cyrus rode up between Gaeren and Daisy, sticking his hand out to pet Gullet. "We should bring him the next time we go hunting. Hawks are supposed to be great hunters."

"I didn't realize Dai—Aeliana went on the hunts," Gaeren said.

Her eyes narrowed when he stumbled over her name. He couldn't stop thinking of her as Daisy, but he'd at least tried using her given name when he spoke out loud.

"I don't anymore. I haven't been able to kill anything."

Once a week, they rested the horses while they hunted, and every few days they broke camp early to forage between cities. It took a lot to feed a group this size, which was one of the many reasons they'd continued at a painfully slow pace. But Gaeren had watched her train in the evenings, both with her magic and her archery. If she hadn't killed anything, it was because she hadn't tried.

"We should go out tomorrow. I'll bring Gullet and give you some tips. It might help get your mind off Felk."

She dragged her gaze away from Gullet's feathers to give Gaeren a glare. "Sylmar would never let you take me."

"But if he did, would you go?"

She stared at him, her face unreadable. "Yes."

"Sylmar," Gaeren called out, still studying Daisy.

The old man grunted from behind them. It was as good a reply as Gaeren was going to get.

"Tomorrow's a rest day," Gaeren said. "Aeliana and I were hoping to hunt." Even as the words left his lips, Gaeren knew the answer would be no. Why would they let someone they only partially trusted take weapons and go out alone in the woods with his sworn enemy, a woman they fiercely protected? But he watched for Daisy to react, and as the silence wore on, he finally saw her confidence falter.

"We're approaching the wetlands," Sylmar said. "The closer we get to your territory, the more advantages you'll have in finding prey. The two of you can go north while we have another party backtrack south."

Gaeren's mouth went slack for a moment. Sylmar actually said yes? Then he grinned at Aeliana, whose face turned red, her eyes narrowing into slits. His mind tuned in to a memory of Larkos groaning about Gaeren's immaturity.

Daisy turned away, and Gaeren's grin faded.

"Well, then, tomorrow we hunt." Gaeren raised his voice in an attempt at cheer, but the words fell flat.

Daisy slouched even deeper in her saddle. "Tomorrow we hunt," she mumbled.

As the land sloped down toward a valley, the forest thinned, providing open lands and a sense of safety that night. Sentries would see anything approaching from a long way off, allowing their watch to be a little more lax. For once, everyone gathered around the fire together, even Daisy. Sylmar had given her the night off in preparation for their morning hunt.

"I hear Jasperus is quite the storyteller," Riveran said. "Velden says the best one involves a giant squid."

Jasperus guffawed. "That's because it's his story."

"Can you blame me?" Velden said. "It's one of your best."

"Let's hear a new one tonight," Daisy said, reaching over to tug on Jasperus' sleeve. "Which one's your favorite?"

"Well, I always like the tragedy of Lovers' Falls."

Half of the group groaned.

"We've heard that a dozen times," Holm complained, even as Iris smacked him lightly on the back of the head.

"It's a beautiful story," she said. "It's not his fault if you can't appreciate it." But then she wrapped her arm through his, and they exchanged a look that confirmed Gaeren's suspicions about them.

"How about the story of King Melchinek," Kendalyhn suggested, her predatory stare locked on Gaeren.

Everyone grew quiet, the pop and sizzle of the fire the only thing breaking the silence of the night.

"I could probably recite it in my sleep." Gaeren grinned at Riveran, attempting to lighten the mood, but Riveran shook his head slightly, and Gaeren's smile fell.

"I doubt you've heard the whole story," Lukai muttered.

"Then tell him," Daisy said, turning to Jasperus. "I haven't heard it either."

A slow smile spread across Kendalyhn's face, and Gaeren had the feeling this was what she'd wanted all along. This story held nothing good for Gaeren or Daisy.

Jasperus shook his head. "I'm not sure it's a good one for mixed company."

Gaeren snorted. "Shouldn't we at least be able to hear each other's legends without fighting?"

"I'll tell it."

Everyone turned as Orra stood, the fire casting a strange glow on her dark skin.

"My version might be different from all of yours, but like Captain Moss and Lady Redwood"—Orra gave a regal nod in Gaeren and Riveran's direction—"I guarantee it's the most accurate."

No one dared argue.

"Everyone can agree that at the time of the Great Divide, Queen Selph Elanesse ruled the Vendarans. During that time, the Vendarans banded together to overcome all they'd lost, but with her husband's death in the Great War, Queen Selph lost much of her motivation to live, to serve, to lead. It wasn't until her son, Melchinek, succeeded the throne with his young wife and bondmate, Amaya, that Vendarans began to thrive." Orra scanned the group as if daring someone to argue, but so far both Recreants and Loyalists seemed to find her story accurate.

"For ten years, they ruled together," Orra continued. "Amaya bore him two children, a daughter named Valyn and a son named Breck."

"What?" Gaeren sat up straighter. "They only had one child."

"Told you he hadn't heard it," Lukai said.

Gaeren turned to Riveran. "Have you heard this?"

"I admit it's hard to swallow the first time you hear it." Riveran refused to hold his gaze. "I'm not sure any of us could verify the truth of either side. But it's worth hearing. It's worth trying to understand."

For a moment, Gaeren wondered if his old friend was still talking about Orra's story.

"May I continue?" Orra asked.

Gaeren nodded, glancing at Daisy. Her eyes held sadness, but as soon as they met his, she steeled her features and turned back to Orra.

"Over time, King Melchinek gave in to blood magic, using the dark spirits to grow his army."

Gaeren clenched his jaw. He wanted to call her out on her lies, but everyone else continued listening with rapt attention, undisturbed over the horror she spewed.

"Eventually, he became so obsessed with his desire for power that he made plans to kill a Star and take its power for himself."

This time it was the Recreants who balked.

"That doesn't make any sense," Jasperus said. "The Stars weren't even communing after the Great Divide."

"They still communed with Queen Amaya," Orra said.

"Why would they do that?" Iris asked.

"Why wouldn't we all know that?" Holm added.

"The events of history have a way of changing over time, depending on who tells the story. Elements that seem unimportant, or unbecoming, are often left out. Now, will you all let me finish?" She eyed them like a stern mother threatening to put them all to bed early. "King Melchinek was the first and last man to kill a Star, but instead of gaining power from the slain Star's blood, it killed him, and the power entered his son, Breck. Queen Amaya ruled in her husband's place until Breck came of age. His power was part of the reason the Elanesse family line held stronger starblood than most, though it grows weaker with every generation."

Her attention rested on Gaeren, reminding him that she spoke of his family line, of him and Enla. Her words were blasphemous, the idea of anyone, especially in his family, killing a Star preposterous. They might not worship the Stars, but his family still honored them. His anger was only slightly tempered by the fact that the Recreants all looked shocked and horrified as well.

"Valyn should have taken the throne," she continued, "but as the siblings grew, she saw that her brother's power far outmatched hers. He could easily kill her and take the throne, so she fled to the Myndren Mountains. She took up a quiet life as a priestess in a Sungazer, where she married Willem Wyndren."

Everyone's focus shifted to Daisy, whose eyes widened in surprise.

CHAPTER 54

"Willem Wyndren," Aeliana muttered. She glanced at Sylmar, who conveniently avoided her gaze. Her heart rate picked up speed as her mind caught up with the history. "You said my mother was a Wyndren. You're saying my family comes from the royal line? A thousand years ago?"

"They're saying your family is the rightful royal line." Gaeren's face scrunched with fury. "I thought the Wyndren line came from some distant cousin."

"No." Aeliana stood, facing Sylmar. "You said we were priests and priestesses—servants of the Sun. You said Mayvus only had some sort of spiritual authority." It had made more sense when they opposed a woman who used blood magic. Now it sounded like a petty family feud.

"I said that's what the royal family believed." Sylmar stood as well, leaning on his staff. "They don't acknowledge the Wyndrens. They say the Wyndrens lost their rights when Valyn left Elanesse."

"No." Gaeren ran a hand through his hair. His bewildered frown settled on the fire. "We don't even say that. I was never even taught about Valyn's existence."

"You're a throne warden, not a king," Sylmar snapped. "Don't assume your family tells you everything."

Gaeren reeled back from Sylmar's words, stirring up a strange thread of empathy in Aeliana's chest. Neither one of them had liked this story's ending.

"You don't care that Mayvus is taking power away from Gaeren's family," Aeliana said, slowly piecing the story together. "You just care that it's not being given to my mother."

The silence that followed was all the confirmation Aeliana needed.

"I came here to get rid of my magic," she said.

Gaeren started, his gaze flipping to her.

"You convinced me to learn it instead. I stayed to find my mother. To free her. But I have no interest in the Vendaran throne. You cannot convince me to pursue that." Her hands shook as she waved the idea away.

Kendalyhn snorted. "I told you she was too weak."

"Is that why you asked for the story? To prove some sort of point?" Gaeren folded his arms across his chest as Kendalyhn's face reddened.

"It doesn't make her weak," Sylmar said. "Emeris always denied interest in the throne as well. Sometimes the ones who want it the least are the ones most suited for it. It's why I thought it best to leave this detail out. When we first found her, it was more likely to scare her away than help convince her to come."

Heat spread from Aeliana's chest to her limbs, her starlock burning in tandem. "Sometimes you seem no different from Arvid and Vera. Out to manipulate me for what you want. You might as well call yourselves Zealots instead of Recreants. You still want a priestess on the throne."

"Zealots?" Gaeren asked.

"I'll explain later," Riveran mumbled.

"We didn't keep it from you because we were trying to manipulate you," Sylmar said. "You are under no obligation to take on your mother's role down the line. But we hope you will. We hope more time with us will make it what you want instead of what you fear. But I knew that fear would drive you away at the start."

His words took the edge off Aeliana's anger, but she still couldn't look at him. "Is there anything else I should know?"

"There's a lot," Sylmar said. "You were raised as a foreigner on blood magic. You know nothing of our people and culture, nothing even of your family history. We're not trying to keep secrets from you. Any question you ask will be answered."

She nodded, knowing that would have to be enough for now.

"Regardless of Kendalyhn's intentions," Orra said, "or Sylmar's reasons for deception, neither of you knew the story in its fullness. Now was the time for it to be told." Her soft voice permeated the air with a false sense of calm.

Aeliana glanced at Gaeren. He watched her for a long moment, a strange sense of understanding passing between them. Instead of his smirk or glare, there was an openness that hinted at his vulnerability.

"It seems like Myndren would be a known harbor for the Wyndrens if all that were true," Gaeren said slowly. "A place a throne warden would be taught to keep a close eye on."

"A lot can get lost in a thousand years," Orra mused.

"But why would Mayvus risk that association?" he pressed.

"Perhaps she's unaware. There are places in the world that call to people because of something intrinsic in them and in that place. For you and Velden it's the sea, for many Wyndrens, it's those mountains." She closed her eyes and tipped her head to the sky. "Before the Great Divide they were the closest place to the Sun."

Aeliana glanced at Gaeren, who shrugged. Others around the fire exchanged similar dumbfounded expressions. If Orra wasn't a Star, she had some sort of ability to tap into the past and future in ways other people never could. And if she was a Star… well, Aeliana wasn't sure what that meant.

"I've never heard of the Star being killed." Skepticism tainted Jasperus' words. "I've always heard that King Melchinek died young, but it was because he'd been sickly all his life."

Everyone turned to Orra, who blinked as if something was caught in her lashes. "Queen Amaya communed with a handful of Stars."

Everyone leaned forward to catch her quiet words.

"Andreas and Lucian—even Reyna. King Melchinek grew jealous of both the time she spent with them and the power they displayed. Witches convinced him that Lucian's death would release his power, but they tricked Melchinek. That night, the people were too busy mourning their king to notice not a single Star danced in the sky.

"As far as I know, that's the last time the Stars came to the earth—not to commune, but to ground themselves from the skies. It was a fast from the Sun's light in order to mourn the loss of Lucian." Orra's eyes were bright with unshed tears. She excused herself from the fire, leaving everyone to contemplate both the accuracy and the meaning of her story.

No one spoke as the fire crackled.

Winex howled in the distance, making Aeliana wonder how Felk was faring and if he'd found a pack. A twinge of remorse nagged at her, and she glanced at Gaeren, studying his unusually sober profile as he stared into the fire. If she could give second chances to dragons and winex, she should be able to give them to a man.

Especially one who had initially shown up to protect her.

She glanced over at the other Vendarans, who'd slowly begun warming up to her once more after Felk had run away. They were still allies—friends, even—but the realization that they'd kept this secret from her stung. How could she trust them to be looking out for her best interests if they couldn't tell her the whole truth?

She understood it. As long as she was a potential brand for Mayvus, she was a liability. The less she knew, the better. But the truth about her identity wasn't something they needed to keep from Mayvus.

Mayvus already knew.

"I'm surprised Sylmar let us go." Gaeren spoke over his shoulder, but Aeliana could still hear the smirk in his voice. It was the only way he knew how to smile, like he was always laughing at everyone.

They trekked down a path that might have once been a run-off from melting snow. The Sun was just starting to rise, and its golden glow reflected off the thin creek ahead. Gullet flew from tree to tree, his beady eyes scanning the forest floor.

"He probably had someone follow us," Aeliana said. None of them fully trusted the Prince of Elanesse, especially after Orra's enlightening story.

"I think someone's been following us for a while now," he said. "Velden goes out each night and comes back to report to Sylmar."

Aeliana stilled. "You think they're checking on Felk?"

"Maybe." Gaeren eyed a tree with a twisted trunk as if he might climb it for a bird's-eye view. He settled himself behind one of the curved roots popping out from the ground. "But Velden was doing that before Felk left."

He gestured for her to join him on the ground, but she hesitated. The space was large enough for two if they squished. Could she even aim properly if they sat that close?

"Come on," he whispered. "I'm only half-winex. I won't bite until the moon is full." He bared his teeth before winking at her.

She crouched behind the same root, hunching until they were shoulder to shoulder and hidden by low-hanging branches. She awkwardly rearranged her bow and readied an arrow, painfully aware of each time her arm rubbed against Gaeren's. He set his bow on the ground behind them as if he had no intention to hunt.

She frowned, glancing back in the direction of camp, wishing there had been a way out of this. The hills behind them rose upward, the redwood and maple forests they'd traveled thick with foliage, hiding any chance of seeing the others. She settled back in, forcing herself not to jerk away when Gaeren's leg settled against hers. The path before them opened up to something similar to the grasslands she'd seen on the way to Islara. Except this grass had murky areas where the creek seemed to bleed out into the lower land. The thick air was filled with the buzz of insects and the trill of birds waking with the Sun.

"There's probably a hundred species of frogs down there that you've never seen before," Gaeren whispered.

"Frogs?" Aeliana followed his gaze. "I thought we were looking for antelope."

He chuckled, then pressed his lips together, cutting off the sound. "I suppose you're not interested in catching frogs anymore." His tone turned wistful, and Aeliana's curiosity flared.

"You said I caught tadpoles." She spoke slowly as his words came back to her. "And you taught me to swim?"

He nodded, then pulled out his dagger, twirling it in his hands so the etched daisy blurred. "Even though the beach was close, we weren't allowed to go to it very often. We swam in the creek instead. You liked to pretend you were Sayhleen." His smile turned softer, the curved edges no longer a smirk.

A thousand questions rose to her mind, but they all felt too personal to ask a near stranger, even if he claimed they'd once been friends. She'd despised him when he'd wanted Durriken dead and when he'd driven away Felk, but now, when knowledge of their family history gave her more reason to hate him, she found herself wanting to give him a chance—hoping he might still give her a chance.

Amidst her swirling thoughts, one question rose to the surface. "What did you see when I disappeared?"

He stopped twirling the dagger, and his jaw clenched. "Your mother was fighting with a woman, probably Mayvus. I didn't know they were sisters back then." His eyes held an accusing glint, as if Aeliana had been the one to keep that secret. "Another woman and man guarded your father. You ran to him, and he used a golden arrow to escape, only the man and woman escaped with you. I knew your father didn't have magic, and they were using…" He trailed off, his eyes straying to her hands.

Instinct made her grip the bow and arrow tighter, but she couldn't hide all her scars. She let him take in the ugly white lines bleeding out from her palms.

"They were using blood magic," she finished for him, tensing, wondering what he thought of the scars. He already treated her like glass, which was more insulting than comforting. She didn't want his pity on top of being sheltered.

"Do you still use it?" he asked.

"Still?" The word came out choked. Stars. Who had told him that? Probably Kendalyhn. "No. I mean, I don't want to. I don't try to." She clamped her jaw down and let him assume the rest.

"So it's never appealed to you?"

She whipped her head to fully face him, their proximity unsettling. His eyes sparked with interest, but she couldn't tell if it was the glint of gossip or genuine curiosity. "Of course not."

"Hmph." He turned to face the wetlands once more. "You're lying," he murmured, his smirk evidence that, if she was lying, he wasn't put out by it.

Her face burned. It hadn't felt like a lie when she'd said it, but she supposed it wasn't the full truth. "Are you using magic on me?"

He shrugged. "It's my secondary spoke. I'm not very good at it, and we have to be touching. But anyone could have seen you didn't even believe that statement yourself."

She scooted away, thankful for any reason to reduce their contact. Even if sharp branches dug into her other side.

"I've been watching you practice," he went on, "and I've been thinking about it. You can't help who raised you. If you were raised with blood magic, if their desire spilled over to you, it's actually more impressive that you fought it. That you rose above it."

This time, the smile he offered was apologetic, maybe for using his magic on her without permission, but she suspected it went deeper than that. That he was apologizing for how she'd ended up being raised by half-lights using blood magic. That he still felt responsible.

"That's a surprisingly understanding perspective. Especially from someone like you."

He burst out laughing, and several birds flew from the tree they'd camped under. Gullet squawked his irritation from his perch a few trees over.

"Someone like me? What did I ever do to make you hate me so much?"

She couldn't help smiling even though the answer came quick enough. "You let Felk think he hurt me to chase him away. You condemned a possibly innocent dragon. How do you know Durriken wasn't fighting his brand, that he wasn't trying to rise above Mayvus' commands?"

Gaeren sighed and trained his attention back on the creek. Not that they had much hope of finding anything after how loud he'd been. "I guess I don't know. But I wasn't about to risk your life to find out." His words carried the weight of a responsibility Aeliana didn't understand. Still, it made her want to be worthy of it.

"I spent a lot of time at the Stargazers," she murmured.

He shot her a questioning glance.

"I suppose that's why I never wanted to use blood magic. The servants of the Stars in each town we lived in had more of a hand in raising me than my guardians." She set her bow and arrow against the tree root and rubbed at her scars, hating the way the memories churned within her.

"So you worship the Stars like Cyrus?" Wariness colored his tone, reminding Aeliana of Orra's story. Only witches worshiped the Stars in Vendaras.

"That's all anyone in Lorvandas worships. I haven't had time to examine my faith since I crossed the barrier, but I'm not a witch."

He hummed his understanding.

It gave her courage to continue. "The first time Arvid and Vera cut me, I thought it was wrong, so I sought forgiveness from the Stars. Every time they took my blood, I took to the Stargazer and prayed for forgiveness. I'm not sure the Stars still offered forgiveness after all my guardians did with my blood, but it didn't stop me from hoping, from asking for it anyway." Her throat grew tight. She wasn't sure why she'd shared that with him. She hadn't even explained it to Cyrus, who seemed bent on drawing her into his own time of worship and prayer.

Gaeren reached over and ran a calloused finger along her scars, and her breath caught at his touch. She hadn't expected a prince to have rough hands, but then he was also supposed to be a sailor. The way he traced each rise of skin left her feeling exposed.

"Why don't you heal them? Now that you have magic to smooth them away."

For a moment, the silly fear that he found them ugly rushed through her, but she didn't care what he thought. "Sometimes scars are best left as reminders. They show us our weaknesses to help us grow stronger."

His hand stilled over her palm, the warmth of his touch like fire even in the muggy heat of the wetlands. He gave her hand a squeeze before finally letting go. "Sometimes the scars that can't be seen end up as unwelcome reminders. Orra would say I was never meant to protect you. That you needed this ripple to prepare you for the challenges ahead."

Goosebumps rose with the loss of his warmth. His strange words still rang true—something she might not have said a few months ago. "She's probably right. I never wanted any of this. But it seems as if the Stars have a purpose in it."

He grinned, and for once the arrogant tilt seemed playful instead of haughty. "Or maybe the Sun. How much do you want to bet that I can convert Cyrus before we reach the Myndren Mountains?"

Aeliana snorted. "He's too devout. Haven't you seen the way he watches Orra?"

"Have you seen the way all the men watch Orra?"

Both their shoulders shook with silent laughter.

As Gaeren turned back to study the creek, Aeliana bit her lip. If he could look past her history with blood magic, who was she to judge him for his attitude toward Durriken? Or for being a Loyalist? Or for being the prince, son of the king and queen bent on annihilating Aeliana's family?

She sighed. There were just too many things dividing them. Even if they got along from this point forward, they would never have the friendship he claimed they'd shared in the past. They'd been children.

"Do you see that?" Gaeren reached for his bow, then hesitated with the arrow. Aeliana followed his gaze. Movement caught her eye —a dark figure, partially hidden in the shadows. The coloring seemed off for an antelope, along with the shape. A few more feet and it would reach the Sunlight, but it didn't move like an animal either.

Just as Gaeren drew back his arrow, Aeliana gasped, pushing his arm down before he even had the chance to aim.

A man ambled toward the water. A cloak covered him from the neck down, and a rough beard hid his face. The rest of his hair was cropped close to his head but stuck up in all directions like he hadn't combed it for days. His skin was lighter than most she'd seen in Vendaras, but she'd heard those from the east coast had fairer skin like Lorvandans. She glanced at her hands. The light copper that had been unusually dark in Lorvandas now seemed pale with her Vendaran companions. But it matched the stranger's. Her mother had come from the east. Maybe this man had too.

He bent forward, scooping up water and splashing it over his face, using it to smooth down his hair. His movements felt exaggerated, intentional, like he wanted to be seen.

"He's waiting for us to approach," Aeliana whispered.

"What?" Gaeren grabbed her, the restrictive motion strangely comforting as his fingers once again warmed her skin.

She shook his hand away along with the distracting thoughts.

"No," he hissed. "You can't talk to him. We have no idea who he is."

"I still don't really know who you are," she pointed out, "and Sylmar sent me off in the woods with you, alone." She stood, keeping a careful eye on the man as she made her way into the valley. The man turned in their direction, but he was too far away for Aeliana to make out his expression. He stayed still as she drew closer, not reaching for any weapons, not calling out for any assistance.

Despite Gaeren's protests, he shadowed her the whole way down the hill.

Too late, Aeliana realized the stranger could have a starlock, and then he might have any number of skills at his disposal, skills that could kill without weapons. Her own starlock warmed, reminding her that she wasn't powerless. She also knew Gaeren wouldn't hesitate to use his magic to protect her, and the thought left her surprisingly comforted. But the stranger's stance remained relaxed, maybe even patient.

When they were a dozen paces away, she stopped, studying the stranger before her. He towered over her even from a distance, unkempt and wary, his cloak muddy and torn. There was something familiar about him, something that tugged at a memory in the back of her mind.

"I just want to talk," the man said, "but I think the conversation would go better if you called off your guards."

Aeliana turned to Gaeren, hand out to smack his bow and arrow back to his side once more, but Gaeren's hands were already down. "We don't have guards…"

She narrowed her eyes, spinning around to scan the ridge they'd come from. So… Sylmar had sent someone after them.

Before she could see anyone, the stranger rammed into her side, and she landed hard on her back, the breath knocked from her. In the back of her mind, she registered the rush of an arrow by her ear. She held up her hands, shielding herself from the blow she anticipated, but it was Gaeren's elbow that bruised her arm as he dropped his bow and arrow and launched himself between Aeliana and her attacker.

The thump of paws on dirt reverberated through Aeliana's ears, followed by a snarl.

Gaeren placed himself over Aeliana as a human shield, but between his arm and side, she caught a flash of silver skin as the man scooted away on his backside, his hands raised in surrender to the strangely familiar winex hovering over him.

"Wait," Aeliana said, even as Gaeren tried shoving her farther behind him. "His hands."

The winex turned, the unmistakable tear mark on his cheek bringing a rush of emotion that clogged Aeliana's throat.

"He attacked you," Felk growled.

The man spun his hands, a glimpse of hope in his eyes. His knuckles and wrists were covered in tattoos.

"No. Back at the Falls—he saved my life." Aeliana pushed Gaeren aside and stood just as an arrow whizzed through the air, penetrating the stranger's side.

CHAPTER 55

THE STRANGER'S eyes widened as he grasped the arrow burrowed in his gut. He staggered back, his pleading gaze resting on Aeliana.

"No." She rushed forward, helping him to the ground. "No, no, no."

"I shouldn't have…" he whispered, trailing off with a low moan.

"Hush," Aeliana said.

Felk pulled on her arm. "Leave him. He can't be trusted."

She shook his hand off. "He needs help." Not that she knew how to help him. Her fingers trembled as she ripped the man's cloak and shirt to expose the wound. There didn't seem to be much blood. That had to be good.

"But he attacked you," Gaeren said.

"Arrow," the man croaked, reaching for his chest as if to instruct Aeliana, but his focus turned to Felk, his eyes intense through his pain. "For her."

Aeliana froze, the man's meaning far too clear. The stranger hadn't attacked her; he'd tried removing her as a target.

Felk and Gaeren both stood, scanning the ridge of the valley as Felk blocked her from whoever had shot the stranger.

"Go," Aeliana said, voice hoarse. "Find them. And get Lukai. Hurry!"

Felk took off in the direction the arrow had come from, but Gaeren hesitated, a strange vulnerability crossing his face. "Daisy…"

"It's all right. You don't need to protect me right now," she said.

His eyes slid shut, and for a moment Aeliana saw the child in him, needing those words, that release of responsibility. Then he practically flew through the woods, his footsteps like thunder between the trees. Out of desperation, Aeliana pushed against the red mark of her bond, willing Lukai to sense the urgency of her need, wishing she had been the one to get shot so he could feel it from afar.

She turned back to the stranger, who already looked paler. Blood trickled down his side like it drew a line connecting the fletching beneath his ribs to the arrow's point protruding from his back.

Even that small bit called to her, and she closed her eyes against its pull, mentally walking through the motions of resisting blood magic. And yet this situation felt desperate, like the night she'd cut herself and bargained with the sprites.

Without blood magic, she'd be forced to sense the injuries deep inside, to stitch together everything the arrow had ripped through. She hadn't done anything that complex. Lukai had only taught her to heal minor injuries and surface cuts.

It would require heavy amounts of energy, the kind she had only used when creating the shield, which she still hadn't been able to fully replicate while practicing with Sylmar. Why couldn't her controlled magic be as powerful as her unbridled magic? Why couldn't it be as strong as blood magic?

She bit the inside of her cheeks, allowing the pain to pull her from her trance. She didn't want to use blood magic. She refused to do it. Instead, she focused on the arrow.

"Oh." She couldn't help the word slipping out when she saw the bloody point. Her hands grew clammy. Why had she ever thought she wanted to be a healer?

"Here." The man grabbed her hand and drew it to the shaft. "Snap." His face twisted up in agony, and she hadn't even touched the arrow. Sweat dripped down into his short beard, and now that she was finally looking, Aeliana recognized his face as well as his hands. He'd let his hair and beard grow unkempt in the last several weeks, but he was definitely the man she'd seen at Lovers' Falls.

He'd saved her life without hesitation, and now she had to do the same for him.

She focused on the arrow and attempted to snap it in two. The man grimaced, and her heart beat faster as the slippery arrow held fast. He reached out a hand and touched the starlock swinging from her neck.

The message came through almost as a reprimand, but she still heeded it.

"Stars protect you," she muttered, closing her eyes and reaching out for the energy in her starlock, drawing it to her without limit. She was more likely to put him out of his misery than heal him in her current flustered state.

First came the euphoria, and when she would have pulled back, she let herself push a little more, reminding her body that this was a good thing. Then came the panic as her mind fought her body, a remembered response that came like breathing as the sense of wrongness built within her. Without knowing how to heal such a deep wound, she had nowhere to put the energy; it simply grew and grew deep inside, threatening to suffocate her like it had when they were still weaning her.

"Please," she whispered, begging the Stars to have mercy. To let the tiniest bit flow into her hands, to steady them as she worked. To guide them, because she had no idea what to do. Strength filled her limbs. That would have to be enough. Before she could second-guess herself, she snapped the arrow's shaft above the fletching.

The stranger groaned at the movement, but instead of following her instinct to apologize and give him time to recover, she tilted him, his weight like a doll's as the energy flowed through her. As soon as he was far enough onto his side, she pulled the point and shaft out in one swift movement.

This time his groan progressed to a scream that made every hair on her body stand on end. Or maybe it was the way blood began to pour from both sides of the wound. Something inside her reared back, ready to pounce on this new source of energy. She gasped at its pull, scooting back as if the distance might keep her from drawing the blood's power.

"Lukai!" She turned in a panic, scanning the trees.

To her surprise, someone stood a dozen paces away, but it wasn't Lukai. Kendalyhn's face creased with anguish, but Aeliana's gaze was drawn to the bow and arrow clutched in the other woman's hands. The fletchings were a perfect match for the arrow Aeliana had just pulled from the stranger's body. Felk hunched next to her, almost like a guard dog holding her at bay.

"I'm sorry," Kendalyhn whispered.

Sorry she'd shot him? Sorry she'd been aiming at Aeliana? No. The stranger had to have been mistaken. Kendalyhn still hadn't warmed up to Aeliana like the others, but she would never attack her. A mix of emotions swept through Aeliana, magnified by her energy store. "Come help me."

Aeliana ripped the man's cloak more, and soon Kendalyhn kneeled beside her, each of them pressing on one side of the wound. But every time they moved their hands to adjust the fabric soaking up blood, more spilled out. The man's breathing grew shallow, the sheen of sweat now covering his entire body. Still, he reached for Aeliana's hand, pushing aside the fabric so he could bring her palm to his wound.

She tried not to be squeamish, but placing her hand directly over his wound and letting the warm blood pour over her fingers left her queasy. Images of Arvid and Vera willfully pouring her blood into their hands, letting it seep into their skin, only intensified her nausea. In some ways, she relished the sickness. It was the only thing keeping her from bringing her other hand forward and cupping both of them beneath his wound.

"Help," the man croaked.

"I'm sorry," she told him. "I haven't learned enough. I don't know what else to do." As the blood ran down her fingers, her desperation grew. Would it be so wrong to use blood magic? What if it was the only way to save him?

She shook her head against the thought. There had to be another way.

While she debated, the man was dying before her eyes.

He pressed his hand on top of hers with a surprising amount of force, then murmured something. Aeliana bent close to hear him.

"Give… to me."

For a moment she didn't understand, but as his grip tightened, sudden clarity spread through her. He wanted her energy because he was a progeny. He could heal himself.

Moving energy was the only thing she'd truly mastered. This was something she could do. She sat up with renewed purpose, closing her eyes to block out all distractions, including Kendalyhn's helpless tears.

Her entire body tingled with the saturation of energy, and as she slowly pushed it through to the stranger, the buzz faded, like a swarm of bees leaving for their hive. At first nothing seemed to change. The wound still poured out blood, so much that her knees now rested in a puddle of it.

But then the flow lessened, and the stranger's breathing gained back its rhythm and strength. Still, Aeliana released her energy, letting it pass from the heat of her starlock through her blood and into the waiting hand of the man who was no longer dying.

Aeliana wasn't sure how long she kneeled over his body, how long she gave him her power. It seemed like moments, but when her magic finally ran out, she felt weary, like it had been hours. The stranger's color returned, and while the wound remained, Aeliana could see that he'd healed himself from the inside out, leaving only superficial wounds still oozing.

Her power depleted, Aeliana sat back on her heels, exhausted, but before she could pull her hand away, the older man squeezed it with renewed force.

"Thank you." He squinted up at her, then over her shoulder. "It appears we have an audience."

Aeliana turned. Velden, Sylmar, Lukai, Kendalyhn, Gaeren, and Cyrus all stood in a semi-circle, gaping at the scene before them. She couldn't blame their shock. Blood soaked everything, like an animal had been slaughtered. It covered her hands and trousers; she even sensed it had splashed on her face—or maybe she'd wiped her brow and spread it across her cheek. Felk sniffed at the air, his eyes darting to look anywhere but at the tempting blood.

Horror washed over her.

"I didn't do blood magic." The words sounded guilty to her own ears. She hadn't, had she? She would know if she'd done it. The stranger had used his magic. She'd just pushed it out to him.

"We believe you." Velden held out a hand as if calming a wild beast. Sylmar scanned the clear skies. He needed the proof, but she couldn't blame him. When no dark spirits came, they all breathed easier. Still, disgust crossed Gaeren's face before he could school his features, and Aeliana's shame heated her cheeks.

"That kind of wound..." Lukai started. "How did you heal it?" There was awe in his voice, but it was mixed with something else. Maybe fear? Hurt? Jealousy?

Aeliana shook her head. "I didn't heal it. I just gave him my magic."

The others studied the stranger, who gave a sheepish grin and half wave. "Hello."

"Let's get you both back to camp," Sylmar said, eyeing the bloody scene. "Maybe after you clean up, we can get the whole story."

CHAPTER 56

GAEREN WATCHED Daisy and the stranger from across camp, unsure whom to keep a closer eye on. What if Kendalyhn was right about Daisy? What if she traveled with these people, biding her time until she could join her aunt and rule alongside her with blood magic? Maybe that was the real reason she'd released the dragon.

He shook away the terrifying image. It couldn't be possible.

But if she hadn't done blood magic, that meant the stranger was more dangerous than he looked. None of the healers in Elanesse could pull off that kind of work, especially not on themselves. And where was the man's starlock?

Lukai finished healing the silent stranger's wounds, and Iris fussed over Daisy, brushing and braiding her hair while giving lots of loud opinions on Sylmar's wisdom in sending her out in the first place. Daisy winced at the woman's rough treatment but still smiled, as if she knew it had been triggered by fear.

Gaeren busied himself by training Gullet with the newest charm he'd added to his starlock's cord. The wooden sphere directed Gullet to Enla, and the block to Riveran, but the roughly star-shaped wooden bead he'd added was intended to guide Gullet to Daisy. Gaeren had had to steal a lock of her hair in the night to train the dumb bird, but as Gullet pecked the bead and then hopped over to Daisy, relief rushed through Gaeren. It was working.

After losing her once, he refused to lose her again. He told himself it was because he needed to keep track of potential threats, but he knew that was a lie. Especially after the panic that had infused him when the stranger said the arrow had been trained on Daisy.

She reached out to pet Gullet, who squawked his appreciation, and when her face lit up with joy, a foreign sense of longing rose inside him. Earning a look like that would be worth five of Lenda's insincere smiles.

Felk sat at the edge of camp even after Daisy urged him to come closer. His eyes darted between Sylmar and Daisy, as if Sylmar were some sort of alpha male who needed to welcome Felk back into the pack. While the others gathered for the midday meal, Gaeren stopped by Felk, passing him a stick with fish and a serving of flatbread.

Felk hesitated, unable to hold Gaeren's gaze.

"Go on," Gaeren said.

Felk grabbed the food, then turned away, sitting on his haunches and picking at the food.

"Thank you for coming back," Gaeren said.

Felk stiffened but didn't reply. Eleven days into the moon's cycle, he was like a full-grown man approaching middle age, with sinewy muscles and a wide jaw. But something about the way he curled around himself still made him seem like a child.

"Aeliana's been sad without you. It's not your fault you fought in a past life. I shouldn't have shown you that. What matters is how you are in this life, and you've been a good friend to her."

"The other winex don't have mamas," Felk said, his brow furrowing in confusion.

Gaeren sighed. "Maybe if they did, more of them would be like you."

"I don't belong with them, not anymore."

Gaeren glanced back at the others. "Do you want to belong with them? Or with us?"

"I want to belong with my ma—with Aeliana."

Felk turned his back to Gaeren and cut off the conversation.

When Gaeren returned to the fire, where the others still circled around to cook more fish, the group was unusually somber. Jasperus and Holm excused themselves to rest up before night watch, while the rest discussed trivial things like the food and weather, their eyes always coming back to rest on the stranger.

Sylmar still ate, likely waiting until after the meal for the interrogation, but Gaeren was done waiting.

"So, what's your name?" Gaeren asked, sitting near the stranger.

The man went rigid, gaze frozen on his food. "I don't—I'm not sure."

Sylmar frowned and set down his plate. "Where are you from?"

Lukai and Velden exchanged wary glances, and Gaeren glanced at Riveran's equally suspicious expression. Was the man an enemy the others didn't recognize? Did that make him a friend or enemy of Gaeren's? Gaeren was beginning to wonder if he knew half of what went on in his family's palace.

"My memories are all jumbled in my mind." The man set his flatbread down on his knee, rubbing his arms even though it wasn't the least bit cold. "I can't grasp any of them. The first thing I remember is waking up in a cave. It glowed with lights in varying colors, like a rainbow lighting the room. When I turned to see the backs of at least ten sprites, I also caught glimpse of them pushing a young woman outside the cave."

Gaeren turned toward Daisy, who choked a bit on her fish, unable to take in the rest of the party's accusing looks.

"Aeliana?" Lukai's voice came out with a growl.

"Yes, they pushed me," she said, "and I was fine. I didn't see him in the cave, but that doesn't mean he wasn't there. It was too dark to see beyond the sprites' bright lights."

Sylmar grunted, and Gaeren suspected she'd be hearing a lot about heightening her awareness during her next lesson with the overbearing mentor.

"I couldn't remember who I was or what I was doing," the man continued, "but I had a compulsion to follow you. To make sure you were all right."

"The sprites let you pass?" Gaeren asked, unable to hide his skepticism. "After they'd pushed her to her death?"

Riveran shook his head, the X on his forehead glinting in the

Sunlight, but Gaeren wasn't sure if Riveran had trouble believing the sprites had let the man pass or if he was warning Gaeren not to give away their experience.

The stranger shrugged. "They parted for me as if they'd expected it. One even said, 'your time has come.' I ran down the path, watching for —for Daisy?"

Several pairs of eyes turned in Gaeren's directions, and his cheeks went hot. Had he called her that out loud in front of the stranger?

"Aeliana," Lukai corrected, scooting closer to her.

The older man took in the exchange with amusement, which gave him a point in Gaeren's favor.

"I watched for Aeliana to surface. When I saw her drag the young man to the shoreline, I slowed, thinking I'd overreacted. But the compulsion only became stronger, urging me to help her."

"You healed Cyrus, didn't you," Aeliana said.

"No, no." The man held up his hands, shaking them as if to wave off her conclusion. "By the time I got there, you had already done that. Nearly killed yourself in the process."

"But then you saved her life," Cyrus prompted. "With magic."

The man hesitated. "I suppose so. It felt instinctual, but I don't really know what I did. I can't recall having done it before." He stared at the soil, digging the toe of his boot at the root of a small fern.

"Why did you leave?" Sylmar asked.

"I panicked. I didn't know who I was. I felt too vulnerable, and instinct made me run."

"Where's your starlock?" Gaeren asked.

The man frowned. "Those are the charms that enhance magic, right?"

Gaeren held back an eyeroll. The story was beginning to smell worse than the fish Velden had caught.

"Do I have one of those?" The man patted down the fresh cloak Lukai had given him, coming up empty.

Iris stood with a huff, joining Jasperus and Holm at the bedrolls. Even Daisy's face held wariness at the false sense of innocence.

"Memory loss is a convenient story." Sylmar crossed his arms over his chest. "It allows you to keep your past loyalties secret while digging for information from us."

The stranger winced. "Are we at war?"

Velden shrugged. "Of sorts. Or we're about to be in one."

"I don't know where my loyalties lie," the stranger admitted. "I would like to think the compulsion to save the young woman means my loyalties lie with her, but I can't blame you for not trusting me. Not if there's a war."

"I've never even met you. How could your loyalties lie with me?" Daisy asked.

"None of you recognize me?" They all shook their heads, and he slumped.

"That doesn't automatically make you an enemy," Gaeren said, surprised at his own words. "I don't recognize you either, and they consider me an enemy."

The stranger glanced around the circle, and Gaeren tried not to be bothered by the fact that no one argued with his statement. He sought out Orra, who quietly took in the whole scene from just outside the circle. Outside of her story the night before, she'd reverted back to her preferred status of "not interfering," which Gaeren found inconvenient most days.

"Have you been following us ever since that night? Even with Durriken's attack?" Daisy asked.

The man nodded, his gaze going back to the dirt.

"If all that's true, why did you attack Aeliana just now?" Gaeren asked.

The stranger winced again, glancing at her. "I didn't attack you. I saw the other woman aiming for us. You said you didn't come with guards, so I assumed her sights were on you."

It was hard to tell in the firelight, but Gaeren swore Kendalyhn's cheeks turned pink. Had the other woman been aiming for Daisy? Or the stranger?

"Well," Aeliana said, "you either have terrible eyesight, or Kenda-lyhn has terrible aim. Except I've seen her with a bow. She wouldn't have hit you unless you were her target."

The man grunted his assent, but Gaeren still didn't relax.

"That same compulsion came over me to protect you," the man said, "and selfishly, I needed you alive to get answers for why that compulsion even exists."

"Why were you following us anyway?" Daisy asked Kendalyhn.

When Kendalyhn glanced at Sylmar, he answered for her. "We knew our group was being followed. We hoped to draw out our pursuer if it seemed you were mostly alone."

Gaeren flexed his fingers into fists. "You used her as bait?"

"It was the only way to make sure we either lost our tail or trapped him before entering open land." Sylmar's face hardened without remorse. "Better to be bait on our own terms than in unknown circumstances. Besides, it worked."

"Well, now that you've caught him, what will you do?" Daisy asked, her irritation evident in the tightness around her mouth. Gaeren understood why they didn't trust him with any of their plans, but they could have at least told Daisy for her own protection.

Sylmar rubbed at his beard, considering. "Kendalyhn?" Her name came out like a question, but everyone else knew it was a command. Well, everyone except the stranger.

Kendalyhn stood, sliding past Gaeren.

"You're Kendalyhn?" The stranger squirmed.

"Just because I shot you doesn't mean I'll use my magic to hurt you." She kneeled next to him.

"I guess I don't have much choice either way." The stranger smiled, but he watched Kendalyhn too closely to truly be at ease. He placed his hand in her open palm.

She closed her eyes, and the others all leaned in a fraction closer, including Gaeren. As Kendalyhn sifted through the stranger's soul and weighed through his intentions, Gaeren also tuned in to the man's memories. He watched them in reverse, the man keeping to himself while maintaining a close proximity to the group. Even the memories surrounding Lovers' Falls held nothing different from what he'd said.

Without warning, the memories cut off like shards of glass. Images of the stranger at various ages splintered across Gaeren's mind, the chaos of the memories painful. He sucked in a breath just as Kendalyhn's jaw went slack and her eyes opened wide. She dropped the stranger's hand and scooted away.

Gaeren leaned back, grasping his temple as if he needed to keep his own memories from splintering the way the stranger's had. Daisy narrowed her eyes at him, far more interested in his reaction than in Kendalyhn's.

"What?" Sylmar asked. "What is it?"

Lukai unsheathed his dagger, but Kendalyhn reached out with a staying hand. "Konram's antithesis," she murmured.

"What?" Daisy glanced at Kendalyhn before turning back to Gaeren.

"Konram is a fable," Gaeren explained. "An old warning for children against using their starlock without training. When Konram came into his power, he became so obsessed with reliving his memories in his mind that he couldn't learn to control it, so he relived his youth that way for the rest of his life, growing old without ever truly living another day."

Daisy flinched away. "You saw the same as Kendalyhn?"

Gaeren hesitated as all eyes turned his way. His noetic skills weren't a secret, but he'd been careful not to use them here among this group. The easiest way to lose people's trust was to delve into their memories without their permission. But now, Kendalyhn's eyes begged him to speak up, to verify that she wasn't going mad with her assessment.

"His past..." Gaeren paused, unsure how to explain it. "It's all fractured. I've never seen anything like it." He wet his lips, trying to think of what could do this to a person—who would do this to a person.

"Marnok," Orra muttered. "He's the mirror-image of Konram, so he can mirror the name until he remembers his own."

Sylmar ignored her. "Can you at least tell who he's been loyal to?"

Kendalyhn shook her head. "There's a mournfulness in these last two moons, a sense of being lost. I saw that with clarity, and it lines up with his explanation. But before that, it's like something went through his soul and crushed who he was." She shuddered.

"Maybe it's the result of an inexperienced noetic unsuccessfully trying to erase a memory," Gaeren suggested, remembering his own unwieldy attempts during training.

"Or an experienced noetic successfully breaking his mind," Velden muttered.

The others all exchanged horrified looks.

"Could Mayvus do that?" Cyrus asked.

"Mayvus is a pneumatic," Sylmar said, "but that doesn't mean she couldn't commission the job."

"Didn't you say Emeris was a noetic?" Cyrus asked. "What if instead of commissioning the job, she used a brand to do it?"

The stranger frowned, taking the information in without comment.

"We'll discuss this at another time." Sylmar changed the subject so quickly it felt like a reprimand. "I admit we can't prove him to be the enemy. He saved one of ours, and we saved him, so we owe him nothing. We'll treat him as a guest in our camp for now."

Sylmar's eyes swung to Gaeren. Maybe he had somehow moved up in the ranks with this new stranger beneath him. Or maybe Sylmar was simply taking stock of how many enemies he was keeping close rather than setting loose.

"We'll take him as far as Elanesse," Sylmar said, turning back to the stranger. "He won't follow us from there."

The stranger slowly nodded his agreement when it became clear Sylmar waited for a response.

"What about Felk?" The question slipped from Gaeren's lips before he could think it through.

Sylmar glanced at him in surprise, then turned to check on the winex, who was patiently sitting a respectful distance from the camp. "He's shown a commendable loyalty to Aeliana," the old man admitted.

Daisy shot Gaeren a surprised look of appreciation. "It could work in our benefit to have a winex with us. He showed restraint." Her hands twisted in her lap while Sylmar considered her words.

The old man frowned, his scars shifting with his mood. "Very well. He can stay for now too."

Sylmar, Lukai, and Velden all threw their dinner remains into the fire, suspicion still marking their faces as they left, but Daisy grinned, beckoning Felk over. He sat next to her, his wide grin revealing his dozens of teeth, now full grown. His body wriggled like that of a child needing to relieve himself.

Kendalyhn studied the stranger as if still parsing out his past. "I know you're telling the truth. It just doesn't make sense."

"I wish it made sense to me too," he muttered.

Daisy's smile resembled more of a grimace as Kendalyhn walked away, leaving Gaeren, Daisy, Orra, Riveran, Cyrus, and the stranger by the fire.

"I'm sorry we almost killed you," Orra said, "but don't give up hope, Marnok."

His eyes brightened. "You think I can get my memories back?"

Orra frowned. "I'd hoped Gaeren could tune in to your past memories and give them back to you." Her gaze strayed to Gaeren, making him feel like a boy caught sneaking in the kitchens for extra cake.

Gaeren shook his head. "I couldn't make sense of them."

Orra hummed, her brow furrowed in concentration. "It seems more like your soul is lost. If we could piece the memories together, they might provide reference points for you to find yourself, but it also might not be enough. We'd almost need to find a way to piece your soul back together before someone could sift through the essence of who you are."

Gaeren winced. Everything about the process sounded painful, especially after tuning in to what was left of the poor man's memory.

The man only nodded. "In that case, I accept the name." He paused, the hint of a smile on his face. "And the apology."

CHAPTER 57

Orra watched as the others settled into their bedrolls. Holm gave Marnok an extra blanket, but Felk denied needing one and volunteered to help with the watch instead.

The stranger settled himself several feet away from the others, keenly aware of their distrust. An itch started inside Orra, a nagging sensation that she could help them be better. If they knew who he was and what he'd done, would they treat him differently? If she restored his memories, would that help their mission?

His ability to heal went far beyond Lukai's. He could be an asset to their team if they knew. But stirring up his past would be painful. So much loss…

She frowned, turning her back on him. Interfering wasn't her way. She couldn't even see the possible paths before him if she interfered, because it was expected that she wouldn't.

And yet her throat ached with the held-back offer. Her hands tingled with anticipation. A single touch could restore his past, good and bad, leaving him free to move forward and to deal with the consequences.

She clenched her fists and squeezed her eyes shut, refusing the temptation. It wasn't her way. And yet, wasn't that exactly what she'd felt the Sun urging her to do by sending Skunk to aid Gaeren? Would helping Marnok be a ripple or a stone?

She settled under her blanket, watching the Stars above, identifying each one by their pattern of dance until her breathing slowed and her muscles relaxed. Did the Stars applaud her self-control? Or was this merely the expectation that she was finally meeting?

It shouldn't matter. It only mattered what the Sun saw in her. Still, it took a long time for her to get their accusing voices out of her head.

Orra played with the braid on her wrist, eyeing the others as they slept. The longer she was with them, the harder it was to focus on her true purpose. Retrieving Aeliana's blood and rescuing Emeris was their cause, their fight, but it had become her own.

Still, she was supposed to be here for something else.

Her attention fell on Aeliana once more as the young woman wrapped a protective arm around the large beast who had previously tried to rip out her throat. Even saving the winex and coddling him was something Orra couldn't have factored in. It put Aeliana on a new trajectory with different outcomes, some better than before, some far worse.

Orra had thought that Gaeren was the one who could help her, but now she wondered if it might be Aeliana. Or maybe the Sun's prophecy had fooled her into thinking it was only one.

If Orra was wrong about them, she needed to be ready to sever ties. The thought sliced through her with more dread than she'd antici-pated, but Aeliana and Gaeren were finite. Long after they were gone, Orra would still hunt for the pieces she'd lost. The arrow needed to matter more. She drew the braid to her lips, wishing it still smelled of hyssop and juniper.

"I won't fail you," she whispered into the night.

CHAPTER 58

As they drew closer to Elanesse, Aeliana sensed the wary mood brought on by Marnok's and Felk's presence shift back to a relaxed camaraderie. Felk became less of a threat as the new moon approached and he became an old winex, spending most of his time resting curled up near Aeliana's bedroll.

Her desire for friendship allowed her to set aside the confusing secrets surrounding her family line. Each night she asked Jasperus for more stories or begged Lukai and Kendalyhn to spill each other's childhood memories. Jasperus and Lukai were far more compliant than Kendalyhn. Their stories gave her and Cyrus a better understanding of Vendaras, even though it didn't change her lack of desire to rule.

Marnok never regained his memories, but he formed new ones, discovering his penchant for detail and a great knowledge of the body. They suspected he'd been a healer, and when they tested his skills, it was clear he was a somatic progeny, despite their inability to find a starlock on him. Each night she trained, he'd watched from a distance, occasionally flexing a hand or closing his eyes in concentration, giving Aeliana the impression he was learning, or relearning, right along with her.

Finally, Marnok stepped forward, offering slight corrections to Lukai's instructions, bringing Aeliana ten times further in her somatic training with a handful of simple tweaks. Her light shields grew to protect her midsection, then her whole body, and eventually a companion—all without needing threats to motivate her.

Even Sylmar had trouble hating him after that.

She couldn't imagine what it would be like to lose her memory. To have no recollection of who she was or where she came from. As much as she longed to be rid of her memories of Arvid and Vera, it sounded disconcerting, like a ship without anchor.

Gaeren even spent time with her, teaching her to use her light shield to stop him from tuning in to her memories or how to defend herself with a dagger. They kept to safer topics, like *Starspeed* or Cyrus' theological debates, rather than addressing their complicated history.

After two weeks, they finally reached the outskirts of Elanesse. Aeliana watched Gaeren adjust his pack as she brushed down her horse. He'd be leaving that night for the palace to secure his ship and ask his sister for reinforcements, and he'd be taking Riveran and Marnok with him.

He took out almost everything, sorting supplies into piles to be left for the rest of their party. Riveran helped him without comment, the two working in tandem as if they had all their lives. Aeliana knew things weren't right between them, but she hadn't ever figured out why. She gave her horse one last pat, then made her way over to Gaeren and Riveran.

"I hear that Orra isn't going with you."

"She was never really with us." Gaeren grinned, the familiar tilt of his lips no longer resembling a smirk. Had his smile changed? Or just Aeliana's perception of it? "She does her own thing, and if it lines up with what we're doing, she'll allow us to participate."

Riveran nodded at Aeliana before heading toward Lukai with a stash of bandages and medicines. The X on his forehead stood out in the glow of the Sun's descent. They'd kept him hidden most of the trip, knowing what other travelers would assume. Would he get a chance to see his wife and baby before joining them on the boat? She supposed Gaeren would be eager to see his bondmate as well.

"Are you offering to take her place?" Gaeren's question startled Aeliana out of her thoughts.

"Whose place?"

"Orra, who else?" He eyed her strangely. "Gullet always likes to have a lady around."

Even though there was a teasing tilt to his smile, she shook her head. She toyed with the end of her braid, and his gaze followed the motion.

"Gullet's probably the only one of you I'll miss," she said. "Besides, I'll wait until we have proof that your parents hold no ill will."

His grin faded. "Either way I'll be back to help you. I know you don't want my help. Maybe you don't even need it. Not like you used to." He looked away.

Aeliana's face heated, and she glanced at Felk, curled up next to her bedroll with a hand over his wrinkled face. "I didn't mean it when I said that. That I didn't want your help. I just—I was mad that night."

He scanned her face as if evaluating the truth of her words. "Either way, I'm with you until we eliminate Mayvus as a threat."

Aeliana envied the confidence in his face, the certainty in his eyes. His goals for justice went far beyond the Recreants' plan to save Emeris. Or at least the plans she knew of. Sometimes Gaeren's eagerness reminded her of Cyrus. Those were the moments where she could think of him as a friend—the moments she wanted to think of him as a friend. Why should the history of their families get to dictate whether or not they could get along?

"And then what?" Her question came out as a whisper, but she knew he heard.

His jaw tightened, either holding in his answer or acknowledging that he had none. He pulled out his dagger, turning it and offering her the hilt. "I want you to have this."

She took a step back and laughed to cover her discomfort. "I already have a dagger."

He raised his eyebrows, glancing at the clunky dagger sheathed at her hip. Her face heated, both at the way his eyes grazed over her and the truth that her dagger was a sorry excuse for a wieldable weapon.

"I'd always meant this to be yours," Gaeren said. "I just—it never seemed like you'd take it before. Or maybe I was worried you'd use it against me." He laughed and ran his free hand through his hair.

Aeliana couldn't hold back her smile, and, against her will, she found herself reaching for the dagger. "It seems like a family heirloom. Hardly something you should pass on to me."

"No, not an heirloom." His smile turned sad. "I had it made for your dedication gift. It's a Vendaran tradition to receive your first weapon at the end of your dedication year. I was only fourteen. A part of me thought that if I had it made, then I would find you. I'd be able to give it to you." He shrugged and looked away once more, blinking fast.

Aeliana hadn't meant to keep the dagger, but she could hardly give it back now. Not after he'd shared something like that. She tightened her grip on the hilt, letting the ridges dig into her skin. "Thank you."

He unhooked the sheath from his belt and passed that over too, then settled back to sorting supplies as Riveran returned. They were almost done, and then Aeliana knew they'd be riding off through the wetlands, approaching their homes. It wasn't a real goodbye. He'd be back the next day, hopefully with news of his ship and reinforcements. But it felt weighted enough that her 'thank you' didn't seem like enough.

"May the Sun's light always shine upon you." The words fell out quickly—awkwardly, since she was used to the Stars' blessing.

Both men paused, making Aeliana wonder if she'd said it wrong. Was it insulting coming from someone who didn't know what to think about the Sun? But then Gaeren's gaze met hers, and he reached over and gave her a fierce hug.

"And may the Stars' light always guide you," he whispered in her ear. He let go before she'd had a chance to process the hug or the words, before she'd had a chance to raise her arms and return the gesture.

She scratched at her palm, unsure what else to say, but Gaeren had already turned back to the supplies, and in moments, he and Riveran were mounting their steeds. Marnok hopped on the back of Riveran's horse, looking as lost as he had the day they'd found him. Aeliana couldn't help feeling sorry for him, wishing they'd been able to help him recover his memories. He hoped to find answers in Elanesse, but they were all just as afraid of what those answers might be.

Orra came close enough to pat the horses and give parting words Aeliana couldn't catch, and the others all waved farewell. As soon as the three men disappeared from view, Aeliana swapped out her old dagger for Gaeren's, testing its light weight against her hip. She couldn't deny it felt better than the old one. She could even pull it out quicker, angling it up and out with just a flick of her wrist. She grinned as she sheathed it once more, thinking more of the man who'd given it to her than the weapon itself.

She tried to ignore the fact that Holm headed out soon after the other men, likely to track them and make sure they went where they'd promised to go, but she couldn't pretend Sylmar didn't call them to break camp. Several others grumbled, but they all obeyed, even an exhausted Felk.

Aeliana turned to Iris. "What are we doing?" she asked. "How will they find us?"

"That's the point, love." Iris gave a small smile. "We don't want them to be able to report our location if they're not as trustworthy as we hope they are."

"But what about Gaeren? And his ship?"

"Holm will watch for their return. If all is well, he'll lead them to our camp." Iris returned to her packing, leaving Aeliana to spin Gaeren's dagger in her palm, letting the ridges dig into the mark of her bond. She couldn't deny the logic even though her heart wanted to trust her new friends. Sylmar was giving them a chance to prove their loyalty.

Iris glanced back at Aeliana, reaching a hand out to tug the braid she constantly encouraged Aeliana to cut. "Be careful not to let Gaeren's presence disrupt your bond."

Aeliana's face heated. She glanced around before leaning in. "My bond? Gaeren and I are barely friends."

Iris shrugged and doused the cookfire. "If you say so." Steam and smoke sizzled around them.

Aeliana's palm itched as she thought about her Lukai. They'd become friends, but they'd agreed that was enough for now. Still, she hadn't put much thought into their bond, not since they'd left Islara. Not since Gaeren had joined them.

Lukai came up beside her and placed her pack on her back. Iris gave her a knowing look and went back to rolling up blankets.

By the time they'd settled in a more hidden location, the Stars were at their dance. Cyrus set up a few feet away from camp to kneel and pray before the Stars, and Orra sat on her bedroll, watching him with a slight frown on her face. After getting Felk's weary body settled next to her bedroll, Aeliana sat by several others around the fire, eyeing Kendalyhn and Lukai, who took watch.

"Maybe Marnok will find someone who recognizes him," Aeliana said. "Someone who can restore his memory."

"Which is exactly why we moved." Jasperus tapped his temple, grinning at her like a proud grandfather.

"I would have liked to be around for that," she murmured. "See his face shift from confused to peaceful, maybe figure out where his starlock is."

"I'm still not convinced he has a starlock." Sylmar's ever-present frown deepened.

"Then how did he heal himself using my magic?"

"I still think that was you." Sylmar eyed her like she might suddenly sprout an extra appendage, one that was capable of far more impressive magic than she was. "Unless he used blood magic."

She held back a groan. Why did it always come back to blood magic? "What if he has a starlock, and it's disguised like Velden's?" She gestured to Velden's earrings. "Maybe it's a button on his cloak or something on his shoe and he's not even aware."

"It's unlikely," Sylmar said. "The starlock gives you the greatest strength the closer it lies to your heart. Only a truly proficient progeny can get away with that trick."

"Why, thank you." Velden beamed, making Sylmar grumble something under his breath.

Jasperus sat back, his face falling into shadows. "I still want to know what fractured his past."

Sylmar hummed his agreement, his gaze settling on the flames. His mind seemed haunted by his own memories as he stroked one of the lumpy scars on his cheek. What kind of injury caused scars like his?

"Each person here has been broken in some way." Velden's unusually serious tone cut into Aeliana's thoughts. "We all made a choice to sacrifice our lives in order to keep Mayvus from gaining power."

Aeliana nodded, then turned to Jasperus. "Yours is the only story I haven't heard. Sylmar said it was one I should hear from your own lips."

Jasperus grasped his starlock and peering at its axe shape. "He probably thought you weren't ready for it at the time. I was actually a Zealot until a year ago, when Mayvus took my son for her army."

Aeliana flinched. "A Zealot?"

"Most Zealots start out as Loyalists. They want leadership, but they see the corruption of the royal family, so they look to the servants of the Sun. As they start to follow Mayvus, they're either unaware of Mayvus' growing connection with the Elanesses, or they're unaware of Mayvus' true motives. My wife and I fell in the second camp."

Aeliana swallowed hard. "How did she take your son?"

"In our country, there are three major schools where men and women are trained after receiving their starlocks. Technically, we should be registering you as a progeny so you can attend one. One of many laws we're breaking." He smirked, but it quickly faded.

As he spoke, Iris joined them by the fire, her hands busy mending one of Holm's shirts.

"Most Recreants hide their starlocks and train at home," Jasperus continued. "The schools are technically under the royal family's authority. But Mayvus scouts the schools to grow her army, calling students into priesthood but training them for warfare."

"So her army is filled with progenies?" Aeliana asked. "How can we match up against that?"

"With strategy." Velden toyed with the fish hooks in his ears. "She takes those who seem the most powerful, but that doesn't always mean the most skilled. Besides, we have our own progenies."

"So she chose your son?" Aeliana asked, turning back to Jasperus.

"Yes." He swallowed, gaze on the fire. "As Zealots, we saw it as a privilege. My wife—" His voice broke. "My wife and I were thrilled at his honored status. He moved up in the ranks of priesthood, but he changed so much." Jasperus' eyes and mouth twitched as he spoke.

Sylmar turned away, but Velden gave a sticky pat to Jasperus' back.

Iris' hands moved faster with her needle and thread as she blinked away tears.

"He changed within a few moons, both in physical strength and power. But his words and thoughts began to change, too. He worshipped the ground Mayvus walked on. On his last visit home, he finally admitted he'd allowed himself to be branded."

Aeliana's chest tightened. "Like my mother?"

Jasperus nodded. "His was voluntary. He wasn't under her control often, but it still left us on edge to know he could be at any time. Especially when he hinted at the use of blood magic. Few people outside our army know or believe that rumor to be true. It's why the royal family is so eager to work with her even though they swear off all blood magic."

Aeliana's gaze drifted to the blackness of the woods, her eyes imagining the trail Gaeren might follow. He would tell them about Mayvus' blood magic. What would they do about it?

"Before he returned to his duties, my wife questioned him about the brand. She asked if he could undo it, and he—he completely lost it. He threw her against the wall. I was so concerned about her that I didn't even see him leave, and I haven't seen him since."

"And your wife?" Aeliana whispered.

"She died two days later from her internal injuries."

The air grew heavy with his loss laid bare.

"I'm so sorry." The words tasted stale on her lips.

"She begged me to forgive him. He's just another victim. I think I have, but some days it's hard to remember. Some days I have to work through it all over again, and I don't always have the strength." He wiped at the wetness clinging to his lashes.

"What's your son's name?" Aeliana asked.

"Brogdon." Jasperus' voice cracked as he added, "After his grandfather."

Silence stretched out for a long moment. "And he still serves Mayvus?"

Jasperus nodded. "He will until he dies, which will likely be soon. As long as Mayvus has brands, she'll be too powerful. Taking out her brands will make her vulnerable, and we need her to be vulnerable."

Fresh horror washed over Aeliana. "How many brands does she have? And how many of them would have to be killed?" Aeliana and her mother might be safe in that plan, but at the cost of how many others?

"Maybe not many," Iris said. "If we can cut out their brands, they could be spared."

Jasperus' jaw clenched. "Unlikely considering they're all under her control."

Aeliana bit her lip. "And there's nothing that can help? Durriken let me cut his out."

Sylmar hummed. "True. That's a unique circumstance. I think it's because stopping you in any way could have killed you, and that conflicted with the orders he'd received from Mayvus."

She'd suspected the same, but what Sylmar saw as a fluke, Aeliana saw as an opportunity. If there had been a way around it with Durriken, why couldn't there be a way around it with someone else?

"What about a bond? Could my desire for Lukai's safety override her control over me as a brand?"

Iris looked up, her eyes apologetic. "Bondmates don't command each other the way brands do. It's not as powerful even if it's more powerful on a deeper level."

Sylmar stared into the fire, stroking his beard, but he said nothing.

"I'd bond myself to Brogdon if I thought it could help. I'd do anything to pull him out of her control. But a brand is far more powerful." Jasperus twisted his starlock in his hands once more. "You know, his starlock is identical to mine. Both in the shape of an axe. Neither of us knew the meaning when he left. I expect it's how one of us will die. Maybe both of us. I still love him, but I'll throw that axe myself if it means protecting our people from that blood witch."

The image left Aeliana reeling, but the words were spoken with an air of confession that she couldn't ignore. "Thank you for telling me your story."

He nodded, and they all sat in somber silence for a few moments before taking turns heading for bed. Aeliana checked on Felk, whose rattled breathing left her anxious. Did some winex die from old age before the cycle was complete? She lay awake long after everyone else had fallen asleep, worrying whether Felk would survive, whether Sylmar would tolerate him in his child state again, whether Felk would still want to be with them after his memories were gone. When she tried to distract herself by thinking of Jasperus' story, it only left her more distraught.

In many ways, it had been Jasperus' way of warning her. If he was willing to sacrifice his son for the greater good of the people, he would do no less with her. Maybe she wasn't as safe as she'd thought. If she became one of Mayvus' brands, Jasperus wouldn't hesitate to kill her for the greater good.

She couldn't decide if she was concerned or grateful.

CHAPTER 59

It DIDN'T TAKE LONG for Gaeren's city to come into view. Torchlights glowed outside homes and inns, increasing in number until the distant shine was like fireflies twinkling in the night. Gaeren's heart swelled with pride and even longing, a strange sensation since he was usually so eager to leave Elanesse.

"I don't suppose you know where you want to be dropped off?" He angled in his saddle until he caught Marnok's troubled face.

"Any tavern will do." The older man sighed, scanning the nearest establishments.

Gaeren and Riveran exchanged a glance as Gullet pecked Riveran's ear. Marnok's memories were as splintered as they'd been the first time Gaeren had checked, making the prince inclined to believe his strange story. But it was still a risk leaving him in the city, where he could spread rumors about dragons and wars in the east or reveal just how unconventional Gaeren's recent companions had been.

"I can help him find a place for the night," Riveran offered, reining Maw to a stop. "Maybe set him up with a few of the merchants who know most everyone in the city. If he's from Elanesse, he'll know before we set sail."

Gaeren nodded his appreciation. This was where he and his old friend parted ways. Even though it was temporary, it stung more than Gaeren had anticipated. The comfortable camaraderie they'd temporarily shared on this journey suddenly felt broken by their nearness to the palace and their past.

"Good luck to you, lost soul." Gaeren grinned at Marnok. "If you ever gain back your memories, it's sure to be a tale I'll want to hear."

Marnok gave him a half-smile, and at Riveran's nudge, Maw took the two men toward the docks.

Gaeren urged Skunk down the main street, where it grew crowded with night revelers. He slipped his hood up and led his horse through smaller streets and back alleys until the palace's long drive came into view. With a grin, he kicked Skunk into a gallop and rode the gelding hard, relishing the last bit of wind and freedom. The guards at the gate fumbled through their shock to open it for him, and Erech's mouth dropped open when Gaeren dismounted and passed over the reins.

"Prince G—I mean, Captain! You're here!"

"Back among the manure and hay, I see," Gaeren said. "How's your mother?"

Erech beamed, and, without warning, an image of a rosy-cheeked infant nestled in his mother's arms crossed through to Gaeren's mind. It was as if the boy couldn't contain his pride or his memories.

"She's well, and so is my new brother. Larkos helped me find the best shell for him." His crooked teeth gleamed in the moonlight, making Gaeren think of Felk.

He was tempted to offer the boy a spot on the ship, but he kept his mouth shut. The pay would be better, but he couldn't bring someone so young to Mayvus' doorstep, not if everything the Recreants had told him were true. He ruffled the boy's hair and sent him off with Skunk.

It wouldn't take long for news of his arrival to reach Enla's ears. His return had probably shown up in a dozen of the paths she'd seen when she'd sifted his soul. She'd find him soon enough. Sweeping past the guards, he made his way through the halls and up the stairs until he reached his parents' chambers. He hesitated at their door, regretting the late hour, then felt ridiculous for letting the guards see his hesitation.

Fist raised, he pounded on the door.

From deep within, his father cursed the guards, whose faces remained stoic.

"What is it?" His father's deep growl came through the wood.

"It's me, Father. I come with news from Islara." Gaeren reached for his dagger before remembering he'd given it to Daisy. He slipped his hand to the pommel of his sword, standing a little straighter.

Silence greeted him, then the creak of hinges. A sliver of torchlight fell on weathered skin and a cloudy blue eye. Gaeren took a step back, gawking at his father's stooped form and sunken cheeks. Had his father contracted whatever ailed his mother?

The King of Elanesse stared past him before wetting his dry lips and barking at the guards. "Send for Enla and Cook. We'll take tea and bread in the sitting room."

"I'm already here." Enla's unusually soft voice came from Gaeren's back.

The grin pulling at his cheeks halted when he saw the haunted look in her eyes. She bent forward, but her embrace carried formality rather than affection. Gaeren tensed.

"Are you all right?" he whispered.

"You've been gone a long time." She pulled back, her eyes studying his. "Too long."

That guilty nerve twinged. "There are things I need to tell you."

His father stepped back, widening the door for the two of them to enter their chambers before he shuffled in toward the sitting room.

By the time refreshments were brought, their mother had made her way to their father's side on the chaise. Gaeren had watched her progress through the room, holding his breath as each step seemed slower than the last. She patted down her greying hair, eyes unfocused and face tense with pain.

"Has the red bush tea helped you some?" Gaeren asked, even though it clearly hadn't.

"You were a dear to send it." His mother's smile seemed forced, her words stilted.

Gaeren and Enla took seats across from their parents, the tea and biscuits between them. Enla's hands folded so tight her knuckles turned white.

Their father grunted, never one for small talk. "What news do you bring from Islara?"

"Mayvus destroyed the entire city."

Enla's face paled, matching her bloodless fingers. She'd probably seen the possibility in her visions and hoped it wouldn't come to pass. His parents showed no reaction.

"You saw this with your own eyes?" his father asked.

"I came upon it within hours. The rubble still smoked from Durriken's fire."

"A terrible beast. She tried to tame him, but his magic is old." His mother's soothing tone eased Gaeren's tension even though he knew she was using her magic on him. It was part of the reason he'd never been able to stand up to his father. Any fight he felt in the king's presence was usually drowned out by the queen projecting unwanted emotion on Gaeren. Even as she manipulated him now, a fire burned beneath his calm, ready for the moment she faltered.

"I saw the memories with my spoke," Gaeren insisted. "Durriken has been branded by Mayvus to do her bidding." He hadn't seen that last part, but he trusted Daisy's word.

Their parents exchanged a glance, and Enla's eyes slid shut.

"Were there any survivors?" his father asked.

"I rescued two children." Their faces swam before his eyes, the boy's cry for his father rising in Gaeren's ears.

A hint of a smile crossed Enla's face.

"It was an unfortunately aggressive show of support." His father frowned, choosing his words too carefully. "Publicly, we're calling it a senseless tragedy. An ancient beast gone mad. Troops have been dispatched to track down the dragon and hold him accountable for his crimes."

With every word his father spoke, the fire of Gaeren's indignation cooled until his insides felt frozen with shock. His mother kept her gaze on the king, nodding along her agreement. Enla's eyes remained shut, her face passive except for a hint of wetness on her lashes.

"What are we calling it privately?" Gaeren forced the question out in an even tone.

His father leaned forward, but his cloudy eyes still seemed distant.

"The Islarans were preparing for war. They'd amassed an army. Mayvus protected us."

The shards of ice in Gaeren snapped. "She killed an entire city. Thousands of our people. Innocents."

"Sacrifices must be made in war," the king said.

Gaeren stood, his parents' indifference heightening his outrage. "We're not at war."

"Sit down." His father's words spilled out with disgust. "You're getting involved in affairs you were never meant to take part in. Your efforts are more likely to reflect poorly on Enla than to do any good. You don't have the stomach for this. You never have."

Gaeren sat, the air rushing out of him. A peace wrapped around him, cocooning the anger in his heart. He tried fighting his mother, blocking the comfort the way his mentors had taught him. Despite the unnatural sense that everything would be fine, his father's words still stuck in his mind, begging the question. "The stomach for it? Why would I want to have the stomach for killing my people? The children of the people I'm supposed to serve?"

"That's not what Father means." Enla placed a hand on his arm, her cool touch calming him further. He shook it off, knowing she'd activated her secondary spoke to help their mother. He'd told Enla he was following a lead to Islara. Had she told Mayvus? Had he played a role in all those deaths?

"I meant what I said," his father barked. "You know what the people say about you?"

Gaeren let out a humorless laugh, thinking of Sylmar's accusation. "I do, actually. That I'm foolish and young, oblivious to what's going on in my country. They're not wrong, but they will be."

Shock flitted across his father's features, digging a knife deeper in Gaeren's soul. Gaeren's new self-awareness surprised the older man, but not news of the dragon's massacre.

They knew what had happened in Islara. They'd known this whole time, and they approved.

"We thought it would help you cope if you didn't have to be directly involved in things." His mother's soothing voice ensured his cooperation and understanding, even though the moment he left the room, his frustration would return. "Early on you showed a distaste for the affairs of the crown. Your mentors confirmed it throughout your training."

Exactly how many people had been a part of this mission to keep Gaeren in the dark?

"With Enla in line," his mother continued, "it didn't seem necessary to push you, so instead we let you drift away from the necessary hard choices that come with ruling."

"Drift away…" He thought of his first year at sea as a cabin boy. He'd been so homesick he'd thought he'd die. When tossed by the waves during storms, he'd begged the Sun to have mercy and return him to the safety of his mother's arms. Only when he'd returned, his mother's arms had no longer felt safe. For the first time, he'd recognized the peace he felt near her had been manipulative.

Enla had changed that year too. She'd started attending council meetings and appointments with dignitaries from the surrounding provinces. She'd stopped laughing.

"You sent me to the sea to keep me away."

"To protect your heart," his mother corrected.

Even the thing he loved was now being tainted by his parents. He thought he'd been willfully ignorant of politics, but they'd manufactured even that.

"Is that why you sent me to Celanoft for my dedication year? You could have picked any Sungazer, but you chose one halfway down the eastern coast."

His father snorted. "Hardly. We chose Celanoft because Mayvus suspected the priestess was a Wyndren plotting for the throne. We sent a spy as your servant, and he confirmed Mayvus' suspicions."

Gaeren's chest expanded, unable to hold the fire building within. "Breck?" He hardly remembered the man. Breck had been a new servant, and hadn't returned from Celanoft. "He was a spy?"

"We should have sent a soldier," his mother admitted. "Breck was killed in the skirmish, and no one knew what happened to you. We thought—we thought you were dead." The break in her voice hinted at love somewhere deep down. It meant little to Gaeren at this point.

"You never even asked me what happened," Gaeren said, but it was the last thing on his mind. His parents were the reason Emeris and Rildan had been caught. His parents were the reason Daisy had been stolen away, taken to Lorvandas and raised by horrid wielders of blood magic.

"You said they'd all disappeared and asked us to investigate." The king leaned forward, eyebrows raised. "We assumed you knew nothing and wanted to keep it that way." It was clear he expected an explanation if Gaeren knew more, but Gaeren wasn't interested in giving his side of the story. Not anymore.

"So now what happens? With Mayvus?" The question showed none of the anger brewing inside him. For once, he was grateful for his mother's interference, the way her projection forced him to discuss the future objectively. He pulled down some of his mental blocks, allowing her comfort to settle his shaking hands.

"Mayvus has been high priestess in the Myndren Mountains for over a decade," his father said. "Her loyalty is unmatched. Because of her demonstration in Islara, we've awarded her full control of the eastern province."

Gaeren's gaze swung to Enla, but her eyes were closed once more, as if guarding her mind, even though their father was a destructive somatic and their mother could only project emotions, not tune in to other's.

Unless Enla was guarding her memories from him.

"The eastern province makes up a quarter of our country." Gaeren weighed his words. There were a dozen smaller provinces between Elanesse and Andel, the southernmost tip of the country. The eastern province was made up of mostly desert, a valley hedged in by Mt. Vescano's range at its southern border, the sea to the north, and the Myndren Mountains in the east. They'd left the province large because so few occupied the desert. Still, it was a lot of land for one woman to control.

"It's no longer a part of our country," his father corrected.

The alarm that slammed through Gaeren grew fuzzy, tempered by his mother.

"Vendaras has grown too large for one king to control." His father's face twitched as he spoke, the words recited like pages read from a book. "The Recreants have been threatening to break up our dynasty for years, so we beat them to it. Instead of having neighboring rulers that despise us, we've chosen a queen who has proven herself an ally."

This time when Enla placed her hand on Gaeren's arm, he didn't push her away. Instead of the false state of calm spreading through his bones, a memory fed into his mind, and he finally understood that her state of concentration was an effort to give it to him. Only it was more like a memory of her thoughts. The words came to his mind with such clarity that he wasn't sure if the thought was Enla's or his own.

You've been gone too long.

CHAPTER 60

GAEREN WAS SENT to bed like a child, the soldiers at his door feeling like guards locking him in. All his plans and expectations lay scattered on the floor, a puzzle he couldn't put together before the Sun's morn. His parents were truly allied with Mayvus. His sister too, whether she wanted to be or not. He had no fleet to offer Daisy and the Recreants. Even if they made it to the Myndren Mountains, they'd be going up against a powerful queen, a woman likely amassing her own army in anticipation of their attack. A woman who expected support from the king she'd recently protected.

He had no idea what to do next.

A tap on his door drew him out of his exhausted half-asleep state. Light poured in through the curtains he'd opened during the night when he'd watched the Stars, wondering if Daisy watched them too. She trusted them like Cyrus, calling on them for aid instead of the Sun. Even though it was the way of the witches, he was tempted to call on them as well. Anything that might fix the mess he was in.

He padded across the room and opened the door. Enla stood before him, an olive dress hugging her form, its color reminiscent of the flecks in Daisy's eyes—the lighter green that flashed when she grew excited.

"Going out?" he asked. He stepped away without expecting an answer, letting her assume she was invited in. The soldiers flanking her took their station by his own guards as she stepped in and shut the door behind her.

"I have a full day of meetings."

"Giving away a few more provinces? Or just solidifying Father's act of desperation?" He sat on a chair by the window, crossing his arms and taking in the grounds below.

The staff milled about the statue of Amaya, the first queen of Elanesse, making the gardens perfect. For some reason, the queen's secretive smile made him think of Orra and her maternal serenity. Both the woman and the statue found ways to make him feel less than. What would Queen Amaya think of the Elanesse and Wyndren families now? She would likely hate that the children of Valyn and Breck fought each other.

"I am not your enemy," Enla said. "I never have been, and I never will be."

Gaeren turned back, taking in the dark circles under her eyes. "The things they say don't even make sense. Mayvus is manipulating them. Do you realize the only reason Mayvus knew Emeris is a Wyndren is because they're sisters? Because Mayvus is also a Wyndren? They gave her a throne."

Enla's face remained passive. "That's exactly why they think she deserves a throne. Because she never asked for it. She defended their right to it."

"Then you knew. How could you let them do something like this?" he muttered.

She sat in the chair across from him with a huff. "You think I have that much power? You weren't here when the dignitaries arrived. I needed you here to help me. I asked you to be here. As it was, I could only stand by and watch as Mother and Father gave a quarter of our kingdom away."

He clenched his jaw, the memories of Islarans' deaths flitting through his mind. They hadn't just given it away like money from their coffers—they'd put people into the hands of a madwoman.

Enla sighed. "Giving Mayvus a portion of the kingdom is Mother and Father's attempt to pacify the long-standing disagreement. They're doing it for our safety."

Her gaze dropped to Gaeren's knee, which had begun bouncing with his agitation.

"Is the warrant for Aeliana Wyndren's arrest also for our safety?" He couldn't help the mocking bite to his words.

"She's the woman I saw, isn't she? The one you found." Enla's eyes glazed over. "I did try to fight that edict. I never knew to search for all these possibilities. I never dreamed things could go this direction."

Gaeren leaned forward, squeezing her hand to pull her out of the paths she sifted. "And you shouldn't. You already sift souls too much. Your duty as the next queen doesn't come before your health and safety."

"You need to go to Lenda." Enla's voice broke through his tortured thoughts, forcing his mind to redirect to the least of his concerns. "Apologize for the way you treated her and show the city that all is well between you."

Gaeren raised his eyebrows.

"When she came back alone, she wasn't very quiet about the way you left her without warning." Enla sighed again. "In the company of another woman."

Gaeren rolled his eyes. "I was with Orra and Riveran."

"The mysterious woman with the light? Did you figure out her source of power?"

"No." The word came out more sullen than he'd intended. "I didn't get the starbridge either. And clearly I wasn't able to assess the loyalties in Islara."

He'd found Daisy, though. His mission had been a success for that reason alone, but how could he tell Enla? What would she do if she heard the strongest pocket of progeny Recreants had settled a few miles from here? That they waited for news from Gaeren? Maybe she already did know. Maybe she'd sent soldiers after them already.

"Oh, and I don't think we should expect to get help from the sprites. Ever."

Enla's eyes narrowed, her gaze traveling over his face. "You've changed. You're not as carefree as you once were."

He squirmed under her gaze. "Maybe responsibilities are finally weighing me down."

Enla shook her head slowly, still contemplating. "Not responsibilities. People. You were tied to me. I felt it when I sifted your soul. You still are, but now there are more." Her eyes took on that faraway look that made Gaeren uncomfortable. "The rope connecting us is still thick, but parts are frayed. Now there's rope to Aeliana, far thicker than the one for Lenda. There are also ropes to Larkos and your men."

He cleared his throat, not wanting to examine the implications.

"There's even one connecting you to Riveran." She blinked rapidly, refocusing on Gaeren.

"What's your point?"

"I don't think Mother and Father can keep you in the dark anymore. Now that you care about how their decisions affect all these people you're tied to, you'll find the answers whether they want you to or not."

He supposed it was a compliment. Enla's way of telling him she approved of the changes in him. But it felt more like a slap. Why hadn't he cared before? How selfish had he always been? And how much of his inward focus had been orchestrated by his parents?

Enla stood. "After you go to Lenda, you can spend your day how you wish. I'll understand if you're not ready to come back here. A lot has changed." She gave him a long searching look, then pulled him to his feet, forcing him into a hug that he didn't resist. "I love you, brother," she whispered.

Her desperate tone startled him as much as the words. Like she was saying goodbye. He hugged her back, memories flooding his mind of the games they'd played as children, the nights they'd stayed up talking about nothing and everything, the pranks they'd played on the servants.

"I love you too," he said.

She pulled away, wiping tears off her cheeks. In the span of a few breaths, she transformed. Her back straightened; her face became stoic once more. She raised her chin as if addressing a commoner. "May the Sun's light always shine upon you."

This time it was Daisy's face who filled his mind, the same expression leaving her lips but holding hope.

"And may the Stars' light always guide you," he mumbled back.

Enla nodded her approval before slipping out from the room.

Guilt pricked at Gaeren as, once again, she failed to check his future. He had no intention of going to see Lenda.

Instead, that afternoon he went to the docks and sought out Larkos, who happened to be checking up on *Starspeed*. His bond mark itched the whole way. As he approached, he saw the ship with new eyes—not just an extravagant gift, but a distraction, a method to keep Gaeren from meddling in the parts of monarchy he couldn't "stomach."

Suddenly the ship's deck seemed too shiny, the sails too pristine. It was more of a toy than a tool.

A cry pierced the sound of water lapping against the hull, and Gullet sank through the sky to land on Gaeren's outstretched arm. Gaeren pulled out the tiny scrap of paper tied around Gullet's leg, but instead of leaving, Gullet hopped on Gaeren's shoulder, as if waiting for Gaeren to write a reply.

He unrolled the scrap to read: *Spoke with Larkos. I'll be ready to sail when you need me.*

Gaeren's limbs loosened. Finally, he had one person on his side. Who would have thought it would be Riveran?

"Just the man I wanted to see." Larkos' deep rumble came from around the mast, bringing a warmth that pricked Gaeren's eyes. "Riveran said you were coming, but I wasn't about to wait around all day."

A slow smile spread on Gaeren's face. Just because the ship had been a bribe didn't mean he couldn't use it for worthy purposes. These men were important. The relationships he'd formed were valuable. And together they would use the ship to make a difference.

Larkos grasped Gaeren's forearm, squinting at the younger man. "You look like you've gone to the Deep and back."

Gaeren laughed, retrieving his hand to muss the hair he hadn't bothered combing. "You always told me I was too pretty for a man. Must be an improvement."

Larkos grunted. "Am I closing the ship up for the season? Or did you convince Enla you deserve another go?"

Gaeren hesitated, tempted to tell Larkos that Enla had approved a voyage to the Northern Sea, that she wanted the salmon found in colder waters. He might even be able to convince Enla to approve it now that his parents suspected he might meddle in politics. The thought should be a relief after weeks of worrying he'd never sail again. But he couldn't trick Larkos or their men into doing what came next.

"Are we alone on the ship?"

Larkos cocked his head. "Aye."

Gaeren headed for the captain's quarters, waving for Larkos to follow. "Good. I have something else in mind."

Larkos leaned back in his chair, which groaned under his weight. The old man's mouth hung open slightly, and Gaeren felt a hint of pride that he'd managed to shock his first mate.

"They've given Mayvus a kingdom?"

"Technically it's a queendom." Gaeren tapped the small desk between them. Normally the close quarters felt safe and secure on *Starspeed*, but today he was plagued by an uneasy restlessness and was eager for answers.

"And she killed an army of Recreants?"

Gaeren shrugged. "I didn't see that for myself, but if the army was there, they didn't survive."

Gullet let out a squawk from his perch on the back of a third chair as if confirming Gaeren's words.

"Sun's fire," Larkos breathed out. "When were they going to tell the people?"

Gaeren frowned at the reminder of his past complacency. "They plan to hold a coronation for her next spring, so you can't tell anyone until they've announced it."

"I meant about Islara."

Gaeren winced. "Probably never. We just arrived, so I expect the news to start trickling in from traveling merchants. They'll make sure it's unrelated to Mayvus being gifted a province. Just a terrible tragedy that we'll mourn as a nation."

Larkos shook his head, his face twisted in disgust.

"I want to go after her." Gaeren leaned forward, his voice dropping to a whisper. "The people I'm traveling with are headed her way for a reason. I think they know how to defeat her. I don't know their plan, but they're a small sect of Recreants, mostly progenies. They've brought the girl with them because she's Mayvus' niece. Her mother's held captive by Mayvus."

"How is bringing Mayvus' niece going to suddenly make Mayvus a good person?"

Gaeren sat back in frustration. "I don't know. They were never willing to discuss their plans in front of me. But they seemed to think Aeliana was key."

They sat for a moment, the slap of water against the ship the only sound between them. The rocking motion calmed Gaeren far more than his mother's magic. He knew his request appealed to Larkos as a Recreant. But deep down, this was far more about protecting Daisy. Despite the fact that she was a Wyndren, and despite the truth that she had plenty of others, including herself, willing and able to provide protection, he couldn't stop himself from looking out for her safety. She needed this boat to get her there. Fast.

"Also, we need to stop Mayvus before Summer Solstice," Gaeren said.

"You just said the coronation was next spring."

Gaeren scrubbed his palms over his face. "I know. But they need to get there before Summer Solstice. Again, I don't know why."

Larkos' gaze turned skeptical. "Look, you're asking us all to commit treason. To assist in warfare against an ally of Elanesse. I can't ask these men to go on a mission like this on a whim. You have to know why." He jabbed his finger against the desk. "Even knowing why isn't enough. You have to believe in the why. And you have to get these men to believe in it too."

"But you're Recreants." Gaeren's voice rose, making Larkos' gaze flick to the door.

"Recreants don't share minds any more than Loyalists. I can't know what Recreants in the south are planning unless they send me a message, and they haven't sent me any message. Which is no surprise. Out of all the provinces, ours is the least trusted. Recreants in Elanesse are more likely to be spies than true Recreants." Larkos stood, signaling that Gaeren was out of time.

Gaeren beat him to the door, blocking it with his body. "But you trust our men. If they believe in this mission, if they want in, we should do it."

"I'm not going to put these men in harm's way. Everything is too risky. Traveling to the Northern Sea is dangerous enough on its own. Icebergs barely poking out the surface but the size of your hull underwater and beasts that aren't wanting to share the water. On top of that, if the wind hits just right, it'll send us straight into the cliffs. There are too many unknowns." Larkos reached for the handle, but Gaeren leaned a hand against the door.

"If you make this decision for them, you're no better than my father. You want a democracy? Prove it. Let these men make the decision for themselves."

Larkos sighed. "I wish it were that simple."

"Maybe it can be," Gaeren said.

Larkos studied him for a long time, something that used to leave Gaeren feeling young, unable to measure up. But something in his first mate's face made Gaeren stand a little taller, a little surer. He needed Larkos to say yes. If the older man refused, Gaeren would probably have to lead Sylmar and Daisy to the royal family's secret pass through the mountains. There was no other way for her to reach the Myndren Mountains by Summer Solstice.

"Fine. Only if"—Larkos held up a hand before Gaeren could express his thanks—"each man makes his own choice. In the past, I've threatened demotion if they didn't take a job. It's the only way to guarantee consistency. But I won't do that here. There are a few men I can't even ask. I'm not confident they'll keep their mouths shut."

Gaeren nodded. "The people I'm bringing are hard workers. Some of them even have experience at sea, and we can train those who don't." He thought of Orra and her stories, then imagined Velden at the bow and Kendalyhn burning food right alongside Breeve. He could get by with a skeleton crew if the Recreants all pitched in.

Larkos held out his hand to seal the deal, then hesitated. "What if the plans they're keeping from you include war against your family?"

Gaeren swallowed hard, glancing at the door but imagining the palace beyond it, where his sister and parents remained unaware of his treasonous actions. "I won't encourage violence against my family, but with the decisions my parents are making, I can't blame others if that's what it comes to. Still, I will defend Enla to my death, and I will ask both you and these other Recreants to spare her life if you can."

Larkos stared him down. "I can't fault you for that. Calia would have my hide if I tried convincing you to do anything less for your sister. I just don't envy the Recreant who comes up against you. Because one will." The sadness in his eyes heightened the gravity of his warning as he brought his hand down to shake with Gaeren.

The sprite's deals warred in Gaeren's mind even as he gripped Larkos' forearm. He would protect Daisy and defend Enla, and he suspected the combination would be his end. The sprite had practically guaranteed it, but as long as both women were safe, the cost wasn't too high.

While Larkos hired dock boys to watch *Starspeed*, Gaeren sent Riveran a message through Gullet, then he hopped down from *Starspeed*, kissing his hand and patting the hull. "See you soon."

After securing a horse from the blacksmith in town, Gaeren headed for the camp he'd left the day before. It was hard to believe it had only been that long. At first, Gaeren thought he was lost among the various paths exiting Elanesse, but then he paid closer attention, retracing Skunk's path from the day before until he found the clearing. He pulled up short, looking at the signs of an abandoned camp, trying to discern when they'd left. It didn't even look like they'd used the fire that day. Had they left yesterday? Right after Gaeren?

He tuned into the wisps of memory around him, confirming that theory, but also catching hold of something more recent, something familiar. His starlock warmed with his suspicion.

"Holm?"

Skunk's ears flattened as if he also sensed the other man's presence, or maybe his horse.

Sure enough, Holm rode into the clearing, his face a bit sheepish. "Had to make sure you were alone."

The lack of faith stung at first. He'd traveled with these people for weeks, gaining and building friendships on top of trust. But hadn't he wanted them to keep Daisy safe from all threats?

"Of course. I'm glad you did," Gaeren said.

"You had a tail on you most of the day."

Gaeren winced. "You mean besides you?"

Holm chuckled.

"That's Enla's doing. I've gotten used to the guards, but I think I lost them just outside the city. I usually do."

Holm nodded. "Well, come on then." With his quiet confidence, he turn his steed and began weaving through the trees. Gaeren followed until he finally caught the scent of smoke on the wind, then the clank of dishes and the stomping of hooves. Voices murmuring.

Then the keening of a dying creature.

CHAPTER 61

"Hush, Felk." Aeliana ran her hand over the winex's forehead. Wrinkles bunched his skin, making him more grey and dusky than silver. He closed his eyes with a moan and curled up on her bedroll. The last time she'd watched his rebirth, it hadn't seemed so painful.

"Mama," he whispered. He hadn't called her that for weeks, and the word sounded strange on his elderly lips. This could have been his fifth life cycle, or it could have been his hundredth. "Tomorrow… tomorrow I won't know you."

She shook her head even though his eyes stayed closed. "Tomorrow you meet me again." She gripped his hand tight in hers, speaking a confidence she didn't feel.

"You remember my last life. You remember how I hurt you?" The lines around his eyes deepened.

She hesitated, unwilling to lie. "I remember. But that was a winex who'd been mistreated. You won't be like that again. Not as long as you stay with us."

"But if I am, you'll kill me. Sylmar will kill me. Anyone here would kill me before they let me hurt you." His wracking cough came out in spasms, and she passed him a cup of water. Most of it spilled down his cheek.

"I could never kill you, Felk," she whispered.

His eyes opened a crack, their blue still as brilliant as they'd been his first day. "You must. I don't want to hurt you."

She hushed him again, bending forward to reassure him, but a commotion at the edge of camp startled her. She turned and squinted, taking in the welcome sight of Gaeren atop a horse. "Gaeren's here. He'll be able to give you memories in the morning."

Felk let out a sigh, then went so still she thought he might already be gone, but it was too soon, and his chest rose and fell with shallow breaths.

She rose to greet Gaeren, who had dismounted and was already surrounded by Holm, Sylmar, Velden, and Lukai. His concerned frown and weary eyes seemed to spread through the group as she worked her way to his side.

"Sylmar was right." He wouldn't hold Aeliana's gaze, and her stomach tightened. "My parents have a warrant out for Aeliana's arrest." The pain in his voice sent a jolt through her.

"They know I'm a Wyndren." She kept her voice even, but he'd known too. And he didn't hold it against her.

Gaeren nodded, still looking everywhere but at her. "They've also aligned themselves with Mayvus."

Lukai inhaled sharply, placing a hand on her arm as if to keep her from getting any closer to the bearer of bad news.

"That doesn't make any sense." Sylmar's frown bunched his scars.

Aeliana's mind raced. This changed things. It would change things for Sylmar's plans. And it would have to change things for Gaeren, wouldn't it?

"Did you tell them about Islara?" Velden asked.

The skin around Gaeren's mouth grew tight. "They already knew."

Aeliana studied Gaeren. The croak of frogs and chirrup of crickets filled the night air, but she waited for him to look at her. When he finally did, his expression was raw, his shame laid bare between them.

"I'm sorry," she said.

He scoffed. "What are you sorry for? My parents—"

"I'm sorry they've put you in such a terrible position."

He swallowed hard and looked away.

"I'm sorry they've disappointed you."

His nod was stiff, and she held back the rest of her words, worried she was misreading the situation—worried she'd read it far too right. He'd have to make a clean break from his family or the Recreants. He couldn't fight against Mayvus without fighting against his family.

She wanted to reach out and squeeze his hand. To ask him about Enla. To find something he could hold on to after such a deep cut. But Iris' words about him interfering with her bond still rang in her ears, and Lukai's hand still held her arm.

"I vowed to protect you long before I knew who you were." Gaeren said the words like they were an apology. "At first I thought your identity changed things. But it doesn't. Not really."

"You can't have it both ways," she whispered, but the words felt loud.

"I know." He stood a little taller, turning to face Sylmar and Velden, even as his eyes flicked back to Aeliana. "I've come here to commit treason. I may not have a fleet, but I'm offering to take you all to the Northern Sea, not as the Prince of Elanesse, but as the Captain of *Starspeed*."

"Everyone knows they're one in the same," Sylmar said, but he stroked his beard thoughtfully.

"True." Gaeren frowned. "I'll probably have to change my ship's name. Maybe paint her. On the plus side, I can grow a beard and get a tattoo. Find a good pirate name. Have any suggestions?"

His lip quirked up in his familiar smirk, and Aeliana couldn't help smiling back. "Maybe Gaeren the Vain or Braggart Brownbeard?"

He put a hand to his chest in mock pain. "You wound me." He took in everyone behind her, and something shifted in his eyes. He hesitated before turning to Sylmar. "I understand if you don't want the added complication of a prince committing treason."

Sylmar's shoulders lifted. "Kendalyhn can sift your soul again." He moved away to find her.

Aeliana stepped closer to Gaeren. "What will you accomplish by going against your family? By joining our cause? What do you want from all this?" She couldn't help the curious questions, but she hoped he couldn't sense her eagerness.

"The same thing I've always wanted." This time, his eyes bore into hers with confidence and a strange warmth she hadn't seen before. She tried remembering what he'd wanted, what Kendalyhn had seen when she'd sifted his soul the first time. Did he want to protect her? To find the starbridge? To go against Mayvus? All those options meant his loyalties lay with them, but for some reason she needed that distinction. For some reason, it mattered.

Sylmar returned with Kendalyhn, who stepped up to Gaeren and held out her open palms. He sighed, then handed his horse's reins to Aeliana and placed his hands in Kendalyhn's, screwing up his face as if he were the one needing to sift through her soul instead of the other way around.

Kendalyhn's eyebrows rose over her closed lids, and Aeliana would have given anything to see what Kendalyhn glimpsed in Gaeren's soul. The moment stretched, and Kendalyhn stepped back, her gaze shooting between Gaeren and Aeliana.

"Well?" Sylmar grunted, shifting his weight more heavily on his staff.

"There's betrayal in his past that wasn't there before. It clouds his motives, but his desire hasn't changed. He wants to protect the people from Mayvus. To find the starbridge. He wants what's best even if his parents don't."

Sylmar squinted, the scars of his face pulling in tight. "He can't be all that noble. Nothing's ever that simple."

"Like I said, his motives are mixed." Kendalyhn glanced at Aeliana, drawing Sylmar's and Lukai's attention too.

Aeliana rubbed the fresh scabs and scars on her palms unsure what to think of Kendalyhn's strange behavior. The woman remained as mysterious as the cuts that continued showing up on Aeliana's skin. Cuts that made her wonder if she was doing blood magic while she slept. Ever since Durriken had been freed, she'd been too afraid to ask Sylmar about it.

"Besides, how can you refuse me? I still have a boat, and you are in need of a boat." Gaeren grinned at Sylmar.

The muscles in Sylmar's face twitched as he debated their options, but clearly this was the best one.

"How soon can we leave?" the older man asked.

Gaeren's smirk bloomed to a full smile. "If we stop for supplies in Bryton or Merrick, we could leave tomorrow afternoon. That will draw less suspicion anyway."

Sylmar nodded, turning back to camp to call out instructions. Kendalyhn left, and Lukai reluctantly followed, glancing over his shoulder at Aeliana and Gaeren, who remained alone at the edge of camp with his horse.

"What about Riveran and Marnok?" Aeliana handed the reins back to Gaeren and stroked the horse's withers.

Gaeren ran a hand through his hair. "I don't know. I think Riveran will come, but I doubt Marnok has had time to fully search for his roots."

"And Enla?"

Gaeren's smile faded. "She has to make her own choices. And I'm not sure they're the same as mine. Once my family realizes I'm gone, I won't be able to return. Not unless we've exposed Mayvus. Even then... this could be unforgivable."

Aeliana bit her lip and turned away. It felt like too big of a risk for him to come. He didn't even know half of the risk because he didn't know about her blood. This moment alone wouldn't last long, not with how little everyone trusted the prince.

But she trusted him.

She almost laughed at the strangeness of the thought. In fact, as rocky as their start had been, sometimes he seemed like the one she could trust the most to tell her the truth, especially if it would be something she didn't want to hear. He had no motives to get her to do what he wanted.

She leaned against the horse, as if revealing her secret to the gelding instead of Gaeren. "Mayvus has my blood," she whispered.

"What?" Gaeren's face paled, his gaze darting to the others still walking away.

"We're guessing she plans to brand me the same way she branded my mother," Aeliana rushed on, unsure which details to spill before they lost their privacy. "My power is strange, unwieldy. Even as Sylmar trains me, it's too strong. They think it has to do with the way my guardians—with the..." She closed her eyes, unable to finish.

"If she branded you, she could control that magic." His hushed voice held sorrow.

Aeliana nodded, still unwilling to look at him. "I just thought you should know the risks before you get more involved. I'd hate for you to get all the way to the Valley of Krahn just to discover it's not a risk you're willing to take on."

"Aeliana?" Lukai's call from up ahead broke the strained silence between Gaeren and Aeliana.

"Coming," she yelled back, taking a step toward her bondmate.

Gaeren stopped her by grabbing her hand, the warmth of his skin sending a trail of hope up her arm. "Thank you," he said. "For telling me."

Her smile faltered when Felk's howl filled the air. "Felk will be reborn tomorrow."

His eyes lit up as he glanced around for the winex. "Can I see him?"

"He's not doing well." Aeliana bit her lip. "It might be difficult to transport him. But I was hoping you could give him some memories after he's reborn. And not the ones of him attacking me."

Gaeren winced. "I can probably come up with a few others. Make him feel like he's at home."

Aeliana slumped. "That would make him the happiest winex in all of Rhystahn."

"You think he'll be the same in his new life?" Gaeren asked.

Aeliana opened her mouth, but her words were drowned out by voices in the distance.

Gaeren's hand tensed in hers. "Run," he whispered before shoving her away.

"Who—?"

"Please—go!" He shoved again, and she tripped, catching herself on a mangrove root. Before she could get too far, Lukai's arms were around her, pulling her into a crouch. The occupants of the camp disappeared in a shimmering wave as Jasperus' face scrunched in concentration, and the voices became clearer as they called Gaeren's name.

"I'm here," Gaeren called, his voice miraculously dozens of feet away, beyond a cluster of mangrove trees. Still, it was too close. How long could Jasperus hold the illusion?

Aeliana squeezed her eyes shut, hoping it was just Riveran and Marnok.

But the voice that answered him was too soft and feminine.

"What are you doing out here, brother?"

CHAPTER 62

"I THOUGHT I told you to stop sifting through my future." Gaeren let his lips curl up as he nudged his sister's ribs. His heart pounded so hard that he felt certain Enla could sense it, even hear it. He itched to glance back through the trees to make sure Daisy couldn't be seen, but that would only draw Enla's attention more.

"Who were you talking to?" Enla's voice held the same teasing lilt as Gaeren's, her guards listening in on every word, but there was an edge of disappointment.

"Just Skunk." He patted the horse's flank, earning a whinny from the beast.

She sighed as if he were an impertinent child. "Why didn't you go to Lenda?"

"You followed me out to the woods just to ask me that?"

"No. There were plenty of people willing to report you leaving the city to Lenda, who then reported it to me. As her future queen, I couldn't stand by and ignore a report of possible treason." Her words came out stilted, like she was saying what she had to instead of what she meant. "But since I'm here, I thought I'd ask why you couldn't follow through on your sister's one simple request."

"So it's treason to want to be by myself for a time? To want to get away from it all?" Gaeren raised his eyebrows, but Enla's face remained rigid.

"It is if you're found in the company of Recreants."

Gaeren laughed, letting it ring through the forest with manufactured ease. "Do you see any Recreants? It's just me and my horse."

"Did you send them to the hidden pass?" Enla's voice rose, startling Gaeren.

"What are you talking about?"

"You wouldn't be stupid enough to take them on your boat. The only other way for them to reach Mayvus from here is through our family's escape route." Her mask cracked for a fraction of a second, her eyes widening in a challenge.

"Are you suggesting that I'm helping Recreants reach Mayvus?" He asked the question slowly, as if angered by her insinuation, but his mind raced with how he might rectify their situation. Now that he'd been caught by Enla, Starspeed was no longer an option. The secret pass through the mountains would be far slower than his boat, but it could still get them there before Summer Solstice.

"You came from Islara," Enla said. "What else am I supposed to think?"

"Even if I were, it would take people almost a moon longer to reach Mayvus through our family's tunnel than it would by boat." He let the words hang in the air for the Recreants to hear. They could do the math —make the decision for themselves. Most likely it would put them at her doorstep within days of Summer Solstice. Hardly enough time to devise a plan to steal back Daisy's blood.

But maybe they already had a plan.

"Are they under some sort of time constraint?" Enla's tone turned curious.

"I'm thinking of my own impatience and laziness." Gaeren's hands shook, so he clenched them into fists. "Why would I want to trek five miles to the Phoenix's Wing, then spend a day hunting for the tiny opening under the tip of the chipped feather just to spend an entire moon trekking the barren border between the desert and the coast? Especially when I could hop on *Starspeed* and let my crew take me there in half the time? I'd be crazy to help Recreants either way, but most especially across land."

There. He'd given them clear directions if they were willing to use them. Even the guards glanced at each other in surprise. The where-abouts of the secret pass weren't exactly public knowledge.

"You know you have to come back with me, right?" Enla's words were barely above a whisper. "Prove to Mother and Father that you're not actively working against them? If you weren't the prince, your suspicious presence out here might be enough for them to throw you in a cell."

"I don't have to prove anything. They'll just keep guards stationed at my room. Like always." Gaeren led his horse past Enla. There was nothing more he could do for Daisy other than leave, but everything inside him resisted walking away. "Besides, it's not about whether I'm actively working against them. It's about whether they're willing to work with Mayvus."

"Don't start this again," Enla's her words came out in small huffs as she worked to catch up with him.

"She practices blood magic. She used a brand on Durriken, but his is only one of many."

Enla flinched but didn't look as surprised as Gaeren had hoped she might. "Father and Mother are reconsidering some of their laws. Brands aren't much different from bonds."

Gaeren reeled back, and his horse nearly knocked him over. He leaned in until the horse blocked them from Enla's guards.

"That's not the only blood magic she does," he whispered fervently. "Not according to the Recreants."

"Whom you now trust?" The accusation in her voice stung more than the judgment on her face.

"The Recreants might be our enemy tomorrow, but today they would stand with us against Mayvus if we asked."

Enla opened her mouth, but Gaeren cut her off before she could argue.

"We're not just up against one Wyndren; we're up against an entire army. They even have a name. Did you know? They call themselves Zealots, and there are thousands of them—men and women who want the Wyndrens ruling instead of us."

The horse danced nervously beside them, clearly not wanting in on their argument. But neither of them moved, Gaeren's words forming a barrier between them.

"Your loyalties put you in danger," she said, her gaze losing focus. "Your thoughts will get you killed."

"Killed? Who will kill me?" His question came out weary. He didn't expect an answer. Her visions didn't work that way. But the answer had to be his parents, and the truth of what they valued left him exhausted.

Enla reached out a hand to grip his arm.

"Why did you go to Lovers' Falls?" Her whisper drove deep into his soul, the pain heightened by his lingering fear over the deal half struck with the sprites. But Enla could only see possibilities in his future, choices and moral dilemmas. She shouldn't know the past.

"How do you—?"

Her grip tightened on his arm. "The paths for your soul are dwindling. If you'd stayed away from there, the options were endless. But now… now too many of them converge or end."

Gaeren glanced over the horse at the guards, but their stoic faces gave no indication that they'd heard.

"You've made yourself sick searching my future." Gaeren pried her fingers from his arm, then held her hand to his face. "I'm here. I'm well. Stop torturing yourself."

"Did you at least take Riveran with you?"

Hearing his name cross her lips brought shadows of memories flooding his mind. Tears and pained cries. Weeks spent sleeping outside her room to hush the name from her lips when the nightmares came. But then more recent memories replaced them. Placing bets on Orra's next antics, laughing by the fire, teasing and training Felk together.

"He found a way to be present." The stiff words were unfair, but they were as much as Gaeren could muster in front of Enla.

Her eyes fluttered shut for a moment. She nodded, then wrenched her hand away, slipping past him toward Elanesse. Once more her chin rose and her back straightened, making Gaeren wonder if her vulnerability had been in his imagination.

They made the rest of the way through the forest in silence, Gaeren stewing over all the half predictions Enla had spouted off. Past the mangrove trees, they joined a second set of guards, and they all mounted horses. When they reached the city limits, a third set of soldiers surrounded them, solidifying Gaeren's suspicion that his days of freely coming and going were gone.

How had he been so blind all these years? In addition to being tyrants, his parents had been forming alliances with an enemy. They likely knew about Mayvus' blood magic and did nothing to stop it. They'd split up Daisy's family and exiled her to Lorvandas. His muscles tensed as he thought about what her childhood must have been like, all because of his parents.

Heat flooded his starlock, matching the way his body warmed with his anger. It no longer mattered what his parents or tutors had told him about the Wyndrens and Elanesses. He would protect Daisy with the same level of loyalty as he had for Enla. The guilty twinge in his gut twisted once more. Maybe even more if Enla continued to insist on working with Mayvus. Was this what the sprites had been warning him about?

He nudged his horse past Enla in the abandoned night streets, forcing her to catch up or be left behind. The guards followed too closely for Gaeren's comfort, but the conversation couldn't wait. Thankfully, Enla followed.

"I can't tell whose side you're on," he hissed. "I need you to be on my side."

"I *am* on your side." The moonlight shone off her face as it crumpled beneath the weight of her burdens. "But I still answer to our parents. In some ways, I still answer to Mayvus. If you'd gone to Lenda, you could have broken your bond. With that last tie severed, you would have been free. You should have listened to me. I told you everything has changed."

Gaeren's mouth went slack. Enla had wanted him to break his bond? The idea was both unthinkable and strangely appealing—absolute freedom that would come with terrible suffering. He doubted it would be as painful for him as it had been for Enla, but the guilt would eat away at him. If that was what Enla had wanted, she could have been more specific with her instructions. He clamped his jaw back down, the memories of her pain flooding his mind. He wasn't sure he could put Lenda through that anyway. Besides, how would freedom from Lenda change anything?

"Now I don't—I don't know." She placed her hands at her temples, the crease on her brow deepening. "The paths split and…" She buried her face in her hands.

"Did you help Aeliana? Or are you sending soldiers to the pass? I need to know if you sent her to her death." He couldn't stop the tremble rising in his voice. "If I just helped you send her to her death."

She rubbed her palms over her face, smoothing out her features and regaining her queenly serenity. But her eyes remained haunted, focused somewhere past even the Stars. "I already sent soldiers. I had to. If your people don't know how to wait them out, it's for the best. The alternatives are far worse."

Gaeren clenched his jaw. He'd get nothing more from his sister. He rode ahead, as irritated with himself as he was with Enla.

By the time they returned to the palace, the faint glow of the Sun's morn lit the sky. Felk had likely just been reborn. He smiled at the thought of the tiny silver baby snuggled in Daisy's arms. While she ran toward Elanesse soldiers.

Gaeren's smile fell.

He tried not to imagine being aboard *Starspeed*, sailing out of the harbor with Daisy and Orra and the others as his crew. It had felt so right when he and Larkos made plans. But now he no longer knew what lay ahead.

CHAPTER 63

A SMILE TUGGED at the edge of Orra's lips as they reached the hidden pass. They'd had to hide and wait two days and a night for the soldiers guarding the pass to return to Elanesse. But now the gentle sounds of night life shifted to the morning raucous of a new day, joined by Felk's childish antics. A large rock in the shape of a wing stretched out from the mountain, obscuring their view of the pass. But once they drew closer, they'd find the chipped feather and the tight opening. Then they'd have to remove packs for the horses to fit, probably blindfold them to convince them the trail led to safety.

"There," Velden called, his voice more whisper than shout. He ran ahead, peering beneath the rock's edge for the promised opening. The others followed, weariness replaced by eager anticipation.

It had been smart of Gaeren to suggest the pass. Or maybe smart of Enla. The young queen's motives still weren't clear, and Orra hadn't been close enough to test them. Regardless, the pass would give them a chance. Orra hadn't used it since its creation. Had forgotten its existence. Funny how things like that could slip someone's mind over time. It was almost noble how Gaeren had given them directions even while knowing his part of the journey had come to an end.

Not that they'd needed directions. Orra could have found it in the dark of night.

For now, they would be safe thanks to Gaeren's sacrifice. He was growing into the role he was meant to have, stretching the limits of what he was told to be, who he thought he was. He might not lead Orra to the arrow, but he would be back. He might even use the starbridges to make the world bigger.

Orra twisted the braid on her wrist. Letting him use the starbridges for the good of the people could slow down her plans, but maybe that was for the best, for now. "It might be what you would have wanted," she murmured. "It might be what the Sun wants."

At that moment the Sun broke through the trees, shining down on Orra with a beam so brilliant it left her breathless. She dropped to her knees, tilting her face up to its warmth. It had been so long since she'd felt the Sun's acceptance, its approval. But it had been equally long since she'd truly sought it. Prayers on behalf of others was one thing, but submission to a will that was not her own... that had become harder the longer she'd been grounded.

Orra stood, taking her place at the back of the line to walk Walnut through the pass.

The future was changing faster than she could keep up with, something that was both alarming and refreshing. Aeliana continued to be a surprise, making choices Orra couldn't have anticipated, hadn't thought to search. For once, Orra lived in the moment, viewing the people around her as more than stones or ripples in time. They weren't just the historical figures of the future she sought—they were closer to companions and friends, something she hadn't allowed herself in ages. Something she hadn't dared to find since she'd lost her last bondmate.

Horses whinnied their impatience, and the sounds of packs being shuffled around echoed through the wing's small cave.

Instead of readying for the pass, Aeliana's gaze shifted back toward the swamps they'd left behind. "What if he comes back and we're gone?"

He wouldn't come back, but Orra knew those words would bring the girl no comfort. "He knew we'd come here. He'll know where to look."

Aeliana gnawed at her lip.

"He led Enla away to keep you safe." Orra reached out, smoothing

Aeliana's hair like she was a child. "He's still protecting you. Don't let his sacrifice go to waste."

Aeliana closed her eyes, and Orra imagined the words sinking in, the truth resting deep in Aeliana's pores. The younger woman joined the others, her brow still furrowed as she chewed her lip.

Orra's smile returned, her heart filling with a hope she hadn't had in several generations.

Some bond marks ran far deeper than the skin.

CHAPTER 64

OVER THE NEXT FEW WEEKS, Gaeren didn't take a single step outside his room without the company of the guards. He recognized them as two of Enla's, the handsome kind who were meant to make her look good even though they were also trustworthy to their core. Still, they were faithful to Enla, and instead of their presence putting him at ease for his safety, they made him wary of his own sister.

Despite spending most of their time in bed, his parents made time to lecture Gaeren over his impropriety, emphasizing that the safest thing for the people was to foster peace between nations, as if Mayvus' new nation had always been something to consider during their reign.

The days blended together as Gaeren was forced to attend council meetings and put on a smile for visitors from the south. Any news from the east came with gifts from the new monarch, while Gaeren heard no more mention of Durriken or Islara.

What use was being a prince if he had no power?

A knock sounded on his door, pulling him from his stupor at his bedroom window. Clothes and books had lain scattered across the floor ever since he'd started refusing to let the maids in his room. The pillows on his bed formed a miniature Mt. Vescano, blocking his view of the door.

The knock came again, signifying that it wasn't Enla, who would have barged in by now.

"Come in," he called, turning back to the window, eyeing the statue of Queen Amaya, swearing her eyes held judgment at they looked up to his.

The door scraped open.

"You have a visitor," one of the guards announced.

Gaeren frowned. Who would be visiting him?

He supposed it could be Lenda. She'd come a few times at Enla's request to keep the people from growing suspicious. With her hand-maiden's watchful eyes and listening ears, Gaeren hadn't been able to ask Lenda about Enla's plan for their bond. Besides, what good would it do? At least the guards hadn't caught Daisy's group. They were likely halfway to Myndren by now, riding along the Northern Sea's coast.

His heart swelled at the thought of being near the open water, dining on fresh fish.

"Prince Gaeren?" The guard spoke again, drawing Gaeren's gaze from the window. Oh, right. A visitor.

"Who is it?"

"I believe he's your first mate." The guard's gaze shifted uneasily. "He, ah, he wouldn't give us his name. He, well, he growled, after which he said something to the effect of 'who else would show up for the boy?'"

The hint of a smile tugged at Gaeren's lips.

"He has tattoos on his arms as well as his shaven head."

"He's bald," Gaeren corrected. "And send him in."

The door burst open before the words had finished leaving Gaeren's lips. The guard tensed, reaching for his sword.

"I have hair where it matters." Larkos patted his chest. He stopped just inside the room, looking around in disgust. "Never would have guessed you lived in a hovel after all the times you've made Breeve swab the deck."

"He's fine," Gaeren said, waving the guard away before pulling a chair from his desk and offering it to Larkos with a flourish. "I thought that if I let it get bad enough, Enla might decide I'm mentally unstable without time at sea."

Larkos squinted after the guard, waiting until the door latched. "Are you in trouble?" he whispered.

"No more than usual." When Larkos remained standing, arms crossed and eyes narrowed, Gaeren shrugged and sat in the chair, propping his bare feet up on the desk. "How did you get all the way down the hall? Enla might be interested in demoting someone for that."

"I'm not sure they would have announced me otherwise. I've been trying to see you for half a moon. I'm guessing I'm on some sort of blacklist."

Gaeren snorted. "That's nothing new. Enla isn't a fan of sailors. Thinks they're all pirates. Besides, if you've come to tell me the ship's ready, it's too late. Enla has me on a leash." He glared at the bottle of wine just out of reach on his sideboard.

Larkos leaned against the desk, knocking Gaeren's feet to the floor. "I'm not playing around. Ever since you told me about the priestess and the girl, strange rumors have been coming through port."

"What kind of rumors?" Gaeren tipped his chair and leaned precariously to grab the bottle and a glass.

"Mostly the same crazy things you told me about a dragon. The people aren't stupid. They know they're not being told the whole story. But instead of finding the truth, they're filling in the gaps with their own ideas. A few say it was the Recreants, but most say it was the king keeping his people in line. Others say it's Mayvus. They whisper about her being a witch, but no one says it too loud. Not after your father made her a queen."

Gaeren poured the wine, watching it swirl in the glass. News had traveled far faster than his father had anticipated. And yet none of it had reached Gaeren before now. Were they continuing to keep him out of the loop?

"What about the girl?" Gaeren tried to keep his tone even, pushing down the terror clawing at his throat, but the effort was a waste thanks to his trembling hands.

Larkos reached for the glass, which Gaeren passed over. Larkos downed the whole cup, not bothering to savor it the way nobles did.

Gaeren shrugged, lifting the bottle to his lips and taking his own long swig.

"No one seems to know about the girl," Larkos said.

Gaeren let his eyes drift shut. At least she had that in her favor.

"The people are riled up, including our men. A few of them had family in Islara."

Memories flooded Gaeren's mind—memories that didn't belong to him. Memories that belonged to mothers and fathers racing their infants to the hope of safety. Children screaming in the streets. Fire burning at their backs. He shuddered, opening his eyes to refocus on the present. The bottle of wine in his hand. The sturdy chair beneath him. The trustworthy man before him.

"Why did you come, Larkos?"

"Unless someone proves it was Mayvus, there's a good chance your father will take the fall. War could be at your doorstep far sooner than you expected."

"Which would turn into a blood bath for my family." Gaeren set down the bottle and scrubbed his palms over his face.

Larkos leaned in. "Did you figure out why your girl is the key to exposing Mayvus?"

Gaeren shoved down the warmth rising at the sound of "your girl." He swallowed hard, reliving Daisy's words about her magic and her blood. She wasn't the key to exposing Mayvus, but she could be the key to Mayvus securing more power. The band of Recreants he'd found had a defensive mission, but Larkos was looking for the upper hand.

"It's not my secret to share."

Larkos grunted, but Gaeren had no idea if it was in irritation or approval.

"I'm not sure you need to share it anyway," the older man confessed. "Riveran brought twenty of your men to *Starspeed*. They're ready to follow you across any sea for their revenge. Through any barrier, to the Deep and back."

A glimmer of hope stirred in Gaeren's chest. "I thought you said they blamed my father."

"The people blame your father because it's easy. He's right here in front of them. Your men know different. They want to get revenge on the right person. Even if they don't want a monarch, they've learned to trust their captain."

Gaeren blinked and looked away as his hope grew. He envisioned the ropes Enla spoke of tethering him to his men growing thicker, holding taut under the tension of impending war.

"I've been a fool, Larkos. I wanted to trust the people I loved, the people I thought loved me."

Larkos hummed. "In a better world, you could. You can't help who you love, but you can choose who to trust. Doesn't make you a fool for wanting someone to be both things."

"I'd rather have the trust of our men than the love of my family." The words sounded harsh to Gaeren's ears, but there was a freeing sensation in speaking that truth.

Larkos' grin grew slowly, and he leaned forward once more, his voice low. "You wanted to go to the old fortress in the Myndren Mountains?"

Gaeren's heart sped up. "Yes."

"If we sail east past Ahmranan's Viewpoint, that would get you a five day's journey from the edge of the valley. Shorter if we can find horses. It would be safer to wait a moon. Those waters are best traveled on the Sun's longest days. Too soon and it's treacherous."

Gaeren shook his head. "I can't wait that long."

Larkos' eyes took on a mischievous gleam. "I never said you had to. I simply said it'd be safer. If you can be out on the veranda tomorrow night at the moon's peak, we can get you to *Starspeed*."

Gaeren eyed him warily even as his chest swelled with his hope. "We'd likely be helping the Recreants start a war."

"Don't you see? You're finally following through. You're an official Recreant." Larkos clapped his hand on Gaeren's shoulder. "War is what these boys have been waiting for. They just needed to know their captain would lead them into it."

CHAPTER 65

AELIANA SLID off her horse's saddle, her boots sinking in the sand. The others did the same, setting up camp the same way they had for the past few weeks every night with the Sun's sleep. The Pass had taken them through a portion of the mountain range, then deposited them into an eternal marshland that hinted at the ocean to come. They'd finally made it through to Northpoint to stock up once more, and everyone was eager to have the swamp at their back and the beach by their side.

A speck in the water grew larger, the form more human as it drew closer. A second silvery shape shadowed the first. As a wave crested, Velden's familiar frame rode it in, the grin on his face contagious. A middle-aged Felk followed, his smile just as big with twice the number of teeth. They each held a net full of fish—the supposed reason for their daily swim. As Velden laughed and shot sprays of water at the others, it was clear the water was where he belonged.

Aeliana took the fish, wrinkling her nose over the smell. "I thought you were unbearably cheery most days, but now you make Velden of the Forest seem positively depressed."

Somehow Velden's grin widened as he squeezed the excess water from his trousers, his webbed fingers absorbing the drops before they fell. He grabbed a vest from his saddle bag and pulled it on as if that tiny bit of fabric suddenly changed him from fish to human.

"I don't hear you complaining when you pick the flaky white flesh off those cod."

"It was an observation, not a complaint."

They settled on the coast, pulling out their knives and starting in on the messy but rewarding work of gutting the fish. Felk attempted to help, but he found the raw fish just as tempting as the cooked, so most of what he prepared ended up in his mouth. As much as Velden's face wrinkled with distaste over the task, he was faster than anyone else, already separating the flesh of a fish and running his knife along its backbone before Aeliana had finished slicing another one's belly.

Aeliana's dagger was less suited to the job, but after taking the weapon from Gaeren, she refused to use anything else. Every time she felt the groove of its hilt or caught the glimmer of the daisy on its pommel, she thought of him and the sacrifice he'd made to help them escape. It felt good to sit in her confusion over his need to protect her even while he was supposed to hate her. The longer she wrestled with it, the more it felt like she could someday figure it out, that the opposing feelings could be parsed out and defined enough to maybe let go of the painful parts.

Even Sylmar had grudgingly admitted Gaeren's word had been true after their escape. They owed Gaeren everything because he'd given them this one last chance to reach Mayvus before Summer Solstice.

"What legend do I get today?" Aeliana asked, not bothering to hide her eagerness.

Velden wasn't as skilled of a storyteller as Jasperus, but he'd traveled farther and experienced far more, making his stories and perspective more interesting. Most of Velden's stories centered around his time in the navy, but occasionally he'd pull out a story from the Sayhleens, something full of history and folklore that no one else knew.

"Have you heard of Lady Merinnia?" he asked.

"Not yet." She winced as she sliced along her own fish's bone, wondering how the two members of their party most squeamish about killing animals got stuck with this part of the food preparation.

"Ah, well, when my mother last visited her family, Lady Merinnia was the Seer of Sayhla." His eyes took on his storytelling glint.

"You can't believe half of what he says," Kendalyhn said, gathering the few fillets they'd already set aside.

"I never do, but it's still fun to listen."

Velden gave a mock frown, pausing to flick a stray fish eye in Aeliana's direction. As Kendalyhn returned to the cookfire, Holm coaxed it to life.

"I'll have you know that Lady Merinnia is basically queen of the Sayhleen, if the noble group ever had such a thing." Velden tilted his chin to peer down his nose at his audience.

Felk raised a fish to his lips, and Velden grimaced.

"Seer, priestess, queen—does the title matter if it's the same outcome?" Aeliana asked. "It seems people are always looking to rule over each other."

Velden shrugged. "Maybe people are always looking for someone to lead them. It doesn't always work out well, but the desire to follow a leader isn't wrong. Good leaders just happen to be rare treasures."

"And I suppose Lady Merinnia is one of those rare treasures."

He bobbed his head back and forth. "Yes and no. Her wisdom surpasses that of any other mortal, but she spends so much time sifting souls, examining the future, that she can't really rule the way you would expect a leader to. It's like her body remains here, but she's already left this world."

Aeliana raised her eyebrows, his words carrying eerie undertones that reminded her of the few things Gaeren had shared about Enla. "She sounds vulnerable."

Velden laughed. "She's not a dragon or winex needing rescuing."

Felk frowned as if trying to determine whether he'd been insulted. Aeliana stuck her tongue out at Velden as Holm came to collect more fillets for the fire. Cyrus sat beside them, joining in to gut more fish after caring for his and Aeliana's horses. The familiar rhythm of making camp at night put Aeliana at ease, allowing her to ignore the danger and unknowns they rode toward each day.

"My mother went to Lady Merinnia once," Velden continued. "It's a rare thing to seek out the Seer, often a life-or-death scenario. Some return with a peace, moving forward confidently in life, affirmed by the Seer. Others return with a madness, unable to speak about what they asked, why it went wrong. Some don't return at all."

"She's as bad as the sprites," Cyrus muttered.

"Yes," Velden said in surprise, pointing his knife at Cyrus. "Exactly. People seek her out when they reach a point of desperation. I'd like to say the outcome isn't always as terrible as it is with the sprites, but my mother made it sound like it could be far worse."

"So why did she go to her?" Aeliana asked, desperate to steer the conversation away from the sprites once more.

Velden shrugged. "She found a silver fish that took her to a world of men and women who only have feet instead of fins, skin instead of scales."

"That's when she found the starbridge," Aeliana breathed the word out.

He nodded. "She was drawn to the world and its people. To one man in particular." He smiled faintly. "Though I'm not sure why. My father was a bit like Gaeren. Too sure of himself. Too interested in himself."

Aeliana laughed even though she no longer found the description apt. "Now I know which qualities you get from your father."

"His good looks for sure." Velden winked. "Though my mother was a beauty even among Sayhleen. Reeled my father in like a siren."

"So Lady Merinnia must have seen good things in your mother's future," Aeliana said.

Velden frowned. "She never told me what the Seer said. It's supposed to be a private affair. A bit like an Awakening in that regard. Although Sayhleen aren't as private about their Awakenings as Vendarans. In Sayhla an Awakening is a rite of passage, celebrated with feasting and dancing. During those celebrations, Paelen's Waters is said to be lit so brightly the Stars are drawn like moths to a flame."

"They still commune with the Stars?" Cyrus asked, sitting straighter.

Velden shrugged. "No more than we do. But I hear they come close enough for their individual dances to be made out in the sky. One might loop here, another might zig-zag there." He let his fingers twirl around Felk's head until the winex's eyes crossed.

Aeliana glanced at Orra, who managed to seem separate from the group while still being mixed in the fray of food preparation and close enough to hear Velden's story. The woman's gaze turned wistful, and she tipped her face to the sky, where it was still too early to catch the Stars in their dance.

"Mama." Felk tugged on Aeliana's sleeve. "I'm going back in the water. I'll see if I can find more."

She glanced down and winced at the pile of fish he'd mutilated. She supposed he should replace what he'd eaten. "Have fun, Felk."

He pecked a fishy kiss on her cheek before taking off down the shoreline, and she resisted the urge to tell him to be careful. He was far too old for her nagging, but the brevity of his life cycle made it hard to stop mothering him.

"Your mother didn't go mad from what she learned," Aeliana said, steering the conversation back to the enigma of the Seer.

"No, but still..." Velden's eyes took on a distant look, his face more somber than Aeliana was used to seeing. "My mother chose to use the starbridge again after speaking with Lady Merinnia. She chose to marry my father and have me. I can't help wondering how much of the future she learned. How much she knew would take place. That's the thing that drives people mad. Knowing too much and being unable to stop it. Not knowing if it was the knowing that made it happen or if that would have been their fate regardless."

"Gaeren said Enla always sees multiple paths," Aeliana said. "That the future isn't set in stone."

Velden hummed his agreement. "I've heard her gift is strong, but the Seer's is the strongest. The strongest even among the Sayhleens' history of Seers. She often sees only two."

The thought didn't settle well with Aeliana, the idea that the future was determined regardless of her actions. Or maybe it was because of her actions. A single choice leading one direction or another. She supposed it shouldn't make a difference that the future might have one path the same way the past only had one, but still, it bothered her.

"You think she saw your mother's death." Cyrus studied Velden, his brow furrowed with empathy.

"I don't see how she couldn't have," Velden said. "And yet my mother chose that path anyway." His smile returned, but there was a sadness to it.

"Then it's a testament to her love for you and your father," Cyrus said. "If that was the path she chose."

"Ever the priest," Velden said with a laugh.

Cyrus' face and ears took on a pink tinge, but Aeliana sensed he was pleased by the slight jab.

They made quick work of the rest of the fish as the Sun slipped past the mountains in the west. Somewhere beyond them, Gaeren was probably being held prisoner in his own home, unable to join their cause, unwilling to expose them. After they rescued her mother, what would come of the Elanesse and Wyndren families?

After dinner, Sylmar ran Aeliana through her regular drills. Now that they'd reached the coast, she'd have little opportunity to practice archery. Endless water and beach stretched north, east, and now west, offering little to no targets. To the south, a hill rested within a few hundred feet of the water, where the grass and minimal brush kept their horses from starving. A dozen feet farther, it was replaced by the Bahlric Desert—a sea of sand instead of water. Prickly trees and bushes that Aeliana couldn't identify dotted the landscape, their frames more like skeletons than foliage. It was an eerie sight but also reassuring. Nothing would be approaching from the south, and if something miraculously did, they would see it from miles away.

"Healing came easier for you before we reached Elanesse, when Marnok was helping," Sylmar mused, studying her over Felk's fevered skin. Supposedly the winex liked being struck with various maladies, but Aeliana couldn't help wondering if Velden's noetic secondary spoke might allow him to project contentment and make the idea more amenable to Felk.

"Maybe I wasn't weaned like you thought," she said. "Maybe my magic gets weaker because my body still continues to normalize. Or maybe I'm not meant to heal any longer. Maybe I'm only meant to create shields."

Sylmar grunted, then gestured toward Felk once more. She hated practicing on anyone, but especially Felk, though she had to admit it was easier adjusting his body since his blood held no magical pull. When she'd drawn the fever from his body and sensed her magic depleting, Sylmar nodded his approval.

"You can finish training with Lukai tonight. If you best him, I'll give you tomorrow night off."

She frowned. He never made an offer without a reason. Maybe Sylmar was testing her bond. Could she even injure Lukai? Did injuring him mean their bond wasn't as strong? A fire swept through her chest as Lukai approached. If Sylmar was testing her bond, she wanted answers as much as he did, so she might as well play along.

When Lukai pulled out his dagger, he raised a teasing eyebrow until Aeliana gripped hers as well. Lukai always told her he hoped it never came to a dagger fight, not because she wasn't formidable but because that meant all her other lines of defense had been exhausted. She wasn't supposed to use magic to simulate what it would be like when her magic drained and she was left to her combat skills.

The problem was that her magic was so rarely drained, it was hard to pretend she knew what that weakness felt like.

Sylmar sat on a rock, settling with his forearms leaning on his staff to watch the show. His eyes narrowed, declaring a challenge for Aeliana. She held his gaze a moment too long.

Lukai lunged, his dagger aiming low for her legs, but she knew it was a feint to get her to swipe for his head and leave her side exposed. She dove left, taking the one-in-two chance that she could draw first blood on his arm, but he also dove left, and her dagger met air.

They danced around each other like this for several moments, their breaths growing heavy and their bodies glistening with sweat. A swim in the ocean afterward would be a nice reward for her and a treat for Felk. The distracting thought made her reaction time a hair slow, and the tip of Lukai's dagger caught her sleeve, the tiny tear almost unnoticeable.

But Sylmar sighed heavily, leaning on his staff to stand.

Lukai and Aeliana paused in indecision, but it hadn't been first blood. Aeliana couldn't let that count for Sylmar. She crouched low once more, and Lukai's grin returned.

"That's right. Wyndrens never quit," he said.

Sylmar turned back, but Aeliana didn't have a chance to evaluate his expression. She let her weight shift to the balls of her feet, dancing to the left then right, her eyes never leaving Lukai's. They remained evenly matched, drawing attention until the entire camp surrounded them, and Aeliana wished she'd given up with the torn sleeve. She could practically hear Iris clucking over the split skirt slowing her down and the loosening braid becoming a liability.

Finally, Lukai hesitated and glanced up. With an instinct that must have been bred into her by Lukai, Aeliana remembered the tell. He stretched his leg high, his boot snapping out to connect with her dagger hand.

Only her hand wasn't there. She slid beneath his raised leg, pulling him down by yanking on his other. She held her dagger at his heel to signal her ability to slice his tendon—a clear win—but his momentum kept him falling, and for some reason he didn't stop his fall with his hands. The crack of his nose hitting dirt made everyone gasp.

"Lukai?" Aeliana abandoned her dagger, crawling to his side to help turn him over.

Blood poured from his nose, and she reeled back, automatically distancing herself from the temptation, but his face was slack, and her bond mark burned with an intensity she'd never felt before.

"What did you do?" Kendalyhn rushed forward, pushing Aeliana out of the way. Her hands settled on Lukai's face and throat, assessing the damage with practiced motions.

Aeliana's palm felt like fire, the pain making her already short breaths come faster and shallower. "Let me heal—"

"You've done enough," Kendalyhn said.

"Please," Aeliana begged.

"Let her try," Sylmar said.

Kendalyhn sat back on her heels, glaring at Aeliana. Blood still poured from Lukai's nose. Reassured that his heart still pumped if he bled, Aeliana leaned forward, placing both hands on his temples, careful not to touch any of the blood.

Her fingers itched to move closer, to draw in the power spilling out of Lukai's body. It was the most starblood she'd seen in any of her training, and it called to her with frightening clarity.

It was no longer of any use to him, so why shouldn't she use it to help save him? Was it really cheating to use his own blood to heal him?

She pulled back shaky hands, scanning the faces of her comrades, desperate for something to center her.

Cyrus stepped forward, kneeling beside her as if he had magic to offer. "The closer you stand, the louder its call." He placed a steady hand on her arm. "Flee while it whispers, or suffer its fall. Better to die without knowing its gall."

She blinked as the words tugged at her memory, some recitation from an old holy book.

"You always have a choice," Cyrus added.

The weaker side of her shoved away his words. The side wanting to test the full limit of her magic, not just the magic in her blood, but the magic she could access from someone else's. The side she still suppressed. Did the others know how hard she had to work at pushing it down?

She scooted farther from Lukai. "I can't do it," she whispered.

"Can't or won't?" Sylmar asked. He turned from Aeliana and shoved his way past Kendalyhn, bending forward to place a hand over Lukai's nose.

A sharp crack was followed by Lukai's gasp, his eyes opening wide. His face was still a bloody mess, purple and blue bruises already forming on his face beneath the stained skin, but the flow of blood stopped, and he gave Sylmar a grateful look.

"You'll have to finish the rest yourself," Sylmar grunted, struggling to stand. "Aeliana," he called over his shoulder, "come with me."

Aeliana wiped her hands on her skirt even though she hadn't touched the blood. She ignored the curious and wary looks of her companions as she walked away, her body feeling drained even though Sylmar had done the work.

She followed him to the beach, the slap of his staff against sand grating on her nerves. Two figures rose from the water, laughing and splashing. Velden and Felk must have missed the sparring. As she and Sylmar approached, Felk lifted his nose to the air before tensing in a crouch. Aeliana imagined herself sniffing for blood, hating how animalistic she felt.

"What happened?" Velden asked, glancing between her and the crowd still gathered around Lukai.

"I broke Lukai's nose." She meant to lighten the mood, but her voice came out flat, her mind still warring over the reaction to his blood. It had taken months—or moons as the Vendarans liked to say—but she'd come to value what the magic in her blood could do, to see it as a gift from the Stars. Only the temptation of the blood magic still tainted the gift, making it less than what it was intended to be.

No matter how much she resisted it, she wasn't sure she could ever be free of its curse, because despite the weaning process, her magic still held frightening strength compared to those around her. If she gave in to the pull of blood magic, even just once, how much damage would her magic do?

Felk laughed, the vibrating tinkle in the air overriding any awkwardness from Aeliana's reaction.

Sylmar's face remained unreadable. "You've earned your day off tomorrow. You're starting to react without thinking in combat. Now you need to learn to do it with magic. It's time you stopped holding back."

Guilt swarmed through her as he saw straight through her tactics. "I'd rather think through my choices. Know if they're right or wrong before I make them instead of having to evaluate it after."

"Your situation is unique." Sylmar's penetrating gaze made her wince. "I never want you to choose blood magic, but at some point you'll need to do magic in the presence of starblood. You can't get around it. I'd rather you tried and failed here, where it's safe. There won't always be time to think. But if you're practicing right reactions, in the moment when it matters, your reaction will be right."

He patted her shoulder, then made his way back to the group, leaving Aeliana more confused than before. Had she been right to hold back her magic this time? Or had fear made her pass up an opportunity?

The ebb and flow of the sea should have calmed her nerves, but her body felt hungry for the blood still spilled on the ground behind her. It called to her even from this distance.

Felk whined, whether because he sensed her distress or felt a similar call to the blood.

"What if he's wrong?" she whispered. "What if I still make the wrong choice?"

CHAPTER 66

THE NEXT MORNING Gaeren asked for a family dinner, surprising Enla into saying yes. They ate in their parents' quarters, his mother even paler than the last time he'd seen her. He stayed on his best behavior, hoping it would deter Enla from sifting his future to discover his plans. Once he left, she'd be sure to sift through all the possibilities, and Gaeren couldn't help wondering what she'd find.

For now, Enla beamed when he bent to pull out his mother's chair and guide her back to her bed. It was an odd role reversal to tuck his parents in, but Gaeren had more memories of nannies and nursemaids tucking him in anyway. Still, Enla's brow knitted as they shut their parents' door and headed back to the main hall. Her anxiety made his plans all the easier, though the four guards following him might make things harder for Larkos.

"Remember when we were young, and we sat out on the veranda to count the Stars?" he asked.

Enla laughed softly. "You mean when you swore there were exactly fifty-two?"

"I counted them dozens of times and always got the same number. How was that not enough for you?" He tucked her hand in his elbow and steered her through the corridors, aiming for the first floor and its excessively large entryway. He soaked in every stone and painting they passed, wondering when he'd see these halls again. For all the times he'd despised the way these walls held him in, he couldn't imagine never being welcome here again.

"How could you possibly keep track with the way they dance?" she asked.

"There's a pattern to their dance."

Her look held disbelief, but she tightened her hold on his arm, more than willing to let him lead her out to the veranda, where they let propriety drop enough to kick off their shoes and drape themselves on the chaise lounges to face the sky. They counted the Stars like they had in the past, Gaeren coming up with fifty-two every single time, but his eyes were more intent on the moon's path across the sky and the guards' determined presence at the stairs leading to the lengthy drive. They would see Larkos from a long way off.

"Do you think it's right that Mother and Father gave Mayvus authority over the eastern province?" Gaeren asked. "She was a power-hungry priestess. Now she's a driven queen. Who's to say she'll stop there?"

"It doesn't matter what I think. It's been done."

"You can undo it."

She sighed but didn't take his bait. Larkos would come, even if she was still here. Gaeren meant to drive her away instead of involving her in his escape, but he was selfish enough to want just a few more moments with her that were unmarred by their disagreements.

"Things were easier when we were children," he mused.

"Perhaps they'll get easier again." Her vague words reminded him of Orra, which was equal parts disturbing and reassuring. When Enla scratched at the scar on her palm, his gut tightened.

"How are things with Croft? I haven't seen him much since I returned."

"Well enough."

"Sounds about as well as things are going for Lenda and me." He knew it was the way of an arranged bond, but he still didn't like it. If he and Enla had been able to choose their bondmates, like Larkos and Calia had, would their bonds be stronger?

For once she didn't scold him or encourage him to lean into his bond with Lenda. Did she still want him to break it? Or had the time for that unclear strategy passed?

"You're right." Enla sat up, pulling her shawl tighter around her shoulders as if the warm summer's night had turned cool. "Things were easier when we were young."

He rolled off his chaise to sit next to her, wrapping an arm around her shoulder so she could lean into him. "I can still give Riveran a beating if you'd like."

She elbowed him hard before fully settling against him. "Why do you continue hating him if I've moved on?"

It was on the tip of his tongue to say he didn't hate Riveran, not anymore. But it felt wrong to admit that possibility to Enla, who had taken the brunt of Riveran's misconduct, when Gaeren hadn't quite been able to admit it even to himself.

"Because you're a better person than me," he said. "That's the answer to a lot of your questions about the things I do."

She snorted, and he grinned. That was the Enla he remembered. He closed his eyes, inhaling the flowery perfume she liked to wear. However long he was forced to stay away, he wanted to remember her like this. Even if he was more likely to be stuck with a final image of her snarling and livid.

"We can't undo the past," Enla said.

Her words triggered Gaeren's own shame. The ways he'd failed Daisy as a child. The ways he was probably still failing her as he bumbled through his efforts to protect her.

"Our only choice is to be vigilant about stepping forward into the future."

Gaeren frowned. "Is that why you don't look at Croft the way you once looked at Riveran? Are you afraid to let yourself love someone who could hurt you? It's not right that Riveran spoiled that for you."

"You don't look at Lenda at all." Enla's quick retort surprised Gaeren. "What spoiled that for you?"

He opened his mouth to say it was Lenda herself who had spoiled it, but he realized that wasn't true. In many ways, Daisy had—or the memory of her had. His focus and drive to right his wrongs had always held higher priority. And now that he'd met Daisy as a woman instead of a child, the space she'd once held in his heart felt too small, too simple.

Enla leaned back, studying his face, which likely gave away his confusion. "A lot of things in life have been spoiled, but not because of Riveran," she whispered. "You can't always believe the lies Mother and Father are forced to tell for the sake of the throne."

Something cold slithered through Gaeren's gut. Lies? About Riveran?

Her words shouldn't surprise him. Lying about the events in Islara wasn't the first time they'd made such a compromise. But for some reason, he'd never connected that terrible possibility to Riveran.

He twisted away from Enla so he could face her, wrapping his hands around her upper arms. "What lies were they forced to tell?"

Enla winced, and Gaeren released her arms, afraid he'd squeezed with too much force. But her pained expression remained.

"Or maybe the better question is, what truth did they cover up with their lies?" His voice shook, the words coming out stilted.

Enla hushed him, yanking him to the stairway, past the guards and down the path. The guards made to follow, but she waved them away. Gaeren knew he should be thrilled. This could work in his favor. But he was too distracted by Enla's secrecy and the clear magnitude of what she had to share.

She stopped near the first set of overarching oak trees, the moon at its zenith and barely filtering through the branches to highlight her raised chin, her eyes like flint. "Riveran didn't break our bond. Mother and Father did."

Gaeren took a step back, his head spinning, heart pounding. "Impossible. The scandal would never be worth it."

"It would if he wasn't worthy of the throne." Enla said the words with a hint of disgust. "He never had an Awakening. He never received a starlock. It didn't matter that his starblood concentration was higher than any other because he wasn't chosen by the Sun."

Gaeren's mind raced through his memories—all the times he and Riveran had played with their adolescent magic. Riveran never could do much, but it was the same for most children on the cusp of adulthood. They all had to wait for their Awakening, for the Stars to gift them with a lock of hair to enhance their magic. It was rare for nobility to not be chosen with their high starblood concentration—impossible for a bond of the royal family, or so he'd thought.

Gaeren turned from Enla, grasping the tree for support, sickened by this revelation, by the fact that he'd allowed the deception to change the way he viewed his friend.

"He and I were never meant to be." Enla's lip wavered. "The Sun didn't choose him. He wasn't worthy of the throne. Mother and Father didn't want to worry everyone with the possibility that their sons and daughters also wouldn't be chosen, that the Sun might be choosing fewer progenies."

Larkos' prediction that magic was being bred out of the people might not be so far off.

"It doesn't matter." Enla pulled her wrap tighter around her shoulders. "The bond was still broken. The real reason doesn't change anything."

"It changes everything," Gaeren whispered. His friend had been faithful. Even worse, Riveran had tried telling Gaeren, but Gaeren had refused to listen.

A flicker of movement down the path caught his eye.

Larkos.

He turned back to his sister, frowning down at her, grateful to at least see a hint of remorse on her face even as he blocked her view of the path. "Maybe he wasn't worthy of this…throne." He waved a hand toward their home. "I don't know. I don't even care. But he was always worthy of your love."

Her eyes glistened with unshed tears, her focus too intent on the disappointment oozing from his every pore to notice the clip-clop of the hooves getting closer. She scratched at the scar on her hand, the one nearly hidden by her new bond.

Daisy's words about scars came back to Gaeren, the idea that some scars were best left as reminders to show weakness and help them grow stronger. Was that why Enla kept her scar? To remind her that Riveran had been a weakness? Or to remind herself that she had been too weak to fight for the man she'd loved?

"Sometimes in order to truly love someone," Enla hissed, "you have to let them go."

He shook his head, even though he knew that was what he was doing with her now, in this very moment. It wasn't the same. It couldn't be.

"I want to be alone," he said. "Even if it's just for a few moments. Have the guards collect me after you're in bed."

Enla pursed her lips, her eyes flashing with indignation.

Gaeren tried channeling the moment they'd had on the veranda, the scent of her perfume, the comfortable safety and warmth of family, but for once his magic failed him, his mind too focused on the here and now.

"Life isn't a fairy tale," she said. "Real happy endings come with a price." She pushed past him, her hair and dress flouncing out to hit him with one last puff of lilac before she rounded the trees and out of sight.

"If the price is too high," he whispered, "there's no happy ending at all. For anyone."

It wasn't possible she heard him. But even if she had, she wouldn't have listened. Her dedication to the throne was probably admirable, but it also scared Gaeren.

He shook his head, turning to the approaching wagon. He raced to meet Larkos before the horses could come any closer. The older man sat up on the bench, his hooded cloak concealing his telltale tattoos and earring, but Thallahan leaned out from the back of the wagon, grinning ear to ear. Arms reached out to haul Gaeren up before Larkos could turn around, but Gaeren didn't have time to examine whom they belonged to.

While empty kegs were tossed over the wagon's edge, a paper and pen were shoved under Gaeren's nose. He signed without question, pressing his signet ring into the soft wax. Thallahan rolled up the note, and the other men shoved Gaeren into a compartment beneath the bench, hidden by hay, momentarily making Gaeren question his own sanity. The space felt large enough for only one, and he folded his limbs together to fit, but as the door shut and he scooted in farther, he bumped against something soft and warm.

"I told them to leave me back at *Starspeed*." Riveran's voice came through the darkness, making tears prick at the back of Gaeren's eyes.

He wished he could see his old friend, but it was enough to know he was there. He'd always been there if Gaeren had been willing to look.

"They couldn't decide if I would attract negative attention or give them clout to get in the grounds," Riveran said. "For some reason, that meant I got stuck riding in here with you."

Gaeren wanted to tell Riveran he wouldn't want it any other way, but his throat grew too raw to speak. He found Riveran's shoulder and clapped a hand on it.

"Did you see Marnok up in the wagon?" Riveran asked.

Gaeren shook his head, then barked out a "no" when he remembered Riveran was as blind in the darkness as he was.

"He checked all the taverns and merchants. Not a single soul recognized him. He's asked permission to sail with us. At first Larkos said no, but then he figured even if you don't trust him, the fact that Marnok knows where we're going is dangerous. He's leaving it up to you to decide if he comes as a sailor or as cargo."

Gaeren's laugh came out harsh as he choked back the knot clogging his throat. He dragged in a breath, fighting the clash of the pain over Enla's lies with the sudden rush of camaraderie with a friend he'd unfairly abandoned.

"You all right?" Riveran asked.

Gaeren squeezed his friend's shoulder tighter. Even though it was his opposite spoke, sending Riveran the memories suddenly felt easier than trying to explain. They came through in reverse order: the heat of Enla's admission, the stubborn hatred Gaeren had carried for the last two years, the pain Gaeren had shared with Enla when he'd returned to address her broken bond, the last moments Riveran and Gaeren had shared as friends before Gaeren had left for school, dozens of childhood memories of running, laughing, fighting, playing—solidifying the foundation Gaeren and Riveran's friendship had been built on.

The memories cut off as Gaeren's hand slipped with the jostle of the wagon. A long pause settled between them before Riveran wrenched him in for a hug that was almost too fierce.

"It was she who betrayed you," Gaeren whispered. "I'm sorry, brother."

"I doubt you have the full story." Riveran let Gaeren go, his voice breaking. Suddenly the darkness felt like a blessing. "It's never completely one person's fault."

"Well, now I'm ready to listen."

A hand rapped on the wood of their compartment.

"Shut up, lovebirds. We're almost at the gate."

CHAPTER 67

THE STOP at the gate took far longer than Gaeren would have liked, but after a fair amount of arguing, Larkos showed the guards Gaeren's seal of approval and convinced them they'd already delivered the ale Prince Gaeren had ordered to a back door per his instructions. It sounded like something Gaeren might have done in his recent state.

A knock came from above, signaling they could talk again, but by now Riveran and Gaeren had grown uncomfortably quiet. Dozens of questions ran through Gaeren's head, questions about Riveran's wife and baby, why his friend had kept quiet about the truth, how the bond had been broken if it wasn't for Riveran's infidelity. As far as Gaeren knew, the only way besides death or unfaithfulness was to cut the bond out. Had his parents forced that on Riveran? Or had they forced the wife on Riveran?

But all of those questions seemed too personal after the gap in their friendship the last two years.

"Why did she tell you?" Riveran asked.

Gaeren's muscles loosened with the question, with the permission to talk again. "I'm not sure. Maybe she'd rather I hate her than you? It's how it felt in the moment. I'm not sure I ever understand my sister's motivations."

Riveran's low laugh sounded forced. "Well, I was sworn to secrecy. Telling you would have been treason."

Gaeren frowned. "Treason against my parents? Or Enla?"

"More likely treason against you." Riveran sighed. "They knew you wouldn't approve of the choice even if I accepted it. I understood the problem. Enla is next in line to the throne. What if her children didn't become progenies? What would that mean for the future of Elanesse?"

Irritation flooded through Gaeren, not just with his sister, but with himself. Because a small part of him did understand the concern. He'd been raised to believe the people needed guidance from someone with greater access to the Sun's power. How had he ever thought something like that was more important than individuals? More important than friendships and people like Riveran? It was bad enough that Enla had gone on thinking it. That Riveran had just accepted it.

"She cried for weeks over you." For once Gaeren's accusations held confusion instead of heat. Had it all been for show?

Riveran cleared his throat. "Just because we agreed it needed to be done doesn't mean it didn't hurt." The other man's emotions were too close to the surface, the memories rising whether Gaeren meant to access them or not. Riveran's anguish, the pain searing through his palm like lightning straight to his heart. A sense of being utterly alone, cut off from half of his own self. It mirrored Enla's pain, drawing out Gaeren's own memories of his failed attempts to remove her memory, to end her suffering.

Riveran's memories kept flowing through Gaeren like a dam had been released. Riveran hiding in Gaeren's mangrove tree for days, then a stranger's home, with a woman sobbing. Night after night of silent meals while the woman's belly grew. A tentative smile, the blossom of a friendship built on mutual need. A baby shoved in Riveran's arms, a sense of responsibility, a commitment to protect.

The visions faded in Riveran's mind, the sense of time slowing and returning to the present rumble of the wagon as unsettling as always.

"The child isn't yours." He'd meant it to be a question, but Riveran had already answered it with his memories.

"Her husband died at sea."

"But now you're her husband. And the child is your son?"

"It's the story we've been asked to tell." Riveran hesitated like the words stuck in his mouth. A lie told so much and for so long it was hard for him to stop. "I provide for her and the child. I will continue to do so until she can provide for herself. Or until she finds someone else. But we never wed. She's always known I still love Enla."

Gaeren squeezed his eyes shut even though the blackness was already absolute. Rage tore through him, the need to let it out in some capacity overwhelming in the tiny hidden chamber. The horses continued their slow plod, unaware that it grated on Gaeren's nerves.

"So you don't even have a bond mark?" How had he not noticed that in all their time together. But the memories he'd seen made it clear. There was no bond in effect. "Maybe it can be undone. If Enla knew you still love her—"

"She knows." Riveran's quiet words silenced Gaeren. "She was the future queen before she was ever mine."

Gaeren shook his head in disbelief. "What happened to my sister?"

A strangled laugh escaped from Riveran. "Nothing. She has remained constant all her years. It's you who's changed. And you can thank her for that. She saw the way her parents were manipulating both of you into becoming a new generation of oppressive rulers. She knew it would break you. So she freed you."

His words echoed everything Enla had said, hardening them to truth in Gaeren's mind. "But she imprisoned herself. She's become just like them."

"She would still sacrifice everything for you," Riveran said.

It was probably an attempt to reassure Gaeren, but it fell short. She already had sacrificed everything for him. Is this what the sprites had meant?

"Despite our bond," Riveran continued, "I always knew she loved you more. I just assumed she could always love us both—a brother and a bondmate. That's not something anyone should have to choose between."

Murmurs came from above, and the horses slowed to a stop.

"I'm sorry." Gaeren's words felt too small, too rushed. It would take a lifetime to make this up to Riveran, and even then it wouldn't be enough.

"You only need to be sorry if you waste what she's given you."

The door to their compartment opened, the moonlight bright

enough to make them squint. Gaeren found Riveran's eyes before his gaze settled on the X. Kendalyhn's admission about what she'd sifted in Riveran's soul came back to him. "And was that because you stole bread for your family?"

Riveran shrugged and looked away. "That's what the magistrate said. It's what Enla told him to say. There were days I had to steal bread because few people wanted me working for them."

"You two gonna stay in there all night?" Breeve asked, yanking on Gaeren's elbow. "I thought we were in a rush."

Gaeren ignored the young sailor, too intent on the parts of Riveran's story that didn't line up. "But that's not why you were caught?"

Riveran shook his head. "No. The man who sold me that book you wanted so badly turned me in for black market trade. Claimed the book had been stolen from him before it was sold to me. That it was a Vendaran artifact meant to be revered in the Sungazers."

"If they believed him, you should have been hanged." Gaeren's mind raced as his guilt rose.

Riveran had been in danger because of him.

"Which is why Enla told the magistrate to mark me as a traitor instead. Keeping me one step away from a hanging was the only way she could protect me."

Gaeren pursed his lips to hold in his bitter response.

Riveran shrugged. "The only thing I don't understand is why Kendalyhn kept that part of the story to herself."

Larkos' frown replaced Breeve's eager face. "I didn't commit treason just to get caught with you two crying in each other's arms on the docks." He pulled on Gaeren's arm with far more force than Breeve. "Move it. Now."

They rushed through the near-empty docks, the hour too late even for revelers but too early for fisherman. As *Starspeed* came into view, a new sense of urgency and energy rushed through Gaeren. He couldn't erase all that had happened in the past. Not for Daisy and not for Riveran. Not even for Enla or himself. But this was the best way he knew how to move forward.

Marnok boarded the boat with them, hesitating briefly when he took in the rigging. He slid a hand over the rope, glancing back at

Gaeren with an almost fearful confusion. When the older man climbed the mainmast with the skill of an experienced sailor, Gaeren knew yet another fractured memory plagued Marnok. Another soul on board whom Gaeren could only hope to help by moving forward.

When he passed Thallahan, he paused, his mind tuning in to another memory. "Aren't you supposed to be getting married in less than a moon? For Summer Solstice?"

Thallahan gave him a sheepish shrug. "We pushed it back. Maybe Harvest Day or Winter Solstice. I promised her we'd wed without threat of war." He winced. "I may have also promised that you'd attend—with a princely gift."

Gaeren laughed. "You realize I no longer have access to the royal coffers?"

"Aye." Thallahan grinned. "You'll find a way."

By the time the Sun peeked over the horizon, Gullet had joined them, but they were far enough out of harbor that no one else would recognize them. Still, Gaeren scanned the waters uneasily. The landmarks of Elanesse and the northwest coastline of Vendaras were interrupted by three unfamiliar specks.

"Are we being followed?" Gaeren reached for the spyglass to identify the ships behind them.

"Ah, that," Larkos muttered, pulling the spyglass from Gaeren's hand. "I might've left that part out."

Gaeren raised his eyebrows and crossed his arms.

"Riveran found twenty of your men," the old man said with a shrug, then scanned the ship, drawing Gaeren's attention to the fact that there were far more than twenty men aboard. "Seems the area he's been living in the past couple of years is full of Recreants. Real ones. Not the ones who give me half-truths to test my loyalty after sailing with the likes of you."

Gaeren frowned, taking in the strangers aboard his ship. A couple even had matching tattoos on their foreheads, labeling them as traitors like Riveran. "This should have been cleared with me. *Starspeed* is—"

"Ah, quit your yapping." Larkos smacked Gaeren on the back hard enough to keep him from arguing again. "You're as bad as Gullet. They'll fight for you, and that's what matters. Even if most of the crew on the other three ships are pirates." He laughed harder, like he'd been waiting to get this one last dig in.

Sailing the Northern Sea against the king's commands. In league with pirates. Well, Gaeren supposed he'd known it would be near impossible to return to Elanesse. This sealed it.

He leaned back over the edge of the boat, taking in the spray of seawater as his homeland disappeared in the morning mist.

"I suppose Calia will never forgive me for stealing you away so soon again."

"She might not forgive me," Larkos said, "but you've got her wrapped around your little finger. She sent cookies and pastries for you, even though she barely gave me a farewell kiss." He rubbed at his bond mark, the smile on his face suggesting his words were an exaggeration.

"What now?" Gaeren asked.

"Now we go in search of real freedom."

"Freedom," Gaeren scoffed. It had once sounded unattainable because of his forced ties to Elanesse, but now it seemed impossible because he would never be free to return. He rubbed at his own bond mark. Enla had wanted him to remove it. Did it even matter at this point? As a traitor, he wouldn't be welcomed home, but they wouldn't bother chasing him down.

"Freedom likely tastes different to every man," Larkos mused. The rising Sun lit up the tattoos covering his bald head. "Could be preference, like how Breeve enjoys his meat burned to a crisp." They both watched the young sailor fumbling with a pack of spices.

"He doesn't like it that way. He's just a terrible cook."

"Aye." Larkos chuckled. "Maybe it depends on how hungry a man is when he sits down for a meal. For some of these men, the freedom they're starving for has the metallic bite of gold."

"Blood also has a metallic bite," Gaeren muttered.

"Now you're confusing the price of freedom versus the taste. But I think it's safe to say that all these men are willing to pay that high of a price. It's why they're here. Even the pirates."

Gaeren frowned down at the crew even though it was Larkos who rankled him. "Sometimes I think you take jobs from me just to see how far you can push me when we're out at sea."

Larkos snorted. "Only sometimes? We just left. I can turn around if you'd rather go back to planning parties with your sister." He used his stocky frame to lean on the wheel, and Gaeren felt the pull against *Starspeed's* rudder.

"I haven't reported you for treason yet, and I listen far more than you might think."

Larkos adjusted the wheel back, his beard shifting with his grin. "That's what I'm counting on. Besides, something tells me we're not getting paid this time."

CHAPTER 68

Aeliana leaned her back against Cyrus, absorbing his warmth as if it might shield her from the night breeze floating in from the sea. He pushed back as though it were a game, something to distract them during their midnight watch.

It had been almost three weeks since they'd left Northpoint, but the water to the north and the desert to the south had remained unchanged. Felk had been born again, much to Sylmar's irritation, and was in his arrogant adolescent phase, though still as loyal as ever.

The next day they'd be abandoning the never-ending grainy coasts of the Northern Sea to head for the canyon separating them from the Myndren Mountains. Supposedly the smooth pebbles would give way to dark rocks, and the hills full of brush would be replaced by treacherous cliffs and caves. But for now, all they saw on the horizon to the north, east, and west was water and sand, and all they saw to the south was the Bahlric Desert. Aeliana shivered, pulling her cloak tighter.

"How is it still so cold when we're only a week from Summer Solstice?" she asked.

"We're not far from the glaciers and icebergs in Ahmranas," Cyrus said, his voice muffled from behind her. "Velden says you can see them from the beach on a clear day, but I wonder if people are seeing the shimmer of the barrier. Still, I should start watching more closely. I could be the first Lorvandan to see the coast of Ahmranas."

"Unless my father saw it," Aeliana whispered, wondering where her father was—if he was dead like Arvid had said or if he still lived, like her mother. Was it truly possible for her to meet her parents after all these years? What would she even say to them?

"I know you're sending me back."

Aeliana frowned, then turned to catch Cyrus' profile. He toyed with the leather necklace, the lump under his shirt still a mystery to Aeliana. Not that the shape of his fake starlock mattered. Only… maybe it did. If he chose it as representation for his life, it could be full of rich meaning.

"Sending you back?" she asked.

"To Lorvandas. When we get the golden arrow." He angled to see her too, his eyebrows raised. "I know you asked Gaeren to take me. Even if he never shows, you'll want me to return home."

She bit the inside of her cheek. "Isn't that what you want?"

"I want to go home to check on Gamps. Maybe find your father. But I can't promise I won't use the arrow to come right back here. I'm not sure I can stay away after being a part of all this." He gestured toward the beaches. "There's so much I can learn from the Vendarans. Maybe then I can take it back to my family—my people." He didn't hold her gaze, and his eyes flashed with something unfamiliar. Apprehension, maybe guilt?

"You're considering their worship of the Sun, aren't you?"

His gaze rested on the sand at their feet, his jaw tightening. "I'm willing to research it further. Even if I continue to disagree, their perspective will give me context for my own faith."

Aeliana hid her smile. Gaeren just might win the unofficial bet he'd placed with her. She reached for the dagger, running her thumb along the daisy on the pommel. "I would be grateful if you sought out my father. I worry about the dangers of Vendaras being too much for someone without magic, but I suppose most of the people here are just like you, only they have inactive starblood."

He nodded, the hint of a smile on his lips.

"Is it wrong for me to want Lorvandans to be right?" Aeliana asked.

"About the Stars?"

She nodded. "The Sun the Vendarans worship sounds frightening, whereas our Stars are friendly."

"I suppose it doesn't matter what we want. We should desire to find the truth." He gazed across the desert. "We haven't always liked everything we learn about Vendaras, but that doesn't mean it's not true."

"That quote you recited, when I was healing Lukai"—Aeliana swallowed down her shame—"was it from *The Song of the Stars*?"

He hesitated. "No, actually. It was from *The Sins of the Stars*."

She nodded more to show acceptance of him quoting such a book than because she understood. She'd never read the book, and the words had seemed familiar. Was it something her parents had read to her as a child?

Kendalyhn and Holm came to relieve them of their watch, and Aeliana was slow to ready herself for bed, the thoughts Cyrus had shared weighing on her mind. She fell asleep debating her own faith but woke to the sound of shouts and growls.

She bolted up, reaching for her dagger while scanning the camp. Her heart sank at the sight of the sinewy forms of several young winex. A few of the creatures brandished crude weapons, but most used their fists. Silver blood spewed from the wounds her comrades had inflicted, but the creatures fought on. Kendalyhn sported a bloody nose, and Lukai remained locked in a tight hold with a winex while another fought him from behind. She sought out Felk's familiar form, but before she could find him among the strangers, a beast skidded to a stop at her bedroll.

"Your turn." His face screwed up as he hissed, and he spun a bloody blade in his hand. Aeliana's stomach dropped when she recognized it as Velden's dagger. The creature lunged at her, and she tripped over her pack in her effort to sidestep him. The blade grazed her arm, and she sucked in a breath as blood seeped from the wound.

The magic of her past called to her, rising up from within. It demanded to be used, to protect her from the enemy standing before her. But the blood seemed to call to the winex too. He closed his eyes and took a deep breath in through his nose, running the blade beneath it.

He grabbed her arm, his hands like ice, then licked Aeliana's wound, making her recoil. A soft, melodious chime fell off his lips, and Aeliana relaxed under his grip. His tone was deeper than Felk's but still so comforting. The winex released her arm and held the dagger over his head. Aeliana knew she should move, but the peace that had settled over her made her a heartbeat too slow.

The dagger came down, but instead of piercing her chest, it went through the silver flesh of another winex, who had thrown himself across her body. He screamed, and the force of the stab brought them both to the ground. Despite the sand, her head hit the ground hard, and through the pain, her focus cleared.

Her attacker swore, bending over her rescuer. She rolled out from under the injured winex and caught sight of Felk's tear-shaped scar as his face contorted in pain.

"No," she whispered. "No, no, no." Her hands brushed his cheek, and his eyes opened. A small smile tugged at his lips, but his breath came out ragged, and the dagger remained wedged in his arm as silver blood pooled beneath him.

Aeliana turned to face the other winex, tightening her grip on her own dagger. A malicious grin crossed his face even though he held no weapon. The starlock warmed at her chest, its gentle reminder filling her with premature relief.

The creature leaped at her, curving his body to avoid her dagger while grabbing at her hair. He wrenched hard, twisting her head and nearly lifting her off her feet. Tears sprang to her eyes, but she slashed out with her dagger, forcing him to drop his hold.

Before she could even consider what magic to use, he was on her again, but she gave the creature a swift kick to his knee. A sickening crack filled the air, and the winex came down with a shriek that halted the battle around them.

The newly injured winex writhed in pain. He tried to rise but crumpled on his twisted knee, scooting away from Aeliana, his youth finally showing in the wake of his rabid assault. For the first time, Aeliana turned her back on a suffering creature, even wondered if he deserved it.

"I'm so sorry, Felk." She bent over him, tucking her dagger back in its sheath. "I'll fix this. I promise."

He moved as if to reply, but she yanked the other dagger from his arm and a scream came out instead. She placed a hand over his wound, letting the heat of the starlock fill her before it surged out to flood Felk's veins, twisting through his injury to find the broken vessels and torn flesh.

Panic and fear drove her power, making her magic as forceful as when she'd first started, but this time with more focus. She sang the lullaby that had once calmed him, partly to calm herself. It had been several days since he was small enough to be sung to sleep, but now he used the hand on his good arm to wipe her tears as he hummed along.

Marnok's instructions for mending guided her more than Lukai's and Sylmar's explanations ever had, and within moments the heaviest flow of blood had stopped, the severed artery healed. A strange relief flooded through her. This was what she should have done for Lukai. This was how her power was intended to work without the temptation of blood magic.

Her power rose, desperate for more nooks and crannies to fill, giving her the same bloated sensation she'd had before weaning. As the lullaby came to an end, the silence around her should have been alarming, but she shut it out by closing her eyes, letting the flow of her magic guide her as she used her blood's power to repair Felk's arm.

She sensed the muscles rebinding and the skin reconnecting beneath her hand, but the wound was deep, and her power drained too quickly. The blood leaking from her arm called to her, reminding her she had another source available, that she could do this faster, with less of a drain on her reserves.

This time she balled her free hand into a fist, half of her focus shifting to resisting the blood magic's pull. Her hands trembled as she held her breath, but at last she sensed that the skin was closed and his pain was a dull ache, a memory of the agony he'd held.

Felk's hand patted her cheek. "It's all right, Mama. Thank you."

She opened her eyes, taking in his solemn gaze. His hand dropped to hers, his grip steady.

For a moment she studied the fresh grey skin covering his injury. Marnok would be proud, and for some reason that mattered to her. She glanced up, wondering how the rest had fared.

Dozens of bulbous eyes stared at her, the winex's silver mouths hanging open. Aeliana's companions could have taken every one of them out in that moment, but instead they held defensive stances, warily glancing between Aeliana and the surprised winex.

One winex still glared at her from his place near her on the ground, his knee bent at an odd angle. He'd dragged himself closer, but his face was contorted with pain, his energy spent. Aeliana sat back on her heels, debating if she had enough energy to heal him—if he was worth it if she did.

She stood on shaky legs, but before she could approach him, he squinted, the hatred in his eyes almost palpable. In one fluid motion, he pulled himself up and lunged at her, teeth bared. The others shouted, no one near enough or prepared to help. Aeliana's starlock warmed with one last bit of strength, surging through her with a desperate force. She reached for her dagger, twisting it forward as if to block the winex's attack, but then let it loose, knowing that with her magic, its aim would be true and its force would be lethal.

It buried to the hilt in the winex's chest as the creature's momentum kept him flying toward her, knocking her down, but his bared mouth went slack.

Aeliana pushed the winex off her, then used a knee against his chest to remove her dagger, his body falling to the sand with a sick thud. Her shoulders slumped, and her hands fell at her sides, the tip of her dagger dripping blood on her skirt. Her companions remained in their defensive stances, but none of the winex moved to attack.

A soft silver hand found its way into her own, and she raised her head to see Felk nod his understanding. The winex that remained went impossibly still.

"You healed him," one winex said, gesturing at Felk.

Aeliana suspected the winex was female, her frame slightly smaller and her voice higher than Felk's.

"He's our friend." Aeliana's grip tightened around Felk's hand. The winex cocked her head in confusion, her large eyes darting between Felk and Aeliana.

"You—?" The same winex spoke up but then turned to Felk. "They stole you. We came to bring you back."

"She didn't steal me. She raised me." Felk stood even taller as the words left his lips.

Several winex backed away as though ready to slink into the brush. Aeliana took in the state of her comrades. Surface injuries were scattered across their bodies, but the winex were in far worse shape. A few winex lay slain, and others had injuries that would never properly heal.

"We can heal your wounded," Aeliana offered before they got too far. The winex stopped.

"Aeliana…" Sylmar's warning tone demanded attention, but Aeliana ignored him.

"You say you came to rescue Felk," she continued, "so it appears this was a misunderstanding. We'll heal your wounded, and Felk can choose to join you if he wishes to be with his kind." The last words pained her, but it was time. She knew she couldn't keep him with her forever, and Felk deserved the opportunity to be with his people.

The self-appointed leader eyed her suspiciously. "Not all came to free. Those with Baljekk"—she gestured to the dead winex at her feet— "came for blood."

"Thank you for your honesty." Aeliana turned and raised her voice, making sure her gaze took in every stunned winex before her. "Those of you wanting peace and healing, you will have it. Those of you wishing for blood may leave, or it will be your own blood that's shed."

The winex exchanged troubled looks, and several rushed off into the desert.

"Would you like help burying your dead?" Cyrus asked the female winex.

She shook her head. "Not our way." The others sneaked away through the brush, the camp quickly becoming deserted of winex.

The female came forward and offered her arm to Aeliana. A gash dripped silver, and Aeliana placed a hand over it, ready to heal.

"No." She gripped Aeliana's forearm, placing them in a handshake of comrades. "Thank you for mercy. If we meet in another moon, forgive me when I don't remember."

She turned to leave, but her gaze rested on Felk, and she waited.

Aeliana held her breath. He should go. She knew he should.

Felk faced her, and the indecision on his face broke her.

"They seem like a good group," she lied. No group of wild winex was good enough for him. He stood taller and spoke clearer. He'd been changed by her influence. Would he last among a group of real winex?

"I'll find you again, Ma." His voice cracked, and she nodded. He wouldn't find her. And if he did, he wouldn't remember her. They both knew that. She reached out a hand to touch the teardrop forever on his cheek.

The female winex turned, loping off through the brush.

"Perhaps I'll find you first." Aeliana gave him a smile, and he buried his face in her shoulder, his arms wrapped tightly around her back. "Now, go," she whispered, gently shoving him away.

He ran after the winex, and her arms ached with the emptiness.

Aeliana turned back to the camp. Lukai finished healing a scratch on Kendalyhn's face, then approached Velden. The others slowly found their bedrolls or went back to taking watch on the berm. The Sun's morn wouldn't come for a few more hours, but Kendalyhn built up the fire, already pulling out pans to cook the morning meal. Before Aeliana could process the normalcy in the wake of the attack, Sylmar stood before her.

"You reacted."

She almost missed his soft words. A light breeze swept in from the sea, and Aeliana hugged herself at the sudden chill.

"Does it make you happy that I was finally willing to take a life?" The question came out bitter as her shock gave way to the reality of what she'd done. Although she wasn't sure Sylmar would count Baljekk as a life. The image of his lifeless eyes, so like Felk's, swam through her mind. She pursed her lips to keep them from trembling.

"No. I'm grateful your training is saving your life." He leaned over his staff, studying her closely. "Even good choices can have consequences that are difficult to bear. Cyrus was right to tell you the motive can change the outcome, but sometimes the motive merely makes the outcome more bearable."

Tears gathered in her eyes, and she nodded. Pushing past him, she settled back in her bedroll, knowing she wouldn't sleep anymore that night.

CHAPTER 69

AELIANA COULDN'T HELP LOOKING for Felk over the next few days. A part of her still hoped to see him even though she knew it was better for him to move on, but the winex either left or remained hidden. As their group traveled away from the coast, the eastern horizon shifted from seashore to cliffs and the sandy desert to sheer rock.

Orra remained in her constant position as a straggler in the back of the group, so Aeliana slowed, thinking the older woman's calming presence might be good for her raw nerves.

Orra nodded when Aeliana approached but said nothing. At first it made Aeliana even more anxious, but soon the rhythm of the waves against the cliffs and the clip-clop of the horses' hooves lulled her to a state of calm. It was almost as if Orra knew and waited for that moment.

"It's never easy to say goodbye to someone you love," she said.

For some reason, Aeliana pictured Gaeren hearing this obvious statement and rolling his eyes. It made the corners of her mouth twinge, and she rested her hand on the dagger, running her thumb over the daisy on its pommel.

As much as she missed Felk, if she was honest, it was Baljekk, the dead winex, who occupied her thoughts more. She'd killed someone. Maybe not a human, but a creature capable of reasoning with her, of speaking. It didn't sit well with her, and she wasn't sure what to do about it. Which made it far easier to talk about Felk.

"You never seemed to disapprove of Felk, but you never spoke to him either," Aeliana said. "What do you think about the winex?"

Orra took so long to reply that Aeliana wondered if she would get an answer. "I think there's far more to them than most mortals realize."

It was another evasive answer, but Aeliana got hung up on the word "mortals." She'd always been fascinated by the fact that winex were immortal in a sense. But in some ways, it sounded as if Orra was excluding herself when referring to mortals.

"Have you ever befriended a winex? Or known someone who has?"

Orra smiled. "No. As far as I know, you are the first."

That news should have been disheartening, because it meant the winex had been mistreated for thousands of years. Instead, it left her warm, knowing she had encouraged change to take place. That she was looking out for those in need and her actions were making a difference.

She kept watching for Felk, but her mind felt more free, able to look ahead instead of only behind.

Jasperus and Holm guided them away from the water through a narrow crevice to the south, and they winded their way into a small canyon. Leaving the open water had been good progress, but riding single file while hedged in between two walls twice their height left Aeliana on edge. Their long trek was coming to an end, but what waited for them? A madwoman who had trapped Aeliana's mother? A massive army they could never defeat?

Summer Solstice was only a handful of days away, and she still didn't feel prepared.

When they broke for the midday meal, Velden rode out ahead of the others. If there were any troops left from the dragon's attack on Islara, they would know by tonight. She sent up a prayer to the Stars that there might be at least one or two factions to instill hope in them again.

Cyrus took himself to a spot in the shade where he lay prostrate on the canyon floor, sending up prayers, though Aeliana couldn't help wondering whom he prayed to. Even Lukai and Kendalyhn tipped their faces to the Sun as if calling upon it for assistance.

Sylmar frowned down at his food, admonishing them between bites. "You all need to eat. We need our strength for tonight and the days to come."

Everyone else continued picking at their food. When they rode out again, no one spoke. Everyone's gaze remained on the canyon's rise, watching for Velden's return. As the Sun sank lower in the sky, the hesitant quiet turned to thick sobriety. Darkness came quick as the canyon walls hid the Sun's light. Shadows loomed like dark spirits, making even the horses a bit skittish. Every rock that fell out of place echoed off the walls, distorting their ability to stay alert for enemies. Aeliana found herself longing for the open sea and sandy desert that she had grown tired of the past few weeks.

Velden should have returned by now if there was nothing to find. But he also should have returned if there was exciting news to share.

"Should anyone else ride ahead to check on him?" Aeliana asked.

Sylmar grunted in response, but the lack of answer implied he was debating the same thing.

After another hour, when the darkness became a hindrance, Sylmar signaled for them all to stop. "Holm, take Jasperus southeast around that peak and see if you can catch sight of Velden. If we don't see him, we'll stay the night here."

The others exchanged glances.

"Is this the end of the canyon?" Aeliana asked.

"This is as far south as it goes." Sylmar scratched at his beard before dismounting. "It continues west through parts of the desert we passed. If we travel a day's ride east, we'll reach the edge of the Myndren Mountains. Mayvus lives on the southeast side, so she should still be another day's ride beyond that. Just south of here, we'll reach the slope of the Valley of Krahn. That's where our troops were meant to gather."

"So close to her home?" Aeliana asked.

"The valley is a safe enough place. Her guards don't often trek beyond the southern edge of the mountains. The population north of the Myndren Mountains isn't large enough to concern Mayvus, which is why we wanted our troops to take the long way through and come around from the north side. It's possible she'd eventually learn of people gathering there, but it's a common location for large groups to set up festivals. Some of our allies typically hold a Summer Solstice celebration there, so she shouldn't grow suspicious. Especially if our numbers have dwindled." His frown deepened.

Holm and Jasperus made their way toward a thin path weaving up the canyon wall. With all of the switchbacks to make the steep incline less severe, it was likely they wouldn't return before the Sun's sleep, but as Aeliana watched them rise, another figure emerged at the top of the canyon.

Sighs of relief went through the others even though he was too far away to make out details. Then, the man they assumed to be Velden began rhythmically pumping his arms.

"What is he doing?" Cyrus asked as Velden added spurts of water like a fountain to the waves, confirming his identity.

Sylmar made a choking noise that sounded suspiciously like a laugh. "He's giving me the count of soldiers. And he's celebrating."

Hope grew in Aeliana's gut. "How many soldiers are there?"

"At least six thousand," Sylmar said. "He's still waving, and each wave represents a faction that survived."

They counted two more waves and spurts.

"Eight thousand? Then most of them left Islara before Durriken arrived." Aeliana's hopes soared.

"We might have a chance after all," Sylmar said.

———

They set up camp while waiting for Velden to make it back down the canyon. He arrived long after most of them would have been asleep, but everyone was eager to hear his news. They sat around the camp-fire, squeezed in tight due to the canyon walls. Kendalyhn served him a bowl of stew, but the questions came too quick for him to eat.

"Only a couple of factions were lost," Velden said. "They left in intervals. Some knew nothing of Durriken because they left days before his arrival. Others left only half a day before he came. Several attempted to turn back and defend the city. Most of them had family in there. But it quickly became apparent that they wouldn't stand a chance against him." His grin faded, and everyone grew quiet as they remembered the horrific scene they'd left behind.

"How did the dragon not see them on his way from the mountains?" Kendalyhn asked.

Velden's face bunched up in thought. "That's the curious part. Several of the soldiers admitted to seeing the dragon flying both directions. He paid no attention to the troops. It's almost as if he didn't care about them."

"That doesn't make sense," Holm said, his face grave in the firelight. "She would've told him to attack the soldiers."

Velden raised a finger, and a sly grin crossed his face. "Unless, maybe, she told him to attack Islara. Maybe he knew exactly what she wanted, but he got around it by doing exactly what she said instead. It does leave room for the possibility that he was never truly working with her."

Aeliana bit her lip, hesitant to show any pleasure at Velden's words. It was hard to be grateful that Durriken only killed the townspeople instead of the soldiers, but still… if he'd been a prisoner to Mayvus, she'd made the right choice by letting the dragon go free. Velden gave her a small nod before finally slurping down some of the stew.

"So they're prepared to launch an attack by the week's end?" Sylmar asked.

"They're all lined up in the Valley of Krahn, waiting for further instruction. They were planning to launch an attack and retrieve Emeris whether or not they saw us in case we'd perished in Islara."

"Tomorrow we'll have to meet with the generals to study their plans." Sylmar leaned against his staff, staring into the fire's light. "They probably have a better idea of how to approach the fortress than we do if they've been scouting it out these past weeks. Realistically, they can do whatever they want to attack her fortress. They're a means of distraction."

"Distraction?" Cyrus asked. "I thought they were helping us get in."

"They are," Sylmar said. "They're helping us get in by distracting her soldiers so we can sneak through a side entrance."

Everyone began talking amongst themselves, less concerned over the details now that their task seemed possible, the threat less intimidating. It was all too new for Aeliana to hold the same confidence. She watched as their shadows flickered against the canyon wall—far more formidable than they actually were. It was exactly how they all felt tonight. Stronger, surer of themselves. But in the morning when the firelight was gone and their shadows receded, what would the Sun reveal? Was this a task they were truly ready for?

"You're quiet," Velden whispered. "I thought you'd be happy to hear they had survived and that your dragon might not be so bad."

She smiled more for his sake than because she actually felt any sense of happiness. "He's not my dragon."

He hummed, bobbing his head back and forth. "You'd be surprised at the memory of a dragon. Your actions won't be forgotten. He owes you his life."

"How do you know about dragons' memories?" Aeliana sat up taller. "They say Durriken is the only one."

"He's the last one," Velden corrected. "There was another when I was young—possibly Durriken's father. They flew together, making their nest in the cliffs on the northeast side of the Myndren Mountains. People could go years without catching sight of them. Made us all wonder if they could cross the barriers. But they still turned up."

"To hunt people?" Cyrus leaned in to join the conversation.

"No, actually." Velden paused to tip his bowl back and take in the last of the stew. "They would take cattle now and then, but until Islara, I hadn't heard of dragons killing people. At least not since the wars. Although Durriken hadn't been spotted for over ten years until recently. Who knows what he was doing in that time?"

"So what about their memories?" Aeliana couldn't stop thinking of the way Durriken had given her his memories, the way she'd sensed his desire for her to know his past. Guilt pricked at her when she realized she'd never told anyone what he'd done. But if he was free now, did it matter anyway? He should be long gone.

"Ah, that's more from legends. Cities used to set out portions of their herds and crops, almost like an offering to stay in the dragons' good will. The dragons each had their regions and were kept happy. Eventually, men were disgruntled at the arrangement, figured dragons could hunt for their own food. Which they did. They hunted among the people's farms." Velden laughed and shook his head. "Except one family continued leaving meager offerings for the dragons. Their farm was never touched."

"It doesn't surprise me," Aeliana said. "His gaze held an intelligence and focus beyond most people's. It was unnerving, but also sort of…" She trailed off, not sure how to describe it.

"Comforting," Velden said. "It's like they see straight through your soul, but they just keep looking, taking you in and assessing without judgment."

His words reminded Aeliana of Kendalyhn's statement that people liked to be truly seen—seen and accepted. She scanned the camp for the other woman, who sat near Lukai, leaning in to whisper something that made him laugh. Something inside Aeliana twinged along with her bond mark, but she shook it off, not ready to examine if a tiny seed of jealousy meant their bond was starting to take.

Excitement kept everyone up later than usual, and if the rustling indicated the others were tossing and turning as much as Aeliana, she assumed hardly anyone slept that night. They all rose early and broke camp while it was still dark. The Sun soon cast light across the sky, but the canyon kept everything hidden for a little longer. Despite the lack of sleep, everyone was in high spirits, eager to join the troops. It made the long climb out of the canyon feel shorter. A few miles from the canyon's edge, the hills parted once more, but this time for a rolling valley filled with trees, grass, and thousands of troops.

A grin split Aeliana's face, making her realize how long it had been since she'd truly smiled. She hadn't been able to imagine a crowd this size, and now that she looked at the waves of people milling about like ants, she still couldn't believe what she was seeing.

"We'll stay together and make camp on the northern edge," Sylmar said. "They're on our side, but we have a slightly different agenda, one they can't all know about in case Mayvus has noetics in her fortress.

This morning I'll—" He cut off as a dark shadow briefly fell over them, making the horses twitch.

Most of her companions drew weapons, but Aeliana's limbs went numb as she turned to the sky. Durriken made a circle high in the sky above them before diving straight at them.

Several of the others loosed arrows, but Aeliana could only stare as Durriken swept past them, his gaze locked on hers. He came close enough for her to hear his snort and feel the rush of air from his wings —close enough for her to see a new black brand darkening his paw.

"I freed you," she murmured. "You're supposed to be free." How had she not considered the possibility of him being rebranded? Mayvus likely had stores of his blood, ready to use at any moment.

The beast turned toward the valley, his wings glinting in the Sun, and then he breathed fire across the scattering troops.

Aeliana slid from her horse with a cry, dropping to her knees as hundreds of men were killed in an instant. Those in the center received the mercy of instant death, but those on the edges ran, tripping and falling as the flames licked their boots. Screams tore through the air, reaching Aeliana with an eerie delay.

"Holm, Iris, Jasperus, take her back into the canyon," Sylmar said.

"No!" Aeliana forced herself to stand. "I'll go with you. He won't hurt me."

"You're right," Sylmar said. "He won't. And I find that just as concerning. I'm not letting him take you straight to Mayvus."

"That's where we're headed anyway," Aeliana argued, pulling herself back up onto her horse. "If you find my mother, you'll find me. But I'm not letting all these men die if she sent him after me." She kicked her horse's sides, relieved that the mare didn't balk at the chaos she aimed for.

Durriken made a second pass and annihilated dozens more. The soldiers scattered, tripping over each other, but there was nowhere for them to hide. Most ran toward Aeliana, toward the canyon, knowing the walls were too narrow for Durriken's wings, but they would never make it in time.

Hooves pounded behind her, and Aeliana hoped her comrades were coming to help her instead of stop her. Her mind raced right alongside her mare, debating her options. She wanted to rescue the soldiers, even if it meant sacrificing herself, but was there a way for her to free Durriken again too? Was it worth it if Mayvus would just brand him again?

As the crowd of troops surged around her, she was forced to dismount to keep making her way closer to the center of the camp, closer to the place where Durriken might see her. She lost sight of Sylmar and the others, swarmed by a sea of strangers. She pressed her hands together, drawing the power up from her center and out of her starlock, letting it build until even her clasped hands couldn't contain it.

The glow that extended from her hands was the biggest light shield she'd made yet, extending on either side of her almost a dozen feet as well as above. The wall of light moved with her, passing through soldiers whose mouths dropped in awe. At first, they fled from the shimmering light, but as they watched her pass through smoldering tents to snuff out flames, a horde gathered around her, desperate for the shield to protect them too.

Initially, she welcomed them. That was the whole point of the shield—to keep people safe. But as the crowd grew, her shield couldn't contain them all. Durriken turned in the sky, headed back for another pass over the troops. He lazily scanned the people until his gaze locked on Aeliana's shield. It drew him in like a beacon, and too late, Aeliana realized the people who could have been fleeing were now fighting each other for a prime spot behind her shield.

"Run!" Her gaze caught on the soldiers at the edges of her shield, their panic making them climb on top of backs or shove down people caught off-balance.

Durriken was nearly upon them, the majestic flap of his wings like the iridescent curve of a seashell. He opened his mouth, his massive chest expanding with inhaled air. In moments, he would breathe fire, knowing Aeliana was safe, knowing he would annihilate everyone outside her shield.

All these people would die, their lives snuffed out in an instant.

Aeliana dropped the shield with a groan, the effort of reversing her magic dizzying. Her knees started to give out, but she reached for a soldier beside her, desperate to see what Durriken did.

The beast's eyes widened, and a strange choking sound left his throat as he held back his flames. His chest nearly brushed the tips of the soldier's swords and shields as he passed, the wind of his wings knocking everyone to the ground.

But they were alive.

It took Aeliana far too long to stand again, but she couldn't help grinning. As long as she was with the people, they were safe. Durriken wouldn't harm them. She tracked him once more, wondering how she could use that knowledge to her advantage, and her smile fell.

Orange flames poured from his mouth like liquid fire dropping down on another faction. She hadn't saved lives; she'd merely exchanged who lived and who died. As long as Durriken was here, he would keep killing. Not because he wanted to, but because he was compelled by Mayvus. Aeliana needed to stop him, not just to save these people, but to save Durriken.

The people around her resumed running, forcing her back as she stubbornly stood her ground, watching as the dragon circled once more. Elbows jostled her side, and people yelled at her for blocking their escape. She ignored them, raising shaking hands far above her head.

"Come and get me," she whispered. "It's me you want."

Once again Durriken scanned the crowd. Aeliana let a burst of light leave her hands, a pathetic attempt at a shield, but exactly what she needed to draw his gaze. She might have imagined it, but she swore she saw sorrow in his eyes as he approached.

The people around her screamed and scattered, leaving Aeliana out in the open. With a touch far gentler than she'd anticipated, the great beast's paws wrapped around her midsection, and her feet left the ground.

CHAPTER 70

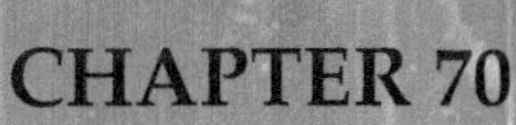

Orra's horse galloped alongside the others, but as they veered left along the edge of the valley to follow Aeliana, Orra veered right, straight to the valley's center. She ignored the shouts of her comrades and closed her eyes, letting go of her reins to press her hands into the mare's withers. She whispered words of strength and speed as energy poured through her palms.

Releasing the light from within was like a flower unfurling in the Sun's rays, stretching, reaching. It sharpened all her senses and bolstered her courage, even though she knew she'd pay for it later. But for now, the Sun's light met her own, and she felt the brief sense of peace and joy. Approval. Acceptance. Her breath caught.

In the distance, she glimpsed Aeliana's shield, pride rippling through her at its width and breadth. Still, after Aeliana's rash choice, every path before the girl held suffering and failure. If Orra didn't intervene, Aeliana's ripples would never expand; her stones would never get thrown. They still might not. Only the Sun knew how Orra's interventions would change things.

She thanked the Sun for its approval, even if it was temporary. Perhaps because this time it was to save a life.

But wasn't that what she'd thought the first time?

She shook away the doubts she didn't have time for, pressing strength into her mare. She increased her stride from an already fast gallop to an otherworldly pace as the horse weaved among the flames and flailing soldiers in the wake of Durriken's fire. Orra closed off her senses to the stench of burning flesh and the sounds of screaming men and women, leaving half her heart behind with them. Her surroundings blurred as she honed in on the dragon's purple hide as he turned to make another pass over the valley, which had become a human herd prepared for slaughter.

As his blue underbelly skirted the tops of the tents, Orra reined in her mare, the sudden stop almost dizzying after the previous rush. The horse felt it too, stumbling for a moment until Orra smoothed a hand over the mare's sides once more, feeding her more energy than Orra wanted to spare. Orra rose to her knees, then balanced on her toes, arms reaching up to gauge the distance she would need to clear not just the tent poles, but Durriken.

The mare danced beneath her, threatening to topple Orra's stance, and the dragon drew closer, his eyes narrowing. He cradled something in his paws, drawing it in protectively toward his chest as he blew out fire along the way, the air from his massive wings doing more work to fan the flame than the fresh fire from his breath. Had he already taken Aeliana?

Orra had even less time than she thought. She crouched and adjusted her footing once more. She would have only one chance to time this right.

For a split second, she hesitated, the voices of her peers echoing through her soul. *It's not our way to interfere.* Was she throwing a stone? Or moving something in the path of a ripple?

But then Durriken was before her, inhaling. She prayed his aim would turn to the side, away from her mare, and she let her blood's energy surge through her as she leaped. Durriken coughed and sputtered in surprise, angling his body as if to block her, but with his low flight and her muscles invigorated by her blood's power, she still managed to grab his wing, one of the only places on his body not armored with scales.

Her grip slipped as his speed increased, and her body slammed into his as he adjusted his angle, clearly trying to throw her off. This close to the beast, she could sense his remembered shock of being grounded with torn wings—the greatest fear of any dragon. But she had no intention of grounding him. She wanted him to fly away.

He rose higher as if sensing that was what she wanted, and she pulled herself up onto his wing, every effort requiring more of the energy in her blood—energy she couldn't replenish as quickly as the others because she had no starlock. Her panic surfaced with the extravagant use of magic after constant suppression. What if she ran out?

She slipped her foot into the groove between his wing and shoulder before launching toward his collar. As she did, he twisted into a barrel roll, nearly dropping her from the sky, but she hung on to the collar, letting her body spin with his. As he righted himself, she wrapped her legs around his neck, pulling herself up and anchoring her foot in his collar to free up her hands.

He growled and threw his head left and right, agitated by her presence, but she leaned forward, placing her hands on the sides of his head just like she had done with her mare, infusing more energy into him, calming him. He stilled enough for her to finally feel safe, but then he banked left, dropping low and angling once more to return for another pass over the soldiers. Flames erupted from his mouth, making Orra cry out as stray sparks in the wind landed on her skin.

"Orra?"

Orra peered around the dragon's scales, catching a brief glimpse of a brown braid. "Hold tight, Aeliana."

"I thought he'd leave." The younger woman's voice was raw from tears. "I thought he'd give up on the soldiers once he had me."

"It depends on the command he was given. We can still fix this." Orra straightened once more.

By now, the surviving soldiers were fighting back, and a volley of arrows flew past them, but Orra closed her eyes and pressed closer into Durriken, letting them glance off his scales. She burrowed deep into his mind, fighting through his resistance, digging through his memories to find the command he'd been given. Her energy waned, and Durriken made another low pass to burn another set of soldiers before she could find what she needed.

Tears stung her eyes, and Mayvus' face swam before her mind, a pale woman with severely angled eyebrows and thin lips pursed in a scowl. "When you see Aeliana and the soldiers, kill everyone else, but spare her and bring her back to me."

Orra's eyes fluttered open, her grip around Durriken's head going slack as her energy drained even more. He banked again, heading toward a new section of soldiers. Despite their distance, Orra made out Sylmar's molten staff. Within moments, everyone she'd arrived with could be aflame.

Orra inched forward, her feet precariously balanced on Durriken's collar. If he flipped now, she would fall. Before he could realize her position, she slipped her hands over his eyes, forcing them closed.

Durriken jerked, and Orra nearly lost her footing. "You see no soldiers," she whispered, cementing the words in his mind as energy spread from her hands to fuse his eyelids shut. "Drop Aeliana, because you don't see her either. Your work here is done." Her plan depended on his desire for a way out of his orders. She was giving it to him, but only if he wanted it.

His trajectory remained unchanged, and Durriken sucked in a deep breath primed for flame. Individual frightened faces came into focus as he skimmed the crowd, including Kendalyhn and Lukai. For a moment Orra thought she'd misread the memory, misunderstood his true motives. Her friends would go up in flames beneath Durriken while she watched on, helpless.

Then Durriken let his air out, the heat of it bringing sweat from every one of Orra's pores. But there was no fire. Orra sagged in relief, adjusting her grip since Durriken's eyes could no longer open. As he flew over the people, he let Aeliana loose, and Lukai and Velden barely broke her fall. Sylmar's mouth dropped open in surprise at the sight of Orra on the dragon's back. Too late he shouted out orders to hold fire. One of the arrows sank into Orra's thigh.

This time when she lost her grip, she couldn't regain it. Her power was gone for now, and she was as subject to gravity as the mortals beneath her.

CHAPTER 71

Aeliana landed hard, her elbow somewhere in Lukai's ribs and her knee on Velden's leg. Both men grunted, and Aeliana moaned, but it could have been worse. As far as she could tell, nothing was broken.

As Durriken passed overhead, another cry rose from the crowd, and Aeliana whipped around in time to see Orra falling from Durriken's back. Her drop was much farther than Aeliana's, and while people reached to break her fall, her head still hit the ground with a sickening crack. Lukai and Velden scrambled to her side, poking and prodding at her neck and limbs.

Aeliana wrapped her arms around herself, trying to process what had happened. She turned back to catch Durriken's frame growing smaller in the distance. How could he have let her go if he was branded? And why had he left?

Iris, Holm, Cyrus and Kendalyhn joined her, and Iris fussed over her cuts and scrapes as if Aeliana couldn't simply heal them with a slight tug from her blood's power. Normally Aeliana would bask in the attention, something she'd never experienced as a child, but now it left her agitated.

"We need to get the wounded to the trees." Sylmar's expression was even grimmer than usual, his face drained of color and the rest of his skin and beard coated in ash. The ash of burned foliage and burned people. The remains of those who were fathers, mothers, siblings, husbands, wives, and children. "No one can be in this valley when he returns. If he flies to the fortress and back, we have at least until mid-morning tomorrow. I wouldn't count on anything more."

"And then what?" Aeliana asked. "We were supposed to have at least a day here to plan before traveling on to her fortress. We can hide from the dragon in the woods, but what if she sends out troops? We're not equipped to fight her anymore."

"We never were," Sylmar said. "Emeris is the only one equipped to fight her. Even if this ends up being a suicide mission for us all, it will be worth it if we can get Emeris out."

His harsh words made them all pause, the wails of the injured filling the silence.

"How many troops do we have left?" Cyrus asked.

Sylmar eyed the smoldering valley. "Maybe a quarter. Enough to march forward and make a plan while we move. They don't have to win this battle. They just need to get us in to Emeris."

Aeliana shivered at the dark truth behind his words.

"And to find Aeliana's blood," Cyrus added.

Sylmar turned to Aeliana. "Yes. That too."

"Come on," Holm said. "Let's spread the word. Wounded to the forest. Those able to fight—camp here. We march out with the Sun's morn." He tugged on Iris' and Kendalyhn's sleeves, and Cyrus joined them.

When Aeliana moved to follow, Sylmar stopped her.

"What did you hope to accomplish by having Durriken take you?" For once his words held no anger or judgment, just curiosity.

"I thought if he took me, he'd leave these people alone." Aeliana couldn't hold Sylmar's gaze. "His orders would be fulfilled. I thought I could protect them. It's my fault Durriken was still alive. It's my fault they're all dead."

Every choice she made seemed to have a miscalculation behind her motive. All the way back to releasing Durriken in the first place. Probably earlier. She wanted to regret her actions. She'd cost people their lives. But when faced with the possibility of protecting an innocent victim, even one as foreboding as Durriken, she would make the same choice again.

She waited for Sylmar's rebuke, wanting the words to inflict the pain she deserved. Instead, his hand brushed her back with the faintest of pats.

"I've been harsh with your training. You were never meant to carry this weight. Bringing you here to find your mother and chase down your blood was too much."

She shook her head but didn't trust her words to come out right. She'd needed his harshness. If she'd stayed back on Bamboo Island waiting for her mother, she never would have agreed to learn magic. She never would have understood the good that could come with it. She probably would have hidden in a hole and bled herself to death, alone and afraid because she didn't understand what was happening to her.

Sylmar grunted. "Mayvus has many resources at her disposal. If it wasn't Durriken, it would have been something else."

It was a poor attempt to absolve her guilt, but it meant more coming from Sylmar. They watched as several soldiers carried and carted wounded across the valley, making their way toward the southwest corner. She wrapped her arms around herself as the moans of the injured met her ears.

"Was there something I could have done differently?" she whispered. "Should I have let Gaeren kill him?"

"We'll never know. None of us escape this life without regrets. Sometimes even the right motivation and the right action don't produce the right outcome." Sylmar's voice grew thick, drawing her curiosity. She peeked up at him, catching a rare vulnerable look on his face. He examined the knot-like marks on his hands, flexing his fingers. Were they tied to some of his regrets?

"The night your mother was kidnapped, I came to warn her," he said.

"In Celanoft?" Aeliana's eyebrows rose. Sylmar rarely spoke of his past. She spent the most time training with him out of everyone but knew the least of his history.

"I came too late to save her." He cleared his throat, gaze still on his scars. "And you. I found Iris, and we teamed up to plan her rescue and to await your father's return, but Mayvus has always been one step ahead of us. I will always have regrets about that night, especially after seeing what it's done to you."

Aeliana pressed her lips together.

He glanced at her, the sorrow on his face making him look decades older. "Did they hurt you much?"

Aeliana stilled. She hadn't gone into detail with anyone about her years in Lorvandas. They had their suspicions after knowing she'd done blood magic, but she'd witnessed and unwillingly participated in hundreds of crimes. She'd wished away all the times they'd bled her. But seeing her past in light of everything she'd done in Vendaras made it seem smaller. Those had been Arvid's and Vera's wrong choices, not hers. Cyrus was right to be grateful for where the Stars had placed her.

She supposed somehow that meant there was purpose even in her choice to help Durriken at great cost, but she wasn't ready to face that. Not yet. But that didn't mean she couldn't ease Sylmar's grief and guilt.

"They didn't hurt me enough to leave scars that can't be healed," she said.

He blinked several times, glancing at her hands—at her scars—then nodded. He reached out once more, this time patting her clasped hands before grasping them tight. "I promise I'm only doing what I think is best for you and for Vendaras. But that doesn't mean you'll always like it. It doesn't mean I'll always do the right thing."

She smiled faintly. "I guess that makes two of us."

They joined the others, and Aeliana got lost in a haze of healing injuries, finding the process both painful and rewarding. Healing one soldier didn't make up for the thousands who'd died, but it felt like a start.

The soldiers soaked up the attention, watching her with something akin to awe while she worked. At first, she thought it was because of her hair. Several reached out to touch her long locks without asking, but other times she caught people staring into her eyes and whispering amongst themselves. Perhaps it was her display of magic or the brief time she'd been caught by the dragon. Would the story become one of Jasperus' legends? Hopefully he would emphasize Orra's success instead of Aeliana's failure.

They worked well into the night, putting out fires and transporting the wounded, eventually transitioning from recovery to preparation despite their exhaustion. Orra eventually woke, and Aeliana found her resting by the fire, her face pinched with pain or worry, her frame looking frail when swallowed up by a blanket.

"It's good to see you up." Aeliana stoked the fire, its source of light and warmth ironic after they'd fled its cause of death and destruction.

Orra smiled wanly in return.

"I hear you blinded Durriken. Wish I'd thought of that in Islara."

"It was a temporary solution." Orra wrapped her blanket tighter around her.

"One that saved hundreds of lives."

Orra shrugged. "He'll still be back. Mayvus won't let him remain blind. And she'll choose her commands more carefully."

"Are you staying with the wounded?" Aeliana asked.

Orra shook her head, then winced. "The little magic I have left would be better spent elsewhere."

Questions about Orra's magic rose to the tip of Aeliana's tongue, questions about how all the Vendarans said she'd glowed like a Star reflecting the Sun's glory, but the woman's gaze glazed over, her limit reached.

The next morning, they began their march, anxiously watching what little sky they could see between the trees for any sign of Durriken. Summer Solstice was three days away, and the fortress was a two-day ride, but Sylmar was determined to make it in less, giving them time to plan in the evenings and to attack earlier than Mayvus might expect from a group recently ravaged by a dragon. The idea that they'd be in Mayvus' fortress in just two days left Aeliana's nerves on edge.

Even though people surrounded her, the ride atop her mare felt lonely, providing too much time to think. She closed her eyes and breathed in the still-lingering scent of charred earth and flesh, forcing herself to bear the weight of the blame.

She couldn't possibly make things right. Hundreds were dead

because of her choices. Even if they managed to stop Mayvus from completing the branding process, even if they freed her mother, that couldn't make up for the destruction she'd let happen.

Seeing the consequences of a wrong decision left her more paralyzed than ever. What would go wrong the next time she made a bad decision? She tried to shake away the thought, to remind herself that failing once didn't mean she should stop trying. But the images of burning soldiers and melting armor filled her vision with far too much clarity.

A screech filled the air, startling her from her mental spiral. When she opened her eyes, a bird descended among the trees, aiming straight for her. But it wasn't just any bird.

"Gullet." She breathed the word out like it might spread hope around her, hope that tentatively grew from deep within her chest. She held out an arm, bracing for the claws she'd only seen dig into Riveran's and Gaeren's shoulders. Sure enough, the bird's force and weight threw her off-balance atop her horse, and his talons pricked her skin.

Still, she laughed, disbelief mounting to relief with such speed that it left her giddy.

"How did you find me?"

With another squawk, he lifted his leg and revealed paper tied beneath his feathers.

"Oh." Aeliana fumbled in her eagerness, struggling to remove the message with one hand. Gullet readjusted several times, eager to be free. When she finally pulled off the paper, he was quick to dismount, taking to the skies. A stab of anxiety shot through her; he was her only connection to Gaeren. But he didn't go far. He settled in a tree, content to watch and wait for her response.

Aeliana didn't waste any time unrolling the tiny scrap. The two words at the top brought tears that blurred the rest of the message.

I'm coming.

CHAPTER 72

AFTER SAILING past Ahmranan's Viewpoint and hiking through the canyon with Riveran's men and the pirate crews, Gaeren itched to reach Daisy's camp. His bond mark itched too.

He'd tried cutting it out several times on *Starspeed*, but each time he did, the betrayal burned, digging up memories of Enla's suffering. Memories he'd shared so deeply with her as he tried to take them from her that they were as strong as any of his own. Bonds weren't meant to be broken, and it went against everything in his nature to do it.

Then he asked Larkos to do it for him, but the older man laughed and backed away, refusing to take part in breaking something so sacred in case Calia found out and had his hide for it. Said it was something Gaeren had to do for himself for the right reason.

In the end, he left it alone. By now everyone in Elanesse had all written him off as a traitor, and the cowardly side of him couldn't help hoping that Lenda might cut out the bond mark herself.

The Valley of Krahn was just over the next hill when the brown blur of Gullet's feathers came into view. He soared through the sky before landing on Riveran's arm with an irritated squawk.

"I thought he was going to stay with Aeliana until we caught up," Gaeren said.

Riveran snorted. "He's a hawk, not a person. Sometimes our

communication isn't perfect." He held up his arm, squinting at Gullet's leg. "Wait, there's a message."

Gaeren tensed as Riveran unrolled the parchment, the back revealing the message Gaeren had written to Daisy.

Riveran's face paled, and his eyes met Gaeren's. "They met up with the troops, but they were attacked by Durriken. They had to keep moving toward the fortress." He passed over the note. "She's asking us to try to catch up. Says they'll have extra horses in the woods southeast of the valley where the wounded are recovering."

Gaeren scanned the message, wanting it to hold more details. Still, a part of him relaxed. At least Daisy was safe. But what about the others?

To the pirates' credit, they didn't even grumble when Gaeren demanded they pick up their pace. A few even gave whoops of excitement at the news of the dragon. But once they crested the hill and the valley came into view, the mood shifted. They skirted the remains of the camp as if it were filled with the diseased instead of the dead. Blackened bodies were grouped in piles, holes started and abandoned as if someone had attempted to take care of the dead but realized the task was too large.

"If we ride hard, we'll catch up with her before the Sun's sleep," Riveran said.

The words comforted Gaeren, who fought against his starlock's pull to seek out the memories around him, knowing he couldn't bear watching everyone slaughtered once again. What would happen when they reached Mayvus' fortress? How could they expect to save Emeris when Mayvus had a dragon once more?

Between the cries of pain and the stench of unwashed bodies, the soldiers were easy to find—too easy, considering Durriken could return. But he wasn't likely to set the entire forest aflame when it led into Mayvus' woods. Those who had stayed to care for the injured were quick to give Gaeren and his men the horses they would need, reassuring them that they were only half a day behind.

Despite pushing the horses farther with his starlock's power, the ride seemed impossibly long, and it was soon after the Sun disappeared behind the treetops that Gaeren finally heard the distant murmur of travelers.

He urged his horse on until he was stopped by sentries, who eventually let him pass. By this point, his nerves couldn't take it any longer, so he dismounted, tossing the reins to Riveran.

"Am I your stableboy now?" Riveran called after him with a laugh.

Gaeren scanned the troops for the long waves of brown hair that would give her away. He supposed he should be grateful that so many lived, but eventually he grew impatient, nosing his way in by a campfire.

"Where's Aeliana?"

The men all pointed east, closer to the front lines. Gaeren picked up his pace, repeating the question as he half ran, half walked down the line of troops.

"Gaeren?"

He turned, tempted to close his eyes in relief but too eager to see her face. She stood, halfway out from a poorly constructed tent, one hand holding open the flap and the other gripping a lantern to reveal that she was wholly intact.

"You're here." Daisy's face bloomed into a smile, and his heart raced, knowing that smile was only for him.

"I wasn't the one fending off dragons." He rushed to her side, ready to wrap his arms around her, to verify the truth for himself that she was unharmed. But their friendship had been tenuous before he left, and they'd been apart for almost a moon. He hesitated, and in that space of time Lukai stepped out behind her. Embracing her felt like crossing a line in front of her bondmate.

"Neither was I." Her gaze dropped, her rueful words falling flat. Lukai awkwardly patted her back, and she stiffened, the change almost imperceptible.

"As long as you're safe." Gaeren's face heated when the words came out more desperate than he intended. "Your people will need you safe," he rushed to add.

"My people?" she scoffed.

Gaeren clenched his jaw to hold back the words threatening to tumble out. This wasn't the time or place to explain he'd had a lot of time on *Starspeed* to think about their families' histories. Especially when so much of his thoughts went back to his parents' role in her kidnapping. If he explained all that had changed for him, he'd have to reveal their part in it. He wasn't ready for that.

Lukai's eyes narrowed, and he stepped closer to Daisy. "How did you get here? And who else did you bring?"

"My crew helped me escape—well, really they helped me commit treason. I've brought men to fight. Recreants from Elanesse who don't want Mayvus enthroned any more than they want my sister as queen."

As he spoke, Riveran and Larkos caught up, with dozens of his other men following. The offering felt pitiful compared to the hordes of men camped out before him, but in light of the damage he'd seen at the Valley of Krahn, every extra fighting hand would count.

Daisy's face broke into a grin, and she set down her lantern so she could embrace Riveran and then Marnok, an easiness to her greetings that left Gaeren regretting his earlier hesitation. He glanced at Lukai, but the other man seemed unperturbed, which only made Gaeren more irritated. He shouldn't be more jealous than her bondmate. He scratched the mark on his palm, then shoved his hands in his pockets, not wanting the extra reminder of his unbroken bond.

"This will raise the people's spirits," Lukai admitted. "Maybe give them hope that infiltrating Mayvus' hold the day after tomorrow might have some measure of success."

"But Summer Solstice is still three days away," Gaeren said. "If Mayvus hasn't branded Aeliana yet, she won't do it before then. We could use the extra day to plan and prepare."

Lukai raised his eyebrows but made no comment on Gaeren's awareness of the branding. "Mayvus knows we're here. If we can get to her earlier, maybe we'll still catch her off guard. We can hope." His words fell flat with his own disbelief.

When another soldier beckoned Lukai back inside the tent, Gaeren turned to look for Daisy. Firelight from campfires danced across soldiers, but every now and then he caught sight of her brown waves peeking out between shirtsleeves and shoulders.

At Sylmar's glare, Gaeren began introductions, which meant

Kendalyhn also came out to sift every man's soul. A few of the pirates resisted, while a few others seemed too eager to place their hands on Kendalyhn. She only had to pull out her knife and threaten to replace one man's hand with a hook to get them all back in line.

Velden slapped Gaeren's back with his slimy webbed hand in lieu of a greeting.

"I almost wish she'd follow through," the older man said. "Unfortunately, we'll need every last one of their thieving hands to pull this off."

"Is it that bad?" Gaeren asked.

Velden bobbed his head back and forth in indecision. "Sylmar is always gloom and doom, but I think he might be right this time. He'll want you in on tonight's meeting. You can decide for yourself if it's hopeless after you hear his plans."

"I doubt anyone wants my opinion. I'm more likely to incite a mutiny if some of these men figure out who I am." Even as he said the words, he realized it might be too late. He hadn't bothered covering his face.

"Aeliana made sure everyone knew how you ensured our escape from Elanesse. There's not a man or woman here who would go up against you now." Velden's gaze sought out Daisy, so Gaeren watched her too, this time noticing the dark circles under her eyes. She'd been through too much in the last few moons, and the worst was yet to come.

He didn't bother saying goodbye to Velden; he headed straight for Daisy. She looked up at him, her eyes brightening through the pain.

"I still can't believe you came," she said.

"The note from Gullet wasn't enough?"

"No, it was. I just…" She trailed off, then looked up at him. "I feel like every time I hope for something to happen, it gets ripped away. I didn't want that to happen with you." She twisted the ends of her hair, not holding his gaze.

"You can't get rid of me that easily." He lightly tapped her shoulder with his knuckles. "I've been chasing you for years; I'm not about to stop now."

She smiled faintly, watching as Marnok made his way through the crowd. The older man stopped various people, asking them each a question. Probably wondering if they knew him before his memory loss.

"I'm scared, Gaeren," she whispered. "Anything could happen in the next couple days. So much could go wrong."

He glanced at her worried eyes, his mind shifting back to their childhood, to the chubby arms reaching out and begging for one more story because the shadows at night were frightening. Only this time, he didn't have a story to cheer her up.

"I think we're all scared," he said.

She nodded, blinking far too fast.

"Come here." He ignored the itch of his bond mark as he took her hand, weaving through the tents and fires until he reached the edge of the camp. He gently nudged her to a fallen log, then sat beside her, still gripping her hand. They sat, and a million questions came to his mind, most too personal to ask out loud.

"How is Durriken helping Mayvus after you freed him?"

A crease formed between Daisy's eyebrows that Gaeren wished he could smooth out.

"She branded him again. I saw it on his paw, and Orra found it when she sifted his soul. Or tuned in to his memories. I still don't understand her magic."

"That makes all of us."

Her lips quirked up, and Gaeren fought for something else to say, something that might keep her smiling. "I'm glad Durriken didn't get to you. Would have wasted all my efforts to keep you safe."

Her smile dropped, and her eyes grew wet. "I wanted him to take me. I offered myself up. Instead, he just kept killing them. All of them." She pulled her hand from his to bury her face in her hands, but it seemed more like she was hiding than crying.

Gaeren's insides twisted, half of him horrified that she had put herself at risk, the other hating the way her guilt weighed her down. At their feet, amidst the grass, a handful of daisies sprouted, their petals unfurling. Gaeren's heart pounded as a dozen memories surfaced from his childhood.

The flowers had grown in a field near Celanoft's Sungazer. He and Daisy had spent hours there over the course of his dedication year. Her baby fingers hadn't been able to form them into chains at first, so she'd insisted he make them for her, fashioning them into necklaces and bracelets, sashes and crowns.

But there were other memories too. Moments she'd been frightened or sad and the flowers had sprouted—even in the dead of winter. He'd never seen magic in a child so young, hadn't known it was possible. Still wasn't sure how such a thing could happen. But he'd known then that she was special, and he knew it even more now.

As her shoulders shuddered, his guilt rose to the surface. Maybe he should use this opportunity to tell her about his parents sending him to her family with a spy.

He glanced back at the camp and saw Orra sitting serenely at its edge, her leg bandaged and eyes closed, lips curved up in a secretive smile. "It's like the ripples," he whispered, finally catching on to what Orra had been suggesting.

"What?"

"Our choices affect others," he said, "but there could be good effects as well as bad ones. And there were choices made before we were here that affected us, too. Each choice ripples out to touch the people and things in its path. When I was home, I found out my parents sent me to Celanoft for my dedication year so my servant could spy on your family."

Her face blanched, so he rushed on.

"My parents' decision resulted in a terrible outcome, one that I will always feel responsible for just like you're carrying a weight you're not meant to bear. Think of the good that still came from my dedication year. I met you." Bolstered by his words, he reached for her hand, wrapping it tight within his. "And I spent my life searching for you instead of taking part in my family's tyranny."

"It's hard to see what good can come from Durriken being branded again." She bit her lip, her gaze on their hands.

"All we can do is keep trying," Gaeren said, the reminder as much for himself as it was for her. "Keep moving forward. We make the best choice that lies right in front of us." He squeezed her hand and she squeezed his back.

"Thank you, Gaeren," she whispered.

The mark of his bond burned between their palms, but he hardly noticed.

CHAPTER 73

AELIANA HESITATED before stepping back into the tent. All the newcomers had been checked by Kendalyhn and offered food, and now Sylmar was eager to finalize their rescue plan. He wanted her there, but she couldn't help feeling she didn't belong.

She was more likely to throw her mother into shock than help bring her out of her branded stupor. Or she might go into shock herself. Sure, she could throw up some light shields, maybe shoot an arrow and throw a dagger, but this was war. As much as she wanted to do her part, she worried she was more of a liability.

An elbow poked her rib, and Aeliana turned to find Iris nudging her farther in.

"Sylmar won't be happy if we're late."

Over a dozen men and women gathered in the tent, most around a small table, which was more like four logs resting on tree stumps. A map stretched across its surface, rocks keeping it from rolling up. Torchlight revealed several familiar faces, and Aeliana's tense muscles loosened.

Cyrus, Kendalyhn, and Lukai huddled over the map, tracing lines with their fingers while Sylmar shook his head. Larkos and Riveran watched from a dark corner while Marnok stood by two strangers in uniforms, one balding with a hooked nose and the other with hair reaching his shoulders—the longest Aeliana had seen on a Vendaran.

Marnok gestured from them to his face, talking emphatically while the men shrugged. Velden's, Holm's, and Jasperus' backs had faced her as they bent over the map, but with the opening of the tent flap, they turned.

"Should she be here?" the bald soldier asked, his attention leaving Marnok to focus on Sylmar.

"She has the most to lose in this battle," Sylmar said.

"And the most to gain," the second soldier said.

"I'm here to make sure Sylmar has a plan that factors in the risks of bringing me along." Aeliana understood their apprehension. She'd felt it every day of this journey when it seemed like no one else had. But now that someone else voiced it, the sting struck deeper. Were they all thinking she was untrustworthy? Was this man the only one willing to speak up?

"She looks and sounds like Mayvus," the bald soldier said in disgust.

"She looks like her mother," Jasperus argued.

"Who looks like Mayvus," the first man pointed out.

"She looks and sounds nothing like Mayvus." Gaeren left the shadows near Riveran and Larkos and stepped closer to her side, his hand on the hilt of his sword.

Aeliana couldn't help the relief flooding through her. She hadn't realized until now that it was his face she'd been searching for, his reassuring presence. One glance at Lukai's passive expression put it all in perspective. She trusted Gaeren to passionately support her, but she also trusted him to passionately disagree with her. When he spoke encouraging words, it wasn't because of a bond—it was because he meant them.

"Mayvus' hair has more gold," Gaeren continued. "Her jaw is broader, and her right ear is higher than her left. She tilts her chin up so high you can see the hair in her nostrils, and she makes an awful noise in the back of her throat every so often, like she might hack up her dinner."

He lifted his chin at a ridiculous angle while snorting and coughing until Aeliana thought he might gag. He stopped in front of Aeliana.

"And when her eyes bore into yours"—Gaeren's look shifted to a

smolder so fast that Aeliana's heart pounded and her palms sweat—
"you assume she might kill you on the spot."

Aeliana's hand tugged at her collar, the heat of all the bodies in the tent finally getting to her. That wasn't exactly where she'd thought he was going with that look, but she supposed it made more sense.

Half the group stared at Gaeren incredulously, but Sylmar let out a raspy chuckle. "Couldn't have described her better myself."

Gaeren grinned. "The benefits of sitting in on horribly boring council meetings."

Holm and Velden shifted from their spots at the table, leaving room for Aeliana, Iris, and Gaeren to step forward while the older men crossed to the other side and flanked Sylmar. In the opposite dark corner, Aeliana thought she caught a glimpse of Orra's crossed arms, but she couldn't make out her face to know for sure.

Velden and Sylmar went back to debating something on the map, and Marnok slid between Aeliana and Iris, his gaze on the map but his thoughts clearly far away.

"Everything all right?" Aeliana whispered.

He hesitated. "They didn't recognize me. None of the people here recognize me."

Aeliana patted his arm. "We'll just have to try another town after this. Keep trying until you find someone."

He shook his head. "If I was on your side, if I was an enemy of Mayvus, don't you think at least one person here would know me?"

The pain on his face made Aeliana's gut twist, but his words sent a shot of alarm through her.

Maybe he was right.

No. He couldn't be. There had to be thousands of people in Vendaras who were either ignorant or ambivalent about this war. Maybe even more who wanted to be rid of Mayvus but weren't ready to fight for it.

"One man thought he recognized me," Marnok said. "Asked if I had a starlock. When I told him no, he said I wasn't the man he thought. Said I should have a sprite starlock around my neck and at least twenty more years on me."

"Maybe you're that man's son," Aeliana suggested.

"The man he knew had no children." His eyes took on a hopeless stare.

"Even if you're right, which I don't think you are," she said, "you're on our side now. And that's what matters."

He nodded and turned back to the map, but his face remained bunched with worry.

"General Nels, if you send your troops east and west," Velden asked, "who'll be taking the center?"

The bald soldier frowned, bending closer to the map. "I'd planned to have a contingency troop in the center, but it was going to spread us thin. Gaeren's men have volunteered to take that role, but we don't expect them to actually hold off Mayvus' army."

Gaeren nodded, his jaw clenched. Fifty sailors would hardly put a dent in her forces.

"And Gaeren's men—what happens when they're not able to hold off the Zealots?" Aeliana asked, following the line traced by the general's hand. If she was understanding the notes he'd scratched on the map's surface, there would be dozens of troops on the edges, leaving Gaeren's men in the center exposed. "Are they being sacrificed for the rest of us to gain entry?"

"Of course not." The general stood straight as if offended by her question. "We want them to lure her men away from her fortress, leaving it vulnerable to our attack. We'll have them safely retreat, over and over, drawing Mayvus' troops back with them. They can bring them all the way back here and let them raze our camp, so long as the rescue team gets through." He glanced at Sylmar, deferring to him for the next phase.

"That rescue team includes most of us," Sylmar said. "What's discussed in here cannot leave this tent in case Mayvus' progenies catch wind of someone's memory or motives."

"Should I leave?" Aeliana asked. "If she brands me, she can control me. I could tell her anything."

"I'm not sure it matters. By the time she feels threatened enough to brand you, we'll be riding on luck and chance." Sylmar paused. "Several people have suggested we leave you behind."

Aeliana stiffened, and a murmur spread among the others. She'd expected him to have protective measures in place—her involvement hinged on him having contingency plans. But he hadn't talked about leaving her behind for months. "You said my mother might need to see me to escape the prison her mind has been in for so many years."

"We can break her out of the physical prison in the fortress. Then we can bring her to you."

The fear she'd tamped down for the last few days broke through the surface. She couldn't stand by and wait for everyone else to risk their lives to save her. "But I've been training. I've progressed so much."

"We can't leave her," Jasperus said. "Who will cut out her brand if Mayvus does the branding ceremony early?"

"Anyone could stay and watch her," Kendalyhn said. "She's a liability who's more likely to turn on us if she's branded than to be helpful."

"Leave her here?" Gaeren asked. "Right where we're guiding Mayvus' troops?"

An argument broke out, everyone's voices clashing, but each of them saying her name, speaking about her, for her. She closed her eyes, trying to drown out the individual voices so she could hear her own thoughts. In two days, they would all be walking or riding to their possible deaths, fighting for their freedom, but also for hers. It wasn't right that they bore the brunt of the danger and the weight of the risks. Not unless she was willing to do the same. Her fear of being a liability hadn't gone away, but facing that fear seemed far better than sitting around waiting for her fate while letting everyone else make sacrifices.

"I want to go." Aeliana's words came out too quietly for anyone to hear. "I want to go," she said again, raising her voice to drown out the others.

They stopped talking, turning to take her in. Her hands shook, so she gripped the edge of the table to hide her fear.

"I can heal people, which is an essential skill on the battlefield. I can give them my energy, which, despite weaning, has been far more than I can use on my own."

Velden's eyebrows dipped at that revelation.

"I can protect people with light shields."

Cyrus, Velden, Lukai, Jasperus, and Holm nodded their approval, but the rest still seemed unconvinced, especially the soldiers she didn't know. They probably wondered if her similarities to Mayvus ran far deeper than her looks.

"Still," Aeliana continued. "We'll need to have a contingency plan. You're right. If she activates the brand, I'll become your enemy. It's been my greatest fear ever since Sylmar and Jasperus explained brands to me."

Sylmar stood taller, no longer leaning on his staff. "We already have a plan."

The mood around the room shifted, her friends suddenly unable to hold her gaze. Even Cyrus looked away, clearly in on whatever plan Sylmar referenced.

Only Gaeren stiffened beside her. "What plan?" he asked.

When none of the Vendarans spoke up, Cyrus sighed. "I told them Aeliana wouldn't do it. It depends on her being willing to give her blood to Jasperus. If Mayvus activates the brand early, Jasperus can brand Aeliana as well, so his brand will compete with Mayvus'."

Aeliana sucked in a breath. "Will that work?" If it could work that easily, why hadn't they told her this before?

"It's blood magic," Gaeren said, shaking his head. "You're no better than Mayvus if you're willing to risk summoning the dark spirits."

Aeliana shrank back even though his accusation was directed at Sylmar. She'd been so quick to be pulled into the idea. Was she still so tempted by blood magic that she wasn't even aware of all the times it tempted her?

"It's a risk worth taking," Sylmar said. "On the battlefield we lie and kill. The boundaries between right and wrong shift depending on the motives behind the action."

Cyrus' eyes met Aeliana's, but the pained expression on his face made it impossible to know if he agreed with Sylmar's words.

"Besides," Sylmar continued, "Jasperus doesn't have a history of blood magic. Even if his actions call the dark spirits, he won't invite them in. He won't be tempted."

His unspoken words rang in Aeliana's ears. She had a history of blood magic. If she called the dark spirits, she might invite them in.

"What about Mayvus?" Aeliana asked. "Wouldn't we just be delivering dark spirits for her to use?"

"We should assume she'll be using them anyway," Sylmar said. "She doesn't need our help for that."

Aeliana shivered, and Gaeren took another step closer to her.

"What would the Sun think of your plan?" Gaeren asked.

"I'm guessing the Sun is just as eager to see Mayvus out of power as we are." Sylmar's voice took on a weary tone. His eyes bore into Gaeren, who clamped his jaw shut and mirrored Sylmar's glare.

"If it's so harmless, why don't you just brand me now?" Aeliana asked.

"We need the brand to be just as strong as Mayvus'," Sylmar said, "so it must be done on the same day. Your question about bonds interfering with brands was a good one. It got me thinking about how a second brand can interfere with the first. A brand will always override a bond. However, a second brand could compete for control. If Jasperus brands you, it won't override her brand, but it will weaken her connection to you. You could fight it."

Aeliana glanced at Jasperus. "So he'll command me to fight it?"

"You have to remember who Mayvus is," Sylmar said. "Once she realizes what he's done, she'll have no qualms about eliminating the threat of his interference."

Aeliana took a step back, understanding sending a cold chill through her chest. She turned to Jasperus. "You'll do it, expecting her to kill you."

He shook his head. "I'll do it, expecting her to brand me next so she can control us both. Which is why I'll need to be killed."

CHAPTER 74

"No." Aeliana backed away from the table. "Absolutely not. If he's killed, I'm no longer branded. It defeats the whole purpose."

"No," Sylmar said. "If he's killed, the part of you that was branded by him is free. Half of your willpower will be free to fight Mayvus."

"How would she get his blood in time to do a brand on him?"

"If you continue to underestimate her, you're better off staying here," he barked.

"I'd rather you killed me than Jasperus." She continued her retreat until she bumped into the tent's frame, her stomach roiling.

Sylmar shook his head. "That's not an option."

"Why not?"

"You're too valuable."

"I'm no more valuable than Jasperus. If anything, I'm less. I'm a liability." She glanced at Kendalyhn for support, but the other woman crossed her arms and looked away.

"You're wrong," Gaeren said. "You have claim to Mayvus' throne."

"Mayvus doesn't hold a throne," Sylmar snapped.

"My parents gave her the eastern province."

Aeliana's stomach dropped.

"She officially became Queen Mayvus around the same time we were walking through human remains in Islara." Gaeren's hand tightened around the pommel of his sword.

Sylmar's face paled above his beard, making his scars stand out. "Why?"

"It was supposed to be a diplomatic move." Gaeren ran a hand through his hair but still kept the other balanced on his sword. "Enla explained it to me, but her reasoning was weak. It all goes back to the story Orra told about two brothers fighting over a throne."

Everyone glanced toward the tent corner, but Orra might have been sleeping in the shadows for how little she reacted.

"I don't want a throne," Aeliana said. "I hardly even want my magic."

"But if those people were given a choice," Gaeren said, pointing out toward the camp, "they'd all rather you had it than Mayvus. Maybe even more than your mother. How fit can she be to rule after ten years as Mayvus' brand?"

General Nels and his soldier exchanged guilty glances. Perhaps Gaeren wasn't too far off in his assessment.

"Why are you telling us this?" Sylmar asked. "She would threaten the throne of your family."

Gaeren shrugged. "It's the truth. Besides, I'm not so sure my family should be ruling."

Like a wave, heads around the tent bent together, murmuring over Gaeren's words.

"None of this," Sylmar shouted over everyone, "changes the fact that Aeliana can only come if she agrees to our contingency plan. She has to be willing to give us her blood so Jasperus can override Mayvus' brand with his own."

Aeliana glanced at Jasperus, noticing that Sylmar had left out the part about Jasperus being forced to do blood magic and then being killed.

"It's all right," Jasperus said. "Even if you don't agree, I plan to do the same for your mother. I'd rather die to save two lives than just one. Perhaps it will undo some of what my son has done."

Instead of convincing her, his logic made her hate the situation even more.

Aeliana slipped the cord from around her neck, setting her starlock on the table. A chill ran through her as she let it go. Half the people bent in for a closer look while half scooted away like it was cursed. "What if I give up my starlock? She can't do much through me without it."

"It would make you too vulnerable." Gaeren stepped forward, his eyes darting between Aeliana and her starlock. "You can't go into battle without it."

A few nodded, but most everyone turned to Sylmar, awaiting his response. The longer he stared at her starlock, the higher Aeliana's anxiety grew. With painstakingly slow movements, he bent forward and picked up the leather cord.

"You are so much like your mother," he said in wonder. He reached into his pocket and retrieved a second cord, an unfamiliar starlock hanging from it. This time everyone bent forward, taking in its dagger shape. Despite being less than the length of Aeliana's pinky, the dagger had intricate vines wrapping around its base, and Aeliana sensed its pointed tip could do significant damage.

"That looks..." Marnok trailed off. "I feel like I've seen that before."

"Is that my mother's?" Aeliana asked.

Iris cleared her throat, blinking fast while staring at the starlock. "When Mayvus came for her, Emeris asked me to take it. She suspected Mayvus would brand her, so she made herself a less valuable prize."

Aeliana reached for the starlock, her mind racing. She ran a finger along the smooth shaft of the blade, then the bumps of the vines and grip. "What if she'd used it to fight instead? Mayvus might not even have her."

"I think we've all asked ourselves that question," Sylmar said. "Which is why I don't think it's wise for you to do the same thing she did." He handed Aeliana her starlock, the warmth of the star in her left hand contrasting the cold metal of the dagger starlock in her right.

"But if my mother had used it, and Mayvus had still caught her..." Aeliana trailed off, imagining the horrors that could have brought. "Mayvus could already be in full power, dominating the entire country. Then we would have been asking ourselves what would have happened if my mother had given it up. We could go in circles playing this game." She tucked her mother's starlock in her pocket, unwilling to let Sylmar carry it a moment longer.

"The fact is," Sylmar said, "Jasperus is ready and willing to make his sacrifice. We could hide you in the woods or leave you here at the camp, but Mayvus has ways of finding you. Eventually she will brand you."

She closed her eyes. She wanted no part of this new plan.

"If we keep you with us, you'll have better protection," Sylmar said. "We can intervene quicker if she brands you, and there's more chance of her staying in her tower if she suspects that you're heading her way. If she brands you and senses you've stayed behind, she might leave, ruining our chances of finding her."

Others in the group nodded, all his points making sense even if Aeliana didn't like the inevitable outcome.

"So I come with you," she said, "but only on the condition that I'm willing to let Jasperus sacrifice himself." She pushed down the rising heat. She was being manipulated to allow something she didn't want, and it felt strangely similar to the ways Arvid and Vera had forced her to give them her blood. Promises that it was for the best, not because it truly was, but because they were threatening to do something worse if they didn't get their way.

Sylmar's beard shifted as his jaw tightened. "I told you that you wouldn't always like my methods."

Aeliana glanced at Jasperus, who gave her an encouraging nod.

"There has to be another way." She shook her head and crossed her arms over her chest.

Lukai cleared his throat, then pulled a vial from his coat pocket. The entire room went still as the glass glinted in the torchlight, drawing attention to the deep brown substance within it.

"There is another way," Lukai said, unable to hold Aeliana's gaze. "I got—this is—" He shook his head, his face turning red as beads of sweat broke out on his face.

Sylmar took the blood from Lukai's outstretched arm. Sharp pain shot through Aeliana's bond mark, and Lukai winced, scratching at his palm as he hunched over the table.

"It's hard to admit the ways you've betrayed your bondmate, isn't it?" Gaeren's voice held a hardness Aeliana hadn't heard since they'd first found him, back when he couldn't trust the Recreants.

"What are you talking about?" she asked.

"He gave me your blood." Sylmar's eyes shone, but his face remained stoic, whether to avoid looking smug or because even this couldn't make him happy.

Aeliana turned to Lukai, whose face pinched with guilt. "How did you—?"

"Training. We often cut each other to practice healing." When Lukai practically choked on the words, Kendalyhn put her arm around him, but he shrugged her off with a moan, as if that interaction sent his bond mark's retaliation over the edge.

Aeliana's palm stung, and when she glanced at it, the skin around the mark appeared red and inflamed. "You would both use my blood without my permission?"

There was a stillness to the air as everyone collectively held their breath.

Sylmar frowned and tossed the vial to the ground, where it bounced on the grass. Then he brought his staff down hard on the vial, breaking the glass and spilling the blood. "No. Even that's a line I'm not willing to cross. It has to be your choice."

A sob broke from Lukai's throat. "Every fiber in me fights to protect you. You have to understand—I don't want to cross that line either, but I want you safe."

Gaeren shook his head, muttering something about bonds that Aeliana couldn't catch.

She stepped forward, reaching out for Lukai, but her hand stopped just above his shoulder. Was she quick to forgive because it was her nature? Or because the bond required it? She let her hand fall and stepped back once more, the reality of what he'd done sitting heavy with her. She couldn't handle addressing it now, especially with an audience.

Her gaze fell on Sylmar, whose brow remained raised in question. His unwillingness to use her blood without permission didn't override his manipulation to get her to hand it over. Was it truly her choice if he made it her only way to help rescue her mother?

A scream threatened to work its way up her throat, but she fought it down before turning away. Tears stung her eyes as she swept the tent flap aside, afraid she might retch. As the cool night air hit her face, she sucked in its freshness, allowing it to calm her pounding heart and settle her stomach.

Most of the troops had gathered around small campfires where they ate a meager meal. The guards on either side of her glanced her way, but they made no comment. They'd likely heard the entire discussion in the tent.

Murmurs started up around her, and, as her eyes adjusted, she saw the stares of the people, followed by the occasional dip of the head. A few even touched their fingers to their foreheads first, something she'd caught Gaeren's men doing before he reminded them he was no longer a prince. A gesture for royalty.

Rumors had spread about her identity as the daughter of Emeris and Rildan, and the curious glances at her hair and dress had shifted to desperate hope as the people examined her features, picking apart the similarities between her and her mother.

Was Gaeren right? Did they see her as an alternate to the throne?

She strode to the edge of camp, swallowing around the lump in her throat and tripping over twigs and stumps she was too distracted to notice in the dim moonlight. When the chatting and laughter blurred to a dull hum, she dropped to her knees and bent forward, burying her face in her hands.

They asked too much of her, and yet they didn't ask enough. It wasn't Jasperus' price to pay tomorrow.

She ripped off her starlock and threw it a dozen steps away. A coldness swept over her, but she fought it, momentarily reveling in its absence. It didn't have to be a part of who she was. She could be strong without it.

Footsteps whispered through the grass behind her. She sat up and turned, almost eager to take her frustration out on someone, but all the anger left her when the shadows shifted to reveal Cyrus approaching. Out of everyone here, he didn't deserve her wrath. He hadn't asked to be a part of this any more than she had.

He stared at her for a moment, then strode past her, bending to search the forest floor before picking up the starlock she'd thrown. When he kneeled in front of her and slipped it back over her head, she couldn't hold his gaze. The starlock settled against her chest, its heat like fire even through the fabric of her shirt, as if it were angry at being cast aside.

"It's a part of you now," he said. "Even if you don't always want it to be. It's a calling from the Stars. They rarely call us to carry light burdens." He tilted his head up to take in the Stars' dance, the reverence on his face almost inspiring.

"Every life that's lost because of me makes the burden heavier," she whispered. "When does it become too much?"

"Gams always liked to remind me that the Stars will never give us more than we can bear. It's written in *The Song of the Stars*." He glanced at her, and his smile held a sorrow that tugged at Aeliana's heart.

"Do you think that was true, even in her final moments?" Aeliana tried keeping her tone even, but the words came out raw and harsh. "When she took the brunt of my guardians' anger instead of me?"

"The Stars sent her Orra, didn't they?" He glanced back toward the camp even though it was impossible to make out individuals. "And they've sent you all these people ready to stand behind you. Or even in front of you."

"I don't want anyone to die for me. Least of all Jasperus. He's lost too much already."

"That's part of the reason he's willing to fill the position." Cyrus winced at his own words, then tugged on the cord around his neck, pulling something dark out from under his shirt. He gripped it tight and hesitated, staring at his fist—not quite willing to reveal what it held. "Maybe the Stars also sent me to give you another option."

Aeliana's heart picked up its pace. "What do you have?"

"I should have shown this to you a long time ago. At first I thought it would be too tempting for you, that it might interfere with your efforts to wean yourself off blood magic. But the longer I had it, the more I started feeling ridiculous for having taken it in the first place. And eventually guilty." He opened his fist for the moonlight to reveal a small vial of dark red blood resting in his palm.

Aeliana sat back on her heels, finally understanding his hesitation. "Whose blood is that?"

"Durriken's."

Aeliana's mouth swung open. "How did you get the dragon's blood?"

The tips of his ears darkened as he lifted a shoulder. "After Orra told me about Gams' last moments, I left camp. Without really thinking about it, I ended up back at Islara's gates, almost like seeing other people's loss might put my own into perspective. But then I also saw Durriken lying there, fast asleep."

Aeliana covered her eyes with her hands. "You didn't."

He laughed, a sound more from relief. "I did. I don't know what possessed me. Curiosity maybe? There was probably a hint of a desire for revenge. But when I got close, I saw his paw. He was branded just like you said. I didn't really know how it worked at that point, but I knew Mayvus had your blood and that gave her power over you. It felt like if we had his blood, it might eventually give us power over him."

Aeliana peeked between her fingers. "So you just went up and cut him?"

He grinned sheepishly. "Pretty much."

"And why exactly did you have an empty vial just sitting in your pocket?"

"There was an apothecary in the building next to him. When I found an undamaged vial that had rolled out on the cobblestone, it seemed like the Stars themselves were insisting I bottle it up." He pulled the leather string over his head, frowning down at the vial. "Every day it grows warm while we travel, like it soaks in the Sun's light even through my tunic. And every night it gets cold, like the energy leaches back out. I understand now why Sylmar and Jasperus are so convinced that branding is more powerful just before the Sun's sleep."

Aeliana shook her head, unable to hold back her smile. "So now what? You want me to give this vial to Jasperus and tell him it's my blood?"

Cyrus winced. "I suppose you could do that. But Sylmar might hold up his end of the bargain to kill Jasperus before checking the brand. Besides, maybe Jasperus won't have to brand you." He rubbed the back of his neck, the rest of his words struggling to get out until they all tumbled through at once. "Not if you first brand Durriken to you."

Aeliana's mouth went dry and she stood, stepping away from Cyrus. "You want me to do blood magic?"

"It's not—" He rose as well, grabbing her forearm as if afraid she might run. "I understand if you don't want to. You have to do what you think is right. But I can't help thinking Sylmar's right. The blood magic attracts the dark spirits, but you still have the choice to let them in."

"What about the rest of what he said? Jasperus doesn't have a history of blood magic, but I do." She balled her hands into fists, hating both the scars and fresh cuts she continued to find on her skin. Cuts she couldn't explain.

Cyrus shook his head. "You have a history of others using your blood for magic. You're tempted to use it because it's all you knew for years, but even with that upbringing, you have always refused the dark spirits. If anything, you're the best person for this task because you've practiced resisting them for years."

"And if I fail, everyone pays for my mistake."

He shrugged, unable to counter her words.

"How does branding Durriken keep Jasperus from branding me?"

"Well, it won't unless you can get Durriken on our side. If you can cut out his brand to Mayvus and get him to fight for us, we not only gain a dragon, but she loses one. If you can turn the tide of the battle before she brands you, Jasperus won't brand you either."

Aeliana bit her lip, staring at the blood still in his hand. "But if I do it too soon, it might push her to brand me earlier."

"I didn't say it was a perfect plan. It's just another option for you."

She inhaled a deep, shaky breath, then took the vial from his hands. She couldn't believe she was even considering the idea. "How do I do it?"

Cyrus hesitated. "Jasperus explained it to me. You choose the place you want his brand marked on you, then cut yourself and pour his blood over your wound. Instead of healing the wound, you use your starlock to seal it. I was hoping that would make sense to you…"

Aeliana nodded, already imagining the difference. Healing felt more like knitting a wound together, but he was talking about covering it or encasing it.

"It forms a mark on your skin, like a tattoo, and simultaneously marks his palm, just like a bond, but it only goes one way." Cyrus' hands rose with his explanation, his gestures becoming wilder with his excitement over the idea. "Durriken will sense a desire to please you without you having that same feeling in return." His description fit with the little Sylmar had told them months ago, but it also laid out exactly what she could expect if Mayvus successfully branded her.

"And then he just does what I ask," Aeliana said. There were so many points it could go wrong. She could lose control cutting herself. The dragon's attachment might be too strong to Mayvus. She might not get close enough to cut out the old brand. And at any point, if Mayvus branded Aeliana, it would be useless.

"I mean, that's the theory." Cyrus' hands dropped, his excitement giving way to uncertainty. "You can always remove the brand when it's all over."

"Free him." Somehow that made the idea more palatable, but she still couldn't see herself using it. By the time she felt the risk was worth it, it might be too late.

"While you're at it, you should consider cutting out your bond. Lukai kind of deserves it after that." He frowned in the direction of the war room tent, shoving his hands in his robe pockets.

"How very… unpriestlike of you." Aeliana laughed, and the tension between them broke. "It's a good plan, Cyrus. One I hope not to use, but still helpful. You're a good friend."

He beamed at her. "Sometimes friends are better than bonds."

Aeliana snorted. "They're far less complicated, that's for sure."

"I'm always going to look out for you, even when you send me back to Lorvandas." His face grew somber, his freckles contrasting more in the moonlight. "Just because you stopped training as a priestess doesn't mean we stopped training together. And that's its own kind of bond. It lasts a lifetime."

"Thank you," she whispered. She could never tell him that deep down, she didn't want to send him back home. He was one of the people she felt safest with. But if she told him that, he would stay, and he needed to go back to Bartholem.

Instead, she pulled out her mother's starlock and placed it over Cyrus' head and tucked it under his tunic. "Now you can still trick the Zealots while safekeeping it for me. I can't have it in my possession when Mayvus brands me."

He patted his chest where it lay. "I'm always praying for you, Aeliana. Whether it's the Sun or Stars out, whether I'm kneeling or riding a horse or sneaking food off the cookfire before Kendalyhn can burn it."

She smiled at the mental image, but a lump grew in her throat at the sincerity behind his words. "Thank you. Both the Sun and Stars know I need it."

***

The next day, they pushed hard as they steadily climbed in elevation toward the Myndren Mountains. Aeliana feared they were bringing the soldiers to a state of exhaustion when they really needed rest before they laid siege to Mayvus' fortress the next day. She urged her mare through the ranks, trying to spread a little bit of her energy to each of the troops to carry them through.

Even though she knew she'd have to eventually give Sylmar her blood, she avoided both him and Lukai until that evening, when Cyrus accompanied her to the hastily constructed war tent once more. She stood outside, gearing up the courage to seal Jasperus' fate when it ironically felt like the far more courageous thing would be to refuse.

Shouts carried across the grass from camp, and they turned, Cyrus' hand going to his hilt. Aeliana scanned the camp, first for intruders but then to see if there was an open path to her bedroll that held her bow and quiver. Crowds blocked her view, but so far she only saw their own people. She stepped away from the tent, weaving through crowd in the hopes of finding the source of everyone's concern, but when people saw her coming, they made way, several whispering her name.

"There you are, love," Iris called, her hand waving over the heads of several shoulders. "General Nels is looking for you. Says he needs you." Her head and shoulders popped out between two beefy arms in the crowd, and she gestured for Aeliana to come closer.

"Me? Why me?"

"There's a winex who's come." Iris beamed. "He's asking for you by name."

CHAPTER 75

GAEREN GRINNED at the full-grown winex snarling at General Nels, enjoying the soldier's discomfort. "He won't hurt you if you put your weapons away."

Felk turned a wary eye on Gaeren, a reminder that Felk hadn't met Gaeren yet this cycle.

"He may have been your pet once, but he's wild now." The general left his blade out, pointed at Felk's chest. The winex stood tall and proud like the men, but his fingers flexed, ready to fight if it came to it.

"He was never my pet," Gaeren said.

A tinkling sound met his ears as Felk threw his head back in laughter. Gaeren paused, slightly stunned, but he recovered far faster than the general, whose arm lowered a good six inches, giving Felk room to step past.

The creature's eyes lit up in the moonlight, reminiscent of how he'd looked in his younger state, and the winex's arms rose to envelop the woman running straight for him. "Mama!"

A murmur started in the crowd behind Daisy.

She ignored them all, laughing as Felk spun her around. That same jealous twinge rose in Gaeren, making him squirm. Now he was jealous of a winex?

She squeezed Felk tight, then pulled back, looking him over. "You've gotten so big again." She held her hand up to his, which was now twice as large as hers. His smile grew, revealing multiple rows of sharp teeth.

The last time Gaeren had seen him, half of those teeth had been missing because of declining health.

Daisy reached out a hand to touch the black tear that stood out on the shine of Felk's silver cheek.

"Are you all right?" Daisy asked. "Have they been treating you well?"

He nodded and ducked his head. "They've accepted me. Even see me as a leader. At first it was because they thought I'd know ways to defeat your kind, but when they finally understood you and I aren't enemies, they wanted me to teach them everything you'd taught me."

Daisy smiled and squeezed his shoulder. "That's wonderful."

"Just so they can forget it with the new moon?" General Nels muttered. "What a waste." He lifted his sword higher.

Daisy turned, leveling the general with a glare even though he towered over her. "You might be gone before the new moon, and Sylmar's still willing to work with you."

A tinkling laughter filled the night air once more, and the general's face went slack.

Gaeren was more prepared this time, and he gave Felk a shove. "You're going to make real enemies if you keep that up."

Felk gave another snarl, throwing out a hand to protect Daisy.

"It's all right," she said, tugging his arm down. "Gaeren is a friend. You knew him in another cycle."

Gaeren held out a hand. "I can show you if you'd like."

Felk cocked his head and narrowed his eyes, but then he gripped Gaeren's hand, his eyes fully closing as Gaeren pushed memory after memory toward the winex. Daisy feeding and training him, wrestling with Gaeren and Riveran, all of them laughing by the campfire. Even their farewell, which had been embarrassingly emotional for Gaeren. Before meeting Felk, he hadn't thought this kind of magic could cross to a winex, hadn't even considered hoping for it. Daisy's ability to have different perspectives and see other options—to see the possible good in everything—had rubbed off on him.

Felk pulled away, his chest heaving as he blinked and regained his bearings. "I don't—I don't remember any of that."

Gaeren nodded. "And yet it all happened."

Wetness clung to the winex's cheeks, and he leaned forward, pulling Gaeren into a hug. "Sorry," he mumbled, then pulled back, awkwardly rubbing his arms and staring at the forest floor.

His face turned more serious than Gaeren ever remembered seeing it, his intelligence far more than it had been when Gaeren had known him. It seemed strange considering the winex couldn't retain their memories, but what if they retained other learned things?

Gaeren glanced over at Marnok, who was possibly the only one not staring at the strange scene before them. The older man's gaze remained intent on the fire, his brow furrowed. He didn't have memories, but he had instinctive knowledge along with general facts. What if their memory loss worked the same?

"I think my clan might have already made enemies." Felk let out a small whine, like a dog on a scent, bringing Gaeren's attention back to the winex, whose wide eyes glanced around the camp, taking in the frightened faces of those huddled around nearby fires. "And I'm not talking about these people."

"So you think," General Nels muttered.

Gaeren glared at the general, then steered Felk and Daisy away from the rest of the camp's prying eyes. This cycle, Felk even walked more like a man, though his hands still had calloused palms like he spent just as much time using the winex lope. They settled near a copse of trees that was mostly in shadow. An eerie glow came from Felk's skin—the reflected moonlight like a small light on their path. To Gaeren's annoyance, the general followed, probably to eavesdrop more than provide protection.

"What happened since you left us?" Daisy asked. "It feels like a lot when it's only been five days."

"We met up with a few other clans," Felk said. "There's a witch in the east who sends her men out to hunt. They kill for sport but gather our blood for the witch."

"Your blood?" Daisy's eyebrows knitted together as she worked her lower lip.

"But you don't have starblood," Gaeren said. Then, because

nothing would surprise him anymore, he added, "Do you?"

Felk shook his head. "Not that I know of. She mixes our blood with some potion. We heard men talking about how it has regenerative properties. It restores life."

Daisy's gaze flicked to Gaeren's.

"That's not possible," Gaeren said, even as he wondered if it could be. What was it about the winex that made them cycle each moon? They were like perennial flowers or, well… the moon. Gaeren couldn't think of much else that functioned the same way. What if it was something in their blood, something that Mayvus could harness and use to renew a body?

"It heals people?" the general asked. "Or raises them from the dead?"

Felk shrugged. "We only hear the soldiers talk. One claimed it brought him back, but another said the man had just been drunk, not dead." His eyes closed to slits, and he leaned back for another laugh. Daisy and Gaeren covered their ears, but the general was too slow. His eyes lost their focus, and he stared past the tree surrounding them.

"Do you remember that we were traveling east to find Mayvus?" Daisy asked.

Felk nodded. "I assume she's the witch."

"It's a good description," Gaeren said with a grin.

Daisy elbowed him before turning back to Felk. "I can't guarantee we'll stop her, but—"

"You can't tell him anything," the general said, finally pulling himself from his stupor. He shifted and stood taller, elbowing his way between Daisy and Felk, who growled.

"I'll tell him anything I please." Daisy's voice took on an edge that made Gaeren's smile widen.

"It's not your decision. The war effort is being run by the Recreants, and I'll not have you putting all my soldiers in harm's way because you assume your pet is loy—" His words cut off with an undignified scream as Felk lifted him by his waist and set him aside with minimal effort. The winex's sinewy muscles bulged in the moonlight, yet another way in which he'd changed from the last time Gaeren had seen him.

"Our clan has been tracking her soldiers. They take the blood in through a side entrance. Part of an old dungeon system to remove dead bodies. They've even taken a few of our winex in there alive." Felk's teeth ground together, the noise putting Gaeren on edge. "We suspect she bleeds them, but it's also possible she plans to breed them."

"Have you tried going in after them?" Gaeren asked.

"Of course not," the general said from behind Felk. "Because the information he's giving you is a setup for a trap."

Felk turned so fast the general jumped back. "I'm not lying," the winex ground out.

Daisy grabbed his arm. "Ignore him."

"We all do," Gaeren added.

Felk turned back and shook his head again. He blinked several times, and at first Gaeren thought the creature was trying to regain control from his anger, but then the winex wiped a tear from his eye. "We haven't gone in yet. The risk is too great. But they have Lilik."

Gaeren glanced at Daisy, who seemed just as lost.

"Who's…" She trailed off. "Oh. Did you—do you have a mate?" Daisy stumbled over the word.

"She's the one who wanted to rescue me." Pride leaked from his words even as more tears fell from his eyes. "And she was the first to stand down when you saved my life." He used his shoulder to wipe his cheeks.

Apparently Gaeren had missed even more than Daisy had.

Daisy patted his shoulder. "Maybe we can help you get her back."

"I hate to agree with the other guy," Gaeren said, jabbing a thumb in the general's direction, "but we can't really take on another agenda for this mission."

Daisy's sympathetic frown shifted to a glare that pinned Gaeren down. "I meant that we could help each other. This could be a way in, both to save Lilik and to find my mother."

Gaeren opened his mouth to argue, but she had a fair point. He'd let Sylmar fight that battle. Besides, anything that potentially upset Sylmar's plans could also prevent the need for blood magic or sacrificing soldiers.

He still couldn't understand why these people were so willing to attempt branding, not when they knew the consequences. Especially for Daisy.

"We should ask Sylmar about this other entrance," Gaeren said. "He had a map of the layout of Mayvus' fortress. The entrance he wanted to use was closer to the back. I don't remember seeing anything else. Doesn't mean it doesn't exist," he rushed to add. "In fact, maybe it's more reliable than his, which hasn't been verified for over a decade."

"If it's more reliable," Daisy mused, "he'll be more likely to agree."

"My clan also brought a peace offering." Felk backed away from Daisy, nearly stepping on General Nels. Felk held out a hand, keeping Daisy at bay until he was a dozen paces away. Then he howled, the forlorn sound raising the hairs on Gaeren's arms.

General Nels straightened, lifting his sword once more and holding it out toward the various shadows surrounding them. Even Daisy tensed, her gaze flicking between Felk and the shadows. Within moments, the shadows shifted, then glinted as moonlight struck the silvery skin of more winex. The general swore as half a dozen emerged, but Gaeren placed a staying hand on the other man's arm.

The winex joining Felk were smaller, their bodies more hunched like the predators Gaeren was used to seeing. They shifted from one foot to the other, slowly closing in on Daisy, Gaeren, and General Nels. Their lips curled in snarls, but they made no move to attack. One by one, they each brought forward a bundle of purple fabric on bolts like ones Gaeren had seen the seamstress hauling through the palace. A wave of homesickness hit him—a startling sensation since he had no desire to be home.

"Um, thank you?" Daisy placed a tentative hand on the pile of fabric.

"We know you plan to attack tomorrow," Felk said. "We hear your sentries talk."

General Nels stood straighter, and Gaeren felt sorry for whichever men had been on duty the last few nights.

"My clan will help you," Felk said, "if you also help them."

"How does purple cloth help us?" Gaeren asked, and General Nels snorted.

Felk stepped forward, tore a strip of fabric from the nearest bolt, then leaned over Gaeren to tie it around his arm. "In battle you will all look like our enemies. This way we know who we shouldn't kill."

Daisy's smile grew until she let out a light laugh. She stepped around the fabric and reached for one of the winex, drawing him into a hug. The general took a step forward, and Gaeren reached for his sword, barely holding back a protest that would earn him yet another glare.

"Thank you," she breathed out.

The winex didn't hug her back but sniffed her shoulder and ear, his teeth far too close to her neck for Gaeren's liking. Even Felk tensed beside him, poised to intervene. But Daisy went down the line, hugging and thanking each of the creatures. A couple hugged her back, but most took the opportunity to learn her scent, the occasional growl sneaking out.

"It does seem like a genuine offer for help," Gaeren admitted, though his hand remained on his sword's hilt.

The general grunted but finally sheathed his weapon. "Six winex against an army of thousands isn't much of an offer."

"Then you haven't seen them in action." Gaeren smiled, recalling the way Felk had protected Daisy. She seemed to attract defenders wherever she went. "Besides, they said they ran into a few clans. I bet they have more like thirty to fifty out in the woods."

"How did you get so much fabric anyway?" Daisy asked, gathering up bolts and shoving them in Gaeren's and General Nels' hands.

Felk let out another small tinkling laugh, which the other winex echoed. The effect was spellbinding, and Daisy, Gaeren, and the general all paused, blinking heavily as they fought to focus.

"We stole it from a trader passing through," Felk said. "If we can't find old nests, we have to make new ones for the eggs we plant. Then we save the rest for our rebirth."

Daisy hesitated, then sighed. "I suppose there's nothing to be done about it for now, but in the future, we're not going to steal, is that understood?"

It was odd to see the massive winex hunch over in shame, as if her words had physically wounded him.

"Yes, Mama," he mumbled.

The other winex grinned, their teeth flashing as they exchanged glances with each other. Leader or not, Felk would be teased relentlessly that night.

"It's too bad they didn't steal uniforms from Mayvus' men while they were at it," General Nels said.

Felk perked up. "You need uniforms?"

The general frowned, addressing Gaeren instead of Felk. "It would be far easier to sneak into the castle with disguises."

Gaeren sighed and turned to Felk. "That's a yes. Do you have some?"

Felk rolled his shoulders and glanced at the other winex. "We've killed some of the soldiers who attacked us. Many of the uniforms are... damaged. But we could bring the ones that aren't. Or the ones that could be fixed."

Daisy shuddered but still nodded. "That would be a great help."

Even Gaeren found the idea of wearing a uniform off a dead soldier less than appealing, but he supposed it was better than showing up in his sailing leathers and tunic.

"I'm surprised they didn't eat the soldiers," General Nels muttered.

"Oh, we did," Felk said, his mouth widening into something too large to be a smile. He leaned closer to the general. "The dried leather of the uniforms is disgusting. So we peel that off and go straight for the meat."

General Nels shrank back, his face growing sickly pale in the moonlight.

"Oh, Felk." Daisy made a face and lightly smacked Felk's arm. "Stop teasing him." When she turned back toward camp, Felk's face drooped with guilt.

Gaeren scanned the other winex, who licked their lips. One even closed his eyes and rubbed his belly. Gaeren's own stomach churned with revulsion and trepidation. He wanted to assume Felk had more influence over these winex than they did over him, but by the time they knew for sure, it might be too late.

CHAPTER 76

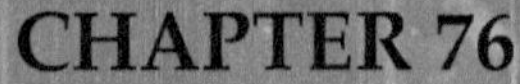

ORRA WATCHED Gaeren and Aeliana return to camp, Felk and General Nels in tow. They deposited bolts of purple fabric just outside the tent where Sylmar still debated his plans. Plans that went awry in almost all of the paths Orra had searched before she'd drained so much of her power.

She bent her legs in until her entire body was in the shadow of the tree she sat against, and she pressed her forehead against her knees. The unease of not knowing was a sensation she would never get used to, and it only occurred more and more with each passing day. What if one day her power didn't return? What if the Sun no longer wished to replenish her blood?

The years the Sun had given her were more than she deserved. She couldn't complain if her time was up.

"Forgive me," she whispered, not sure if she spoke to the Sun or Bryton or the generations in the wake of the stone she'd so carelessly thrown.

Tomorrow, if all went well, she would hold the golden arrow once more. But then what?

"Hungry?"

Orra jolted at Gaeren's question, the surprise on his face a mirror of her own. It wasn't often that someone could sneak up on her. She'd grown weaker than she'd realized. He held out flatbread, one of the many Kendalyhn and Breeve had burned.

She took the food but merely turned it in her hands.

"Aeliana's worried about you." Gaeren took a seat next to her, munching on his own bread. "Sent me to check on you."

A smile tugged at Orra's lips. She should be looking out for Aeliana, but everything had gotten muddled. Had she dealt with Durriken to protect Aeliana or to ensure her own access to the golden arrow? Or was it something she did simply because she sensed the Sun calling her to? Did it make a difference why she did it? Or only that she'd done it?

"Well, I guess I'll tell her you're just as moody as always." Gaeren brushed the crumbs from his hands and stood.

"Have you finished reading *The Sins of the Stars*?" she asked.

He nodded. "Even lent it to Cyrus, though I'm sure he thinks it's heretical. It didn't tell me as much as you could. If you ever decide to speak plainly instead of in riddles."

She closed her eyes and leaned her head back against the tree. "There are parts missing from the text, that's certain. But there are parts you missed because you only look for what you want to see."

"Such as?"

"How did your parents bond you to Lenda?" She peeked between her lashes to catch him studying his hand.

"By joining our blood and fusing it on our skin." He said the words slowly, like he was hearing them for the first time.

"Is that not a form of blood magic?"

"It's different. It…" He trailed off.

She opened her eyes fully and smiled up at him. "What about Lovers' Falls? You tuned in to Aeliana's blood to find her."

His mouth hung open.

"It's magic that uses blood, and while it might catch the attention of the dark spirits, it doesn't call them the same way it does when Mayvus uses blood magic. The intention behind it matters because it's indicative of your response to the dark spirits. They are attracted to the blood, but they're also attracted to the darkness brewing in the progeny that spills it."

"Are you suggesting blood magic can be good?"

She lifted a shoulder. "Spilling blood for magic is rarely an act of love. And it will always attract darks spirits. But the Sun gave us blood to house the power of the light given to us. One could argue that every time magic is used, it's a form of blood magic since that's where the power resides. It's our choices that will determine if it's used for right or wrong."

"That perspective... no one else seems to agree. Even those who approve of blood magic speak in terms of it tapping into higher power rather than harnessing it for right or wrong." His words held more curiosity than accusation, his brow knitted with the thoughts tangled in his mind.

"Even these Recreants," she said, "who are willing to use blood magic as a last resort, might find my definitions disturbing. But the Sun wants us to do right things—not just for the sake of doing them. We need to do the right things for the right reasons."

She swallowed hard, the rush of the truth being revealed pricking at the back of her eyes. It had been on the tip of her understanding for hundreds of years. But the Sun saw fit to give her understanding now. For this moment. For her needs as well as Gaeren's. "The Stars sinned, not because they separated the people or because they put up barriers. It wasn't the actions themselves that were wrong. They sinned because they did those things without consulting the Sun. They did it for their own purposes, which were guided by fear instead of love."

"That's not how the story is told." Gaeren frowned at her.

"And yet it's the way the story goes." She said the words firmly, more like a reprimand. "You came to the text with your preconceived ideas and found ways for the words to fit what you already believed. You should have come with an open mind and heart. You should have let it speak to your soul. It wouldn't hurt to read it again."

She studied him a moment longer, and he shifted under her gaze.

"It seems your pull toward the starbridges has lessened," she said.

He barked out a laugh. "It's all but disappeared. I no longer need them to find Aeliana or protect her. I thought they could protect my family, or at least appease my sister, but it appears my family doesn't want protection."

"If you didn't have people to protect or wars to be fought, would you want them?"

He hesitated. "Maybe to see lands and people beyond this one. But somehow I suspect your reason for wanting them is far more noble than mine."

She smiled, even though his words weren't accurate. Her reason was likely the most selfish of all. "And yet our two goals aren't mutually exclusive."

She glanced over his shoulder to the camp beyond, where Sylmar exited his tent and glared at everyone within view before stomping over to Aeliana. After exchanging a few words, Aeliana pointed toward Orra and Gaeren, and Sylmar squinted in their direction.

"You should help Aeliana with the uniforms Felk just delivered," Orra suggested as Sylmar made his way toward their tree. "Maybe show the others Felk can be trusted. Sylmar's about to send you away anyway."

Gaeren stood and turned, starting at Sylmar standing less than a foot away.

"Go on," the older man said. "I need to have a word with Orra."

Gaeren gave her a questioning glance.

"I'll be fine," she said, finally munching on the flatbread he'd given her.

Sylmar snorted, then sat beside her, groaning as his stiff joints made it more of a fall than anything else.

Gaeren took off, and Orra watched as he sat beside Aeliana, far closer than he needed to. She swallowed the burned bits of bread and tore off another piece, popping it into her mouth.

"I told you to leave Aeliana out of your mischief," Sylmar said.

Orra turned to face him as she chewed, studying the scars lining his face. The memories leaking off them spoke of sacrifice and honor, but she knew better than to bring up his past. He wore the scars as a mask for his soft side, letting only the harshness shine through.

"Aeliana is central to everything," she said. "I can't leave her out of my plans any more than you can."

He let out a huff. "And what are your plans?"

She ripped apart the bread even though her appetite was gone. "To find the starbridges."

"What does that have to do with Aeliana?"

Orra smiled. "Maybe nothing."

She took a bite of the bread without tasting it.

Maybe nothing. Or maybe everything.

Aeliana and Gaeren had already thrown stones and caused ripples, but they still had more to throw, more waves to cause. Orra was content to watch their ripples expand and move things in place to ensure maximum impact. That was the part she had to play.

"I know you're after the starbridges," Sylmar said. "It was all over Gaeren's memories when Kendalyhn sifted his past. I didn't trust you when you showed up, not when I knew what you'd done. But I kept you close, waiting for you to show your true motives. Only you saved Aeliana."

Orra returned his stare, not even blinking.

"What will you do if you get them tomorrow?" he asked. "Why do you even want them?"

There were several answers she could give, but none she was willing to say. "You talk about how much motive matters, but say little of your own motives. Why are you so determined to remove Mayvus from power?"

Sylmar went still. She knew how he'd gotten his scars, and not just the ones dotting his skin. The more he dug for her secrets, the more she could expose his own.

He stood. "I'll leave you to your brooding, then."

As he walked away, Orra closed her eyes and tilted her head toward the Stars. Did they watch her from above? Did they still despise her for her choices? Or did they root for her to reverse what she'd done wrong?

"I'm not doing it for them." She lifted the braid to her lips. "I'm doing it for you."

She winced, still not sure if she had her motivation right.

CHAPTER 77

THE NEXT MORNING, Aeliana rose before the Sun.

They weren't planning to leave for the Myndren Mountains until mid-morning, but she couldn't fall back asleep. She sat at the edge of their camp as dawn approached, her gaze traveling over the hundreds of people she could see with thousands more stretching beyond them in the woods, all resting for maybe their last time in this world. She tried to remind herself that they'd planned to move forward with this attack long before she'd arrived. They pushed on out of loyalty to her mother and their country, not any loyalty to her.

But that didn't lessen the weight on her chest.

If anything, the thought of her mother made the burden heavier. She hadn't let herself think much about what success might mean, but now she let the hope of her family flood in and warm her from head to toe. The few glimpses she had from her childhood seemed almost brighter than when she'd first dredged them up for Velden, the faces clearer. But it was probably her imagination filling in the gaps, her hopes for the memories to solidify and become available in the present.

She patted her shirt pocket, making sure the vial of Durriken's blood was still there, ready to soak in as much warmth and rays of the Sun's light as possible.

Others around camp began stirring, forcing Aeliana out of her thoughts. She made her way to the war tent, and, without ceremony, she cut her palm and gave Sylmar a vial of blood. He tried apologizing, but she refused to hear it. She told herself it didn't matter, that Jasperus wouldn't need to use her blood because she had her own backup plan to brand Durriken.

But that still didn't sit well with her either.

Gaeren stood at his bedroll two fires away, his eyes seeking out hers. He grinned and ran a hand through his disheveled hair, making it stick up more.

She supposed she ought to get this one last task out of the way. She picked up two purple strips of cloth and headed toward Gaeren. Several people greeted her, the awe she'd grown accustomed to in their eyes now clouded with the sober truth of what they planned to do in mere hours.

By the time she reached Gaeren, he was fastening the buttons of his new shirt—one of the uniforms Felk had given them. Her gaze dropped to the skin and hair of his chest, then to the fabric in her hands as her cheeks burned. "Do you have a moment?"

"Of course."

She led him through the maze of bedrolls to the edge of camp, where they found a decent enough log. As soon as they sat, she tied one of the purple strips around his arm. It was one of the widest she could find, so it would hopefully be the most visible. She dreaded the thought of any of the soldiers being taken down by Felk's friends, or even worse, Felk himself.

When she finished, she patted the tie, then continued staring at it, gripping his arm as if she needed the connection to say what was on her mind. But her mouth stayed closed, her mind a jumble of words she didn't know how to put together.

Gaeren's voice startled her.

"You once told me there was something wrong with your magic." He studied the ground. "That it was pushed to an unhealthy limit by Arvid and Vera, and now you can't seem to rein it in."

She nodded, trying to shift from the hard thing she had to ask to this new topic, which sounded equally difficult.

"I don't think that's quite right." He pointed at their feet, where more than a dozen daisies grew, some still sprouting, others unfurling by their shins.

Her face heated. "They grow when I'm distressed. The first time it happened, Vera told me about the magic in my blood. It was the first time she took my blood, too." Several more blossomed as she spoke, as if the memory spurred on more heartache that required more release of her magic. "It's a curse."

"No, that's not right." Gaeren's jaw tightened and his brow furrowed. "It happened hundreds of times when you were a child. It started from a place of joy. Maybe Arvid and Vera twisted it into something else, but I wouldn't have called you Daisy if it weren't for—" He let out a frustrated sigh and tousled his hair. "I wish you remembered."

Aeliana thought of Felk and the mix of joy and sorrow on his face after Gaeren had shared their memories. "Can you show me?"

His eyes softened, the vulnerable expression quickly replaced by the mask of his normal smirk.

"You were an impetuous child. Don't say I didn't warn you." He placed his hand over hers, solidifying her hold on his arm, spreading his warmth through each of her fingers.

Her mind flooded with hazy images. She gasped, squeezing his arm tighter as the visions made her dizzy. Warmth brushed her forehead, then the weight of his forehead against hers served to both anchor her and bring clarity to the images.

A dimpled toddler towered over where Aeliana lay before launching on top of her with earsplitting giggles. The same toddler standing, arms reaching to her waist—begging to be lifted up. The weight of the child on her back as she ran through the forest. As the images revolved, Aeliana realized she was seeing everything from Gaeren's perspective as a boy, and the toddler with curly brown hair was her. They splashed in the creek and rolled down grassy hills, each place oddly familiar. A field of daisies spread before her, and a chain of them grew in her hands —Gaeren's small boyish hands—before she let the toddler take it. Her younger self held it up to her neck and fastened it like fine jewelry.

A peacefulness settled over her, a feeling she hadn't remembered ever experiencing, a comfort and warmth that brought new meaning to the word "home." Her chest tightened as her parents came into view, their kiss making Gaeren duck his head, which let Aeliana see herself as a toddler, racing for her parents, who then welcomed Gaeren into their family's hug.

The daisies kept returning, some in the field where they spent most afternoons, but some by the creek or the house, forming as the toddler grew excited or burst into laughter. Her chubby hands always scooped them up, offering them to the nearest family member as a physical token of her love.

The images seemed to go on forever until at last her mother shoved her—or Gaeren—aside, telling him to take Aeliana to the creek. Cold fear laced through her bones as they ran and hid, as she made one last daisy chain to distract her younger self. The last images left her breathless as Arvid and Vera came into view, and a blinding light took them all away.

When the images disappeared, it took Aeliana several moments to reorient herself to the woods with pines instead of oaks, the rising Sun instead of the blackness of night. Her cheeks were wet with tears, and Gaeren's forehead still pressed against hers. She stayed that way for a moment, wishing she didn't have to break the contact and feel his absence. His breathing shifted, and she knew he'd pulled himself from his own memories, and still they sat, hands clasped against his armband, foreheads pressed together, breath mingling.

"I never stopped looking for you," he whispered, finally breaking the spell. He pulled back and used his thumbs to wipe the tears off her cheeks, even though his own lashes were wet. "I promised your mother I'd keep you safe. But more than that, I promised myself. If I couldn't keep you safe, how could I keep a queen safe—an entire nation?" He dropped his hands and looked away.

"I'm safe now," she said.

He let out a short, bitter laugh, a reminder of what was to come that afternoon. Stars, it made the thing she'd brought him out here to ask that much harder.

"Thank you for sharing that with me." She squeezed his hand, waiting for him to meet her gaze. "I needed to see that, to know. The safety I felt—that's what I'm fighting for tonight."

"The safety you felt was mine." His sad smile made her long for his smirk. "It was my memory, so you felt my feelings. I've never felt more at home than the days I spent with your family. With you." His expression shifted into something unreadable, and he pulled his hand from hers, scratching at his palm. He looked away, and she realized how close they were. How the distance likely didn't feel strange to him when he saw her as a little sister, but how it felt uncomfortably intimate to her, especially considering they were each bonded to someone else.

Her bond mark itched, but she ignored it and held out the second strip.

He took it without comment, frowning as he tied it almost too tightly around her upper arm.

"I have a favor to ask of you," she said. "It's not fair for me to ask, especially after what you showed me, but it's for the good of Vendaras, and I know you care about Vendarans."

He eyed her warily, not making any promises.

She sighed and forged ahead. "Obviously our goal is to find my mother and my blood before Mayvus can brand me. If everything goes right, that's how this night will end. And you know how fond I am of Sylmar's backup plan."

A hint of Gaeren's smirk returned, bolstering her courage.

"I know you don't want them doing blood magic either." The weight of the vial in her pocket suddenly tripled with her guilt. Hopefully she wouldn't have to use it, but if she did, Gaeren might never forgive her. "So, if things don't go as planned, I think you should keep Jasperus from branding me."

He laughed. "I doubt I could stop him unless I killed him, and that's exactly what you're trying to avoid."

She brought her gaze to his and lifted her chin. "You could stop him if you kill me."

His head jerked back, his smile fading.

"You were willing to kill Durriken if it meant saving hundreds more lives."

He shook his head and held up his hands, but she grabbed his hands and spoke over his arguments.

"If Mayvus brands me, she won't hesitate to use me to kill all the rest of you." She blinked away the tears threatening to spill. "I can't live with that. You would be saving me. You would be protecting me from a future I can't live with."

He winced, and she knew she'd found the right way to make him understand.

"This is the best way you can protect me. You can protect me from myself."

He turned away, placing his elbows on his knees and scrubbing his palms over his face.

"It shouldn't come to it," she said, scooting closer and placing a hand on his back, "but if it does, you're the only one I trust to follow through. It has a higher chance of success than Sylmar's backup plan anyway." Every muscle in her body tensed until he turned to face her, his grave face suddenly years older.

"How can you expect me to make a promise like that?" he asked.

She bit her lip. "I don't expect you to, but I hope you will."

He closed his eyes. Aeliana studied the log they sat on, tracing the curve of the knot between them.

"Can you at least promise," she asked, "that if it looks like there's no other way, that if she's going to use me to kill the others, that you'll seriously consider it?"

He let out a long breath and opened his eyes. "If it's the only way for me to stop Mayvus from using you to kill…" He shook his head as if he couldn't believe what he was saying. "Then I will kill you first."

She slumped over with her relief. "Thank you," she whispered.

He wrapped his arm around her and tucked her head under his chin, sending a new sort of warmth straight to her belly.

"Don't expect me to say you're welcome."

Gaeren could hardly look at her the rest of the morning. Sylmar gave some sort of rousing speech that Aeliana barely heard, then had her step on a stump next to him and raise a fist in solidarity. The crowd of men and women cheered, but instead of feeling bolstered, she felt sick, wondering how many would return that night.

The majority of the troops were heading south in multiple waves, making a wide berth along the coast of Vendaras to approach the fortress from the southeast. One group would be splitting off for the western gate while the other settled at the eastern gate. Aeliana's group would be leaving last, as they planned to watch the eastern gate get breached before making their way through the dungeon's entrance.

Aeliana smoothed down the ill-fitting black leather uniform and its mauve vest. She strapped on her bow and quiver and mounted her mare before lining up with Sylmar, Cyrus, and Velden, her hands shaking against the reins.

"You could still stay here." Aeliana leaned over toward Cyrus. "The prayers you offer up will likely be as effective as your sword and far less dangerous to your health."

"I could," Cyrus said. "But when we get the golden arrow and I return home, I would never hear the end of it from all my older brothers." He urged his horse forward, joining Kendalyhn, Lukai, and Holm in the front. He should be safe enough with three experienced fighters, two of whom were progenies. Aeliana almost convinced herself it was true, but then she remembered Gams on the floor of the Stargazer, her body writhing in pain.

"If you convince everyone you care about to stay back," Sylmar said, "none of them will be there to help you."

"And none of them will be there to get hurt by me." Aeliana's mare pranced uneasily, likely sensing Aeliana's nerves.

Velden sent a squirt of water in her direction. "Most of us have been risking our lives for far less noble causes since before you were born."

Marnok, Jasperus, Iris, and Orra rode past, Orra still looking too sickly to come along, but, like Cyrus, she refused to be left behind. Seeing them all in the uniforms of Mayvus' soldiers was like having strangers in camp. The red on black held a foreboding quality that left her on edge. She focused on the purple armbands, counting them all off.

She watched as Gaeren said farewell to his men, charging Larkos and Riveran to look after the young sailors while Gaeren came to protect—or kill—her. Every man and woman prepared to march bore a purple armband. After delivering uniforms the night before, Felk and his clan had left to spread the word among the clans they'd joined, promising to meet Aeliana just outside Mayvus' gates.

Now she nervously wished they'd agreed to travel the rest of the way together.

Gaeren was the last of their dozen to mount up, and he took the final spot next to Aeliana.

The beauty of the surrounding land belied the darkness Mayvus' fortress held. With summer fully underway, the rolling fields of grass and warm babbling brooks hinted at a tranquility none of the travelers could tap into.

It only took a couple of hours to reach the coastline, where Velden lifted his nose to the salty scent. As the Sun reached its zenith, Aeliana's group left their horses behind and trekked another quarter mile, following the coast to the forest dividing the fortress from the sea. From this point, they could see the sheer black rock wall of the Myndren Mountains stretching to the sky, but the pines blocked their view of the nearby fortress walls.

Any closer and Mayvus would realize she was under attack.

If she wasn't already anticipating it. Mayvus had her blood. She knew they were coming for it. Did it really matter if they were a day early?

They came across two sentries who were easily dispatched by Kendalyhn's arrows, then they eventually left the shore to settled in a copse of trees. Waves lapped in the distance behind them, but the small valley at the base of the Myndren Mountains stretched out five hundred feet before them. Murmurs of distant shouts and laughter carried on the wind. From Aeliana's vantage point, she mostly saw rock where the fortress blended in with the mountain's side. She shifted to the left and crouched until she could see more through the gap of foliage.

Her jaw dropped as she took in Mayvus' fortress. The fierce black structure's height seemed to defy gravity. Even though she knew it was carved into the mountain's wall, there had to be at least fifteen levels spanning the base to the highest tower, and that was just what she could see above the outer walls. Beyond the walls, a roiling sea of armed men camped at the fortress' base. Their weapons remained sheathed, and drinks flowed freely—their Summer Solstice celebration already well underway a day early.

If that many were housed outside the gates, how many more were inside them?

Guards posted at the edge of their camp scanned the woods, and she froze as the one nearest turned her way.

"Relax, Aeliana," Lukai whispered. His breath tickled her ear. "They can't see us from here. The forest is too dense."

Her anger flared at his nearness and confidence, as if he hadn't betrayed her to Sylmar. The sensation battled with her bond mark, which insisted he was safety, that she wanted him close. It didn't even matter that he was right. On top of the forest being thick, at least one hundred feet of fields separated them from the guards. They were safe for now. Aeliana backed up, and her stomach gave a lurch when she saw her own dagger pulled out, her knuckles white where she clutched its grip. She didn't even remember pulling it from her boot.

Gaeren eyed her from across the others, his eyebrows raised as he took in her dagger. She could practically hear him asking if she was willing to use it, which made her think of the only time she had, when it had sunk into the chest of a winex. She scowled as she replaced the dagger.

Gaeren squeezed between Kendalyhn and Holm until he stood near Aeliana.

"No sign of Felkie?" he asked, his teasing tone putting her more on edge than at ease.

"Don't let his clan hear you call him that," she said.

Gaeren snorted. "He called you 'Mama.' He dug his own grave."

Aeliana shivered, the jest hitting too close to home. "He'll come. His mate is in there."

"Well, if he doesn't come soon enough," Sylmar said, "we stick with our original plan. The pirates fall back in the center line while we sneak through from the west. We use the dungeon entrance with or without the winex."

"What if Felk was lying?" Kendalyhn asked, probably voicing everyone's concerns. "If he doesn't show up, isn't it likely to be a trick?"

"You sifted his soul," Sylmar said. "Of all people, you should know best that his loyalty to Aeliana is greater than any new loyalty to his clan."

Eleven pairs of eyes turned Aeliana's way. She swallowed hard, not sure if she should defend Felk or let Sylmar's words be enough. Kendalyhn scowled and resumed watching the fortress' base, turning her back on Aeliana.

As time passed, Sylmar's agitation grew. Finally, shouts met Aeliana's ears as the news of an attack rolled through the soldiers like a wave. Velden's eyes closed, his hand grasping General Nels' handkerchief. The general was supposed to be near the western gates. Once they saw the eastern gate fall, and once Velden sensed the general's men had breached the western gates, they'd be free to follow the wall back around the eastern edge toward the dungeon's northeastern entrance near the sea.

The entrance would be difficult to find without Felk.

"They're making good progress," Lukai announced from his lookout point in a tree. "Oh, the eastern gate is already breached!"

Aeliana risked peeking through the edge of the forest line to see the last of the gate get raised as their soldiers surged toward it. She couldn't help noticing that just as many Zealots poured out to attack Recreants as Recreants moved in to attack Zealots.

"The western gate..." Velden frowned, making Aeliana wonder how far his pneumatic skills could sense what General Nels was experiencing through the handkerchief.

"Are they through?" Sylmar asked. "We need to go in—now."

Velden shook his head. "I thought maybe—there are Zealots outside the gates, fighting. But I can't tell..."

Aeliana peeked through the trees, trying to make sense of the blur of black and red mixing with browns and greens. It seemed like her eyes played tricks on her as the black and red quickly multiplied, outnumbering the Recreants in a matter of moments.

Something was wrong.

"Oh no." Velden's eyes opened wide, his panic confirming her fears. "The western gate wasn't breached; it was opened by the Zealots. They had a counterattack ready. They're sweeping their slaughter toward the east, right at us."

CHAPTER 78

"Do we need to retreat?" Gaeren calculated how quickly he could get Daisy to *Starspeed*. It hadn't been part of any of their plans, but they'd underestimated Mayvus. This was an impossible feat.

"No. We need to go in," Sylmar said.

"You said we needed both gates breached," Daisy argued.

Velden shook his head. "We needed the soldiers leaving from both gates. This isn't the way we thought it would happen, but it's still taking them away from the fortress. If they're coming this way, our only option is to go in."

A high-pitched howl broke through the heat of the afternoon, sending a host of birds flying from the forest canopy. Even though Felk's call had been expected, everyone stiffened, weapons drawn. In the distance, shouts from the camp grew louder. Daisy let out a relieved sigh and peeked through the trees once more.

"Sweet Stars," she murmured.

"Is Felk all right?" Gaeren asked, unable to see past her shoulder.

"He's been recruiting," she said in awe.

Gaeren leaned past her, expecting to see a few dozen winex heading for the soldiers. Instead, he took in the sight of Felk standing tall amidst a swarm of hundreds of sinewy silver bodies filling the field that separated their forest hideout from the retreating soldiers.

Dozens of winex loped past Felk, snarling in some sort of frenzy, like the nearness of that many men brought on a hunger for their flesh.

"That's impossible." Gaeren's eyes burned as the Sun reflected off the waves of silver skin. He'd never seen so many winex in his life, let alone in one place at one time. The others around them took turns peeking through the trees, their excitement overriding their need to be quiet, especially since the winex howls drowned out any noise their own voices might have made.

"He said he'd found a few clans," Daisy said. "And Mayvus was taking their blood. Maybe she was helping their population grow over time so she could use their blood. Except they don't have starblood. So she wouldn't want them for more magic." The crease between her brow deepened. "That's still probably a bad sign, isn't it?"

"For now we'll be grateful. Let the other possibilities be a problem for tomorrow." Gaeren grinned at her.

"If we live until tomorrow," she muttered.

"Pull that dagger out if you're worried."

She frowned, pulling an arrow from her quiver instead.

Felk howled again.

"That's our signal." Sylmar raised a hand, beckoning them all forward. Cyrus, Holm, Jasperus, and Iris moved past him, swords and daggers drawn. Gaeren joined Velden, Lukai, and Sylmar, their weapons ready, starlocks humming with anticipation. Kendalyhn, Orra, Marnok, and Daisy split, flanking the others with their bows drawn tight.

They moved as one, but when they stepped through the trees, the two winex nearest turned, their snarls turning to wild growls that drew several others. The winex snapped their jaws and flashed their multiple rows of teeth, inching closer.

"Felk?" Daisy called.

Over the heads of the other winex, Felk turned and howled again.

The winex shook their heads as if to clear them, then eyed the purple bands on everyone's arms. One leaned in to sniff Daisy, and Gaeren stepped toward her, tightening his grip on the hilt of his sword. But the winex leaned away before turning back to follow the crowd. As he did, Felk bounded through the winex like a fish swimming upstream, then skidded to a stop before Daisy.

"Come," Felk said, turning to run alongside the winex toward the massive outer wall of the fortress. The horde of winex filled the path, forcing Gaeren and the others to break formation to follow Felk. Gaeren couldn't take his eyes off the roiling mass of silver backs as he and Aeliana caught up to their friend.

"How did you convince them all to come?" Gaeren asked.

Felk didn't slow his pace. "How did you convince your men?"

"They were already looking for an excuse to go up against Mayvus," Gaeren said. "They would have come with or without me."

"Then our situations are not so different," Felk shouted over his shoulder before darting right at the wall where the other winex turned left.

For a moment, Gaeren and the others hesitated, watching the winex travel toward the open gate. By now Mayvus' soldiers had seen them, and arrows were flying. The winex came anyway, crawling through the gate like ants swarming a loaf of bread.

The ones who were too impatient to get through the gate clambered over the wall, and screams echoed across the distance. Large numbers of winex were left behind, already dead or dying from the arrows. They had been efficient, but at a great cost. They'd functioned more like a hive fighting for the greater cause. The winex jumped off the wall, teeth bared as they likely landed on Zealots beyond the wall.

Gaeren couldn't make out any of his men from this distance, but he studied the place where they should be, praying the Sun might keep them safe.

"Felk's clans might actually make it harder for the soldiers to fake the need to retreat," Daisy said.

Gaeren let out a strangled laugh. "I can't decide if that's a good or bad thing."

Felk whined, and they turned back to follow him along the outer wall, nearer to the sea and farther from the melee.

Even though the ocean's waves grew louder, the forest grew denser, this portion of the wall not maintained as well as the entrance. When Felk finally stopped, Gaeren had to squint to see how the cracks in the stone made up a door. Felk pulled on a few divots in its surface, sliding it open with a grinding motion that made most everyone wince.

Sunlight poured into the hall, revealing an intricate smooth stone floor that would have fit in Gaeren's palace if it had been given a festive rug. The walls were dark and rough, and the blackness beyond the Sun's light was a gaping maw. Gaeren tuned in to his surroundings, hesitant to use up magic he could no longer replenish once he entered Mayvus' dungeons but not willing to step into the unknown.

Faint impressions remained—the squeals of winex being dragged forward, the grunts of soldiers as they fought the wild beasts. Nothing pleasant, but nothing unexpected or alarming. Felk lifted his nose to sniff the air, and a tremor ran through his body as if he sensed or smelled the same things as Gaeren. He whined and stepped forward, but Sylmar placed a hand on his arm.

"Felk alone frees the winex so he can explain the purple bands," Sylmar reminded them, his gaze taking in each of their group. This had been one of his stipulations when they'd agreed to both accept help from Felk and offer help in return. "Kill any soldiers you need to, but if you can save one to question, that would be better. The more information we can gather, the sooner we can find what we came for."

Gaeren smiled as Daisy exchanged her bow for the dagger, its daisy flashing in the Sun's light. Kendalyhn, Marnok, and Orra made similar swaps, but Kendalyhn inched her way to the center of the line with Gaeren. The two of them were Sylmar's weapons to gain information by sifting souls and tuning in to memories.

Felk led the way. His bare feet and hands were silent on the stone, but he let out an occasional whine that echoed off the walls, like he couldn't contain the shared sorrow of whatever they were about to encounter. The farther they went in, the more the blackness engulfed them, forcing them to rely on Felk's eyes and nose to guide them. Water dripped from somewhere deeper in, and sweat beaded on Gaeren's brow, more from the dank air than any exertion. They passed a dozen halls and doors, making turns according to Felk's intuition. The passageway banked left, and soon an echo of whimpers greeted them. Felk's whining intensified, and his pace increased.

A pinprick of light grew larger until they reached an oak door. Its small window revealed torchlight, and silver blood glinted in patches on the floor. Velden picked the lock on the door, and Gaeren tensed as several of the others stepped into the chamber. No one cried out for battle, but Felk let out a small howl, and fists banged on iron from within the room.

"Hush," Daisy whispered, and Gaeren craned his neck to see beyond Holm's hulking form. A narrow hallway stretched before them, ending at the base of a staircase that rose into more blackness. A single cell door revealed several pairs of silvery hands gripping the bars. He couldn't make out more than a handful of emaciated bodies, but before he could stop himself, he tuned in to the presence of at least a dozen more behind them, most too injured to be a threat, but a few shackled and still brimming with hatred.

"We've come to rescue you," Felk whispered, and the banging grew louder, punctuated by more howls and whines.

"Make them stop," Sylmar said with a growl. "Unless you want them slaughtered by the guards."

"We want at least one guard to come, right?" Gaeren asked, glancing toward the stairs.

"Six will come," Orra murmured from his left.

He turned to squint at the strange expression on her face. "Do you know exactly what's going to happen?"

She shook her head. "My power has become as unpredictable as Enla's. I could search the future for hundreds of ways to find Mayvus, but I can't guarantee which ways will hold success. But every path holds six guards."

"That's convenient for no one," he muttered. Still, six guards was helpful information.

Velden bent down to pick the lock but cried out and stepped back as several winex hands scratched at his.

"He won't hurt you," Felk said. "We're taking you home."

"Felk?" The hesitant voice came from deeper in the chamber, and Felk's eyes slid shut.

"Lilik? Yes, it's me."

A new set of hands came through the bars, and Felk gripped them in his own. A strange purring sound came from within the cell, and the rest of the hands pulled away, allowing Velden to work at the lock once more.

"They've taken our eggs." Lilik's voice came from inside, her words rushed with panic. "If they've buried them, I don't know where."

The other winex picked up their howls again. A click sounded from the top of the stairs, nearly drowned out by their cries.

"I told you I'd snuff your light if you kept up that racket," a man called.

Footsteps thudded on the stone, but Gaeren couldn't make out if it was a single soldier or the six Orra had predicted. Jasperus beckoned Gaeren and Holm forward just as the man's boots came into view.

His threats turned to mumbles as his knees and torso hit the light, but his eyes barely had time to widen before Jasperus' sword sliced through his gut. The man fell to his knees with a groan and reached for his wound as Jasperus pulled his sword back.

When the soldier reached for the dagger at his side, Jasperus sliced the blade across the man's throat, finishing the job. But the man's cry had sent up the alarm, and more boots and shouts could be heard from above. Since the soldiers were forced to come down single file, the next one walked into the same trap as the soldier before him, but the others caught on and were quicker to fight back. Gaeren and Jasperus were each left to parry with a soldier while Holm and Lukai dispatched the final two guards.

The soldier before Gaeren was older but still quick on his feet, matching every thrust with his own blocks and advances. The scuff of their boots echoed on the walls, joined by their grunts and the howls of the winex. More than once, Gaeren could have sent the soldier to his death, but he did the math, watching as Jasperus finished off the seventh soldier.

They needed this one for information.

The soldier feinted left, leaving his weapon exposed. When he did it a second time, Gaeren was ready to disarm him, but Sylmar's molten staff slammed between them, knocking both of their swords from their hands. Gaeren recovered faster, only falling to one knee, while the soldier fell to his backside, scrambling back on his hands and feet.

Gaeren's face heated as he reached for his sword, but the soldier paled, his own sword far out of reach.

"S-Sylmar?" the man asked. "What are you doing here?"

"Miklous." Sylmar gave an almost respectful nod in the soldier's direction. "I see they've demoted you to guard duty."

Daisy and the others came closer, several holding their noses against the reek of blood and bowel spilled on the floor. Velden and Felk remained behind, likely still working at the lock.

Miklous recovered and managed a sneer. "After you left, Mayvus wasn't sure she could trust me."

Gaeren stood and turned to Sylmar, eyebrows raised. "After you left?"

Miklous laughed, then slowly stood, his breaths still heaving from their fight. "Have you not told them of your time with Mayvus?"

Gaeren stiffened and glanced at Daisy, whose face held an equal measure of shock.

"We're well aware that he switched sides," Iris said, stepping forward.

Miklous raised his hands in defense as Sylmar shoved his still glowing staff closer to the soldier's face.

"Maybe you're not all aware…" Miklous' black eyes glittered as he focused on Daisy. "I'm guessing there's a lot of things you didn't tell the child."

Daisy frowned, glancing at Sylmar.

"He's not the only former Zealot," Jasperus said. "Mayvus has a way of making enemies even among her followers."

Miklous scanned the group, his gaze lingering on each face as though assessing who had once been a Zealot. "So she does."

"Where is she?" Sylmar asked.

"It looks like you brought friends, so by now she could be anywhere." He shrugged. "She could be at the south tower, assessing her defenses. She could be at the northern keep, hiding away with her sister. Or she might have already left. Durriken comes quickly when she calls."

Daisy's eyes slid shut.

"Gaeren," Sylmar snapped, angling his head at Gaeren while keeping Miklous at bay with his staff. "Tune in to his memories."

Miklous smiled and closed his eyes.

Gaeren complied, doubting he'd find anything of value with Miklous' confident defiance. He stepped forward and placed a hand on the soldier's wrist, rushing his way through the man's memories. Mayvus' face sprang before his mind countless times, but nothing that would give a clue as to her current whereabouts.

He stepped away and shook his head, his starlock burning with his annoyance. What a waste of magic.

"Check his hands," Sylmar said.

Miklous laughed again, holding out his hands for inspection. "What, you think she got rid of my brand?" A dark mark rested on his palm, not unlike the bond mark on Gaeren's palm. But this one looked crudely done, the mark having bubbled up far larger and darker. Like Durriken's brand had been.

Sylmar's face hardened, his scars looking harsher in the torchlight.

"She knows you're here with me. So, yes"—Miklous leaned forward, feigning a conspiratorial whisper—"she could even be headed this way." He barked out a deeper laugh, sending a chill through Gaeren's chest.

Before Gaeren could even think to ask a question, Sylmar's staff shifted to a shimmering sword, then swung down on Miklous' arm, cleaving his hand from his wrist. Gaeren jumped back but still felt a spray of blood hit his face.

Miklous howled, cradling his stump to his chest as blood spurted and leaked across the floor and then his clothes. The others all took a step back, wary either of the blood or Sylmar's rage. Sylmar's sword shifted back to a staff, but he ignored Miklous, bending down to poke at the soldier's severed hand.

Blood dripped from the hand, quickly draining it of color, but the mark also paled, the magic of the brand fading with it. Sylmar leaned on his staff and rose to his feet. "Thank you for that demonstration."

Panic clawed up Gaeren's throat, and he turned to Daisy, who tucked her hand against her chest. Her eyes held fear, but then her face hardened with resolve as she caught his gaze. He shook his head and backed away, but she reached out her hand and snaked it around his wrist.

"Which is better, killing me or taking my hand?" she hissed.

"I don't want to do either."

"You promised." Her grip tightened on his wrist, and he looked away.

"I know. I did. I will." He clenched his teeth, not sure how to say that it was all a last resort he didn't expect to have to do. He didn't see how he could ever cut off her hand, let alone kill her. It was too much to ask.

Miklous' screams drowned out any more explanation Gaeren might have given.

"You're crazy." Miklous' body shook even as he stumbled back to the floor. "She always said you were."

The hall filled with the shuffling of feet and whimpers only slightly held at bay. Then the shuffling shifted to a collective sniffing, and the whimpers turned to howls.

"Felk," Sylmar called without looking back. "Did you explain the purple bands to our friends?"

"Yes," the winex said from the back of the hall. "They've all agreed."

"Good." Sylmar pointed his staff at the stairway. "Felk can take the winex out to join the soldiers. It's time to resume our search."

Daisy bit her lip, standing on tiptoe to get one last glimpse of Felk, but he pushed forward until he could give her a hug.

"Thank you," he said. "Stay safe."

She choked out a laugh. "Sending your people into battle doesn't feel like a fair trade for picking a couple of locks."

"We would have come anyway," Felk said. "This is our fight as much as yours. Maybe an alliance like this can break through the next cycle."

Daisy's smile wavered. They all knew how unlikely that was.

"We'll remember your faithfulness even if you don't," Gaeren said, surprising himself as much as them. "I can't imagine that won't count for something with the new moon. Maybe you'll have the patience to let me give you a memory or two. That's all it would take."

Felk nodded in his direction, but Jasperus and Holm were already leading the way up the stairs, stepping over the broken bodies of the soldiers. The others all followed, Gaeren and Kendalyhn taking their place in the center of the line with Daisy close behind.

As Gaeren reached the top of the stairs, Sylmar's voice rang out from below as he addressed the winex. "You see our purple bands? This man doesn't have one. He was one of your captors, and he's now the first of your victims."

The frenzied snarls of starved winex joined with Miklous' screams in echoing off the walls.

CHAPTER 79

AELIANA COULDN'T STOP SHAKING as they made their way through the guards' room. She'd known she wasn't prepared to face Mayvus, but she'd thought she was prepared for battle. Watching the others take down soldier after soldier wore on her and made her question if she could kill when the need arose. And then to have Sylmar mutilate and discard Miklous…

As they spread through the guards' room, checking the closets and washroom for any lingering men, she positioned herself near Sylmar. "You didn't have to do that," she murmured.

"I did." Sylmar shifted, planting his staff between them and forcing her to stop and look up at him. "Now we know that if cutting out your mother's brand won't work, we can cut off her hand."

She shivered even though she'd suggested the same thing to Gaeren. "That's not what I meant. You didn't have to feed him to the winex."

He grunted. "They would have fed on him anyway. This way they're more likely to follow the rule about the purple armbands."

Aeliana's stomach churned as she recalled the sound of teeth on flesh and the fade of whimpers.

"It makes me wonder what other lines you're willing to cross." She moved to sidestep him and join the others, who checked the adjoining soldiers' dormitory.

His eyes burned with fury, and he grabbed her arm. "I told you I'm doing what I think is best for you and for Vendaras. I warned you that you won't always like it."

She shook his hand off. "How long did you serve Mayvus? How much of her ways are still ingrained in your methods? Did you partake in blood magic too?"

His beard shifted as his jaw clenched, and he swallowed hard and looked away. "You may not have known my history, but that doesn't mean I've kept it secret. When this is over, you'll get your answers. The important thing is that now we're both working to stop her."

"Fine." She forced the word out before joining the others now at the door to the main hall.

"I think we should split up," Holm said, turning from the door. "Miklous wasn't wrong. She could be in a number of places now. She could keep moving as we search, sending us in circles."

Marnok frowned. "Is it worth it to weaken whichever party inevitably finds her?"

"I doubt she's left if she knows Aeliana is here," Sylmar said. "There's a small chance she's overseeing the battle, but the odds are much higher that she's with Emeris or even preparing for the branding ceremony."

Aeliana squirmed, tightening her hold on her dagger so the grip rubbed against her palm. The bond mark was bad enough, but having a brand like Miklous' would feel like some sort of leech living under her skin.

"I could take a few of us to the south tower, and if she's not there, we could meet you at the northern keep," Holm said.

"I'll go with you," Orra said, placing a hand on his back.

"Thank you." Holm tugged at his too-tight vest.

Aeliana got the impression he would have picked anyone else before Orra.

"It's not a bad idea to have more archers up on the parapets," Gaeren said. "Maybe Kendalyhn should join them. You already have disguises. If you relieve one of Mayvus' soldiers at an arrowslit, you can help the people still attacking the castle." He shifted from one foot to the other. "At least whichever ones haven't started the intentional withdrawal."

Aeliana didn't need magic to sense the weight of his thoughts—the burden of the men he'd left behind. She hated the idea of splitting up, but his fear became her own. She patted the vial in her chest, the insanity of attempting to brand a dragon no longer seeming so ridiculous.

"Holm, Marnok, Kendalyhn, and Orra can head for the southern tower," Sylmar conceded. "Send word immediately if she's there. Aid those on the ground if you can, but if it's too late—for any reason—come help us instead."

Gaeren's jaw tightened, but he nodded along with everyone else.

When Holm opened the door, they split ways, Holm taking his three archers and Sylmar leading the others toward the northern keep. The halls were strangely deserted, but Aeliana supposed the soldiers had all been called to arms. They went past dozens of doors, some open to reveal disheveled bed chambers or a paper-strewn war room or chancery, but most remained closed.

Sylmar had spent hours studying the maps of Mayvus' fortress, but he ran through them like someone who had known the halls well. What had he done for Mayvus before defecting? And why hadn't he told Aeliana? She couldn't help feeling misled, like the truth had been kept from her in order to manipulate her. He'd always been gruff, but she'd at least trusted him to look out for her.

Now she didn't know what to think.

Sylmar and Velden cut down the few men they came across, and Iris and Cyrus did the same to those who came up from behind. Most had been sent out to fight, just as they'd hoped, but it still became glaringly clear that Aeliana was being coddled in the center of the group. As much as she hated it, she wasn't about to volunteer to step forward and take out the next person who rounded the corner. Not after stepping across bodies and slipping on the blood of fallen men.

Men who looked exactly like Gaeren, Cyrus, or Lukai in the uniforms they'd stolen. Some with Sun-bleached hair like Gaeren's, their mouths frozen in shock instead of a smirk. Some with freckles like Cyrus, though none as pale or red-haired. One had Lukai's golden curls and upturned nose, the devastating sight of his broken body on the floor making her regret holding her bondmate's actions from the night before against him.

Eventually the halls turned to stairs leading to the tower in the north, the keep that might hold Aeliana's mother and aunt. The stone here was darker and rougher, more like the dungeons where they'd found the winex. She supposed they were in the older areas of the fortress, but she couldn't help imagining that those stones had also soaked in more blood, had held more of the dark spirits over the years.

The stairs opened up to a final hall filled with heavy oak doors. By now the Sun was lower in the sky, its light spilling through windows, highlighting the dust in the air as if to give false hope that the area was abandoned. Sylmar slowed down, sending Velden, Jasperus, and Lukai out through the rooms ahead. As each was determined to be clear, they inched forward. Sweat ran down Aeliana's brow. They were taking too long. If Mayvus felt threatened, she could be performing the branding ceremony right now.

She studied the scars on her palms, eyeing the dark mark of her bond, wondering if Mayvus would brand over it or use the other palm. Or was that something determined by the Stars? Or Sun? She squeezed her hands into fists, letting her fingernails dig into both scars and bond. When she glanced up, Gaeren was studying her, his face unreadable.

A shout came from the room ahead—it sounded like Jasperus— then the sound of steel on steel. Sylmar, Cyrus, and Gaeren rushed forward, but Iris held Aeliana back in the hall.

"They need our help," Aeliana said.

"You can help them far more by surviving, love," Iris said. "They might need you to heal them."

If they survived.

Aeliana wanted to add the words, but they stuck in her throat as the sounds of grunts and reverberating metal grew louder. Lukai and Velden came from two other rooms, following the sounds of the skirmish, confirming Aeliana's suspicion that it was Jasperus who'd first cried out.

She closed her eyes, imagining blades slicing through each of her comrades, wounds too deep to be healed by her limited magic. A coldness swept over her, and she shivered, trying to redirect her thoughts, but with the goosebumps came an overwhelming sense of familiarity.

She opened her eyes and stood straighter, leaning into the sensation with fresh understanding.

"The dark spirits," she whispered.

Iris stiffened. "What?"

"Someone's doing blood magic."

Before Iris could stop her, Aeliana rushed toward the fight.

CHAPTER 80

Orra's head ached as possibilities flashed through her mind. She hadn't meant to use the magic, hadn't wanted to waste it. But in her weakened state, it was harder to control it. She followed Holm across the battlements, crouching low to avoid arrows flying from their own people at the fortress' base. But her mind sifted through a hundred scenarios, her eyes seeing various avenues of death and destruction instead of the stones beneath her feet.

Splitting up had been the only way to keep everyone alive at the time, but even then, too many of the paths still held death.

"We should go back," Marnok hissed. "All of these soldiers are occupied fighting. There's no sign of Mayvus."

Orra's mind went in reverse, starting the process over again, sifting through all the options stemming from Marnok's suggestion. She shook her head to clear it, then winced as pain lanced through the back of her neck. She hadn't had enough time in the Sun's light. Wasn't sure she ever could anymore. Not if she wanted to reach her previous potential.

"What about Gaeren's idea?" Kendalyhn asked. "Should we steal parapets and use up our arrows? It's not like they'll be any good once we join the others. Unless Mayvus is riding her dragon." Her mouth turned down.

Orra's mind raced in a different direction, flying through the fortress walls to calculate the number of scenarios in which that might happen. She grasped the sides of her head and squeezed her eyes shut, willing her mind to settle and focus, to hold the magic at bay until it could be put to better use.

"Are you all right?" Marnok asked. He placed a hand on her arm, and she sensed his efforts to push his energy into her. He still wasn't aware of the extent of his power or what left it limited, but that wasn't her secret to reveal. And it made no difference, because his energy couldn't touch her. Their magic was like oil and water, something that used to make her feel empowered but now left her lonely.

"I'll be fine," she said.

"Those three," Kendalyhn whispered, pointing at three soldiers kneeling at arrowslits, their quivers nearly empty. "They were terrified to go into battle, even scared to come out on the parapets. They're only here because desertion means being fed to Durriken."

Orra's chest ached, and her mind grew desperate to search that truth out for herself. Dragons didn't typically eat humans, but did this one? Had she been wrong about him? She no longer trusted herself or her magic, let alone her intuitions.

They all rushed forward, and Holm spoke with more authority than Orra had ever heard from him.

"Take your break. Refill your quivers. Then relieve the next group." He gestured at the soldiers to the right, but the three frightened men were already gathering their supplies. One hesitated, looking at Orra a little too long, the fuzz on his upper lip revealing his youth.

"Go on," she said. "Maybe the fight will be over before you have to return."

His face brightened, then he schooled his features. "They've started retreating, but Zane wants us to follow. Says the queen wants us to defeat them all. When our arrows can no longer reach, we're to head to the outer courtyard."

Orra nodded and took his place against the wall facing the bailey. "Then I'll see you there."

She didn't wait for him to reply. She wedged herself against the stone until she could see through the arrowslit. The destruction below teased her mind, making her want to weigh out the options and dig through each scenario, but she reined in her power, focusing on the truth of the moment and what needed to be done. A blanket of bodies stretched from the inner courtyard to the gate, a patchwork of black and red leather, grey skin and brown. The Sun glinted off pools of red and silver blood, like jewels sewn on. She swallowed hard, then switched to an arrowslit at the opposite wall. The trail of bodies extended past the gate, thinning out as the carnage drew closer to the forest line, where a number of soldiers and winex still fought.

"It's almost too late already," Marnok said, his voice muffled as he leaned against the arrowslit beside her. Most of the soldiers were getting too far from the castle wall to take aim at them, but not all.

Orra nocked an arrow and pulled back on her bow, letting her eyes hone in on a target. "Forgive me for what I must do," she murmured, "and may the Sun have mercy on your soul." She let the arrow fly but set her sights on another before it hit.

Three more hit their targets before Kendalyhn gasped.

"Aren't those Gaeren's men?"

Orra pulled away from the wall to see Kendalyhn peering over the opposite edge toward the bailey and inner walls. Four men held enemy shields over their heads, shields they'd clearly stolen since their leathers were brown instead of black. They went against the flow of men exiting the castle, cutting them down before the soldiers could realize the shields hid their enemy. Arrows glanced off the bronze-plated wood, but Orra winced as one struck a calf and the man stumbled. She caught a glimpse of Breeve and Larkos as the men righted themselves.

"What are they doing?" Holm asked, his nervous tick returning.

Orra couldn't help smiling. "Going against orders."

Kendalyhn let out a huff of air but raised her bow, taking out a few of Mayvus' soldiers heading toward the sailors.

"Hey!" A soldier to their right pulled back from the battlement's edge. "Watch your aim!" He glared at Kendalyhn, who shrugged apologetically. The soldier's glare turned suspicious, but he soon went back to his arrowslit.

"We can't stay here much longer," Marnok whispered. "Otherwise, we'll end up fighting all the soldiers up here on top of those down below."

Orra peeked over the edge again, watching as Larkos, Breeve, Riveran, and Thallahan all made it safely into the main hall. Not that they would be very safe in there.

Holm licked his lips, glancing at the Sun. "Maybe we should get the sailors from below before joining the others in the northern keep."

It was a solid plan, but would it prevent them from getting to Emeris? Would it keep Aeliana alive? Would it stop Orra from getting the golden arrow?

"Good idea," Marnok said. "They'll want to defend Gaeren, and we could use the extra hands."

Orra resisted the urge to search out the possibilities. It was a waste of magic, effort that relied on her own power. She knew now that she should seek out the Sun. She didn't need to see all the possible paths if she saw the path the Sun wanted her to take. But it had been too long since she'd truly communed with the Sun. She wasn't sure she'd see the right path. Not after all her years of failures.

Kendalyhn grumbled but followed the others as they wound their way through the battlement stairs and past servant's quarters. Thanks to their stolen uniforms, they didn't get a second glance from the soldiers they passed—not until they reached a lower level near the main hall.

"You don't want to go down there," one soldier said, gesturing behind him. "They set winex on the fortress. Don't know how they did it. Winex!" The man shook his head and kept walking, not bothering to notice whether or not they took his advice. Orra and Marnok exchanged glances, then all four of them adjusted their purple bands, ensuring their visibility.

Another hall and staircase later, the frenzy of the winex feasting echoed across the stone. Orra's stomach turned, her thoughts aligning more with Mayvus' soldier. She didn't want to go down there.

Sweat dripped down Holm's face as they approached the south entrance to the main hall.

"I think we should find a way around that room," he whispered.

"I'll check," Kendalyhn said. "If the sailors are still there, and if I can get their attention, I'll have them come this way. If not, maybe I can see where we can reach them faster."

Holm's quick nod sent Kendalyhn through the door, leaving Orra with Marnok and Holm.

"They're probably not even in there," Marnok said, voicing Orra's thoughts. "They've probably already headed toward the northern keep. It's not like they'd sit around in the hall with all those winex."

With each moment that passed, Orra hoped they'd made the right choice. By now, they could have been in the northern keep, aiding the others and finding the golden arrow.

When Kendalyhn slipped back through the door, she was on her knees. She pulled the door shut behind her and stood. "The banister barely hid me, but the slats allowed me to see the entire room. They're not there."

"Then we go to the northern keep," Holm said. They all turned back toward the passageways, gauging which way might get them there the fastest.

A click rang through the hall, followed by a hiss erupting from behind them.

When Orra turned, she caught a glimpse of a winex down on all fours as he slinked his way through the doorway Kendalyhn had just vacated. His licked his lips before baring his dozens of sharp, pointy teeth.

"We have purple bands," Marnok said, lifting his arm toward the winex. "We'll honor our agreement if you honor it too."

"Felk made a promise," the winex said with a cackle. "He does not speak for me."

Kendalyhn frowned. "We're helping to free you from Mayvus."

"Or we helped you." The winex shrugged and continued advancing.

Kendalyhn pulled out her dagger, but before he got within range, Marnok loosed an arrow. At that short distance, the arrow drove deep into the winex's belly, making it hunch over and groan in pain.

"Let's go." Marnok led the way up the stairs as the winex fell to his knees.

The winex let out a soft howl, and they all paused, holding their breath. A returning howl sounded from the main hall. Kendalyhn's eyes widened, and she raced past Orra, through a servants' door instead of the standard halls. The cramped passageways felt like a trap, the darkness in favor of the winex—but only if the winex had seen and followed.

The rumble of footsteps sounded behind them, occasionally fading as they gained distance, then rising as the crowd of winex likely grew to a stampede. The grunts and howls grew more muffled, but soon they couldn't tell if the winex were only in the main rooms beside them or if they were also in the tight passageways following them.

When the servants' corridor finally spilled out into a larger hall, they all blinked against the light streaming in through the window at the hall's end. In the back of Orra's mind, she breathed a sigh of relief that the Sun still shone. They still had time.

The faint scuffling of the winex grew louder.

Before them, the passageway split around a large iron door. As Holm pulled them to the right, the door's hinges creaked, and it opened.

A tall soldier with skin so pale it seemed translucent frowned down at the four of them, taking in their disheveled uniforms and fast breathing, his eyes narrowing on the purple bands. A dozen others stood behind him, their polished uniforms showing no sign of battle, though all their palms held deep black branding marks.

"What are you doing up here?" the first man asked. "Only generals are allowed in these quarters, and you can't all be messengers." He pulled a sword from his belt, and the rest followed, brandishing their weapons as though ready to run the newcomers through without hearing an explanation.

Orra closed her eyes, searching through the possibilities ending in life, but she was too distracted by the feral growls hitting her ears. She turned to see silver skin rounding the corner and the frenzied winex picking up their pace.

The soldier swore, dropping his sword to pull the iron door back in its place. But half the men inside pushed forward, perhaps unaware of the winex and eager to do battle, forcing the doors back open.

"Come on," Holm shouted, pulling Kendalyhn's arm to the right.

The four of them raced out through a different door onto another battlement. As the door shut behind them, Orra caught sight of the winex leaping on Mayvus' soldiers.

They all paused for a moment, heaving deep breaths and licking their dry lips.

"Let's go," Holm said. "Whichever group survives, they'll be after us."

CHAPTER 81

THE SCENT of blood filled Aeliana's nostrils before she registered the battle around her. Two soldiers lay near the entrance, while two others fought Gaeren and Cyrus, their blades moving at vicious speeds on her left. To her right, Lukai crouched over Jasperus, healing a wound on his side while Velden fended off two other soldiers' swords with his own.

Beyond them all, Arvid and Sylmar faced off, Arvid's hands already drenched in the blood of a third dead soldier at his feet.

Aeliana shivered, wondering if he was taking advantage of the dead soldier's blood or if he'd killed the soldier himself to extract more power.

The goosebumps on her skin rose higher as the familiar sense of dread settled around her. Arvid would let the dark spirits fuse with him. He'd let them take over, knowing they could do far more damage than he could do on his own. She had to stop him before he reached that point.

And she had to resist the spirit's pull on her.

She drew out her dagger with a shaking hand. He would see her coming and probably force her to turn the dagger on herself. He'd always preferred using her blood to his own.

She tossed the dagger behind her and stepped forward, ignoring Iris' calls of protest. The men would have protested too if they weren't already busy fighting for their lives. She winced as a sword tip came deathly close to Gaeren's neck, another slicing the air near Cyrus' liver. But their distraction cleared a path for her to make her way to Arvid.

He reached for the wall behind him, letting it crumble just so he could send the stones flying toward Sylmar, whose molten staff became a shield. Cold wind blew in through the missing portion of the wall, brushing across Aeliana's face and stinging her cheeks, reminding her of just how high up the cliff's face they'd traveled within the fortress walls.

The men didn't speak, their glares intently focused on each other, assessing one another's power and weaknesses. Aeliana did the same with fresh eyes. The last time she'd watched Arvid use blood magic, it had felt like an unlimited well he could draw from, but now she understood it better.

His magic was as limited as Sylmar's, maybe even more so, because his either remained stuck at the hub of the Wheel, forcing him to manipulate objects around him, or he skipped to the rim, creating fire that could harm himself as much as Sylmar.

But as long as he could draw blood from the soldier, his magic would last longer.

She glanced at the soldier's body, then gauged the distance to the fresh gap in the wall. The stones continued crumbling, the gap now from her ankles to her chin. She couldn't fight Arvid, not like Sylmar could, but she could weaken him.

Arvid seemed to have similar plans for Sylmar, and he shifted, placing Sylmar in a sideways dance that put the old man in front of the gap. Sylmar showed no concern, and Aeliana suspected he welcomed the change. Through the gap, the setting Sun's rays hit the older man's back, likely replenishing his blood's power.

With Arvid's back to her, it was the perfect time to make her move. She crept forward, drawing Sylmar's attention. When his eyes met hers, he shook his head, eyes wide. Arvid turned right, forcing Aeliana to drag the soldier's body left, out of his view, attempting to reach the room's new balcony, which was still several feet away. Even with her starlock pushing energy into every muscle she had, it wouldn't be an easy thing.

She passed on Sylmar's side, but there was no way she could hide now.

Arvid let out a yell, and she winced, waiting for the strike, but it never came. A glance up revealed the two men grappling, whatever magic they might be using lost beneath chokeholds, elbows, and knees. She kept dragging, the scrape of leather and flesh on stone making her stomach heave. Blood spread across the floor with the dead soldier, beckoning her to draw on it. If there was ever a time to lean into such strong magic, it was now, when her friends needed her help. The temptation slowed her progress.

She held her breath, but instead of smelling the blood's allure, she tasted its metallic tang, the sensation making her mouth water. When she reached the edge, the distance below was dizzying, and she froze, waiting for her vision to still as she gripped the broken stones jutting out from the wall.

Sylmar grunted from behind her, and when bones cracked, both men hollered, jarring her from her stupor. She glanced back to see them separated once more, Sylmar's nose bleeding into his beard and Arvid's left arm tucked in close to his chest.

She bent down, shoving the corpse as close to the edge as she dared to get. When the body's weight finally shifted and pulled the soldier over the lip, she nearly tumbled with it, falling flat on her stomach with her palms scraping against the jagged edges of the floor.

She scrambled back, running into someone she didn't anticipate. She whipped around, reaching for the dagger she no longer had, then instinctually lifted a knee, aiming for a groin.

Gaeren sidestepped her at the last moment, crying out in surprise before angling her away from Arvid and Sylmar.

"Are you all right?" He gripped her elbows and held steady.

"Sorry." Her breath came out in ragged gasps. She glanced back at Arvid's hands, where the blood had dried up, and hopefully the magic with it. "We need to get rid of the bodies. He's using them."

Gaeren followed her gaze, catching on without more of an explanation. He pulled Lukai from Jasperus' side, and then together they grabbed the two closest dead soldiers. After skirting Arvid and Sylmar, they tossed the bodies over the edge like sacks of potatoes. They each returned for another, eliminating Arvid's sources of power far quicker than Aeliana could have. Jasperus sat against the wall, no longer bleeding, but still spent from his injury. Of the two soldiers who had been fighting Velden, only one remained upright, now forced to defend himself against Cyrus' attacks while still battling Velden.

He wouldn't last long.

Aeliana bit her lip, studying the blood still on the floor, hoping it wasn't enough for Arvid to use. As if he could hear her thoughts, he started laughing, and Gaeren stumbled at the room's edge, the last of the dead soldiers in his arms.

"Gaeren!" Aeliana shouted. Her heart lurched as he dropped the man like all the others, then bent forward as if a string might be connecting them before barely catching himself against the wall's sharp edge. When he turned back around, his face held a grimace. His right hand gripped his forearm, now drenched in blood from a deep gash, and he took a few uneven steps toward Aeliana.

Arvid intercepted him, wrapping an arm around the prince's neck.

Aeliana tensed, watching their motions as if underwater, her eyes demanding the scene to reverse. But there Arvid stood, holding a knife to Gaeren's neck, stretching his other hand over the fresh cut on Gaeren's arm. The others all went still, the room finally void of any enemies beyond Arvid, and yet the balance of power shifted in his direction.

"They really do find the highest starblood concentration for their line." Arvid's eyes rolled back in his head for a moment, and Gaeren grew more limp under his grip. "It's rare to find anything so pure."

Even Sylmar glanced around the room, clearly at a loss for what to do. If they attacked Arvid, it was Gaeren who would get hurt. If they didn't attack, Arvid would continue drawing power from Gaeren's blood until nothing was left.

When Sylmar's gaze landed on Aeliana, it seemed there was an apology in his eyes.

She shook her head. "No. Stop."

Arvid turned, swinging Gaeren in front of him like a puppet, using him as a shield. Her gaze dropped to Gaeren's arm, to the blood seeping out.

"They've been teaching you." Arvid's grin widened. "You know how this works. Probably found yourself wanting their blood. Afraid I won't leave enough for you?"

She winced and stepped back, hating the way his words picked at her past, like a scab hiding a gruesome wound. "Never."

His grin quickly fell, and the point of his knife dug into Gaeren's neck, droplets of blood falling like the sprinkling of rain. "You could have been as great as Mayvus by now if you'd stuck with us. They've weakened you." His fingers tightened on Gaeren's forearm, widening his wound so the blood spilled over, making the prince moan in his half-conscious state. "A small taste of this, and you could see how far blood magic could take you."

She closed her eyes, unsure if it was to block out the temptation or to focus better. Gaeren's blood practically sang to her, Arvid's words ringing with a truth she'd never sensed in the past. If anything, that should make her more wary. The only reason he'd offer her power would be if he knew it would break her in some way.

She took a step closer.

"No, Aeliana," Lukai hissed from behind her.

The words she'd heard Cyrus recite from *The Sins of the Stars* came back to her.

"The closer you stand, the louder its call." She muttered the quote almost like an incantation, then took another step forward. The scent of Gaeren's blood grew stronger, permeating the air in a way that heightened her other senses. In all her training with Lukai, she'd never been exposed to this much starblood. She was heady with it, the reverent words coming more like a childhood rhyme. "Flee while it whispers or suffer its fall."

Another step brought her close enough to touch Gaeren's arm. Arvid adjusted his grip, leaving space for her to place her hand over Gaeren's wound. When she did, she sensed her blood's itch to draw his energy into herself, like the leeches she'd used years before.

She hardly murmured the last words, but Cyrus joined in, his voice drowning out hers. "Better to die without knowing its gall."

She hesitated as his voice echoed across the stone walls. She'd tasted its gall. The family she'd killed, the ways Arvid and Vera had used her blood. She'd been a pawn in their hands. Now it was her move to make. Using Gaeren's blood would be her choice. Her own invitation to the dark spirits.

She should run, save herself from the dangers of blood magic. But how could she save herself and leave Gaeren at Arvid's mercy?

"How much more could I do with blood magic?" she asked, finally opening her eyes.

The protests of her comrades were like the buzzing of insects in her ears.

Arvid's grin returned. "Why don't we find out?" He licked his lips, glancing down at the blood on her hand, waiting for it to be used. Waiting for her to invite the dark spirits in just as he always had.

She gripped Gaeren's arm tighter. It would be so easy to use his blood. Outside of Gaeren's body, it was no longer any use to him, but for her? She shivered. Now that she knew how to control its power and guide it, she could do so much with it—far more than Arvid—but it would come at a cost.

Instead of drawing Gaeren's power into her starlock, she fought against the starblood's natural flow. She let her power flow out, driving his energy source back in. She sensed the wound knitting beneath her hand long before she could see it. Arvid shifted, lowering his knife and loosening his grip on Gaeren in anticipation of Aeliana's blood magic being the death of the prince.

"I used to think you took my blood because you were greedy. You wanted more than what you already had." The blood remained on Aeliana's hands, its energy no more or less than before she'd begun, and the blood in Gaeren's veins flowed strong.

She shoved him aside, careful to let him fall on the stones exposed to the Sun, hoping in his weakened state he might play dead just a bit longer. "But the truth is, your magic was never as strong as mine. Blood magic was the only magic you could do. So you tricked me into using it to weaken me. To keep me enslaved without a need for chains."

Arvid twitched under her gaze, but he didn't disagree.

"I never wanted any part of it, and I still don't."

Arvid raised his knife once more, but Aeliana let her starlock's power reach out through her, forcing Arvid to loosen his grip until the knife clattered to the ground. She grabbed the knife for herself, its foreign grip still giving her a sense of power now that it was in her control.

For a moment, his eyes widened, a strange panic she'd never seen on either of her guardians' faces overtaking him.

But then the cold rush returned, taking Aeliana's breath out of her lungs. Darkness flooded the room, momentarily blocking out even the Sun's rays. It swept over Gaeren, who shivered and scooted back against the wall, then it rested on Arvid, pausing as if to take a breath. Only it was Arvid who took the impossibly long breath, sucking in the dark spirit as if it gave life to his body, when in reality it brought him just shy of death. The darkness retreated, absorbing into Arvid until his skin seemed leached of color and warmth. He stretched his neck and flexed his fingers, reveling in the new sense of power.

He stood near the wall's edge, the broken stones framing him as the Sun's light filtered in.

Aeliana's heart raced, her small victory now a waste of effort.

"You've made a mistake," Arvid said, his voice deeper, his smile wider. "Not just in refusing the blood magic, but in thinking righteous choices are rewarded. Refusing to do blood magic won't save your friends." He held out a hand, and something black coiled out from his fingers, burrowing into Jasperus' side.

Jasperus slid farther down the wall, and Iris rushed to gently lower him, lifting his shirt. The skin remained intact, but a blackness spread in his vessels like a poison working its way through him.

The others inched away from Arvid, but Aeliana stepped closer.

"You're right. I can't compete with your dark spirits."

His laugh bounced painfully off the walls.

"But you are still a man." She flicked her wrist and released the dagger just like Lukai had shown her, just like she'd done when fighting the winex. It flew through the air with surprising accuracy, and Aeliana held her breath. She hadn't imagined being able to take a human life in this way, but now that the moment was here, she was ready for the weight of it, just like she'd been ready with Baljekk.

Only Arvid batted the knife away like a child's toy, and it fell and clinked against the stone.

"I'm no longer just a man when I have this in me." Arvid gestured to himself, and his form flickered, allowing Aeliana to see the dark spirit permeating every part of his body, fused with his soul, feeding on it like maggots.

Aeliana frowned, pulling her bow from her back instead. The others each readied their weapons as well, their movements slower, slightly more wary. Arvid wanted Aeliana alive, but the others didn't matter. This fight needed to be hers.

"Leave," she whispered, glancing at the others' uncertain faces. "Take Jasperus and go before Arvid injures you or uses you."

Iris dragged Jasperus toward the doorway until Lukai and Velden helped her lift him, but Sylmar spun his molten staff, forcing Arvid to face him once more.

Aeliana sent an arrow flying at Arvid's chest, but he caught it, tossing it out the gap before summoning his knife. Still, his gaze remained on Sylmar's spinning staff, an almost youthful arrogance to his eagerness. Blackness shot out from his hands once more, snuffing out Sylmar's staff like a candle's flame.

Sylmar tripped in his surprise, catching himself on the wall and letting his staff clatter to the floor. Arvid released another dark wave that caught Sylmar's hand against the stone like a fly in a spider's web before he could summon his starlock's energy another way. Velden joined the fray, pulling at the blackness, but it only spread to his webbed hands, weaving through both their veins like paint spreading on a canvas. Cyrus rushed to Velden's side, stripping fabric from his tunic before attempting to wipe the blackness away.

Aeliana readied another arrow, which made Arvid laugh.

"We could do this all day, but you're running out of time." He glanced meaningfully at the Sun over his shoulder, which was now at eye level.

Too late, Aeliana realized it was a ploy. When she flicked her gaze back to Arvid, his black ropes had yanked Cyrus in front of him like a shield. He sliced Cyrus' upper arm, then held his knife at the younger man's neck. With his free arm, he trapped Cyrus against his chest and caught the blood pooling beneath the wound.

Arvid's eyes widened as he sensed the lack of starblood.

"Did you and your dark spirit forget Cyrus is human?" Aeliana almost felt like laughing, but Cyrus groaned, then twisted away from Arvid's knife until he had an arm free. He shoved his hand against Arvid's throat, using it more as a handle to push Arvid toward the tower's opening than to actually choke him.

Arvid latched onto Cyrus' wrist, pulling the younger man with him. Blackness oozed out from his hands, but it hovered, more like the dark spirit assessed its safety with Arvid. As they reached the opening, Arvid placed one hand on the surrounding stone for balance, ready to drive Cyrus over the edge. Aeliana steadied the arrow at her cheek and took one final shot. This time the older man wasn't watching to defend it, and this time the dark spirit sensed Arvid wasn't worth it. The arrow struck Arvid's wrist. He lost his grip and balance, scrabbling for purchase. He nearly pulled Cyrus with him as he tumbled over the edge, but Gaeren snatched Cyrus' feet to stop his fall.

Both men landed hard, Cyrus' torso hanging over the edge of the gap. Aeliana rushed forward, helping them get clear of the opening. Her hands shook as she peered over the edge, thankful she couldn't see the evidence of her actions.

She closed her eyes anyway, her mind reliving the moment of the arrow entering Arvid's flesh with a thunk before he disappeared over the edge. She'd killed him. Just like Baljekk and just like the children at the farm.

No, the children at the farm had been killed by the dark spirits. The dark spirits Arvid had welcomed in. Numbness crept through her, replacing the guilt that warred with justification.

"Are you all right?" Gaeren tugged on her sleeve, his concerned eyes taking in every part of her face.

"Of course. It's Cyrus who was in danger."

"That's not what—" Gaeren cut off, placing a hand on her cheek, the warmth of his skin seeping into the icy chill left from the arrow's flight from her bow. "You had to do it. You did the right thing. Doesn't mean it was easy."

She looked away, her gaze resting on Cyrus' pale face, his freckles standing out like targets for the enemy.

"Are you all right?" This time the question came slower from Gaeren's lips, like he wanted her to assess each word individually before she gave her answer. He would only accept the truth.

"None of us will be after tonight." She kept her eyes on Cyrus. "But my friend is alive. The weight will grow lighter." When she glanced at Gaeren, he nodded slowly.

Fresh panic hit her, and she patted at the pocket of her shirt. The vial of blood still sat there, mercifully intact. Shouts rose through the room as Sylmar called the others back in. Velden wrapped seaweed around Sylmar's hand, and the blackness leached from the injury to the plant.

"Give this to Jasperus," Velden said, handing a bit of the plant to Cyrus. With all the noise, it took a moment for Aeliana to notice the small door in the room and the quiet pounding that came from behind it.

She stepped forward, placing her ear against the wood.

"Please." The weak cry sounded feminine, and the soft pounding came again, like the fist of an arm that no longer had the strength to rise off the wood. "Please, help."

"Mother?" Aeliana called.

The room went silent, on both sides of the door.

"Mother, is that you?"

The pounding turned frantic, the sobs beyond it equally panicked.

Velden rushed to Aeliana's side, working to pick the lock.

It wasn't the right time to care, but Aeliana couldn't help smoothing a hand over her messy braid and down her soiled uniform. Her face felt caked with mud, more likely blood. What would her mother think of her?

When the door opened, a woman tumbled out, her hair short and matted and her dress stained. Still her body remained hale and hearty and her green eyes clear. She trained them on Aeliana as she righted herself, soaking in every detail as Aeliana did the same.

"My baby," her mother breathed out before wrapping her arms around Aeliana.

Aeliana swallowed around the lump in her throat, unable to respond.

When they pulled back, Aeliana finally understood why the people had stared. She probably got her nose and ears from her father, but her mother's lips had the same uneven tilt, and her eyebrows held the same downward curve. Her mother's wrinkles served as the fastest way to tell them apart—until Aeliana caught sight of her mother's palm. An ugly black bump rose like Miklous' had.

Her brand.

CHAPTER 82

GAEREN WAS SHOVED ASIDE as Sylmar stepped forward, yanking Daisy and her mother apart.

"She's still branded to Mayvus," Sylmar said.

"She's not—she doesn't always control me," Emeris said, her gaze still fixed on Daisy. "She has too many brands for that. I can feel the difference when she does. But you're right. She'll know you're here soon."

"Exactly what you'd say if she was controlling you," Sylmar muttered. He didn't waste time pulling out a knife and reaching for her palm.

Without warning, her eyes glazed over and her fist drove into his neck, making him cough and sputter.

"I'm sorry." She shook her head, her eyes widening with horror. "I've tried cutting it out dozens of times over the years, but it's not possible. That's something she always has control over."

Sylmar exchanged a glance with Jasperus before pulling out a vial. "Let's try the other hand." He sliced before she could argue, and everyone breathed a little easier when the blood dripped into the vial, sensing the plan might actually work.

Gaeren shifted, exhaustion hitting him fresh now that they'd finally slowed down, and Emeris' gaze fell on him.

She squinted. "Gaeren? You've… well, you've grown into a man." She ignored Sylmar as he healed her palm and stepped away. "How in Rhystahn did you get caught up in all this?"

Her use of his real name instead of "Henri" left him reeling, too distracted by his own questions to answer hers.

"You knew who I was?" he asked. "When I came for my dedication year?"

She shrugged. "We suspected, and then we had it confirmed."

"Then why did you let me stay? Why did you let my parents bring Breck as a spy into your midst?"

Emeris sighed and glanced over Gaeren's shoulder. He followed her gaze to see Jasperus holding out his palm while Daisy argued with Sylmar.

"We fed Breck several lies," she finally said. "First to test him, then to weaken Mayvus. But I kept your identity a secret, even from Iris, especially once I saw how attached you grew to Aeliana. I was determined to protect you as much as her. Eventually Mayvus caught on." She gestured around the room, her hand trembling. "Which is why it's all come to this."

Gaeren finally took in her odd mix of health and suffering. Soiled clothes and dirt under long nails hinted at days, if not weeks, without bathing, but his own battle sweat smelled too much to detect anything on her. Still, beneath the dirt she was well fed, her eyes bright. In all these years, Mayvus hadn't broken her. Or maybe Mayvus hadn't been willing to because she needed Emeris strong enough to use her.

Behind them, Jasperus groaned. Emeris took up the same cry, each holding their hand in front of them as they dropped to their knees. Jasperus' forearm bubbled up black, making Gaeren wince. Emeris' palm did the same, her mark mirroring Jasperus'.

He glanced at Daisy, who wrung her hands, eyes wide. He could practically see her calculating the amount of time she had left before the same mark started bubbling up on her hand. Only it could be a brand from Mayvus instead of Jasperus. She flinched as Lukai grabbed her hand and leaned in to whisper, stroking her hand with his own.

Gaeren turned away.

"Are you all mad?" Emeris croaked out, holding on to the wall as she tried to stand.

"I can sense her." Jasperus' voice came out pained. "It's so strong. Like I'm having my Awakening all over again."

Gaeren imagined the sensations he must be feeling, the rush of energy and its constant presence, a sense of insignificance in the midst of a newfound importance.

"You shouldn't have done that," Emeris whispered, her eyes unfocused.

"I can sense more than her, too. I can sense Mayvus." Jasperus stood, wild eyes darting around the room as though looking for the nearest exit. "If I can sense her, she'll sense me soon. She'll know what we've done."

"Command Emeris to cut out her old brand," Sylmar said. "Quickly."

Emeris stood, eyes narrowing at Jasperus. She rushed at him, bare feet slapping on stone, arms outstretched. Gaeren reached for her arm to hold her back, but she slipped to the side and his fingers only grazed her sleeve. Her hands were on Jasperus' neck before anyone could stop her, squeezing so hard Gaeren thought the old man's neck might snap.

Sun's fire, Mayvus didn't waste any time.

Gaeren and Lukai each grabbed one of Emeris' arms, pulling her grip back enough to let Jasperus gasp in breaths.

"Cut out..." He wheezed out the command. "Your old brand."

She hesitated, and Gaeren and Lukai took the opportunity to wrestle her to the floor, pinning her down as she thrashed against them. Sylmar sat on her back, and Velden kneeled by her face.

"I'm sorry," Velden said as he pulled out a knife and worked at her palm.

Her screams shifted from anger to pain, and blood pooled beneath her hand. Gaeren tried to imagine himself cutting a brand out of Daisy. It would be far better than killing her, but would it even be possible? It was taking four men to hold Emeris down, and that was with Jasperus already counteracting Mayvus' brand.

Daisy had been right to ask for her death, but he still didn't know if he could do it. He doubted he could even cut off her hand.

Before long, Emeris' screams subsided, and Lukai wrapped his hands around her raw flesh. It felt like a waste to heal her now. They should be saving their magic for whatever was coming. But Daisy kneeled next to him, tears in her eyes as she thanked him.

Emeris' gaze held fresh clarity, like she hadn't just been possessed to kill the people around her. "I'm sorry," she said, over and over, even as Cyrus passed over Emeris' starlock and Daisy settled it around her mother's neck.

"I don't think Emeris can handle us cutting out Jasperus' brand too," Sylmar said. "Not tonight."

Jasperus nodded his understanding. It would have made him less of a target, but it didn't matter if he planned to brand Daisy anyway. Mayvus would just have two reasons to brand him instead of one. Sylmar would have two reasons to kill him instead of one.

Gaeren didn't look toward Daisy, afraid his face would give away his doubt in his ability to follow through on his promise.

Gaeren released Emeris' other arm, awkwardly standing by as she and Daisy hugged once more.

Where was Mayvus? And where was Daisy's blood?

He peered out the broken wall, examining the fight below. Most of the people he saw were fallen, the fields surrounding the fortress oddly empty. Had Mayvus' entire army chased the pirates and Recreants into the woods? He squinted at the battlements, wondering if his eyes were tricking him. Was that... Riveran? The man disappeared back inside the building, but Gaeren felt even more certain as he thought about the X he'd seen on the man's forehead.

Except what was Riveran doing there?

"Were all the soldiers and sailors supposed to retreat with the pirates?" he asked, turning to beckon Sylmar. The old man joined him at the edge, and Gaeren pointed out the door where Riveran had disappeared. "I saw Riveran there. Is that where he should be?"

Sylmar frowned. "No. None were supposed to remain."

Gaeren rushed to the other wall, leaning through one of the real windows. The Sun had nearly hit the horizon. From this angle, he could also see the gatehouse, oddly empty. Even if they'd chased away most of the Recreants, Mayvus never would have approved of the Zealots abandoning that post. He frowned, trying to piece together how all the soldiers could have made it to the fields and forests beyond that fast. Movement caught his eye as a line of black and red crossed a battlement, the soldiers headed right for Riveran and the northern keep Emeris had been trapped in.

Gaeren's gaze snapped to Sylmar, his sudden understanding reflected on the old man's slack face. "We thought we were tricking them by leading them away from the castle, but we ended up setting a trap for ourselves. Whatever soldiers are left, they're coming here."

Sylmar yanked on Emeris' collar, pulling her upright to stand beside him. "Where is Mayvus?"

Gaeren ran back to the hall and the spiral stairs they'd come from. The clink of metal could be distantly heard, the sound getting louder as soldiers grew closer. "They're coming," he called to Sylmar, who swore.

"By now she's probably on the balcony attached to her rooms," Emeris said. "She knew you were coming, and she knew she'd need to brand Aeliana early. But she'll hold off as close to the Sun's sleep as she can to let her blood be at its peak state of energy. She'll want the brand to be as strong as possible." She gave an apologetic look to Daisy.

"This way," Sylmar said, leading them all out to the hall. Only a few doors remained this high up on the tower. Once the Zealots reached their level, they'd be impossibly overrun.

"We need to block the passage," Gaeren said.

"What about Orra and the others?" Daisy asked. "We could use their help."

Gaeren frowned. Riveran and more of his men might be down there too. They might already be dead. By blocking them off, he could be surrounding them with the enemy and sealing their graves.

"Gaeren's right," Sylmar said. "Our priority is to keep Mayvus from branding Aeliana and to get both her and Emeris to safety. We can't do that with an army on our heels. Velden, take the others through the door to the west with the dragon crest on it. Those are

Mayvus' rooms. If she's not in there, Emeris is right. She'll be on the balcony."

Sylmar held out a hand to Gaeren before planting his feet in the doorway to the stairs.

"I don't have that kind of power," Gaeren reminded him. "I deal in memories. I haven't developed my rim magic yet."

Sylmar's brow rose. "You have starblood like any other progeny. Give your power to me."

Gaeren eyed the doorway, then glanced at the others making their way down the hall. Sylmar could have asked Velden or Lukai—even Daisy. She threw him a desperate glance.

He nodded once, his heart doubling its speed as the relief spread on her face.

"I know your family isn't used to sharing things with others," Sylmar said with a hint of dry irritation, "especially those below their station, but I can't do this alone without killing myself. And as you said, you deal in memories. Your powers may not be needed tonight."

Gaeren narrowed his eyes but took Sylmar's hand, letting his starlock burn as he sent his blood's supply toward the other man. It stung for him to give up his power, but it stung worse knowing his power was seen as expendable.

The stones in the archway rattled as if something in them had come to life, the noise competing with the rhythmic stomp of boots on stone. Gaeren peered down the steps, wondering if he would see torchlight at any moment or maybe the flash of weaponry or armor.

The pull on his power faded, as if Sylmar had hit a point of saturation. Gaeren loosened his grip, but Sylmar squeezed tighter, heat forming between their hands. Two stones broke from the arch, flying to the floor with more force than simple gravity before smashing to pieces. Gaeren sensed another pull on his starlock's power, shocked at how quickly Sylmar might drain him.

Sylmar leaned heavily against the wall of the arch, his hand shaking where it braced against stones. The stones rattled louder, several more loosening and falling.

Gaeren stepped back to avoid being hit, watching the rubble grow and fill the doorway as their energy drained. Sylmar stepped back with him but traced the wall with his hand, loosening key stones as he went, and more stones showered down. Gaeren coughed as the dust rose, and he pulled Sylmar back despite the older man's resistance.

"I think that's enough," Gaeren shouted over the din. "You're going to bring down the whole tower."

Sylmar shook his head but didn't waste the energy to reply. More stones flew, building a river of rock more than a wall against the incoming soldiers. Shouts grew over the sound of grinding stone, and through the gaps, Gaeren made out faces, one of them distinctly familiar with a black X.

"Riveran!" Gaeren tried to shake off Sylmar's hand, to cut off the flow of power, but his grip was inhuman, his focus unmatched.

Riveran pawed at the stones, pushing a few out of his way to widen the opening that revealed his nose up to the ceiling. His hands clawed at more stones, but with Sylmar's adjustments, they remained wedged, cutting Riveran off from the safety of the tower.

Riveran's gaze rested on Gaeren's, his eyes pained.

"We have to help them," Gaeren shouted, forcing Sylmar to release his hand.

"It's too late," Sylmar said, his voice weak. He leaned his forehead against the wall, his lips dry and face pale above his beard.

Riveran gave Gaeren a nod, then turned. Gaeren caught glimpse of a glint of steel before the final stones fell and cut them off completely. Silence echoed around them, choking Gaeren as much as the dust settling over their bodies.

Gaeren fell to his knees, vaguely aware of his sudden weakness. They'd cut Riveran off along with the enemy, possibly burying them all alive. Their deaths could come at the hands of soldiers or even other sailors in the chaos. All because Gaeren had wanted to protect himself.

"Your actions have given the others a chance," Sylmar rasped out, patting Gaeren's back, likely more for his own support to stand than to comfort Gaeren. "We've given Aeliana and Emeris a chance to stop Mayvus. We've given all of Vendaras a chance at freedom."

His words stirred up the dying embers in Gaeren's chest. They hadn't lost everything yet. He'd made promises he needed to keep. A promise to himself to protect Daisy, and a promise to Daisy to kill her if need be. He stood on shaking legs, pulling Sylmar up beside him, reaching for the staff the man had lost.

They slowly made their way down the hall toward the others.

It was time to break one of his promises, but he still wasn't sure which one.

CHAPTER 83

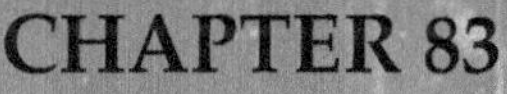

BEYOND THE BATTLEMENT, Orra saw the northern keep where it practically grew out of the mountain. She'd been present when this keep was first built, after the split of the family of Elanesse. It had started as a refuge for Valyn Elanesse, but as her piety grew and the threat on her life lessened, it had turned into a Sungazer. She and Willem Wyndren had settled down, content with their life as servants of the Sun.

Their descendants had chosen different paths, growing bitter over the throne they felt entitled to. Now the keep was a shadow of the great house of worship it had once been, the ceiling closed off and the rooms filled with weaponry. Usually clouds covered these mountains, almost as if the Sun wanted nothing to do with what the fortress had become. Orra closed her eyes to bask in the Sun's rays, wondering if maybe its presence today was a sign that it approved of their plans.

That it still might approve of her.

Warmth filled her chest, spreading out toward her limbs.

Kendalyhn nudged her side, breaking her concentration. "We don't have time to rest. Up the stairs."

They crossed the battlement at a crouch. The door to the keep was already open, which Orra took as a bad sign. Their group was aiming for stealth, so it had likely been left that way by Zealot soldiers unconcerned about giving away their location. They went in one by one, taking the steps two at a time.

The moment Orra crossed the doorway, the entire tower rumbled. She gripped the stone frame, trying to find purchase.

"Are they bringing the whole thing down?" Marnok's eyes widened as he looked back at Orra.

"No." Orra traced her fingers over the stone, sensing Sylmar's work. "They're blocking the top of the stairs. It's Sylmar, not the soldiers."

"Why would they—?" Marnok cut off, his voice turning resigned. "There are Zealots between us, aren't there? Zealots in front of us and either Zealots or winex behind."

Orra turned back, still able to see the door leading back to the larger fortress building across the battlement. As if they'd heard Marnok, the door across the battlement flew open, and a horde of winex poured out like fleas.

Orra shut the northern keep's door behind her. "Seal it, Kendalyhn."

"I'm not—I'm a pneumatic. I can't do that kind of magic," Kenda-lyhn said.

"Then give your energy to Marnok so he can seal it."

"But that would drain both of us."

Orra pushed past the younger woman, not waiting to see if she obeyed. She kneeled down, placing a palm on the lowest step. Her mind traveled through the possibilities without her permission, seeking out all the ways they could overtake the soldiers above, all the ways people would die if they didn't. Every way she looked ended in failure. Every way without her interference ended in death.

Even if she did something, she wasn't sure it would change things. The end result still might not include the golden arrow.

But this time, it was like the Sun itself urged her on with a whisper of hope. Her throat grew tight with the familiarity of it. It had been so long since she'd felt not just the Sun's presence or possible approval, but its guidance. The overwhelming presence of it both stung and reas-sured her. No matter what happened, in life or death, the Sun would not abandon her.

She brought the braid to her lips and kissed it. "I'm sorry. I promise I'll try again."

Then she placed both palms on the step and reached out, searching for the smallest of seeds. Her mind drove through the cracks of the steps, the mud holding stone upon stone until she found a tiny sapling, more like a weed sprouting in the dank corner of the fourth stair up, grown by water that dripped when it rained and by the Sun's morning light. She fed her energy to the sapling until it grew and twisted, its vines wrapping along the steps and up the wall.

Holm gasped and jumped back, but Marnok made his way up the steps, careful to avoid stepping on her creation.

"Earth," Kendalyhn breathed from behind her. "You control earth. You have rim magic. But you have no starlock. You really must be a Star."

Orra ignored the younger woman, instead focusing on the vine as it thickened and stretched, winding its way up the stairs before splitting in a dozen directions, climbing the walls until it covered the stairs above and below, continuing to creep up to the enemy above. The vine was blind to the soldiers it would encounter, but Orra could sense them. Thorns grew from each of the vine's tips, thrashing out like claws on a whip.

The first soldier's scream made them all jump as it echoed down the stairwell. Orra closed her eyes and leaned into that first step, letting her forehead rest on the stone of the second. Her power leaked from every pore, congealing at her palms before finding a home in the vine that still grew and lashed out at soldiers.

As the vine spread farther, it wrapped around ankles and wrists and necks, yanking them off balance or squeezing air from their lungs. The crack of bones and skulls on stone mixed with panicked shouts and horrified screams. Something warm and wet dripped down the center of the stairwell, plinking against Orra's hands.

The cramped stairwell left the soldiers trapped, unable to pass the vines and dead soldiers blocking their escape down. Still, they tried, trampling each other in their fear, putting themselves in the path of Orra's deadly vine. She kept it growing out and up, overlapping itself

until it was thick enough to entangle men and bury bodies, all the way
to the stair's end.

And something else… something good.

Orra stretched and reached, her hands beginning to tremble, her
breaths coming in short gasps. Another power met her own at the top
of the stairs. She halted the vine, holding it steady, pausing as if to sniff
out the other source. Only remnants of magic remained, but her power
was too weak to trace its signature, and three souls remained at the
top, three people not yet tainted by Mayvus' magic and influence. She
let her vine pass over them before turning back around, crawling
through the bodies sprawled across the steps, slicing through any that
still held life. At this point it was a mercy, silencing the moans and
cries of a battlefield.

When the last of them faded, Orra collapsed across the steps, her
eyes open but not seeing. Only Stars danced before her vision, and for
a moment she smiled as they darted to and fro.

"My friends," she murmured.

But then the vision cleared, and Kendalyhn's face swam before her,
at least three different versions of it.

"Orra?" The word reverberated in her head like when they'd sat in
the canyon, and Orra closed her eyes against the pain in her temple.

"Leave me," she said.

"I don't—I'm not sure our lock will hold." Kendalyhn's voice grew
more frantic, which only hurt Orra's ears more. "It's not something
either of us have done before."

"I'll take her," Holm said.

Hands gripped Orra, and she sensed the change in gravity, like
taking flight. Then she sensed nothing more.

CHAPTER 84

AELIANA RUSHED THROUGH MAYVUS' rooms, barely noticing the elaborate bedding and drapes, a strange contrast to the rest of the fortress' barren rooms. Every time the floor shook, they paused, wary of what might be happening back at the stairs with Gaeren and Sylmar. Eventually, when the rumbling stopped, Aeliana passed Velden, sensing a pull that guided her through the rooms until she reached the balcony door. Pink and orange light streamed through the glass panels of the door, highlighting their loss of time.

A hand brushed Aeliana's back, startling her. "You don't need to face her," her mother whispered. "I'm no longer branded. I can take care of this."

Aeliana frowned. "I'd rather you protect Jasperus than me." Both women turned to see the soldier limping through the doorway, his eyes glazed over. In some ways, he already seemed half dead, but Aeliana shook that thought away.

The rumbling behind them grew louder, and Aeliana's fear for Gaeren drowned out any worry for herself. Velden joined them by the door, his eyebrows raised in question. Lukai, Jasperus, Cyrus, and Iris fanned out behind them.

"Remember, we go for the blood, not Mayvus," Velden said. "We're not ready for Mayvus."

"She controls every spoke now." Her mother frowned. "Her pneumatic skills are natural, but all the rest are bought with brands. She has dozens of brands. I thought she'd quit when she had one of every kind, but she grew greedy. Wanted all points on the spoke. Wants to eventually access all parts of the rim."

"More powerful than we think," Aeliana said. "Got it." She took a step forward, but her mother grabbed her arm.

"Let me get your blood." There was a desperation to her tone that made Aeliana pause. The idea of having a mother who wanted to fight her fights left her homesick for something she'd never truly had. And Sylmar had said her mother knew something, that her mother could defeat Mayvus. It was the whole reason they'd wanted to rescue her.

"Do you know how to stop her?" Aeliana asked.

Her mother nodded. "It has to be me. I can stop all of this." Her hands shook, and her eyes twitched.

Her mother was too weak, and Aeliana had her own plans. She pulled out her dagger even though she was a far better shot with her arrows. It didn't matter how well she used weapons tonight. It was all about blood and timing. She glanced back at the hall, which had gone eerily silent. Hopefully Gaeren was still coming, but if not… she reached for the vial in her pocket for the hundredth time. This time it held a heat she didn't remember, a warning that this was the peak time to use it.

"Next time. For now, it's more important for you to stay alive and protect Jasperus," Aeliana said again, gently pushing her mother toward the ailing soldier. "Sylmar plans to have him brand me the same as you."

Her mother hesitated, but Velden patted her back, guiding her away from the door. When her mother glanced over her shoulder at Aeliana, she looked more like a lost child than a found mother.

As the Sunlight brushing her hands turned more red than pink, Aeliana pulled on the handle and opened the door.

A cool breeze met her face, making her suck in a sharp breath. Goosebumps ran along her arms and legs, and instinct made her want to wrap her arms tightly around herself, but instead she held out her dagger.

Mayvus was nowhere in sight.

The others joined her on the balcony naturally formed by the rock wall. Its surface was larger than she'd anticipated, maybe one hundred feet by one hundred feet, but a dead end nonetheless. The breeze picked up into a wind that whipped loose strands from Aeliana's braid into her face. She strode to the walled edge on the southern side but didn't need to lean out to see the desperation of their situation. The surrounding forest was like a small grass field. Beyond the trees a tiny strip of beach represented their morning trek. The view made her dizzy, and she reached out to grip the stone of the balcony's balustrade.

"If we can't go down, maybe we can go up," Cyrus said, his eyes riveted on the cliff wall behind them to the north, a thoughtful look on his face. The way up to the heights of the Myndren Mountains was closer than the way down.

"Proper equipment and the strength of our best day would still only give us slim chances of scaling that wall." Velden hacked at the smooth, hard stone with his sword as if to illustrate his point. The stone remained flawless. "Besides, we have to find the vial before we can escape."

The tip of the Sun sank below the horizon.

Dusk.

Aeliana closed her eyes, wishing she were a pneumatic who could see the future, even wishing she were already branded so she could sense Mayvus in some way. Lead her companions to her. The distant rush of air met her ears, and she hushed her companions, who were already silent.

As it grew louder, she turned in a full circle, honing in on the direction it came from. When she opened her eyes, she was facing west, but nothing had changed. She squinted past the black rock wall still bordering them on the right, angling to see where the wall turned beyond the balcony and what else might be up in these mountains. Just as she opened her mouth to warn the others, fire erupted from the side, flashing out to hit the wall, nearly reaching them.

The others all dropped, but Aeliana stepped forward, waiting for Durriken to round the wall's edge. When he did, a rush of air blew over Aeliana with the flap of his glorious purple wings. His eyes widened, and he slowed his approach.

A woman sat on his back, her long white dress almost a mirror image of her mother's, but where her mother's was soiled and torn, Mayvus' was pristine. The exposed skin of her arms held dozens of welts—marks of her brands. Durriken perched on the balcony's western edge, his wings nearly hitting Aeliana as he kept himself mostly still in flight, the stones beneath his paws already breaking off from the little weight he put on them.

Mayvus slid from his back, lifting her chin and peering down her nose with dark eyes. She turned back to Durriken, whispering some sort of instruction too low for the others to hear. Durriken's wings flapped harder as he rose, then he dove toward the lower levels of the fortress.

Aeliana swallowed hard, hoping most of their people had already retreated toward camp. She tightened her grip on the vial of blood, debating if she should go ahead and brand him anyway. How many lives could she save by contradicting Mayvus' orders? Except it was blood magic. Blood magic that would summon dark spirits.

Mayvus cleared her throat.

The noise reminded Aeliana of Gaeren's unflattering description of Mayvus as a witch. She smiled and stood straighter, drawing Mayvus' attention.

"All this trouble," Mayvus said. "Caused by you."

"Hello, Auntie Mayvus," Aeliana said, grateful her voice didn't shake like her hands, which she kept pressed against her sides even as she tightened her grip on her dagger.

Mayvus grimaced, then glanced beyond Aeliana. "I see you've found your mother. I've taken good care of her over the years. You're welcome."

Her mother snorted. "You've taken care of yourself."

Mayvus quirked one eyebrow, her slow steps toward Aeliana more nerve-wracking than if she'd charged. "One might argue the two go hand in hand."

Feet pounded from behind them, and Sylmar and Gaeren rushed

out from Mayvus' rooms. Sylmar's face reached a shade of red so dark it was almost purple, his scars standing out white.

"We've come for Aeliana's blood," he said.

Mayvus paused, her gaze resting on Sylmar. "Is that all you've come for? I know the way your mind works, dear. You never settle for less than everything."

"Things have changed," Sylmar said. "I've changed."

She laughed, but before she could respond, Sylmar's staff shifted to fiery blades that shot out toward Mayvus. So much for going after the blood first.

Aeliana winced in anticipation of the blood and screams, but the blades froze in the air, a handsbreadth from Mayvus' face and torso. Their tips turned a pale blue as icicles formed on their edges, and they all clattered to the ground, smashing into dozens of pieces.

Aeliana's mouth hung open, her mother's warning coming back to her. Mayvus had far more power than they'd realized. Even Sylmar's face showed defeat as he leaned heavily on Gaeren.

Aeliana narrowed her eyes at both men, the sheen of sweat covering their skin, their shaking limbs. What had they done back in the tower? How much magic had they already used?

"I'll forgive that less-than-appreciative welcome if we can come to a quick agreement." Mayvus smoothed down her dress, her hands showing no weakness over the previous display. "You all surrender, and no one gets hurt. I have no reason to want you dead. I want my niece by my side and the Prince of Elanesse as my ally." She smiled sweetly at Gaeren.

"I'm no friend of yours." He spat on the stone floor and wiped his mouth.

Aeliana's chest swelled at his show of defiance until she noticed the blood on his hand and cheek. His gaze bore into hers as if desperate to tell her something. Hopefully that he was ready to follow through.

"If you want me by your side, why won't you give me my blood?" Aeliana asked, turning to Mayvus. "It's far better to have a willing accomplice than a branded one."

Mayvus laughed. "I highly doubt you'd be willing. Arvid told me of your resistance." She took another step forward, crossing over the broken daggers without concern. "He also told me of your power. Possibly natural, but more likely developed by their incessant use of your blood. It's given me ideas for how to use my brands." Her smile widened. "And my winex."

"The winex aren't yours," Aeliana said, the heat in her belly driving the words forward. She eyed Mayvus' sleeves and waist, trying to see where the woman might be storing Aeliana's blood. They were mere feet apart, her aunt's proximity both terrifying and promising.

"Such a soft heart," Mayvus murmured. "Arvid and I will break you of that soon enough."

"Arvid is dead," Aeliana said.

This finally caught Mayvus off guard. She narrowed her eyes. "You're speaking truth. I suppose it's possible." She shrugged. "I never branded him, so I can't test it. Probably felt like quite the accomplishment, killing a man who wasn't even a progeny."

Aeliana resisted the guilt that swarmed through her. "Where's my blood?"

"Ah, and now we come back to the reason you're here," Mayvus said. "The reason I wanted you to come." She pulled a vial out from a side pocket of her dress, the setting Sun gleaming off the glass. Everyone stood a little straighter, the atmosphere thickening. Now that they knew where the blood was, there was no reason for them to hold back. With nine of them and one of her, it should be easy.

At the same moment, a rush of wind blew over the western side of the balcony, followed by Durriken's iridescent wings and scales. He grasped the wall, slipping and pulling down portions of the facade as if the balcony's edge were made of crumbs instead of stone. Puffs of steam and smoke left his nostrils as he growled his irritation, but he held his position as a dozen soldiers climbed off his back.

"Sweet Stars," Aeliana muttered as her friends rushed forward without hesitation. Only her mother and Jasperus held back, scooting against the door leading back to the tower.

Mayvus moved to the western edge of the balcony, the melee of fighting now a river between her and Aeliana. When Aeliana moved forward to help, Sylmar shoved her back, taking a cut to his arm because of his distraction.

Blades clashed, and Aeliana's frustration mounted.

She reached out, trying to sense which of her friends had wounds she could address from this distance, but enough blood was being spilled that it was hard to sense friend from foe. She pulled energy into her core, letting it build and ready for a light shield, but everyone moved so quickly that she was just as likely to protect the enemy as her friends.

Mayvus stepped to the side as if watching a play unfold. Her arm dropped, the vial resting against her side as she closed her eyes. Her lips twisted in a wicked grin.

Aeliana frowned, then studied the soldiers more closely. Between the weapons they gripped and the rapid thrusts and parries, it was hard to tell, but it seemed like they all had small black welts on their hands.

Mayvus' branded.

Which meant she was controlling them. She was distracted.

A ridiculous idea raced through Aeliana's mind, the details crystal clear, as if she'd already done it. It was just as despicable as branding Durriken, and yet somehow it felt more just. She would only be doing to Mayvus what Mayvus intended to do to her.

Aeliana inched forward, making a wide perimeter south around the soldiers until she reached the farther edge of the balcony. She scooted closer on all fours until she was tucked under the curve of the balustrade, where she crept until she was within arm's reach to either slice Mayvus' arm or grab the vial. Which was the safer bet?

She caught a glimpse of the leather cord around Mayvus' neck, her starlock encased in a clear sphere. Its shape was identical to her mother's.

Aeliana hesitated. Had the Stars assigned a duplicate? Or had she copied Aeliana's mother's the way Velden had copied his own? Aeliana's heart sank. Marnok had recognized her mother's starlock, but what if he was actually recognizing it as Mayvus'?

Where were Marnok and the others?

Durriken let out a huff of hot breath that brushed Aeliana's arm. He eyed her as he adjusted his grip, keeping up a strange dance to maintain his hold on the balcony's edge. Would Mayvus sense her presence through him? If she opened her eyes, she would see Aeliana, and it would all be over.

Aeliana licked her lips to get rid of the trickling beads of sweat.

The whistle of an arrow made Aeliana jump, her head hitting stone on the ledge above her. She couldn't waste any more time. She turned to slice Mayvus' arm.

Her aunt still had her eyes shut, lips curled in eager anticipation.

Aeliana didn't hesitate over the brands decorating the woman's skin like sets of tattoos. She'd barely broken the skin when Mayvus' eyes flew open, her smile shifting to a frown. Instead of losing her grip on the vial, she tightened her fist, blood streaming down her arm as her boot met Aeliana's wrist, knocking the dagger to the stone floor. Then Mayvus' hand was on Aeliana's hair, wrenching Aeliana to her feet. Aeliana screamed, more from frustration than pain, and thrashed out wildly, hoping to knock the vial from Mayvus' hands.

"We're almost out of time if we want the strongest brand anyway," Mayvus said. "Summer Solstice would have been better, but what's a day going to do at this point?" She flicked the cork off the vial, then swirled it, using some sort of somatic energy to adjust the clotted remnants until they thinned into a sticky red substance once more.

Aeliana panicked. Why hadn't she branded Durriken? Why hadn't she stuck to the plan?

In order to pour the blood on the wound Aeliana had inflicted, Mayvus had to release her. When she did, Aeliana slapped at Mayvus' hand, knocking the blood out from the vial in a wide arc away from Mayvus' arm. Her relief didn't even have time to rise before the droplets froze in the air, tiny rubies glinting in the Sun, which now barely showed above the horizon.

Aeliana stared in horror as Mayvus swept them up in her hand and smeared them over her arm. A tingle started on Aeliana's right palm, and she scrambled away from Mayvus. With Mayvus' distraction, her branded soldiers had lost their edge, and several lay on the floor with vacant expressions. Iris was also down, but Lukai bent over her, hopefully able to fix her ailments. Velden, Gaeren, and Cyrus still fought

Mayvus' soldiers, but on the east side of the balcony, Sylmar rushed toward Jasperus, ready to counteract Mayvus' brand with their own.

Aeliana ignored the way the itch on her palm grew to a burn. She stepped away from Mayvus, reaching for Cyrus' arm and shoving him toward Jasperus. "Stall them." Her voice came out harsh. "Stop them any way you can."

She followed him to the eastern side of the balcony, putting as much distance as possible between her and Mayvus, while pulling out the vial of Durriken's blood. As she stepped over a soldier, she pulled a dagger from his belt and sliced open her itchy palm. Even if it was too late to brand Durriken, maybe this would interfere with Mayvus' attempts.

She turned back to Mayvus, hesitating over whether to stoop as low as this witch. But she saw her mother crawling along the same balustrade Aeliana had just sat at, reaching for Aeliana's dagger with its daisy pommel.

As soon as her mother grasped it, she lunged, but her body was weak. The dagger sliced open Mayvus' shoulder, and the two women crashed into each other, falling to the stone floor, where they rolled several feet. Mayvus' eyes rolled wildly, and she stopped, knocking Aeliana's mother against the stone so hard her head made an audible crack.

"You're going to get us both killed," Mayvus shouted.

Aeliana forced herself to look away, to let her mother's interference distract Mayvus but not her. She poured the blood over her palm, then stumbled as it bubbled and burned, forming dozens of tiny black marks. She moaned and reached out to the wall for support, trying to remember what Cyrus had told her to do. Her starlock burned against her skin, instinctually insisting that she heal the wound. At the same time, the blood oozing out from her wound called to her, demanding to be used, offering to aid her in defeating Mayvus once and for all.

Durriken growled from his perch on the balcony's edge, shifting his grip and shaking his left paw in irritation.

Aeliana's gaze fell on her mother, who was held back by a soldier while Mayvus resumed her branding ceremony, hand over her arm and eyes shut tight.

"No," Aeliana whispered, running Cyrus' instructions through her mind once more. "Seal it."

Instead of letting the power flow through her arm to knit it back into place, she let it spread like a bandage, covering the wound and encasing it. The bubbles on her hand grew, connecting until there were two large shiny marks instead of several tiny dots. Two separate brands? One incomplete brand? "Please work," she whispered.

If it didn't…

A coldness swept through her, one that started in her mind, but soon it was as visceral as the wind. Her actions had summoned the dark spirits. It wouldn't be long before they came, demanding payment, expecting reward. She'd seen it often enough for Arvid and Vera, but she felt sick knowing this time they were coming for her.

She sought Gaeren out from among those still fighting. He pulled a sword from between a soldier's ribs, its blade slick with blood. Then, as if he sensed her watching, he turned to catch her gaze.

"Please," she whispered, but conflict still warred behind his eyes.

As the marks on her right palm solidified, a cooling sensation swept over them, and Aeliana suddenly felt invaded, like someone else occupied her mind. The Sun slipped behind the horizon, leaving an orange glow in the sky. In the distance, blackness drifted, like the wings of a bird.

Or the trail of a dark spirit.

Durriken? She paused, waiting for his confirmation. He huffed from the other side of the balcony and adjusted his paws with a rumble deep in his chest. His eyes shifted between Mayvus and Aeliana, his head cocking in confusion.

"Aeliana."

Her gaze snapped to Mayvus, the command leaving her aunt's lips but also reverberating through her mind.

"Aeliana, come to me."

And Aeliana did.

CHAPTER 85

As Daisy took slow steps toward Mayvus, Gaeren's breath hitched. Her eyes held no emotion, the purpose driving her moments ago vanished. This was what he'd been waiting for. This was the moment she wanted him to kill her. He lifted his sword, gauging whether he could reach her before she reached Mayvus.

Did it matter? He couldn't imagine running her through. And not just because she was the Daisy of his childhood, but because it still went against every instinct in his body, even after all he'd learned about her blood magic and family line. Maybe especially because of everything he'd grown to learn about her. At this point, if Mayvus commanded Daisy to kill Gaeren, he wasn't sure he could defend himself.

Not if it meant hurting her.

"I sense the power raging inside your veins." Mayvus took a deep breath in through her nose, as though she could also smell it. "Why don't you use it? It's such a waste."

Gaeren glanced at the remaining soldiers in the center of the balcony—only three left to fight Velden, Lukai, and Iris, who stood once more, her defensive posture a bit unsteady. Velden and Lukai alone could take the soldiers while he snuck south around them toward Daisy. But if he was within distance to strike Daisy, maybe he should strike Mayvus instead.

"I only use what I need," Daisy said, her wooden voice sending a shudder through Gaeren. "That way I don't make too much."

Mayvus laughed. "Too much? There's no such thing." By now Daisy had reached her aunt, and Mayvus patted her on the head like an obedient child. "You are mine. You protect me above all else. But you also protect yourself. Because keeping your power safe helps keep me safe."

Daisy nodded, her eyes blank.

Mayvus flipped Daisy's hand to examine it next to her arm. She traced the outline of a fresh mark on Daisy's palm. "This one is clearly mine. But who does this belong to?"

Sun's fire. Had Jasperus already finished? Was Gaeren too late? Gaeren inched backward, attempting to block Mayvus' view of Sylmar huddled over Jasperus. From behind him, he caught Sylmar's and Cyrus' heated whispers.

"It's not what she wanted," Cyrus was saying.

"It doesn't matter what she wanted," Sylmar countered, his whispers holding far more conviction. "Now she's under Mayvus' control. This is the only way to counteract it."

"It's my brand for Durriken," Daisy said.

Gaeren nearly tripped. Durriken? She'd told him she would never do blood magic again, and she'd branded Durriken? Her answer kept the attention off Jasperus, but it left Gaeren distracted too.

Durriken shifted on the balcony stones, and Mayvus' laugh rang out again, covering the whimper that left Jasperus' lips when Sylmar cut his palm.

"You branded Durriken? Why would you bother doing that? I already control Durriken, and now I control you."

Gaeren closed his eyes, trying to process what Daisy had done. She'd done blood magic, but she wanted Gaeren to keep Jasperus from doing the same. Maybe it wasn't that she wasn't willing to do blood magic. Maybe it was that she wasn't willing to ask someone else to do it for her. Or maybe she was only willing to do it for a specific reason or purpose. Was there ever a good reason for blood magic? Orra's words came back to him, more like a prophecy than a memory.

Jasperus would be doing it out of fear, but Daisy—Daisy had done it out of love.

"Or it could be Jasperus' brand," Daisy said.

Gaeren went still, as did Cyrus, Jasperus, and Sylmar behind him. Even Velden, Lukai, and Iris paused in their advance on the other soldiers, their breathing overriding the sound of steel on steel and boots on stone.

"Jasperus?" Mayvus turned, her brow raised as she scanned the others. When she saw Gaeren, her eyes narrowed. She held out a hand, and the force of a vicious gale of wind knocked Gaeren aside like he was little more than a leaf. He landed on his side, and his wrist bent too far beneath him, his body barely clinging to the balcony's balustrade.

Mayvus' laugh held surprise as she flexed her hand and studied it. "So much power."

Gaeren read her lips more than he heard her words, as the wind she'd created stole them from the air. It stopped as suddenly as it had started, making Gaeren's ears ring with the new silence.

Cyrus and Sylmar braced themselves in front of Jasperus, but between their legs, Gaeren caught sight of Jasperus struggling to open the vial of Daisy's blood.

Mayvus watched too. "No. It's not the fool who stole my brand from your mother. He didn't finish the job yet." Her brows rose, and she leaned in toward Daisy. "Kill him."

Daisy stepped forward, but Mayvus put out a hand.

"Wait." Mayvus squinted at the soldiers who had stopped fighting Lukai, Velden, and Iris to watch Mayvus' power unfold. "Brogdon?"

One of the soldiers straightened, and Daisy flinched.

"Didn't you have a Recreant father named Jasperus?" Mayvus asked.

The young man stepped forward, his shoulders tight. "Yes, Your Majesty." His voice boomed out with the same intensity as Jasperus', and Gaeren stiffened at the title. Other subtle similarities grew more evident the longer Gaeren stared. The tilted nose and droopy ears. Sinewy limbs on a petite frame. But the amber eyes that held warmth in Jasperus' face were cold in Brogdon's.

"Your father is attempting treason." Mayvus steepled her fingers over her lips and lifted her chin. "You can't allow him to live."

"Yes, Your Majesty," Brogdon repeated. Instead of a sword, he raised an axe, and Daisy's face blanched.

"No," she whispered.

Mayvus frowned in her direction but still swept a hand out toward Jasperus' self-proclaimed bodyguards. Another rush of wind swept across the balcony, sending Sylmar and Cyrus sprawling and leaving Jasperus wide open for Brogdon's lunge.

Gaeren scrambled to his feet and stretched out his fingers, barely grasping leather ties on the soldier's arm. He pulled back, knocking Brogdon's attack off-kilter, but the axe still burrowed into Jasperus' gut where he sat on the floor.

The old man gasped in pain, and the vial rolled from his hands, unopened and forgotten on the stone tile. Gaeren rushed forward, both to hide the vial and to hold Jasperus upright.

Brogdon remained bent over, blinking down at his father in confusion. A leather cord dangled from his neck, the small axe starlock swinging in the remaining breeze of Mayvus' wind.

"My boy," Jasperus whispered, his bloody hands reaching out to touch Brogdon's face.

Brogdon's face shifted, a softness crossing his features, followed by horror. "Papa?" He reached for Jasperus' face, then the wound. "Papa..." He trailed off, running trembling fingers through his own hair and leaving streaks of blood.

Jasperus pulled his son's hands back to his chest. He sucked in a breath and shut his eyes as he moaned.

"I'll fix this. I can heal you." Without warning, Brogdon pulled the axe out. All three men groaned at the sight and sound of Jasperus' insides shifting. The blood pooled beneath him, but Brogdon shoved his hand against it, eyes closing in concentration. A somatic progeny? Or was he doing blood magic?

"Brogdon," Mayvus called out, "don't waste your time on the Recreant traitor."

Brogdon pulled his hands away, making Jasperus groan louder. The young soldier stood, his eyes blank once more. "Yes, Your

Majesty." He returned to her side, leaving Gaeren to hold Jasperus' hand.

"I'm sorry," Gaeren said, his eyes grazing Jasperus' wounds as his own stomach heaved. His mentors had never bothered going over the healing arts with Gaeren, at least not since they'd discovered his secondary spoke wasn't somatic.

Jasperus' hand tightened around Gaeren's, a surprising level of strength in his grip as the light faded from his eyes. "I forgive..." Jasperus started, his breath coming in ragged huffs. "I love him."

Gaeren nodded, then glanced at the others to see who could take his place at Jasperus' side. Who could heal him? Or at the very least comfort him in his death? But Velden, Lukai, and Iris had lifted their swords once more, and Sylmar and Cyrus had eyes on Mayvus, likely trying to figure out how they could still save Daisy.

"He must—he must know." The desperation in Jasperus' voice made Gaeren turn back, and the other man stared at him with an uncomfortable intensity. "Tell him."

Gaeren nodded again, Jasperus' words finally clicking. "I'll make sure Brogdon knows he's forgiven. He's not the one who killed you. It was Mayvus."

A sigh escaped Jasperus' lips, one that almost sounded like the word "yes." His entire body relaxed, and his hand went limp against Gaeren's. The stillness of Jasperus' body left Gaeren feeling equally empty.

He closed his eyes, trying to block out the fight surrounding him. Heat and the hiss of steam at his back suggested Durriken and Velden had rejoined the battle. Things were coming to a swift end, and they were out of options. They hadn't gotten the blood from Mayvus. Daisy had branded Durriken, but not before Mayvus branded her. Jasperus had been killed before he could brand Daisy.

The only option left was for Gaeren to take out Daisy's brand. He could try just cutting off her hand. The thought still made him sick, but it would keep her alive—for now. But could he even manage that precise of a cut in this havoc? Killing her was the better guarantee. She would want him to go for the sure thing.

He turned to face the chaos. He'd lost track of half of their people, their wounded—or maybe dead—bodies mixed among the Zealots. Emeris had somehow gotten free from her soldier, but she lay on the floor near the balcony's edge, weakened, likely from Jasperus accidentally draining her power as he died. Sylmar and Velden were left to use the remains of their magic on Mayvus and Durriken on the western side of the balcony, and Daisy sat on the balustrade, unknowingly feeding Mayvus unbridled power.

It would be too easy to run his sword through Daisy. Mayvus wasn't even watching for him, didn't suspect that he would kill his own friend. It would be even easier to wrap his arms around her and take her over the balcony's edge. The thought of holding her in their last moments seemed almost merciful, but he knew it was more for his own comfort than hers.

He shifted to stand, and his boot kicked the vial of Daisy's blood, making it clink against the stone. Something pulled in Gaeren's gut, a sliver of hope mixed with a sickening dread. The Sun had gone to sleep, but it hadn't been gone for long. The blood in the vial would still be strong.

Gaeren had another option, if he was willing to do it.

If he failed, Mayvus would likely brand him. And if he succeeded, any last hope of restoring relationships with his family were gone. Either way, he would be going against all his training and generations of values upheld. Worst of all, he'd be breaking the promise Daisy had asked him to make.

But it would give her a chance to live. He would be keeping his promise to himself to protect her.

He prayed to the Sun that Orra was right and that his childhood priest had been wrong. Then he took his knife and sliced his palm before cracking the vial and spilling the blood over his wound. It burned and bubbled like acid, bringing an immediate physical pain that matched the panic and desperation he'd felt when he'd tried to erase Enla's memories, when their minds had melded and nearly broken and his mentor had managed to loosen and untie the mental strands between them.

But he didn't have his mentor, and he wasn't a somatic progeny. Without someone to seal the brand for him, it could take hours to settle, and he didn't have hours. A shiver ran across his neck, like when they'd fought Arvid. Were the dark spirits already coming?

He tucked his hand against him like a broken wing and stumbled toward Sylmar, but Durriken's fire divided them, nearly singeing Gaeren before he quickly threw himself to the ground. Did that mean Velden was also out of commission?

Through smoke and flame, he caught sight of Lukai and Cyrus rushing toward Daisy, swords still bloody from their most recent kills. In the back of his mind, he wondered if one of them had killed Brogdon, if there was another promise he couldn't keep.

He pulled himself to his feet and grabbed Lukai's arm as he passed, clumsily feeding him the memory of what he'd done, how he'd thought through the possibilities, started the branding process, and how now it slowly sealed.

Lukai's eyes widened, his mouth dropping open in horror. Still, he placed his hand over Gaeren's, the soothing sensation of the burn being wrapped in a coolness so the fire could burrow down deep, unable to be sensed or touched.

"You're mad," Lukai whispered.

"I'm desperate," Gaeren said, his voice ragged from the pain and smoke. He coughed against it, then watched as the skin of his palm smoothed over, the strange bump so much like his bond mark but so much bigger and uglier. He could never hide this from Enla or his parents. They might have taken him back before, but now… even after cutting this out, he wouldn't be able to hide it. "It doesn't matter," he murmured.

"What?" Lukai asked.

"Nothing," Gaeren said. Then he closed his eyes and reached out for Daisy.

CHAPTER 86

AELIANA LIFTED her eyes to the darkening sky. The Stars were just beginning to show, their faint patterns visible against the purple of twilight. Only tonight they didn't seem to dance. The few she could see flickered, bundling together. Were they disappointed in her? Did they regret giving her a starlock?

You've done well.

Mayvus' affirmation filled Aeliana's mind even as her aunt's ice nearly killed Sylmar. Where did ice fall on the Wheel of Magic anyway? Or did Mayvus' brands allow her to tap into new magic?

Her mind distantly registered thunderous fire from Durriken. She knew she should be horrified by the things happening, but they no longer concerned her. The shouts of her comrades seemed faded, both in her hearing and in her mind. The dark spirits drawing closer felt harmless. Those things simply didn't matter anymore. Even the burn that grew and intensified in her left palm didn't matter.

Daisy, can you hear me?

Aeliana tensed, her hearing perking up like that of a hound on a trail.

She'll sense me soon. Fight her control. Listen to me and fight her before she knows your loyalty is divided.

Warmth flooded her chest and spread to her limbs, awareness resuming with an awful jolt. The sounds around her magnified, the horror of the grunts and screams of friend and foe echoing in the night air.

Her mother stood before her, Aeliana's dagger in her hand. Aeliana blinked down at it, trying to think why her mother would try to harm her, then realized Mayvus held Aeliana out like a shield. Her mother was desperate to get to Mayvus. Was she desperate enough to go through her daughter?

Her mother licked her lips, and Aeliana's gaze shot between the dagger starlock around her neck and the dagger in her hand.

Something was wrong.

Aeliana could feel it even through the haze of not one but two brands. She prayed to the Stars that Mayvus' distraction would keep her from sensing all the wrongness too.

"Don't ever harm your mother," Mayvus whispered in her ear. "I need her."

The command made her sick with a need to obey, and yet she also felt sick over her desire to go against anything Mayvus might say. Her gaze swung to Gaeren, who crouched halfway across the balcony. Had he really branded her? After all his hatred for blood magic, after her history with it? He was supposed to kill her, but this was more likely to kill him.

He nodded at her.

Resist. Take away the source of her power.

A whimper escaped Aeliana's lips. She was the source of Mayvus' power. She couldn't take that away because Mayvus had commanded her not to. The commands competed in her mind, not perfect contradictions, but still impossible to reconcile.

"Aeliana." Her mother's brow furrowed, drawing Aeliana's attention. "Please, daughter. Don't stop me from saving us all."

Her words triggered a response, her body prioritizing Mayvus' command before her mind could process her options. She tackled her mother, and the dagger flew from her mother's hand, clattering against stone.

"No," her mother said, pushing Aeliana aside as she clawed her way toward the blade. But Aeliana was faster, stronger. Her hands raked across her mother's neck, drawing blood, and the brand on her palm stung. She hadn't meant to disobey. She hadn't realized it was possible to. Still, she reached for her dagger before her mother could, then clambered back and stood to ensure she couldn't accidentally harm her mother more. Just like Mayvus had commanded.

"Good girl." The words filled Aeliana's ears and mind as Mayvus stroked the back of her hair.

Now, Daisy. Resist her while she's comfortable. Take away her power.

Aeliana turned to Mayvus and lifted her dagger. For a single breath, she hesitated, watching as Mayvus' eyes narrowed before scanning the others, seeking out the source of Aeliana's resistance.

The brand was still too strong for Aeliana to hurt Mayvus, but Gaeren's command finally took hold, understanding dawning. In one quick motion, she sliced the leather cord of Mayvus' starlock and tugged it from her aunt's neck.

Mayvus snarled and reached for her starlock, but Aeliana stepped back and cut the cord of her own before tossing them both toward Gaeren. Mayvus' hands went to her chest and neck, patting them down as if she felt the same nakedness as Aeliana, the same weakness.

Cold fright swept through Aeliana, followed by relief. Mayvus could no longer use her power. Her aunt stumbled away, getting lost in the chaos.

It felt like a battle won, but Cyrus still fought on the other side of the balcony, wearing down one of the soldiers. Lukai practically held Gaeren up near its center. Her mother lay at her feet, the recent grapple over the dagger filling Aeliana with shame. Sylmar's and Velden's efforts to restrain Durriken came to a standstill as the dragon shook his head as though waking from the same dazed state as Aeliana.

A cold hand circled her wrist and took the dagger from her grip. Aeliana blinked up into the determined eyes of her mother.

"Which one is Mayvus'?" her mother asked, turning Aeliana's palms up.

Aeliana held her hands up, examining the small red bond mark on her left palm next to a slightly larger black bump that looked raw and misshapen, like a child had tried drawing a triangle. She didn't remember it from before, so that one must be Gaeren's. Her right hand held two marks, the first being a much larger portion of raised skin covering a quarter of its surface. That one had to be Durriken's. But the second was small like Brogdon's, the skin smooth and the shape a perfect circle, like that brand had been done by the brander a thousand times.

Because it had.

"This one." Aeliana flinched and cried out as her mother wasted no time digging the brand out of her hand, half of her pain from the clear disregard for Mayvus' desires. But Mayvus' power had diminished with the absence of her starlock, and Gaeren's wish for her to cut out the brand was stronger.

Blood sprayed both Aeliana and her mother, and in Aeliana's pain, she fought to restrain the pull of blood magic to heal herself. Lukai was there in an instant, wrapping his arms around her and placing his hand over hers, healing the skin her mother tore loose.

"Get down," Gaeren called.

The three dropped to their knees as a gust of wind threatened to pull them to the balcony's edge. They linked their arms while still managing to completely remove the brand.

"The Sun and Stars are not the only source of power in this world," Mayvus said, her voice coming out like a growl.

Aeliana turned, squinting against the dust rising in the air with Mayvus' storm. Blood streamed from her aunt's hand, which she raised toward the skies. She was beckoning the dark spirits, inviting them in.

Durriken shifted along the edge of the balcony, adjusting his perch to be closer to Aeliana. His wings beat more frantically, and his eyes rolled in panic. Their connection was weak with her starlock gone, but it was still there.

Free me, too. Free me!

The rumble of words was so deep, Aeliana almost didn't understand them, but her heart seemed to sense their meaning. She took the dagger from her mother and stepped closer to Durriken.

"No, Daisy!" Gaeren called.

She hesitated, sensing the words he shouted from within. It was a command as much as a warning, and she couldn't resist.

I'm sorry. I just—is it safe? This time his words were spoken only in her mind.

She turned to study him from across the balcony. "Safer than the alternative." She gestured toward Mayvus, who managed to ward off Sylmar's and Velden's attacks while waiting for her spirits to empower her.

Gaeren nodded.

She turned back to Durriken, who struggled to lift his right paw toward her without completely losing his grip on the wall, and his wings beat so powerfully Aeliana lost her balance. Lukai came up behind her to steady her as she leaned out to cut Durriken's paw.

"What if you take the whole paw?" he asked. "Like Miklous?"

Durriken's growl was more like a hiss, the heat of his breath sending steam at them both.

Aeliana ignored the question. "Heal him too," she pleaded, and to her relief, Lukai placed a trembling hand on the dragon's paw, healing it as she cut.

They hadn't gotten halfway through before the air around them turned to ice and the Stars above were blotted out. Even cold-blooded Durriken shivered in the wind, losing his grip and plummeting half a story before his wings caught him back up.

Mayvus' laugh rose above her wind until it shifted to a gurgle and choke. Aeliana turned around and immediately wished she hadn't. The dark spirit clawing its way into Mayvus' mouth was twice the size of any Aeliana had seen. It filled every space of Mayvus, pulling color from her while healing her wounds and returning her strength. When her throat was clear once more, she let out a sigh of bliss.

She opened her eyes, and her black irises latched onto Aeliana.

The transition hadn't ever been this way with Arvid. But maybe this spirit was too big to fit in such a small woman. Maybe it leaked out through every pore and socket.

"You've stolen my brand and my starlock." Mayvus took a step toward Aeliana, the motion so smooth Aeliana doubted her feet touched the stone. Her teeth and tongue were blackened by the spirit's touch. "And now you try to steal my dragon?"

A growl started in Durriken's throat.

Resist her. Aeliana tried to push the same thoughts on Durriken that Gaeren had pushed on her, but she didn't have her starlock. She didn't know if it would work.

"I had plans for you," Mayvus said. "But plans can change. Durriken, take her to your cave and hold her there."

Durriken rose above Aeliana, his eyes glazed over with the command infused with the power of blood magic and a dark spirit.

Better my paw than my life. The pause and the rumbled words were all Aeliana needed to drop her dragger and pull Lukai's sword from his sheath. It was heavier than she'd expected after only training with daggers and bows, but she could still lift and swing.

The blade sliced through Durriken's right foreleg, severing it just above the joint. The appendage holding Mayvus' brand landed at Aeliana's feet with a sickening thud. Instead of reaching for Aeliana, Durriken let out a cry, then dropped, barely giving her and Lukai enough time to roll out of his way. The entire northern keep shuddered under his weight.

Mayvus briefly stumbled but quickly caught herself as the others still scrambled for purchase.

"The whole tower's going down," Velden shouted, pulling Iris to her feet while swinging her arm across his shoulder. "We have to get out of here."

Lukai rushed to help Emeris, but Aeliana went straight for Durriken's snout, where mournful cries escaped. She placed a hand on his scales.

His eyes opened, and he stilled.

I'm sorry. She hoped Durriken could still sense her words through his pain. The tower shifted beneath them, making Aeliana slide closer to Durriken's wing.

Warmth touched her back and hands lifted a leather cord over her head. She felt her starlock's heat before she even saw it. "Yes," she breathed out, bending forward to heal Durriken's stump. She couldn't give him back his paw, but at least she could do this. As his wound closed over and her power waned, her mind flooded with his memories. Flying back to his home after she'd freed him, content to live out his days in peace rather than vengeance. Waking with the pain of another brand forming on his paw. Misjudging Mayvus' power.

"She had no right. I'm so sorry."

A simmering growl came from Durriken's mouth, more like a hum.

"She probably has stores of your blood to do it all over again."

The growl intensified.

"Can you still command him?" Gaeren leaned in to ask. "Can he take us all to safety?"

Aeliana frowned, searching for Mayvus. Sylmar's staff was in one piece again, and he drove Mayvus back with its molten frame, but she returned a wind that knocked him aside.

"I doubt it. Besides, if we run now, we just have to do this all over again," Aeliana said. If they'd defeated Arvid and his dark spirit, they could defeat Mayvus and hers too. Aeliana's mind sped through the fight with Arvid, the way he'd still needed blood magic. Mayvus would eventually need more—she couldn't drain all of her own blood. "We can weaken her. Besides, we asked for this war. He didn't."

She leaned against Durriken's forearm. *You're free. I have the right to command you, but I release you of it. Go where you want to go, live how you want to live. Just never serve Mayvus again.*

Durriken stirred.

Aeliana stepped away, trading the warmth of the dragon's breath for the warmth of Gaeren's hand. Aeliana didn't know if her command could be enough to prevent Mayvus' control if she branded him again, but maybe keeping him branded would allow Aeliana to protect him in some way.

She reached for her dagger, tucking it back into its sheath. The tower shifted again, making her stumble, and Gaeren caught her, pulling her in against his chest.

Durriken struggled to his three paws, testing out his balance, which only made the tower shift again. He let his wings spread, then flapped them harder, sending several others on their backsides once more.

Thank you.

Durriken took off, first gliding down from the tower, then flapping his wings and rising higher into the night sky. The tower went still, its foundation no longer sturdy but the threat of collapse momentarily halted. Gaeren released Aeliana, and they turned as one to face Mayvus.

Sharp pain stabbed into Aeliana's side. She hunched forward as Gaeren did the same.

"You let him go?" Mayvus stood over Aeliana, her piercing voice pounding into Aeliana's skull with the same force as the magic.

Aeliana tried to see what was causing her pain, but Mayvus was relentless, white sparks flying from her fingertips as she spoke, like nails driving in each word.

"Ten years it took me to catch him and brand him, and you let him go. Twice. Remember how well that worked out last time?"

The wind picked up around Aeliana as she fell to the stone floor, curling up in a ball with her eyes closed. The white light kept coming, kept hitting her in just the right spot to set her nerves on fire once more. She cried out, no longer able to hear Mayvus' words, especially with the intolerable wind. How could one woman control so much power, so much magic?

They had to get rid of the bodies, just like they'd done with Arvid. They could do it. Aeliana squinted at her companions, trying to see who might be free to start the process, but her vision blurred with each white light that struck her.

Suddenly, the fiery currents stopped, and so did Mayvus' tirade, but the wind grew louder, like Mayvus was working it up to a tropical storm.

Aeliana came to her knees, summoning her blood's energy, letting it shift and grow until she sent it out like a wall, a shimmering light that encompassed everyone near her, protecting everyone behind her on the east side of the balcony.

"Mother?" Aeliana called, scanning her companions still on the west side of the shield, still not safe.

Her mother's hand lifted, but she was too far for Aeliana to reach her, too near to Mayvus.

"How do we defeat her?" Aeliana asked.

Her mother sat up, eyes sad. Her lips moved, but the words couldn't reach Aeliana over Mayvus' wind.

Aeliana fought her way forward, the shield forced to press against the wind while everything behind her remained calm and still. "Get rid of the dead," she called out.

Gaeren and Lukai were quick to obey after their experience with Arvid. The others followed, sending all the bodies behind her shield over the balcony's edge. As she passed more, they removed them as well.

Soon Aeliana would reach Mayvus' side, and then what? The nearer she got, the more her shield flickered. Mayvus' white bolts of light were back, penetrating the shield and weakening it.

"How do we defeat her?" she asked again.

"You have to—"

This time Aeliana caught half of her mother's words, the tail end getting sucked away by Mayvus' wind. Aeliana pressed forward more, her mother nearly in reach.

Mayvus' face contorted, the volley of sparks hitting the shield multiplying, and the flickers growing longer, the occasional wind and bolt getting through.

Aeliana winced, pushing as much of her power into the shield as she could, ensuring that once she stepped past her mother, they'd both be safe on the other side.

Her mother's breath caught with the change of environment, her hair settling around her face as the wind died to stillness. "You have to kill me."

Aeliana's shield faltered, and Iris let out a yelp as one of Mayvus' sparks got through to her thigh. Aeliana infused her shield with more power, but while stronger in the center, its canopy grew smaller, the edges thinner.

"What do you mean?" Aeliana asked, certain she'd misheard.

"If she dies, I die." Her mother pulled Aeliana's dagger from her sheath, holding it out so the daisy on the pommel was level with Aeliana's hand. "But if I die, so does she."

Aeliana's shield flickered as she backed up. "No. I can't. There has to be another way."

Her mother smiled, then shifted her grip. "It's all right."

Too late, Aeliana realized what her mother meant to do. She dropped her shield, then reached out to pull the dagger back, to keep her mother from taking her own life, but Mayvus' white bolt hit her mother's leg first.

The dagger fell from her mother's hand as she dropped to her knees. Mayvus dropped as well, seeming weaker after her efforts to break down Aeliana's shield.

Aeliana grabbed her dagger to keep it out of her mother's reach but then hesitated. Was it true? If she went after Mayvus, would she be endangering her mother?

They had to find a way to weaken Mayvus, to bind her magic until they could get answers. She sheathed her dagger and put up the shield once more, driving it toward Mayvus, imagining it wrapping around the woman like a cocoon.

The black depths of Mayvus' eyes faltered, and for a moment, Aeliana detected fear, either from the dark spirit or Mayvus. It gave her confidence that this could work, that by placing the shield around Mayvus, she would protect everyone else outside of it.

The blackness leached from her aunt's eyes, the dark spirit pulling away to its own sense of safety. Mayvus backed up on the balcony, eyes wide with terror, but her gaze rested beyond Aeliana.

Before Aeliana could see what frightened her, blue and purple scales streaked past her, the wind knocking Aeliana over and making her lose grip on her shield.

But it didn't matter. Durriken's sharp teeth clamped around Mayvus' pale form, and blood dripped in a trail across the balcony as he took his prize.

I want no debt with your kind. Now we are equal.

CHAPTER 87

HER MOTHER'S screams made Aeliana turn back, but Lukai was already bent over Emeris, calming her out of her distraught state while assessing her wounds. Blood seeped across her white dress, new spots forming as fast as Lukai could address them.

"How is she still hurting you?" Lukai asked.

"It's not her." The mumbled words coming from her mother's lips made Aeliana seek out Durriken's form as he disappeared around the west side of the cliffs. Where would he take Mayvus? And what would he do to her?

She bit her lip. Was her mother right? Was she dying because Mayvus was dying? Because Durriken was killing her?

She scanned the balcony, which seemed oddly quiet now that Durriken and Mayvus were gone, taking her dark spirits and wind-storm magic with her. Velden was bent over Iris, who was back on the ground but moving and talking. She should be fine.

Loud sobs tore through the air from the eastern edge of the balcony, where Brogdon's arms were wrapped around Jasperus. Sylmar's beady gaze watched both Brogdon and the other remaining soldier, who had dropped his weapons and allowed Cyrus to bind his wrists.

"Are you all right?" Gaeren's spoken question echoed in Aeliana's mind, a strangely comforting sensation instead of the invasiveness she'd expected.

"I think so." Her hands still shook, and her legs threatened to give out, but she was mostly intact. She should be thrilled at the turn of events. Durriken had just solved their problems with one clamp of his jaw. "I'd feel better if I could see evidence that she's truly gone."

Gaeren screwed up his face. "You've seen what Durriken's capable of. I think it's safe to say Mayvus is dead or will be soon."

"That's not—" She cut off, glancing at her mother once more. If what she'd said was true, it might not be something for Aeliana to share, not even with Gaeren. "Then we should remove your brand."

He winced as he ran a hand through his hair. "Sorry about that."

"No." She placed a hand on his arm, waiting until he caught her gaze. "You needed to do it. I needed your help. Thank you for being willing."

He nodded, then pulled her dagger from her sheath. Without hesitation, he sliced at the mark on his hand, his face screwing up in either concentration or pain. Sweat poured down his temple, and Aeliana took pity on him, pulling the dagger from his hand so she could finish the job. While she worked, she let the magic in her blood flow through her fingers, healing his wound as she went.

Tendrils of temptation wove up from his blood, more like a whisper in the back of her mind than the shouts she used to hear.

As the last of the brand was cut out, she felt the ties between them break. It should have been a relief, but a small part of her longed for the connection.

Gaeren rubbed the raw spot she'd left behind, the skin a shiny white and bright pink over a lump of flesh. It was almost as if he missed the connection too.

"I can try to smooth out the scars more in a couple days, but you might be better off having Lukai do it. Or even Marnok, if we can find him." She didn't want Gaeren to suggest what it might mean that the others had never caught up.

"This type of scar can't be healed. It's its own branding mark, a warning that I use blood magic."

She couldn't help reeling back. "So I'll have the same when I remove Durriken's brand?"

He nodded. "Although you should keep that for a bit, at least to have a sense of where he is. Especially if you want confirmation that Mayvus is dead."

She swallowed hard, not liking the practical truth in his words. "Thank you, Gaeren. For doing something you hate so much when you could have just killed me."

His laugh came out strangled. "You hear how backwards that sounds, right?"

She grinned back, but her mother's moans made her turn.

"I can't keep up with whatever's injuring her," Lukai said.

Aeliana kneeled to help him. Between the two of them, they managed to stay on top of the wounds, but they still kept appearing, as if some phantom dagger kept plunging through her side. The others helped move her to the bed in one of Mayvus' rooms, where Iris was placed beside her in order for Velden to set her broken arm and bind her cracked ribs.

Gaeren lit several lanterns, placing them throughout the room before approaching Brogdon and his fellow soldier, who had been bound and left in the corner. Aeliana watched from her mother's bedside as he gestured toward Jasperus, then placed a hand on Brogdon's shoulder, whatever words he said managing to bring the ruthless soldier back to tears.

Sylmar pulled up a chair next to Aeliana. "Do we need to cut out his brand as well?" He gestured toward Brogdon. Something about his question felt like another test. It was a decision he would have made in the past, maybe with Jasperus, but now he came to her.

"If Mayvus is dead, it can't hurt him anymore."

He gave a noncommittal hum. "Your mother seems to think Mayvus is still alive."

Aeliana turned to look at her mother's pale skin, her lips still mumbling incoherently in her sleep. Her wounds had finally stopped reappearing, allowing her to rest beside Iris. "Then yes, we should free him, along with anyone else who's branded."

Sylmar shrugged. "A brand could be a good way to learn if our enemy returns."

She felt sick over the truth of his words, the reason for his line of questioning. The ease at which he would leave someone at Mayvus' whim for the sake of information. The pain of his lies swept through her once more. "And what about you? Are you my enemy?"

He sighed, leaning back in his chair and resting his staff over his knees. "I was at one time. Like Jasperus, I changed my ways, proved my loyalty." He stretched out his palms. "Mayvus never branded me because we were already bonded."

Aeliana stiffened as she took in his familiar scars. "Bonded? You and Mayvus?" Jasperus' explanation of cutting out brands and bonds came back to her. "You cut out your bond mark."

He nodded. "As well as all the brands Mayvus had helped me perform over the years." He gestured to the rest of the scars on his arms and face.

Aeliana recoiled at the thought of him having so many brands in so many places, but she supposed he would have matched his bondmate. She imagined Mayvus' brand and the pain she'd felt cutting it out, how she'd needed her mother's help. How had he cut out so many? Who had helped him?

"What changed? Why did you cut them all out?"

Sylmar hesitated. "I thought it was Mayvus who changed, but I suppose it was me. She'd always had a strange obsession with the Stars. She didn't worship them like the witches—not that I'm comparing your worship to the witches." He glanced at Cyrus through the open door, where the priest-in-training was already saying prayers over Jasperus' body and preparing him to return to the Stars. "Mayvus worshiped them as something to aspire to or obtain. She wanted to be a Star."

"And you didn't see that as a problem from the beginning?"

He scowled. "Bonds play tricks on your mind and your heart. They make you overlook faults in your bondmate when maybe those things should be seen."

Aeliana scanned the room for Lukai, whose head was bent with Velden. The two men gestured wildly back at the tower stairs, Lukai eager to leave the tower and search for the others while Velden wasn't ready to move the patients. Gaeren joined in on the conversation, hopefully to find some sort of compromise.

"So what made you turn on her?"

He flinched, making Aeliana realize that, even after all these years, he harbored guilt over the decision. Guilt bred by the bond he'd once shared with Mayvus.

"She wanted you," he said. "I knew she wanted your mother's magic. Emeris was the prize she patiently waited for. But you—you were the prize she hadn't anticipated. When her spies told her of your magic, she became obsessed. Refused to wait until you were grown."

Goosebumps rose on Aeliana's arms, and the memories Gaeren had shown her came back. The daisies she'd grown as a toddler. "Children aren't supposed to have magic."

"And yet you did." Sylmar blinked, his eyes suspiciously wet. "I don't know why. I'm not sure anyone knows. But it made you her target. Suddenly I saw each of her brands—each of my brands—as individuals. People who were once children like you. People who had parents who loved them, families who needed them." He cleared his throat and looked away.

Aeliana couldn't help smiling. "There is a soft side to you."

He shrugged. "It wasn't right. And when I cut out my bond, I could see it even more clearly. It wasn't just that I couldn't be a part of it. I had to put a stop to it."

His lips pursed, and Aeliana knew she wouldn't get anything more out of him. But it had been enough.

"If Durriken didn't put a stop to her, we'll find another way," she said.

He nodded. "As long as you and your mother let me stay on, I'll help you rebuild. Not just this tower, but this group of people. Hundreds are probably waking up like Brogdon just did. Your people will all be broken."

Her breath hitched. "My people? I thought we agreed that I wasn't fit to rule."

He grunted and shook his head, but before he could argue, shouts came from the tower stairs.

Everyone turned, but Gaeren shouted back, "Riveran?"

Another indecipherable yell carried through the stone hall, and Gaeren took off running.

CHAPTER 88

Gaeren ran for the hall where he and Sylmar had cut off the others. He'd assumed the worst for his men, but that shout had sounded distinctly like Riveran.

The stones were still there, blocking off the spiral stairway, but voices sounded on the other side, and light peeked through the upper left corner of the doorway.

"Gaeren?"

The deep muffled tone was like the song of the Stars to Gaeren's ears.

"Yes, it's me!" Gaeren crawled up on the rubble, pulling at loose stones and finding leverage for some of the bigger ones. "How are you still alive?"

"Always a good question."

A laugh bubbled up in Gaeren's throat. "Who else is with you?"

Lukai and Velden joined him, pawing at the highest rocks until Riveran's shaved head could be seen. Gaeren reached out to rub it, and Riveran gasped, adjusting to peer over the stones at Gaeren.

"I have Larkos and Thallahan here." His eyes clouded over. "Breeve is here too, but he—he didn't make it."

Gaeren's joy deflated. The fourth-generation sailor hadn't lived to bring about a fifth generation. Images of the younger man's apron-clad mother and laughing siblings rushed through his mind. He never should have let Breeve come.

"He took after his father," Riveran said, his voice cracking. "He's a war hero, and his mama's going to hear exactly how brave he was."

Gaeren nodded. "And she'll be getting a nice lump sum from the treasury—" He cut off, realizing that was no longer a promise he could make.

"Maybe your family will take you back," Riveran said. "They'll have to see that Mayvus was wrong, that they were wrong to ally with her."

Gaeren shook his head. "Enla would have already seen this outcome. Even if it was one of many, she couldn't have ignored Mayvus' depravity in it. She knew. I still can't go home." He didn't bother mentioning the blood magic he'd done. He'd tell Riveran eventually, but not here and not now.

"Well, we'll find a way to take care of Breeve's mother," Riveran said.

Gaeren nodded.

"Orra and some of the others were down there too," Riveran said. "She did something, something that saved us all. But she's weak."

The concern in his voice made Gaeren work faster at the rubble until finally Riveran could get through. When Gaeren's old friend pulled him in for a hug, all the fears he'd had pent up for the last few weeks came out in a death grip punctuated by a shuddering dry sob.

"I forgot what saps you two are." Larkos gazed at them from the stairway, his arms resting on the half wall that still remained. "Now get over here. I'm a lot fatter than Riveran, and I'm not gonna fit through this tiny hole."

Despite his complaining, Larkos let Thallahan go through first, probably on account of the younger sailor's left eye being matted closed with blood. More blood oozed from the wound as he crossed the threshold, and Gaeren suspected the eye was lost. Hopefully his bride would consider an eye patch roguishly handsome.

Next Larkos passed Breeve's body through, and Gaeren carefully carried it out to the balcony. Cyrus still kneeled by Jasperus, hands raised to the Stars. Gaeren didn't understand Cyrus' faith, but he couldn't deny that it was the Stars who would come and burn up Jasperus' body, returning his starlock to the heavens. Calling on them for aid at this time wasn't a terrible idea.

"I know Breeve isn't a progeny," Gaeren said as he laid Breeve next to Jasperus, "but I think he would have liked knowing he had a progeny's funeral pyre."

Cyrus' lips lifted in a sad smile. "Hundreds will be gathered up by the Stars tonight. Maybe not their bodies, like the progenies, but in spirit. It's an honor either way."

Gaeren nodded. "Do you mind praying for him as well?"

"I'll pray, but he doesn't really need our prayers anymore. He's with the Stars." He inclined his head toward Gaeren. "Or the Sun. Either way, when I pray over the dead, it's for all the lives they've touched, all the people left behind."

The lump returned in Gaeren's throat as he thought of Breeve's family. "Even better."

When Gaeren returned to the hall, they'd gotten Larkos out along with Kendalyhn, and they were in the process of passing Orra's unconscious form through. Gaeren took her to the settee in Mayvus' main room, where Daisy immediately fussed over her.

Seeing Orra reminded Gaeren of their secondary objective.

"Did anyone find the golden arrow?" he asked.

Daisy remained bent over Orra, her hands assessing for wounds to heal, but she shook her head. "I don't think anyone's had the time to look."

By the time Gaeren made it back to the hall, Holm and Marnok had made it through, informing everyone that the only things left on the stairs were corpses and the fading howls of the winex, who would hopefully give up scratching at the door with the Sun's morn.

"So much for a truce with the winex," Kendalyhn muttered as they all gathered in Mayvus' main room.

"We can't expect a complete turnaround in one generation," Daisy said. "At least not in one of their generations. Maybe within ours."

Velden and Holm began exchanging stories of what had happened on the balcony and the staircase while others gave in to their need for sleep, curling up on the floor or simply sitting against a wall and leaning on each other. Cyrus finally joined them, shutting the door on the balcony and the horrors they would have to face in the morning.

Gaeren knew he should sleep, but first he made a quick search of the room, only pausing in surprise to catch Holm's retelling of Orra's significant use of magic. He eyed the woman still lying unconscious on the settee, her pale face looking close to death. In spite of all her secrets, he felt confident she was the only one who was meant to find the starbridges. A wave of curiosity rushed through him, but it wasn't the same level of desire he'd once had. The starbridges didn't hold the same appeal, but he would still seek them out for her.

"Try the loose stone behind the bed," Sylmar said, his eyes barely open as he watched from the corner.

Gaeren hesitated, but Sylmar wasn't one to joke around. It took three of them to move the bed with Emeris and Iris on it, but once they did, the stone Sylmar spoke of became obvious. Gaeren worked his fingers into the gap, sliding the stone out until it revealed a barrel-sized gap behind the stone. At first it seemed empty, but when Gaeren reached down, his fingers brushed warm metal that hummed.

Behind him, Orra murmured, stirring on the settee.

Gaeren pulled a golden arrow out and held it up for everyone to see. The ancient words etched on its side glimmered in the lantern's light, drawing the others around him in a tight circle.

Cyrus whispered the foreign words as he leaned over Gaeren's shoulder.

"What does it mean?" Gaeren asked, passing it over to Daisy.

Cyrus hesitated. "I was never very good at the old language."

"Divided in war. United in hope. Reconciled in love." Orra's voice rang through the room with surprising strength, drawing everyone's gaze. She was sitting on the settee, stroking the braid on her wrist, her face a sickly grey. Her clear eyes focused on the golden arrow. "Its pull is so much stronger when Aeliana holds it."

Daisy frowned thoughtfully. "But nothing is ever just one thing. Back in the Stargazer, you said something else. Separated by strife, merged by faith, and..." She trailed off, her brow furrowing.

"Restored by sacrifice," Orra finished.

"I still don't know what it means," Gaeren said.

"Perhaps you're not meant to." Orra's words came out on a grunt as she attempted to stand, and Gaeren rushed forward to help her. Cold hands pressed into his arm as she leaned into him, practically pushing him toward the balcony. "Hurry, there's not much time."

"Time for what?" he asked.

"I need to be on the balcony, and you need to stay here," she whispered. "The Stars are coming."

Gaeren paused. "It's not safe to be out there. We all need to stay inside."

"That's what I just said." Orra stepped away from him, holding on to the door leading out to the balcony, her breath coming in gasps as she pulled it open with both hands. "Stay here."

Her body was still too frail for Gaeren's liking, but she held up a hand to ward him off when he approached.

"No one else come out until morning."

Then she shut the door behind her.

CHAPTER 89

ORRA TURNED to face the moon, relishing the minimal bits of the Sun's light reflecting off it. It wasn't enough to heal her, but it gave her comfort. Bright lights flashed in the sky, the start of the Stars' descent. They would each have to make several trips after a night like this. It could take all week for them to gather the last of the starlocks, to burn up the last of the bodies.

She hobbled her way past Mayvus' dead soldiers. Some had starlocks, so the Stars would come, but they were likely to stay longer near Jasperus. This was her chance.

They'd be angry at Orra's presence, but they wouldn't deny her a chance to speak. Not after tonight.

Would they?

She sat by Jasperus' body, placing a hand over his starlock. She shivered in the night air, desperate for warmth. She would even welcome the fire of a Star burning her up, if such a thing were possible.

The heat started at her back, tempting her to turn, but she kept her place at Jasperus' side, hand wrapped around the solid warmth of the axe-shaped starlock. The Star who had given it to him would come to retrieve it, burning up the metal encasing the Star's hair and saving the lock of hair for the next chosen progeny.

When the heat shifted to a burn, tears stung Orra's eyes, but not because it hurt. It felt like going home.

"Sheen?" The already high voice rose in surprise from behind her.

Reyna. Of course it would be Reyna.

Orra turned. "I go by Orra now."

Reyna's dark skin glowed in the night, a stark contrast to Orra's faded color. When she'd reflected the glory of the Sun, she'd had darker skin too, but every year she grew paler. Is that how it would end? Would she simply disappear?

"Changing your name doesn't change what you did." Reyna frowned, her gaze on Orra's hand, which still clutched the starlock. The Star's dark hair only reached her calves. How many starlocks had she given out in the last thousand years?

"I'm not here to discuss the past," Orra said. "We need to talk about the future."

Reyna stepped forward, holding out her hand. "Give me the starlock."

"Will you listen?"

"I listened to you a thousand years ago. Nearly helped you. Andreas is an outcast because of you. I shouldn't have to remind you what happened to Bryton and Lucian."

Orra winced at the sound of Bryton's name on Reyna's lips. "It's time for me to fix things."

A bitter laugh rang out from Reyna. "You mean interfere? You're still interfering?"

"My mere presence is an interference. All of us were interfering when we communed with the people. It wasn't about whether or not we interfered—it was about whether or not we were guided by the Sun."

Something in Reyna's face shifted, her confidence wavering.

Orra stood straighter. "You're communing again, aren't you?"

The vulnerability disappeared, a hardness hiding Reyna's true response. "We've chosen a select few."

"Who is 'we'?"

Reyna shook her head. "We're testing if the people are ready for it, and these ones are."

Orra's fingers tightened around the starlock until they felt numb. "Everyone is ready for it. Always. There was no reason to stop."

Reyna's voice turned cold. "You are the reason we stopped."

Orra was running out of time. "Please, Reyna. I need your help. Where are the other pieces? I'm certain the stone was here recently, but I don't know about the fish or the dagger. If I can find them—if I can reunite them—we can change this. We can save these people and this world. We can right my wrongs."

Reyna reached over, her hand wrapping around Orra's until Orra hissed from the heat and let go of the starlock. It dropped into Reyna's other hand, the metal glowing and bubbling until it dripped through her fingers and to the balcony's floor, leaving behind a small curled lock of black hair—Reyna's hair. She tucked the lock in her dress pocket.

Orra backed away, knowing what would come next. Reyna wrapped her arms around Jasperus, placing her forehead against his. She whispered words, a soft song, and her skin's glow brightened until Orra could no longer look.

She shielded her eyes from both the light and the heat as Reyna's inferno enveloped Jasperus' body. When the heat receded and the glow faded, Orra blinked into the blackness. Dark ash covered her skin. If she'd been a mere human, even a half-light, she would have been burned up in Reyna's glow like Breeve had been. Released to the Sun along with Jasperus.

Instead, she was left alone to mourn all she'd lost.

CHAPTER 90

As NIGHT GAVE way to morning, Aeliana kept watch over her mother and Iris. No one was confident in the tower's stability, so Sylmar was determined to evacuate them all once the winex left with the Sun's morn. She only agreed after Marnok reassured her the two women could survive the move.

She tried not to think about Jasperus and Breeve being burned up on the balcony and—if rumors of that process were true—Orra as well. She tightened her grip on her mother's hand and let her gaze roam over the bodies sprawled throughout the room, all their chests rising and falling with life.

Holm sat next to Iris' side of the bed, his head bent by hers and his arm half wrapped around her, somehow aware to be gentle even in his sleep. Kendalyhn and Lukai slept on the settee, their hands lightly touching in a way that made Aeliana's bond mark tingle, which was silly after all they'd been through.

Velden and Sylmar started to stir even though they'd been the last to succumb to sleep. Their murmurs and plans for the day woke Marnok, who stepped over Gaeren and Cyrus. He kneeled next to Thallahan, whose eye was beyond healing but could still benefit from Marnok's magic. Larkos and Riveran leaned against each other by the wall as if they'd been keeping watch over the room before falling asleep.

Most were awake by the time the Sun's light filtered through the window, but everyone sat a little straighter when the balcony door opened and Orra walked through.

Larkos broke the silence by swearing.

"How did you survive?" Gaeren asked.

Orra glanced over, but it was like she didn't see or hear him. "We have to find them all. It's the only way."

"All the starbridges?" Gaeren asked.

She nodded. "All the pieces. We have to reunite them."

"What's she talking about?" Sylmar asked.

Aeliana let go of her mother's hand to reach into her pocket and grasp the golden arrow.

Orra shuddered, then scanned the room until her searching gaze landed on Aeliana.

"I'll take Cyrus home," Gaeren said, "and then I'll bring it back to you. I swear on the Stars."

Orra stilled, then nodded.

"We can search for the stone while you're gone." Sylmar's grunted words left everyone stunned.

"How do you know about the stone?" Orra asked.

"Stone?" Gaeren asked. "Is that the circle? Is that what takes people to Ahmranas?"

Sylmar nodded. "Last I saw it was hidden in that loose stone behind the bed. It's where Mayvus always kept it. It's how I knew where the arrow would be. I'd hoped we'd find both."

Something in Orra deflated, and Gaeren helped her back to the settee, shooing away Kendalyhn and Lukai.

"I suppose there's no reason for us to wait," Cyrus said, but his gaze strayed to Aeliana, begging her to change her mind.

"You need to check on Bartholem. And if you can find my father—"

Her mother stirred on the bed, but her eyes remained closed as a soft moan escaped her lips. Marnok stepped away from Thallahan, shifting his focus to her mother.

Riveran twisted his hands. "If you can wait until Gullet returns, I'd like to come with you."

"What about your... wife?" Gaeren asked.

Aeliana smiled at the genuine concern in his voice. Something had changed between the two men.

Larkos stood, pushing off the wall. "Thallahan and I will gather our remaining men. Paint *Starspeed* and give her a new name. We'll get what we can to take care of Riveran's wife and Breeve's mother. Maybe bring them back here if that seems safer."

"Can you check on Erech, too?" Gaeren asked. "Make sure he and the stableboys are taken care of before you leave?"

Larkos nodded. They both turned to Aeliana, and suddenly everyone was looking at her for direction, as if she were the one in charge.

"Does that mean the rest of you will stay?" she asked. "Help my mother rebuild?"

"Iris and I won't leave Emeris' side," Holm said. He stood, then inclined his head while touching his fingers to his forehead. It was the same motion the soldiers had done back in the forest, the same she'd seen Gaeren's men do before him.

"Kendalyhn and I will be here as well," Lukai added, making the same motion. It made her squirm.

"You can't get rid of Sylmar and me even if you want to," Velden said. Thankfully, he shot water from his hand to her face instead of bowing.

"Marnok?" Aeliana asked, nudging his back where he was bent over the bed.

"I'll stay if you'll have me," he said, his fingers pressed against her mother's wrist.

"That sounds… good." Uncertainty colored her tone, but the others all stood, dividing as if she'd given orders.

Riveran stepped out onto the balcony, whistling for Gullet to return.

Sylmar took Velden to the stairwell, eager to make sure the winex were gone and to find General Nels for a report. Gaeren's men followed. Suddenly everything was happening too fast for Aeliana. She thought they'd get a break after Mayvus was gone, but it seemed as if it was all just beginning.

"Mayvus?" The murmur came from her mother's lips.

"What?" Marnok asked as he and Aeliana both leaned in.

Her mother's eyes fluttered open. "Where is Mayvus?"

"Durriken took her," Aeliana said. "We think she's dead."

Her mother frowned, her gaze resting on Marnok, her eyes widening as she reached up to touch his face. "It's not possible."

Marnok shushed her, bringing her hand back to her side. "You sustained several injuries last night. I'm doing my best to heal them, but it's like they keep coming back. We'll figure it out though. Don't worry."

"Thank the Sun," she murmured.

"Yes," Marnok agreed. "The Sun has seen fit to let you live another day."

She shook her head. "No. Thank the Sun you're alive."

Marnok's hands stilled, his eyes widening. "You know me?"

Her mother laughed. "Of course I know you." Then she paused, taking in his pained expression. "Do you not remember me?"

"Aeliana?" Sylmar called through the doorway, competing with Marnok's response. "We need you downstairs."

She hesitated, watching her mother draw Marnok in closer, placing her palms on his face.

"I can show you who you are." Her mother and Marnok went so still that it was like magic held them in place. Was this what it had looked like when Gaeren had given her memories?

"Aeliana?" Sylmar's voice came louder.

"Coming!" She rushed through the doorway, throwing one last glance back at her mother and Marnok, who were still locked in their strange embrace.

Passing through the stairway was like walking through an open graveyard in a jungle, with Orra's vines still clinging to the dead bodies and nearly blocking Aeliana's path to the battlement below. But when she got there, her heart leaped in her chest, the horrific journey worth it.

Felk stood tall with Lilik at his side.

Before she could process anything more, she was lifted off the ground and into Felk's arms, his sinewy limbs squeezing her tight.

"You're alive," he said.

"As I told you," Sylmar grumbled as Felk set her down.

No other winex were around, which left her relieved, even though she knew she could trust Felk to protect her.

"How do the winex fare?" she asked.

Velden snorted. "They were fine when we checked on them in the middle of the night. Ravenous, but fine."

Felk's face drooped. "I'm afraid there's division in their ranks. There are too many of them to get organized and not enough who stand by the promise I made. I don't think you should go near any of them this cycle."

"But we found our eggs," Lilik said, her teeth bared as she beamed. "We can build a nest, start our own clan."

Aeliana glanced back at the stairs toward all the goodbyes she was preparing to say. "Where will you go?"

Felk hesitated. "We were hoping to stay here. We thought maybe if we nested near you, maybe you could give us memories. Maybe we could build on our cycles instead of forgetting them."

"We want more for our offspring," Lilik added.

"That sounds like a terr—" Sylmar started, but Aeliana cut him off.

"Of course. You'll always be welcome here."

This time it was Lilik who picked Aeliana up off the ground, the female winex's hold just as tight.

"Thank you," Lilik whispered as she set Aeliana down. "We'll go get our eggs. There's a courtyard I saw on the east end of the fortress that I think would be perfect."

"Aeliana." Sylmar's voice came out in a warning growl, but she ignored him.

"Make it your home, then. As long as I can come visit." Aeliana smiled as they loped across the battlement and disappeared through a door to head below, then turned back to Sylmar. "Was that all you needed from me?"

Sylmar glared, and Velden gave her a wink.

She headed back up the stairwell, holding her breath as she stepped through the battlegrounds. Before she reached Mayvus' rooms, she ran into Marnok, who rushed toward her, his face white with shock.

"Marnok?" She reached a hand out to steady him, but he let out a cry and backed away.

He scanned her face like she was a ghost, then shook his head in disbelief.

"What happened? Did my mother give you your memories?"

He scrubbed his hands over his face. "Too many memories."

Aeliana's heart sank. "Are you—will Sylmar think of you as an enemy?"

Marnok shook his head. "No, but I can't stay here."

"Why not?" She reached for his arm, but he pulled away.

"I have to—I just can't." He shook his head and backed away from her, toward the stairs.

"Please stay," she begged. "I'm sure we can work it out. I know we can trust you. I still have so much to learn from you. You're the only one who can seem to show me how to heal."

Her words seemed to make him recoil more. "I'll come back. There are things I need to do. More questions I need answered. But I promise I'll come back when I'm ready."

It wasn't the answer Aeliana wanted, but she had no choice as he disappeared down the stairwell. Where would he even go?

When she reached Mayvus' main room, her mother was sitting up in bed, eating a portion of a broth Kendalyhn still cooked over the fireplace. The others gathered around the fire, soaking in its warmth and passing around two shared bowls to fill their stomachs.

Her mother made a face at Aeliana before Aeliana could even ask the question.

"It was a lot for him to take in," her mother said.

"Why? Who is he?"

"An old friend," she said. "But he's lost so much. It will be up to him to share his past when he's ready."

Riveran stepped in from the balcony, Gullet squawking from his shoulder. "I'm ready whenever you are."

Gaeren and Cyrus stood, looking expectantly at Aeliana before she remembered the golden arrow still rested in her pocket. She let her fingers wrap around the arrow, sensing its hum.

Orra stiffened on the settee, closing her eyes in concentration.

Aeliana pulled it out, surprised at how hard it was to even consider passing it over. She'd hunted this arrow with her guardians for years, imagined it being the key to her freedom from magic, from their evil.

It had been, but not in the way she'd imagined. It had led to so much more.

"We'll take good care of it." Cyrus gently pried it from her hand. Then he pulled her in for a hug. "You're more than the magic in your blood, Aeliana. You always have been. You get to choose what you make of your magic."

She smiled and stepped back. "Make sure you tell your brothers about the warrior priest you've become." Her smile fell. "And tell Bartholem I'm sorry."

"I expect he'll tell me about Orra singing Gams to the Stars. I doubt he'll feel you have anything to apologize for." He stepped away and stood by Riveran, who gave her the same odd bow and salute as the others earlier.

She didn't have time to examine why it bothered her before Gaeren was wrapping her in his arms. Her bond mark twinged as his hold tightened, every line of their bodies pressed against each other. His lips barely brushed her ear as he whispered his farewell.

"I'll come back for you, Daisy."

When she pulled away, the loss of his warmth sent a pang through her chest. The intensity in his eyes left her fumbling for the right words. "Bring my father if you can, but either way, come back soon."

The tilt of his lips returned, the familiar secretive smile that made it easier for her to shove him away, back toward Cyrus and Riveran. Cyrus held out the arrow, and all three men touched it.

Aeliana reached back to steady herself against the bed and found her mother's hand instead, the comforting squeeze far more solid than the bed's frame.

Cyrus uttered the words on the arrow, and the room filled with a blinding light.

THE END

AUTHOR'S NOTE

Looking for the next book?

Book 2 (of 4) will be coming to Kickstarter in Fall 2024 and to other retailers in Spring 2025. Sign up for my newsletter or follow the campaign by going to my website, which you can find at www.karynenorton.com or by using the QR code.

Still want more?

If the 600+ pages of *Blood of the Stars* were not enough, I have some extra goodies to tie you over until Book 2 releases! You can find the prequel, audio glossary, high-resolution maps, coloring pages, and a fun magic quiz at www.karynenorton.com/extras or by using the QR code. As the series progresses, more bonus content will be added, but it will always be available at the same site.

GLOSSARY

This glossary of terms is not exhaustive, but should address the pronunciation and importance of any names/terms used multiple times. Some explanations and terms are missing or left intentionally vague to reduce the risk of spoilers. For the audio glossary, check the bonus content available at www.karynenorton.com/extras.

Aeliana (a-lee-AH-nuh) - a young Vendaran woman with unusual magic who was stolen across the barrier to Lorvandas as a child and raised by two Vendarans who use blood magic

Ahmranas (ahm-RAHN-us) - the country/continent north of Lorvandas and Vendaras with people who value physical strength over intelligence

Andel (an-DELL) - a large seaport on the southern coast of Vendaras

Arvid (AR-vid) - a man from Vendaras who serves Mayvus and doesn't have enough blood to be a progeny, so he resorts to blood magic for his power

Awakening - an event that reveals if a half-light is deserving of a starlock; if the half-light survives their Awakening, they receive a starlock and will begin training in magic

Bahlric Desert (BALL-rick) - a large desert north of the Myndren Mountains in Vendaras

Bamboo Island - a small island off the western coast of Vendaras;

it's the drop-off point for the strabridge that connects Lorvandas to Vendaras

Barrier - a shimmering barrier between all the continents that was put in place by the Stars during the Great Divide

Bartholem (bar-THALL-em) - Cyrus' grandfather, the priest

Bond mark - a raised red mark on the left palm that indicates someone is bonded to someone else; typically between couples

Bondmate - the person someone is bonded to; typically a spouse or betrothed

Brand - a raised black mark on either palm that indicates someone is being controlled by the person who branded them

Breeve - an adolescent sailor on Gaeren's ship who is known for burning food

Calia (Kuh—LEE-uh) Larkos' wife, who has doted on Gaeren for the past several years

Celanoft (SELL-uh-nahft) - a city on the east coast of Vendaras where Emeris served as a priestess; the city where Gaeren went for his dedication year; the city where Aeliana lived before being stolen away

Croft (CRAHFT)- Enla's current bondmate

Cyrus (SY-ruhss) a priest-in-training who befriends Aeliana

Daisy - Gaeren's nickname for Aeliana

Deep - slang for the afterlife apart from the Sun/Stars

Dehvlon (DEV-lawn) - the country/continent east of Vendaras with people who value intelligence over physical strength

Della (DEL-uh) - Cyrus' grandmother, the priestess

Durriken (DUR-ih-kin) - the dragon

Elanesse (el-uh-NESS) - the capital of Vendaras on the northwest coast near the swamps; Gaeren's family name

Emeris (EM-er-iss) - Aeliana's mother; a priestess who is well loved by the people

Enla (EN-luh) - Gaeren's sister and next-in-line for the throne

Erech (AIR-ick) - stableboy/cabin boy

Fay - the woman Thallahan wants to marry

Felk - the winex Aeliana befriends

Fernandus (fur-NAN-dus) - the Elanesse family priest

Gaeren (GAIR-en) - the prince of Elanesse and eventual throne warden to his sister who will be queen

Gahldric Valley (GAHL-drick) - the city where Cyrus and his family live and where they serve in their Stargazer

General Nels - the head of the Recreant army

Great Divide - an event that took place a thousand years ago, when the Stars split the land and divided people groups by waters and barriers in order to prevent fighting

Gullet - the hawk that's always with Riveran

Half-light - a descendant of the Stars; someone with starblood in their veins, a person born of a human and a Star

Holm - he spied for Aeliana's parents years ago; now he's part of Sylmar's rescue team; Iris' bondmate; a Vendaran half-light with no magic

Iris - she was a maidservant for Emeris years ago; now she's part of Sylmar's rescue team; Holm's bondmate; a Vendaran half-light with no magic

Islara (Iz-LAHR-uh) - city near the heart of Vendaras

Jasperus (JASS-pur-us) - former Zealot; now he's part of Sylmar's rescue team; a constructive somatic progeny

Kendalyhn (KEN-duh-lin) - parents were killed by Mayvus; now she's part of Sylmar's rescue team; a destructive pneumatic progeny

Lady Merinnia (Muh-RIN-ee-uh) - a Seer on Sayhla Island

Larkos (LAR-cohs) Gaeren's first mate; he has been feeding Gaeren Recreant political ideas for years; he is loyal to his captain, but not the crown

Lenda (LEN-duh) - Gaeren's bondmate

Lilik (LIL-ick) - Felk's mate

Lorvandas (Lor-VAHN-dus) - the country/continent where humans live

Lovers' Falls - a significant waterfall near the heart of Vendaras where the sprites live

Loyalists - people who support the royal family of Elanesse

Lukai (LOO-ki) - Aeliana's bondmate; he's part of Sylmar's rescue team; a constructive somatic progeny

Marnok (MAHR-nock) - a man found with no memories or allegiances, but who joins Sylmar's rescue team

Maw - Riveran's horse

Mayvus - Emeris' sister and Aeliana's aunt; a high priestess who has risen to power on the eastern side of Vendaras

Miklous (ME-clows) - a man branded by Mayvus

Mt. Vescano (Veh-SCAH-no) - a volcano at the southern tip of the Myndren Mountains

Myndren Mountains (MIN-drin) - the large mountain range running through Vendaras

Noetic - progenies who are able to tune into the mind

Orra (OR-uh) - a woman with mysterious magic who asks Gaeren to help her find a starbridge

Paelen's Waters (PAY-lehn) - the sea surrounding Sayhla Island

Pneumatic - progenies who are able to sift through the soul

Progeny - a half-light who has survived their Awakening and received a starlock; someone training in magic

Recreants - people who are opposed to the royal family of Elanesse and wish for democracy

Reyna (RAY-nuh) - a Star

Rhystahn (RIH-stahn) - the known world that contains the countries/contintents of Dehvlon, Ahmranas, Vendaras, Lorvandas, and Sayhla Island, and was a single continent prior to the Great Divide

Rildan (Rihl-dahn) - Aeliana's father

Riveran (RIH-vur-ehn) - Gaeren's best friend from childhood turned enemy and Enla's former bondmate

Sayhla Island (SAY-luh) - the country/continent south of Lorvandas where people live who have been cursed by the sprites to be bound to the water

The Sins of the Stars - a book accounting the Great Divide

Skunk - Gaeren's horse

Somatic - progenies who are able to adjust the body

The Songs of the Stars - a book containing songs sung by the Stars

Sprites - large winged creatures who live in Lovers' Falls and grant wishes for a high price

Starblood - blood that can house magic; comes from someone who is half-human and half-Star

Starbridge - an object that can transport people across the barriers

Stargazer - a tower with an open roof built to worship the Stars

Starlock - the conduit for a progeny's magic that allows them to develop stronger magic along one of the spokes

Stars - different from the static stars in the sky; they can take human form; they are worshiped by Lorvandans as loving creators

Starspeed - Gaeren's ship

Sun - worshiped by Vendarans as a distant and fearful creator

Sungazer - a tower with an open roof built to worship the Sun

Sylmar (SIHL-mahr) - a progeny with advanced power who's leading a mission to rescue Emeris; a destructive somatic progeny who has accessed metal on the rim of the Wheel of Magic

Thallahan (Thal-uh-han) - Gaeren's second-mate who is hoping to get married after this voyage

Valley of Krahn - a valley near Mayvus' fortress where the Recreant troops will gather before their attack

Valorian (Vuh-LORE-ee-ehn) - a city in south Vendaras

Velden (VEHL-dehn) - a man with webbed fingers/toes whose mother was Sayhleen and whose father was Vendaran; a constructive pneumatic progeny who has accessed water on the rim of the Wheel of Magic

Vendaras (Vehn-DAHR-us) - the central country/continent in Rhystahn whose people are all half-lights

Vera (VAIR-uh) - a woman from Vendaras who serves Mayvus and doesn't have enough blood to be a progeny, so she resorts to blood magic for her power

Walnut - Orra's horse

Wheel of Magic - the way magic is explained and defined, with the basic magic starting at the hub of the wheel before expanding to the spokes and eventually the rim; please see diagram in front of book for more details

Winex (WIHN-ex) - creatures that wax and wane with the moon

Wyndren (WIHN-drehn) - Aeliana's family name, descending from Valyn and thought (by some) to be the right rulers of Vendaras

Zealots - people who believe Mayvus should be on the throne

KICKSTARTER ACKNOWLEDGMENTS

The following people all contributed to this book's creation and success by being among the first buyers. I can't even explain how encouraging it was to have 405 people say "I believe in this" before it was even out in the world. I'm so thankful for the Kickstarter community and for all of your generosity. I hope this story lived up to your expectations!

A.
A. L. LORENSEN
A.M. REYNWOOD
AARON HUGHEY
ABIGAIL
ADAM DAVID COLLINGS
ADRIANA WALKER
AIDEN DANA'AN
AKGAMR73
ALEX GRADE
ALEX HARLEQUIN
ALEXANDRA CORRSIN
ALY BENOIT
ALYSSA CORMIER
AMANDA BALTER
AMANDA DAVID VANHOOSE
AMANDA ESCHMEYER
AMANDA REYNOLDS
AMANDA THOMPSON
AMANDA W
AMY SUMMERFIELD
ANDREA KIDDER
ANNIE HAYES
ANTHONY KOZAK
ARIEL
ASHTON SMITH
AUSTIN ZHU

AUTHOR KATIE CHERRY
AUTHOR MEDIA
BARBARA MIDDELKOOP-MEIJSEN
BECKY
BEEGREEN
BEN DIDONATO
BETH CULP
BETHANY RICHARD
BILL BATEMAN
BILLYE HERNDON
BLAINE WILLIAMS
BONNIE GROSS
BOWDEN JONES
BRAD ROYLSTON
BRANDON
BRENDAN PEASE
BRETONNS
BRIANA PEREZ
CAITLIN MILLSAPS
CAMILLA
CANDACE
CARISSA PARKER
CARLY ARAVE
CARMEN PADILLA
CAROLINE M.
CATRINA ANKARLO

Celya Briz
Chad Bowden
Chase
Cheryl Smith
Cheyenne Heckermann
Chiara Heinzl
Christopher Davis
Christopher Wesselstam
Cinder Nickleson
CJ Milacci
CoffeeMH
Colin Letch
Colleen Villasenor
Constance Lopez
Corinne B
Covington
Cris-André Pedersen
Cristal Juarez Lopez
Crunchy
Dan Begallie
Dana Whitley
Daniel Bishop
Daniel Kenner
Danielle Cage
Danielle Tantone
Darlene N. Böcek
Dave
David
David Collick
David DeHaan
Davidnn12345
Davin Greenwood
Dead Fish Books
Deann Fox
DeEtta
Deidra Joy

Derrick Smythe
Destinee the Farmgirl
Devlin Pierce Moyers
Dona
Doug & Erin Williams
Dru Kuhlman
E. A. Hendryx
Eliza Kontiokari
Elizabeth Frazier
Elizabeth Mellas
Elizabeth Moody
Elyce de Reefe
Emilie Garneau
Emma
Eric Nabeta
Erik Westin
Eris
Erisnyx
Felicia
Fenixspartan
Fiddlehead Press
Francesco Tehrani
Gabrielle Wright
Gaby I.M.
Georgianna Myers
Gerald P. McDaniel
Gerald Rose
Gordon Sturgeon
Grace Ward
Grey
Grey Alder
Habibah
Helen J Roberts
Hestand Meredith
Holly Frandsen
HotHawks003

Irinel Finco
J F Rogers
JA Andrews
Jacob Watt
Jacqueline McCarthy
Jake Stoddard
James McGinnis
James McKlemurry
Janelle Amundsen
Janette Fletcher
Jason Joyner
Jayme Johnson
Jean Sitkei
Jeff Hedrick
Jeffrey Johnson
Jenna
Jenna Albert
Jenni McKinney
Jennifer Dyer
Jerome
Jessica Lucille
Jessica Mc
Jessica Snoots
Jim Rubart
John Idlor
John McDougall
John Powell
Jonah Pavlicek
Jonathan Norton
Joseph Morgan
Joshua Fowler
Jürgen Falch
Justin Vonsik
Kaitlyn Maxwell
Kandi J Wyatt
Karen

Karen Bulgarelli
Karen Grunst
Karen Hawbecker
Kate
Katelyn
Katherine Malloy
Katherine Pawlik
Katherine Shipman
Kathi
Kathy Brasby
Katie Briggs
Katie Cross + Kaley Mills
Katie Robles
Katie W.
Kelly
Kelsey Stenberg
Kent M. Smith
(HyruleBalverine)
Kenyon Wensing
Kevin
Kevin Norton
Kimberly
Kindly Athena
Kristin Flanagan
Kristin Hendrick
Kristopher
Kristy VW
Krystal Bohannan
Krystal Markham
Kurtis Boulianne
Kyle Sullivan
Lady D
Larry
Lauren Brochu
Lauren Pamperin
Laurie Christine

Lee Alexander
Leigh Mumford
Leonora Teale
LGlaser
Liliyana Greer
Lisa Flower
Lisa Thibault Pietsch
Lissette Buckley
Liz Delton
Liz M
Logan Burlew
Lorlen12
Luke Nabeta
Lyle Martin
Mackenzie Cocke
Madi
Malcolm Coon
Malia Jenks & Dylan Lusk
Margaret
Maria Mejia
Marie Lynch
Marisa Davis
Marisa Davis
Mary Allen
Mary Grove
Matthea Ross
Matthew M.
Matthew Redman
Max Stone
Megan Malicoat
Megan N. Quinn
Melanie Marttila
Melissa
Melissa Banian
Melissa Marr
Meredith Carstens

Merrie Destefano
MF Caram
Michael B Mitchell
Michael Harleman
Michael J. Sullivan
M
Michelle Coffey
Mike Brown
Mike G.
Mike Rogers
Mike Vance
Mindy Hite
MJ
Monica Arsenault
Morgan
Natalie Munford
Natalie Shepard
NeonPixxius
Nichole Haratyk
Nicola Thompson
Nicole Allen
Nicole Sanders
Nicole Talbot
Nikki K
Noemi Hernandez
Orel
Paige Lynn
Pamela Hart
Petra Fruzsina Unger
Phillup Foster
Qavee
R. Lennard
Rachel Newhouse
Rachel Strehlow
Rajasekaran Senthil
Kumaran

REAPERNX

REBEKKA THORUD

RENE NOBELEN

RENEE

RINGMASTER

R.M. KROGMAN

ROB HALL

ROBBY HAENTZE

ROBERT CLODFELTER

ROGER NASH

SADIE B.

SAMANTHA G

SAMANTHA MCCULLOCH

SANCHEZ CARLOS

SANDRA K. LEE

SARA COLLINS YOUNG

SARA LAWSON

SARA REED

SARA WILDE

SARAH

SARAH CLIFFORD

SARAH DYE

SARAH HENNE

SARAH SMYTH

SARAH L. STEVENSON

SARAH T

SCOTT WILLIAMS

SEAMUS SANDS

SHANNON DAVIDSON

SHANON BROWN

SHARINA

SHAY HARRIS

SHEENA O'LOUGHLIN

SOUTHERNRHAPSODY

STEFANIE MARTIN

STEFKE

STEPHANIE

STEPHANIE

STEPHANIE CAIN

STEPHANIE ROY

STEPHEN BALLENTINE

STEVEN "WAFFLES" LANE

SUSAN

SUZY MORGAN

TABITHA

TANA REEVE

TANYA

TESSA

THEAH

THERESA HOLLAND

THERESA WILLIAMS

TIFFANY NOBLE

TIFFANY SMITH

TISH THAWER

TOM WEAVER

TRENTON NASH

TRISTAN AMANT

TYLER

TYLER O'DONNELL

VALERIE LILY

VICKI DEVICO

VICKIE GRIDER

VIRGINIA KUHLMAN

WESSEL

WILL

WINSTON CRUTCHFIELD

WINTER DORR

WOUTER DE WIT

XENABELLE

YOLANDA ANGUIANO

ZANE

AUTHOR'S
ACKNOWLEDGMENTS

Oh, so you're someone who likes to read acknowledgments? Me too. It's fascinating to see how many people it takes to put a story out in the world.

I'll start with a quick shout out to the members of Fantasy Faction and some even older critique partners who have stepped in and out of my writing life. You may not have helped with this particular book or version, but you helped mold me into the writer I am today.

Specific big thanks to Melissa and Laura for all your mad editing skills. Also St. Jupiter, for putting together exactly what I wanted on the cover when I had no idea what that was. Rachael, your maps are phenomenal, and I can't wait to see the rest of the world come to life with your artwork.

Paul and Jake, thanks for being amazing critique partners and for not being afraid to tell me when you didn't like things. Constance - thanks for all your encouraging words and your ability to read lightning fast. I promise there will be (slightly) more romance coming!

Candace, Carli, and Katie - I don't know where I would be on this journey without you. I'm so grateful for all our writing and marketing discussions. Knowing we have each other's backs is a game changer in this crazy publishing world.

Jim and Thomas - taking your Book Launch Blueprint course was like opening up a world of possibilities. It was far less about marketing and far more about understanding why I write and why I'm publishing. Your encouragement and instruction was a major pivot point in my career that I will always look back on as a game changer.

Melissa, I'm so thankful that you took me under your wing all those years ago. You gave me confidence when I needed it, and your constant effort to invest in me and my career has always been so encouraging.

Janice, I wouldn't be putting any of this out in the world if it weren't for your gentle nudges to consider indie publishing, and I'm a better writer and person for all our exchanges about books, writing, publishing, faith, and life in general. Thank you for all you do.

I'll always be thankful for my family—for parents who raised me to read and who value creativity, for a sister who keeps me grounded in reality and a brother who pushes me to think even more outside the box.

Most especially, I'm thankful for my kids, who never complained when I needed a writing day, and for Jon, who gave me those writing days (and weekends) and encouraged me to keep pursuing this path at every step. I love getting to live life with you all.

Thank you, Jesus, for all of the above. May the words I write be pleasing to you, O Lord, my rock, and my redeemer.

ABOUT THE AUTHOR

Karyne Norton hasn't found the key to time travel, cloning, or infinite lives, so she's taking a break from nursing and photography to focus on raising four human beings while writing fantasy and science fiction. She's a contributing author for Putting the Science in Fiction by Writer's Digest. *Blood of the Stars* is her first novel.